Green Eyes

Dr Ezawa had made some remarkable discoveries about the Voodoo beliefs that persisted in the Louisiana bayou country – like how to create zombies by injecting corpses with the dirt from old slave graveyards, the eyes of the awoken dead blazing with a brilliant green luminosity and their souls tormented by strange visions and superhuman abilities …

The Jaguar Hunter

Fourteen stories – including 'Radiant Green Star', winner of the 2001 Locus Award for Best Novella – make up this classic collection. Beginning with the Nebula Award-winning title story, in which a poor Honduran hunter is coerced into tracking the forbidden 'Black Jaguar of Barrio Carolina', and moving through futuristic war, menacing wind spirits, parallel worlds, and a six-thousand-foot dragon, this collection proves that Shepard is neither strict fantasist nor strict realist, but one of the most intriguing writers in any genre.

Vacancy

A washed-up actor, a mysterious motel and a Malaysian 'woman of power' form the central elements in a riveting account of a rootless man forced to confront the impossible – but very real – demons of his past.

Also by Lucius Shepard

Novels
Green Eyes (1984)
Life During Wartime (1987)
The Golden (1993)
Viator Plus (2010, expanded from 2004 novella)

Novellas
Kalimantan (1990)
The Last Time (1995)
A Handbook of American Prayer (1999)
Colonel Rutherford's Colt (2002)
Valentine (2002)
Aztechs (2003)
Floater (2003)
Louisiana Breakdown (2003)
Softspoken (2007)
Vacancy (2009)
Ariel (2009)

Collections
Barnacle Bill the Spacer: And Other Stories (1997)
The Jaguar Hunter (2001, expanded from 1987)
Nantucket Slayrides: Three Short Novels (with Robert Frazier) (1989)
The Ends of the Earth: Fourteen Stories (1991)
Two Trains Running (2004)
Trujillo and Other Stories (2004)
Dagger Key: And Other Stories (2008)
Skull City and Other Lost Stories (2008)

Lucius Shepard
SF GATEWAY OMNIBUS

**GREEN EYES
THE JAGUAR HUNTER
VACANCY**

GOLLANCZ
LONDON

This omnibus copyright © Lucius Shepard 2015
Green Eyes copyright © Lucius Shepard 1984
The Jaguar Hunter copyright © Lucius Shepard 1987, 2001
Vacancy copyright © Lucius Shepard 2009
Introduction copyright © SFE Ltd 2015

All rights reserved

The right of Lucius Shepard to be identified as the author
of this work has been asserted by him in accordance with the
Copyright, Designs and Patents Act 1988.

First published in Great Britain in 2015 by
Gollancz
An imprint of the Orion Publishing Group
Orion House, 5 Upper St Martin's Lane,
London WC2H 9EA

An Hachette UK Company

A CIP catalogue record for this book is
available from the British Library

ISBN 978 0 575 08989 1

1 3 5 7 9 10 8 6 4 2

Typeset by Jouve (UK), Milton Keynes

Printed and bound by CPI Group (UK) Ltd, Croydon, CR0 4YY

The Orion Publishing Group's policy is to use papers
that are natural, renewable and recyclable products and
made from wood grown in sustainable forests. The logging
and manufacturing processes are expected to conform to
the environmental regulations of the country of origin.

www.orionbooks.co.uk
www.gollancz.co.uk

CONTENTS

Introduction from The
Encyclopedia of Science Fiction   ix

Green Eyes   1

The Jaguar Hunter   225

Vacancy   607

ENTER THE SF GATEWAY ...

Towards the end of 2011, in conjunction with the celebration of fifty years of coherent, continuous science fiction and fantasy publishing, Gollancz launched the SF Gateway.

Over a decade after launching the landmark SF Masterworks series, we realised that the realities of commercial publishing are such that even the Masterworks could only ever scratch the surface of an author's career. Vast troves of classic SF and fantasy were almost certainly destined never again to see print. Until very recently, this meant that anyone interested in reading any of those books would have been confined to scouring second-hand bookshops. The advent of digital publishing changed that paradigm for ever.

Embracing the future even as we honour the past, Gollancz launched the SF Gateway with a view to utilising the technology that now exists to make available, for the first time, the entire backlists of an incredibly wide range of classic and modern SF and fantasy authors. Our plan, at its simplest, was – and still is! – to use this technology to build on the success of the SF and Fantasy Masterworks series and to go even further.

The SF Gateway was designed to be the new home of classic science fiction and fantasy – the most comprehensive electronic library of classic SFF titles ever assembled. The programme has been extremely well received and we've been very happy with the results. So happy, in fact, that we've decided to complete the circle and return a selection of our titles to print, in these omnibus editions.

We hope you enjoy this selection. And we hope that you'll want to explore more of the classic SF and fantasy we have available. These are wonderful books you're holding in your hand, but you'll find much, much more ... through the SF Gateway.

www.sfgateway.com

INTRODUCTION
from The Encyclopedia of Science Fiction

Lucius Shepard (1943–2014) was a US author about the discovery of whose first appearances in print there was some initial confusion. Only around 1995 was it discovered that he was the credited author of four stories and four articles in *Collins Magazine* (variously retitled *Collins, the Magazine to Grow Up With* and *Collins Young Elizabethan*) between 1952 and 1955, the first actual piece of fiction being "Camp Greenville" (January 1953 *Collins, the Magazine to Grow Up With*), where he is listed (accurately) as being nine years old. Some confusion was later caused by the claim that a family member may have written and placed these stories under Shepard's name, even though their innate competence, and their clear prefigurations of Shepard's adult voice, make it perfectly plausible that they were in fact essentially written by a precocious child between the ages of nine and twelve. Making the picture even murkier, Shepard himself preferred to claim (or not bother to deny) a birth date of 1947, but his actual birth in 1943 (which fits the *Collins* statement) has been confirmed by the 1945 census in Florida, where his parents then lived, and by the US Public Records Office record of his 1993 residence in Seattle, Washington. His first acknowledged work was poetry, and his first book was a poem, *Cantata of Death, Weakmind & Generation* (1967), whose rhetorical gumption tends to drown content.

Shepard began to publish adult prose fiction of genre interest only with "The Taylorsville Reconstruction" for *Universe 13* (1983) edited by Terry Carr, assembled with other early work as *Skull City and Other Lost Stories* (2008). Between the mid-1960s and the beginning of the 1980s, he had lived in various parts of the world, travelled widely, became – according to his testimony – marginally and incompetently involved in the fringes of the international drug trade, and in about 1972 started a rock band which went through various incarnations over the following years. Some of the experiences of this long apprenticeship are directly reflected in stories like "A Spanish Lesson" (1985); but the abiding sense of authority generated by all his best work depends upon the born exile's passionate fixation on place. It is no accident that – aside from the Latin American Magic-Realist tradition whose influence upon him is often suggested – the writer whom Shepard seems at times most to resemble is Joseph Conrad, for both authors respond to the places of the world with imaginative avarice and a hallucinated intensity of portrayal;

both create deeply alienated protagonists whose displacement from the venues in which they live generates constant ironies and regrets; and both tend to subordinate mundane resolutions of plot to moments of death-like Transcendence characteristic of Horror in SF.

Kalimantan (1990) evokes, for instance, Conrad himself as well as Graham Greene in a dark quest tale whose structure and pacing directly homage *Heart of Darkness* (1899); Shepard sets the action in Borneo and incorporates at its centre a not altogether convincing transference to an SF Alternate History. *Kalimantan* is typical of his mature work, and overflows any normal or necessary description of an SF text. The Dragon Griaule sequence – comprising "The Man Who Painted the Dragon Griaule" (1984), *The Scalehunter's Beautiful Daughter* (1988), *The Father of Stones* (1988), *Liar's House* (2004) and *The Taborin Scale: A Novella of the Dragon Griaule* (2010), all assembled, along with the novel-length "The Skull", as *The Dragon Griaule* (2012), similarly embeds an undeveloped SF premise, for it may be that the immense dragon Griaule is an Alien from another planet; what seems to have been the sequence's final instalment, the posthumous *Beautiful Blood* (2014), neither affirms nor denies that premise. But the all-encompassing dragon just as closely resembles the eponymous City in William Carlos Williams's *Patterson* (1946–1958); and in the end any SF implications are drowned out in a fantasy narrative whose claustrophobic intricacies are as entangling as the town of Macombo depicted in Gabriel García Márquez's *One Hundred Years of Solitude* (1967). In this land of darkness and fixity, using storylines primarily to expose an extraordinarily rich thematic compost, Shepard created a series of parables in which human Arts can reach fruition solely through a Transcendence that, like the dragon's itself, may be indistinguishable from death.

Shepard's first full-length novel was *Green Eyes* (1984) [see below]; his second novel, *Life During Wartime* (1987), similarly embeds SF elements – a Near Future setting, advanced forms of Drug manipulation – into a Latin American venue which, essentially, absorbs these elements into a horrified, dense presentation of a Vietnam War conducted, this time, in the Western Hemisphere. "R&R" (1986), which was published previously and which won a Nebula Award, shapes the first part of the book, and a hallucinated, obsessed journey into the heart of darkness in search of some underlying transformation dominates its last sections. A later novella, *Aztechs* (2003), is set in the same general universe: America and Mexico are now separated by a laser fence; the Artificial Intelligence that runs the mysterious AZTECH corporation seems to be laying the groundwork for its becoming a Messiah figure, perhaps as the head of something like a Cargo Cult; but as with many later Shepard narratives, the ending is abrupt and inconclusive. His third full-length tale, *The Golden* (1993), which won a Locus Award, is a Vampire story, set in a vast edifice specifically modelled on Piranesi's *Carceri d'Invenzione* ["Imaginary Prisons"] (1749); the final pages of the story, set in sunlight as the surviving vampires head for Asia, are compellingly surreal.

Many of Shepard's works fall short in length, though not intensity, of full-length novels; it is at points a difficult judgement call to distinguish one category from the other, but any attempt to do so lends point to the argument that he was most comfortable with the shorter form; his later publishing career, in which several of these works were given separate release, confirms the sense that the novella was central to his work. Earlier long tales of interest are assembled with shorter fiction in *The Jaguar Hunter* (1987) [see below], *The Ends of the Earth* (1991) and *Barnacle Bill the Spacer and Other Stories* (1997). Later major collections – including *Trujillo and Other Stories* (2004), *Dagger Key and Other Stories* (2007) and *Five Autobiographies and a Fiction* (2013), the latter containing only fiction despite the title – also incorporate longer works, but most of Shepard's novellas were by now appearing as separate volumes. They rank among the finest Fabulations composed by an American writer in recent years, and in addition to the awards mentioned above they were variously honoured: a 1993 Hugo Best Novella Award for "Barnacle Bill the Spacer" (1992), a Locus Award for "Radiant Green Star" (2000) and a Shirley Jackson Award for *Vacancy* (2009) [see below]. Most of them are not SF, except for *Kalimantan* and *Aztechs*, both discussed above, though *Viator* (2004; expanded as *Viator Plus* 2010) is a study in Perception housed in a Pocket Universe-like stranded ship, told with an effect of driven Equipoise that marks almost all his best work. Shepard clearly felt comfortable with SF; and the genre benefited from the publication of a dozen tales which assimilate SF into a wider imaginative world; but certainly, despite his aesthetic influence on the genre in the years since his explosive debut (for which he received a John W. Campbell Award in 1985), Shepard could best be described as a writer of Fantastika. There is some sense that his large oeuvre has gone relatively unrecognized; there is certainly no question that his work has received insufficient attention from academic critics, perhaps because its explosive ambiguities of texture and narrative do not paraphrase well. As with other major writers whose work is not easily reducible to thematic studies, including Jack Vance and Gene Wolfe, this lack of attention travesties the field as a whole.

In his final decades, Shepard began to publish considerable non-fiction, most notably a regular column on SF Cinema for *The Magazine of Fantasy and Science Fiction*, beginning with the December 2000 issue of that journal and continuing until the September-October 2013 issue; his views about American cinema, and American culture in general, were conveyed there with jeremiad intensity. Much of this material, and other work, was assembled as *Weapons of Mass Seduction: Film Reviews and Other Ravings* (coll 2005);

but despite the importance of this work, it pales beside the transformative intensity of his fiction. In any purely literary sense, Shepard was one of the two or three finest writers ever to work in the field.

The first text presented here, *Green Eyes* (1984), easily stands comparison with other first novels published in 1984 as the famous Ace Specials series edited by Terry Carr; they include William Gibson's *Neuromancer*, Kim Stanley Robinson's *Wild Shore* and Howard Waldrop's *Them Bones*. The storyline is instantly entangled in the clutches of a jungle-like world, the American Deep South where a research organization has successfully created Zombies by injecting cadavers with bacteria from a graveyard. As an SF premise, this is unremarkable; but Shepard presents the transformation of dead bodies into representative human archetypes, and the escape of one of them into bayou country, with a gripping closeness of touch; the almost synaesthesiacal epiphany at the end, already characteristic of his work, also tests true.

The Jaguar Hunter (1987) brings together 13 prime examples of Shepard's astounding early production – almost 30 stories, some of considerable length, in four years – including "The Man Who Painted the Dragon Griaule" (1984), the self-contained beginning of the Griaule sequence, a teaser for anyone who wishes to explore that visceral world. Other stories include three set in Viet Nam, which haunt the mind with history, and four in South America, where monsters and artefacts breed in the heart of the heart of the country. Every story, no matter how distant from normal reality, reads as though its author had been there; and was reporting back from the front. Some of the news is bad. Some of the news makes us look again at the world.

The final story here presented is the award-winning *Vacancy* (2009), a kind of ghost story, though the ghost is called (or comes on her own hook) from Malaysia, and the American she visits turns out to be harrowed by memories of a life (or maybe lives in a dozen worlds) anything but vacant. In the end, there is no escape. But this is what Shepard tells us always, everywhere in his vast oeuvre: that what we do adds up. Nothing else really matters: dreams, evasions, lies. As with all of his best tales, the end of *Vacancy* is life.

For a more detailed version of the above, see Lucius Shepard's author entry in *The Encyclopedia of Science Fiction*: http://sf-encyclopedia.com/entry/shepard_lucius

Some terms above are capitalised when they would not normally be so rendered; this indicates that the terms represent discrete entries in *The Encyclopedia of Science Fiction*.

GREEN EYES

This book is for my Mother
For all the usual and well-deserved reasons,
And for Kim,
for reasons not so usual.

Thanks to Marta Randall for shelter, to Mary Steedly for fast fingers, to Laura Scroggins for the bacteria, to James Wold for lots of stuff, and especially to Terry for the opportunity.

I have no more desire to express
The old relationships of love fulfilled
Or stultified, capacity for pain,
Nor to say gracefully all that poets have said
Of one or other of the old compulsions.
For now the times are gathered for confession.

                                                          Alun Lewis

BIAP Interview No 1251
Host Name: Paul Pelizzarro
BIAP Name: Frank Juskit
Length of Interview: fifty-seven minutes
Interpretation: None. See video.
Comments/Personal Reactions/Other: I am, as usual, both saddened by the death and repelled by the patient's actions, by my dutiful response; in fact, by the nature of the work: the tricks we play and the patients themselves, comic in their weakness, horrible in their desire for life and the flash of ardor that ends them ... Green fireballs lodged in their eye sockets, their minds going nova with the joy of a lifetime crammed into a few minutes. Still, I find that the patients in their compressed, excited states are far more interesting than any of my acquaintances, and I believe that even relative failures such as Mr Juskit would – had they lived a full span at this accelerated pace – have accomplished a great deal more than they have related. Their repellent aspects, in my opinion, are outweighed by the intensity of their expression. For this reason I wish to withdraw my resignation tendered yesterday, 24 October 1986.

Therapist's Signature: *Jocundra Verret*

Staff Evaluation: *Let's assign Verret to a slow-burner as soon as possible, but not just the first one that comes along. I'd like to see a photograph and data sheet on each new slow-burner, and from that material I'll make an appropriate selection.*

A. Edman

CHAPTER 1

From *Conjure Men: My Work With Ezawa at Tulane*
by Anthony Edman, MD, PhD.

… I did not see my first 'zombie' until my second day at Tulane when Ezawa permitted me to witness an interview. He ushered me into a cubicle occupied by several folding chairs and switched on a two-way mirror. The room beyond the mirror was decorated in the style of a turn-of-the-century bordello: red velvet chairs and sofa perched on clawed feet, their walnut frames carved into filigree; brass urns holding peacock plumes; burgundy drapes and maroon-striped wallpaper; a branching chandelier upheld by a spider of black iron. The light was as bright as a photographer's stage. Though 'zombies' – at least the short-termers – do not see clearly until the end, they react to the color and the glare, and ultimately the decor serves to amplify the therapist's persuasive powers.

In passing, I should mention that I considered the lack of a suitable chair within the observation cubicle a personal affront. Being a compactly built man himself, it might be assumed Ezawa had simply committed an oversight and not taken my girth into account; but I cannot accept the proposal that this meticulous and polite gentleman would overlook any detail unless by design. He had exerted all his influence to block my approval as psychiatric chief of the project, considering my approach too radical, and I believe he enjoyed watching me perch with one ham on, the other off, for the better part of an hour. Truthfully, though, what I was to see beyond the mirror banished all thought of my discomfort, and had it been necessary to balance on a shooting stick and peer between the shoulders of a crowd, I would still have felt myself privileged.

The therapist, Jocundra Verret, sat on the edge of the sofa, her hands folded in her lap. She was a shade under six feet tall, slender, impassively beautiful (therapists are chosen, in part, on the basis of physical attractiveness), and dressed in a nurse's white tunic and slacks. She looked younger than her twenty-five years, long-limbed, solemn and large-eyed. Dark brown hair wound through by strands of gold fell to her shoulders, and her skin had the pale olive cast of a Renaissance figure. The most notable feature of her appearance, though, was the extent of her makeup. Lipstick, eyeliner and mascara had been applied so as to transform her face into an exotic mask, one which evoked the symmetry of design upon a butterfly's wing. This gilding the lily was an essential part of the therapist's visual presentation, and similar makeup was utilized during the early stages of a slow-burner's existence, gradually being minimized as their perceptions sharpened.

Jocundra's movements were graceful and unhurried, and her expressions developed slowly into distant smiles and contemplative frowns, giving the impression of a calm and controlled personality. I later learned in my work with her that this impression was half a lie. Indeed, she viewed the world as a system of orderly processes through which one must maneuver by reducing experience to its logical minimum and analyzing it; but her logical bias, her sense of orderliness, her passivity in engaging life – these traits were counterbalanced by a deep romantic strain which caused her to be high-strung and, as has been publicized, occasioned her to acts of recklessness.

I asked Ezawa whether it was difficult to recruit therapists, and he replied that though the combination of physical beauty, lack of squeamishness, and a scientific background was uncommon, the turnover rate was low and there was a waiting list of applicants. I further asked if he had observed a general similarity of history or personality among the therapists, and he said with a trace of embarrassment that many had a history of checkered academic careers and interest in the occult. Jocundra was fairly typical in this regard. She had done undergraduate work in physics, switched to anthropology in graduate school, and had been involved in a study of voodoo cults before joining the project. Ezawa, for whom the truth appeared to consist of microbiological data, exhibited little interest in the psychological puzzles posed by our subjects, none whatsoever in the therapists, and constantly sought to downplay the mysterious aspects of the project. In light of this, I found curious his use of the term 'zombie' rather than the official 'Bacterially Induced Artificial Personality' or its acronym: it signalled some backsliding from his position of scientific rigor.

'I must admit,' he said, 'the process has elements in common with a voodoo recipe. We *do* isolate the bacteria from dirt taken from the old slave graveyards, but that's simply because of the biodegradable coffins ... They permit the decomposing tissues to interact with microorganisms in the soil.'

Once the bacteria was isolated, Ezawa explained, a DNA extract from goat's rue was introduced into the growth medium and the bacteria was then induced to take up chromosomes and DNA fragments from the goat's rue, thereby mediating recombination between the two types of DNA. The resultant strain was injected via a heart pump into the cerebellum and temporal lobes of a corpse less than an hour dead, whereupon the bacteria began pre-transcriptional processing of the corpse's genetic complement, bringing the body sufficiently alive so it could begin the post-transcriptional processing. Twenty-four hours after injection the 'zombie' was ready for the therapist.

An orderly entered the room beyond the mirror, pushing a pale, heavy-set man in a wheelchair: jowly, middle-aged, with receding brown hair and a five o'clock shadow. He wore a green hospital gown. The orderly assisted him onto the sofa, and the man struggled feebly to rise, kicking aside the coffee table. His name, I saw from Ezawa's clipboard, had been Paul Pelizzarro, a vagrant, though he would soon begin to recall a different name, a different history. Random fragments of the transforming DNA in the recombinant bacteria coded for an entirely new personality, or so Ezawa expressed it. When I suggested that the personality might not be entirely new, that we might be observing wish-fulfilment on the cellular level, he gave me a startled look, as if suddenly suspecting I was addled – or so I characterized it at the time, though in retrospect it is clear he knew far more than I about the nature of our subjects and could not possibly have been surprised by my obvious interpretation. Perhaps he was simply reacting to my perspicacity.

Pelizzarro sat unmoving, head resting on his shoulder, eyes dull, mouth open. On being revivified they are all intractable and lax, blank slates, much like the zombies of folklore. They are told by the orderly that they have died and been brought back to life by means of an experimental process, and that he is taking them to someone who will help. It is the therapist's job to make the 'zombie' want to please her – or him – by stimulating a sexual response, initiating a dependency.

'Naturally,' said Ezawa, 'the sexual response has the side effect of increasing acetylcholine and norepenephrin production at the neuromuscular junctions ... improves the motor control.' He switched on the audio. The orderly had left, and the interview had already begun.

Jocundra stood in front of the 'zombie,' swaying her hips like a starlet tempting a producer.

'Why won't you talk?' she asked.

He rolled his head from side to side, pushed at the cushions, still too weak to stand. When his hand impacted with the plush of the sofa, his breath came out in a soft grunt.

Jocundra stepped behind him and trailed her fingers along his neck, stimulating the spinal nerves. He froze, his head cocked as if listening to an ominous whisper; his eyes flicked back and forth. He seemed terrified. Jocundra moved around the sofa and posed before him once again.

'Do you remember your death?' she asked coldly. 'Or anything afterwards?'

The 'zombie' floundered, flailed his arms; his lips drew back, revealing rows of perfect white teeth, small and feminine-looking in contrast to his fleshiness. 'No!' His voice was choked. 'No! God, I ... I don't!'

'Maybe I should just leave. You don't seem to want to talk.'

'Please ... don't.' He lifted his hand, then let it fall on to the cushion.

I was to learn that each therapist employed a distinctive method of relating to the 'zombies', but – perhaps only because Jocundra was the first therapist I observed – I have never found another style more compelling, more illustrative of the essential myth-construct at the heart of the therapist-'zombie' relationship. I have mentioned that her movements were graceful and unhurried under normal conditions; when working, however, they grew elegant and mesmerizing, as if she were displaying invisible veils, and I was reminded of the gestures of a Balinese dancer. The 'zombie', then, would perceive her initially as a blurred silhouette, a shadowy figure at the centre of a dim candleflame, an unknown goddess weaving a spell to attract his eye until, at last, his vision cleared and he saw her there before him, taken human form. Jocundra utilized the classic feminine tactic of approach and avoidance to augment her visual and tactile presentation, and, in this particular interview, once the 'zombie' had begged her not to leave, she sat beside him on the sofa and took his hand.

'What's your name?' she asked.

He appeared to be stunned by the question, but after several seconds he answered, 'Frank. Frank Juskit.' He peered at her, searching for her reaction, and managed a smile. 'I was a … a salesman.'

'What sort of salesman? My uncle's a salesman, too.'

'Oh, I was just an old horse trader,' he said, assuming a character at once pompous and self-deprecating. A mid-western accent nagged at his vowels, becoming more acute as he grew more involved in telling his story. 'At the end, there, I didn't do much selling. Just kept an eye on the books. But I've sold franchises and factories, swampland and sea coasts. I've worked land contracts and mortgages and tract developments. Hell, I've sold everything every which way and backwards!'

'Real estate?'

'Yes, ma'am! Both real and surreal!' He clapped his hands together and attempted a wink which, due to his lack of muscle control, came off as a grotesque leer. 'And if I couldn't sell it, I bought it! I turned landfills into shopping malls, tree-lined suburbs into neon wastes. I swallowed quiet suburbs and shat out industrial parks. I was the evil genius of the board room! I sharked through the world with blood on my teeth and a notary's seal for a left eye! And when I get down to Hell, I'll sell the devil two bedrooms and a bath overlooking the Promised Land and take over the goddamned place myself …'

Ezawa has labeled these outbursts 'ecstatic confessions,' but I find the term inexact and prefer 'life story.' Because the 'zombie's' senses are dim, his motor control limited, he must compress the variety of his synthesized experience into a communicative package in order fully to realize himself. The result is a compact symbolic structure, one summing up a lifetime of creative impulse: a life story.

'This is typical,' said Ezawa. 'I doubt we'll learn anything of value. Do you see the eyes?'

I looked. There were flickers of phosphorescent green in the irises, visible to me at a distance of ten feet; they were faint at first, but quickly increased in frequency and brilliance.

'It's the impingement of the bacteria on the optic nerve,' said Ezawa. 'They're bioluminescent. When you see it you know the end's near. Except in the case of the slow-burners, of course. Their brains retard the entire process. We have one out at Shadows who's been showing green for two months.'

At Jocundra's questioning, Mr Juskit – I came to think of him by his assumed name, convinced by the assurance of his memories – detailed a final illness which led to a death he had previously failed to remember. The flickerings in his eyes intensified, glowing like swampfire, blossoming into green stars, and he made the fisted gestures of a company president exhorting his sales force. As he gained control of his muscles, he seemed more and more the salesman, the Napoleon of the board room, the glib, nattering little man born of the union between a vagrant and the bacterial DNA. When I had first seen him in the room beyond the mirror, dazed, dull, barely conscious, I had been struck by the perversity of the situation: an unprepossessing, half-dead man was being danced for by a lovely woman in a nurse's uniform, all within a gaudy room which might have been the private salon in a high class whorehouse. The scene embodied a hallucinated sexuality. But now there was a natural air to the proceedings, a rightness; I could not imagine any room being made unnatural by Mr Juskit's presence. He dominated his surroundings, commanding my attention, and I saw that Jocundra, too, was no longer weaving her web of elegant motion, no longer the temptress; she leaned toward him, intent upon his words, hands folded in her lap, attentive as would be a dutiful wife or mistress.

Mr Juskit began to address her as 'babe,' touching her often, and, eventually, asked her to remove her tunic. 'Take it off, babe,' he said with contagious jollity, 'and lemme see them puppies.' So convinced was I of his right to ask this of her, of its propriety in terms of their relationship, I was not taken aback when she stood, undid her buttons and let the tunic drop onto her arms. She lowered her eyes in a submissive pose. Mr Juskit pushed himself off the sofa, his hospital gown giving evidence of his extreme arousal, and staggered toward her, a step, arms outstretched and rigid, eyes burning a cometary green. Jocundra leapt aside as he fell to the floor, face downward. Tremors shook him for nearly half a minute, but he was dead long before they ceased.

Ezawa opaqued the mirror. I had been leaning forward, gripping the edge of the mirror, and I believe I stared wildly at him. Seeing my agitation, no doubt thinking it the product of disgust or some allied emotion, he said, 'It frequently ends that way. The initial sexual response governs them, and during the final burst of vitality they commonly attempt to embrace the therapist or ... ask favors.' He shrugged. 'Since it's their last request, the therapists usually comply.'

But I was not disgusted, not horrified; instead I was stunned by the sudden extinction of what had seemed a dynamic imperative for the last half hour or thereabouts: Mr Juskit's existence. It was unthinkable that he had so abruptly ceased to be. And then, as I gained a more speculative distance from the events, I began to understand what I had witnessed, its mythic proportions. A beautiful woman, both Eve and Delilah, had called a man back from the dead, lured him into vivid expression, coaxed him to strive for her and tell his secrets, to live in a furious rush of moments and die one breath short of reward, reaching out to her. The 'zombie'-therapist relationship, I realized, made possible a new depth of scrutiny into the complete range of male-female interactions; I was eager to take up residence at Shadows and begin my investigations of the slow-burners. *They* were the heart of the project! The scene I had just witnessed – the birth, life and death of Frank Juskit while in the company of Jocundra Verret – had transmitted an archetypal potency, like the illustration on a tarot trump come to life; and though I had not yet met Hilmer Magnusson or Donnell Harrison, I believe at that moment I anticipated their miraculous advent.

CHAPTER 2

BIAP Interview No 1251
Host Name: Paul Pelizzarro
BIAP Name: Frank Juskit
Length of Interview: fifty-seven minutes
Interpretation: None. See video.
Comments/Personal Reactions/Other: I am, as usual, both saddened by the death and repelled by the patient's actions, by my dutiful response; in fact, by the nature of the work: the tricks we play and the patients themselves, comic in their weakness, horrible in their desire for life and the flash of ardor that ends them ... Green fireballs lodged in their eye sockets, their minds going nova with the joy of a lifetime crammed into a few minutes (that is how I imagine it, though I'm certain Dr Ezawa will quarrel with such an unscientific appraisal). I have long since become accustomed to the slight difference in body temperature and the other salient differences between the patients and the ordinary run of humanity, but I doubt I will ever grow callous enough to be unaffected by those final moments.

At times like these I realize how much my work has distanced me from friends and family. Still, I find that the patients in their compressed, excited states are far more interesting than any of my acquaintances, and I believe that even relative failures such as Mr Juskit would – had they lived a full span at this accelerated pace – have accomplished a great deal more than they have related. Their repellent aspects, in my opinion, are outweighed by the intensity of their expression. For this reason I wish to withdraw my resignation tendered yesterday, 24 October 1986.

Therapist's Signature: *Jocundra Verret*

Staff Evaluation: *Let's assign Verret to a slow-burner as soon as possible, but not just the first one that comes along. I'd like to see a photograph and data sheet on each new slow-burner, and from that material I'll make an appropriate selection.*

A. Edman

CHAPTER 3

10 February 1987

The road to Shadows was unmarked, or rather the marker – an old metal Grapette sign – had been overgrown by a crepe myrtle, and a live oak branch, its bark flecked with blue-green scale, had cracked off the trunk and fallen across the bush, veiling it in leaf spray and hanks of Spanish moss. But Jocundra caught a glint of metal as she passed and slammed on the brakes. The van fishtailed and slewed onto the shoulder, and the man beside her was thrown forward against the safety harness. His head bounced on the back of the seat, then he let it loll toward her and frowned.

'I'm sorry,' she said. 'These brakes are awful. Are you all right?' She touched his leg in sympathy and felt the muscles jump.

The silence between them sang with tension. Crickets sawed, a jay screamed, the thickets seethed and hissed in a sudden breeze, and all the sharp sounds of life seemed to be registering the process of his hostility toward her. His frown softened to a reproving gaze and he turned away, staring out at the clouds of white dust settling around the van.

'We should be there in another half hour,' she said. 'And then I'll fix us some lunch.'

He sighed but didn't comment.

Heat rippled off the tops of the bushes, and every surface Jocundra touched was slippery with her sweat. A mosquito whined in her ear; peevish, she slapped at it and blew a strand of hair from her eyes. She backed up, setting his head bouncing again, and headed down a gravel track whose entrance was so choked with vegetation that vines trailed across the windshield, and twigs bearing clusters of yellow-tipped leaves tattered at the side vent and swatted her elbow. Rows of live oaks arched overhead and the road was in deep shade, bridged by irregular patches of sunlight falling through rents in the canopy. Once it had been a grand concourse traveled by gleaming carriages, fine ladies and fancy gentlemen, but now it was potholed, ferns grew in the wheel ruts, and the anonymous blue vans of the project were its sole traffic.

The potholes forced her to drive slowly, but she could hardly wait to reach Shadows and hand him over to the orderlies. Maybe an hour or so of being alone would make him more amiable. She leaned forward, plucking her dress away from her damp skin, and glanced at him. He just stared out the window, his fingers twitching in his lap. The brown suit they had issued him at Tulane was too short in the arms, exposing knobbly wrists, and when she had first seen him wearing it she had thought of the teenage boys from her home town dressed in their ill-fitting Sunday best, waiting for the army bus to carry them off to no good future. He was much older, nearly thirty, but he had the witchy look that bayou men often presented: hollow-cheeked, long-nosed, sharp-chinned, with lank black hair hanging ragged over his collar. Not handsome, but not ugly either. Large hazel eyes acted to plane down his features and gave him a sad, ardent look such as you might find in an Old Master's rendering of a saint about to die of wounds gotten for the love of Christ. His irises were not yet showing a trace of green.

'You know, I was born about forty miles from here,' she said, embarrassed by the artificial sunniness in her voice. 'Over on Bayou Teche. It's beautiful there. Herons and cypresses and old plantation homes like Shadows …'

'I don't want to talk.' His voice was weak but full of venom; he kept his eyes turned toward the window.

'Why are you so angry?' She put her hand on his arm, probing the hollow of his elbow. 'I'm just trying to be friendly.'

He looked at her, eyes wide, confused, and she wondered how it would be, her own flesh cool and numb, and the fingers of a more vital creature firing the nerves, sending charges into the midnight places of the brain. She pictured mental lightnings striking down in a landscape of eroded thoughts, sparking new life, new memories; but it would be nothing so dramatic. Things dawned slowly upon them. Every sensation, it seemed, held for them a clue to their essential wrongness, their lack of true relation to the world, and they struggled to arrange the murky shapes and unfamiliar smells and ringing voices into structures which would support them.

Breath whistled in his throat, but he didn't speak; he leaned back and closed his eyes.

His name – his 'zombie' name – was Donnell Harrison, though the body had once hosted the dreams and memories of Steven Mears, a carnival worker dead of alcohol poisoning at the age of twenty-nine. He did not remember Mears' life, however; he remembered having been a poet and living with his wife Jean in a mountain cabin. 'The air was clarity,' he had said. 'The rain fell like peace.' Almost singing the phrases, he had told her how his wife had died, crushed beneath a roofbeam during a storm. His hand had clawed at the armrest of the sofa as he strained to express the emotion swelling in him, and Jocundra had imagined that his skin contained not flesh and blood, but was tightly stretched over a cool darkness lit by a tendril of green fog, the magical analogue of a tungsten filament at the center of a light bulb. She had listened to the tapes so often since the initial interview that she had memorized his final outburst.

'Old men, old liars drowsy with supper and the hearth, their minds grazing on some slope downward of illusion into death, they'll tell you that the wild north king visits the high country disguised as a wind, blowing up spectacles of lightning-flash and hosannas of cloud. But this storm was animal, a wave of black animal breath bigger than the beginning. All its elements infected the land, making it writhe like the skin of a flea-infested dog, setting St Elmo's fire to glimmer in the pinetops, decaying the stones into thunder, rotting the principles of ordinary day until the light caught fire and roared ...'

Then, at the realization of loss, understanding the magnitude of the tragedy he had invented for himself, he had broken off his life story and sunk into a depression. Jocundra had not been able to rouse him. 'Slow-burners always go through a fugue,' Edman had told her. 'It's as if they realize they're in for the long haul and better get their act together, slow their pace, reduce their intensity. Don't worry. Sooner or later he'll come around.' But Jocundra was not sure she believed Edman; all his advice to her reeked of bedside manner, benign assurances.

The potholes became so wide she had to ease down into them and use the four-wheel drive to climb out. The live oaks thinned and swamp country began. Stretches of black, earth-steeped water were ranked by gaunt cypresses, their moss-bearded top branches resembling the rotted crosstrees of a pirate fleet mouldering in the shallows. Gnats blurred the air above a scaly log; a scum of rust-colored bubbles clung to the shoreline reeds. It was dead-still, desolate, but it was home ground to Jocundra, and its stillness awakened in her a compatible stillness, acting upon her tension like a cold compress applied to a fevered brow. She pointed out the landmark sights to Donnell: a wrinkle in the water signaling the presence of a snake, dark nests in the cypress tops, a hawk circling over a thicketed island. Prodded by her touch, he lifted his head and stared, using – she knew – some vague shape or color of what he saw to flesh out his life story, adding hawks or a pattern of cloud to the sky above his mountain cabin.

The swamp gave out into palmetto glades and acacia, stands of bamboo, insects whirling in shafts of sunlight, and they came to an ironwork gate set into a masonry wall. A tarpaper shack stood beside it. The security guard logged their arrival on his clipboard. 'Y'all have a nice day,' he said, winking at Jocundra as if he knew nice days were not in the cards.

The grounds were gloomy and gently rolling. A flagstone path bordered with ferns and azalea meandered among enchanted-looking oaks, which fountained up at regular intervals. They overspread the lawn, casting a dark green shade upon the stone benches beneath them; thin beams of sun penetrated to the grass as a scatter of gold coins. And at the center of the gloom, glowing softly like the source of the enchantment, was a two-story house of rose-colored brick with white trim and fluted columns across the front. A faceted glass dome bulged from the midpoint of its gabled roof. Two orderlies hustled down the steps as Jocundra pulled up and helped Donnell into his wheelchair.

'If you'll take Mr Harrison to the suite,' she said, 'I'll see he gets checked in.' And paying no attention to Donnell's alarmed reaction, she walked out along the drive.

From the bench nearest the gate, the brightness of the brick and trim made the house appear to be rippling against the gloom, as if while she had been walking it had reverted to its true form – a black castle, a gingerbread house – and in turning back she had caught it unawares. It was an unlikely place for scientific work, though its gothic atmosphere bolstered the image Edman had fostered; he had suggested that Shadows would be an Experience, spoken about it in terms suited to the promotion of a human potential group rather than demystifying it as he usually did any hint of the occult. She had talked to other therapists who had been at Shadows, but most had seemed traumatized, unwilling to discuss it. Even the microbiologists had been hazy at her briefing, saying they knew little about the new strain of bacteria with which Donnell had been injected. 'He'll be longer lived,' Ezawa had said. 'Better motor control, sharper senses. Watch his visual development especially, and keep in mind he won't be easy to fool. He's no short-termer.'

No doubt about that, she thought, as she began strolling back to the house. Before lapsing into his depression, Donnell had displayed a subtle good humor, a joyful appreciation of life apparently grounded in a realistic assessment of its pleasures and pains, this far different from the short-termers: cloudy, grotesque creatures who clutched and stared until you feared you would burn up under the kindling glare of their eyes. They had many of the qualities of the zombies in her father's lurid bedtime stories: dazed, ragged men and women stumbling through plantation fields at midnight, penned in windowless cabins fifty or more to a room, stinking, shuffling, afraid to touch each other, sustained on water and unsalted bread. 'They ever get a taste of salt,' her father had said, 'they'll head straight for the buryin' ground and try to claw their way back into Hell.' Sometimes the straw boss would send them after runaway slaves, and the slave would scramble through the swamp, eyes rolling and heart near to bursting, hearing the splash of the zombie's footsteps behind him or seeing its shadow rear up from the weird fogs wreathing the cypress, reaching for him with rotting fingers and arms rigid as gibbets. Let the slave escape, however, and the zombie would wander on, singlemindedly searching until years later – because a zombie lives as long as the binding magic holds; even if its flesh disintegrates the particles still incorporate the spirit – maybe a hundred years later, the image of its quarry grown so amorphous that it would react to any vaguely human form, the zombie spots a lighted window in a house on the bayou and is drawn by the scent of blood ... Her father had banged the bottom of the bed, jumped up in mock terror, and she had lain awake for hours, shivering, seeing the tortured faces of zombies in the grain of the ceiling boards.

But there was no such witchery involved with Donnell, she thought; or if there was, then it was witchery of an intensely human sort.

She had a moment of nervousness at the door; her stomach grew fluttery, as if crossing the threshold constituted a spiritual commitment, but she laughed at herself and pushed on in. No one was in sight. The foyer faced large cream-colored double doors and opened onto a hallway; the walls were painted pale peach, and the doorways ranging them were framed with intricate molding. Ferns splashed from squat brass urns set between them. Church quiet, with the pious, sedated air common to sickrooms and funeral homes.

'Jocundra!' A lazy, honeysuckle voice.

From the opposite end of the hall, a slim ash-blonde girl in hospital whites came toward her, giving a cutesy wave. Laura Petit. She had been an anomaly among the therapists at Tulane, constantly encouraging group activities, parties, dinners, whereas most of them had been wholly involved with the patients. Laura punctuated her sentences with breathy gasps; she batted her eyes and fluttered her hands when she laughed. The entire repertoire of her mannerisms was testimony to filmic generations of inept actresses playing Southern belles as shallow, bubbly nymphs with no head for anything other than fried chicken recipes and lace tatting. But despite this, despite the fact she considered the patients 'gross,' she was an excellent therapist. She seemed to be one of those people to whom emotional attachment is an alien concept, and who learn to extract a surrogate emotionality from manipulating friends and colleagues, and – in this case – her patients.

'That must have been yours they just wheeled in,' she said, embracing Jocundra.

'Yes.' Jocundra accepted a peck on the cheek and disengaged.

'Better watch yourself, hon! He's not too bad lookin' for a corpse.' Laura flashed her Most Popular smile. 'How you doin'?'

'I should check in ...'

'Oh, you can see Edman when he makes his rounds. We're real informal here. Come on, now.' She tugged at Jocundra's arm. 'I'll introduce you to Magnusson.'

Jocundra hung back. 'Is it all right?'

'Don't be shy, hon! You want to see how your boy's goin' to turn out, don't you?'

As they walked, Laura filled her in about Magnusson, pretending genuine interest in his work, but that was camouflage, a framework allowing her to boast of her own triumph, to explain how she had midwifed the miracle. Dr Hilmer Magnusson had been their initial success with the new strain: the body of a John Doe derelict now hosting the personality of a medical researcher who, less than a month after his injection, had casually handed them a cure for muscular dystrophy: a cure which had proved ninety-five percent effective in limited testing.

'One day,' said Laura, her voice rising at the end of each phrase, turning them into expressions of incredulity, 'he asked me for his Johns Hopkins paper, the one he remembered first presentin' the process in. Well, I didn't know *what* he was talkin' about, but I played along and told him I'd send for it. Anyway, he finally got impatient and started workin' without it, complainin' that his memory wasn't what it used to be. It was incredible!'

Things, Jocundra observed, had a way of falling into place for Laura. Doors opened for her professionally, attractive men ditched their girlfriends and came in pursuit, and now Magnusson had produced a miracle cure. It was as if she were connected by fine wires to everything in her environment, and when she yanked everything toppled, permitting her passage toward some goal. The question was: were her manipulative skills intellectually founded, or had she simply been gifted with dumb luck as compensation for her lack of emotionality? It was hard to believe that anyone of intelligence could erect such a false front and not know it was transparent.

Slashes of sunlight fell from louvred shutters onto the carpet, but otherwise Magnusson's room was dark, suffused by an odor of bay rum and urine. At first Jocundra could see nothing; then a pair of glowing eyes blinked open against the far wall. His pupils had shrunk to pinpricks; his irises flared green and were laced with striations of more brilliant green, which brightened and faded. The glow illuminated a portion of his face, seamed cheeks tattooed with broken veins and a bony beak of a nose. His wheelchair hissed on the carpet, coming close, and she saw that he was an old, old man, his facial muscles so withered that his skull looked melted and misshapen.

Laura introduced them.

'Jocundra. Such a charming name.' Magnusson's voice was weak and hoarse and expressed little of his mood. Each syllable creaked in his throat like an ancient seal being pried up.

'It's Creole, sir.' She sat on the bed facing him. There were food stains on his bathrobe. 'My mother was part Creole.'

'Was?'

'Both my parents died several years ago. A fire. The police suspected my father had set it.'

Laura shot her a look of surprise, and Jocundra was surprised at herself. She never told anyone about the police report, and yet she had told Magnusson without the slightest hesitation.

He reached out and took her hand. His flesh was cool, dry, almost weightless, but his pulse surged. 'I commiserate,' he said. 'I know what it is to be alone.' He withdrew his hand and nodded absently. 'Rigmor, my great-grandmother, used to tell me that America was a land where no one ever need be alone. Said she'd had that realization when she stepped off the boat from Sweden and saw the mob thronging the docks. Of course she had no idea to what ends the Twentieth Century would come, the kinds of shallow relationships that would evolve as the family was annihilated by television, automobiles, the entire technological epidemic. She had her vision of families perched on packing crates. Irish, Poles, Italians, Arabs. Plump girls with dark-eyed babies, apple-cheeked young men in short-brimmed hats carrying their heritage in a sack. Strangers mingling, becoming lovers and companions. She never noticed that it all had changed.' Magnusson attempted an emphatic gesture, but the effect was of a palsied tremor. 'It's terrible! The petty alliances between people nowadays. Worse than loneliness. There's no trust, no commitment, no love. I'm so fortunate to have Laura.'

Laura beamed and clasped her hands at her waist, a pose both virtuous and triumphant. Magnusson studied the backs of his hands, as if considering their sad plight. Several of his fingers had been broken and left unset; the nail of his right thumb was missing, exposing a contused bulge of flesh. Jocundra was suddenly ashamed of her presence in the room.

'Perhaps it's just my damned Swedish morbidity,' said Magnusson out of the blue. 'I tried to kill myself once, you know. Slit my wrists. Damned fool youngster! I was discouraged by the rain and the state of the economy. Not much reason, you might think, for self-destruction, but I found it thoroughly oppressing at the time.'

'Well,' said Laura after an uncomfortable silence. 'We'll let you rest, Hilmer.' She laid her hand on the doorknob, but the old man spoke again.

'He'll find you out, Jocundra.'

'Sir?' She turned back to him.

'You operate on a paler principle than he, and he will find you out. But you're a healthy girl, even if a bit transparent. I can see it by your yellows and your blues.' He laughed, a hideous rasp which set him choking, and as he choked, he managed to say, 'Got your health, yes ...' When he regained control, his tone was one of amusement. 'I wish I could offer medical advice. Stay off the fried foods, take cold showers, or some such. But as far as I can see, and that's farther than most, you're in the pink. Awful image! If you were in the pink, you'd be quite ill.'

'What in the world are you talkin' about, Hilmer?' Laura's voice held a note of frustration.

'Oh, no!' Magnusson's bony orbits seemed to be crumbling away under the green glow of his eyes, as if they were nuggets of a rare element implanted in his skull, ravaging him. 'You're not going to pick my brain anymore. An old man needs his secrets, his little edge on the world as it recedes.'

'Ezawa thinks he might be seein' bioenergy ... auras.' Laura closed the door behind them and flexed the lacquered nails of her left hand as if they were blood-tipped claws. 'I'll get it out of him! He's becoming more and more aroused. If his body hadn't been so enervated to begin with, he'd already be chasin' me around the bed.'

Laura went down to the commissary to prepare Magnusson's lunch, and Jocundra, in no hurry to rejoin Donnell, wandered the hallway. Half of the rooms were untenanted, all furnished with mahogany antiques and the walls covered with the same pattern of wallpaper: an infancy of rosebud cottages and grapevines. Cards were set into brass mounts on the doors of the occupied rooms, and she read them as she idled along. Clarice Monroe. That would be the black girl, the one who believed herself to be a dancer and had taught herself to walk after only a few weeks. Marilyn Ramsburgh, Kline Lee French, Jack Richmond. Beneath each name was a coded entry revealing the specifics of treatment and the prognosis. There were two green dots after Magnusson's name, signifying the new strain; his current prognosis was for three months plus or minus a week. That meant Donnell would have eight or nine months unless his youthfulness further retarded the bacterial action. A long time to spend with anyone, longer than her marriage. The Thirty Weeks War, or so Charlie had called it. She had seen him a month before. He had cut his hair and trimmed his beard, was deeply tanned and dressed in an expensive jacket, gold chains around his neck, a gold watch, gold rings ... the petered-out claim of his body salted with gold. She smiled at her cattiness. He wasn't so terrible. Now that he had become just another figment of the French Quarter, working around the clock at his restaurant, clinking wineglasses with sagging divorcees and posing a sexual Everest for disillusioned housewives to scale, he bore little resemblance to the man she had married, and this was doubtless the reason she could now tolerate him: it had been the original she disliked.

She had been standing beside Magnusson's door for less than a minute when she noticed her right side – that nearest the door – was prickly with ... not cold exactly, more an animal chill that raised gooseflesh on her arm. She assumed it was nerves, fatigue; but on touching the door she discovered that it, too, was cold, and a vibration tingled her fingertips as if a charge had passed through the wood from an X-ray machine briefly in operation. Nerves, she thought again. And, indeed, the cold dissipated the instant she cracked the door. Still, she was curious. What would the old man be like apart from Laura's influence? She cracked the door wider, and his scent of bay rum and corruption leaked out. White hallway light spilled across shelves lined with gilt and leather medical texts, sweeping back the darkness, compacting it. She leaned on the doorknob, peering inside, and the sharp shadows angled from beneath the desk and chair quivered, poised – she imagined – to snick through the blood and bone of her ankles if she trespassed. Feeling foolish at her apprehension, she pushed the door wide open. He sat in his wheelchair facing the far wall, a dim green oval of his reflected stare puddled head-high on the wallpaper. The uncanny sight gave her pause, and she was uncertain whether or not to call his name.

'Go away,' he whispered without turning.

A thrill ran across the muscles of her abdomen. His head wobbled and his hand fell off the arm of the chair, half a gesture of dismissal, half collapse. He whispered once more, 'Go away.' She jumped back, pulling the door shut behind her, and she leaned against the doorframe trembling, unable to stop trembling no matter how insistently she told herself that her fright was the product of stress alone. His voice had terrified her. Though it had been the same decrepit wheeze he had spoken in earlier, this time it had been full of potent menace, the voice of a spirit speaking through a cobwebbed throat, its whisper created by the straining and snapping of spider silk stretched apart by desiccated muscles. And yet, for all its implicit power, it had been wavering and faint, as if a wind and a world lay between them.

CHAPTER 4

February 11–24 March 1987

Every morning at nine-thirty or thereabouts an astringent odor of aftershave stung Donnell's nostrils, and the enormous shadow of Dr Edman hove into view. Sometimes, though not this morning, the less imposing shadow of Dr Brauer slunk by his side, his smell a mingling of stale tobacco and sweat, his voice holding an edge of mean condescension. Edman's voice, however, gave Donnell a feeling of superiority; it was the mellifluous croon of a cartoon owl to whom the forest animals would come for sage but unreliable advice.

'Lungs clear, heart rate … gooood.' Edman thumped Donnell's chest and chuckled. 'Now, if we can just get your head on straight.'

Irritated by the attempt to jolly him, Donnell maintained a frosty silence. Edman finished the examination and went to sit on the bed; the bedsprings squealed, giving up the ghost.

'Had a recurrence of that shift in focus?' he asked.

'Not lately.'

'Donnell!' said Jocundra chidingly; he heard the whisk of her stockings as she uncrossed her legs behind him.

He gripped the arms of the wheelchair so his vertigo would not be apparent and concentrated on Edman's bloated gray shape; then he blinked, strained, and shifted his field of focus forward. A patch of lab coat swooped toward him from the shadow, swelling to dominate his vision completely: several pens clipped to a sagging pocket. By tracking his sight like a searchlight across Edman's frame, he assembled the image of a grossly fat, middle-aged man with slicked-back brown hair and a flourishing mustache, the ends of which were waxed and curled. Hectic spots of color dappled his cheeks, and his eyes were startling bits of blue china. Donnell fixed on the left eye, noticing the pink gullies of flesh in the corners, the road map of capillaries: Edman hadn't been sleeping.

'Actually' – Donnell thought how best to exploit Edman's lack of sleep – 'actually, I had one just when you came in, but it was different …' He pretended to be struggling with a difficult concept.

'How so?' Papers rustled on Edman's clipboard, his ballpoint clicked. His eyelids drooped, and the blue eye rolled wetly down.

'The light was spraying out the pores of your hand, intense light, like the kind you find in an all-night restaurant, but even brighter, and deep in the light something moved, something pale and multiform,' Donnell whispered melodramatically. 'Something I soon realized was a sea of ghastly, tormented faces …'

'My God, Donnell!' Edman smacked the bed with his clipboard.

'Right!' said Donnell with mock enthusiasm. 'I can't be sure, but it may have been …'

'Donnell!' Edman sighed, a forlorn lover's sigh. 'Will you please consider what our process means to other terminal patients? At least do that, if you don't care about yourself.'

'Oh, yeah. There must be thousands of less fortunate stiffs just begging for the chance.' Donnell laughed. 'It really changes your perspective on the goddamn afterlife. Groping, bashing your head on the sink when you go to spit.'

'You know that's going to improve, damn it!' The blue eye blinked rapidly. 'You're retarding your own progress with this childish attitude.'

'What'll you give me?' Jocundra stroked his shoulder, soothing, but Donnell shrugged off her hand. 'How much if I spill the secrets of my vital signs?'

'What would you like?'

'Another whore.' Donnell jerked his head toward Jocundra. 'I'm bored with this one.'

'Would you really prefer another therapist?'

'Christ, yes! Dozens! Orientals, Watusis, cheerleaders in sweatsocks for my old age. I'll screw my way to mental health.'

'I see.' Edman scribbled furiously, his eye downcast.

What gruesome things eyes were! Glistening, rolling, bulging, popping. Little congealed shudders in their bony nests. Donnell wished he had never mentioned the visual shift because they hadn't stopped nagging him since, and he had begun to develop a phobia about eyes. But on first experiencing it, he had feared it might signal a relapse, and he had told Jocundra.

Edman cleared his throat. 'It's time we got to the root of this anger, Donnell.' Note-taking had restored his poise, and his tone implied an end to games. 'It must be distressing,' he said, 'not to recall what Jean looked like beyond a few hazy details.'

'Shut up, Edman,' said Donnell. As always, mere mention of his flawed memory made him unreasonably angry. His teeth clenched, his muscles bunched, yet part of his mind remained calm and watchful, helpless against the onset of rage.

'Tall, dark-haired, quiet,' enumerated Edman. 'A weaver … or was she a photographer? No, I remember. Both.' The eye widened, the eyebrow arched. 'A talented woman.'

'Leave it alone,' said Donnell ominously, wishing he could refine his patch of clear sight into a needle beam and prick Edman's humor, send the fluid jetting out, dribbling down his cheek, then watch him go squealing around the room, a flabby balloon losing flotation.

'It's odd,' mused Edman, 'that your most coherent memories of the woman concern her death.'

Donnell tried to hurl himself out of the wheelchair, but pain lanced through his shoulder joints and he fell back. 'Bastard!' he shouted.

Jocundra helped him resettle and asked Edman if they could have a consultation, and they went into the hall.

Alone, his anger ebbing, Donnell normalized his sight. The bedroom walls raised a ghostly gray mist, unbroken except for a golden fog at the window, and the furniture rippled as if with a gentle current. It occurred to him that things might so appear to a king who had been magicked into a deathlike trance and enthroned upon a shadowy lake bottom among streamers of kelp and shattered hulls. He preferred this gloom to clear sight: it suited his interior gloom and induced a comforting thoughtlessness.

'... don't think you should force him,' Jocundra was saying in the hall, angry.

Edman's reply was muffled. '... another week ... his reaction to Richmond ...'

A mirror hung beside the door to Jocundra's bedroom, offering the reflection of a spidery writing desk wobbling on pipestem legs. Donnell wheeled over to it and pressed his nose against the cold glass. He saw a dead-gray oval with drowned hair waving up and smudges for eyes. Now and again a fiery green flicker crossed one or the other of the smudges.

'You shouldn't worry so about your eyes,' said Jocundra from the door.

He started to wheel away from her, upset at being caught off guard, but she moved behind his chair, hemming him in. Her mirror image lifted an ill-defined hand and made as if to touch him, but held back, and for an instant he felt the good weight of her consolation.

'I'd be afraid, too,' she said. 'But there's really nothing to worry about. They'll get brighter and brighter for a while and then they'll fade.'

One of the orderlies sang old blues songs when he cleaned up Donnell's room, and his favorite tune contained the oft-repeated line: 'Minutes seem like hours, hours seem like days ...'

Donnell thought the line should have continued the metaphorical progression and sought a comparative for weeks, but he would not have chosen months or years. Weeks like vats of sluggish sameness, three of them, at the bottom of which he sat and stewed and tried to remember. Jocundra urged him to write, and he refused on the grounds that she had asked. He purely resented her. She wore too damn much perfume, she touched him too often, and she stirred up his memories of Jean because she was also tall and dark-haired. He especially resented her for that. Sometimes he took refuge from her in his memories, displaying them against the field of his suffering, his sense of loss, the way an archeologist might spread the fragments of an ancient medallion on a velvet cloth, hoping to assure himself of the larger form whose wreckage they comprised: a life having unity and purpose, sad depths and joyous heights. But not remembering Jean's face made all the bits of memory insubstantial. The hooked rugs on the cabin floor, the photograph above their bed of a spiderweb fettering a windowpane stained blue with frost, a day at a county fair. So few. Without her to center them they lacked consistency, and it seemed his grief was less a consequence of loss than a blackness welling up from some negative place inside him. From time to time he *did* write, thinking the act would manifest a proof, evoke a new memory; the poems were frauds, elegant and empty, and this led him to a sense of his own fraudulence. Something was wrong. Put that baldly it sounded stupid, but it was the most essential truth he could isolate. Something was *very* wrong. Some dread thing was keeping just out of sight behind him. He became leery of unfamiliar noises, suspicious of changes in routine, convinced he was about to be ambushed by a sinister fate masquerading as one of the shadows that surrounded him. There was no reasonable basis for the conviction, yet nonetheless his fear intensified. The fear drove him to seek out Jocundra, she in turn drove him to thoughts of Jean, round and round and round, and that's why the weeks seemed like goddamn centuries, and the month – when it came to be a month and a little more – like a geologic stratification of slow, sad time.

One summerlike afternoon Jocundra wheeled him out to the stone bench nearest the gate and tried to interest him with stories of duels and courtship, of the fine ladies and gentlemen who had long ago strolled the grounds. He affected disinterest but he listened. Her features were animated, her voice vibrant, and he felt she was disclosing a fundamental attitude, exposing a side of herself she kept hidden from others. Eventually his show of boredom diminished her enthusiasm, and she opened a magazine.

High above, the oak crowns were dark green domes fogged by gassy golden suns, but when he shifted his field of focus he could see up through the dizzying separations of the leaves to the birds perched on the top branches. His vision was improving every day, and he had discovered that it functioned best under the sun. Colors were truer and shapes more recognizable, though they still wavered with a seasick motion, and though the brightness produced its own effects: scrollworks of golden light flashing in the corners of his eyes; transparent eddies flowing around the azalea leaves; a faint bluish mist accumulating around Jocundra's shoulders. He tracked across the glossy cover of her *Cosmopolitan* and focused on her mouth. It was wide and lipsticked and full like the cover girl's; the hollow above her lips was deep and sculptural.

'How do I look?' The lips smiled.

Being at such an apparently intimate distance from her mouth was eerie, voyeuristic; he covered his embarrassment with sarcasm. 'What's up in the world of bust enhancement these days?'

The smile disappeared. 'You don't expect me to read anything worthwhile with you glowering at me, do you?'

'I didn't expect you could read at all.' Flecks of topaz light glimmered in her irises; a scatter of fine dark hairs rose from her eyebrow and merged with the hairline. 'But if you could I assumed it would be crap like that. Makeup Secrets of the Stars.'

'I suffer no sense of devaluation by using makeup,' she said crisply. 'It cheers me up to look nice, and God knows it's hard enough to be cheerful around you.'

He turned, blinking away the patch of clear sight, considering the blurs of distant foliage. It was becoming increasingly difficult for him to maintain anger against her. Almost without his notice, as subtly as the spinning of a web, threads of his anger had been drawn loose and woven into another emotion. Its significance escaped him, but he thought that if he attempted to understand it, he would become more deeply ensnared.

'I have a confession,' she said. 'I read through your notebook this morning. Some of the fragments were lovely ...'

'Why don't you just look in the toilet after I go ...'

'... and I think you should finish them!'

'... and see if my shit's spelling out secret messages!'

'I'm not trying to pry out your secrets!' She threw down her magazine. 'I thought if you had some encouragement, some criticism, you might finish them.'

Halting footsteps scraped on the path behind him, and a scruffy, gassed voice asked, 'What's happenin', man?'

'Good morning, Mr Richmond,' said Jocundra with professional sweetness. 'Donnell? Have you met Mr Richmond?'

Richmond's head and torso swam into bleared focus. He had a hard-bitten, emaciated face framed in shoulder-length brown hair. Prominent cheekbones, a missing lower tooth. He was leaning on a cane, grinning; his pupils showed against his irises like planets eclipsing green suns.

'That's Jack to you, man,' he said, extending his hand.

The hair's on Donnell's neck prickled, and he was tongue-tied, unable to tear his eyes off Richmond. A chill articulated his spine.

'Another hopeless burn-out,' said Richmond, his grin growing toothier. 'What's the matter, squeeze? You wet yourself?'

A busty, brown-haired woman came up beside him and murmured, 'Jack,' but he continued to glare at Donnell, whose apprehension was turning into panic. His muscles had gone flaccid, and unable to run, he shrank within himself.

The brown-haired woman touched Richmond's arm. 'Why don't we finish our walk, Jack?'

Richmond mimicked her in a quavery falsetto. '"Why don't we finish our walk, Jack!" Shit! Here they go and stock this place with these fine bitches, and they won't do nothin' for you 'cept be polite!' He bent down, his left eye inches from Donnell's face, and winked; even when closed, a hint of luminous green penetrated his eyelid. 'Or don't you go for the ladies, squeeze? Maybe I'm makin' you all squirmy inside.' He hobbled off, laughing, and called back over his shoulder. 'Keep your fingers crossed, sweetheart. Maybe I'll come over some night and let you make my eagle big!'

As Richmond receded, his therapist in tow, Donnell's tension eased. He flicked his eyes to Jocundra who looked quickly away and thumbed through her magazine. He found her lack of comment on his behaviour peculiar and asked her about it.

'I assumed you were put off by his manner,' she said.

'Who the hell is he?'

'A patient. He belongs to some motorcycle club.' Her brow knitted. 'The Hellhounds, I think.'

'Didn't you feel ...' He broke off, not wanting to admit the extent of his fright.

'Feel what?'

'Nothing.'

Richmond's voice drifted back from the porch, outraged, and he slashed his cane through the air. The rose-colored bricks shimmered in the background, the faceted dome atop the roof flashed as if its energies were building to the discharge of a lethal ray, and Donnell had a resurgence of crawly animal fear.

After the encounter with Richmond, Donnell stayed closeted in his room for nearly two weeks. Jocundra lambasted him, comparing him to a child who had pulled a sheet over his head, but nothing she said would sway him. His reaction to Richmond must have been due, he decided, to a side effect of the bacterial process, but side effect or not, he wanted no repetition of that stricken and helpless feeling: like a rabbit frozen by oncoming headlights. He lay around so much he developed a bedsore, and at this Jocundra threw up her hands.

'I'm not going to sit here and watch you moulder,' she said.

'Then get the fuck out!' he said; and as she stuffed wallet and compact into a leather purse, he told her that her skin looked like pink paint, that twenty dollars a night was probably too high but she should try for it, and – as she slammed the door – that she could go straight to Hell and give her goddamn disease to the Devil. He wished she would stay gone, but he knew she'd be harassing him again before lunchtime.

His lunch tray, however, was brought by the orderly who sang, and when Donnell asked about Jocundra, he said, 'Beats me, Jim. I can't keep track of my own woman.'

Donnell was puzzled but unconcerned. Coldly, he dismissed her. He spent the afternoon exploring the new boundaries of his vision, charting minuscule dents in the wallpaper, composing mosaic landscapes from the reflections glazing the lens of the camera mounted above the door, and – something of a breakthrough – following the flight of a hawk circling the middle distance, bringing it so close he managed to see a scaly patch on its wing and an awful eye the color of dried blood and half filmed over with a crackled white membrane. An old, sick, mad king of the air. The hawk kept soaring out of his range, and he could never obtain a view of its entire body; his control still lacked discretion. It was a pity, he thought, that the visual effects were only temporary, though they did not suffice of themselves to make life interesting. Their novelty quickly wore off.

The orderly who brought his dinner tray was tanned, fortyish, with razor-cut hair combed over a bald spot and silken black hairs matting the backs of his hands. Though he was no more talkative than the singing orderly, Donnell suspected he could be drawn into a conversation. He flounced pillows, preened before the mirror, and took inordinate pleasure in rubbing out Donnell's neck cramp. Gentle, lissome fingers. On his pinky he wore a diamond ring, an exceptionally large one for a person earning orderly's wages, and Donnell, seeking to ingratiate himself, to learn about Jocundra, spoke admiringly of it.

'It belonged to my grandmother,' said the orderly. 'The stone, not the setting. I've been offered eighteen thousand for it, but I held onto it because you never know when hard times might snap you up.' He illustrated the snapping of hard times by pinching Donnell's leg, then launched into an interminable story about his grandmother. 'She had lovers 'til she was sixty-seven, the old dear. Heaven knows what she did after that!' Titter. He put on a dismal face. 'But it was no picnic being raised by a dirty old woman, let me tell you.' And he did.

Donnell had been hoping to weasel information about Jocundra during the course of the conversation, but the orderly showed no sign of allowing a conversation, and he was forced to interrupt. The orderly acted betrayed, said he had no idea where she was, and swept from the room with a display of injured dignity that evoked the angry rustle of taffeta.

Then it dawned on Donnell. She wasn't coming back. She had deserted him. How could she just go without telling him, without arranging a replacement? Panicked, he wheeled out into the hall. As he headed for the foyer, hoping to find Edman, a ripple in the carpet snagged his wheels and canted him into one of the potted ferns; the brass urn toppled and bonged against the floor. The door beside it opened, and a thin blond woman poked out her head. 'Shh!' she commanded. She knelt by the fern, her nose wrinkling at having to touch the dirt. She had the kind of brittle prettiness that hardens easily into middle-aged bitchdom, and as if in anticipation of this, her hair was done up into a no-nonsense bun and tied with a dark blue ribbon.

'Have you seen Jocundra?' asked Donnell.

'Jocundra?' The woman did not look up, packing down the dirt around the fern. 'Hasn't she left?'

'She's left?' Donnell refused to accept it. 'When's she coming back?'

'No, now wait. I saw her on the grounds after supper. Maybe she hasn't gone yet.'

'Laura!' A querulous voice leaked out the open door; the woman wiggled all five fingers in a wave, a smile nicked the corners of her mouth, and she closed the door behind her.

It had been easy to tell Jocundra to leave when he had not believed it possible, but now he was adrift in the possibility, all solid ground melted away. He skidded down the ramp into the parking lot. The lanterns above the stone benches were lit, bubbles of yellow light picking out the blackness, and fireflies swarmed under the oaks. Toads ratcheted, crickets sizzled. She would be – if she hadn't left – at the bench near the gate. The flagstones jolted the wheels, his chest labored, his arms ached, a sheen of sweat covered his face. Something flew into his eye, batted its wings, clung for a second and fluttered off. A moth. He crested a rise and spotted Jocundra on the bench. She wasn't wearing makeup, or was wearing very little, and she looked hardly more than a girl. He had always assigned her the characteristic of sophistication, albeit of a callow sort, and so her youthfulness surprised him. Her melancholy expression did not change when she saw him.

'I don't want you to leave,' he said, scraping to a halt a couple of feet away.

She laughed palely. 'I've already left. I just went into New Orleans for the day.' She regarded him with mild approval. 'You made it out here by yourself. That's pretty good.'

'I thought you'd gone,' he said, choosing his words carefully, not wanting to appear too relieved. 'I didn't much like the idea.'

'Oh?' She raised an eyebrow.

'Listen.' He balked at apology, but gave in to the need for it. 'I'm sorry. I know I've been an asshole.'

'You've had good reason to be upset.' She smoothed her skirt down over her knees, then smiled. 'But you *have* been an asshole.'

'Could it be my nature,' he said, rankled.

'No, you're not like that,' she said thoughtfully. She slung her bag over her shoulder. 'Let's go on in.'

As she wheeled him toward the house, Donnell felt strangely satisfied, as if some plaguing question had been put to rest. The fireflies pricking the dark, the scrape of Jocundra's shoes, the insect noises, everything formed an intricate complement to his thoughts, a relationship he could not grasp but wanted to make graspable, to write down. Near the house another moth fluttered into his face, and he wondered – his wonder tinged with revulsion – if they were being attracted by the flickers in his eyes. He pinched its wings together and held it up for Jocundra's inspection.

'It's a luna moth,' she said. 'There was this old man back home, a real Cajun looney. He's blind now, or partially blind, but he used to keep thousands of luna moths in his back room and study their wing patterns. He claimed they revealed the natural truth.' She shook her head, regretful, and added in a less enthusiastic voice, 'Clarence Brisbeau.'

'What's wrong?' Donnell loosed the moth and it skittered off, vanishing against the coal-black crowns of the oaks.

'I was just remembering. He scared me once. He got drunk and tried to kiss me. I was only thirteen, and he must have been almost sixty.' She stared after the moth as if she could still see it. 'It was spooky. Stripes of light were shining between the boards of the cabin, dead moths on the floor, thousands clinging to the walls. Every time he gestured they fluttered off his arms. I remember him walking toward me, dripping moths, talking.' She adopted an accent, like French, but with harsher rhythms. '"I'm tellin' you, me," he said. "This worl' she's full of supernatural creatures whose magic we deny."'

CHAPTER 5

March 25–17 April 1987

'Now don't laugh, but I've been thinking about our patients in terms of spirit possession.' Dr Edman folded his hands across his stomach and leaned back; the leather chair wheezed.

Jocundra was sitting across a mahogany desk from Edman in his office: a curious round room whose roof was the glass dome. Shafts of the declining sun struck through the faceted panes, and dust motes swirled idly like the thoughts of a crystal-skulled giant. Recessed bookshelves ringed the room – you entered by means of a stair leading up through a trapdoor – and the volumes were mired in shadow; though now and then the light brightened, crept lower on the walls, and the odd gilt word melted up from the dimness: Witchcraft, Psychologica, Pathology. A chart of the brain was tacked up over a portion of the shelves, and Edman had scribbled crabbed notes along arrows pointing to various of the fissures. The shelf behind his head held an array of dusty, yellowed human crania, suggesting to Jocundra that he was the latest in a succession of psychologist-kings, and that his own brain case would someday join those of his predecessors.

'During a voodoo ritual,' Edman continued, 'the celebrants experience tremors, convulsions, and begin to exhibit a different class of behaviors than previously. They may, for example, show a fondness for gazing into mirrors or eating a particular food, and the *houngan* then identifies these behaviors as aspects belonging to one of the gods.'

'There *is* a rough analogue …' Jocundra began.

'Bear with me a moment!' Edman waggled a finger, summoning a thought. 'I prefer to regard this so-called spirit possession as the emergence of the deep consciousness. A rather imprecise term, easily confused with Jungian terminology, but generally indicative of what I'm after: the raw force of the identity to which all the socialized and otherwise learned behaviors adhere, barnacling it with fears and logical process and so forth, gradually masking it from the light and relegating it to a murky existence in the …' He smacked his head, as if to dislodge an idea. 'Ah! In the abyss of forethought.' He scribbled on his notepad, beaming at Jocundra. 'That ought to wake up the back rows at the next convention.' He leaned back again. 'My thesis is that we're stimulating spirit possession by microbiological means rather than hypnagogic ones, elevating the deep consciousness to fill the void created by the dissipation of learned behaviors. But instead of allowing this new and unfocused identity to wander about at will for a few hours, we educate and guide it. And instead of a *houngan* or a *mama loi* to simply proclaim the manifestation, we utilize trained personnel to maximize their potential, to influence their growth. Of course if we had a *mama loi* on the staff, she'd say we had conjured up a god.' He chuckled. 'See what I'm after?'

'It's hardly a scholarly viewpoint.' Jocundra found the idea of playing voodoo priestess to Donnell's elemental spirit appealing in the manner of a comic book illustration.

'Not as such! Still, a case might be made for it. And wouldn't it be a surprise package if we learned there were exact correlations between personality types and the voodoo pantheon!' Edman pursed his lips and tapped them with his forefinger. 'You must be familiar with anthropological studies in this area ... Any input?'

'Well,' said Jocundra, unhappy at having to supply grist for Edman's mill, 'the voodoo concept of the soul has some resonance with your thesis. According to doctrine all human beings have two souls. The *ti bon ange*, which is more or less the conscience, the socialized part of the mind, and the *gros bon ange*, which is the undying part, the immortal twin. It's been described as the image of a man reflected by a dark mirror. You might want to read Deren or Metraux.'

'Hmm.' Edman bent to his notepad. 'Tell me, Ms Verret. Do you like Donnell?' He cocked an eye toward her, continuing to write. 'You must have some personal reaction.'

Jocundra was startled by the question. 'I think he's brilliant,' she said. 'You've seen his work.'

'It seems quite competent, but that's not what I'm driving at. Suppose Donnell wasn't your patient, would you be attracted to him?'

'I don't believe that's relevant,' she said defensively. 'Not to the project or ...'

'You're right, of course. Sorry.' Edman took another note and favored her with a paternal smile. 'I'm just an old snoop.'

'I'm *concerned* for him, I'm not happy he's going to die.'

'Please! Your private concerns are just that. Sorry.'

Edman opened a file drawer and rummaged through it, leaving Jocundra a little flustered. The sun was going down, staining the faceted panes to ruby, empurpling the shadows along the wall, and these decaying colors – augmented by the glutinous sound of Edman's breath as he bent over the file, taxed by even this slight exertion – congealed into a perverse atmosphere. She felt soiled. His question had not been idle curiosity; he was constantly prying, hinting, insinuating. Her opinion of him had always been low, but never so low as now. She pictured him alone in the office, entertaining fantasies about the therapists, fondling himself while watching videos of the patients, feeding upon the potential for sickness which the project incorporated.

At last he unbent, his pale face mooning above the desk. 'The microbiology people think Magnusson's the key ...' He paused, his attention commanded by a clipping in a manila folder; he clucked to himself and closed it. 'Did you know they've been letting him work on material related to the bacterial process?'

'Yes, Laura told me.'

'Ah! Well, he *is* important. But because of Donnell's youth, his human focus, it's possible he's going to give us a clearer look into the basis of consciousness than even Magnusson. Now that he's in harness it's time to lay off the whip and break out the sugar, although' - Edman fussed with papers - 'although I wonder if it isn't time for another forced interaction.'

'He's working so smoothly now, I'd hate to disrupt him ... and besides, he didn't react well to Richmond.'

'None of them react well to Richmond!' Edman laughed. 'But I keep thinking if we could override this fear reaction of theirs, we might proceed by leaps and bounds. Even Richmond seems reluctant for intimate confrontation. He enjoys facing down his own fear, but his contacts are kept on the level of ritual aggression.'

Edman rambled off onto other matters, talking mainly to himself as he dealt with his files; he admitted to using his sessions with the therapists as a means to order his thoughts, and Jocundra knew her active participation was not required. She wondered how he would wed his latest theory to his previous one: that of cellular wish-fulfilment. He considered Richmond weighty evidence in support of the latter because, unlike the rest of the slow-burners - all of whom had murky backgrounds - the body had a thoroughly documented past. Richmond, born Eliot Vuillemont, had been the heir of a prominent New Orleans family, disinherited for reasons of drug abuse. This young man, Edman argued, who had lived a life of ineffectual rebellion, whose college psychiatric records reflected a history of cowardice and repressed violence, had chosen as his posthumous role the antihero, the apocalyptic lone wolf; the new personality was a triumphant expression of the feebly manifested drives which had led to his death by overdose. Edman posited that the workings of memory chemically changed portions of the RNA - those portions containing the bioform of our most secret and complex wish, 'the deepest reason we have made for being' - and intensified their capacity for survival. It was, Jocundra thought, a more viable theory than his latest, but she had no doubt both would soon appear in published form, welded together into a rickety construct studded with bits of glitter: a Rube Goldberg theory of the personality.

'I believe. I'll bring it up in staff tonight.' Edman reached inside his lab coat and pulled forth a red memorandum book. 'The seventeenth looks free.'

Jocundra looked at him questioningly, realizing she must have missed something. Edman smiled; he slipped the book back into his pocket, and it seemed to her he had reached deep within his body and fed his heart a piece of red candy.

'I won't take any more of your time, Ms Verret. I was saying that I thought this fear reaction needed to be examined under group conditions, and I proposed we have a party for our green-eyed friends. Invite the staff from Tulane, arrange for some sort of music, and just see if we can't get the patients to pass off their fear as another side effect of the process. At the very least it should be a memorable social occasion.'

The main hall was thronged with doctors, technicians, students and administration people wearing sport jackets and summer dresses, most gathered around the groupings of sofas which roughly divided the room into thirds; and scattered throughout the crowd were the five patients – Richmond had not yet arrived. A three piece band played cocktail jazz on the patio, and several couples were dancing. The room was huge. Carved angels flowed from the molding, spreading their wings in the corners of the ceiling, and the space whose sanctity they guaranteed was the size of a country church, filled with the relics of bygone years. Gilt chairs and statuettes and filigreed tables occupied every spare nook, and every flat surface was cluttered with *objets d'art*, the emphasis being upon ceramic figurines of bewigged lords and ladies. The French doors were flanked by curio cabinets, except for those beside which stood a grand piano, its finish holding a blaze of sunlight. Paintings and prints and photographs hung in rows to the ceiling, presenting scenes of the countryside, historical personages, hunts, groups of shabbily dressed blacks. One print depicted a masque whose participants were costumed as demons, beasts, and fanciful birds. Passing it on the way to the punch bowl, Jocundra decided that this masque had much in common with Edman's party: though the mix of music and conversation suggested a trivial assemblage, most eyes were fixed on the patients and most talk concerned them, and there was an underlying air of anticipation, as if the partygoers were awaiting a moment of unmasking so they could determine which of them was not masked, which was truly a demon, a beast, or a fanciful bird.

Knots of people were clumped along the refreshment table, and Jocundra eavesdropped as she ladled punch.

'... the greater their verbal capacity, the more credibly they fabricate a past reality.' A fruity male voice.

Jocundra moved down the table, examining the sandwich trays, hoping for some less Edmanesque commentary.

'... and Monroe looked like the devil had asked her to tango!' Laughter, a babble of voices.

'Listen to this!' The click and whirr of a tape recorder, and then the tiny, cornpone-accented voice of Kline French:

'... Ah'm quite an afficionado of the dance, though of course Ah've only been exposed to its regional privations.'

Clarice Monroe had been sketching scenes for a ballet on one of the sofas, and French had been maneuvred into approach by his therapist and had asked to see her sketch.

FRENCH: 'This appears to be an illumination of an African myth ... Am Ah correct?'
MONROE (*tremulously*): 'It's the Anansi, the Ashanti god of lies and deceit.'
FRENCH: 'And this young lady has fallen into his clutches?'
MONROE: 'She's the sorceress Luweji. She's traveled through the gates of fire ...'
FRENCH: 'Represented by these red curtains, I presume?'
MONROE: 'Yes.' (*Silence*)
FRENCH: 'Well, it seems quite wonderful. Ah hope Ah'll have the privilege of attendin' its triumphant celebration.'

Jocundra spotted French through the press of bodies. He was being wheeled along, nodding his massive head in response to something his therapist was saying. His shoulders were wide as a wrestler's; his eyes sparked emerald in a heavy-jawed, impassive face, and made Jocundra think of an idol ruling over a deserted temple or – perhaps closer to the truth – one of those James Bond villains whose smile only appears when he hears the crunching of a backbone. The doctors said they had rarely had a patient with such muscle tone, dead or alive, and there had been a rumour at Tulane that his body had been introduced to the project via a government agency. But whatever his origins, he now believed himself to be a financial consultant; the administration followed his market analyses with strict attention.

'There goes French,' said someone beside her. 'I bet he's chasing Monroe again.' Giggles.

'He's out of luck. I think she had to go potty after the last time.' Laughter unrestrained.

Balancing the punch, slipping between couples, Jocundra threaded her way toward Donnell. He was sitting across the room from the punch bowl, scowling; he had gotten some tan lately, his hollows were filling in, but his social attitudes had not changed much. He had rejected every advance so far, and no one was bothering to talk to him anymore. Jocundra was beginning to feel like the loser in a garden show, watching the crowd encircle the winners, sitting alone with her dispirited, green-eyed plant.

'I know, I know,' she said, handing him the punch. 'Where have I been?'

'Where the hell *have* you been?' He sipped the punch. 'God, this is awful! Let's get out of here.'

'We have to stay until Edman comes. He should be here soon.' A lie. Edman was monitoring the video, overseeing the big picture.

Marilyn Ramsburgh's therapist signalled to Jocundra, and she signalled him back No. Donnell was not ready for Ramsburgh. She was, as far as Jocundra was concerned, the most physically alarming of the patients. Frail, white hair so thin you could see the veined scalp beneath, hunched in her chair, hands enwebbed with yarn, her pupils shrunk to almost nothing. She was due to be 'discharged' soon, taken back to Tulane for 'a few final tests,' and lately she had been chirping about hugging her grandchildren again, promising to write everyone, and had presented Edman with a beautiful hand-woven coverlet worked into a design of knights battling in a forest illuminated by violet will o' the wisps: a token of her gratitude.

Squabbling noises on the patio, a woman's squeal, and Richmond came into view, swinging his cane to clear a path; his therapist, Audrey, trailed behind him. He limped along the refreshment table, picked up a sandwich, had a bite, and tossed the remainder on the floor; he dipped a ladleful of punch, slurped, and spewed it back into the bowl. 'Fuckin' fruit juice! Jesus!' Punch dribbled off his chin onto a torn T-shirt emblazoned with a crudely painted swastika and letters spelling out Hellhounds MC. Greasy strands of hair fell down over his eyes, and he glared between them at the crowd like a drunken Indian.

The crowd retreated from the refreshment table, from Richmond, but three men and an overweight girl in a yellow sun dress bravely held their positions. Noticing them, Richmond hooked his cane over an arm, limped forward and grabbed the girl's breast, slipping his free arm around her waist and pulling her close. She shrieked and lifted her hand to slap him.

'Go ahead, bitch,' said Richmond, nonchalant. 'Lessee what you got.'

The girl's mouth puckered, opened and shut, and she let her hand fall. Richmond cupped her breast at different angles, squeezing it cruelly. 'Damn, mama!' he said. 'I bet you give Grade A.'

'Let her go, Jack.' Audrey tried to pull his hand loose, but he shook her off. 'C'mon back to the room.'

'Cool. How 'bout all three of us go and we play a little ring-around-the-rosy?' He tightened his hold on the girl's waist and flicked her nipple with his thumb. Her eyelids lowered, her head drooped to one side, as if she were experiencing a sweet wave of passion.

One of the men, a skinny guy in a madras jacket, did a shuffle forward and said, 'Uh, Mr Richmond ...'

'Hey, little savage!' said Richmond good-naturedly. 'Guess you wonder what's gonna happen to your squeeze.'

The girl spun free. Richmond made no effort to hold her, but as she staggered back, he clawed at the top of her dress. He was too weak to rip the material, but his fingers hooked one of the straps, and in her struggle it came away in Richmond's hand – a little yellow serpent. Her right breast bounded out, pale and pendulous, the imprint of his fingers already darkening to bruises. Richmond sniffed at the strap. 'Warthog,' he said, identifying the odor. The skinny guy covered the girl with his jacket, and she flung her arms around him, sobbing.

Richmond grinned at the crowd, nodded; then he whirled about and brought his cane down on the punch bowl, shattering it. The punch gushed out, floating cookies off the trays, puddling in the paper plates. He swung again and again, snake-killing strokes, his hair flying, red droplets spraying from the tablecloth, until a sugary dust of pulverized glass lay around his feet. No one spoke. Jocundra could hear the punch dripping onto the carpet.

'Why you citizens just stand there and let me fuck with your women?' asked Richmond, hobbling away from the table. The crowd parted before him, reforming at the rear. 'I mean this *is* the real world, ain't it?' He spotted Donnell and headed toward him. 'Hey, sweets! You lookin' gorgeous today. How come you think these chickenshits is lettin' me crow?'

Donnell gripped the arms of his wheelchair, but didn't freeze up. 'Keep your mouth off me, asshole,' he said.

'Hostility!' Richmond was delighted. 'Now I can relate to some hostility.' He moved closer, tapping the crook of his cane on his palm.

Jocundra set down her punch, preparing to help Audrey restrain him; it was certain no one else would help. The crowd had packed in around them, penning the four of them against the wall, and their faces were the faces of intent observers. Tape recorders whirred, clipboards were in evidence. Jocundra saw that all the patients had pushed into the front rank, and each was exhibiting extreme tension. Magnusson sucked his gums, Ramsburgh plucked feverishly at her knitting, French's fingers drummed on his leg, and the pretty dark face of Clarice Monroe peeked over a shoulder, blinking and stunned. It was, thought Jocundra, one of Ramsburgh's tapestries come to life: a mysterious forest, a myriad faces peering between the branches, the spirits of trees, goblins, ghostly men and women, and a few whose glowing eyes served as the structural focus of the design.

Magnusson rolled a foot forward. 'They're observing us, sonny. That's why they're letting you foul the air.'

Forgetting about Donnell, Richmond spread his arms in a gesture of false heartiness. 'Damn if it ain't Doctor Demento!'

'And they've good reason to observe.' Magnusson glanced from one patient to another. 'Feel around inside yourselves! Find anything solid, anything real? We're not who we were!'

For a moment, silence; then French spoke. 'Ah don't believe I see what you're drivin' at, Doctor.' He kneaded his leg with the heel of his palm.

'Don't listen to that old maniac,' creaked Ramsburgh. 'He was 'round the other day trying to poison me with his ravings.' She frowned at Magnusson; his eyes blazed out from the mottled ruin of his face, and they stared at each other like hellish grandparents gloating over an evil thought.

'Your mind's poisoned, Hilmer!' Ramsburgh's hands danced among her needles and yarn. 'Your arteries are hard, and your brain's a dried-out sponge! Time you came to grips with the fact and left the rest of us in peace.'

'Old woman,' said Magnusson gravely. 'Don't you feel the winnowing of your days?'

Edman eased through the crowd and seized the handles of his wheelchair. 'I think you've had too much excitement, Doctor,' he said with professional cheer. He started to wheel him away, but the old man locked his hands onto the wheels and the chair wouldn't budge.

'Don't you see it's a hoax?' Again he glanced at the other patients. 'By God, you'll see!' he said to Donnell. 'You'll have a glimpse over the edge before you fall.'

Laura knelt beside him, prying at his fingers. 'Stop this, Hilmer!' she said. 'Stop this right now.'

Gasping, reddening with the effort, Edman wrangled the chair sideways, and for a split second Jocundra found herself looking into Magnusson's eyes, except it was not merely looking: it was falling down luminous green tunnels so bright they seemed to be spinning, whirlpools sucking her under, and the pattern of gristle and discoloration surrounding them made no sense at all.

'It's so clear.' Magnusson shook his head in wonder, then he gazed sternly at Jocundra. 'No sorrow is too great to bear,' he said, 'and this one cannot be averted.'

Jocundra thought she understood him, but her understanding fled the instant he turned away and she felt disoriented.

Edman gave way to two black orderlies, who lifted Magnusson's wheelchair, bearing him aloft like a king on a palanquin.

'Hey, niggers!' shouted Richmond, and swung his cane at the nearest orderly; but Audrey wrapped her arms around him from behind and his swing went awry. They swayed together, struggling.

'No hope for you, sonny.' Magnusson beamed at Richmond from on high. 'You're a dead man.'

'Out!' bawled Edman; he waved his fist, abandoning control. 'Everybody out! Staff in my office!'

As the orderlies carried Magnusson off, he called back. 'Two years, Edman! Three at the most! They'll probe your every hollow, but they'll never find it!'

A babble arose, cries of alarm, milling, and Jocundra was later to reflect that when psychiatrists lost their cool they did not stoop to half measures. She had intended to wait until the crowd thinned, but Dr Brauer rushed up, poked his face into Donnell's, bleated 'Harrison!' then shouted at Jocundra to move it. There were more shouts of 'Move it!' and 'Let her through!' A hefty red-haired woman tried to get out of her path, snapped a high heel and tumbled head first over the arm of a sofa; her skirt slid down around her hips, exposing thighs dimpled by cellulite. A doctor and an orderly tugged at Clarice Monroe, contending for the right to escort her; French's wheelchair sideswiped Ramsburgh's, and she jabbed at his therapist with a plastic needle. Dodging, swerving, Jocundra pushed Donnell along a tunnel of consternated faces and into the hall. Three doctors had backed the girl whom Richmond had assaulted against the wall; she was straddling a fern, holding the madras jacket together. Tears streaked her face. She nodded in response to a question, but the nod may have had no significance because she continued to bob her head while they scribbled on their clipboards.

Donnell's room was sunny, a breeze shifted the curtains, leaf shadow jittered on the carpet. Jocundra could not think what to say, what lie would soothe him, so she left him at the writing desk and collected the laundry, watching him out of the corner of her eye. He straightened a stack of paper, picked up a pen, doodled, laid it down.

'He's really ...' He picked up the pen again.

'Pardon?' She tossed his bathrobe into the hamper.

'What's the matter with him? Is he just naturally crazy or is it something to do with the process?' He kept fidgeting, his hands moving aimlessly from pen to paper to notebook.

'He's very, very old.' Jocundra knelt beside him, happy for the opportunity to comfort him. 'He was probably senile before the process was applied, and it wasn't able to restore him fully.' She rubbed the bunched muscles in his shoulder.

He bent his head, allowing her easier access to his neck. 'I can't wait to get out of this place,' he said.

'It'll be sooner than you think,' she said, wishing it weren't so harshly true. She had begun to hate herself for lying, but she had no better thing to tell him. 'Please don't let it depress you. I want you to get well.'

A poignant sadness rose in her, as if the words 'I want you to get well' had been a splash of cold water on the hot stones of her emotions. But the sadness didn't seem attached to his dying. It seemed instead a product of the way the light slanted down, the temperature, the shadows and sounds: a kind of general sadness attaching to every human involvement, one you only felt when the conditions were just right but was there all the time. She thought the feeling must be showing on her face, and to hide it she pretended to cough.

'God,' he said, 'I wish I was well now.' He looked over at her, eyes wide, mouth downturned, the same expression he had worn during the drive from Tulane. 'Ah, Hell. I guess there's some virtue to having died …' He trailed off.

She knew he had been about to refer to her as that virtue, to make a joke of it, to address lightly his attraction for her, but he left the punchline unsaid and the last words he *had* said hung in the air between them, taking on the coloration of all the fear and sickness in the room. Shortly afterward she excused herself and went into the bathroom. She sat on the edge of the sink for almost fifteen minutes, expecting to cry, on the verge of crying, tears brimming, but the sob never built to critical in her chest, just hung there and decayed.

CHAPTER 6

From *Conjure Men: My Work With Ezawa at Tulane*
by Anthony Edman, MD, PhD.

... It was as close as I have ever come to striking a colleague, but Brauer – in his capacity of ambitious underling, thirsting for authority – seemed determined to make a case for my bungling the interaction, allowing the patients too much leeway, and my temper frayed. I forced myself to calm, however, and reminded him that we had achieved exactly the desired result: despite Magnusson's unexpected outburst, or because of it, we had brought the patients' fear of one another into the open where it could be treated with and analyzed.

'Within a week they'll be forming associations,' I told him. 'Monroe and French are obvious, Harrison and Richmond ... Now that Richmond's found someone who'll face up to him, someone more or less his own age, he's bound to make friendly overtures. It's inevitable. Perhaps we've suffered a few flesh wounds, but now they'll have to accept their fear as a side effect of the process and deal with it.'

My show of unruffled confidence bolstered staff morale, and, in effect, dismasted Brauer who continued his outraged sputterings, but to no avail. I explained to staff that our loss of control only added authenticity to the proceedings. Had we not, I asked them, reacted in the manner of concerned medical personnel, of doctors responsible for the welfare of patients making a difficult mental adjustment? We had shown them our humanity, our imperfect compassion. I admitted my own loss of control was, like theirs, a response to the possibility that the patients might understand their true natures; still, I felt that any damage caused by our actions or by Magnusson's could be turned to our advantage if we did not attempt a cover-up, if we allowed Magnusson to remain at Shadows, and not – as Brauer suggested – hide him from the world in a cell at Tulane. Let him say what he will, I advised, and we will simply put on a sad face and express pity over his senility, his general deterioration. *We* will be believed.

Of course, it did not prove necessary to debunk Magnusson; just as Ramsburgh had defended herself, so the patients – in defense of their threatened identities – arrived at this conclusion on their own, separate and unanimously.

We had taken a vast step forward as a result of the group interaction. The patients began to speak openly of their fearful reaction to one another, and we analyzed their reports, gaining further insights into the extent of their perceptual abnormalities. For example, it was during the period immediately following the interaction that Harrison revealed the fact he was seeing bio-energy: '... Raw mists of a single color sheathing the upper body, showing patches and glints of secondary colors, all fading in a matter of seconds.' His perceptions, in particular, gave me cause to ponder Magnusson's pronouncement concerning my own illness, though at the time I assumed his diagnosis to be a vindictive rather than an accurate one. But while such insights provided clues to the developmental processes of these phenomenal strangers who were the BIAP patients, they shed no direct light upon the essential mystery of their existence; and the illumination of this mystery must be, I felt, the primary goal of the project. So, instead of pursuing a hands-off policy in the wake of Magnusson's revelations to the group, I continued as planned to set up problematic situations which would, I hoped, stimulate the patients to more profound depths of self-discovery.

Throughout the hullabaloo which eventuated after the media's disclosure of the project, my detractors have labeled me a manipulator, and while I do not accept the term with its overtones of maleficence, I submit that all psychotherapy is manipulation; that as psychiatrists we do not heal people, but manipulate their neuroses into functional modes. Any psychiatrist worth his salt is at heart a sophist who understands he is lost in a great darkness and who utilizes theories not as doctrinal cant, but as guideposts to mark the places he has illumined in his dealings with specific patients. Thus, also, did ancient alchemists incise their alembics with arcane symbols representing the known elements. I have been accused of ruthlessly swaying the courses of lives to satisfy my academic whimsies. This charge I deny. I maneuvred both patients and therapists as would a man lost in a forest strike flint and steel together to make a light. And we *were* lost. Before my arrival the project had an unblemished record of failure in every area, especially as regards the unraveling of the patients' intrinsic natures. This memoir is not the proper framework in which to detail all we *did* unravel after my arrival, but I must point out the various papers and monographs of my detractors as evidence of my successes (the more scholarly reader may wish to avail himself of my own soon-to-be-published *The Second Death* and its speculative companion, *Departed Souls: A Psychoanalytic Reassessment of Animist Beliefs*).

My detractors have addressed with especial venom what one of them has termed my 'unprofessional obsession with Jocundra Verret,' and have laid the blame for all consequent tragedy at my feet. In this I admit to some complicity, yet if I am to shoulder the blame, then surely I must take credit for all that has been gained. While I do not discount my colleagues' responsibility, and while Ms Verret herself has testified that she acted for reasons of her own, if they are insistent I will accept full blame and credit, and leave history to confer final judgement on the worth of my contribution. Yes, I took chances! I flew by the seat of my pants. I was willing for all hell to break loose in order to learn the patients' secrets, and perhaps a measure of hell was necessary for the truth to emerge. We were cartographers, not healers; it was our duty to explore the wilderness of this new human preserve, and I could not accept as Brauer seemingly could my role as being merely that of babysitter to the undead.

Though my case study of the relationship between Harrison and Verret – and never has a courtship been so thoroughly documented as theirs, recorded on videotape and footnoted by in-depth interviews of the participants – though this study revealed much of value, as the weeks passed I came to regard the relationship primarily as a star by which I navigated, one whose unwavering light signaled the rightness of my course. This may seem an overly romantic attitude for a member of my profession to hold, and perhaps it was, but I believe I can justify having held it in terms of my own emotional needs. The pressures on me were enormous, and I was only able to cope with them by commuting to and from New Orleans on the weekends and spending the nights in my own home. Project officials screamed for results, my colleagues continually questioned my concern for the patients' well-being. *My* concern? Because I refused to indulge in banal Freudian dissections and quasi-metaphysical coffee klatches with these second-rate theoreticians, did I lack concern? I stimulated the patients, encouraged them, tried to provide them with a pride in their occupations. Should I, instead, have pampered them, patted them on the head and admired the fact that they actually breathed? This was Ezawa's attitude: having made them, he was well pleased, looking upon them as mere monuments to his cleverness.

But, of course, the greatest pressure was that exerted by the patients themselves. Imagine, if you will, indwelling with a group of brilliant and charismatic individuals, thoroughly dominant, whose vivid character suppresses and dulls your own. It was a constant strain to be around them; I cannot think of a single person who did not suffer a severe depression at some time or another as a result. They were mesmeric figures: green-eyed monsters with the capacities of angels. Harrison's poems, Monroe's ballet, even Richmond's howled dirge ... these were powerful expressions, dispiriting to those of us incapable of emulating them, especially dispiriting because of the wan light their productions appeared to shed on the nature of creativity, demystifying it, relegating it to something on the order of a technological twitch, like the galvanic response of a dissected frog. And yet neither could we totally disabuse ourselves of mystical notions concerning the patients. At times it seemed to me that we were a strange monastic order committed to the care and feeding of crippled, green-eyed saints whose least pronouncement sent us running to examine the entrails for proof of their prophetic insight. All the therapists stood in awe of them, or – as did Laura Petit – maintained an artificial distance; all, that is, except Jocundra Verret.

Watching Verret and Harrison, observing the relaxed attitude they had adopted with each other, their reponses increasingly warm and genuine, I felt I was witnessing the emergence of some integral shape from the chaotic sphere of Shadows: a sweet, frail truth which – despite its frailty – underlies our humanity. Always a beautiful woman, Verret grew ever more beautiful; her skin glowed, her hair shone and her walk – previously somnolent, head down, arms barely aswing – grew sprightly and girlish. I often pointed out to her during our sessions that she – every bit as much as the residual RNA – was a determining factor in Harrison's personality, that just as the *mama loi* identifies the possessing spirit in a voodoo rite, so she was 'identifying' Harrison, evoking the particular complex of his behaviors to conform with her own needs. He was, after all, trying to please her, molding himself to suit her requirements as a man. Given Harrison's perceptual abilities, his concentrated focus upon her, it is likely he was being influenced by her on levels we can only begin to guess at, and the extent of her influence is equally unfathomable. She preferred, however, to downplay her role of creatrix, insisting he was something more mysterious and self-determining. I am certain she did not know what was happening, not at first, hiding her feelings behind the pose of duty.

Although I had detected this potential in Verret at our initial meeting, still it dazzled me that love could arise between two such ill-matched individuals and under such intimidating circumstances. Their relationship provided a breath of normalcy amidst the abnormal atmosphere of Shadows, one which I inhaled deeply, rising to it as a miner trapped in a gas-filled tunnel would lift his head at the scent of fresh air. I became more and more interested to learn how far this affair might progress, interested to the point of adding my own thread to the tapestry they were weaving.

Manipulate? Yes, I manipulated. And despite the ensuing events, I would do so again, for it is the function of psychiatry to encourage the living to live, and thus did I encourage Harrison and Verret.

One day, while lunching in the commissary, I was joined by Laura Petit and Audrey Beamon. Petit had with her a Tarot deck and proceeded to tell Beamon's fortune, and, thereafter, insisted on telling mine. I chose the Hierophant as my significator, cut the cards and listened as Laura interpreted their meanings. I could see the cards were ordinary, showing no pattern; I had not concentrated during the shuffle or the cut. Laura was not aware of my familiarity with the Tarot and therefore did not realize I learned more of her character from the reading than of my fate. Punctuating her delivery with

'Oh dears' and 'Now, wait a minutes,' she twisted the meanings of the cards, telling me a glittering tale of my future – fame after struggle – and told me also by the flattering, insinuating nature of her interpretation that here was a clever ally whom I could entrust with any mission, no matter how underhanded. Afterwards, she laid a card face up on the table: the Devil, a great, shaggy, horned figure crouched on a black stone to which a naked man and woman were chained. 'I *really* think you should have chosen this as your significator, Dr Edman,' she said, fluttering her lashes and giggling. Despite the apparent triviality of the comment, her identification of me with this awesome masculine figure, this cruel master, signaled her willingness to enlist in my cause, to submit, and, as well, displayed her sly delight in what she presumed we were really doing: all the subterfuge and nastiness of the project. All right, I thought, if I am to be Satan, then Laura will be my imp. I would put her simpering guile to use. And I did, though I am certain my manipulation was not the sole casual agent of the affair.

The character and climate of Shadows, no doubt, exerted an influence on my actions. This great manor house glooming on the edge of the swamp amid sentinel oaks and penitential moss, inhabited by dead men come to life again ... here were both magical setting and characters, the stuff from which great drama arises, and perhaps, unconsciously, I was trying to spark such a drama, obeying the commands of some inner theatricality which the house had stirred in my depths, my 'deep consciousness.' Perhaps, were I to be injected with the Ezawa bacterium after death, I might well reincarnate as a playwright. But each morning before rounds as I took my constitutional, I would look back at the house and experience a thrill of excitement and fear. From a distance its windows appeared dead black as if it contained not furniture and walls and lives, but only a ripe and contaminating darkness. We inhabited that darkness, and I alone of all the project dared strike matches and dispel the gloom. Most of my colleagues, I believe, feared what would be revealed and satisfied themselves with behavioral studies. But this was an experiment, not a behavioral clinic; we were there to learn, not to footnote extant knowledge. And what did we learn? We uncovered new forces, we took a step along what may be an endless path towards divinity, we redirected the entire thrust of psychoanalytic theory, and, as with all knowledge, we found that deeper and more compelling mysteries yet lay beyond those we had reduced to the security of fact.

CHAPTER 7

April 18 – May 3, 1987

'You should come on a run with me sometime,' said Richmond; he lay back, arms behind his head, and pondered the passing clouds. 'Cruisin' through some half-ass town, pullin' up to the fountain in the park or whatever they got for a public eyesore. 'Bout forty or fifty of you. The cops ain't to be found, man. You know, they got sudden problems out on the highway, and you are in *control* of the situation. That's when the ladies will do some flockin' around. The ladies dig on a Harley, man! They wanna run their fingers 'long your gas tank, you understand?'

'Uh huh,' said Donnell, too exhausted to do more than listen to Richmond. He had managed to walk almost a hundred yards, and as a result his legs trembled, his chest hammered, and sweat was trickling into his eyes; but the accomplishment gave him a feeling of serenity.

'Dig it, man. After we blow outta here, we'll head on down to the Gulf, place I know, do some money trips, and then get the fuck outta Dodge City! Put our shit nationwide!' He held out his hand to be slapped five.

Donnell propped himself up on an elbow and accommodated him, amused by Richmond's adoption of him as a sidekick. His function, it seemed, was to agree, to share Richmond's enthusiasm for drugs, violence, and sleazy sex – those things he considered the joys of life – and to confirm Richmond's wisdom in all areas except that of intellectual wisdom, dominion over which he accorded to Donnell. He did not particularly like Richmond, and he still had a nervous reaction to him, but the vivid stories shored up his confidence in his own memories.

'There's a feelin', man,' said Richmond, solemn as a priest, 'and don't nothin' else feel like it. That goddamn four-stroke's howlin' like a jet, and your ol' lady's got her tits squashed against your leathers, playin' with your throttle. Whoo! Sex and death and sound effects!'

Audrey and Jocundra were sitting on a bench about thirty feet from where they were lying, and Donnell concentrated on Jocundra. He lowered his head, looked up at her through his brows, and brought her aura into focus: an insubstantial shawl of blue light, frail as the thinnest of mists, glimmering with pinpricks of ruby and gold and emerald-green.

'Takes a commitment, though,' said Richmond soberly. 'If you gonna ride with the 'hounds, you gotta kill a cop.'

'You killed a cop?' Donnell was surprised to learn that Richmond was capable of mortal violence; he had sensed an underlying innocence, a playfulness, and had assumed most of the bloody tales to be lies or exaggeration.

'Naw, I was just runnin' probate, but the day's gonna come, man.' Richmond plucked a handful of grass and tossed it up into the breeze, watched it drift. 'My ol' lady says I ain't got what it takes to be a one-percenter, but what the hell's she know? She works in a goddamn massage parlor, punchin' ol' farts' hornbuttons for fifty bucks a pop. That don't make her no damn expert on my potential!'

Donnell let the aura fade and studied Jocundra. He constantly was finding new features to examine – a nuance of expression, the glide of a muscle – and it was beginning to frustrate him to the point of physical discomfort. Through an unbuttoned fold of her blouse he saw the curve of her breast molded into a swell of beige silk, and he imagined it was as near to him as it appeared, warm and perfumed, a soft weight nudging his cheek. He suspected she was aware of his frustrated desire, and he did not think she was put off by the fact he wanted her.

Wheels crunched on the flagstones, footsteps, and Magnusson rolled up, his therapist beside him. 'Go have a talk with your friends, Laura,' he said. She started to object, then tossed her head in exasperation and stalked off.

'Fine ass,' said Richmond. 'But no tits. Ain't none of 'em got tits like ol' Audrey.'

'Gentlemen!' Magnusson's lips pursed spasmodically as if he were trying to kiss his nose. 'I've given up attempting to enlist your support, but I've made a decision of which you should be aware.' He glared at them, squeezing the arms of his chair: a feeble old king judging his unworthy subjects. 'May the third, gentlemen. I want you to mark that date.'

'Why's that, Doc?' asked Richmond. 'You havin' a party?'

'In a manner of speaking, yes. Mr Harrison! I'm determined you'll listen to me this time.'

Donnell avoided the old man's eyes. His nervous reaction was becoming more pronounced, and as often happened around Magnusson, his vision was playing tricks, shifting involuntarily.

'As I told you last week, it's obvious to me that the life span of the bacteria within the host should be on the order of a day or thereabouts. No more. Well, I believe I've deduced the reason for our longevity, though to be sure I'd have to take a look inside an infested brain.'

Richmond's back humped with silent laughter.

'Your brain would do nicely, Mr Richmond. Dissection may well prove its optimal employment.' Magnusson cackled, 'Initially, they wouldn't give me brain data. Said all the patients had recovered, and there was no such data. But I succeeded in convincing Brauer to assist me. Surely, I said, there must have been early failures, animal experiments. If I could see those files, I told him, no telling what insights they might elicit.'

Out of the corner of his eye, Donnell saw Magnusson embedded in a veil of red light, an aural color so deep that the old man's head showed as featureless and distorted as the darkness at the heart of a flawed ruby.

'There's too much data to relate it all,' said Magnusson, 'so let me take a tuck in my argument. Each of us has experienced perceptual abnormalities, abilities the uninformed would categorize as "psychic." It's clear that some feature of our brain allied with these abilities is retarding the bacterial process. Three of the case studies Brauer loaned me revealed extensive infestation of the dopamine and norepenephrine systems. I didn't dare ask him about them, but I believe they were like us, and that the seat of the retarding factor, and therefore of 'psychic' potential ...'

'Doc, you borin' the shit outta me!' Richmond stood, only a little awkwardly, and Donnell envied his ease of mobility.

'You won't have to put up with me much longer, Mr Richmond.' A loose cough racked Magnusson's chest. 'I'm being discharged on May the fourth. Ezawa himself will be on hand to oversee my ... my liberation.' He sucked at his teeth. 'Mr Harrison. I want you to promise me that on May the third you'll look closely at your bedroom walls. A simple duty, but your assumption of it will both guarantee my peace of mind and substantially prove my point.'

Donnell nodded, wishing Magnusson away.

'Your nod's your bond, I suppose. Very well. Look closely, Mr Harrison. As closely as only you can look.' He wheeled off, calling for his therapist.

'Senile old bastard,' said Richmond.

'Every time he's around,' said Donnell, 'it's like something's crawling up my spine. But he doesn't sound senile to me.'

'So what. I get weird vibes off you, and you ain't senile,' said Richmond with his usual eccentric logic. 'Just 'cause you get weird vibes off a dude don't mean they gotta be one way or another ...' He lost the flow of his argument. ''Course maybe I'm just used to weirdness,' he continued moodily. 'Where I grew up there was a cemetery right across the street, and all kinds of weird shit was goin' on. Funerals and shit. Especially on Thursdays. How come you think Thursdays is such a big day for funerals, man?'

'Probably a slow business day.' Donnell picked up his cane.

'I'm gonna head on back with the cooze. Who knows!' Richmond waggled his tongue in a parody of lust. 'Tonight might be the night me and ol' Audrey get down and do the low yo-yo!'

As Richmond sauntered off, his limp barely evident, Donnell levered himself up with his cane. His first step sent pains shooting from his feet into his knees.

'Hi.' Jocundra came up beside him. 'Should I bring the chair?'

'I can deal with it.' He linked arms with her, and they walked toward the house at a ceremonial pace. His skin was irritated to a glow each time her hip brushed him.

'Was Dr Magnusson bothering you again?'

'Yeah. He says he's being discharged May the fourth.'

'That's right.'

Donnell stepped on a pebble, teetered, but she steadied him. 'Where's he going to end up?' he asked. 'He can't take care of himself.'

'A home for the elderly, I suppose,' she said. 'I'll find out from Laura if you like.'

Her smile was sweet, open, and he smiled back. 'It doesn't matter.' He started to tell her of his promise to Magnusson, but thought better of it, and told her instead about Richmond having to kill a cop.

Toward the end of April, Jocundra dreamed that Donnell came into her room one night while she was asleep. Within the logic of the dream, a very vivid dream, she was not surprised to see him because she knew – just as in reality – that he often waked before her and would sometimes become lonely and ask her to fix breakfast. This time, however, he did not wake her, merely sat beside the bed. The moon was down, and he was visible by the flickers in his eyes: jagged bursts of green lightning sharply incised upon the darkness, yet so tiny and short-lived they seemed far away, as if she were watching a storm at the extreme edge of her horizon. After a minute he reached out and rested his fingers briefly on the inside of her elbow, jerking them back when a static charge crackled between them. He sat motionless for a few seconds, and she thought he was holding his breath, expecting her to wake; at last he stretched out his hand again and brushed his fingertips across the nipple of her left breast, teasing it erect beneath her nightgown, sending shivery electricities down into the flesh as if he were conducting the charges within his eyes. Then he cupped her breast, a treasuring touch, and the weight of his hand set a pulse throbbing between her legs.

She had another dream immediately afterward, something about clowns and chasing around a subdivision, but she most remembered the one about Donnell. It disturbed her because she was not certain it had been a dream, and because it brought to mind a talk she had had with Laura Petit several days before. Donnell had requested a morning alone to begin a new project – a story, he said – and so Jocundra had picked out a magazine and gone onto the grounds. Laura had accosted her in the parking lot, saying she needed a friendly ear, and they had walked down to the stone bench near the gatehouse.

'I'm losin' touch with Hilmer,' said Laura. 'He wants to be alone all the time.' Strands of hair escaped from her barrette, there were shadows around her eyes, and her lipstick was smeary.

Jocundra was inclined to sympathy, but she couldn't help being somewhat pleased to learn that Laura was not impervious to human affliction. 'He's just involved with his work,' she advised. 'At this stage you have to expect it.'

'He's not workin',' said Laura bitterly. 'He wanders! All day long. I can't keep track of him. Edman says to let him have the run of the house, but I just don't feel right about it, especially with the cameras breakin' down so much.' She gave Jocundra a dewy, piteous look and said, 'I should be with him! He's only got a week, and I know there's somethin' he's hidin'.'

Appalled by the depth of Laura's self-interest, her lack of concern for Magnusson, Jocundra opened her magazine and made no reply.

Suddenly animated, Laura pulled out a file from her pocket and began doing her nails. 'Well,' she said prissily, 'I may not have *totally* succeeded with Hilmer, but I've done my job properly ... not like that Audrey Beamon.'

Jocundra was irritated. Audrey, though dull, was at least no aggravation. 'What's your problem with Audrey?' she asked coldly.

'It's not *my* problem.' Registering Jocundra's displeasure, Laura assumed a haughty pose, head high, gazing toward the house: a proud belle watching the plantation burn. 'If you don't want to hear it, that's fine! But I just think you should know who you're associatin' with.'

'I know Audrey quite well.'

'Really!' Laura hmmphed in disbelief. 'Well, then I'm sure you know she's been doin' it with Jack Richmond.'

'*Doing* it?' Jocundra laughed. 'Do you mean sex?'

'Yes,' said Laura primly. 'Can you imagine?'

'No. One of the orderlies is telling you stories to get you excited.'

'It wasn't any orderly!' squawked Laura. 'It was Edman!'

Jocundra looked up from her magazine, startled.

'You can march right up there and ask him if you don't believe me!' Laura stood, hands on hips, frowning. 'You remember when the cameras went out a whole day last week? Well, they didn't go out ... not for the whole day. Edman wanted to see what might happen if people didn't know they were bein' observed, and he got an eyeful of Audrey and Richmond!'

After Laura flounced off, Jocundra whimsically considered the prospect of green-eyed babies and thought about Laura's capacity for lying – no doubt vast; but she decided it was perfectly in keeping with Edman's methods to have done what Laura said. She tried to imagine Audrey and Richmond making love. It was not as difficult to imagine as she had expected; in fact, given Audrey's undergraduate reputation at Tulane – the sorority girl run amok – she probably would find Richmond fascinating. Further, Jocundra recognized that her own fascination with Donnell had allowed her to relax the role of therapist and become his friend; and if you could become the friend of a man such as Donnell, if you could put aside the facts of his life and see the person he really was – something which had been no chore to do because he *was* both fascinating and talented – well, then it might even be less of a chore to become his lover.

The dream, however, shone a new light on all this. Jocundra realized the boundaries of her friendship for Donnell were fraying, and she was glad of the realization. Now that it was out in the open she could deal with it, and dealing with it was important. There certainly was no future in letting it develop. The more she thought about the dream, the more convinced she was that Donnell had actually entered her room, that she had convinced herself she was asleep, observing him from the cover of sleep, from a dreamlike perspective. Self-deception was a particular talent of hers, and had already led her to a terrible marriage. Charlie had not wanted to be married, but she had persuaded him. He had been her first lover, and after the rite of passage was unsatisfactorily concluded, feeling sullied, ruined, the ghost of her Catholic girlhood rearing up like a dead queen out of a sarcophagus, she had seduced herself into believing she could love him. From a painfully ordinary and unattractive present she had manufactured the vision of a blissful future, and had coached herself to think of Charlie foremost, to please him, thinking these submissions would consolidate her vision, yet knowing all the while that he was not only her first lover, but also her first serious mistake. And now, it seemed, this same self-deception was operating along a contrary principle: disguising the growth of strong emotion as symptoms of friendship and responsibility.

To deal with it Jocundra let the routines of Shadows carry her away from Donnell. She attended staff meetings religiously and took every opportunity to join the other therapists for conversation and coffee; but when forced to be alone with Donnell she found these measures were not sufficient to counter the development of an attachment. She began to lie awake nights, brooding over his death, counting the days left him, wishing they would pass quickly, wishing they would pass slowly, experiencing guilt at her part in the proceedings. But despite her worries, she was satisfied that she could eventually cultivate a distance between herself and Donnell by maintaining an awareness of the problem, by adherence to the routines, and she continued to be thus satisfied until May the third arrived and all routines were shattered.

> *'I was born in Rented Rooms Five Dollars*
> *Down on Adjacent Boulevard,*
> *You know that funky place got no fire escape,*
> *No vacancies, and a dirt front yard.*
> *My mama was Nobody's fool,*

He left her for a masseuse down in New Orleans,
Take the cash and flush the credit cards
Was the best advice he ever gave to me ...'

Four doctors were holding conference in the main hall, but Richmond's raucous voice and discordant piano stylings flushed them from the sofa, set them to buttoning their lab coats and clipping their pens in a stiff-necked bustle toward the door. 'Turkeys!' snarled Richmond. He hammered out the chords, screaming the words after them, elbowing Donnell, urging him to join in the chorus.

'Early one mornin' with light rain fallin'
I rode off upon my iron horse,
You seen my poster and you read my rap sheet:
Armed and dangerous, no distinguishin' marks,
Wanted for all the unnatural crimes
And for havin' too much fun,
He leads a pack of one-eyed Jacks,
He's known as Harley David's son!
Aw, they say hell hath no fury
Like a woman scorned,
But all them scornful women catch their hell
From Harley David's son!'

The door slammed; Richmond quit pounding and noodled the keys, a musical texture more appropriate to the peaceful morning air. Sunlight laid a diagram of golden light and shadow over the carpet, the lowest ranks of the paintings were masked in reflected glare, and ceramic figurines glistened on end tables beside the French doors. Jocundra and Audrey were sitting on a sofa, talking, at ease, and their voices were a gentle, refined constant like the chatter of pet birds. The old house seemed to be full of its original atmosphere, its gilt and marble and lacquer breathing a graciousness which not even Richmond's song could disrupt. And yet Donnell detected an ominous disturbance in the air, fading now, as if a gong had been struck and the rippling note had sunk below the audible threshold. He felt it dooming through his flesh, insisting that the peace and quiet was an illusion, that today was May the third, Magnusson's May the third, and thereafter nothing would be the same. He was being foolish, he told himself, foolish and suggestible. He did not understand half of what Magnusson spouted, and the other half was unbelievable, but when he tried to finalize his disbelief, to forget about Magnusson, he could not. The old man's arguments – though they sounded insane – were neither disassociative nor rambling, not senile.

'Hey!' Richmond nudged him and handed him a piece of paper. 'Check it out.'

Donnell was glad for the distraction. He read the lines, then used the piano bench as a table on which to scrawl changes. 'Try this.' He passed the paper back to Richmond, who frowned and fingered the chords:

> *'Cold iron doesn't stop me*
> *And you ain't got no silver gun ...'*

Richmond clucked his tongue. 'Lemme see how it works together.' He sang the song under his breath, filling with the chords.

The song was Richmond's sole creation, and Donnell approved of it; it was, like Richmond, erratic and repetitive and formless. The choruses – there were dozens, detailing the persona of a cosmic outlaw who wore a three-horned helmet – were sung over a major chord progression; Richmond talked the verses in a minor blues key, telling disconnected stories about cheap crooks and whores and perverts he had known.

The slow vibration in the air ended, sheared off, as if a circuitbreaker had engaged, and Donnell suddenly believed it *had* been in the air, a tangible evidence of Magnusson's proof, and was not a product of suggestion or sensory feedback from his own body.

'This here's the best goddamn one yet!' Richmond poised his hands above the keyboard. 'Dig it!'

'I think Magnusson's done something,' said Donnell.

Richmond snorted. 'You hearin' voices or something, man? Shit! Listen up.'

> *'If you hear a rumblin',*
> *It's too late to run,*
> *Cold iron doesn't stop me*
> *And you ain't got no silver gun,*
> *Then your girlfriend's breast starts tremblin'*
> *And she screams, "Oh God! Here he comes!"*
> *Half beast, half man, half Master Plan,*
> *It's Harley David's son!*
> *Aw, I'll kiss your one-eyed sister,*
> *Hell, I'll lick her socket with my tongue!*
> *I'm Christ-come-down-and-fucked-around,*
> *I'm Harley David's son!'*

'Now that ...' said Richmond proudly. 'That's got it. What'd you say about the last one?'

'The archetypal power of good graffiti.'

'Yeah.' Richmond plinked the keys. 'Arche*typ*al!'

The main doors swung open and Laura Petit wandered in, stopped, and trailed her fingers across the gilt filigree of a table. The same slow, rippling vibration filled the room, more forcibly than before, as if it hadn't died but had merely grown too weak to pass through walls and now could enter. Audrey waved, and Laura walked toward the sofa, hesitant, looking nervously behind her. She asked something of Jocundra, who shook her head: No. 'Please!' shrilled Laura. Audrey stood, beckoned to Jocundra, and they all went into the hallway, closing the door after them. The vibration was cut off.

'Squeeze, you might have a point about the Doc.' Richmond shut the piano lid and swiveled around to face the door. 'There was some strange bullshit walked in with that little lady!'

'What is it?' Audrey shut the door to the main hall.

Laura was very pale; her Adam's apple worked. 'Hilmer,' she said, her voice tight and small; she looked up to the glass eye of the camera mounted above the door and was transfixed.

Jocundra sprinted ahead, knowing it must be bad.

Magnusson's door stood ajar; it was dark inside. Sunlight through the louvered shutters striped a heraldic pattern of gold diagonals across the legs of the shadowy figure on the bed. She leaned in. 'Dr Magnusson?' Her words stirred a little something within the darkness, a shiver, a vibration, and then she saw a flicker of fiery green near the headboard, another, and another yet, as if he were sneaking a peek between his slitted eyelids. 'Are you all right, Doctor?' she asked, relieved, thinking Laura had overreacted and nothing was seriously wrong. She turned on the ceiling light.

It was as if she had been watching someone's vacation slides, the projectionist clicking from scene to scene, narrating, 'Here's grandpa asleep in his room ... kinda pretty the way the light's falling through the shutters there,' click, the screen goes black, and the next slide is the obscene one which the neighbor's teenage kid slipped in as a prank. Click. Magnusson's room was an obscenity. So much blood was puddled in the depression made by his head and shoulders, streaked over the headboard and floor, that at first she could not bring her eye to bear on the body, tracking instead the chaotic sprays of red. A mild heated odor rose from the glistening surfaces. She clutched the doorknob for support, tucking her chin onto her chest, dizzy and nauseated.

'Oh, Jesus!' said Audrey behind her. 'I'll get Edman.'

Laura snuffled.

Jocundra swallowed, gathering herself. Magnusson lay on his side, his right arm upflung across his face and wedged against the headboard, concealing all except his forehead and the corner of his right eye. She switched off the lights, and the green flickers were again visible. God, she thought, what if somehow he's alive. She switched the lights back on. It was becoming easier to bear, but not much. She stepped around the bloody streaks and stopped a foot from the bed. His chest was unmoving. She knelt beside him and was craning her neck, trying to locate the wound, when his arm came unwedged and dangled against her knee. The shock caused her to overbalance. She tipped forward and planted her hand on the bed to stabilize. Blood mired between her fingers, and her face bobbed to within inches of a neat slice in his throat. Its lips were crusted with a froth of pink bubbles. One of them popped, and a clear fluid seeped from the wound.

Laura screamed – an abandoned, throat-tearing scream – and Jocundra threw herself back and sat down hard on the carpet, face to face with Magnusson. Folds of waxy skin sagged from his cheeks, and the bacteria were in flux within his eyes. Spidery blobs of luminescence spanned the sockets, their edges eroding, gradually revealing sections of his liverish whites and glazed blue irises. Jocundra was spellbound. Then she felt something soaking her slacks and realized that the horrid paste sticking them to her thighs was a spill of Magnusson's blood. She scrambled up and started for the door. And stopped. Laura had fallen to her knees, sobbing, and behind her stood Richmond and Donnell.

'There's been an accident,' Jocundra said, obeying the stupid reflex of lies. She pushed them away and tried to shut the door, but Richmond knocked her hand aside and jammed the door open with his foot.

'No shit!' he said, peering into the room. 'Ol' Doc musta tripped or somethin', huh?'

Jocundra decided she couldn't worry about Richmond; she took Donnell's arm and propelled him along the hall. 'I think he killed himself. It's going to be a madhouse in a minute. You wait in the room and I'll find out what I can.'

'But why would he kill himself?' he asked, as she forced him through the door. 'He was getting out.'

'I don't know.' She helped him lower into the wheelchair. 'Let me go now. I've got to make my report.' A flash of memory showed her the old man's eyes, his throat, something still alive after all that blood, and she shuddered.

Donnell blinked, looking at the wall above his writing desk. 'Yeah, go ahead,' he said distractedly. He wheeled over to the desk and picked up a pen.

'What's the matter?'

'Nothing.' He opened a notebook. 'I'll figure it out.'

She knew he was holding something back, but she was in no mood to pry and no shape to field his questions. She reassured him that she would return quickly and went into the hall. Agitated voices lifted from Magnusson's room; Laura was still sitting outside the door, collapsed against the ornate molding like a beggar girl beneath a temple arch. Jocundra leaned against the wall. From the moment she had seen Magnusson, she had been operating on automatic, afraid for either herself or for Donnell, and now, relieved of pressure, she began to tremble. She put her hand up to cover her eyes and saw the brown bloodstains webbing the palm; she wiped it on her hip. She did not want to think anymore, about Magnusson, about herself or Donnell, and so, to occupy her mind and because no one else would be likely to bother, concerned only with their experiment gone awry, she hurried down the hall to find if anything could be done for Laura.

DON'T TELL JOCUNDRA was written on the wall in crudely printed letters about the size of a fist; the letters were not of a color but were indented into the wallpaper, and it had taken only a slight shift in focus to bring them clear. Beneath the first line was a second message: THE INSTANT YOU ARE ALONE, LOOK UNDER YOUR MATTRESS.

Donnell didn't hesitate. He felt around under the mattress, touched something hard and thin, and pulled out a red account ledger from which an envelope protruded; the words READ THIS NOW! were printed on the envelope, and inside were five typewritten pages and a simple plan of the first floor and basement. There were only a few lines on the first page.

> I am dying early for your benefit, Mr Harrison, and I hope you will therefore give my rationality the benefit of the doubt and act at once upon my instructions. If you have learned of my death shortly after its event, then these instructions apply; if more than twenty minutes have elapsed, you must use your own judgement. Leave your room immediately. Do not worry about the cameras: they are currently malfunctioning. Follow the diagram and enter the room marked X. All personnel will be doubtless involved in frantic inessentials, but if you happen to be observed, I am certain you can supply an adequate excuse. The ledger and the letter will clarify all else.

Donnell cracked the bedroom door. An orderly rushed past and into Magnusson's room; Jocundra was hunkered next to Laura outside the room, but she had her back to him and was blocking Laura's view. No one else was in the hall. He eased out the door and wheeled toward the foyer, expecting her to call out at any second; he passed the foyer, continued along the hall and turned the corner. The door leading to the basement was the first on his left. He stood, wobbly on his cane, and shoved the wheelchair back into the front hall so they could not tell where he had gone. The stairs were steep, and each step jolted loose pains in his hips and spine. A dimly lit corridor led off the stair; he entered the second door and twisted the latch. Gray-painted walls, two folding chairs facing a large mirror, and a speaker and switches mounted beside the mirror. Breathing hard, he sat and fumbled out the remainder of Magnusson's letter.

> In the event it is Dr Edman who reads this: sir, you are a great ass! If, however, it has reached your hands, Mr Harrison, you have my congratulations and my thanks.
>
> The ledger contains my notes on the bacterial process which enlivens us and an appendix which attempts a description of certain psychophysical abilities you will soon enjoy, if you do not already. Whereas the medical notes might be digested best at a time affording you a degree of leisure, I suggest you look over the appendix after concluding this letter.
>
> I am not sure what has compelled me to give my posthumous counsel, but I have been so compelled. Perhaps it is because we are microbiologically akin, or because I believe that *we* should have a voice in determining the course of these mayfly existences. Perhaps an arc of destiny is involved. But most assuredly it is because I have seen (mark the verb!) in you a future of greater purpose than my past has proved. There is a thing you must do, Mr Harrison. I cannot tell you what it is, but I wish you its accomplishment.
>
> I have chosen this precise time to die because I knew Dr Ezawa would be in residence and would – being a good research man – wish to perform the autopsy at once. The laboratory next to this room is the only place suitable for such work. If you will turn on the wall switches beside the mirror, in due course you will see and hear all the proceedings …

Donnell hit the switches. A light bloomed within the mirror, and a wide room dominated by two long counters became visible; a lamp burned on the nearest counter, illuminating beakers, microscopes and a variety of glass tubing. No one was in sight. He turned back to the letter.

> … though it is likely your view will be impaired as the doctors crowd around, shoving each other aside in their desire for intimacy with my liver and lights. I doubt you will be disturbed; the basement will be off-limits to all but those involved in my dissection, and the room you occupy has no video camera. It was, I suspect, designed as an observation post from which to observe the initial recovery phase of creatures like ourselves, but apparently they chose to sequester that portion of the project at Tulane. In any case, it will take some hours at least to restore the video, and if you exercise caution you should be able to return upstairs unnoticed.

Enough of preamble. Hereafter I will depend a list of those things I have learned which may be pertinent to your immediate situation.

1) If you concentrate your gaze upon the cameras, you will sooner or later begin to see bright white flashes in the air around them: cometary incidences of light which will gradually manifest as networks or cages of light constantly shifting in structure. I am convinced these are a visual translation of the actions of electromagnetic fields. When they appear, extend your hand toward them and you will feel a gentle tugging in the various directions of their flow. The ledger will further explore this phenomenon, but for now it will suffice you to know that you can disrupt the system by waggling your fingers contrary to the flow, disrupting their patterns ...

The laboratory door swung open, a black arm reached in and switched on the overhead fluorescents; two orderlies entered wheeling Magnusson's corpse on a dolly. Then a group of lab-coated doctors squeezed through the door, led by Dr Brauer and an elderly Japanese man whose diminished voice came over the wall speaker. '... matter who gave him the scalpel, but I want to know where it has vanished to.' He stalked to the dolly and pinched a pallid fold of flesh from Magnusson's ribs. 'The extent of desanguination is remarkable! There can't be more than two or three pints left in his body. The bacteria must have maintained the heart action far longer than would be normal.'

'No wonder Petit's so freaked,' ventured a youngish doctor. 'He must have gone off like a lawn sprinkler.'

Ezawa cast a cold eye his way, and he quailed.

Seeing his creator filled Donnell with grim anger, righteous anger, anger based upon the lies he'd been told and funded by the sort of natural anger one feels when one meets the wealthy or the powerful, and senses they are mortals who have escaped our fate. Ezawa had an elegant thatch of silky white hair and eyebrows to match; his eyes were heavy-lidded and his lips full, pursed in an expression of disapproval. Moles sprinkled his yellow cheek. He had a look of well-fed eminence, of corporate Shintoism, of tailor-made pomposity and meticulous habits and delicate sensibilities; but with a burst of insight Donnell knew him for a pampered soul, a sexual gourmandizer of eccentric appetites, a man whose fulfilled ambitions had seeded an indulgent nature. The complexity of the impression confused Donnell and lessened his anger.

'Actually,' said Ezawa, 'it's quite an opportunity being able to get inside the brain before termination of the cycle.'

'I don't suppose,' said the youngish doctor, obviously seeking to re-establish himself, 'that there's any chance he's still alive?'

'Anyone connected with this project should realize that the clinical boundary for death may never be established.' Ezawa smiled. 'But I doubt he will have any discomfort.'

The two orderlies lifted Magnusson onto the counter and began cutting away his pyjamas and robe; one held his shoulders down while the other pulled the soaked cloth from beneath him laying bare his emaciated chest. Troubled by the sight, Donnell went back to the letter.

> ... I must admit I had misgivings as to my sanity on first learning this was the case. I am, be it illusion or not, a scientist, and thus the parameters of my natural expectation were exceeded. But each time I have done as I described, the result has been the same. I cannot rationalize this as being the result of miraculous coincidence.
>
> 2) You possess, as do we all, a commanding presence. I realize you are prone to deep anxieties, insecurities, but nevertheless you can exert a profound influence on our nursemaids. Argue forcefully and you will achieve much. This may sound simplistic, but in this way did I convince Brauer to bring me files, various materials, and, eventually, to allow me access to the laboratory where I secured my means of exit from this world.
>
> 3) Trust your intuitions, especially as regards your judgements of people. I have discovered I can discern much of a person's general character and intent by simply looking at his or her face. It may be there is a language written in the wrinkles and muscular movements and so forth. But I have no clear idea of the process. The knowledge simply comes unbidden to my brain. It is my contention that when we stumble across someone we cannot read – our fellow patients, for example – it causes us nervousness, trepidation. I have only been able to read the other patients on one occasion: during Edman's social. And then it was as if a light shone upon all of us, perhaps engendered by our group presence. This particular ability is extremely erratic, but I would trust it when it occurs.
>
> There is more, much more, all sounding equally mad. The ledger contains all the proof of which I have been capable.
>
> I am not overborne by the prospect of my imminent death. This body is vile and stinks in my nostrils, and the condition of death seems far more mutable to me than it did when I began these investigations. That is what most astounds me about the project personnel: they have raised the dead and see nothing miraculous about it, treating it as merely an example of technological prestidigitation. Ah, well, perhaps they are correct and I am totally deluded.
>
> Use this information as you see fit, Mr Harrison. I will not instruct you further, though I will tell you that had I the strength I would have long ago left Shadows. I believe that outside these walls I might have been capable of vital action, but within them I could not see in what direction I might act.
>
> Goodbye. Good luck.

Donnell folded the letter. The exhilaration of his race down the hall had worn off, and his muscles were cramping from the exertion. His mind was fogged with gloomy, half-formed thoughts. The doctors blocked his view of the body, ringing the counter, leaning forward, peering downward and inward like gamblers around a dice table, and over the wall speaker came the tinny reproduction of a splintering whine as Ezawa broke into Magnusson's skull.

CHAPTER 8

May 3 – May 17, 1987

'Looking onto the top of the brain,' said Ezawa, 'I find the usual heavy infestation of the visual cortex ... Is the recorder on?'

Dr Brauer assured him it was; some of the doctors whispered and exchanged knowing glances. Between their shoulders Donnell saw a halation of green radiance, but then they crowded together and blocked his view entirely.

'In addition,' Ezawa continued, 'I see threadlike striations of bioluminescence shining up through the tissues of the cerebral cortex. All right.' He brushed a lock of hair from his eyes with the back of his hand, which contained a scalpel. 'I'm now going to sever the cranial adhesions and lift out the brain.'

The doctors attended Ezawa with the silent watchfulness of acolytes, bending as he bent to his labor, straightening when he straightened, bending again to see what he had removed. 'Let's get some shots of this,' he said. The doctors moved back, enabling one of the orderlies to obtain good camera angles, and Donnell had a glimpse of the brain. It was resting on Magnusson's chest, a gray convulsed blossom with bloody frills and streaks of unearthly green curving up its sides, like talons gripping it from beneath. He looked away. There was no need to watch any more, no need to puzzle or worry. Form had been given to the formless suspicions which had nagged him all these weeks, and he was surprised to discover that he had already accepted a death sentence, that this crystallization of his worst fears was less frightening than uncertainty. Veils of emotion were blowing through him: anger and revulsion and loathing for the glowing nastiness inside his own skull, and – strangely enough – hope. An intimation of promise. Perhaps, he thought, riffling the pages of the ledger, the intimation was simply an instance of the knowledge springing – as it had to old Magnusson – unbidden to his brain.

Flashcubes popped. He wondered if they would pose with their bloody marvel, link arms and smile, get a nice group shot of Ezawa and the gang to show at parties.

Ezawa cleared his throat. 'On the ventral and lower sides I find a high concentration of bacteria in those areas traversed by the catecholamine pathways. Patches of varying brightness spreading from the hindbrain to the frontal cortex. Now I'm going to cut along the dorsal-ventral axis, separating the upper and lower brain.'

The doctors huddled close.

'God! The entorhinal system!' Brauer blurted it out like a hallelujah, and the other doctors joined in an awed litany: 'I told Kinski I suspected ...' 'Brain reward and memory consolidation ...' 'Incredible!' The babble of pilgrims who, through miraculous witness, had been brought hard upon their central mystery.

'Doctors!' Ezawa waved his scalpel. 'Let's get an anatomical picture down on tape before we speculate.' He addressed himself to the recorder. 'Extremely high concentrations of bacteria in the medial and sulcral regions of the frontal cortex, the substantia regia, the entorhinal complex of the temporal lobe. It appears that the dopamine and norepenephrine systems are the main loci of the bacterial activity.' He began to slice little sections here and there, dropping them into baggies, and Magnusson's chest soon became a waste table. He held up a baggie containing a glowing bit of greenery to the ceiling lights. 'Remarkable changes in the ventral tegumentum. Be interesting to run this through the centrifuge.'

Donnell switched off the speaker. A wave of self-loathing swept over him; he felt less than animal, a puppet manipulated by luminous green claws which squeezed his ventral tegumentum into alien conformations. The feathery ticklings inside his head were, he hoped, his imagination. Magnusson was right: logic dictated escape. He could not see what was best for himself unless he left behind this charnel house where crafty witch doctors chased him through mazes and charted his consciousness and waited to mince him up and whirl his bits in a centrifuge. But he was going to need Jocundra's help to escape, and he was not sure he could trust her. He believed that her lies had been in the interests of compassion, but it would be necessary to test the depth of her compassion, the quality of the feelings that ruled it. Having thought of her for weeks in heavy emotional contexts, it amazed him he could think so calculatingly of her now, that – without any change in his basic attitude, without the least diminution of desire – he could so easily shift from needing her to using her.

With Brauer assisting, Ezawa opened Magnusson's chest and they examined the organs. Bastards! Donnell switched off the mirror. He flipped through the ledger, skimming paragraphs. It was a peculiar record, a compendium of scientific data, erratic humour, guesswork, metaphysical speculations, and he drew from it a picture of Magnusson not as the cackling old madman he had appeared, but as he had perceived himself: a powerful soul imprisoned in a web of wrinkled flesh and brittle struts of bone. One of the last entries spoke directly to this self-perception:

... Over the past months I have had contact with thirteen fellow patients, half of them now deceased, and in each case, as in my own, I have noticed we exhibit – manifest both in our work and our behavior – an obsession with nobility, with regal imagery; it seems to comprise part of our innate self-image. I suspect a psychiatrist might countenance this as a result of the death trauma, suggesting we had linked the myth of Christ arisen to our deep insecurity at having died and been reborn so changed and incomplete. But I sense in myself and the others nothing that reflects the gentle Christian fabrication; rather the imagery is of a pagan sort and the feeling of nobility is one of a great brooding spirit, half-animal, his perceptions darkening the trivial light of day. When I feel this spirit moving within me, I cannot believe otherwise than that all my illusory dry-as-dust memories of sorting test tubes and sniffing after some crumb of scientific legend have been foisted on me by the process of my life at Shadows, and that they are a veneer covering a reservoir of more potent memories.

All of us now alive embody this spirit in individualistic fashion: Richmond, who poses as the hoodlum warrior; Monroe, with her alter ego the sorceress Luweji; French, the corporate duke; Harrison, the bleak poetic prince; Ramsburgh, the mad dowager who knits coverlets and shawls which depict Druidic scenes of haunted woods and graven altars. I believe that this common tendency is of extreme importance, though I am not certain in what way; but lately I have experienced a refinement of these feelings.

One night, a splendid windy night, I went unaccompanied onto the grounds and sat in my wheelchair atop a rise close to the house. Everything, it seemed, was streaming away from me. The wind poured in a cold, unbroken rhythm off the Gulf, the oaks tossed their shadowy crowns, and silver-edged clouds raced just beneath the moon, which was itself a disc of silver, almost full. I was the single fixed point in that night's flowing substance. Black leaves skittered across silvery falls of moonlight, and my clothes tugged and snapped as if they wished to be rid of me. Time was going on without me, I thought, and I was becoming timeless once again. That was all the rectitude of life and death, then, this process of becoming timeless. My whole attention was focused outward upon the flow of night and wind, and I felt myself grown stern and intractable in relation to the petty scatterings of these inessential things, felt my little rise swell into a lofty prominence, and felt my flesh to be the sounding of a music, fading now, but soon to sound anew after the indrawing of an ancient breath. Dreams, you might say, fantasies, an old man's maunderings on mystery as his second death approaches. But it is dreams which make us live, and mystery, and who is to say they will not carry us away when life is done.

They took Laura back to Tulane under sedation. ''Bye,' she said at the door, weakly, staring into Jocundra's eyes with puzzled intensity, as if wondering at their strange color, and then repeated, ''Bye,' looking down to the floor, saying it the way you might say a word you had just learned, trying out its odd shape in your mouth.

Like everyone else, Jocundra assumed Laura had been in the room when Magnusson slit his throat – if such was the case: the missing scalpel permitted the possibility of alternate scenarios, though it was generally held that Laura, in her distracted state, had picked it up and mislaid it. But unlike everyone, Jocundra did not believe the violence of the death was wholly responsible for Laura's condition. That alone could not have transformed her into this pale doll creature who was led by the elbow and helped to sit in Ezawa's gray Cadillac, who pressed her face against the smoked glass window and gazed wanly back at the house. Her apparent callousness toward Magnusson must, Jocundra thought, have masked real feelings which had most contributed to her breakdown.

'She'll be fine,' said Edman at the staff meeting later in the day. 'You knew there'd be some trauma.'

But Jocundra had not known there was a potential for collapse, for derangement, and she was outraged. 'The end will be difficult,' a vastly paternal Edman had told her at the briefing before she left Tulane. 'But you'll take from it something very human and strengthening.' And she had swallowed it! She wanted nothing more to do with lies or with Edman, who was the father of lies; she would prepare as best she could for the inevitable crash of Donnell's ending, and afterward she would wash her hands of the project.

For the next two weeks she intensified her commitment toward cultivating a distance between herself and Donnell, and attempted as well to create distance between herself and the project, though this did not prove easy. The atmosphere of Shadows had grown more muted and clandestine than ever. It was as if there had been a unity in the house, some league now dissolved by Magnusson's death, and no one could be certain of the new alignments which might emerge. The therapists passed each other in the hall with averted eyes; French and Monroe hid behind their bedroom doors, and Richmond wandered by himself. The doctors broke off whispered conferences whenever anyone of lesser authority came near and withdrew to the upstairs offices. Even the ubiquitous ferns in their brass pots seemed instruments of subterfuge, their feathery fronds capable of concealing sensitive antennae. Yet despite this divisiveness, or because of it, everyone pried and eavesdropped and agitated. Once Dr Brauer pulled Jocundra aside and heaped invective upon Edman who, he said, spent most of his time on the telephone to Tulane, begging the administration to keep hands off, not to disrupt the process.

'But don't you think a disruption is necessary? Haven't the patients been exposed to enough of Edman's incompetence?' When she shrugged, unwilling to join in any power struggle, he drew his sour, thin features into a measly smile and asked, 'How's Harrison doing?'

'Frankly,' she said, furious at his false concern, 'I don't care who runs this damned place, and as for Harrison, he's dying!'

For several days Jocundra worried that Donnell had learned something about his own situation from Magnusson's death. She picked up a change in him, a change too slippery and circumstantial to classify. On the surface it appeared to have affected him in a positive way: he redoubled his efforts at walking; his social attitudes improved, and he went poking about the house, striking up conversations with the orderlies; he finished his story and started a new one. But when they talked – and they talked far less often than before – the exchanges were oddly weighted. One afternoon he sat her down and had her read his story. It was a violent and involuted fantasy set upon a world with a purple sun, specifically within a village bounded by a great forest, and it dealt with the miserable trials of an arthritic old tradesman, his vengeance against an evil queen and her black-clad retinue, eerie magic, grim conclusions for all. The circuitous plot and grisly horrors unsettled Jocundra. It was as if a curl of purple smoke had leaked out of the manila folder and brought her a whiff of some ornate Persian hell.

'It's beautifully written,' she said, 'but there's too much blood for my taste.'

'Yeah, but will it sell?' He laughed. 'Got to make a living somehow when I get out of here. Right?'

'I prefer your poetry.' She shut the folder and studied a fray in her skirt.

'No money in poetry.' He walked to the desk and stood over her, forcing her to look at him. 'Seriously, I'd like to have your opinion. I want to live in the city for a change, travel, and that takes money. Do you think I can earn it this way?'

She could only manage a puny, 'Yes, I suppose,' but he appeared satisfied with her answer.

Donnell's new independence allowed Jocundra to cultivate her distance. Though the cameras continued to break down – 'Like some damn bug's in the wires,' said the maintenance man – the orderlies kept track of his comings and goings, and each morning she put on shorts and a T-shirt, took a blanket and found a sunny spot in which to pass the day. She pored over graduate school catalogs, thinking she might go after her doctorate at Michigan or Chicago, or maybe Berkeley. Within a couple of years she could be doing her field work. Africa. Thatched huts on a dusty plain, baobab trees and secretary birds, oracular sacrifices and tattooing rituals, great fireball sunrises, the green mountains still full of gorillas and orchids and secret kingdoms. Each noon she could almost believe that Shadows was the seat of a lost African empire or some empty Eden; the grounds were deserted, the only sounds were those of insects and birds, and the sunlight hung in gauzy shafts straight down through the canopy, as if huge golden angels were beaming down from their orbiting ark to seed civilization. She drowsed; she read ethnography, the French theorists, rediscovering an old emnity for the incomprehensible Jacques Lacan, reacclimating her mind to the rigorous ingrown language of academics. But after a while, after a shorter while each day, it grew boring in the sun and Donnell would stray into her thoughts. Drowsy, nonspecific thoughts, images of him, things he had said, as if he were brushing against her and leaving bits of memory clinging.

May the 18th was her mother's birthday. She had forgotten it until an orderly in the commissary asked her for the date, but all through dinner she thought about what her family might have done to celebrate. Probably nothing. Her father might have given her mother a present, mumbled a tepid endearment and gone out onto the porch to twang his guitar and sing his sad, complaining songs. Her mother would have tidied the kitchen, put on her frumpy hat and scurried off to church for a quick telling of the beads, for fifteen minutes of perfumed darkness at the chipped gilt feet of the Virgin. The Church had been her one stab at individualism, her single act of rebellion against her husband, who had been an atheist. Not that he had tried to dominate her. She had slipped into his shadow like a fearful mouse who had been searching her whole life for such a shelter and would be happy to scuttle around his feet forever. It annoyed Jocundra when she noticed incidences of her mother's character in herself.

After dinner she had intended to go to the staff meeting – the big showdown, it was rumored, between Brauer and Edman – but Donnell asked her to stay and talk. He had her sit on the bed and himself leaned against the windowledge, his cane propped beside him. For a long time he was silent, merely staring at her, but finally he said, 'We're having a private conversation. The cameras quit working.'

His stare unnerved Jocundra; it was calm and inquisitive and not the usual way he looked at her. 'How do you know?'

'It doesn't matter.' He gave a sniff of amusement. 'They have enough data on my psychological adjustment, and besides, my adjustment's complete. I'm ready to leave right now.'

She laughed edgily; though his tone was casual, everything he said had the weight of a pronouncement. 'You're not strong enough, not yet.'

'I want to tell you something about yourself.' The curtain belled inward, eerily swathing his face in lace; he brushed it away. The ceiling lights diminished the green in his eyes to infrequent refractions. 'You're not totally aware of it, because you try to constrain it, but I don't think you can totally deny it either. You feel something for me, something like love, though maybe that's too extreme a word for what you feel because you have been somewhat successful in denying it.'

He paused to let her respond, but she was at first too confused to answer, then annoyed that he would assume so much, then curious because he exhibited such assurance.

'Of course I'm in love with you.' He mumbled it as if it were hardly worth mentioning. 'I know it's part of the program for me to love you, that you've …' He ran his cane back and forth through his hands. 'I don't guess that's important.' He stared at her, his mouth thinned, his eyebrows arched, as if what he saw offered a prospect both mildewed and glorious. 'Do you want to deny anything?' he asked.

'No,' she said, and was surprised at the buoyancy she felt on saying it.

'The day Magnusson died,' he said, 'I went down to a little room next to the lab and watched them chop him up.'

'You couldn't have,' she said, coming to her feet.

'The usual heavy infestation of the visual cortex,' he said. 'Remarkable changes in the ventral tegumentum.'

She started to go to him, but then she thought how he must despise her for lying, and she sat back down, heavy with guilt.

He picked up a paper sack from the windowledge and walked to the bed. 'I'm going to do something about it. It's all right.'

'I'm sorry.' The foolish sound of the words caused her to laugh, and the bitter laugh dynamited the stoniness of her guilt and left her shaky.

'Magnusson gave me his notes before he died,' he said. 'I think there's a chance I can use them to prolong my life. I'm not sure, but I'll never find out here. I'm going to leave.'

'You can't!'

'Sure I can.' He plucked a set of keys out of the paper sack: she recognized them as the standard set issued to orderlies, keys to the vans and the pantry and various other rooms. 'The staff is in conference,' he said. 'The orderlies are playing poker in the lab. None of the phones or cameras are working. And the gate.' He smiled. 'It's taken care of, too.'

His arguments were smooth, logical, insistent. He had, he said, a right to go where he chose, to spend his time as he wished. What was the future in remaining here to be probed and tested and eventually dissected? He needed her help. Where did her true responsibilities lie? To herself, to him, or to the project? She had no contrary argument, but the thought of being cast adrift with him made her afraid.

'If you're worried about my loss to the scientific community,' he said, 'I can assure I'm not going to cooperate any more.'

'It's not that,' she said, hurt. 'I'm just not sure what's right, and I don't think you are either.'

'Right? Christ!' He lifted a small tape recorder out of the sack; the cassette within it bore Edman's handwriting on the label. 'Listen to this.'

'Where'd you get that?'

'Edman's office. I told him I wanted to see how life looked from inside a crystal ball. It thrilled his tiny soul to have the beast sniffing round his pantry. These were lying about like party favors on the shelves, so I collected a few.' He punched down the play switch, and Edman's voice blatted from the speaker:

'April 27th … (a cough) … Despite all reason to the contrary, romance blooms between Harrison and Verret. I expect one morning I will walk onto the grounds and find a valentine containing their initials carved upon an oak. I've today received the package of information concerning Verret's divorce proceeding. In layman's terms, it might be said that Verret seems to have a penchant for losers. Her husband, one Charles Messier, a musician, apparently misused her physically: the divorce was granted on the grounds of physical and mental cruelty. I haven't had time to study it in detail, but there are obvious similarities between the two men. Artistic avocation, both four or five years older than Verret, a general physical resemblance. Of course I am not yet clear how large a part these similarities play in what is now transpiring, but I am convinced we will soon begin to learn. The relationship is, I believe, at a stage of breakthrough … (a sigh) … I must admit to feelings of paternity toward Harrison and Verret in that I have served as their matchmaker … (a laugh) … It does not seem wholly improbable that we may one day be treated to the pageant of a nuptial, one of those such are consummated between prisoners and their loving correspondents – or, more aptly, between terminal patients and their fiancées. I can easily imagine it. Verret, beautiful in white beneath the arching oaks. Harrison, his eyes ablaze, the lustful groom. And the priest intoning sonorously, "What Ezawa hath joined, let no man put asunder …"'

'Is *that* right?' Donnell smashed down the off switch. 'To have this fat vulture perch in his crystal cave and drool over our libidos!'

Jocundra ejected the cassette and read Edman's inscription: 'Harrison, Verret – XVII.' She turned it over in her hand; it was like holding a jar containing her appendix, a useless organ which once had poisoned her, but was now trivial, powerless. Leaving offered no secure hope, but neither did it offer the hopelessness of Shadows. They had no choice. At the very least, Edman was dangerously unethical, and it was probable he was mad, cunningly mad, passing his madness off as a clever form of sanity, infecting everyone and fooling even himself. It was, she thought, a little dreamlike to be doing something so extreme.

'We'll need money,' she said. 'I've got credit cards and … Why are you looking at me that way?'

'For a minute I thought I'd lost you,' he said.

*

The engine caught, exploded to a roar, then died as Jocundra's foot slipped off the clutch. Overanxious, she failed twice to restart it, but finally succeeded and backed the van until it was facing the drive and headed out. The headlights veered across the grounds, spotlighting a menagerie of leafy shapes, and the side mirror showed the house receding against the darkness, doll-sized, a lantern-lit confection of rose and white topped by a rhinestone bauble. Jocundra's throat was dry. She had almost lost her resolve half a dozen times before they reached the parking lot, and Donnell's plan for the gate – what little he had revealed of it – did nothing to bolster her confidence; her hands and feet, though, honored her commitment, working the gearshift and pedals seemingly without her cooperation. She pulled up close to the gate. Branches of the magnolia bush beside it scraped Donnell's door. He slumped down, pretending unconsciousness. The headlights sprayed between the bars, playing over the glistening tarpaper of the gatehouse and the guard sidled forth, sleepily scratching his ribs. 'What you want?' he called. He yawned and blinked away the glare, settling his holster around his hips: a pudding-faced, pot-bellied man wearing chinos.

'I've got an emergency!' Jocundra called back, hoping to inject an appropriate desperation into her voice. 'One of the orderlies! It's his heart!'

'I don't see no doctor with you. Can't let you by without no doctor.' He waved her back to the house.

'Get out!' hissed Donnell. 'Convince him!'

She climbed out. 'Please,' she said, pressing against the bars. 'He's had a coronary!'

The guard's eyes flicked to her breasts. 'I wish they'd get them damn phones straightened out. Awright.' He punched a button set into the masonry, and the gate whined open a foot. He slipped inside, and she stepped out of his way, standing at the front of the van while he slapped the magnolia branches aside and shone the flashlight in the window to check on Donnell. Jocundra heard a rustle from the bush behind him and saw a pair of blazing green eyes emerging from the welter of white blossoms and waxy leaves. 'This ol' boy ain't no orderly,' said the guard, and something swooshed through the air and struck his neck, then struck again. Jocundra jumped back, coming up against the gate, and the guard fell backwards out of sight behind the van. In a moment Richmond stood, stuffing the guard's gun into his belt. Jocundra moved out onto the road, putting the bars between them.

'You better be scared, lady,' he said, and laughed. 'When you motherfuckers made me, you created a monster.'

He ducked back into the bush, then came around the front of the van, holding his guitar. Underlit by the headlights, his face was seamed and gruesome; his eyes effloresced. Donnell climbed down, limped to the gate, and pushed the button. The iron bars swung open. 'Pull it on through,' he said to Richmond.

As Richmond drove the van out, the moon sailed from behind the clouds and everything grew very sharp and bright. The gate whined shut. Pearly reflections rippled over the side of the van; the road arrowed off toward the swamp, a bone-white strip vanishing between dark walls of cypress, oak and palmetto. Fresh mosquito bites suddenly itched on Jocundra's arm, as if the moon had broken through her own cloudiness, her confusion, illuminating her least frailty. She did not want to be with Richmond. The road was a wild, unreckonable place crossed by devious slants of shadow.

The guard moaned.

'Hurry up!' yelled Richmond.

Donnell was doing something to the lock mechanism, molding voluptuous shapes in the air around it with his hands; he stopped, apparently satisfied, stared at it, then stepped over to the wall and jabbed the control button several times.

The gate remained shut.

'Man, I can handle this road at twice the speed,' said Richmond from the back of the van. 'She's drivin' like a fuckin' old lady.'

'She's got a license,' said Donnell patiently. 'You don't.'

'Listen, man!' Richmond stuck his head up between the seats. 'It was cool you runnin' the show when we was inside 'cause you could deal with the cameras and shit, but I ain't ...' He nearly toppled into the front as the van hit a pothole, then he fell back. 'Look at this shit! She's gonna kill our ass!'

'Quit yelling in her ear, damn it! How the hell can she drive when you're yelling at her!'

Hearing them argue, Jocundra had a moment of hysteria, a happy little trickle of it eeling up from her depths, and all the unhappy particulars of the situation were bathed in a surreal light. There they sat like TV hoodlums planning a spree of Seven-11 stick-ups and high times, fighting over who was boss – to further this impression they were both wearing sunglasses which Richmond had stolen from the orderlies – and there she sat, the mute flunky, the moll. At length they agreed on a compromise: Donnell would serve as the mastermind, while Richmond would take charge in situations calling for swift action and street smarts. Donnell asked her if she knew a place nearby where they could be safe for a couple of days.

'The swamp,' she said. 'It's full of deserted shanties and cabins. But shouldn't we get as far away as possible?'

'Jesus!' said Richmond, disgusted. He scrunched around on the floor; his guitar banged hollowly. 'I'm gonna lay back for a while. You deal with her, man.'

'You weren't listening,' said Donnell exasperated.

'I'm sorry. I was concentrating on the road.'

'We're going to switch license plates. They'll expect us to run, I think, so we're going to stay nearby, maybe pick up another car. The swamp won't do. We need someplace near a town, within a couple of hours' drive. That's how long the gate and the phones should stay out.'

'Well, over on Bayou Lafourche there's a stretch of motels,' she said. 'Mostly dumps. I doubt they pay much attention to who their customers are.'

'Make it some place near a liquor store,' said Richmond. 'I need to get fucked up!'

When they reached the state highway, Jocundra boosted the speed to fifty and raised her window. Wind keened in the side vent. White houses bloomed phosphorescent among the brush and scrub pine; gas stations with broken windows and boarded-up restaurants. Near the town of Vernon's Parish they passed a low building with yellow light streaming from its doors and windows, a neon champagne glass atop it, surrounded by cars. Black stick figures, armless and faceless, jostled in the doorway, and their movements made them seem to be flickering, pulsing to the blare of light around them like spirits dancing in a fire. Then they were gone, the moon was occluded, and a wave of unrelieved darkness rolled over the van. Richmond chorded his guitar.

> *'Past the road to Vernon's Parish*
> *Our tailpipe was sprayin' sparks.*
> *The preacher in the Calvary Church*
> *Felt cold fingers 'round his heart ...'*

The song and the air of stale, forced confinement in the van reminded Jocundra of traveling with Charlie's band. When he had described it to her, it had sounded romantic, but in reality it had been greasy food and never enough sleep and being groped by Quaaluded roadies. The only good part had been the music, which served to mythologize the experience. She glanced at Donnell; he rested his head wearily against the window as Richmond's cawing voice wove into the rush of the highway.

> *'Now if you see a fiery fall*
> *Of comets in the East,*
> *Or the shadow slinkin' 'cross the moon*
> *Of some wiry, haggard beast,*
> *If you feel your blood congeal*
> *And you've the urge to call a priest,*
> *Never fear, it'll disappear,*
> *You can rest tonight in peace.*

*'Well, you might want to run outside
And fall down on your face,
You might scream or you might pray
Or you might vacillate,
You might give the United Way,
But no matter what you done,
I tell you, straight,
You can't escape the fate
Of Harley David's son!
Oh, the days they've swept away from me
Like fires through a slum.
But when I die I'll roam the night,
The Ghost of Harley David's son!*

'Bullshit song,' said Richmond, dejected. He leaned between the seats. 'But what the hell, squeeze! It sure feels good to be hittin' the highway again.' He punched Donnell's arm and grunted laughter. 'Even if we never did feel it before.'

CHAPTER 9

May 17 – May 19, 1987

A stand of stunted oaks hemmed in Sealey's Motel-Restaurant against the highway. Bats wheeled in the parking lot lights, and toads hopped over the gravel drive and croaked under the cabins, which were tiny, shingle-roofed, with peeling white paint and ripped screen doors. Mr Sealey – Hank Jr according to the fishing trophy on the office desk – was squat and glum as a toad himself, fiftyish, jowly, wearing a sweat-stained work shirt and jeans. He hunched in a swivel chair, showing them the back of his seamed neck and gray crewcut hair, and when they asked for a room he spun slowly around; he closed his right eye, squinted at Jocundra through the trembling lowered lid of his left, clucked his tongue, then tossed them a key and resumed tying a fishing fly large and gaudy enough to be a voodoo fetish. Donnell pictured him clad in scarlet robes, dangling said fly into a fiery pit from which scaly, clawed hands were reaching.

'Don't want no screechin' or bangin' after midnight,' grumbled Sealey. 'Take Cabin Six.'

The cabin, twelve dollars for two singles and a cot ('You got to tote the cot yourself') was no bargain, being the home of moths and crickets and spiders. 'All things small and horrible,' said Donnell, trying to cheer Jocundra, who sat eyeing with disfavor a patch of mattress, one of several visible through holes in the sheet, dotting it like striped islands in a gray sea. For light there was a naked light bulb hung from the ceiling, fragments of moth wings stuck to its sides; between the beds stood an unfinished night table whose drawer contained no Bible but a palmetto bug; the walls were papered in a faded design of flesh-colored orchids and jungle leaves, and mounted cockeyed above the bathroom sink was a flyspecked Kodachrome of Lake Superior.

Though it was poor and pestilent, Richmond made Cabin Six his castle. He cracked the twelve-pack he had bought from Sealey, chugged the first can, belched, and threw himself on the bed to chord his guitar and drink. After three beers he suggested they go for a ride, after five he insisted upon it, but Jocundra told him they were low on gas. Disgruntled, he paced the cabin, interrupting his pacing to urinate out the door and serenade the other cabins with choruses of his song. But when Donnell reminded him that rest was necessary, he grumpily agreed, saying yeah, he had to fix up some stuff anyway. Sitting on the bed, he shook his guitar until a rolled-up piece of plastic fell out; he unrolled it, removing a scalpel. Then he emptied the security guard's gun and began to notch the tips of the bullets. At this Jocundra turned to face the wall, drawing her legs into a tight curl.

'Sleep?' Donnell perched on the edge of her mattress.

'Yes,' she murmured. 'You should, too.'

'I want to go over Magnusson's notes a while.'

Dark hairs were fanned across her cheek. He started to brush them away, a tender response to her vulnerability, but he suddenly felt monstrous next to her, like a creature about to touch the cheek of a swooning maiden, and he drew back his hand. He had a sensation of delicate motion inside his head, something feathery-light and flowing in all directions. His breath quickened, he grasped the bedframe to steady himself, and he wished, as he always did at such moments, that he had not witnessed the autopsy or read Magnusson's morbid self-descriptions. He stayed beside Jocundra until the sensation abated, then stood, his breath still ragged.

'You wanna kill the light, squeeze,' said Richmond. 'I'm gonna fade.' He poured the bullets into an ashtray.

Donnell did as he was told, went into the bathroom and switched on the light. Gray dirt-streaked linoleum peeled and tattered like eucalyptus bark, shower stall leaning drunkenly, chipped porcelain, the mirror stippled with paint drippings, applying a plague to whomever gazed upon it. The doorframe was swollen with dampness, and the door would not close all the way, leaving a foot-wide gap. He hooked his cane over the doorknob, lowered the toilet lid, sat and tried to concentrate on the ledger. According to Magnusson the bacterial cycle was in essence a migration into the norepenephrine and dopamine systems; since his 'psychic' abilities increased as the migration progressed, he concluded that these systems must be the seat of such abilities. So much Donnell could easily follow, but thereafter he was puzzled by some of Magnusson's terminology.

> ... each bacterium carries a crystal of magnetite within a membrane that is contiguous with the cytoplasmic membrane, and a chain of these magnetosomes, in effect, creates a biomagnetic compass. The swimming bacteria are passively steered by the torque exerted upon their biomagnetic compass by the geomagnetic field; since in this hemisphere the geomagnetic field points only north and down, the bacteria are north-seeking and tend to migrate downward, thus explaining their presence in the sediment underlying old graveyards. Of course within the brain, though the geomagnetic field still affects them, the little green bastards are bathed in a nutrient- and temperature-controlled medium so that movement downward is no longer of adaptive

significance. They're quite content to breed and breed, eventually to kill me by process of overpopulation.

Richmond's heavy snores ripped the silence, and Donnell heard footsteps padding in the next room. Jocundra eased through the gap in the door; she had changed into jeans and a T-shirt. 'Can't sleep,' she said. She cast about for a clean place to sit, found none, and sat anyway beside the shower stall. She spread the folds of the shower curtain, examining its pattern of hula girls and cigarette burns, and grimaced. 'This place is a museum of squalor.'

She asked to see the ledger, and as she leafed through it, her expression flowing from puzzlement to comprehension, he reflected on the difference between the way she looked now – a schoolgirl stuck on a problem, barely a teenager, worrying her lower lip, innocent and grave – and earlier when she had entered the cabin; then she had appeared self-possessed, elegant, masking her reaction to the grime beneath a layer of aristocratic reserve. She had one of those faces that changed drastically depending on the angle at which you viewed it, so drastically that Donnell would sometimes fail to recognize her for a split second.

'I didn't believe you … about extending your life,' she said excitedly, continuing to pore over the ledger. 'He doesn't come right out and say it, but the implication – I think – is that you may be able to stabilize the bacterial colony …'

'Magnetic fields,' said Donnell. 'He was too much in a hurry, too busy understanding it to see the obvious.'

'There's a lot here that doesn't make sense. All this about NMR, for example.'

'What?'

'Nuclear magnetic resonance.' She laughed. 'The reason I almost flunked organic chemistry. It's a spectroscopic process for analyzing organic compounds, for measuring the strength of radio waves necessary to change the alignment of nuclei in a magnetic field. But Magnusson's not talking about its analytic function.' She turned a page. 'Do you know what these are?'

There were three doodles on the page:

Beneath them Magnusson had written:

What the hell are these chicken-scratchings? Been seeing them since day one. They seem part of something larger, but it won't come clear. Odd thought: suppose the entirety of my mental processes is essentially a letter written to my brain by these damned green bugs, and these scribbles are the Rosetta Stone by which I might decipher all.'

'I see them, too,' said Donnell. 'Not the same ones, but similar. Little bright squiggles that flare up and vanish. I thought they were just flaws in my vision until I saw the ledger, and then I noticed this one ...' He pointed to the first doodle. 'If you turn it on its side it looks exactly like an element of the three-horned man Richmond drew on his guitar.'

'They're familiar.' She shook her head, unable to remember where she had seen them; she gave him a searching look. 'This is going to take time, and Richmond doesn't have much time.'

'Neither do I.'

'Maybe we should go back to Shadows. With all the resources of the project ...'

'Richmond knows he's nearly terminal,' said Donnell sharply. 'He won't go back, and I have my own reasons not to.'

For the first time since Magnusson's death, he had an intimate awareness of her unencumbered either by doubts about her motives or by the self-loathing he felt when he was brought up against the fact of his bizarre existence. Her face was impassive, beautiful, but beneath the calm façade he detected fear and confusion. By escaping with him, she had lost herself with him, and being lost, as she had rarely been before, she was at a greater remove from her natural place in the world than was he, to whom all places were unnatural.

'What are you thinking?' she asked.

'This and that,' he said. He took back the ledger and read from the appendix. '"Mitochondria research has long put forward the idea that human beings are no more than motile colonies of bacteria, so why do I shudder and think of myself as a disease in a borrowed brain?" That, too.'

The subject obviously distressed her. She looked away and ran her eye along the mosaic of dirt and faded pattern spanning the linoleum. 'There wasn't anyone at Shadows who'd subscribe to a purely biological definition of the patients,' she said. And she sketched out Edman's theories as an example, his fascination with the idea of spirit possession, how he had snapped up the things she had told him about the voodoo concept of the soul, the *gros bon ange* and the *ti bon ange*.

'The part about your influence on me,' he said. 'Do you buy that?'

A frail pulse stirred the air between them, as if their spirits had grown larger and were overlapping, exchanging urgent information.

'I suppose it's true to an extent,' she said. 'But I don't think it means anything anymore.'

*

Sleep did not come easily for Donnell. Lying on the cot, he was overwhelmed by the excitement of being away from Shadows, by the strange dissonance everything he saw caused in his memory, at first seeming unfamiliar but then wedding itself to other memories and settling into mental focus. Triggered by his excitement, he experienced a visual shift of an entirely new sort. The moonlight and the lights of the other cabins dimmed, the walls darkened, and every pattern in the room began to glow palely – the grain of the boards, the wallpaper, the spiderwebs, the shapes of the furniture – as if he were within a black cube upon whose walls a serpentine alphabet of silver smoke had been inlaid. It frightened him. He turned to Jocundra, wanting to tell her. Both she and Richmond were black figures, a deeper black than the backdrop, with fiery prisms darting inside them, merging, breaking apart: like the bodies of sleeping gods containing a speeded-up continuum of galaxies and nebulae. The screen mesh of the door was glowing silver, and the markings of the moths plastered against it gleamed coruscant red and blue. Even when he closed his eyes he saw them, but eventually he slept, mesmerized by their jewel-bright fluttering.

He waked to the sound of running water, someone showering. Richmond was still snoring, and the sun glinted along spiderwebs, glowed molten in the window cracks. Bare feet slapped the linoleum, the floor creaked under a shifted weight. He rolled over, and looked through the gap in the bathroom door. Jocundra was standing at the window, lifting the heft of her hair, squeezing it into a sleek cable. Water droplets glittered on her shoulders, and she was wearing semi-transparent panties which clung to the hollows of her buttocks. She bent and toweled her calves; her small breasts barely quivered. A feeling of warm dissolution spread across Donnell's chest and thighs. Her legs were incredibly long, almost an alien voluptuousness. She straightened and saw him. She said nothing, not moving to cover herself, then she lowered her eyes and stepped out of sight behind the door. A minute later she came out, tucking her blouse into a wraparound skirt. She pretended it had not happened and asked what they were going to do about breakfast.

That day, as her mother would have said, was a judgement upon Jocundra. Not that it began badly. Richmond went out around ten to scout the area for a change of cars, promising to return at noon, and she buried herself in Magnusson's notes, fearful that she had misread them the night before. She had not. The bacteria were passively steered by the geomagnetic field toward the dopamine and norepenephrine systems, and there they starved to death; the two systems were centers of high metabolic activity, and in performing their functions of brain reward and memory consolidation and – at least so said Magnusson – running the psychic machinery, they used up all the available energy. Of course the bacteria bred during their migration, and their breeding rate was so far in excess of their death rate that eventually they put too much of a burden upon the brain's resources. What Magnusson did not say, but what was implicit, was that if the bacteria could be steered more rapidly back and forth between centers of low and high metabolic activity, this by a process of externally applied magnetic fields, then the excess might be killed off and the size of the colony stabilized.

She discussed with Donnell various lines of investigation, how much money they would need – a lot! – and tried again to convince him to return to Shadows.

'I don't expect you to understand,' he said. 'But I *know* that's not the way.' He had just taken a shower, and with his hair sleeked back, his sunglasses, he looked alert and foxy, every jut of his features pointed toward some dangerous enterprise: a small-time hood plotting a big score. 'Maybe New Orleans,' he said. 'Not as much problem getting money there. Libraries, Tulane.'

She marvelled at the changes in him. There was such an air of purpose and calculation about his actions, it was as if he had thrown off a cloak of insecure behaviors and revealed himself to have been purposeful and calculating all along. He was, she knew; still uncertain about a great many things, but he seemed confident they would work themselves out and she no longer felt it necessary to soothe his doubts and fears. In fact, when Richmond did not return at noon, he undertook to soothe hers by leading her on a tour of the cabin, describing to her the things she could not see: the weird spindly structures fraying at the edges of spiderwebs, insect eggs joined together and buried in a crack like crystals in a rock, a fantastic landscape of refracted light which he saw within a single facet of a dead fly's compound eye. Then he led her outdoors and described what Magnusson believed to be the geomagnetic field.

'I can see it better at night,' he said. 'Then it's not as translucent, more milky white, like the coil of a huge snake lying across the sky, fading, then reappearing in a new configuration.' He scuffed his foot against the cabin steps. 'I can always tell how it'll look before I look. Magnusson says that's because the bacteria are interpreting its movements, conveying the knowledge as intuition.' He took off his sunglasses and looked at her with narrowed eyes. 'Human fields are different. Cages of white fire flickering in and out. Each bar a fiery arc. When I first saw one, I thought of it as a jail to keep the soul in check.'

Two o'clock, three, four, and Richmond did not return. He had been preparing for violence, and Jocundra was certain he had met with it. Even Donnell's confidence was sapped. He brooded over the ledger while Jocundra kept watch. A few cars passed, several stopping at Sealy's Restaurant: a building of white concrete block just up the road. Once Sealey himself crossed from the office to the restaurant, pausing to spit on a clump of diseased agave that grew on an island at the center of the parking lot. Palmetto bugs frolicked over the floor, the cabin stank of mildew, and Jocundra's thoughts eddied in dark, defeated circles. When Richmond finally did return, drunk, at dusk, he announced that he had not only found a car – it would be safe to pick up in the early morning – but he had also arranged a date for the movies with Sealey's day-shift waitress.

'Good ol' country girls,' he said, rubbing his groin, grinning a tomcat grin; then he looked pointedly at Jocundra and said, 'Ain't like them downtown bitches think their ass is solid silver.'

Both Jocundra and Donnell argued vehemently against it, but Richmond was unshakable. 'I ain't got my cooze with me like you, man,' he said to Donnell. 'Now you can come with me if you want, but you sure as shit ain't gonna stop me!' He put on his Hellhounds T-shirt and a windbreaker, slicked back his hair and tied it into a ponytail.

The neon sign above the restaurant – a blue script Sealey's – hummed and sputtered, attracting clouds of moths which fluttered in and out of its nimbus like spotches in a reel of silent film. Jocundra pulled up to the side entrance, and a rawboned blond girl wearing a tube top and cut-offs skipped out and hopped in the back of the van with Richmond. 'Couldn't get but a six-pack,' she said breathily; she leaned up between the seats. 'Hi! I'm Marie.' Her face was long-jawed and dopey, heavy on the lipstick and mascara. Introductions all around, Jocundra eased out onto the highway, and then Marie poked Donnell's arm and said, 'Sure was a weird wreck you guys had, y'know. The light hurt your eyes, too?'

Donnell tensed and said, 'Uh, yeah,' but Marie talked right through his answer. 'Jack here says he don't never take his glasses off, even when he gets, y'know …' She giggled. 'Friendly.'

The Buccaneer Drive-In was playing TRIPLE XXX LADIES NO CHARGE, and the lot was three-quarters full of vans and pickups and family cars, most honking and whooping, demanding the show begin at once. The first feature was *Martial Arts Mistress*; it detailed the fistic and amorous exploits of a melon-breasted, bisexual Chinese girl named Chen Li, who slept her way up the ladder of the emperor's court so she ultimately could assassinate the evil prime minister, he who had seduced and killed her sister. The film's highlight was a kung fu love battle between Chen Li and the minister, culminating with them both vaulting impossibly high and achieving midair penetration, after which Chen Li disposed of her nemesis by means of a secret grip bestowing unendurable pleasure.

Jocundra might have found it amusing, but Richmond's performance eliminated any possibility of enjoyment. As he and Marie scrunched between the seats, he snorted into her neck and grabbed her breasts, causing giggles and playful slaps, and as the middle of the film approached, he drew her down under a blanket. Rummaging, whispers, a sharply indrawn breath. The van shuddered. Then the unmistakable sounds of passionate involvement, topped off by hoarse exclamations and suppressed squeals. Jocundra sat stiffly, staring at the writhing Oriental shapes, doing for technicolor sex what Busby Berkley had done for the Hollywood musical. Marie made a mewling noise; Richmond popped a beer, glugged, and belched. Feeling imperiled, isolated, Jocundra glanced at Donnell, seeking the comfort of shared misery. He had flipped up his sunglasses and was holding Magnusson's ledger close to his face, illuminating the page with the green flashes from his eyes.

At intermission, the theater lights blazed up, cartoon crows bore fizzing soft drinks to save a family of pink elephants stranded in a desert, and people straggled toward the refreshment stand. Marie declared she had to visit the ladies' room and asked Jocundra to come along; her tone was light but insistent. Some teenagers hassled them outside the bathroom and beat on the door after they entered. The speaker over the mirror squawked, 'Five minutes until showtime,' and blared distorted circus music. Bugs fried on the fluorescent tubes; the paper towels soaking on the floor looked like mummy wrappings, brown and ravelled; and a lengthy testimonial to the joys of lesbianism occupied most of the wall beside the mirror.

Marie removed lipstick, eyeliner and mascara from her purse, and began to repair the damage done her face by Richmond. 'Did they really shoot them boys fulla snake poison?' she asked abruptly. 'That why Jack's, y'know, a little cooler than average?'

Jocundra restrained a laugh. 'Uh huh,' she said, and splashed water on her face.

'I heard about 'em changing people's blood,' said Marie. 'But I never did hear about 'em replacin' it with snake poison. Is yours the same way?'

'It's only temporary.' Jocundra affected nonchalance, patting her face dry.

Two women banged the door open, jabbering, and disappeared into grimy stalls.

Marie tugged at her cut-offs, turned sideways to judge the effect. 'Well, it don't bother me none. I just thought ol' Jack was shittin' me. He's one crazy dude.' She winked at Jocundra and wiggled her hips. 'Anyway, I like 'em crazy! Guess you do, too.'

Jocundra was noncommittal.

Marie adjusted her tube top. 'He asked me to come along with y'all.' Then seeing Jocundra's stricken expression, she hastened to add, 'But don't worry, I'm not. It ain't Jack, y'understand. He's just fine.' She headed for the door, pausing for a final look into the mirror; she had, by dint of painstaking brushwork, transformed her eyes into cadaverous pits. 'I just know there'd be trouble between you and me,' she shot back over her shoulder, tossing her hair and switching her rear end. 'I can tell we ain't got nothin' in common.'

Marie said she had better be gettin' on home, it had been fun but her mother was sick and would worry – a lie, thought Donnell; her mood had changed markedly since visiting the ladies' room, and she was not as tolerant of Richmond's affections. They left during the credits of the second feature and dropped her at a white stucco house a mile from the motel. The front yard was lined with lawn decorations for sale: stone frogs, plastic flamingos, mirrored balls on pedestals, arranged in curved rows facing the road, like the graduation grouping of an extraterrestrial high school. Richmond stole one of the mirrored balls and stared gloomily at his reflection in it as they drove towards the motel. Donnell suggested they try for the car, and Richmond said that he was hungry.

'I'd like to go back to the room,' said Jocundra firmly.

Richmond hurled the ball against the side of the van. Silvery pieces flew into the front seat, and Jocundra swerved.

'Be fuckin' reasonable!' yelled Richmond. 'You been stickin' to the room so damn much, Sealey's gonna think we kidnapped you! I ain't boostin' no car 'less I eat.'

Sealey's was frigid with air conditioning, poorly lit by lights shining through perforations in the ceiling board. A plate glass window provided a view of highway and scrub. The kitchen was laid out along the rear wall, partitioned off from two rows of black vinyl booths, interrupted by the entrance on one side, a waitress station and cash register on the other. A long-nosed, saw-toothed fish was mounted above the grill, and there were photographs stapled beneath the health classification, all yellowed, several of children, one portraying a younger, less bulbous Sealey in Marine blues. At the end of the aisle a jukebox sparkled red and purple, clicking to itself like a devilish robot. They took the booth beside it. Sealey remained behind the register, indifferent to their presence until Richmond called for service; then he stumped over to them. Donnell asked to see a menu.

'Ain't got no menus,' said Sealey. 'I got burgers and fries, egg salad. I got fish, beer, Pepsi, milk.'

He clanged his spatula on the grill as he cooked, clattered their plates on the table, and dumped their silverware in a pile. He folded his arms and glowered at them.

'You folks leavin' tomorrow?'

'Yeah,' said Donnell, and Jocundra chipped in with, 'We'll be getting an early start.'

'Well, I don't mind,' said Sealey, regarding them with a mix of superiority and distaste.

'What kind of fish is that?' asked Donnell, pointing to the trophy above the grill, meaning to placate, to charm.

Sealey pitied him with a stare. 'Gar.' He scuffed the floor in apparent frustration. 'Damn,' he said; he scratched the back of his neck and refolded his arms. 'It ain't that I don't need the business, and I don't give a damn what you do to each other …'

'We ain't doin' shit, man,' said Richmond.

'But,' Sealey continued, 'that don't mean I got to like what's goin' on.'

'I think you've got the wrong idea,' said Jocundra meekly.

Sealey sucked on a tooth. 'If you was my daughter and I seen you with these two in some motel …' He shook his head slowly, staggered by the prospect of what he might do were such the case, and stumped back to the register, muttering.

His professed hunger notwithstanding, Richmond did not eat. He fed quarters to the jukebox, syrupy country and western music welled forth, and he danced in the aisle with an imaginary woman. 'Broken dreams and heartsick mem-o-rees,' he howled, mocking the sappy lyrics as he dry-humped his invisible partner. He ordered beer after beer, taking pleasure in stirring Sealey off his stool, and each time the man brought him a fresh bottle, Richmond would weave threats and insults into his rap. 'Some people you can just fuck with their minds and they'll leave your ass alone,' he said, squinting up at Sealey. 'But some people's so dumb and ugly you gotta terrorize them motherfuckers.' Sealey either ignored him or did not catch his drift; he retook his seat behind the register and thumbed through a magazine whose cover showed soldiers of different eras marching beneath a tattered American flag.

It would soon be necessary, thought Donnell, to part company with Richmond; he was becoming uncontrollable. Richmond would not mind them deserting, he only wanted to flame out somewhere, but the idea bothered Donnell; he felt no loyalty whatsoever to Richmond, and this lack reflected on his inhumanity. They should share a loyalty founded on common trials, the loyalty of prisoners and victims, yet they did not; the bonds of their association were disintegrating, proving to be as meager as those between strangers traveling on a bus. Perhaps loyalty was merely a chemical waiting to be released, a little vat of sparkling fluid hidden away in some area of his brain as yet uninfested by bacteria, and when the bacteria spread to it, he would light up inside with human virtues.

'Some people you gotta waste,' said Richmond, deep into his rap. 'You gotta go to war with 'em, otherwise they won't let you be.' He had untied his pony tail, and his hair spilled down over his sunglasses; his skin was drawn so tightly across his bones that whenever he smiled you could see complex knots of muscle at the ends of his lips. 'War,' he said, savoring the word, and drank a toast to it with the last of his beer.

Jocundra nudged Donnell's leg; her lips were pressed together, and she entreated him silently to leave. Donnell glanced at the wall clock; it was after one. 'Let's go, Jack,' he said. 'We want to hit New Orleans before dawn.'

They were halfway along the aisle, slowed by Donnell's halting pace, when a grumbling roar came from the highway and a motorcycle cop pulled up in front. 'Just keep goin',' said Richmond. 'Dude's just comin' off shift. He was in this afternoon.' He laughed. 'Looks like a damn nigger bike ... all them bullshit fenders and boxes stuck all over.'

The cop dismounted and removed his helmet. He was young with close-cropped dark hair and rabbity features; his riding jacket was agleam with blue highlights from the neon sign. The record ended, the selector arm chattered along the rack, stopped, and began clicking.

'Couple of burgers?' asked Sealey as the cop pushed on in, and the cop said, 'Yeah, coffee.' He gave them a brief onceover and sat at the booth beside the entrance.

They waited at the cash register while Sealey tossed two patties on the grill and brought the cop his coffee; he sipped and made a sour face. 'I can't get used to this chicory,' he said. 'Can't a man get a regular cup of coffee 'round here?'

'Most of my customers are dumb coon-ass Cajuns,' said Sealey by way of apology. 'They can't live without it.' He moseyed back to the register and took Jocundra's money.

Donnell glued his eyes to the countertop.

'Hey, Officer,' said Richmond. 'What kinda piston ratio you runnin' on that beast?'

The cop blew on his coffee, disinterested. 'Hell, I don't know diddley 'bout the damn thing. I'm on temporary with the highway division.'

'Yeah?' Richmond was aggravated. 'Man don't know what he's ridin' don't belong on the road.'

Surprised, the cop glared at Richmond over the edge of his cup, but let it pass.

'Seems like ever since them sand niggers raised the price of gas,' said Richmond nastily, 'every cheap son of a bitch in the country is gettin' hisself up on a Harley.'

The cop set down his coffee. 'Okay, buddy. Show me some ID.'

'No problem,' said Richmond. He reached for his hip pocket, but instead sneaked his hand up under his wind-breaker and snatched out the security guard's gun. He motioned for the cop to raise his hands, and the cop complied. 'ID!' Richmond laughed at the idea. 'You askin' the wrong dudes for ID, Officer. Hell, we ain't even got no birth certificates.'

Looking at the gun made Donnell lightheaded. 'What are you going to do?' he asked. Jocundra backed away from the register, and he backed with her.

'Ain't but one thing *to* do man,' said Richmond. He moved behind the cop, jammed the gun in his ear, and fumbled inside the leather jacket; he ripped off the cop's badge and stuffed it into his jeans. Then he stepped out into the aisle, keeping the gun trained head-high. 'If we don't want the occifer here to start oinkin' on his radio, I'm gonna have to violate his civil rights.'

'You could break the radio,' said the cop, talking fast. 'You could rip out the phone. Hey, listen, nobody drives this road at night …'

Richmond flipped up his sunglasses. 'No,' he said. 'That ain't how it's gonna be, Porky.'

The cop paled, the dusting of freckles on his cheeks stood out sharply.

'Them's just contact lenses,' said Sealey with what seemed to Donnell foolhardy belligerence. 'These people's in some damn cult.'

'That's us,' said Richmond, edging along the aisle toward the register. 'The Angels of Doom, the Disciples of Death. We'll do anything to please the Master.'

'Watch it!' said Donnell, seeing a craftiness in Sealey's face, a coming together of violent purpose and opportunity.

As Richmond crossed in front of the register, the partition beneath it exploded with a roar. Blood sprayed from his hip, and he spun toward the door, falling; but as he fell, he swung the gun in a tight arc and shot Sealey in the chest. The bullet drove Sealey back onto the grill, and he wedged between the bubbling metal and the fan, his head forced downward if he were sitting on a fence and leaning forward to spit. A silvered automatic was clutched in his hand.

The explosiveness of the gunshot sent Donnell reeling against Jocundra, and she screamed. The cop jumped, up, unsnapping his holster, peering to see where Richmond had fallen. A second shot took him in the face, and he flew backward along the aisle, ending up curled beneath a booth. His hand scrabbled the floor, but that was all reflex. And then, with the awful, ponderous grace of a python uncoiling from a branch, Sealey slumped off the grill; the grease clinging to his trousers hissed and spattered on the tiles. Everything was quiet. The jukebox clicked, the air conditioner hummed. The cop's hamburgers started to burn on the grill, pale flames leaping merrily.

Jocundra dropped to her knees and began peeling shreds of cloth from Richmond's wound. 'Oh, God,' she said. 'His whole hip's shot away.'

Donnell knelt beside her. Richmond's head was propped against the rear of a booth; his eyelids fluttered when Donnell touched his arm and his eyebrows arched in clownish curves with the effort of speech. 'Oh …' he said; it didn't have the sound of a groan but of a word he was straining to speak. '… ooh,' he finished. His eyes snapped open. The bacteria had flooded the membrane surfaces, and only thready sections of the whites were visible, like cracks spreading across glowing green Easter eggs. 'Oh …' he said again.

'What?' Donnell put his ear to Richmond's mouth. 'Jack!'

'He's dead,' said Jocundra listlessly.

Richmond's mouth stayed pursed in an O shape, but he was not through dying. The same slow reverberation shuddered Donnell as had when Magnusson had died, stronger though, and whether as a result of the reverberation or because of stress, Donnell's visual field fluctuated. White tracers of Richmond's magnetic field stitched back and forth between the edges of his wound, and flashes erupted from every part of his body. Donnell got to his feet. Jocundra remained kneeling, shivering, blood smeared on her arms. The night was shutting down around them, erecting solid black barriers against the windows, sealing them in with the three dead men.

A car whizzed past on the highway.

The light switches were behind the register, and Donnell's cane pocked the silence as he moved to them. He had a glimpse of Sealey open-mouthed on the floor, his chest red and ragged, and he quickly hit the switches. Moonlight slid through the windows and shellacked the formica tables, defining tucks and pleats in the vinyl. The cash drawer was open. He crumpled the bills into his pocket, turned, and was brought up short by the sight of Richmond's corpse.

Richmond was still propped against the booth, his legs asprawl. He should have been a shadow in the entranceway, half his face illuminated by the moonlight, but he was not. A scum of violent color coated his body, a solarized oil slick of Day-Glo reds and yellows and blues, roiling, blending, separating, so bright he looked to be floating above the floor: the blazing afterimage of a man. Even the spills of his blood were pools of these colors, glowing islands lying apart from him. Black cracks appeared veining the figure, widening, as if a mold were breaking away from a homunculus within, and prisms were flitting through the blackness like jeweled bees. The reverberation was stronger than ever; each pulse skewed Donnell's vision. Something was emerging, being freed. Something inimical. The colors thickened, hardening into a bright sludge sloughing off the corpse. Donnell's skin crawled, and the tickling sensation reawakened in his head.

He took Jocundra by the arm; her skin was cold, and she flinched at his touch. 'Come on,' he said, pulling her toward the door. He stepped over the writhe of color that was Richmond and felt dizzy, a chill point of gravity condensing in his stomach, as if he were stepping over a great gulf. He steadied himself on the door and pushed it open. The air was warm, damp, smelling of gasoline.

'We can't go,' said Jocundra, a lilt of fear in her voice.

'The hell we can't!' He propelled her across the parking lot. 'I'll be damned if I'm going to wait for the police. You get the ledger, the clothes. Clean everything out of the cabin. I'll check the office and see if Sealey wrote anything down.'

He was startled by his callousness, his practicality, because he did not recognize them to be his own. The words were someone else's, a fragmentary self giving voice to *its* needs, and he did not have that other's confidence or strength of purpose. Any icy fluid shifted along his spine, and he refused to look back at the restaurant for fear he might see a shadow standing in the door.

CHAPTER 10

May 20, 1987

According to the map it was eight-five miles, about two hours' drive, to the town of Salt Harvest, and there they could catch the four-lane to New Orleans; but to Jocundra the miles and the minutes were a timeless, distanceless pour of imaginary cherry tops blinking in the rear view mirror, the wind making spirit noises through the side vent, and memories of the policeman's face: an absurdly neat concavity where his eyes and nose had been, as if a housing had been lifted off to check the working parts. Cypresses glowed grayish-white in the headlights, trees of bone burst from dark flesh. Rabbits ghosted beneath her wheels and vanished without a crunch. And near the turn-off a little girl wearing a lace party dress stepped out onto the blacktop, changing at the last second into a speed limit sign, and Jocundra swerved off the road. The van came to rest amid a thicket of bamboo, and rather than risk another accident, they piled brush around it and slept. But sleep was a thing seamlessly welded to waking, the continuance of a terrible dream, and in the morning, bleary, she saw shards of herself reflected in the fragments of the mirrored ball that Richmond had broken.

They started toward New Orleans, but the engine grated and the temperature indicator hovered near the red. A mile outside Salt Harvest they pulled into Placide's Mobile Service; junked cars resting on a cracked cement apron, old-fashioned globe-top pumps, a rickety, unpainted shack with corroded vending machines and lawn chairs out front. Placide, a frizzy-haired, chubby man chewing an unlit cigar, gazed up at the sky to receive instructions before allowing he would have a look at the van after he finished a rush job. Miserable, they waited. The radio news made no mention of the killings, and the only newspaper they could find was a gossip rag whose headlines trumpeted *Teen's Pimples Found to be Strange Code.*

'Somebody must have seen them by now!' Donnell kicked at a chair in frustration. 'We've got to get out of here.'

'The police aren't very efficient,' she said. 'And Sealey didn't even check us in. They may not know there was anyone else.'

'What about Marie?'

'I don't know.' She stared off across the road at a white wooden house by the bayou. A tireless truck in the front yard; shade trees; children scampering in and out of the sunbeams which penetrated the branches. The scene had an archaic air, as if the backing of a gentle past were showing through the threadbare tapestry of the present.

'Don't you care?' he asked. 'Aren't you worried about being caught?'

'Yes,' she said tonelessly, remembering the yellow dimness and blood-smeared floors of the restaurant. 'I ...'

'What?'

'You just don't seem bothered by what happened.'

'Bothered? Guilty, you mean?' He thought it over. 'The cop bothers me, but when Sealey pulled the trigger' – he laughed – 'oh, he was a happy man. He'd been waiting for this chance a long time. You should have seen his face. All that frustrated desire and obsession blowing up into heaven.' He limped a little way across the apron. 'It was Sealey's crime. Richmond's maybe. But it's got no moral claim on me.'

Around five o'clock a sorrowful Placide delivered his report: a slow leak in the oil pan. Ten or fifteen more miles and the engine would seize up. 'I give you fifty dollars, me,' he said. Jocundra gave him a doubtful look, and he crossed himself.

They accepted his offer of a ride into town, and he let them off at the Crawfish Cafe where, he said, they could learn the bus schedules. A sign above the door depicted a green lobsterlike creature wearing a bib, and inside the lighting was hellishly bright, the booths packed with senior citizens – tonight, Sunday, being the occasion of the cafe's Golden Ager All-U-Can-Eat Frog Legs and Gumbo Creole Special $2.99. The smell of grease was filmy in Jocundra's nostrils. The waitress told them that a bus left around midnight for Silver Meadow ('Now you be careful! The shrimp fleet's in, and that's one wild town at night.') and there they could catch a Greyhound for New Orleans where she had a sister, Minette by name, who favored Jocundra some though she wasn't near as tall, and oh how she worried about the poor woman living with her madman husband and his brothers on Beaubien Street like a saint among wolves ... Try the shrimp salad. You can't go wrong with shrimp this time of year.

The senior citizens, every liver spot and blotch evident under the bright lights, lifted silvery spoons full of dripping red gumbo to their lips, and the sight brought back the memory of Magnusson's death. Jocundra's stomach did a queasy roll. An old man blinked at her and slipped a piece of frog into his mouth, leaving the fork inserted. The tinkle of silverware was a sharp, dangerous sound at the edge of a silence hollowed around her, and she ate without speaking.

'Do you want to go back?' Donnell asked. 'I can't, but if you think it's better for you there, I won't stop you.'

'I don't see how I can,' she said, thinking that she would have to go back to before Shadows, before the project began.

He toyed with a french fry, drawing circles in the grease on his plate. 'I need a more isolated place than New Orleans,' he said. 'I don't want to lose it in public like Richmond.'

'You're nothing like Richmond.' Jocundra was too exhausted to be wholeheartedly reassuring.

'Sure I am. According to Edman, and it seems to me he's at least partially right, Richmond's life was the enactment of a myth he created for himself.' The waitress refilled Jocundra's coffee, and he waited until she finished. 'He had to kill someone to satisfy the myth, and by God he did. And there's something I have to do as well.'

She looked up at him. 'What do you mean?'

'Magnusson told me I had something special to do, and ever since I've felt a compulsion to do it. I have no idea what it is, but the compulsion is growing stronger and I'm convinced it's not a good deed.'

White gleams of the overheads slashed diagonally across the lenses of his sunglasses. For the first time she was somewhat afraid of him.

'A quiet place,' he said. 'One without too many innocent bystanders.'

More senior citizens crammed into the cafe. They huddled at the front waiting for a seat, and the waitress became hostile as Donnell and Jocundra lingered over their empty plates. Jocundra wedged Magnusson's ledger into her purse; they tipped the waitress generously, leaving the overnight bag in her keeping, and walked out into the town.

The main street of Salt Harvest was lined with two-story buildings of dark friated brick, vintage 1930, their walls covered by weathered illustrations of defunct brands of sewing machines and pouch tobacco, now home to Cadieux Drugs, Beutel Hardware, and the Creole Theater, whose ticket taker – isolate in her hotly lit booth – looked like one of those frowsy, bewigged dummies passing for gypsy women that you find inside fortune-telling machines, the yellowed paint of their skin peeling away, their hands making mechanical passes over a dusty crystal ball. The neons spelled out mysterious red and blue and green words – HRIMP, SUNOC, OOD – and these seemed the source of all the heat and humidity. Cars were parked diagonally along the street, most dinged and patched with bondo, windshields polka-dotted by NRA and SW Louisiana Ragin' Cajun decals. Half of the streetlights hummed and fizzled, the other half were shattered. Dusk was thickening to night, and heat lightning flashed in the southern sky.

Groups of people were moving purposefully toward the edge of town, and so as not to appear conspicuous, they fell in at the rear of three gabbling old ladies who were cooling themselves with fans bearing pictures of Christ Arisen. Behind them came a clutch of laughing teenage girls. Before they had gone a hundred yards, Donnell's legs began to cramp, but he preferred to continue rather than go contrary to the crowd now following them. Their pace slowed, and a family bustled past: mom, kids, dad, dressed in their Sunday finery and having the prim, contented look of the well-insured. Some drunken farmers passed them, too, and one – a middle-aged man whose T-shirt read *When Farm-boys Do it They Fertilize 'Er* – said 'Howdy' to Jocundra and offered her a swig from his paper sack. He whispered in his buddy's ear. Sodden laughter. The crowd swept around them, chattering, in a holiday mood, and Jocundra and Donnell walked in their midst, tense, heads down, hoping to go unnoticed but noticeable by their secretive manner: Jews among Nazis.

The night deepened, gurgling and croaking from the bayou grew louder as they cleared the city limits, and they heard a distorted amplified voice saying, 'CHILDREN, CHILDREN, CHIL ...' The speaker squealed. A brown circus tent was pitched in a pasture beside the bayou, ringed by parked cars and strung with colored bulbs; a banner above the entrance proclaimed What Jesus Promised, Papa Salvatino Delivers. The speaker crackled, and the voice blatted out again: a cheery, sleazy voice, the voice of a carnival barker informing of forbidden delights.

'CHILDREN, CHILDREN, CHILDREN! COME TO PAPA SALVATINO! COME BEFORE THE NIGHT CREEPERS AND THE GHOST WORMS SNIFF YOU OUT, COME BEFORE THE DEVIL GETS BEHIND YOU WITH HIS SHINBONE CLUB AND SMACKS YOU LOW. YEAH, THAT'S RIGHT! YOU KNOW YOU GONNA COME, CHILDREN! YOU GOTTA COME! 'CAUSE MY VOICE GONNA SNEAK LIKE SMOKE THROUGH THE CRACK IN YOUR WINDOW, CURL UP YOUR STAIR AND IN YOUR EAR, AND HOOK YOU, CROOK YOU, BEND YOU ON YOUR KNEE TO JEEESUS! YES CHILDREN, YES ...'

A furious, thumping music compounded of sax, organs and drums built up under the voice, which continued to cajole and jolly the crowd; they streamed into the entrance, and the tent glowed richly brown against the blackness of field and sky. As Donnell and Jocundra hesitated, a police car pulled up next to the field and flashed its spotlight over the rows of parked cars; they joined the stragglers walking towards the tent.

At the entrance a mousy girl asked them for three dollars each admission, and when Jocundra balked, she smacked her gum and said, 'We used to do with just love offerin's, but Papa fills folk so brimful of Jesus' love that sometimes they forgets all about givin'.'

Inside, radiating outward from a plywood stage, were rows of folding chairs occupied by shadowy figures, most standing, hooting and clapping to the music. The mingled odors of sweat and liquor and perfume, the press of bodies, the slugging music, everything served to disorient Donnell. He squeezed Jocundra's hand, fending off a visual shift.

'And lo!' a voice shouted in his ear. 'The blind and the halt shall be first anointed.' A gray-haired man, tall and lean, his hair cut short above the ears and left thick on top, giving him a stretched look, beamed at Donnell. 'We'll get you a seat down front, brother,' he said, steering him toward the stage. Jocundra objected, and he said, 'No trouble at all, sister. No trouble at all.' His smile seemed the product of a wise and benign overview.

As he led them along, people staggered out of their chairs and into the aisle. Deranged squawks, angry shouts, and scuffles, a few cries of religious fervor. A Saturday-night-in-the-sticks-and-ain't-nothin'-else-to-do level of drunkenness. Hardly sanctified. Donnell was grateful when the usher shooed two teenagers off the first row and sat him down beside a fat lady. 'Ain't it hot?' she cried, nudging him with a dimpled arm the size of a ham. ''Bout hot enough to melt candles!' The edges of the crimson hibiscus patterning her dress were bleeding from her sweat, and each crease and fold of her exuded its own special sourness. 'Oh, Jesus yes!' she screeched as the saxophonist shrilled a high note. She quivered all over, and her eyelids slid down, false lashes stitching them to her cheeks.

The music ebbed, the organist stamped out a plodding beat on the bass pedals, and the saxophonist played a gospel fanfare. The lights cut to a single spot, and a paunchy, balding man, well over six feet tall, slouched onto stage. His walk was an invitation to buy drugs, to slip him twenty and meet the little lady upstairs; his face was yellow-tinged, puffy, framed by a hippie-length fringe of brown hair. He wore a powder-blue suit, a microphone dangled from his hand, and his eyes threw back glitters of the spotlight.

'CHILDREN, CHILDREN, CHILDREN,' he rasped. 'ARE YOU READY FOR PAPA'S LOVE?'

There were hysterical Yesses in response, a scatter of Nos, and one 'Fuck you, Papa!'

He laughed. 'WELL, THEM THAT SAY YEA, I AIN'T WORRIED 'BOUT THEM. AND AS FOR THE REST, YOU GONNA LEARN THAT OL' PAPA'S JUST LIKE POTATO CHIPS AND LOVIN'. YOU CAN'T DO WITH JUST ONE HELPIN'!' He bowed his head and walked along the edge of the stage, deep in thought. 'I'M HERE TO TELL YOU I'M A SINNER. DON'T YOU NEVER LET NO PREACHER TELL YOU HE AIN'T! HELL, THEY'S THE WORST KIND.' He shook his head, rueful; then, suddenly animated, he dropped into a crouch, and his delivery became rapid-fire. 'BUT IN HIS INFINITE COMPASSION THE LORD JESUS HAS FILLED ME WITH THE SPIRIT, AND I AIN'T TALKIN' 'BOUT THE IMMATERIAL, PIE-IN-THE-SKY,

SOMETHIN'-YOU-GOTTA-HAVE-FAITH-IN SPIRIT! NOSIR! I'M TALKIN' 'BOUT THE REACHABLE, TOUCHABLE, GRABAHOLD-OF-YOU-AND-MAKE-YOU-FEEL-AGREEABLE POWER OF GOD'S LOVE!'

Faint Praise Gods and Hallelujahs; the crowd rustled; the fat lady raised her hands overhead, palms up, praying silently.

'I'M TALKIN' 'BOUT THE SAME SPIRIT THAT SOON ONE MORNIN'S GONNA LIFT US ON ANGELS' WINGS INTO THE LIGHT OF THE RAPTURE WHERE WE WILL LIVE IN ECSTASY 'TIL HIS EARTHLY KINGDOM IS SECURE HALLELUJAH!'

'Hallelujah!' chorused the crowd. Donnell was beginning to relax, his senses settling; he stretched out his legs, preparing to be bored. Papa Salvatino paced the stage: a downcast, troubled man. The organ rippled out an icy trill.

'OH, CHILDREN, CHILDREN, CHILDREN! I SEE THE PATHS BY WHICH YOU'VE TRAVELED GLEAMIN' IN MY MIND'S EYE. SLIMY SERPENT TRACKS! YOU BEEN DOWN IN THE MUCK OF SHALLOW LIVIN' AND FALSE EMOTION SO LONG YOU'RE TOO SICK FOR PREACHIN'!' He pointed to the fat lady beside Donnell. 'YOU THERE, SISTER RITA! I SEE YOUR SIN SHININ' LIKE PHOSPHOR ON A STUMP!' He pointed to others of the crowd, accusing them, and as his gaze swept over Donnell, his yellow face, gemmed with those glittering eyes, was as malevolent as a troll's.

'BUT IT AIN'T TOO LATE, SINNERS! THE LORD'S GIVIN' YOU ONE LAST CHANCE. HE'LL EVEN GET DOWN IN SATAN'S DIRT AND TEMPT YOU. HE'S OFFERIN' YOU A ONE-TIME-ONLY-GUARANTEED-YOUR-SOUL-BACK-IF-YOU-AIN'T-SATISFIED TASTE OF SALVATION! AND I'M HERE TO GIVE YOU THAT TASTE! THAT SOUL-STIRRIN' TASTE OF HOSANNAH-IN-THE-HIGHEST AMBROSIA! 'CAUSE EVEN IF HE CAN'T SAVE YOU, THE LORD JESUS HIMSELF WANTS YOU TO HAVE BIG FUN TONIGHT DOWN ON THE BAYOU!'

The crowd was on its feet, waving its arms, shouting.

'YOU WANT THAT TASTE, CHILDREN?'

'Yes!'

'WHAT'S THAT YOU WANT?'

'A taste!' called the organist, prompting the crowd, and they hissed raggedly, 'A taste!' The saxophone brayed, the drummer bashed out a shuffle beat, and the organist unleashed a wash of chords. Papa Salvatino shed his jacket. 'AMEN!' he shouted.

'Amen!'

Donnell turned and saw open-mouthed, flushed faces, rolling eyes; people were shouldering each other aside, poising to rush the stage.

'THY WILL BE DONE!' Papa leapt high and came down in a split, gradually humping himself upright, and did a little shimmy like a snake standing on its tail. 'I WANT THE SICK ONES FIRST AND THE WHOLE ONES LAST! ALL RIGHT, CHILDREN! COME TO PAPA!'

The crowd boiled toward the stage, bumping Donnell's chair, and once again the gray-haired usher loomed before him. He helped Donnell up. Jocundra pried at his grip, protesting, and Donnell struggled: but the usher held firm and said, 'You come with him if you want, sister. But I ain't lettin' you stand in the path of this boy's salvation.'

After much shoving, many Biblically phrased remonstrations directed at people who would not move aside, the usher secured a choice spot in line for Donnell, fourth behind Sister Rita and a thin, drab woman with her arm draped around a teenage boy, a hydrocephalic. He grinned stuporously at Donnell. His hair was slicked down, pomaded, a mother's idea of good grooming; but the effect was of a grotesque face painted on a balloon. He let his head roll around, his grin broadening, enjoying the dizzy sensation. A pearl of saliva formed at the corner of his mouth.

'Jody!' The thin woman turned him away from Donnell, and by way of apology smiled and said, 'Praise the Lord!' Her hair was piled up in a bouffant style, which accentuated her scrawniness, and her gray dress hung loosely and looked to be full of sticks and air.

'Praise the Lord,' muttered Donnell, struck by the woman's sincerity, her lack of pose, especially in relation to the fraudulence of Papa Salvatino; his face was a road map of creepy delights and indulgences, and masked an unaspiring soul who had discovered a trick by which he might prosper. The nature of the trick was beyond Donnell's power to discern, but no doubt it was the cause of the anticipation he read from the shadowy faces bobbing in the aisle below.

The music lapsed into a suspenseful noodling on the organ, and Jocundra leaned close, her face drawn and worried. 'Don't let him touch your glasses,' she whispered. She pointed to the rear flap of the tent, which was lashed partway open behind the drum kit, and he nodded.

'What's ailin' you tonight, Sister Rita.' Papa clipped the microphone to a stand and approached. 'You look healthier than me!'

'Oh, Papa!' Sister Rita wiggled her hips seductively. 'You know I got the worst kind of heart trouble.'

Papa laughed. 'No need to get specific, sister,' he said. 'Jesus understands full well the problems of a widow woman.' He placed his hands palms inward above her head and began to knead the air, hooking his fingers, shaping an invisible substance.

Astounded, Donnell recognized the motions to be the same as he had used to disrupt the lock on the gate at Shadows. He brought Sister Rita's magnetic field into focus, and saw that Papa was inducing the fiery arcs to flow inward toward a point at the top of her head; and as they flowed, they ceased flickering in and out, brightened and thickened into a cage of incandescent wires. Her back arched. Her arms stiffened, her fingers splayed. The rolls of fat rippled beneath her dress. And then, as all the arcs flowed inward, a brilliant flash enveloped her body, as if the gate to a burning white heaven had opened and shut inside her. In Donnell's eyes she existed momentarily as a pillar of pale shimmering energy. He felt the discharge on every inch of his skin, a tingling which faded with the same rapidity as the flash.

Sister Rita wailed and staggered to one side. His smile unflagging, the gray-haired usher led her toward the stairs, and the band launched into a triumphant blare. Fervent shouts erupted from the crowd.

'PRAISE JESUS!' Papa bawled into the mike. 'I'M STOKED FULL OF GOD'S LOVE TONIGHT!'

But if Papa were truly a conduit for the Holy Spirit, then the Spirit must consist of a jolt of electromagnetism channelled into the brain reward centers. That, thought Donnell, would be how Magnusson would have interpreted the event. Papa Salvatino must be psychically gifted, and in effect was serving his flock as a prostitute, bestowing powerful orgasms and passing them off as divine visitations. Donnell glanced down at Sister Rita. She was sprawled in her chair, gasping, her legs spread and her skirt ridden up over swollen knees; an elderly woman leaned over her from the row behind and was fanning her with a newspaper.

The music lapsed once more, the crowd stilled, and Papa began working on the hydrocephalic. The thin woman closed her eyes and lifted her arms overhead, praying silently, the ligature of her neck standing out in cables with the ferocity of her devotion. Things were not going as well as they had for Sister Rita. Papa's eyes were nearly crossed with the strain, sweat beaded his forehead, and the hydrocephalic's head was sunk grimacing on his chest. His field was more complex than Sister Rita's, hundreds of arcs, all of them fine and frayed, woven eratically in a pattern similar to a spiderweb. Instead of slowly fading and rematerializing, they popped in and out with magical quickness. Whenever Papa touched them, they flared and sputtered like rotten fuses. The thing to do, thought Donnell, would be to meld the arcs together, to simplify the pattern; but Papa was doggedly trying to guide them inward, and by doing so he was causing them to fray and divide further. A bubble of spittle burst on the boy's lips, and he moaned. The crowd was growing murmurous, and the organist was running out of fills, unable to build to a climax.

Papa withdrew his hands, spread his arms, and addressed the darkness at the tent top, his lips moving, apparently praying, but his gaze darted back and forth between the crowd and the thin woman.

A feeling of revulsion had been building inside Donnell, a feeling bred by the stink of the tent, the raucous music, the slack-jawed faces, but most of all by Papa Salvatino: this big yellow rat standing on its hind legs and mocking the puny idea which sustained his followers in their fear. With a rush of animosity, and with only a trace of amazement at his own incaution, Donnell stepped forward, hooked his cane onto his elbow, and placed his hands above the boy's head. The fiery arcs tugged at his fingers, and he let them guide his movements. Two of the arcs materialized close together, and he urged them to merge into a single bright stream, setting it coursing inward toward the boy's scalp, a spot to which it seemed to gravitate naturally. As more and more of the arcs were joined, the boy's great head wobbled up. He smiled dazedly and lifted his arms and waggled his fingers, as if in parody of the thin woman's charismatic salute. Dimly, Donnell was aware of Jocundra beside him, of marveling shouts from the crowd. And then a heavy hand fell on his shoulder, spinning him around.

'Blasphemer!' shouted Papa, clutching a fistful of Donnell's shirt; his cheeks were mottled with rage. He drove his fist into Donnell's forehead.

Donnell fell against the drum kit, cracking his head on the cymbal stand. His sunglasses had snapped in the middle, and one piece dangled from his ear. He did not lose consciousness, but everything had gone black and he was afraid he had been blinded. Footsteps, pounded the boards, screams, and a man's voice nearby said, 'Oh God, lookit his eyes!' He groped for his cane, feeling terribly exposed and helpless, and then he saw his cane outlined in glowing silver a few feet away, lying across a silver sketch of planks and nails. He looked up. The tent had been magicked into a cavernous black drape ornamented with silver arabesques and folds, furnished with silver-limned chairs, and congregated by ebony demons. Prisms whirled inside the bodies of most, masked the faces of others with glittering analogues of human features; and in the case of two, no, three, one standing where Papa Salvatino had been, the prisms flowed through an intricate circuitry, seeming to illuminate the patterns of their nerves and muscles, forming into molten droplets at their fingertips and detonating in needle-thin beams of iridescent light, which spat throughout the crowd. Yet for all their fearsome appearance, the majority of them edged away from the stage, huddling together, afraid. Curious, Donnell held up his hand to his face, but saw nothing, not even the outline of his fingers.

Jocundra, a gemmy mask overlaying her features, knelt beside him and pressed the cane into his hand. The instant she touched him, his vision normalized and his head began to throb. She pulled him upright. The band had fled, and Papa Salvatino was halfway down the steps of the stage.

'Abomination!' he said, but his voice quavered, and the crowd did not respond. They crushed back against the tent walls, on the verge of panicked flight. Most were hidden by the darkness, but Donnell could see those in the front rank and was fascinated by what he saw.

They were more alien to him now than their previous appearance of ebony flesh and jeweled expressions had been. Lumpy and malformed; protruding bellies, gaping mouths, drooping breasts; clad in all manner of dull cloth; they might have been a faded mural commemorating the mediocrity and impermanence of their lives. Wizened faces topped by frumpy hats; dewy, pubescent faces waxed to a hard gloss with makeup; plump, choleric faces. And each of these faces was puckered or puffed up around a black seed of fear. As he looked them over one by one, bits of intelligence lodged in his thoughts, and he knew them for bad-tempered old men, vapid old women, thankless children, shrewish wives, brutal husbands. But the complications of their lives were only a façade erected to conceal the black ground which bubbled them up. He took a step forward. Jocundra tried to drag him toward the rear flap of the tent, but he shook her off and limped to the front of the stage. Papa backed along the aisle.

'Why are you so afraid?' Donnell asked the crowd. 'It's not just my eyes. That's not what drives you to seek salvation.' He spotted a portly, sport-jacketed man trying to push through to the entrance. 'You!' he called, pointing, and knew the substance of the man's life as if it had rushed up his finger: pompous, gluttonous, every dependency founded on fear and concealing a diseased sexuality, a compendium of voyeurism and the desire to inflict pain. 'Don't be afraid,' he said derisively, the way a murderer might taunt his victim, and was amazed to see the man swallow and inch toward the stage, his fear lessening. 'Come closer,' said Donnell. 'Tonight, verily, you will bear miraculous witness.'

He singled out others of the crowd, coaxing them nearer, and as he did, he felt a distance between his voice and his cautious soul, one identical to that he had experienced when he persuaded Jocundra to leave the scene of the murders at Sealey's. But in this instance the distance was more profound. The element of his consciousness which spoke dominated him totally, and his own fear was swept away by the emotional charge of the words. Disgust, pity and anger met in his mind and pronounced judgement on the crowd, on the culture that had produced it, comparing it unfavorably to a sterner culture existing beneath the flood of his memory like a submerged shoal, unseen, undefined, known only by the divergence of waves around it; but he did not question its reality, rather acted as its spokesman. He could, he thought, tell the crowd anything and they would listen. They were not really listening, they were reacting to the pitch and timbre of his voice, his glowing eyes. Their fear had taken on a lewd, exultant character, as if they had been eagerly awaiting him.

'Lo,' he said, spreading his arms in imitation of Papa Salvatino, 'the Lord

God has raised me up from the ramshackle kingdom of the dead and sent me to warn you. Not of Kingdom Come but of Kingdom Overthrown, of Satan's imminent victory!'

Hesitant, they shuffled forward, some coming halfway along the aisle, soothed by the familiar Biblical cadences, but not yet ready to embrace him fully. The ease with which they could be swayed delighted him; he imagined an army carrying a green-eyed banner through the world, converting millions to his cause.

'Do you remember the good old days?' he asked with a wistful air, hobbling along the edge of the stage. 'Those days that always seem just to have vanished or perhaps never even were. Days when the light was full of roses and lovers, when music played out every window and the kids weren't into drugs, when Granny baked her bread fresh each morning and the city streets were places of excitement and wonder. Whatever happened to those days?'

They didn't know but wanted to be told.

'You began to hear voices,' he said. 'You began to have visions, to receive reports, all of which conjured against that peaceful world. Radio and newspapers preaching a gospel of doom, a spell binding you to its truth. And then along came Satan's Eye Itself. Television.' He laughed, as at some fatal irony. 'Don't you hear the evil hum of the word, the knell of Satan? Television! It's the ruling character of your lives, like the moon must have been for Indians. An oracle, a companion, a signal of the changing seasons. But rather than divine illumination, each night it spews forth Satan's imagery. Murders, car crashes, mad policemen, perverted strangers! And you lie there decomposing in its flickering, blue-gray light, absorbing His horrid fantasies.'

He stared over their heads as if he saw a truth they could not see, staring for so long that many followed his gaze.

'You'll go home tonight and look at your sets and say, "Why, it's a harmless entertainment, a blessing when the kids are sick." But that logic's Satan's sales pitch, brothers and sisters. What it really is is the transmission of Armageddon's pulse, the rumormonger of the war foretold by Scripture, the power cell of Satan's dream for mankind. Take a closer look. Turn it on, touch the glass and feel the crackle of His force, catch a whiff of His lightning brain. It's the thing you fear most, the thing which has seduced you, which is lifting you to its jaws while you think it's preparing to give you a kiss. Know it, brothers and sisters! Or be consumed. And when you truly know it, save yourself. Break the glass, smash the tubes!'

'Break the glass!' shouted someone, and another shouted, 'Break it! Break it!'

'Break the glass,' said Donnell softly. 'Smash the tubes.' And the crowd, though unfamiliar with the litany, tried to repeat it.

'Hallelujah!' said Donnell.

They knew that one and were nearly unanimous in their response. He had them say it again, letting them unite within the sound of the word, and then held out his hands for silence.

'Break the glass, smash the tubes, and …' He made them wait, enjoying the expectancy on their faces. 'And … renew the earth! Oh, brothers and sisters, don't you remember when you used to walk to the edge of town and into the woods and fields? What's taken their place?'

They weren't sure. 'Evil!' someone suggested, and Donnell nodded his approval.

'Right enough, brother. Gas stations and motels and franchise restaurants. Defoliated zones of sameness! Places that have lost their identity and might be anywhere on God's earth. Why, put a good Christian down in one and he might think he was in Buffalo as like as Albuquerque. But you know where he really is? Those bright little huts tinkling with jingles are the anterooms of Hell-on-earth, an infection of concrete and plastic spreading over the land, reducing everything to the primary colors and simple shapes of Satan's dream. Arby's, Big Boy, McDonald's, Burger King! Those are the new names of the demons, of Beelzebub and Moloch.' He shook his head, disconsolate. 'Satan's nearly won, and he would have already except for one thing. God has a plan for Salt Harvest. A master plan, a divinely inspired plan! Do you want to hear it?'

Yes, indeed. The boldest of them were three-quarters of the way down the aisle, waggling their hands overhead, praising God and begging His guidance.

'Salt Harvest! Listen to the name. It's a natural name, an advertising man's dream of organic purity, a name that bespeaks the bounty of the sea and of God, redolent of Christian virtue and tasty gumbos. How many people live here?'

They argued briefly, settling on a consensus figure of between fifteen and eighteen thousand.

'And things aren't going too well, are they? The economy's depressed, the cannery's shut down, the kids are moving away. Am I right?

'Now bear with me, brothers and sisters. Hear me out, because like every great plan this one's so simple it might sound foolish until you get used to it. But imagine! Eighteen thousand Christian souls united in a common enterprise, all their resources pooled, digging for every last cent, competing with Satan for the consumer dollar and the souls of the diners. You've got everything you need! Cannery, shrimp boats, good men and women, and God on your side. Salt Harvest. Not a town. A chain of franchise restaurants coast to coast. I'm not talking about a dispensary of poisoned meat, a Burger Chef, a Wendy's, a Sambo's. No! We'll stuff them full of Gulf Shrimp and lobster, burgers made from the finest Argentine beef. We'll outcook and undersell

Satan and his minions, drive them into ruin. Instead of pimply, dope-smoking punks, we'll staff our units with Christian converts, and in no time our logo, the sign of the fish and the cross, will not only be familiar as a symbol of God's love but of gracious dining and quality cuisine. We'll snip a page from Satan's book and have a playland for the kids. They'll enter through the Pearly Gates, ride Ferris wheels with winged clouds for cars, cavort with actors dressed as cute angels and maybe even the Messiah Himself. A chapel in the rear, ordained ministers on duty twenty-four hours a day. Every unit will shine with a holy beacon winking out the diamond light of Jesus Christ, and soon the golden arches will topple, the giant fried chicken buckets will fill with rainwater and burst, and we'll bulldoze them under and build the Heavenly City in their place! Oh, there've been Congregationalists and Baptists and Methodists, but we'll have something new. The first truly franchised religion! That's real salvation, brothers and sisters. Economic and spiritual at the same time. Hallelujah!'

'Hallelujah!' Their chorus was less enthused than before; some of them weren't quite sold on his idea.

'Praise the Lord!'

'Praise the Lord!' They were coming round again, and after a few more repetitions they were held back from the stage by the thinnest of restraints. A man in a seersucker suit stumbled along the aisle, keening, almost a whistling noise like a teakettle about to boil, and fell on all fours, his face agonized, reaching out to Donnell.

Overwhelmed with disgust, Donnell said, 'I could sell you sorry fuckers anything, couldn't I?'

They weren't sure they had heard correctly; they looked at each other, puzzled, asking what had been said.

'I could sell you sorry fuckers anything,' he repeated, 'as long as it had a bright package and was wrapped around a chewy nugget of fear. I could be your green-eyed king. But it would bore me to be the salvation of cattle like you. Take my advice, though. Don't buy the crap that's slung into your faces by two-bit wart-healers!' He jabbed his cane at Papa Salvatino, who stood open-mouthed in the aisle, a litter of paper cups and fans and Bibles spreading out from his feet. 'Find your own answers, your own salvation. If you can't do that,' said Donnell, 'then to Hell with you.'

He took a faltering step backward. His fascination with the crowd had dulled, and the arrogant confidence inspired by his voice was ebbing. He became aware again of his tenuous position. The crowd was massing back against the tent walls, once more afraid, in turmoil, a clot of darkness sprouting arms and legs, heaving in all directions. Whispers, then a babble, angry shouts.

'Devil!' someone yelled, and a man countered, 'He ain't the Devil! He was curin' Alice Grimeaux's boy!' But someone else, his voice hysterical, screamed 'Jesus please Jeesus!'

'Yea, I have gazed into the burning eye of Satan and been sore affrighted,' intoned Papa Salvatino. 'But the power of my faith commands me. Pray, brothers and sisters! That's the Devil's poison: Prayer!'

The gray-haired usher came up behind him, grabbed a chair, held it overhead and advanced upon the stage while Papa exhorted the crowd. Dark figures began to trickle forward between the chairs, along the aisle. Jocundra stood by the drum kit, pale, her hand poised above the cymbal stand as if she had meant to use it as a weapon, transfixed by the sight of the Army of Our Lord in Louisiana bearing down on them. Donnell felt his groin shriveling. Ordinary men and women were slinking near, gone grim and wolfish, brandishing chairs and bottles, a susurrus of prayer – of 'Save us sweet Jesuses' and 'Merciful Saviors' – rising from them like an exhaust, ragged on by Papa Salvatino's blood-and-thunder.

'Pray! Let your prayer crack Satan's crimson hide! Shine the light of prayer on him 'til he splits like old leather and the black juice spews from his heart!'

A meek hope of countering Papa's verbal attack sparked in Donnell, but all he could muster was a feeble 'Ah ...' An old lady, her cane couched spear-fashion, her crepe throat pulsing with prayer, came right behind the gray-haired usher; a tubby kid, no more than seven or eight, clutching his father's hand and holding a jagged piece of glass, stared at Donnell through slit black eyes; Sister Rita, two hundred pounds of blubbery prayer, cooed to the Savior while she swung her purse around and around like a bolo; the man who had tried to worship Donnell had himself a pocket knife and was talking to the blade, twisting it, practicing the corkscrew thrust he planned to use.

'Let's fry Satan with the Holy Volts of prayer!' squalled Papa Salvatino, 'Let's set him dancin' like a rat on a griddle!'

Donnell backed away, his own sermon about fear mocking him, because fear was gobbling him up from the inside, greedy piranha mouths shredding his rationality. He bumped against Jocundra; her nails dug into his arm.

'God, I'm healed!' somebody screeched, and two boys sprinted down the aisle. Teenagers. They darted in and out of the crowd, knocked the gray-haired usher spinning, and reeled up to the stage. One, the tallest, a crop of ripe pimples straggling across his cheeks, raised his arms high. 'Holy Green-eyed Jesus!' he shouted. 'You done cured my social disease!' The other doubled up laughing.

'Goddamn it, Earl!' A barrel-shaped man in overalls dropped his chair and rushed the boys, but they danced away. He lunged for them again, and they easily evaded him.

'Witness the work of Satan!' cried Papa. 'How he turns the child against the father! Child!' He pointed at the tall boy. 'Heed not the Anti-Christ or he will bring thee low and set maggots to breed in the jellied meats in thine eyes!'

'Shut up, you big pussy!' The boy avoided his father's backhand by a hair and grinned up at Donnell. 'You done made my hot dog whole!' he shouted. 'Praise the fuckin' Lord!'

A ripple of laughter from the front of the tent, and a girl yelled, 'Git him, Earl!' More laughter as the big man fell, buckling one of the chairs.

The laughter disconcerted the crowd, slowed their advance. Donnell turned to Jocundra, thinking they might be able to hide amongst the cars; but just then she seized him by both hands and yanked him through the *rear* flap. He sprawled in the cool grass, shocked by the freshness of the night air after the pollution inside. She hauled him to his feet, her breath shrill, rising to a shriek as somebody jumped down beside them. It was Earl.

'Them Christians get their shit together, man,' he said, 'and they gonna nail you up. Come on!'

He and Jocundra hoisted Donnell by the elbows and carried him between the rows of parked cars to a van with a flock of silver ducks painted on its side. Earl slid open the door, and Donnell piled in. His hand encountered squidgy flesh; a girl's sulky voice said, 'Hey, watch it!' and somebody else laughed. Through the window Donnell had a glimpse of people streaming out of the tent, imps silhouetted against a blaze of white light; Then the engine caught, and the van fishtailed across the field.

'Whooee!' yelled Earl. 'Gone but not forgotten!' He banged the flat of his hand on the dash. 'Hey, that's Greg and Elaine back there. And I am ...' He beat a drumroll on the wheel. 'The Earl!'

Headlights passing in the opposite direction penetrated the van. Elaine was a chubby girl wriggling into a T-shirt, forcing it down over large breasts, and Greg was a longhaired, muscular kid who regarded Donnell with drugged sullenness. He pointed to his own right eye. 'Papa Salvatino do that to you, man?'

Elaine giggled.

'He's been sick,' said Jocundra. 'Radiation treatments.' She refused to look at Donnell.

'Actually it was bad drugs,' said Donnell. 'The residue of evil companions.'

'Yeah?' said Greg, half-questioning, half-challenging. He took a stab at staring Donnell down, but the eyes were too much for him.

'You shoulda seen the dude!' The van veered onto the shoulder as Earl turned to them. 'He talked some wild shit to them goddamn Christians! Had ol' Papa's balls clickin' like ice cubes!'

Elaine cupped her hand in front of Donnell's eyes and collected a palmful of reflected glare. 'Intense,' she said.

Greg lost interest in the whole thing, pulled out a baggie and papers and started rolling a joint. 'Let's air this sucker out,' he said. 'It smells like a goddamn pig's stomach.'

'You the one's been rootin' in it.' Earl chuckled, downshifted, and the van shot forward. He slipped a cassette into the tape deck, and a caustic male voice rasped out above the humming tires, backed by atonalities and punch-drunk rhythms.

> '... Go to bed at midnight,
> Wake at half-past one,
> I dial your number,
> And let it ring just once,
> I wonder if you love me
> While I watch TV,
> I cheer for Godzilla
> Versus the Jap Army,
> I think about your sweet lips
> And your long, long legs,
> I wanna carve my initials
> In your boyfriend's face.
> I'm gettin' all worked up, worked up about you!'

The singer began to scream 'I'm gettin' all worked up' over and over, his words stitched through by a machine-gun bass line. Glass broke in the background, heavy objects were overturned. Earl turned up the volume and sang along.

Jocundra continued to avoid Donnell's gaze, and he couldn't blame her. He had nearly gotten them killed. A manic, sardonic and irrationally confident soul had waked in him and maneuvred him about the stage; and though it had now deserted him, he believed it was hidden somewhere, lurking behind a mist of ordinary thoughts and judgements, as real and ominous as a black mountain in the clouds. Considering what he had done, the bacterial nature of his intelligence, it would be logical to conclude that he was insane. But what logic would there be in living by that conclusion? Whether he was insane or, as Edman's screwball theory proposed, he was the embodiment of the raw stuff of consciousness, the scientific analogue of an elemental spirit, it was a waste of time to speculate. He had too much to accomplish, too little time, and – he laughed inwardly – there was that special something he had to do. A mission. Another hallmark of insanity.

Earl turned down the tape deck. 'Where you people headin'?'

Jocundra touched Donnell's arm to draw his attention. 'I've thought of a place,' she said. 'It's not far, and I think we'll be safe. It's on the edge of the swamp, a cabin. Hardly anyone goes there.'

'All right,' said Donnell, catching at her hand. 'I'm sorry. I don't know what happened.'

She nodded, tight-lipped. 'Can you take us as far as Bayou Teche?' she asked Earl. 'We'll pay for the gas.'

'Yeah, I guess so.' Earl's mood had soured. 'Jesus fuckin' Christ,' he said sorrowfully. 'My ol' man's gonna kill my ass.'

CHAPTER 11

May 21 – May 23, 1987

A tributary of Bayou Teche curled around the cabin, which was set on short pilings amid a palmetto grove, and from the surrounding darkness came a croaking, water gulping against the marshy banks, and the electric sounds of insects. Yellow light sprayed from two half-open shutters, leaked through gaps in the boards, and a single ray shot up out of a tin chimney angled from the roof slope, all so bright it seemed a small golden sun must be imprisoned inside. The tarpaper roof was in process of sliding off, and rickety stairs mounted to the door. Jocundra remembered the story Mr Brisbeau had told her, claiming the place had been grown from the seed of a witch's hat planted at midnight.

'This is the guy who kept the moths? The guy who molested you?' Donnell had put on a pair of mirrored sunglasses – a gift from Earl – and the lenses held two perfect reproductions of the cabin. 'How the hell can we trust him?'

'He didn't molest me, he just …'

Before she could finish, the door flew back, giving her a start, and a lean old man appeared framed in the light. 'Who's there?' he asked, looking out over Jocundra's head, then down and focusing on her. Gray streaks in his shoulder-length white hair, a tanned face seamed with lines of merriment. His trousers and shirt were sewn of flour sacking, the designs on them worn into dim blue words and vague trademark animals. He squinted at her. 'That you, Florence?'

'It's Jocundra Verret, Mr Brisbeau,' she said. 'I've got a friend with me.'

'Jocundra?' He was silent, the tiers of wrinkles deepening on his brow. 'Well,' he said, 'better you come in than the damn skeeters.'

He had them sit on packing crates beside a wood stove while he boiled coffee and asked Jocundra about herself. The cabin was exactly as she remembered: a jackdaw's nest. Waist-high stacks of yellowed magazines along the walls interspersed by even taller heaps of junk. Dented cookware, broken toys, plastic jugs, boxes, papers. Similar junkpiles occupied the room center, creating a miniature landscape of narrow floorboard valleys meandering between surreal mountains. Beside the door was a clothes-wringer, atop it a battered TV whose screen had been painted over with a beach scene. The wood stove and a cot stood on opposite sides of a door against the rear wall, but they were so buried in clutter they had nearly lost their meaning as objects. The walls themselves were totally obscured by political placards and posters, illustrations out of magazines, torn pages of calendars. Layer upon layer. Thousands of images. Greek statues, naked women, jungle animals, wintry towns, movie stars, world leaders. A lunatic museum of art. Mildew had eaten away large areas of the collage, turning it into gray stratifications of shreds and mucilage stippled with bits of color. The light was provided by hurricane lamps – there must have been a dozen – set on every available flat surface and as a result the room was sweltering.

Mr Brisbeau handed them their coffee, black and bittersweet with chicory, and pulled up a crate next to Jocundra. 'Now I bet you goin' to tell me why you so full of twitch and tremble,' he said.

Though she omitted the events at the motel and in Salt Harvest, Jocundra was honest with Mr Brisbeau. Belief in and acceptance of unlikely probabilities were standard with him, and she thought he might find in Donnell a proof for which he had long been searching. And besides, they needed an ally, someone they could trust completely, and honesty was the only way to insure that trust. When she had done, Mr Brisbeau asked if he could have a look at Donnell's eyes. Donnell removed his glasses, and the old man bent close, almost rubbing noses.

'What you see wit them eyes, boy?' he asked, settling back on his crate.

'Not much I understand,' said Donnell, a suspicious edge to his voice. 'Funny lights, halos.'

Mr Brisbeau considered this. 'Days when I'm out at the traps, me, even though ever'ting's wavin' dark fingers at me, shadows, when I come to the fork sometimes the wan fork she's shinin' bright-bright. Down that fork I know I'm goin' to find the mus'rat.' He nudged a bale of coal-black muskrat skins beside the stove. 'Maybe you see somethin' lak that?'

'Maybe,' said Donnell.

Mr Brisbeau blew on his coffee and sipped. He laughed. 'I jus' tinkin' 'bout my *grand-mere*. She take wan look at you and she say, "Mon Dieu! The black Wan!" But I know the Black Wan he don't come round the bayou no more. He's gone long before my time.' He squinted at Donnell, as if trying to pierce his disguise, and shook his head in perplexity; then he stood and slapped his hip. 'You tired! Help me wit these furs and we fix you some pallets.'

The back room was unfurnished, but they arranged two piles of furs on the floor, and to Jocundra, who was suddenly exhausted, they looked like black pools of sleep in which she could drown.

'In the mornin',' said Mr Brisbeau, 'I got business wit ol' man Bivalaqua over in Silver Meadow. But there's food, drink, and me I'll be back tomorrow night.'

He glanced quizzically at Jocundra and beckoned her to follow him into the front room. He closed the door behind them.

'Wan time I get crazy wit you,' he said, 'and twelve years it takes to forgive? Don't you know, me, I'm just drunk. You my *petit zozo*.' He held out his arms to her.

His entire attitude expressed regret, but the lines of his face were so accustomed to smiling that even his despondency was touched with good humor. Jocundra had the perception of him she had had as a child, of a tribal spirit come to visit and tell her stories. She entered his embrace, smelling his familiar scent of bourbon and sweat and homemade soap. His shoulder blades were as sharp and hard as cypress knees.

'You was my fav'rite of all the kids,' he said. 'It lak to break my heart you leavin'. But I reckon that's how a heart gets along from one day to the nex'. By breakin' and breakin.''

Jocundra lay on her side, waking slowly, watching out the window as gray clouds lowered against a picket line of cypresses and scrub pine. At last she got up and smoothed her rumpled blouse, wishing they had not left the overnight bag in Salt Harvest. She heard a rummaging in the front room. Donnell was sitting beside one of the junkpiles, his sunglasses pushed up on to his head.

'Morning,' she mumbled, and went out back to the pump. A few raindrops hollowed conical depressions in the sandy yard, and the sweet odors of rot, myrtle and water hyacinth mixed with the smell of rain. The roof of an old boathouse stuck up above the palmetto tops about fifty feet away; a car rattled on the gravel road which passed in front of the cabin, hidden by more palmettos and a honeysuckle thicket.

She had expected Donnell would want to discuss the events in Salt Harvest, but when she re-entered he insisted on showing her the things he had extracted from the junkpiles. An armadillo shell on which someone had painted a mushroom cloud, five-years-back issues of *Madame Sonya's Dream Book*, and a chipped football helmet containing a human skull. 'You suppose he found them together?' he asked, deadpan, holding up the helmet. She laughed, picturing the ritual sacrifice of a losing quarterback.

'What's he do with this stuff?' He flipped through one of the issues of the *Dream Book*.

'He collects it.' Jocundra lit the stove for coffee. 'He's kind of a primitive archaeologist, says he gets a clearer picture of the world from junk than he could any other way. Most people think he's crazy, and I guess he is. He lost his son in the Asian War, and according to my father, that's what started him drinking. He'd pin up photos of the president and target-shoot at them for hours.'

'Something funny's happening,' said Donnell.

She glanced at him over her shoulder, surprised by his abrupt change of subject. 'Last night, you mean?'

'The last few days, but last night especially.' He riffled the pages of the book. 'When I picked this up earlier, I had no idea what it was, but then I had a whole raft of associations and memories. Stuff about palmists, seances, fortune-tellers. That's how my memory has always worked. But lately I've been comparing everything I see to something else, something I can't quite put my finger on. It won't come clear.' Discouraged, he tossed the book onto a junkpile, dislodging a toy truck. 'I guess I should tell you about last night.'

His account took the better part of two cups of coffee, and after mulling it over, Jocundra said. 'You have to consider this in light of the fact that your thrust has been to supply yourself with a past, and that your old memories have been proved false. You remember my telling you about the *gros bon ange?* Back at the motel?'

'Yeah. The soul.'

'Well, you began to see the black figures almost immediately after I told you about them. It's possible you've started to construct another past from materials I've exposed to you. But,' she added, seeing his distress, 'you're right. It's not important to speculate about the reality of what you see. Obviously some of it's real, and we have to get busy understanding it. I'll ask Mr Brisbeau to pick up some physics texts.' She plucked at her blouse. 'And some clothes.'

'Oh, yeah. Here.' He reached behind his packing crate. 'It might not fit, but it's clean.' He pulled forth a dress, a very old, dowdy dress of blue rayon with a design of white camellias. 'Try it on,' he suggested.

In the back room, Jocundra removed her jeans and blouse, and then, because it was so sweaty, her bra. The dress had been the property of someone shorter and more buxom. It was flimsy and musty-smelling, and she linked the mustiness with all the women she had known who had been habituated to such dresses. Her mother, musty aunts and neighbor ladies sporting hats adorned with plastic berries, looking as if they had dropped in from the 1930s. The skirt ended above her knees, the bodice hung slack, and the worn, silky material irritated her nipples.

'I must look awful,' she said, coming out of the back room, embarrassed by Donnell's stare.

He cleared his throat. 'No,' he said. 'It's fine.'

To cover her embarrassment, she pretended interest in the camellia pattern. Striations of blue showed through the white of the petals; misprintings. But they had the effect of veins showing through pale, lustrous skin. The blossoms had been rendered with exaggerated voluptuousness, each curve and convolution implying the depth and softness of flesh, as if she were gazing at the throat of a seductively beautiful animal.

Throughout the morning and into the afternoon, they puzzled over the ledger. According to Magnusson, if the Ezawa bacterium existed in the southern hemisphere it would tend to be south-seeking, following the direction of the geomagnetic field in those regions; but it would – like its northern counterpart – migrate downward. However, if a south-seeking bacterium could be transported to the north, then it would migrate upward. It seemed evident to her that a north-seeking bacterium could be induced to become south-seeking by exposure to brief, intense pulses of a magnetic field directed opposite to the ambient field, thereby reversing the magnetic dipolar movement of the magnetosome chain. If necessary the bacterium's north-seeking orientation could be restored by a second pulse delivered anti-parallel to the first. Thus the colony could be steered back and forth between areas of stimulus and deprivation in the brain and its size controlled. Of course the engineering would be a problem, but given the accuracy of Magnusson's data, the basic scenario made sense.

The rain sprinkled intermittently, but by midafternoon the sun was beginning to break through. They walked down to the tributary in back of the cabin, a narrow serpent of lily-pad-choked water that wriggled off into the swamp. Droplets showered from the palmetto fronds when they brushed against them. The sun made everything steamy, and to escape the heat they went into the boathouse, a skeletal old ruin with half its roof missing. Spiders scuttling, beetles, empty wasp nests. The grain of the gray boards was as sharply etched as printed circuits. A single oar lay along one wall, its blade sheathed in spiderweb, and Mr Brisbeau's *pirogue* drifted among the lily pads at the end of a rotting rope. They sat on the edge of the planking and dangled their feet, talking idly, skirting sensitive topics. He had rarely been so open with her; he seemed happy, swinging his legs, telling her about dreams he'd had, about the new story he had begun before leaving Shadows.

'It had the same setting as the first. Purple sun, brooding forest. But I needed a castle so I invented this immense bramble, sort of a briar patch thousands of feet high growing from the side of a mountain, with the tips of the highest branches carved into turrets.' He flipped up a lily pad with the end of his cane; long green tendrils trailed from the underside, thickening into white tubules. 'I never had a chance to work out the plot.'

A tin-colored heron landed with a slosh in the lily pads about thirty feet away, took a stately step forward and stopped, one foot poised above the surface.

'You should finish it,' said Jocundra; she smiled. 'You're going to have to do something for a living.'

'Do you really think I can?' he asked. 'Survive?'

'Yes.' She flicked a chip of rotten wood onto the lily pads and watched a water strider scuttle away from the ripples. 'You were right to leave Shadows.

Here there won't be so much pressure, and it'll be easier to work things out. And they *can* be worked out.' She hesitated.

'But what?'

'Given the ledger, everything you're seeing, everything you can do, I'm convinced a solution is possible. In fact, I'm surprised one of these geniuses at Tulane hasn't stumbled on it. If you have the data at hand, it's hardly more than a matter of common sense and engineering. But equipment and materials will be expensive. And the only way I can see of getting the money is to find a bargaining position and force the project to fund us.'

'A bargaining position.' He stirred the water with his cane. 'What say we sell Edman a new diet plan? Harrison's Magnetotactic Slimming Program. Reorients your fat molecules to be south-seeking and sends them down to Latin America where they're really needed.'

'It's Ezawa you'd have to sell.'

'Even easier. One jolt of Papa Salvatino's Love Rub and he'd be putty in our hands.'

Rainclouds passed up from the south. Big drops splatted on the lily pads, and the sun ducked in and out of cover. Donnell complained of leg cramps, and Jocundra supported his arm as they walked to the cabin. She stopped at the pump to wash off the grime of the boathouse, and as she bent to the gush of water, he rested his hand on her waist. She turned, thinking he had lost his balance. He put his other hand on her waist, holding her, not pulling her to him. His expression was stoic, prepared for rejection. The light pressure of his hands kindled a warmth in her abdomen, and it seemed to her she was building toward him the way the edges of a cloud build, boiling across the space between them. When he kissed her, she closed her eyes and opened her mouth to him as if it were the most natural thing in the world. Then she drew back, dizzy and a little afraid. A pine branch behind his head flared and was tipped with gold, the sun breaking through again.

Tentatively, he fingered the top button of her dress. 'It's all right,' she said, trying to gloss over his awkwardness. Still tentative, he began undoing the buttons. Static charges crackled wherever he touched the cloth, delicate stings. She wondered how the material could have accumulated such a charge, and then, recalling other occasions when he had touched her, other instances of static, she wondered if he might be their cause. It didn't bother her. All his strangeness was common to her now, a final accommodation had been reached. As if a pool of electricity were draining around her, the dress slid from her shoulders, popping and clinging to her skin as it fell away.

Twilight gathered in the back room. Jocundra lay with her face turned to the ceiling, her arm flung across Donnell's hip. The fur tickled, and as she shifted position, he absently caressed her leg. Through narrowed eyes she watched the gaps between the boards empurple, imagining the cabin adrift in an unfeatured element of purple, a limbo where time had decayed matter to this one color. The intensity of her response to him perplexed her. She had not known how much she had wanted him. The desire had been buried in some anthracitic fold of herself, and she had seen but a single facet of it, unaware that it would take only the miner's pick of opportunity to expose a significant lode. Sex for her had always involved a token abandonment, a minimal immersion in the act, and she was beginning to realize that she had been programmed to expect no more. Her mother's attitude toward sex had been neatly summarized the day before Jocundra's wedding; she had called Jocundra aside, thinking her still a virgin, and presented her with a gift-wrapped plastic sheet. 'Sometimes,' she had whispered, peering around to be sure no one would overhear, baring a horrible secret, 'sometimes there's an awful mess.'

A moonless dark embedded the cabin, the wind blew warm and damp through the cracks, and as Donnell's hand smoothed down the curve of her belly, the easy rise of her passion made her feel fragile and temporary, a creature of heat and blackness stirred from shapelessness by the wind and left to fade. Her arms went around his back, her consciousness frayed. Some childish part of her, a part schooled to caution by the dictates of a timorous mother, was unwilling to be swept away, fearful of committing to an uncertain future. But she banished it. Exulting in the loss of control, she cried out when he entered her.

Mr Brisbeau returned shortly before noon the next day, earlier than planned and in a surly mood. He unloaded provisions from a burlap sack, tossing canned goods into a wooden storage chest, making an unnecessary racket, and then, with bad grace, thrust two parcels into their hands. Shirts and jeans for Donnell, blouses and jeans for Jocundra. Their appreciation did not lighten his surliness. He stood by the wood stove, squinting angrily at them, and finally said, 'That ol' man Bivalaqua he's nothin' but talk-talk, tellin' me 'bout the holy show over in Salt Harvest.'

Jocundra opened her mouth to say something, but Mr Brisbeau cut her off. 'Why you takin' my hospitality and don't offer to cure me lak that Grimeaux boy?'

'I didn't cure him,' said Donnell, nettled by the accusatory tone of his voice. 'Nobody could cure him.'

A frown carved the lines deeper on the old man's face.

'Look.' Donnell sat up from the cot, where he had been going over the ledger. 'I'm not even sure what I did. Last night was the first time I've ever done anything like that.'

'It can't hurt to try,' said Jocundra, coming over to him. 'Can it? We might learn something that'll help.'

Mr Brisbeau's magnetic field was distinguished by a misty patch about the size of a walnut behind his right temple, floating amid the fiery arcs like a cloud permanently in place. When Donnell mentioned it, Jocundra dug among the junk and located a pencil and suggested she take notes while he described the process. Each time one of the arcs materialized near the misty patch, it would bend away to avoid contact. On impulse, Donnell began inducing arcs to enter the patch, but they resisted his guidance and tore away from his grip. Rather than the gentle tugging he had expected, they exerted a powerful pull, and the harder he strained at them, the more inelastic they became. After perhaps a half hour of experiment, he tried to direct two of the arcs to enter the patch from opposite sides, and to his amazement they entered easily. The patch glowed a pale whitish-gold, and the arcs held steady and bright, flowing inward toward each other.

'Damn!' said Mr Brisbeau, clapping his hand to his head. 'Feel lak you plug me in or somethin'.'

Within a few minutes the arcs began to fade, and this time Donnell introduced four pairs of them into the patch, setting it to glowing like a little gold spider. But for all his success at manipulating the field, Mr Brisbeau's sight did not improve. He said, though, he felt better than he had in months, and whether due to the treatment or to his satisfaction with Donnell's effort, his mood did brighten. He withdrew a bottle of bourbon and a jar of cherry juice from the storage chest, mixed and added sugar to taste, humming and chuckling to himself. 'Cherry flips,' he said, handing them each a glass. It tasted awful, bad medicine and melted lollypops, but he downed half a dozen while Donnell and Jocundra nursed their drinks.

His eyes red-veined from the liquor, he launched into the tale of Bayou Vert, the legendary course of green water appearing now and again to those lost in the swamp, which – if they had the courage to follow – would lead them to the Swamp King's palace and an eternity of sexual delights among his beautiful, gray-haired daughters.

'Long gray hair lak the moss, skin white lak the lily,' he said, kissing his fingertips. He scooted his crate next to Jocundra and put his arm around her waist. 'But can't none of 'em shine lak Jo' here, can they?' His fingers strayed near her breast, and her smile froze. 'One time,' he went on, 'fool me, I'm sick with the fever, and the hurricane she's shreddin' the swamp and I'm out at the traps. That's when I see Bayou Vert. Jus' a trickle runnin' through the flood. But I tink it's the fever, and I'm too scared to follow.'

It had been drizzling, but now the sun broke through and slanted into the cabin, heating the air, shining off the veins of glue between the pictures on the walls, melting the images of dead presidents and centerfolds and famous buildings into an abstract of color and glare. Mr Brisbeau took to staring at Jocundra, madly doting; his narrative grew disconnected, lapsing in midsentence, and his hand wandered onto her thigh. Donnell was on the verge of interrupting, hoping to spare her further molestation, when the old man jumped up and staggered toward the door, sending avalanches of fragments slithering down the junkpiles.

'*Le Bon Dieu!*' he shouted; he teetered on the top step and fell with a thump in the sand.

By the time they reached the door, he had climbed to his feet and was gazing off at the treeline. Tears slithered down the creases of his cheeks.

'Look there,' he said: 'Goddamn and son of a bitch! Look there!' He pointed. 'I ain't seen that chinaberry for tree-four years. Oh, goddamn, jus' look at that!' He went a step forward, stumbled, and fell again, but crawled on all fours to the edge of the palmettos and pitched face downward beside a stubby, bluish-green shrub. 'Indigo,' he said wonderingly. 'I tink she's gone from here.'

'You can see?' Jocundra turned to Donnell, and mixed with the excitement, he thought he detected a new apprehension in her face. He looked down at his hands, shaken by the realization that he had done something material to Mr Brisbeau.

'Firs' I tink it's the drinkin' and mem'ries givin' me sight of you, girl.' The old man wiped his eyes. 'But I mus' be seein', 'cause I lose my good-time feelin' when I fall.' He pulled himself up and brushed the crust of mucky sand off his shirt; then, struck by a thought, he said, 'Me, I'm goin' to bring ol' man Bivalaqua so you can touch his migraine.'

'We can't have people coming here,' said Jocundra. 'We'll have the police …'

'The Cajun he's not goin' to give you away,' said Mr Brisbeau adamantly. 'You know better'n that, girl. And besides, the boy he jus' wither up if he try to hide his gift.' He walked over to the steps and stared up at Donnell; his eyes were still brimming. 'I thank you, boy, but how'm I goin' to thank you for true?' Then he grinned. 'Come on! We ask *Le Bon Dieu!* I'm taking you to see Him.' He started toward the boathouse, staggered, and fetched up against the cabin; he turned and went back to the bluish-green shrub. He plucked off a leaf.

'Goddamn,' he said, holding it up to the sun so the veins showed. 'Indigo.'

Mr Brisbeau poled the *pirogue* into a channel barely wider than the boat. Clouds of mosquitoes descended upon them, and thickly leaved bushes arched overhead, forming a buzzing green tunnel. The branches scratched their arms. They passed along the channel for what seemed to Donnell an inordinate length of time, and bent double to avoid the branches, breathing shallowly, he lost his sense of perspective. Up and down were no longer consistent with the colors of earth and sky. Whenever they passed beneath an opening in the brush, the water reflected a ragged oval of blue and the sun dazzled the droplets tipping the leaves; it was as if they were gliding through a mirrored abyss, one original likeness hidden among the myriad counterfeits. Fragments of dried wasp nest fell on his neck and stuck in the sweat; purplish-veined egg masses clung to holes in the bank, and the dark, web-spanned gaps between the roots of the bushes bristled with secretive movement. Just below the surface at the edge of the bank were fantastic turrets of slime tunnelled by black beetles.

Then they were gliding out into a vaulted chamber canopied by live oaks, pillared by an occasional cypress. Here the water forked in every direction, diverging around islands from which the oaks arose; their branches bridging between the islands, laden with stalactites of Spanish moss, some longer than a man, trailing into the water. The sun's beams withdrew, leaving them in a phantom world of grays and gray-greens so ill-defined that the branches appeared to be black veins of solidity wending through a mist of half-materialized forms. An egret flapped up, shrinking to a point of white space. Its flight was too swift to be a spirit's, too slow for a shooting star's, yet had the quality of both. Mr Brisbeau's pole sloshed, but otherwise there was a thick silence. The place seemed to have been grown from the silence, and the silence seemed the central attribute of the gray.

Mr Brisbeau beached the *pirogue* upon the bank of an island where three small crosses had been erected; a muskrat skin was nailed to each one. He climbed out and knelt before them. Kneeling, he was a head taller than the crosses: a giant come to his private Calvary. The skins were mouldering, scabbed with larval deposits, but the sight of him praying to this diseased trinity did not strike Donnell as being in any way grotesque. The silence and the great arching limbs abolished the idea of imperfection, and the decomposing skins were in keeping with the grand decomposition of the swamp.

Now and then Mr Brisbeau's voice carried to Donnell, and he realized it was more of a conversation than a prayer, a recounting of the day's events salted with personal reaction.

'... You remember the time Roger Hebert smack me wit the oar, sparks shootin' through my head. Well, that's the way it was 'cept there wasn't no pain ...'

Sitting in the boat for so long had caused Donnell's hip to ache, and to take his mind off the discomfort he played tricks with his vision. He discovered that if he brought the magnetic fields into view and shifted his field of focus forward until it was dominated by the white brilliance of a single arc, then the world around him darkened and the *gros bon ange* became visible. He looked out beyond the prow and glimpsed a glowing tendril of green among the silvery eddies. He turned his head, blinking the sight away. He did not want to verify or acknowledge it. It dismayed him to think Jocundra might be right, that he might be able to see anything he wished. Anything as ridiculous as Bayou Vert. Still, he was curious.

'What's off there?' he asked, pointing out the direction of the green current to Jocundra.

'Marshlands,' she said. 'A couple of towns, and then, past that, Bayou Rigaud.'

'Rigaud.' The word had a sleek feel, and important sound.

He steadied the boat for Jocundra as she moved forward to sit beside him. 'Why do you want to know?' she asked. But the old man's voice lifted from the shore and distracted his attention.

'If I was you, me,' he said contentiously, talking to the centermost cross. 'I'd end this boy's confusion. You let him see wit the eyes of angels, so what harm it goin' to do to let him know your plan?'

CHAPTER 12

May 30 – 26 July 1987

One night after patients had begun to arrive in numbers, Donnell and Jocundra were lying on their bed in the back room surrounded by open textbooks and pieces of paper. The bed, an antique with a mahogany headboard, and all the furniture – bureau, night table, chairs – had been the gifts of patients, as were the flowers which sprouted from vases on the windowsills. Sometimes, resting between sessions, Donnell would crack the door and listen to the patients talking in the front room, associating their voices with the different flowers. They never discussed their ailments, merely gossiped or exchanged recipes.

'Now how much lemon juice you addin' to the meal,' Mrs Dubray (irises) would ask; and old Mrs Alidore (a bouquet of Queen Anne's lace and roses) would hem and haw and finally answer, 'Seem lak my forget-list gets longer ever' week.'

Their conversations, their gifts and their acceptance of him gave Donnell a comforting sense of being part of a tradition, for there had always been healers in the bayou country and the people were accustomed to minor miracles.

'I think I'm right,' said Jocundra.

'About what?' Donnell added a flourish to the sketch he had been making. It was a rendering of one of the gold flashes of light he saw from time to time, similar to those Magnusson had drawn in the margins of his ledger; but this one was more complex, a resolution of several fragments he had seen previously into a single figure:

'About you being a better focusing agent for the fields than any device.' Jocundra smacked him on the arm with her legal pad. 'You aren't listening.'

'Yeah I am,' he said, preoccupied by the sketch. 'Go ahead.'

'I'll start over.' She settled herself higher on the pillows. 'Okay. If you transmit an electrical charge through a magnetic field, you're going to get feedback. The charge will experience a force in some direction, and that would explain the changes in light intensity you see. But you're not just affecting the fields. To cure someone as hopeless as Mr Robichaux, you have to be affecting the cells, probably on an ionic level. You aren't listening! What are you doing?'

'Doodling.' Dissatisfied, Donnell closed his notebook. It did not feel complete. He could not attach the least importance to the gold flashes, yet they kept appearing and it bothered him not to understand them. 'I'm listening,' he said.

'All right.' Jocundra was miffed by his lack of enthusiasm for her explanation. 'Now one basic difference between a cancer cell and a normal cell is that the cancer cell produces certain compounds in excess of normal. So, going by Magnusson's notes, one likelihood is that you're reducing the permeability of the nuclear membranes for certain ions, preventing the efflux of the compounds in question.'

Donnell rested his head on the pillow beside her. 'How's that relate to my being the focusing agent?'

'NMR.' She smoothed down his hair. 'Magnusson's stuff on it is pretty fragmentary, but he appears to be suggesting that your effect on the cameras was caused by your realigning the atomic magnetic nuclei of the camera's field and transmitting a force which altered the electrical capacitance of the film. I think you're doing more or less the same thing to the patients.' She chewed on her pencil. 'The fact that you can intuit the movements of the geomagnetic field, and that you're able to do the right things to the patients without any knowledge of the body, it seems to me if you had enough metal to generate a sufficiently powerful field, two or three tons, then you'd be able to orchestrate the movements of the bacteria with finer discretion than any mechanical device.'

Donnell had an image of himself standing atop a mountain and hurling lightning bolts. 'Just climb upon a chunk of iron and zap myself?'

'Copper,' she said. 'Better conductivity.'

'It sounds like magic,' he said. 'What about the wind?'

'There's nothing magical about that,' she said. 'The air becomes ionized under the influence of your field, and the ions are induced to move in the direction imposed on the field. The air moves, more air moves in to replace it.' She shrugged. 'Wind. But understanding all this and being able to use it are two different things.'

'You're saying I should go back to the project?'

'Unless you know how we can buy three tons of copper with a Visa card.' She smiled, trying to make light of it.

Something was incomplete about her explanation, just as there had been about his sketch, and he did not believe either would come to completion at Shadows. 'Maybe as a last resort,' he said. 'But not yet.'

The majority of the patients were local people, working men and housewives and widows, as faded and worn as the battered sofas they sat upon (Mr Brisbeau had tossed out the junk and scavenged them from somewhere); though as the weeks passed and word spread, more prosperous-looking people arrived from faraway places like Baton Rouge and Shreveport. Most of their complaints were minor, and there was little to be learned from treating them. But from the difficult cases, in particular that of Herve Robichaux, a middle-aged carpenter afflicted with terminal lung cancer, Jocundra put together her explanation of the healing process.

When medical bills had cost him his home, with the last of his strength Robichaux had built two shacks on a weed-choked piece of land near the Gulf left him by his father, one for his wife and him, the other for his five children. The first time Donnell and Jocundra visited him, driven by Mr Brisbeau in his new pickup, the children – uniformly filthy and shoeless – ran away and hid among the weeds and whispered. Their whispers blended with the drone of flies and the shifting of wind through the surrounding scrub pine into a sound of peevish agitation. In the center of the weeds was a cleared circle of dirt, and here stood the shacks. The raw color of the unpainted boards, the listless collie mix curled by the steps, the scraps of cellophane blowing across the dirt, everything testified to an exacerbated hopelessness, and the interior of the main shack was the most desolate place of Donnell's experience. A battery-operated TV sat on an orange crate at the foot of the sick man's pallet, its pale picture of gray figures in ghostly rooms flickering soundlessly. Black veins of creosote beaded between the ceiling boards, their acrid odor amplifying rather than dominating the fecal stink of illness. Flies crusted a jelly glass half-full of a pink liquid, another fly buzzed loudly in a web spanning a corner of the window, and hexagrams of mouse turds captioned the floors. Stapled on the door was a poster showing the enormous, misty figure of Jesus gazing sadly down at the UN building.

'Herve,' said Mrs Robichaux in a voice like ashes. 'That Mr Harrison's here from Bayou Teche.' She stepped aside to let them pass, a gaunt woman enveloped in a gaily flowered housecoat.

Mr Robichaux was naked beneath the sheet, bald from chemotherapy. A plastic curtain overhung the window, and the wan light penetrating it pointed up his bleached and shrunken appearance. His mouth and nose were so fleshless they seemed stylized approximations of features, and his face communicated nothing of his personality to Donnell. He looked ageless, a proto-creature of grayish-white material around which the human form was meant to wrap.

'Believe,' he whispered. He fingers crawled over Donnell's wrist, delicate as insects' legs. 'I believe.'

Donnell drew back his hand, both revolted and pitying. A chair scraped behind him: Jocundra settling herself to take notes.

The area of the magnetic field around Robichaux's chest was a chaos of white flashes; the remainder of the field had arranged itself into four thick, bright arcs bowing from his head to his feet. Donnell had never seen anything like it. To experiment he placed his hands over the chest. The attraction was so powerful it locked onto his hands, and the skin of his fingers – as well as the skin of Robichaux's chest – dimpled and bulged, pulled in every direction. He had to wrench his hands loose. They disengaged with a loud static pop, and a tremor passed through the sick man's body.

Donnell described the event to Jocundra, and she suggested he try it again, this time for a longer period. After several minutes he detected a change in the field. The pulls were turning into pushes; it was as if he had thrust his hands into a school of tiny electric fish and they were swimming between his fingers, nudging them. After several minutes more, he found that he could wiggle the top joints of his fingers, and he felt elements of the field cohere and flow in the direction of his wiggle. A half hour went by. The four bright arcs encaging Robichaux began to unravel, sending wispy white streamers inward, and the pyrotechnic display above his chest diminished to a barely perceptible vapor.

Sweat poured off Robichaux, his neck arched and his hands clawed the sheet. Whimpers escaped between his clenched teeth. A spray of broken capillaries appeared on his chest, a webbing of fine purplish lines melting up into view. He rocked his head back and forth, and the whimpers swelled to outright cries. At this, Donnell withdrew his hands and noticed the wind had kicked up outside; the room had grown chilly. Jocundra was shivering, and Mrs Robichaux knelt by the door. 'Holy Jesus please, Holy Jesus please,' she babbled.

'What happened?' Jocundra's eyes were fixed upon the sick man, who lay gasping.

Donnell turned back to Robichaux; the field was reverting to its previous state. 'I don't know,' he said. 'Let me try again.'

The cure took three days and two nights. Donnell had to work the field an hour at a time to prevent its reversion; then he would break for an hour, trembling and spent. Her husband's torment frightened Mrs Robichaux, and she fled to the second cabin and would not return. Occasionally the eldest boy – a hollow-cheeked eleven-year-old – poked his head in the window to check on his father, running off the instant Donnell paid him the slightest attention. Mr Brisbeau brought them food and water, and waited in the pickup, drinking. Donnell could hear him singing along with the radio far into the night.

The first night was eerie.

They left the oil lamp unlit so Donnell could better see the field, and the darkness isolated them in a ritual circumstance: the healer performing his magical passes; the sick man netted in white fire, feverish and groaning; Jocundra cowled with a blanket against the cold, the sacred witness, the scribe. Crickets sustained a frenzied sawing, the dog whined. Debris rustled along the outside walls, driven by the wind; it kicked up whenever Donnell was working, swirling slowly about the shack as if a large animal were patrolling in tight circles, its coarse hide rubbing the boards. Moonlight transformed the plastic curtain into a smeared, glowing barrier behind which the shadows of the pines held steady; the wind was localized about the cabin, growing stronger with each treatment. Though he was too weak to voice his complaints, Robichaux glared at them, and to avoid his poisonous looks they took breaks on the steps of the shack. The dog slunk away every time they came out, and as if it were Robichaux's proxy, stared at them from the weeds, chips of moonlight reflected in its eyes.

During their last break before dawn, Jocundra sheltered under Donnell's arm and said happily, 'It's going to work.'

'You mean the cure?'

'Not just that,' she said. 'Everything. I've got a feeling.' And then, worriedly, she asked, 'Don't you think so?'

'Yeah,' he said, wanting to keep her spirits high. But as he said it, he had a burst of conviction, and wondered if like Robichaux's belief, his own belief could make it so.

The second day. Muggy heat in the morning, the slow wind lifting garbage from the weeds. Weary and aching, Donnell was on the verge of collapse. Like the rectangle of yellow light lengthening across the floor, a film was sliding across his own rough-grained, foul-smelling surface. But to his amazement he felt stronger as the day wore on, and he realized he had been moving around without his cane. During the treatments the sick man's body arched until only his heels and the back of his head were touching the pallet. Two of the man's teeth shattered in the midst of one convulsion, and they spent most of a rest period picking fragments out of his mouth. The fly in the web had died and was a motionless black speck suspended in midair, a bullet-hole shot through the sun-drenched backdrop of pines. The spider, too, had died and was shriveled on the windowsill. In fact, all the insects in the cabin – palmetto bugs, flying ants, gnats, beetles – had gone belly up and were not even twitching. Around noon the eldest boy knocked and asked could he borrow the TV 'so's the babies won't cry.' He would not enter the cabin, said that his mama wouldn't let him, and stood mute and sullen watching the heaving of his father's chest.

On the second night, having asked Mr Brisbeau to keep watch, they walked down to the Gulf, found a spit of solid ground extending from the salt grass, and spread a blanket. Now and again as they made love, Jocundra's eyes blinked open and fastened on Donnell, capturing an image of him to steer by; when she closed them, slits of white remained visible beneath the lids. Passion seemed to have carved her face more finely, planed it down to its ideal form. Lying there afterward, Donnell wondered how his face looked to her, how it displayed passion. Everything about the bond between them intrigued him, but he had long since given up trying to understand it. Love was a shadow that vanished whenever you turned to catch a glimpse of it. The only thing certain was that without it life would be as bereft of flesh as Robichaux's face had been of life: an empty power.

Jocundra rolled onto her stomach and gazed out to sea. An oil fire gleamed red off along the coast; the faint chugging of machinery carried across the water. Wavelets slapped the shore. Sea and sky were the same unshining black, and the moonlit crests of the waves looked as distant as the burning well and the stars, sharing with them a perspective of great depth, as if the spit of land were extending into interstellar space. Donnell ran his hand down her back and gently pushed a finger between her legs, sheathing it in the moist fold. She kissed the knuckles of his other hand, pressed her cheek to it, and snuggled closer. The movement caused his finger to slip partway inside her, and she drew in a sharp breath. She lifted her face to be kissed, and kissing her, he pulled her atop him. Her hair swung witchily in silhouette against the sky, a glint of the oil fire bloomed on her throat, and it seemed to him that the stars winking behind her were chattering with cricket's tongues.

On the afternoon of the third day, Donnell decided he had done all he should to Mr Robichaux. Though his field was not yet normal, it appeared to be repairing itself. His entire chest was laced with broken capillaries, but his color had improved and his breathing was deep and regular. Over the next two weeks they visited daily, and he continued to mend. The general aspect of the shacks and their environ improved equally, as if they had suffered the same illness and received the same cure. The dog wagged its tail and snuffled Donnell's hand. The children played happily in the yard; the litter had been cleared away and the weeds cut back. Even Mrs Robichaux gave a friendly wave as she hung out the wash.

The last time they visited, while sitting on the steps and waiting for Mr

Robichaux to dress, the youngest girl – a grimy-faced toddler, her diaper at half-mast – waddled up to Donnell and offered him a bite of her jelly donut. It was stale, the jelly tasteless, but as he chewed it, Donnell felt content. The eldest boy stepped forward, the other children at his rear, giggling, and formally shook Donnell's hand. 'Wanna thank you,' he muttered; he cast a defiant look at his brothers and sisters, as if something had been proved. The toddler leaned on Donnell's knee and plucked off his sunglasses. 'Ap,' she said, pointing at his eyes, chortling. 'Ap azoo.'

Robichaux was buttoning his shirt when Donnell entered. He frowned and looked away and once again thanked him. But this time his thanks were less fervent and had a contractual ring. 'If I'm down to my last dollar,' he said sternly, 'that dollar she's yours.'

Donnell shrugged; he squinted at Robichaux's field. 'Have you seen a doctor?'

'Don't need no doctor to tell me I'm cured,' said Robichaux. He peered down inside his shirt. The web of broken capillaries rose to the base of this neck. 'Don't know why you had to do this mess. Worse than a goddamn tattoo.'

'Trial and error,' said Donnell without sympathy. It had come as a shock to him that he did not like Mr Robichaux; that – by gaining ten pounds and a measure of vigor – the characterless thing he had first treated had evolved into a contemptible human being, one capable of viciousness. He suspected the children might have been better off had their father's disease been allowed to run its course.

'It ain't that I ain't grateful, you understand,' Robichaux said, fawning, somewhat afraid. 'It's just I don't know if all this here's right, you know. I mean you ain't no man of God.'

Donnell wondered about that; he was, after all, full of holy purpose. For a while he had thought healing might satisfy his sense of duty unfulfilled, but he had only been distracted by the healing from a deeper preoccupation. He felt distaste for this cringing, devious creature he had saved.

'No, I'm not,' he said venomously. 'But neither are you, Mr Robichaux. And that little devil's web on your chest might just be an omen of worse to come.'

'... Since the great looping branches never grew or varied, since the pale purple sun never fully rose or set, the shadow of Moselantja was a proven quantity upon the grassy plain below. Men and beasts lived in the shadow, as well as things which otherwise might not have lived at all, their dull energies supplied, some said, by the same lightless vibrations that had produced this enormous growth, sundered the mountain and sent it bursting forth. From the high turrets one could see the torchlit caravans moving inward along the dark avenues of its shadow toward the main stem, coming to enlist, or to try their luck at enlistment, for of the hundreds arriving each day, less than a handful would survive the rigors of induction …'

'What do you think?' asked Donnell.

Jocundra did not care for it, but saw no reason to tell him. 'It's strange,' she said, giving a dramatic shudder and grinning. She emptied the vase water out the window, then skipped back across the room and burrowed under the covers with him. Her skin was goose-pimpled. It had been warm and dead-still the night before, but the air had cooled and dark, silver-edged clouds were piling up. Sure signs of a gale. A damp wind rattled the shutters.

'It's just background,' said Donnell petulantly. 'It has to be strange because the story's very simple. Boy meets girl, they do what comes naturally, boy joins army, loses girl. Years later he finds her. She's been in the army, too. Then they develop a powerful but rather cold relationship, like a hawk and a tiger.'

'Read some more,' she said, pleased that he was writing a love story, even if such an odd one.

'War is the obsession of Moselantja, its sole concern, its commerce, its religion, its delight. War is generally held to be the purest natural expression of the soul, an ecological tool designed to cultivate the species, and the cadres of the Yoalo, who inhabit the turrets of Moselantja, are considered its prize bloom. Even among those they savage, they are revered, partially because they are no less hard on themselves than on those they subjugate. As their recruits progress upward toward the turrets, the tests and lessons become more difficult. Combat, ambush, the mastery of the black suits of synchronous energy. Failure, no matter how slight, is not tolerated and has but one punishment. Each day's crop of failures is taken to the high turret of Ghazes from which long nooses and ropes are suspended. The nooses are designed not to choke or snap, but to support the neck and spine. The young men and women are stripped naked and fitted with the nooses and lowered into the void. Their arms and legs are left unbound. And then, from the clotted darkness of the main stem, comes a gabbling, flapping sound, and the beasts rise up. Their bodies are reminiscent of a fly's but have the bulk of an eagle's, and indeed their flights recall a fly's haphazard orbiting of a garbage heap. Their wings are leathery, long-vaned; their faces variously resemble painted masks, desiccated apes, frogs, spiders, every sort of vile monstrosity. Their mouths are all alike, set with needle teeth and fringed with delicate organelles like the tendrils of a jellyfish. As with any great evil, study of them will yield a mass of contradictory fact and legend. The folk of the plain and forest will tell you that they are the final transformation of the Yoalo slain in battle, and this is their Valhalla:

to inhabit the roots and crevices of Moselantja and feed upon the unfit. Of course since the higher ranks of the Yoalo model their energy masks upon the faces of the beasts, this is no doubt a misapprehension.

'There are watchers upon the battlements of Ghazes, old men and women who stare at the failed recruits through spyglasses. As the beasts clutch and rend their prey, these watchers note every twitch and flinch of the dying, and if their reactions prove too undisciplined, black marks are assigned to the cadres from which they had been expelled. Many of the recruits are native-born to Moselantja, and these are watched with special interest. Should any of them cry out or attempt to defend themselves or use meditative techniques to avoid pain, then his or her parents are asked to appear the next day at Ghazes for similar testing. And should *they* betray the disciplines, then their relatives and battle-friends are sought out and tested until the area of contagion is obliterated. Occasionally a seam of such weakness will be exposed, one which runs throughout the turrets, and entire cadres will be overthrown. Such is the process of revolution in Moselantja …'

As he read, Jocundra tried to force her mind away from the unpleasant details, but she could not help picturing the hanged bodies in stark relief against the purple sun, rivulets of blood streaming from their necks as the beasts idly fed, embracing their victims with sticky insect legs. When he had finished, she was unable to hide her displeasure.

'You don't like it,' he said.

She made a noncommittal noise.

'Well,' he said, blowing on his fingers as if preparing to crack a safe. 'I know what you *do* like.'

She laughed as he reached for her.

A knock on the door, and Mr Brisbeau stuck in his head. 'Company,' he said. He was hung over, red-eyed from last night's bottle; he scowled, noticing their involvement, and banged the door shut.

Hard slants of rain started drumming against the roof as they dressed. In the front room a broad-beamed man was gazing out the window. Dark green palmetto fronds lashed up behind him, blurred by the downpour. He turned, and Jocundra gasped. It was Papa Salvatino, a smile of Christian fellowship wreathing his features. He wore a white suit of raw silk with cutaway pockets, and the outfit looked as appropriate on him as a lace collar on a mongrel.

'Brother Harrison!' he said with sanctimonious delight and held out his hand. 'When I heard you was the wonder-worker down on Bayou Teche, I had to come and offer my apologies.'

'Cut the crap,' said Donnell. 'You've got a message for me.'

It took a few seconds for Papa to regain his poise, a time during which his face twisted into a mean, jaundiced knot. 'Yes,' he said. ''Deed I do.' He assessed Donnell coolly. 'My employer, Miss Otille Rigaud … maybe you heard of her?'

Mr Brisbeau spat. Jocundra remembered stories from her childhood about someone named Rigaud, but not Otille. Claudine, Claudette. Something like that.

'She's a wealthy woman, is Miss Otille,' Papa went on. 'A creature of diverse passions, and her rulin' passion at present is the occult. She's mighty intrigued with you, brother.'

'How wealthy?' asked Donnell, pouring a cup of coffee.

'Rich or not, them Rigauds they's lower than worms in a pile of shit,' said Mr Brisbeau, enraged. 'And me I ain't havin' their help in my kitchen!'

Papa Salvatino beamed, chided him with a waggle of a finger. 'Now, brother, you been cockin' your ear to the Devil's back fence and listenin' to his lies.'

'Get out!' said Mr Brisbeau; he picked up a stove lid and menaced Papa with it.

'In good time,' said Papa calmly. 'Miss Otille would like the pleasure of your company, Brother Harrison, and that of your fair lady. I've been authorized to convey you to Maravillosa at once if it suits. That's her country place over on Bayou Rigaud.'

'I don't think so,' said Donnell; he sipped his coffee. 'But you tell her I'm intrigued as well.'

'She'll be tickled to hear it.' He half-turned to leave. 'You know, I might be able to satisfy your curiosity somewhat. Me and Miss Otille have spent many an evenin' together, and I've been privy to a good bit of the family history.'

'Don't bullshit me,' said Donnell. 'You're supposed to tell me all about her. That's part of the message.'

Papa perched on the arm of the sofa and stared at Donnell. 'As a fellow professional, brother, you mind tellin' me what you see that's givin' me away?'

'Your soul,' said Donnell; he stepped to the window and tossed his coffee into the rain. At this point his voice went through a peculiar change, becoming hollow and smooth for half a sentence, reverting to normal, hollowing again; it was not an extreme change, just a slight increase in resonance, the voice of a man talking in an empty room, and it might not have been noticeable in a roomful of voices. 'Want to know what it looks like? It's shiny black, and where there used to be a face, a face half spider and half toad, there's a mass of curdled light, only now it's flowing into helical patterns and rushing down your arms.'

Papa was shaken; he, too, had heard the change. 'Brother,' he said, 'you wastin' yourself in the bayou country. Take the advice of a man who's been in the business fifteen years. Put your show on the road. You got big talent!' He shook his head in awe. 'Well' – he crossed his legs, leaned back and sighed – 'I reckon the best way to fill you in on Otille is to start with ol' Valcours Rigaud. He was one of Lafitte's lieutenants, retired about the age of forty from the sea because of a saber cut to his leg, and got himself a fine house outside New Orleans. Privateerin' had made him rich, and since he had time on his hands and a taste for the darker side of earthly pleasures, it wasn't too surprisin' that he fell under the influence of one Lucanor Aime, the leader of the Nanigo sect. You ever hear 'bout Nanigo?'

Mr Brisbeau threw down the stove lid with a clang, muttered something, and stumped into the back room, slamming the door after him. Papa snorted with amusement.

'Voodoo,' he said. 'But not for black folks. For whites only. Valcours was a natural, bein' as how he purely hated the black man. Wouldn't have 'em on his ships. Anyway, ol' Lucanor set Valcours high in his service, taught him all the secrets, then next thing you know Lucanor ups and disappears, and Valcours, who's richer than ever by this time, picks up and moves to Bayou Rigaud and builds Maravillosa.' Papa chuckled. 'You was askin' how rich Miss Otille was. Well, she's ten-twenty times as rich as Valcours, and to show you how well off he was, when his oldest girl got herself engaged, he went and ordered a cargo of spiders from China, special spiders renowned for the intricacy and elegance of their webs, and he set them to weavin' in the pines linin' the avenue to the main house. Then he had his servants sprinkle the webs with silver dust and gold dust, all so that daughter of his could walk down the aisle beneath a canopy of unrivalled splendour.'

The wind was blowing more fiercely; rain eeled between the planking and filmed over the pictures and the walls, making them glisten. Jocundra closed and latched the shutters, half-listening to Papa, but listening also for repetitions of the change in Donnell's voice. He didn't appear to notice if himself, though it happened frequently, lasting a few seconds, then lapsing, as if he were passing through a strange adolescence. Probably, she thought, it was just a matter of the bacteria having spread to the speech centers; as they occupied the various centers, they operated the functions with more efficiency than normal. Witness his eyes. Still, she found it disturbing. She remembered sneaking into Magnusson's room and being frightened by his sepulchral tone, and she was beginning to be frightened now. By his voice, the storm, and especially by the story. Fabulous balls and masques had been weekly occurrences at Maravillosa, said Papa; but despite his largesse, Valcours had gained an evil reputation. Tales were borne of sexual perversion and unholy rites; people vanished and were never seen again; zombies were reputed to work his fields, and after his death his body was hacked apart and buried in seven coffins to prevent his return. The story and the storm came to be of a piece in Jocundra's head, the words howling, the wind drawling, nature and legend joined in the telling, and she had a feeling the walls of the cabin were being squeezed together and they would be crushed, their faces added to the collection of pasted-up images.

'Valcours' children spent most of their lives tryin' to repair the family name,' said Papa. 'They founded orphanages, established charities. Maravillosa became a factory of good works. But ol' Valcours' spirit seemed to have been reborn in his granddaughter Clothilde. Folks told the same stories 'bout her they had 'bout him. And more. Under her stewardship the family fortune grew into an empire, and them-that-knowed said this new money come from gun-runnin', from white slavery and worse. She was rumored to own opium hells in New Orleans and to hang around the waterfront disguised as a man, a cutthroat by the name of Johnny Perla. It's a matter of record that she was partners with Abraham Levine. You know. The Parrot King. The ol' boy who brought in all them Central American birds and set off the epidemic of parrot fever. Thousands of kids dead. But then, right in the prime of life, at the height of her evil doin's, Clothilde disappeared.'

Papa heaved another sigh, recrossed his legs, and went on to tell how Clothilde's son, Otille's father, had followed the example of his grandparents and attempted to restore the family honor through his work on behalf of international Jewry during World War II and his establishment of the Rigaud Foundation for scientific research; how Otille's childhood had been scandal after scandal capped by the affair of Senator Millman, a weekend guest at Maravillosa, who had been found in bed with Otille, then twelve years old. Donnell leaned against the stove, unreadable behind his mirrored lenses. The storm was lessening, but Jocundra knew it would be a temporary lull. July storms lingered for days. The damp air chilled her, breaking a film of feverish sweat from her brow.

'The next few years Otille was off at private schools and college, and she don't talk much 'bout them days. But around the time she was twenty, twenty-one, she got bitten by the actin' bug and headed for New York. Wasn't long before she landed what was held to be the choicest role in many a season. Mirielle in the play *Danse Calinda*. 'Course there was talk 'bout *how* she landed the part, seein' as she'd been the playwright's lover. But couldn't nobody else but her play it, 'cause it had been written special for her. The critics were unanimous. They said the play expanded the occult genre, said she incarnated the role. Them damn fools woulda said anything, I expect. Otille probably had 'em all thinkin' slow and nasty 'bout her. She'll do that to a man, I'll guarantee you.' He smirked. 'But the character, Mirielle, she was a strong, talented woman, good-hearted but doomed to do evil, bound by the ties of a black tradition to a few acres of the dismal truth, and ol' Otille didn't have no trouble relatin' to that. Then, just when it looked like she was gonna be a star, she went after her leadin' man with a piece of broken mirror. Cut him up severe!' Papa snapped his fingers. 'She'd gone right over the edge. They shut her away in a sanatorium someplace in upstate New York, and the doctors said it was the strenuousness of the role that had done her. But Otille would tell you it was 'cause she'd arrived at certain conclusions 'bout herself durin' the run of the play, that she'd been tryin' to escape somethin' inescapable. That the shadowy essence of Valcours and Clothilde pervaded her soul. Soon as they let her loose, she beelined for Maravillosa and there she's been for these last twelve or thirteen years.' He puffed out his belly, patted it and grinned. 'And I been with her for six of them years.'

'And is she crazy?' asked Donnell. 'Or is she evil?'

'She's a little crazy, brother, but ain't we all.' Papa laughed. 'I know I am. And as for the evil, naw, she's just foolin' with evil. The way she figures it, whichever she is she can't deny her predilection, so she surrounds herself with oddballs and criminal types. Nothin' heavy duty. Pickpockets, card sharps, dopers, hookers ...'

'Tent show hucksters,' offered Donnell.

'Yeah,' said Papa, unruffled. 'And freaks. You gonna fit right in.' He worried at something between his teeth. 'I'll be up front with you, brother. Goin' to Otille's is like joinin' the circus. Three shows daily. Not everybody can deal with it. But gettin' back to her theory, she figures if she insulates herself with this mess of lowlife, she'll muffle her unnatural appetites and won't never do nothin' *real* bad like Valcours and Clothilde.' He fingered a card out from his side pocket and handed it to Donnell. 'You wanna learn more 'bout it, call that bottom number. She's dyin' to talk with you.' He stood, hitched up his trousers. 'One more thing and I'll be steppin'. You're bein' watched. Otille says they on you like white on rice.'

Donnell did not react to the news; he was staring at the card Papa had given him. But Jocundra was stunned. 'By who?' she asked.

'Government, most likely,' said Papa. 'Otille says you wanna check it out, you know that little shanty bar down the road?'

'The Buccaneer Club?'

'Yeah. You go down there tomorrow. 'Bout half a mile past it's a dirt road, and just off the gravel you gonna find a stake out. Two men in a nice shiny unmarked car. They ain't there today, which is why I'm here.' Papa twirled his car keys and gave them his most unctuous smile. 'Let us hear from you, now.' He sprinted out into the rain.

Jocundra turned to Donnell. 'Was he telling the truth?'

He was puzzled by the question for a moment, then said, 'Oh, yeah. At least he wasn't lying.' He looked down at the card. 'Wait a second.' He went into the back room and returned with a notebook; he laid it open on top of the stove. 'This,' he said, pointing to a drawing, 'is the last sketch I made of the patterns of light I've been seeing. And this' – he pointed to a design at the bottom of the card – 'this is what my sketch is a fragment of.'

Jocundra recognized the design, and if he had only showed her a fragmentary sketch, she still would have recognized it. She had seen it painted in chicken blood on stucco walls, laid out in colored dust on packed-earth floors, soaped on the windows of storefront temples, printed on handbills. The sight of it made all her explanations of his abilities seem as feckless as charms against evil.

'That's what I want to build with the copper,' said Donnell. 'I'm sure of it. I've never been ...' He noticed her fixation on the design. 'You've seen it before?'

'It's a *veve*,' said Jocundra with a sinking feeling. 'It's a ritual design used in voodoo to designate one of the gods, to act as a gateway through which he can be called. This one belongs to one of the aspects of Ogoun, but I can't remember which one.'

'A *veve*?' He picked up the card. 'Oh, yeah,' he said. 'Why not?' He tucked the card into his shirt pocket.

'What are you going to do?'

'I'm going to wait until morning, because I don't want to appear too eager.' He laughed. 'And then I guess I'll go down to the Buccaneer Inn and give Otille a call.'

Donnell dropped in his money and dialed. A flatbed truck passed on the road, showering the booth with spray from its tires, but even when it had cleared he could barely make out the pickup parked in front of the bar. The rain dissolved the pirate's face above the shingle roof into an eyepatch and a crafty smile, smeared the neon letters of the Lone Star Beer sign into a weepy glow.

'Yes, who is it?' The voice on the line was snippish and unaccented, but as soon as he identified himself, it softened and acquired a faint Southern flavor. 'I'm pleasantly surprised, Mr Harrison. I'd no idea you'd be calling so quickly. How can I help you?'

'I'm not sure you can,' he said. 'I'm just calling to make a few inquiries.'

Otille's laugh was sarcastic; even over the wire it conveyed a potent nastiness. 'You obviously have pressing problems, or else you wouldn't be calling. Why don't you tell me about them? Then if I'm still interested you can make your inquiries.'

Donnell rubbed the phone against his cheek, thinking how best to handle her. Through the rain-washed plastic, he saw an old hound dog with brown and white markings emerge from the bushes beside the booth and step onto the road. Sore-covered, starved-thin, dull-eyed. It put its nose down and began walking toward the bar, sniffing at litter, unmindful of the pelting rain.

'I need three tons of copper,' he said. 'I want to build something.'

'If you're going to be circuitous, Mr Harrison, we can end this conversation right now.'

'I want to build a replica of the *veve* on your calling card.'

'Why?'

At first, prodded by her questions, he told half-truths, repeating the lies he had been told at the project, sketching out his plan to use the *veve* as a remedy, omitting particulars. But as the conversation progressed, he found he had surprisingly few qualms about revealing himself to her and became more candid. Though some of her questions maintained a sharp tone, others were asked with childlike curiosity, and others yet were phrased almost seductively, teasing out the information. These variances in her character reminded him of his own fluctuations between arrogance and anxiety, and he thought because of this he might be able to understand and exploit her weaknesses.

'I'm still not quite clear why you want to build this precise *veve*,' she said.

'It's an intuition on my part,' he said. 'Jocundra thinks it may be an analogue to some feature of my brain, but all I can say is that I'll know after it's built. Why do you have it on your card?'

'Tradition,' she said. 'Do you know what a *veve* is, what its function in voodoo is?'

'Yes, generally.'

'I'm quite impressed with what I've heard about you,' she said. 'If anyone else had called me and suggested I build the *veve* of Ogoun Badagris out of three tons of copper, I would have hung up. But before I commit ... excuse me.'

The hound dog had wandered into the parking lot of the bar and stood gazing mournfully at Mr Brisbeau's tailgate; it snooted at something under the rear tire and walked around to the other side. Donnell heard Otille speaking angrily to someone, and she was still angry when she addressed him once again.

'Come to Maravillosa, Mr Harrison. We'll talk. I'll decide whether or not to be your sponsor. But you had better come soon. The people who're watching you won't allow your freedom much longer.'

'How do you know?'

'I'm very well connected,' she said tartly.

'What guarantee do I have they won't be watching me there?'

'Maravillosa is my private preserve. No one enters without my permission.' Otille made an impatient noise. 'If you decide to come, just call this number and talk to Papa. He'll be picking you up. Have that old fool you're staying with take you through the swamp to Caitlett's Store.'

'I'll think about it,' said Donnell. Gray rain driven by a gust of wind opaqued the booth; the lights of the bar looked faraway, the lights of a fogbound coast.

'Not for too long,' said Otille; her voice shifted gears and became husky, enticing. 'May I call you Donnell?'

'Let's keep things businesslike between us,' he said, irked by her heavy-handedness.

'Oh, Donnell,' she said, laughing. 'The question was just a formality. I'll call you anything I like.'

She hung up.

Someone had drawn a cross in blue ink above the phone, and someone else, a more skilful artist, had added a woman sitting naked atop the vertical piece, wavy lines to indicate that she was moving up and down, and the words 'Thank you, Jesus' in a word balloon popping from her lips. As he thought what to do next, he inspected all the graffiti, using them as background to thought; their uniform obscenity seemed to be seconding an inescapable conclusion. He walked back to the truck, cold rain matting his hair.

After Donnell described the conversation, proposing they see what Maravillosa had to offer, Mr Brisbeau grunted in dismay. 'Me, I'd sooner trust a hawk wit my pet mouse,' he said, digging for the car keys in his pocket.

'She sounds awful,' said Jocundra. 'Shadows can't be any worse. At least we're familiar with the pitfalls.'

'She's direct,' said Donnell. 'You have to give her that. I never knew what was going on at Shadows.'

Jocundra picked at an imperfection of bubbled plastic on the dash.

'Besides,' said Donnell, 'I'm convinced there's more to learn about the *veve*, and Maravillosa's the place to learn it.'

Rain drummed on the roof, the windows fogged, and the three of them sat without speaking.

'What's today?' asked Donnell.

'Thursday,' said Mr Brisbeau; 'Friday,' said Jocundra at the same time. 'Friday,' she repeated. Mr Brisbeau shrugged.

Donnell tapped the dash with his fingers. 'Is there a back road out of here, one the truck can handle?'

'There's a track down by the saw mill,' said Mr Brisbeau. 'She's goin' to be damn wet, but we can do it. Maybe.'

'If Edman still spends his weekends at home,' said Donnell, 'we'll give him a chance to make a counterproposal. We'll leave now. That way we'll catch whoever's watching by surprise, and they won't expect me to show up at Edman's.'

'What if he's not home?' Jocundra looked appalled by the prospect, and he realized she had been counting on him to reject Otille's offer.

'Then I'll call Papa, and we'll head for Caitlett's Store. Truthfully, I can't think of anything Edman could say to make me re-enter the project, but I'm willing to be proved wrong.'

She nodded, downcast. 'Maybe we should just call Papa. It might be a risk at Edman's.'

'It's all a risk,' he said, as Mr Brisbeau switched on the engine. 'But this way we'll know we did what we had to.'

As Mr Brisbeau backed up, the right front tire jolted over something, then bumped down, and Donnell heard a squeal from beneath. He swung the door open and climbed down and saw the old hound dog. The truck had passed over its neck and shoulders, killing it instantly. It must have given up looking for food and bellied under the wheel for shelter and the warmth of the motor. One of its eyes had been popped halfway out of the socket, exposing the thready structures behind, and the rain laid a glistening film upon the brown iris, spattering, leaking back inside the skull. Bright blood gushed from its mouth, paling to pink and wending off in rivulets across the puddled ground.

Mr Brisbeau came around the front of the truck, furious. 'Goddamn, boy! Don't that tell you somethin'?' he shouted, as if it had been Donnell's fault he had struck the dog. 'You keep up wit this Rigaud foolishness, and you goin' against a clear sign!'

But if it was a sign, then what interpretation should be placed upon it? Pink-muzzled, legs splayed, mouth frozen open in a rictus snarl; the grotesque stamp of death had transformed this dull, garbage-eating animal into something far more memorable that it had been in life. Donnell would not have thought such a miserable creature could contain so brilliant a colour.

CHAPTER 13

From *Conjure Men: My Work with Ezawa Tulane*
by Anthony Edman, MD, PhD.

... Though Ezawa's funding was private, he had been required by regulation to notify the government of his work with recombinant DNA. Government involvement in the project was minimal, however, until the death of Jack Richmond. The morning after his death – I had not yet learned of it – Douglas Stellings, our liaison with the CIA, visited me without appointment. I was not happy to see him. We had managed to keep news of the escape from the other patients, but Staff was in shock and the general reaction was one of utter despondency, of resignation to failure. Not even Dr Brauer could bestir himself to muster a sally against me. We had all been expecting a breakthrough, but with the exit of Magnusson, Richmond and Harrison our little stage had been robbed of its leading players, and we of our central focus. And so, when Stellings appeared, I greeted him as the bereaved might greet a member of the wake, with gloomy disinterest, and when he notified me of the deaths, I could only stare at him.

Stellings, a thin, fit man given to punctuating his phrases with sniffs, was wholly contemptuous of me, of Staff, in fact of anyone with less that CIA status. 'We've told the locals to back off,' he said. Sniff. 'The Bureau's taking care of it ... under our supervision, thank God!' As he glanced at the display of aboriginal crania behind my head, a tic of a smile disordered his features, which were, to my mind, pathologically inexpressive. 'Get your people up here,' he commanded. 'I want to see videos of Harrison.'

Until late in the evening we reviewed Harrison's last four days of tape. After a few initial questions, Stellings withheld comment; then, around midnight, he asked that three particular segments be rerun. The first showed Harrison sitting at his desk; he leaned forward, resting his head in his left hand, propped his right elbow on the desktop and wiggled his fingers. He gave the impression of being deep in thought. Shortly thereafter the image broke up and the screen went blank. The second section was similar, except that Harrison was limping along the downstairs hall, and the third, recorded the night of the escape, was identical to the first.

'Cameras are always screwing up,' muttered someone.

Stellings ran the tape back to the beginning of the third segment, then ran it forward again. 'He's peeking at the camera,' he said. 'He's looking up and sideways so you won't notice, masking his eyes behind his fingers. And then he waggles his fingers, we count to ten' – he counted – 'and the camera malfunctions. Got it?'

'Just like Magnusson,' breathed Dr Leavitt in tones of awe, tones which sounded false to my ear.

'What about Magnusson?' snapped Stellings.

'He exhibited similar finger-eye behavior prior to video malfunctions,' said Leavitt – earnest, deeply respectful Leavitt. 'I mentioned it to Dr Brauer, but he didn't assign it much importance.'

'You people ought to be in short pants,' said Stellings with disgust.

'Why wasn't I appraised of this?' I asked of Brauer. I was, I admit, delighted to see him squirm, though I realized that the downfall of a Brauer only permits the rise of a Leavitt; and Leavitt, our learning expert, whose primary contribution had thus far been a study of the patients' acquisition of autobiographical detail from their exposure to television, was if anything more of an opportunist than Brauer. Of course I had not noticed Harrison's behavior myself, but there sat Brauer, narrow-eyed, licking his lips, the image of a crook set up to take the rap.

Stellings dismissed everyone excepting myself and called his superiors. He recommended that all measures be taken to remove the FBI from the case, thus beginning the jurisdictional dispute which, in effect, allowed Harrison and Verret to find refuge at the home of Clarence Brisbeau. At the moment Harrison stood upon the stage of the revival in Salt Harvest, not one agent or officer was searching for him. All the hounds had been frozen at point, waiting until their masters could untangle their leashes, and by the time the CIA had won dominance and Harrison had been located, the decision had been made to permit his continued freedom. The idea was, as Stellings put it, to 'let him roll and see if he comes up sevens.' Harrison would certainly prove uncooperative if captured; therefore it would be more profitable to monitor him. Brisbeau's cabin was not an optimal security situation, but its isolation was a positive factor, and neither Stellings nor his superiors expected Harrison to run. Besides, there would be other slow-burners; the more Harrison inadvertently revealed, the more effectively we would be able to control them. When it was learned that Harrison was practising a form of faith healing, the CIA, in a master stroke of bureaucratic efficiency, sent him patients from their hospital, all of whom experienced miracle cures; and it was then – awakened by this luridly mystical image of sick spies being made whole by the ministrations of a 'zombie' healer – that I came out of the fog which had lowered about me since the escape and began to be afraid.

The surveillance devices planted within Brisbeau's cabin malfunctioned most of the time, but on days when no patients visited and Harrison's electrical activity was at a minimum, we were sometimes able to pick up distorted transmissions; and from them, as well as from our extant knowledge and agents' reports, we pieced together the science underlying Harrison's abilities. Stellings evinced little surprise upon learning of the cures or any other of the marvels; his reactions consisted merely of further schemes and recommendations. Yet I was shaken. Harrison had been alive five months, and he was already capable of miracles. And listening to one particular exchange between him and Verret, we caught a hint of some new evolution of ability.

VERRET: What is it?
HARRISON: Nothing. Just the *gros bon ange*. I'm getting better at controlling it *(laughter)* or vice versa.
VERRET: What do I look like?
HARRISON: You've got a beautiful soul. *(Verret laughs)*. What I was reacting to was that all the bits of fire were swarming about in the black, coalescing at random, and then, whoosh! they all converged to form into your mask. It wasn't the same as usual, though the features were the same. Are the same. But the colors are different. Less blue, more gold and ruby.
VERRET: I wonder...
HARRISON: What?
VERRET: A second ago I was thinking about you... very romantically.
HARRISON: Yeah? *(A rustling sound.)*
VERRET: *(laughing)* Do I feel different? *(A silence.)* What's wrong?
HARRISON: Just trying to shift back. It's hard to do sometimes.
VERRET: Why don't you not bother? I don't mind.
HARRISON: *(His voice becomes briefly very resonant, as if the transmission were stabilizing.)* It'd be like two charred corpses making love. *(A long silence.)* There. Are you okay?
VERRET: *(shakily)* Yes.
HARRISON: Oh, Christ! I wasn't thinking. I didn't mean to say that. I'm sorry.
VERRET: You've no reason to be.

Thereafter Harrison's electrical activity increased, and the transmission distorted into static.

The capacity to manipulate magnetic fields, to affect matter on the ionic level, and now this mysterious reference to the voodoo term for the soul. I realized we had no idea of this man's potential. My imagination was fueled by the sinister materials of the project, and I was stricken by a vision of Harrison crumbling cities with a gesture and raising armies of the dead. I suggested to Stellings that we bring him in, but he told me the risks were 'acceptable.' He did not believe, as I was coming to, that Harrison might be one of the most dangerous individuals who had ever lived. Of course Stellings had no knowledge of Otille Rigaud ... or did he? Perhaps there was no end to the convolution of this circumstance. It seemed to unravel by process of its own laws, otherworldly ones, like a cunning tapestry of black lace worked with tiny figures, whose depicted actions foreshadowed our lives.

And then came the night of 26 July 1987, a night during which all my fears were brought home to me. I had been asleep for nearly an hour, not really asleep, drowsing, listening to the rain and the wind against the dormer window, when I thought I heard a footfall in the corridor. Though this was hardly likely – my security system being extensive – I sat up in bed, listening more closely. Nothing. The only movement was the rectangle of white streetlight cast on the far wall, marred by opaque splotches of rain and whirling leaf shadow. I settled back. Once again I heard a sound, the glide of something along the hallway carpet. This time I switched on the bedside lamp, and there, framed in the door, was a preposterous old man with shoulder-length white hair and wearing a loose-fitting shirt decorated, it seemed to my bleary eyes, with the image of a blue serpent (I later saw this was actually the word *Self-rising*, the imprint of a flour company). 'Goddamn, he's a big one, him,' said the old man to someone out of sight around the corner. A second figure appeared in the doorway, and a third, and I understood why my burglar alarms had failed. It was Verret, troubled-looking, and beside her, disguised by a pair of mirrored glasses, was Harrison. He had gained weight, especially in the shoulders, but he was still gaunt. His hair had grown long, framing his face, giving him a piratical air.

'Edman,' he said.

The word was phrased as an epithet, containing such a wealth of viciousness I almost did not recognize it as my name.

His movements revealing no sign of debility, he picked up a straight-backed chair, carried it to the bed and sat next to me. How can I tell you my feelings at that moment, the effect he had upon me? I have stated that the patients were charismatic in the extreme, but Harrison's personal force was beyond anything of my experience. To put it simply, I was terrified. His *anima* wrapped around me like an electrified fist, immobilizing and vibrant, and I stared helplessly at my agog reflection in his mirrored lenses. The wind rattled the window, branches ticked the glass, as if heralding his presence. I wondered how Verret and the old man could be so at ease with him. Did they not notice, or had they become acclimatized to his aura of power? And what of *his* patients? Were all faith healers equally potent beings? Could it be that the power to heal was in part conferred by the faithful upon the healer, and this exchange of energies immunized the patients against awe? It is, I believe, a testament to the rigorous discipline of my education that, despite my fear, I was able to make a mental note to investigate the subject.

'Any successes lately with the new strain?' he asked.

I am not sure what I expected him to say, a threat perhaps, an insult, but certainly not this. 'Two,' I managed to gasp.

Expressionless, he absorbed the information. 'Edman,' he said, 'I need money, a place to work unimpeded, and a guaranteed freedom of movement. Can you supply it?'

I wish I had said that I could offer no guarantees, that the CIA was involved and I no longer had substantive control of the project; then he might have accorded me a measure of confidence. But as it was, I obeyed the reflexes of my office and said, 'Come back to the project, Donnell. We'll take care of you.'

'I bet,' he said, and here his voice became resonant for the space of a few syllables, the voice of a ghost rather than a man. 'I should be taking care of you. You're quite ill, you know.' He turned to the old man and gestured toward the door. 'See if there's anything around we can use, okay?' And then to Verret: 'He's totally untrustworthy. One second frightened, the next scheming. Do you have any money?' he asked, turning back to me.

I pointed to my trousers hanging on the clothes rack. Verret went over and emptied my wallet of bills. I felt sudden hostility toward her, seeing her as the betrayer of our mutual cause, and I commented on her thievery.

'Thief?' She lashed out at me. 'You ghoul! Don't call me names!'

'Don't waste your breath on him.' Harrison regarded me with displeasure. 'He's just random molecules bound together by the stickum of his education.'

Normally I would have been infuriated by such a description, but he said it with kindness, with pity, and for the moment I accepted it as accurate, a sad but true diagnosis. This, and the fact that during our encounter I was prone to fits of depression, a characteristic I had associated with Harrison, led me to wonder whether or not his energies were materially affecting my thought processes.

Verret left to join the old man in his search, and Harrison gazed at me thoughtfully. 'Get up,' he said. He pushed back his chair and stood.

I was afraid he was about to harm me. My fear may seem to you irrational; I was, after all, a much larger man, and I might well have been able to overpower both him and Verret, though the old man had a wiry, dangerous look. Yet I was very afraid.

'I'm not going to hurt you,' he said, thoroughly disgusted. He removed his sunglasses. 'I'm going to try to cure you.'

As he moved his hands above my head, concentrating his efforts at the base of my skull, I lost track of the storm, the others in the house, and was caught up in the manner of my healing. Mild electric shocks tingled me from head to foot, my ears were filled with oscillating hums. Once in a while violent shocks caused my muscles to spasm, and after each of these I experienced a feeling of – I am hesitant to use the term, but can think of no other – spirituality. Not the warm *bona fides* of Jesus as advertised by the Council of Churches. Hardly. It was a cold immateriality that embraced me, that elevated my thoughts, sent them questing after a higher plane; it was less a palpable cold than a mental rigor, one implying an icy sensibility in whose clutch I foundered. I had an image of myself lying in a gold-green scaly palm, tiny as a charm. Was this the biochemistry of salvation in action, an instance of Harrison's effect releasing spiritual endorphins? Or was it the overlapping of his sensibility with my own? I only know that each sight I had of the flashes within his eyes gave credence to my newfound apprehension of the supernatural.

'Sorry,' he said at last. 'It's going to take too long. A day or more, I'd guess.' He smiled. 'Maybe you should have one of the new patients check you over.' (And I would have, had not the project been taken from me.) He must have forgotten that Verret had left the room, for he half-turned and spoke over his shoulder, assuming her presence, saying, 'If this works out, we should think about setting the others loose. There's no …' Then, realizing she was elsewhere, a puzzled expression crossed his face.

'What is the *gros bon ange*?' I blurted. 'What are you intending to do?' I was still frightened, but the character of my fear had changed. It was the unknown quantity he represented that assailed me, and I was desperate to understand.

'The *gros bon ange*?' His voice became resonant and hollow again, gusting at me like a wind from a cave, merging with the howling wind outside. 'A dream, a vision, or maybe it's the shadow a dog sees slipping out of an open coffin.' Then his voice reverted to normal, and he described what he had seen.

I am not sure why he humored my question. Boredom, perhaps, or it may have been simply that he had no reason to hide anything from me. There were, he said, three types, the most commonplace a black figure in which prisms of light whirled chaotically. The second most common type seemed to exert a measure of control over its inner fires (his term), able to form of them faces, simple patterns; and the rarest, a type of whom he had seen only three, were capable of wielding extensive control, even to the point of sending bursts of light shooting from their fingers.

'As to what I intend,' he said, 'I intend to live, Edman. I'm going to build the *veve* of a voodoo god out of copper. Three tons of copper.' He laughed. 'I don't suppose you know about *veves*, though.'

Indeed, I assured him, I did know, having done quite a bit of reading on the subject of *vaudou*, this at the urging of Ms Verret.

'Oh?' He scratched the back of his neck. 'Tell me about Ogoun Badagris.'

'One of the aspects of Ogoun,' I said, 'who is essentially the warrior hero of the pantheon. I believe that Ogoun Badagris is associated with wizardry. A *rada* aspect.'

'Rada?'

'Yes. *Rada* and *petro* are more or less equivalent to white and black magic. Good and evil.'

'And which is *rada*?'

'Good,' I said.

'Well,' he said softly, more to himself than to me, 'I guess I should be thankful for that.'

He went on to tell me of a plan he had, hardly a plan, more a vague compulsion to act in some direction, and though the action was as yet unclear, as the days passed the parameters of the deed were defining themselves. Something decisive, he said, something dangerous. It was evident to me that he was evolving past the human, and I was in mortal terror of the vibrant devil he was coming to be. I lay half hypnotized, helpless before him, the tongues of his words tasting me, licking me prior to taking a bite. Finally Verret and the old man returned; he was carrying a brandy bottle and she a coil of rope. Without further ado they gagged me and lashed me to the bed, and afterwards Harrison asked me to break free if I could. Ordinarily I would have pretended to struggle, but at his behest I shook the bed in earnest.

And then they were gone, gone to Maravillosa, swallowed up and gone beyond the reach of the CIA, the project, and for all I know beyond the hand of God Himself. We had no word of them until news came of Harrison's actions on Bayou Rigaud.

I may well have met Otille Rigaud; however, from all reports, it is unlikely I would have forgotten the occasion. She was a woman who traveled freely through the various strata of society, and the mention of her name was sufficient to cause highly respected citizens to cough, make their excuses, and leave the room. I wish that I had met her. Though many have tried to explain the events which occurred upon Bayou Rigaud, she alone might have illuminated them. Stacked on my writing table at this moment is page after page of dubious yet accurate explanation. Data sheets, medical records, government documents. For example, here we have the results of an autopsy performed on an unidentified body, citing one hundred and seventy separate fractures caused by the instantaneous degeneration of bone tissue, blood clots, cell damage, crushed spinal ganglia, and so forth. Appended is a telephone-book-sized study exploring the victim's agony, which must have been substantial, and speculating on the nature of the forces that came into play. I will quote from the summary section.

... Movements of the Ezawa bacteria within the brains of Subjects One and Two created electrical currents which interacted with the electrical functions of the neurons, thereby enabling them to intuit the direction of the geomagnetic field. The copper device, aside from its function of conductivity, seems to have acted as a topological junction, its design such that all possible formulae of energy manipulation – the vibrational and rotational states of electrons, spin states of magnetic nuclei – were reduced to the choreographed movements of an electrical field (either Subject One or Two) within the geomagnetic field. Together with the device, the subjects became dynamos. They provided the current fed through the device, which in turn fed a magnetic field back through their bodies. Dependent on the exact choreography, the field could attain a potential strength of at least several hundred thousand times that of the geomagnetic field.

'The energies redirected through the bodies of both subjects must have been of sufficient strength to disrupt in coherent fashion their atomic structures. Bulman hypothesizes there may have been a particular reaction involved with the hemoglobin. Electrons were raised to higher energy states, unipolar fields were created at the fingertips of the subjects, and photons transmitted along the lines of the fields. The emission of light visible in the tapes resulted from energy loss when the electrons dropped back to lower energy states. Essentially, the physical damage sustained by Subject One occurred when his nuclei absorbed enough radiation to flip their orientation and align with Subject Two's field, this being a structural irony his component particles could not maintain …

All well and good. But none of this speaks to the absolute question: Can the events on Bayou Rigaud be taken at face value, or were more consequential historical actions involved? It may be unanswerable. It may be that when we peer over the extreme edge of human experience, we will find nothing but mute darkness. Or, and this is my conviction, it may be that there is a process of nature too large for us to perceive, an ultimate conjoining of the physics of coincidence and probability, wherein an infinite number of events, events as minuscule as two people meeting in the street and as grandiose as a resurrection, combine and each take on radiant meanings so as to enact an improbable and magical fate. But my own answer aside, I prefer above the rest that given me by an old Cajun woman whom I interviewed preparatory to beginning this memoir. At the very least, it does not beg the question.

'*Le Bon Dieu*. He got riled at all the funny doin's down on Bayou Rigaud,' she said. 'So He raised up The Green-eyed Man to do battle wit His ancient enemy.'

CHAPTER 14

July 27–28 July 1987

The oak tree sheltering Caitlett's Store looked as if it had undergone a terrifying transformation: a hollow below its crotch approximating an aghast mouth, swirled patterns in the bark for eyes, thin arms flung up into greenery. Mr Brisbeau parked the truck beside it, keeping the motor running, while Jocundra and Donnell slid out. Someone cracked the screen door of the store and peeked at them, then let it bang shut, rattling a rusted tin sign advertising night crawlers. Nothing moved in the entire landscape. The marshlands shone yellow-green under the late afternoon sun, threaded by glittering meanders of water and pierced by the state highway, which ran straight to the horizon.

'Are you going back to the cabin?' Jocundra asked Mr Brisbeau.

'The damn gov'ment ain't puttin' me on their trut' machine,' he said. 'Me, I'm headin' for the swamp.'

'Goodbye,' said Donnell, sticking out his hand. 'Thank you.'

Mr Brisbeau frowned. 'You give me back my eyes, boy, and I ain't lettin' you off wit "goodbye" and "thank you."' He handed Donnell a folded square of paper. 'That there's my luck, boy. I fin' it in the sand on Gran Calliou.'

The paper contained a small gold coin, the raised face upon it worn featureless.

'Pirate gold,' said Mr Brisbeau; he harumphed, embarrassed. 'Now, me, I ain't been the luckiest soul, but wit all my drinkin' I figure I cancel it out some.'

'Thank you,' said Donnell again, turning the coin over in his fingers.

'Jus' give it back nex' time you see me.' Mr Brisbeau put his hands on the wheel. 'I ain't so old I don't need my luck.' He glanced sideways at Jocundra. 'You wait twelve more years to come around, girl, and you have to whisper to my tombstone.'

'I won't.' She rested her hand on the window, and he gave it a pat. His fingers were trembling.

'Ain't sayin' goodbye,' he said, his face collapsing into a sad frown; he let out the clutch and roared off.

Jocundra watched him out of sight, feeling forlorn, deserted, but Donnell gazed anxiously in the other direction.

'I knew the son of a bitch would be late,' he said.

The interior of the store was dark and cluttered. Shelf after shelf of canned goods and sundries, bins of fish hooks and sinkers, racks of rods and reels. The fading light was thronged with particles of dust, and their vibration seemed to register the half-life of some force that radiated from a tin washtub of dried bait shrimp set beneath the window.

'Cain't wait here 'less you buy somethin',' said the woman back of the counter, so they bought sandwiches and went outside to eat on the steps.

'Funny thing happened last night,' he said, breaking a long bout of chewing. 'I was talking to Edman while you were searching the house, and I felt you behind me. I could've sworn you'd come back in the room, but then I realized I was feeling you walk through the house. It's happened before, I think, but not so strongly.'

'It's probably just sexual,' she said.

He laughed and hugged her.

'You folks cain't wait here much longer,' said the woman from inside the door. 'I'm gonna close real soon, and I don't want you hangin' round after dark.'

'There must be some kind of feedback system in operation,' said Jocundra after the woman had clomped back to the counter. 'I mean considering the way your abilities have increased since you began healing. I'd expect more of an increase while you're on the *veve*. Even though you'll be trimming back the colony, you'll be routing them through the systems that control your abilities.'

'Hmm.' He rubbed her hip, disinterested. 'It was really weird last night,' he said. 'Sort of like the way you could tell the Gulf was beyond the pines at Robichaux's. Something about the air, the light. A thousand micro-changes. I knew where you were every second.'

The sun was reddening, ragged strings of birds crossed the horizon, and there were splashes from the marsh. A Paleozoic stillness. The scene touched off a sunset-colored dream in Jocundra's head. How they sailed down one of the channels to the sea, followed the coast to a country of spiral towers and dingy portside bars, where an old man with a talking lizard on a leash and a map tattooed on his chest offered them sage advice. She went with the dream, preferring it to thinking about their actual destination.

'That's him,' said Donnell.

A long maroon car was slowing; it pulled over on the shoulder and honked. They walked toward it without speaking. There were bouquet vases in the back windows, a white monogrammed R on the door. Jocundra reached out to open the rear door, but Papa Salvatino, his puffy face warped by a scowl, punched down the lock.

'Get in front!' he snapped. 'I ain't your damn chauffeur!'

'You're late,' said Donnell as he slid in. Jocundra scrunched close to him, away from Papa.

'Listen, brother. Don't you bê tellin' me I'm late!' Papa engaged the gears; the car shot forward. 'Right now, right this second, you already at Otille's.' He shifted again, and they were pressed together by the acceleration. 'We got us a peckin' order at Maravillosa,' Papa shouted over the wind. 'And it's somethin' you better keep in mind, brother, 'cause you the littlest chicken!'

He lit a cigarette, and the wind showered sparks over the front seat. Jocundra coughed as a plume of smoke enveloped her.

'I just can't sit behind the wheel 'less I got a smoke,' said Papa. 'Sorry.' He winked at Jocundra, then gave her an appraising stare. 'My goodness, sister. I been so busy scoutin' out Brother Harrison, I never noticed what a fine, fine-lookin' woman you are. You get tired of sharpenin' his pencil, give 'ol Papa a shout.'

Jocundra edged farther away; Papa laughed and lead-footed the gas. The light crumbled, the grasses marshaled into ranks of shadows against the leaden dusk. They drove on in silence.

The house was painted black.

On first sight, a brief glimpse through a wild tangle of vines and trees, Donnell hadn't been certain. By the time they arrived at the estate, clouds had swept across the moon and he could not even make out the roofline against the sky. A number of lighted windows hovered unsupported in the night, testifying to the great size of the place, and as they passed along the drive, the headlights revealed a hallucinatory vegetable decay: oleanders with nodding white blooms, shattered trunks enwebbed by vines, violet orchids drooling off a crooked branch, bright spears of bamboo, shrubs towering as high as trees, all crammed and woven together. Peeping between the leaves at the end of the drive was the pale androgynous face of a statue. Things crunched underfoot on the flagstone path, and nearing the porch Donnell saw that the boards were a dull black except for four silver-painted symbols which seemed to have fallen at random upon the house, adjusting their shapes to its contours like strange unmelting snowflakes: an Egyptian cross floating sideways on the wall, a *swastika* overlapping the lower half of the door and the floorboards, a crescent moon, a star. He assumed there were others hidden by the darkness.

Papa led them down a foul-smelling, unlit corridor reverberating with loud rock and roll. Several people ran past them, giggling. At the end of the corridor was a small room furnished as an office: metal desk, easy chairs, typewriter, file cabinets. The walls were of unadorned black wood.

'Wait here,' he said, switching on the desk lamp. 'Don't you go pokin' around 'til Otille gives you the say-so.'

The instant he left, Jocundra slumped into a chair. 'God,' she said; she opened her mouth to say something else, but let it pass.

Shrieks of laughter from the corridor, the tangy smell of cat shit and marijuana. Oppressed by the atmosphere himself, Donnell had no consolation to offer.

'The ends of the earth,' she said, and laughed despondently. 'My high school yearbook said I'd travel to the ends of the earth to find adventure. This must be it.'

'The ends of the earth are but the beginning of another world,' someone intoned behind them.

The gray-haired usher from Papa Salvatino's revival stood in the door; neither his beatific smile nor his shabby suit had changed. At his side was a crewcut, hawk-faced young man holding a guitar, and lounging beside him was a teenage girl, whose costume of a curly red wig and beige negligee did not disguise her mousiness.

'This here's Downey and Clea,' said the usher. 'I'm Simpkins. Delighted to have you back in the congregation.'

Downey laughed, whispered in Clea's ear, and she grinned.

Jocundra was speechless, and Donnell, struck by a suspicion, shifted his visual field. Three black figures bloomed in the silver-limned door; the prismatic fires within them columned their legs, delineated the patterns of their musculature and nerves, and glowed at their fingertips. Simpkins and one of the other two, then, along with Papa, must have been the three figures Donnell had seen in Salt Harvest, and he thought he knew what their complex patterns indicated. He shifted back to normal sight and studied their faces. Clea and Downey were toadies and boot-lickers, but each with a secret, a trick, an ounce of distinction. Simpkins was hard to read.

'So you're Otille's little band of mutants,' said Donnell, walking over to stand behind Jocundra.

'How'd you know that?' asked Clea, her voice a nasal twang. 'I bet Papa told you.'

'Lucky guess,' said Donnell. 'Where's the other one? There's one more besides Papa, isn't there?'

Simpkins maintained his God-conscious smile. 'Right on all counts, brother,' he said. 'But if half what we been hearin's true, we can't hold a candle to you. Now Downey here' – he gave Downey's head a friendly rub – 'he can move things around with his mind. Not big things. Ping-pong balls, feathers. And then only when he ain't stoned, which ain't too often. And Sister Clea ...'

'I sing,' said Clea defiantly.

Downey snickered.

'And when I do,' she said, and stuck out her tongue at Downey, 'strange things happen.'

'Sometimes,' said Downey. 'Most times you just clear the room. Sounds like someone squeezin' a rat.'

'It's true,' said Simpkins. 'Sister Clea's talent is erratic, but wondrous things do happen when she lifts her voice in song. A gentle breeze will blow where none has blown before, insects will drop dead in midflight …'

'She oughta hire out to Orkin,' said Downey.

'And,' Simpkins continued, 'only last week a canary fell from its perch, never more to charm the morning air.'

'That was just a coincidence,' said Downey sullenly.

'You're just jealous 'cause Otille kicked you outta bed,' said Clea.

'Coincidence or not,' said Simpkins, 'Sister Clea's stock has risen sharply since the death of poor Pavarotti.'

'And what's your speciality, Simpkins?' asked Donnell.

'I suppose you'd classify me as a telepath.' Simpkins folded his arms, thoughtful. 'Though it never seemed I was pickin' up real thoughts, more like dreams behind thoughts …'

'Simpkins once had a rather exotic vision which he said derived from my thoughts,' said a musical voice. A diminutive, black-haired woman swept into the room, Papa and a heavy-set black man at her heels. 'It was a pretty vision,' she said. 'I incorporated it into my decorating scheme. But his talent failed him shortly thereafter, and we never did learn what it meant.' She walked over to Donnell; she was wearing a cocktail dress of a silky red material that seemed to touch every part of her body when she moved. 'I'm Otille Rigaud.' She gave her name the full French treatment, as if it were a rare vintage. 'I see you've been getting to know my pets.' Then she frowned. 'Baron!' she snapped. 'Where's Dularde?'

'Beats me,' said the black man.

'Find him,' she said, shooing them off with flicks of her fingers. 'All of you. Go on!'

She gestured for Donnell to sit beside Jocundra, and after he had taken a chair, she perched on the desk in front of him. Her dress slid up over her knees, and he found that if he did not meet her stare or turn his head at a drastic angle, he would be looking directly at the shadowy division between her thighs. She was a remarkably beautiful woman, and though according to Papa's story she must be nearly forty, Donnell would have guessed her age at a decade less. Her hair fell to her shoulders in serpentine curls; her upper lip was shorter and fuller than the lower, giving her a permanently dissatisfied expression; her skin was pale, translucent, a tracery of blue veins showing at the throat. Delicate bones, black eyes aswim with lights that did not appear to be reflections. A cameo face, one which bespoke subtle understandings and passions. But her overall delicacy, not any single feature of it, was Otille's most striking aspect. Against the backdrop of her pets, she had seemed fashioned by a more skillful hand, and when she had entered the office, Donnell had felt that an invisible finger had nudged her from the ranks of pawns into an attacking position: the tiny ivory queen of a priceless chess set.

'You have a wonderful presence, Donnell,' she said after a long silence. 'Wonderful.'

'Compared to what?' he said, annoyed at being judged. 'The rest of your remaindered freaks?'

'Oh, no. You're quite incomparable. Don't you think so, Ms Verret? Jocundra.' She smiled chummily at Jocundra. 'What an awful name to saddle a child with! So large and cumbersome. But you *have* grown into it.'

Jocundra registered surprise on being addressed, but she was not caught without a reply. 'I'm really not interested in trading insults,' she said. She opened her purse and pulled out a manila folder. 'These are our cost estimates. Shouldn't we get down to business?'

Otille laughed, but took the folder. She carried it back to the desk, sat, and began to examine it.

A tap on the door, and Papa leaned in. 'Otille? They spotted Dularde in the ballroom, but there's so damn many people, we can't catch up with him.'

'All right. Don't do anything. I'll be down in a minute.' She waved him away. 'These don't seem out of line,' she said, closing the folder. 'And I'm quite impressed with you, Donnell. But I think we should both sleep on it and see how we feel in the morning. Then we can talk. Agreed?'

'Fine by me,' he said. 'Jocundra?'

She nodded.

'I apologize for getting off on the wrong foot,' said Otille, scraping back her chair and standing. 'I have to deal with so much falsity, I end up being false myself. And I suppose my theatrical background has affected me badly.' She tipped her head to one side, considering an idea. 'Would you like to hear something from my play? *Danse Calinda?*'

Donnell shrugged; Jocundra said nothing.

Otille adopted a distracted pose behind her chair. 'I'll do a brief passage,' she said, 'and then we'll find Dularde.' As she spoke the lines, she darted about the room, her hands fidgeting with her dress, papers on the desk, straightening furniture, and all her movements had the electrified inconsistency of someone prone to flashes of otherworldly vision.

'"... And then coming back from Brooklyn Heights, the cabbie was talking, looking at me in the rear view mirror, winking. He was very friendly, you know how they are when they think you're from out of town. But anyway as he was talking, the skin started dissolving around his eye, melting, rotting away, until there was just this huge globe surrounded by shreds of green flesh staring at me in the mirror. And I was afraid! Anyone in their right mind would have been, but all down Broadway I was mostly afraid that if he didn't keep his eye on the road we were going to crash. Isn't that peculiar? I'm terribly hot. Are you hot?"' She walked over to the wall and pretended to open a window. '"There. That's better."' She fanned herself. '"I know you must think I'm foolish running on like this, but I talk to so few people and I have ... I was going to say I have so many thoughts to express, so many tragic thoughts. So many tragic things have happened. But my thoughts aren't really tragic, or maybe they are, they're just not nobly tragic. The only thing noble I ever saw was a golden anvil shining up in the clouds over Bayou Goula, and that was the day before I came down with chicken pox. No, my thoughts are like the radio playing in the background, pumping out jingles and hit tunes and commercials and the news bulletins. Flash. A tragic thing occurred today, ten thousand people lost their lives, then nervous music, typewriters clicking, and moving right along, on the last leg of her European tour the First Lady presided over a combined luncheon and fashion show for the wives of the foreign press. Ten thousand people! Corpses, agony, death. All that breath and energy flying out of the world. You'd think there'd be a change in the air or something, a sign, maybe a special dark cloud passing overhead. You'd think you would *feel* something ..."'

Donnell had been absorbed by the performance, and when Otille relaxed from the manic intensity she had conjured up, he felt cut off from a source of energy. 'That was pretty good,' he said grudgingly.

'Pretty good!' Otille scoffed. 'It was a hell of a play, but the trouble was I tended to lose myself in the part.'

Otille's pets and the black man she had called Baron were waiting by the doors of the ballroom. Though the doors were shut, the music was deafening and she had to raise her voice to be heard. 'I really hate to interrupt things on account of Dularde,' she said, looking aggrieved.

Downey and Clea and Papa put on expressions of concern, displaying their sympathetic understanding of Otille's position, but Simpkins' smile never wavered, apparently feeling no need to cozy up. The black man stared at Jocundra, who hung back from the group, ducking her eyes, lines of strain bracketing her mouth.

'Is this important?' asked Donnell. 'We're tired. We can meet him in the morning.'

'I won't be awake in the morning,' said Otille angrily; she turned to the others. 'Please try to find him once more. I'll wait here.' She gestured to the Baron, and he flung open the doors.

Music, smoky air and flashing nights gusted out, and Donnell's immediate impression was that they had pierced the hollow of a black carcass and stumbled onto an infestation of beetles halfway through a transformation into the human. Hundreds of people were dancing, shoving and mauling each other, and they were dressed in what appeared to be the overflow of a flea market: feathered boas, ripped dinner jackets, sequined gowns, high school band uniforms. Orange spotlights swept across them, coils of smoke writhing in the beams. As his eyes adjusted to the alternating brilliance and dimness, he saw that the ceiling had been knocked out and ragged peninsulas of planking left jutting from the walls at the height of about twenty feet; these served as makeshift balconies, each holding half a dozen or more people, and as mounts for the spotlights and speakers, which were angled down beneath them. Ropes trailed off their sides, and at the far end of the room someone was swinging back and forth over the heads of the crowd.

'... party!' shouted Otille, as her pets infiltrated the dancers, pushing their way through.

'What?' Donnell leaned close.

'It's Downey's party! He just released ...' Otille pointed to her ear and drew him along the hall to where the din was more bearable. Jocundra followed behind.

'He's just released his first record,' said Otille. 'We have our own label. That's him playing.'

Donnell cocked an ear to listen. Beneath the distortion, the music was slick and heavily synthesized, and Downey's lyrics were surprisingly romantic, his voice strong and melodic.

'... *Just like a queen upon a playin' card,*
A little cheatin' never hurt your heart,
You just smile and let the deal go on
'Til the deck's run through ...
See how they've fallen for you.'

'It's one of the benefits of living here,' said Otille. 'I enjoy sponsoring creative enterprise.' She strolled back down to the doorway, beckoning them to follow.

The shining blades of the spotlights skewed wildly across the bobbing heads, stopping to illuminate an island of ecstatic faces, then slicing away. Some of the dancers – both men and women – were naked to the waist, and others wore rags, yet they gave evidence of being well-to-do. Expensive haircuts, jewelry, and many of the rags were of good material, suggesting they had been ripped just for the occasion. Five minutes passed, ten. Jocundra stood with her hand to her mouth, pale, and when he asked her what was wrong, she replied, 'The smoke,' and leaned against the wall. Finally Downey and Papa returned, Simpkins behind them.

'I think I saw him,' said Downey. 'But I couldn't get close. It's like the goddamn stockyards out there.'

'Somebody said he was headed this way,' said Papa; he was huffing and puffing, and it was clear to Donnell that he was exaggerating his winded condition, making sure Otille noticed how diligently he had exerted himself on her behalf.

'I guess we'll have to stop the dancing,' said Otille. 'I'm sorry, Downey.'

Downey waved it off as inconsequential.

'Now, hold up,' said Papa, earnestly addressing the problem. 'I bet if all of us, maybe Brother Harrison here as well, if we all got out there and kinda formed a chain, you know, about five or six feet apart, and went from one end to the other, well, I bet we could flush him that way.'

Otille glanced shyly up at Donnell. 'Would you mind?'

What he read from Otille's face angered Donnell and convinced him that this was to be his induction into petdom, the first move in a petty power play which, if he were nice, would bring him treats, and if he weren't, would earn him abusive treatment. When he had met Otille, her face had held a depth of understanding, intimations of a vivid character, but now it had changed into a porcelain dish beset with candied lips and painted eyes, the face of a precious little girl who would hold her breath forever if thwarted. And as for the rest, they would go on happily all night trying to tree their kennelmate, delighting in this crummy game of hide-and-seek, woofing, wagging their tails, licking her hand. Except for Simpkins; his smile in place, Simpkins was unreadable.

'Christ!' said Donnell, not hiding his disgust. 'Let me try.'

The ballroom darkened, and the world of the *gros bon ange* came into view. It was laughable to see these black, jeweled phantoms flailing their arms, shaking their hips, flaunting their clumsy eroticism to the accompaniment of Downey's song. He scanned the crowd, searching for the complex pattern that would single out Dularde; then Otille could loose her hounds, and he and Jocundra could rest. He wondered what Dularde's punishment would be. Banishment? Gruel and water? Perhaps Otille would have him beaten. That would be well within the capacity for cruelty of the spoiled brat who had batted her lashes at him moments before. He swung his gaze up to the makeshift balconies, and there, at the far end of the room, were two figures holding hands and kicking out their legs in unison on the edge of a silver-trimmed platform. Glittering prisms twined in columns around the legs of the taller figure, delineated the musculature of his chest, and fitted a mask to his face.

'There,' said Donnell, adding with all the nastiness he could muster, 'is that your goddamn stray?'

He pointed.

As he did, his elbow locked sharply into place, and his arm snapped forward with more force than he had intended. The lights inside Dularde's body scattered outward and glowed around him so that he presented the silhouette of a man occulting a rainbow. He wavered, staggered to one side, a misstep, lost his grip on his partner, fought for balance, and then, just as Donnell normalized his sight and drew back his arm, Dularde fell.

Hardly anyone noticed. If there were cries of alarm, they could not be heard. But Otille was screaming, 'Turn off the music! Turn it off!' Papa and Simpkins and Downey echoed her, and several of the dancers, seeing it was Otille who shouted, joined in. The outcry swelled, most people not knowing why they were yelling, but yelling in the spirit of fun, urging others to add their voices, until it became a chant. 'Turn off the music! Turn off the music!' At last it was switched off, and someone could be heard above the hubbub calling for a doctor.

Otille flashed a perplexed look at Donnell, then pressed into the crowd, Papa Salvatino clearing a path before her. Downey craned his neck, gawking at the spot where Dularde had fallen. Simpkins folded his arms.

'My, my,' he said. 'We're purely havin' a rash of coincidences. Ain't we, Brother Downey?'

Their bedroom was on the second floor, as were those of all the pets, and though the furnishings were ordinary, Jocundra had spent a sleepless night because of the walls. They were paneled with ebony, and from the paneling emerged realistically carved, life-sized arms and legs and faces, also ebony, as if ghosts had been trapped passing through the tarry substance of the boards. Everywhere she rested her eyes a clawed hand reached for her or an angelic face stared back, seeming interested in her predicament. The faces were thickest on the walls of the alcove leading into the hall, and these, unlike the others, were agonized, with bulging eyes and contorted mouths.

Donnell, too, had spent a sleepless night, partly because of her tossing and turning, but also due to his concern over the man who had fallen. She didn't fully understand his concern; he had taken worse violences in stride. She tried, however, to be reassuring, telling him that people commonly survived far greater falls. But Dularde, said Otille, when she came to visit early in the afternoon, had suffered spinal injuries, and it was touch and go. She did not appear at all upset herself and insisted on showing them the grounds, which were fantastic in their ruin.

It had rained during the night, the sky was leaden, and peals of distant thunder rolled from the south. They walked along the avenue of pines where long ago Valcours Rigaud's daughter had wed beneath a canopy of gold and silver spiderwebs. Now the webs spanned even between the trunks, creating filmy veils dotted with the husks of wasps and flies. Otille slashed them down with her umbrella. The entire landscape was so overgrown that Jocundra could only see a few feet in any direction before her eye met with a plaited wall of vines, an impenetrable thicket of oleander, or the hollow shell of a once mighty oak, itself enwrapped by a strangler fig whose sinuous branchings had spread to other trees, weaving its own web around a series of gigantic victims. The world of Maravillosa was a dripping, parasitical garden. Yet underlying this decay was the remnant of artful design. Scattered about the grounds were conical hills fifteen and twenty feet in height, matted with morning glory and ivy, saplings growing from their sides, like the jungle-shrouded tops of Burmese temples. Paths entered the hills, curving between mossy walls, and at the center they would find broken benches, fragments of marble fountains and sundials, and once, a statue covered in moss and vines, its hand outheld in a warding gesture, as if a magician had been struck leafy and inanimate while casting a counterspell.

'Valcours,' said Otille bemusedly, rubbing away the moss and clearing a circular patch of marble.

From atop one of the hills, between walls of bamboo and vines, they had a view of the house. Black; bristling with gables; speckled with silver magical symbols; a ramshackle wing leading off behind; it had the look of a strange seed spat from the heart of the night and about to burst into a constellation. Beyond the hills lay an oval pool bordered in cracked marble and sheeted with scum, enclosed by bushes whose contours were thrust up into odd shapes. Valcours, Otille explained, had been fascinated with the human form, and the bushes overgrew a group of mechanical devices he had commissioned for his entertainment. She hacked at a bush with her umbrella and uncovered a faceless wooden figure, its head a worm-trailed lump and its torso exhibiting traces of white paint, as well as a red heart on its chest. A rusted *epee* was attached to its hand.

'It still worked when I was a child,' she said. 'Ants lived inside it, in channels packed with sand, and when their population grew too large, traps were sprung and reservoirs of mercury were opened, flooding the nests. The reservoirs were designed to empty at specific intervals and rates of flow, shifting the weight of the figure, sending it thrusting and lurching about in a parody of swordsmanship. The only ants to survive were those that fled into an iron compartment here' – she tapped the heart – 'and then, after it had been cleaned, they were released to start all over.' She cocked an eyebrow, as if expecting a reaction.

'What was it for?' asked Jocundra. The apparent uselessness of the thing, its death-powered spurts of life, horrified her.

'Who knows what Valcours had in mind,' said Otille, stabbing the dummy with her umbrella. 'Some plot, some game, But I hated the thing! Once, I was about eight, it scared me badly, and after it had stopped moving, I took out the iron compartment and dropped it in the bayou.' She sauntered off along the rim of the pool, scuffing algae off the marble. 'I've ordered the copper,' she said over her shoulder. 'You can stay if you like.'

'How long will it take?' asked Donnell.

'A week to get here, then a few weeks for construction.' She started walking toward the house. 'You can think about it a few more days if you wish, but if you do stay, I hope you understand that it's a job. You'll have to keep yourself available to me five days a week from noon until eight. For my experiments. Otherwise, you're on your own.' She turned and gave Donnell a canny look. 'Are you sure you've told me everything about the *veve*, why you're building it?'

'I hardly know myself,' he said.

'I wonder how it relates to *Les Invisibles*,' she said.

'*Les Invisibles?*'

'The voodoo gods,' said Jocundra. 'They're sometimes called *Les Invisibles* or the *loas*.'

'Oh,' he said derisively. 'Voodoo.'

'Don't be so quick to mock it,' said Otille. 'You're about to build the *veve* of Ogoun Badagris out of three tons of copper. That sounds like voodoo to me.'

'It's quite possible,' said Jocundra, angry at Otille's know-it-all manner, 'that the *veve* is an analogue to some mechanism in the brain and can therefore be used by mediums as a concentrative device, one which Donnell – because of his abilities – can use in a more material way.'

'Well,' Otille began, but Jocundra talked through her.

'If you're a devotee of voodoo, then you certainly know that it's a very social religion. People bring their day to day problems to the temple, their financial difficulties, lovers' quarrels. It's only reasonable to assume they're receiving some benefit, something more than a placebo of hope, that there are valid psychological and even physiological principles embedded in the rituals.'

'Oh, my,' said Otille, rolling her eyes. 'I'd forgotten we were keeping company with an academic. Let me tell you a story, dear. There was a man in Warner's Parish, a black man, who was on the parish council and who believed in voodoo, and his colleagues put pressure on him to disavow his beliefs publicly. It was an embarrassment to them, and they weren't too happy about having a black on the council in any case. They threatened to block his re-election. Well, the man thought it was important to have a black on the council, and he made the disavowal. But that same night hundreds of men and women came into town all possessed by Papa Legba, who was the man's patron *loa*. They were all dressed up as Legba, with moss for gray hair, canes, tattered coats and pipes, and they went to the man's house and demanded he give them money. It was a mob of stiff-legged, entranced people, all calling out for money, and finally he gave it to them and they left. He said he'd done it to make them go away, which is true no matter how you interpret the story. The people of the parish put it off to a bunch of crazy backwoods niggers getting excited about nothing, but as a result the man kept his post and satisfied his god. And of course it hasn't happened since. Why should it? The necessary had been accomplished. That's the way *Les Invisibles* work. Singular, unquantifiable events. Impossible to treat statistically, define with theory.'

Otille smiled at Jocundra, and Jocundra thought of it as the smile of a poisoner, someone who has seen her victim sip.

'Hardly anyone notices,' said Otille.

Behind the house was a group of eight shotgun cabins, each having three rooms laid end to end, and here, said Otille, lived her 'friends.' Slatternly women peered out the windows and ducked away; slovenly men stood on the porches, scratched their bellies and spat. To the west of the cabins was a graveyard centered by a whitewashed crypt decorated with *rada* paintings – black figures holding bloody hearts, sailing in boats over seas of wavy blue lines – this being home to Valcours' seven coffins. And at the rear of the graveyard, through a thicket of myrtle, was the bayou, a grassy bank littered with beer cans and bottles, a creosote-tarred dock, and moored to it, a black sternwheeler: an enormous, grim birthday cake of a boat with gingerbread railings and a smokestack for a candle. It had originally belonged to Clothilde, Otille's grandmother.

'It was to have been her funeral barge,' said Otille. 'She had planned to have it sailed down the Gulf carrying her body and a party of friends. My father used to let us play on it, but then he found out that she had boobytrapped it in some way, a surprise for her friends. We never could find out how.'

Jocundra was beginning to think of Maravillosa as an evil theme park. First, the Black Castle studded all over with silvery arcana; then the Bacchanal of Lost Souls with a special appearance by the Grim Reaper; the Garden of Unholy Delights; the cabins, an evil Frontier-land where back porch demons drooled into their rum bottles and groped their slant-eyed floozies, leaving smoldering handprints on their haunches; and now this stygian riverboat which had the lumbering reality of a Mardi Gras float. Somewhere on the grounds, no doubt, they would find Uncle Death in a skeleton suit passing out tainted candy, black goat rides for the kiddies, robot beheadings. Perhaps, she thought, there had once been a real evil connected with the place, a real moment of brimstone and blood, but all she could currently discern were the workings of a pathetic irrationality: Otille's. Yet, though Maravillosa reeked of an impotent dissolution rather than evil, Otille the actress could bring the past to life. Leaning against the pilot house, her black hair the same shade as the boards, making it seem she was an exotic bloom drooping from them, she told them another story.

'Have you heard of Bayou Vert?' she asked.

Donnell perked up.

'They say it runs nearby. It's extraordinary that a place like this could create a myth of Heaven, even such a miserable one as the Swamp King's palace. Gray-haired swamp girls don't sound very attractive to me.' She let her eyes contact Jocundra's, her lips twitching upward. 'Clothilde wrote me a letter about Bayou Vert, or partially about it. Of course she died long before I was born, but she addressed it to her grandchild. The lawyer brought it to me when I was sixteen. She said she hoped I would be a girl because girls are so much more adept at pleasure than boys. They have, in her phrase, "more surfaces with which to touch the world." She instructed me in the use of … my surfaces, and confessed page after page of her misdeeds. Mutilations, murders, perversions.' Otille crossed to the railing and gazed out over the water. 'She said that she had fertilized the myth of Bayou Vert – it had been old even in Valcours' day – by spreading rumors of sightings, new tales of its wonders, tales about the Swamp King's black sternwheeler that conveyed the lucky souls to his palace. Then she poured barrels of green dye into the water, sending swirls of color down into the marshes, and waited. Almost every time, she said, some fool, a trapper, a fortune hunter, would come paddling up to the boat, and there he'd find Clothilde, naked, gray wig in place, the handmaiden of Paradise.' Otille ran her hand over the top of a piling and inspected the flecks of creosote adhering to her palm. 'They must have had a moment of glory on seeing her because they could never say anything. They just looked disbelieving. Happy. She'd make love with them until they slept, and they slept deeply, very, very deeply, because she gave them drugged liquor. And after they woke, too groggy yet to feel anything, she said they always had the most puzzled frowns when they looked down and saw what she had done with her knife.'

The clouds were breaking up, the sun appearing intermittently, and the beer cans on the bank winked bright and dulled, as if their batteries were running low.

'Come on,' said Otille sadly. 'There's lots more to see.'

CHAPTER 15

July 29–14 August 1987

Those first weeks at Maravillosa, Jocundra had time on her hands. She wandered the corridors, poking into the cartons and crates that were stacked everywhere, exploring the various rooms. The motif of ebony faces and limbs emerging from the walls was carried out all through the house, but in the downstairs rooms most of the faces had been painted over or disfigured, and it was common to see nylons fitted over a wooden leg, coffee cups hooked to fingers, a black palm holding a soiled condom. The furniture was wreckage. Footless sofas, stained mattresses, cushionless chairs, everything embedded in a litter of beer cans and wine bottles. And here Otille's 'friends' could be found at any hour of the day or night. Drinking, making love, arguing. Many of the arguments she overheard involved the virtues of religious cults and gurus; they were uninformed, usually degenerating into shoving matches, and their most frequent resolution was the use of sentences beginning with, 'Otille said …' It soon became clear that this interest in religion only mirrored Otille's interest, and that the 'friends' hoped by arguing to gain some tidbit of knowledge with which to intrigue her.

To pass the time further, Jocundra decided to put together an ethnography of the estate and went about securing an informant. Danní ('It's really Danielle, but there's so many Danielles who's actresses already, so I dropped the endin', you know, just said 'to 'elle with it,' kept the i and accented it. I think it sounds kinda perky, don't you?') was typical of the women. Pretty, though ill-kempt; blond and busty; accustomed to wearing designer T-shirts and jogging shorts; an aspiring actress in her mid-twenties. She had come to Maravillosa in hopes that Otille would 'do something' for her career. 'You see what she's done for Downey, don't you? I mean he's almost a star!' She identified the other 'friends' as gamblers in need of a stake, poets looking for a patroness, coke dealers with a plan, actors, singers, dancers, musicians and con artists. All young and good-looking, all experts on Otille's past and personality, all hopeful of having something done.

'But what do you do for her?' asked Jocundra one day. 'I understand you provide her with companionship, an audience, and she gives you room and board …'

'And actin' classes,' Danní interrupted. 'I wouldn't be here if it wasn't for the classes.'

'Yes, but knowing Otille, it seems she'd expect more for her money.'

'Sometimes she entertains,' said Danní, uncomfortable, 'and we help out.' When Jocundra pressed her, Danní became angry but finally said, 'We sleep with the bigwigs she brings out from New Orleans! Okay?' Ashamed, she refused to meet Jocundra's eyes. 'Look,' she said after a petulant silence. 'Otille's a terrific actress. Bein' taught by her, it's ... well, I'd sleep with the Devil himself for the chance. You learn so much just watchin' her! Here.' She affected a pose Jocundra recognized as a poor caricature of Otille. 'Baron!' she snapped. 'Bring Downey to me at once. If he's not here in ten minutes, I'm not going to be responsible!' She relaxed from the pose and grinned perkily. 'See?'

The hierarchy of the pets was, according to Danní, the main subject of study among the 'friends'; they spent most of their energy trying to associate themselves with whomever they believed was in the ascendancy. Going to bed with Otille's favorite was the next best thing to going to bed with Otille herself: a rare coup for a 'friend,' so rare it had been elevated to the status of a myth. Clea was currently much in demand, and Papa, because of the reliability of his gift, was always ranked first or second. Simpkins was scarcely more than a 'friend' himself, and Downey, due to his star quality, could have his pick regardless of his status in Otille's eyes. Even Clea had a crush on him. And as for the Baron, he was apparently neither 'friend' nor pet and Danní was of the opinion that he had some sort of hold over Otille.

'I used to be Downey's girl,' said Danní one day while they were having coffee in Jocundra's room. 'I used to live right down the hall. Otille even invited me upstairs a couple of times. Boy, is that gorgeous! But then' – she made a clownishly sad face – 'she took a fancy to him again, and I got kicked back down to the cabins.' She sipped her coffee. 'That could be what happens to you pretty soon, at least the way I hear it.'

'I know Otille's after Donnell,' said Jocundra. 'But I doubt she'll succeed.'

'You'd better not doubt it,' said Danní, 'Men don't stand a chance with Otille. She'll have him doin' lickety-split before ...' She gave herself a penitential slap on the cheek. 'I'm sorry. I'm just used to dealin' with the others, and you're so nice and all. I shouldn't be talkin' to you like that.'

'I'm not offended,' said Jocundra. 'I admit I worry about it.' She sloshed the dregs of her coffee. 'We're in a difficult position with Otille.'

Danní took her hand and said it would probably be all right, that she understood.

Despite the difference in their backgrounds, Jocundra enjoyed Danní's company. Having a girlfriend made the wormy atmosphere of the house easier to bear, and Danní, too, seemed to enjoy the relationship, taking special pleasure in helping Jocundra search for clues to the estate's history among the crates and cartons. One morning, while digging through a dusty crate in a downstairs closet, they found an old book, a diary, embossed with the gilt letter A and bearing another gilt design on the foreleaf; this last, though wormtrailed beyond recognition, was obviously the remains of a *veve*.

'I bet that's, you know, what's his name ...' Danní banged the side of her head. 'Aime! Lucanor Aime. The one who taught ol' Valcours his tricks.'

The initial entry was dated 9 July 1847, and graphically described a sexual encounter with a woman named Miriam T, which sent Danní into fits of giggles. There followed a series of brief entries, essentially a list of appointments kept, saying that the initiate had arrived and been well received. Then Jocundra's eye was caught by the words *les Invisibles* midway down a page, and she went back and read the entire entry.

Sept. 19, 1847. Today I felt the need for solitude, for meditation, and to that end I closed the temple and betook myself to the levee, there spending the better part of the afternoon in contemplation of the calligraphy of eddies and ripples gliding past on the surface of the river. Yet for all my peaceful reverie, I could not arrive at a decision. Shortly before dark, I returned to the temple and found Valcours R waiting in the robing room ...

'Valcours!' breathed Danní. 'I don't know if we should be lookin' at this.' She shuddered prettily.

... his noxious pit bull at his feet, salivating on the carpet. Suddenly, my decision had been made. As I met Valcours' imperturbable stare, it seemed I was reading the truth of his spirit from his wrinkled brow and stonily set mouth. Though by all he is accounted a handsome man, at the moment his handsomeness appeared to have been remolded by some subtle and invisible agency, as by a mask of the clearest glass, into a fierce and hideous countenance, thus revealing a foul inner nature. Without a word of greeting, he asked for my decision.

'No,' I said. 'What you propose is the worst form of *petro*. I will not trifle with *les Invisibles*.'

He exhibited no surprise and merely pulled on his gloves, saying, 'Next Saturday I will bring three men to the temple. Together we will penetrate the mysteries.'

'Keep your damned mysteries to yourself!' I shouted.

'Sunday,' he repeated, smiling. Then he inclined his head in one of those effete bows I find so irritating and left me, his accursed dog at his heels.

It is in my mind now that I should work spells against him, though by doing so I would in effect be practicing *petro* of the sort he wishes me to practice.

And yet, it would be strictly in the service of the temple, and thus not a violation of my vows, only of my self-esteem. Be that as it may, there is an aura of significant evil about Valcours, such as I have not met with in all my experience, and it is time our association came to an end, one way or another.

Thereafter the diary continued in ordinary fashion, lists of appointments and more sex with Miriam T, until a third of the way through the volume, at which point the entries ceased.

Aime's account only posed new mysteries, and reading it had knotted Jocundra's muscles and set her temples to throbbing, as if it had contained the germ of an old disease. She begged off the rest of the morning, telling Danní she wanted to lie down a while, while Danní insisted on coming along and giving her a massage.

'There ain't nothin' like a massage for tension,' she said; she winked slyly. 'I learned all about it out in Hollywood.'

She accompanied Jocundra back to the room, had her remove her blouse and unhook her bra and lie flat on her stomach. At first the massage was relaxing. Danní straddled her, humming, rubbing out the tension with expert hands, but then she slipped a hand under to cup Jocundra's breast, kissed her shoulder and whispered how beautiful she was. Shocked, Jocundra rolled over, inadvertently knocking Danní off the bed.

'I thought you wanted me,' sobbed Danní, completely unstrung, her facial muscles working, tears glistening in her eyes. 'Don't you like me?'

Jocundra assured her she did, just not that way, but Danní was inconsolable and ran from the room.

Their relationship deteriorated swiftly. Jocundra tried to convince Danní to leave Maravillosa, pointing out that Otille had never given substantial help to any of the 'friends', and offered to lend her money; but Danní rejected the offer and told her she didn't understand. She began to avoid Jocundra, to whisper asides to her companions and giggle whenever Jocundra passed by, and a few days later she made an ineffectual play for Donnell. That, Jocundra realized, had been Danní's objective all along, and she had been foolish not to anticipate it. The pathos of the 'friends', of this talentless child-woman and her imitation of Otille, her Otille-like manipulations, caused Jocundra to wonder if she had not underestimated the evil influence of the place. Donnell was becoming moody and withdrawn again, as he had not been since leaving Shadows, refusing to talk about what transpired during the days; and one night toward the end of the second week, waiting for him to return, staring out of their bedroom window, she had a new appreciation of Maravillosa.

Screams, some of them desperate sounding, arose from the cabins. Torches flared in the dark thickets behind them. The half moon sailed high, sharp-winged shadows skimming across it, and the conical hills and the vine-shrouded trees washed silver-green under the moonlight had the look of a decaying city millennia after a great catastrophe.

Morning sunlight shafted from the second-story windows, the rays separate and distinct, leaving the lower half of the ballroom sunk in a cathedral dimness, but revealing the wallpaper to be peeling and covered with graffiti. Crudely painted red and green *veves*, including that of Ogoun Badagris, occupied central positions among the limericks and sexual advertisements. Otille held her acting classes in the ballroom, and wooden chairs were scattered throughout, though only five were now taken, those by Otille, Donnell, and the rest of the pets. Except for Otille and Donnell, they sat apart, ringed about Clea, who was hunched over a chewed-up yellow guitar, looking pale and miserable. Without her wig, she lacked even the pretense of vivacity. She wore a slip which showed her breasts to be the size of onions, and passing her in the door, Donnell had caught a faint rancid odor that reminded him of spoiled milk. Around her feet were half a dozen cages filled with parakeets and lovebirds.

'What are you going to play for us, dear?' Otille's voice rang in the emptiness.

'I ain't ready yet,' said Clea, pouting.

Simpkins sat with folded arms; Papa leaned forward, his hands clasped between his knees, affecting intense interest; and Downey sprawled in his chair, bored. The birds hopped and twittered.

'Allrighty,' said Clea bravely. 'Here goes nothin.''

She plucked a chord, humming to get the pitch, and raised a quavering soprano, souring on the high notes.

> 'Beauty, where have you fled tonight,
> In whose avid arms do you conspire …'

'Aw, God!' said Downey, banging his heels on the floor. 'Not that. Sing somebody else's song!'

'I wanta sing this,' said Clea, glowering at him.

'Let her alone, Downey,' said Otille with maternal patience. She put her hand on Donnell's arm. 'Downey wrote the song when he thought he was in love with me, but then he entered his narcissistic period and he's ashamed to have written anything so unabashedly romantic.' She turned again to Clea. 'Go ahead, dear.'

'We're behind you, sister,' said Papa. 'Don't be bashful.'

Donnell wondered if anyone could possibly buy Papa's cheerleading act. His face was brimful of bad wishes, and by course of logic alone it was obvious that Clea's failure would improve his lot. She lifted her reedy voice again, and it seemed to Donnell to be the voice of Maravillosa, the sad, common sound of the dead trees and the 'friends' and the ebony faces, of Otille herself, of the sullen and envious relationships between the pets, the whine of a supernatural nervous system which governed them all. Even if no one were there to hear it, he thought, the sound would go on, arising from the wreckage of evil. A futile transmission like the buzz of a half-crushed wasp.

Clea faltered, a high note shrilled. 'I can't sing when he's grinnin' at me,' she said, gesturing at Downey. 'He's makin' me too nervous.'

'Oh, hell!' said Downey. 'Lemme help her.' He stalked over and took the guitar from her.

'If it won't interfere,' said Otille. 'Will it interfere?'

Clea could not hide her delight. She blushed, casting a furtive glance at Downey. 'Maybe not,' she said.

He pulled up a chair beside her, picked a fancy introduction of chords, and this time the song had the courtly feel of a duet between a country girl and a strolling balladeer.

> '... Beauty is everywhere, they say,
> But I can't find a beauty like thine.
> Beauty, I love you so much more
> Than I do truth, which only lasts for a moment,
> While you live forever,
> Eternal and fleeting,
> And without you no truth
> Has any meaning...'

Some of the birds were fluttering up in their cages, chirping, agitated; others perched on the bars, trilling, throats pulsing in a transport of song. Donnell felt Otille tense beside him, and he focused on Clea. Her magnetic field was undifferentiated by arcs, a nimbus of white light encompassing her and Downey and sections of all the cages. Through the glow, she looked like an enraptured saint at prayer with her accompanying angel. The face of her *gros bon ange* was ecstatic, a mosaic of cobalt interlaced by fine gold threads. Nearing its end, the song grew more impassioned and the white glow spread to surround the cages and every one of the birds was singing.

> '... Beauty, you've come only once to me,
> And now you've gone, you seem so rare and inviting,
> A chalcedon lady,
> Gold glints in your dark eyes,
> Admitting no imperfections,
> Miraculous diamonds

*Clasped round your slim throat,
Where the pulse beats in the hollow
And the blue veins are showing
Their cryptic pattern
Leading to somewhere,
An infinite gleaming
Trapped here forever
Here in my song,
Pure paragon.'*

Otille was disappointed at song's end. She praised Clea's effort, acknowledged the result, but her displeasure was evident.

'Lemme have a crack at them birds, Otille,' said Papa. He popped his knuckles, eager to get started.

'We all know what you can do, Papa,' said Otille. 'It will prove nothing to see it again. I was hoping for something more … more out of the ordinary.'

Clea hung her head. Downey picked out a brittle run of blue notes, uninvolved.

'It's obviously a matter of mood,' said Simpkins. 'When poor Pavarotti was struck down, I recall Sister Clea as bein' in a snit, whereas today, makin' music with her heart's desire …'

'He's not!' squawked Clea; she leapt up and pointed at him, fuming. 'Lessee what you can do with 'em! Nothin', I bet!'

Downey smiled, strummed a ripple of chords.

'If I begin to tweet,' said Simpkins, 'then indeed we have a proof positive of Sister Clea's talent. But frankly I'm more interested in seein' what Brother Harrison can achieve with our feathered friends.'

Otille pursed her lips and tapped them with an ivory finger. She cocked one eye towards Donnell. 'Would you mind?' she asked.

Donnell stretched out his legs and folded his arms in imitation of Simpkins, returning his bland smile. Simpkins was obviously a force to be reckoned with, despite his failed gift, and Donnell did not want to establish the precedent of following his orders by proxy. 'I'll pass,' he said. 'I didn't come here to kill birds.'

'You don't have to *kill* them,' said Otille, as if that were the furthest thing from her mind. 'I'm much more interested in the variety of psychic powers than their repetition. Why don't you just see what you can do. Experiment. I won't hold it against you if nothing happens.'

But you will if I don't try, thought Donnell. 'All right,' he said. He took Clea's place in the midst of the cages, and she and Downey settled into chairs.

The birds appeared none the worse for wear, bright-eyed and chirping, swinging on their perches. Their plumage was beautiful – pastel blues and pinks, snowy white, bottle greens – and their magnetic fields were hazy glimmers in the air, easy to influence at a distance like the fields of telephones and cameras. He found if he reached out his hand to a cage, the birds within it stilled, quieted, and their fields glowed. But he could produce no other effect. The two cages closest to him contained nine birds, and by spreading his fingers magician style he managed to still all nine controlling each with one of his fingers, feeling the tug of the fields. He doubted, though, that this would satisfy Otille. Then following Otille's advice – 'Experiment' – and wondering why it had never occurred to him to try before, he maintained his hold on the fields and shifted his focus into the darkness of the *gros bon ange*.

Bits of whirling blackness and jeweled fire hung in the silver cages. Tentatively, he pushed a forefinger against one of the fields, stroking it, and a thread of iridescent light no thicker than a spiderweb shot from his fingertip. He withdrew the finger, startled; but since the bird displayed no ill effects, its fires undimmed, he tried it again. Eventually nine threads of light connected his fingertips with the nine birds, and the refractions inside their bodies flowed in orderly patterns. The pressure of their fields against his hands increased, and when he involuntarily crooked a finger, one of the birds hopped down off its perch. He repeated the process, and soon, feeling omnipotent, the ringmaster of the magical circus, he had gained enough control to send them marching about the cages. Tiny jewelbox creatures hopping onto silvery feeders and swings, twittering and parading around and around.

Clea gasped, someone knocked over a chair, and someone else contributed slow, ironic applause. 'Thank you, Donnell,' said Otille. 'That's quite sufficient.'

He relaxed his control, brought the ballroom back into view and saw Otille smiling at him. 'Well,' he said, stung by the pride of ownership in her face, 'was that out of the ordinary enough?' Then he glanced down at the cages.

He had not killed the birds. Not outright. That would have been merciful compared to what he had done. The delicate hues of their feathers were dappled with blood, and freed from his control, their cries had grown piercing, stirring echoes in the sunlit upper reaches of the room. Their beaks were shattered, crimson droplets welling from the cracks; their wings and legs were broken; and the membranes of their eyes had burst and were dripping fluid. All lay flapping on the floors of the cages except for a parakeet, its legs unbroken, which clung to its perch and screamed.

'Papa,' said Otille. 'Will you and Downey take the undamaged ones to my office?'

Downey was frozen, grim-faced; Clea buried her head in his shoulder. Papa hesitated, eyeing Donnell nervously.

Three, no, four of the birds had quit fluttering, and Donnell sat watching them die, stunned.

'Simpkins,' said Otille. 'Take the others out to my car.'

'Yes, ma'am,' said Simpkins. He came over to the cages, and as he bent down, he whispered, 'Poor Dularde never knew what hit him, did he, brother?'

Sick of his snide comments, his contemptuous air, Donnell jumped up and swung, but Simpkins easily caught his wrist and with his other hand seized Donnell's throat, his fingers digging in the back of the Adam's apple. 'I ain't no goddamn parakeet, brother,' he said. He tightened his grip, and Donnell's mouth sprang open.

'Simpkins!' Otille clapped her hands.

'Yes, ma'am.' Simpkins released Donnell and hoisted the cages, once again bland and smiling.

Donnell headed for the door, holding his throat.

'Where are you going?' called Otille.

He didn't answer, intent on finding Jocundra, on washing away the scum of Otille and her pets. But he turned back at the door, waylaid by a thought. Why, while he was killing the birds, had their ... their what? Make it their souls. Why not? Why had they showed no sign of injury? He stared at the bloody heaps of feathers, blinking and straining until the cages gleamed silver. They were empty. Then movement caught his eye. Up above Simpkins' head rising and falling and jittering like jeweled sparks in a wind, the souls of the slain birds were flying.

Near the end of the second week, Jocundra ran into the Baron in the hall outside his room. He was adjusting his doorknob with a screwdriver, muttering, twisting the knob. He had never said a word to her, and she had intended to pass without greeting, but he called out to her and asked to borrow her for a few seconds.

'You just stand there,' he commanded. 'Give that doorknob a twist to the right when I tell you, then step inside quick.'

He went into the room and began prying with the screwdriver at a narrow ceiling board. 'Someone,' he said, grunting, digging at the board, 'someone been sneakin' round, so I'm rigging myself a little security.' He was wearing jeans and a ripped New Orleans Saints jersey, and his arm muscles bunched and rippled like snakes. His eyes, though, had a liverish tinge. She had presumed him to be in his forties, but now she reckoned him a well-preserved sixty.

He put down the screwdriver and held up his hands beneath the board. 'Do it,' he said.

She twisted the knob. The hallway door slammed shut, almost striking her as she stepped inside, and a second door dropped from the ceiling and would have sealed off the alcove if the Baron had not caught it. He staggered under the weight. 'Sucker must weigh a hunnerd, hunnerd and fifty pounds,' he said.

He noticed Jocundra's bewilderment. 'All the rooms like that. Ol' Valcours he liked to trap folks.' He chuckled. 'And then he give 'em a hard time.' He pushed the door back into place until it clicked, then he stared at her in unfriendly fashion. 'Don't you recognize me, woman?' She looked at him, puzzled, and he said, 'Sheeit! Mama Zito's Temple down on Prideaux Street. I was the damn fool used to stand out front and drag folks in for the service.'

'Foster,' she said. 'Is that right?' She remembered him as a hostile, arrogant man who had drunk too much; he had refused to be her informant.

'Yeah, Foster.' He picked up his screwdriver. ' 'Cept make it Baron, now. That damn Foster name never done me no good.' He stepped around her, opened the hallway door, and twisted the knob to the left until it clicked twice. 'You ever get to Africa?' he asked.

'No,' she said. 'I quit school.'

'Yeah, well, I figured you didn't make it, seein' how you hangin' with that green-eyed monkey.' He registered her frown. 'Hey, I got nothin' against the monkey. It's just that since he come the boy have put a charge into Otille, and that ain't good.'

'What's your relationship with Otille?'

'You writin' another paper?'

'I'm just curious.'

'That's good,' he said. 'You keep an edge on your curious, 'cause this one damn curious place. Huh! Curious.' He walked over to his drawer and took out a shirt. 'I'm Otille's friend. Not like one of them raggedy fuckers down at the cabins. I'm her *friend*. And she's mine. That's why she take to callin' me Baron after the death god, 'cause she say can't nobody but death be a friend to her. 'Course that's just the actress in her comin' out.' He stripped off the jersey and shrugged into the shirt; a jagged scar crossed his right chest, and the muscles there were somewhat withered. 'She don't make me do no evil, and I don't preach to her. We help each other out. Like right now.' He brandished a fist. 'I'm watchin' over you and the monkey.'

'Why?'

'You think Otille's mean, don't you? Sheeit! She got her moods, ain't no doubt. But there's folks 'round here will cut you for a nickel, squeeze you for a dime. Take that smiley son of a bitch Simpkins ...'

'Baron!' Otille stood in the door, her face convulsing.

The Baron calmly went on buttoning his shirt. 'I be down in a minute.'

'Have you seen Donnell?' asked Jocundra, hoping the question would explain her presence to Otille.

Otille ignored her. 'Bring the car around,' she said to the Baron.

'Nothin' to get excited 'bout, Otille,' he said. 'Woman's just helpin' me fix my door.' When she remained mute, he sighed, slung his coat over his shoulder and strode out.

'I don't want you talking to him,' said Otille in measured tones. 'Is that clear?'

'Fine.' Jocundra started for the door, but Otille blocked the way. Her temples throbbed, nerves jumped in her cheek, her coral mouth thinned. Only her eyes were unmoving, seeming to recede into black depths beneath her milky complexion, like holes cut in a bedsheet. It amazed Jocundra that when she next spoke, her voice was under control and not a scream.

'Would you like to leave Maravillosa?' she asked. 'I can have you driven anywhere you wish.'

'Yes,' said Jocundra. 'But if I left, Donnell would go with me, and even if he stayed, then I'd stay because I'd be afraid you'd hurt him.'

'Bitch!' Otille lashed out at the wall with the side of her fist. 'I'm not going to hurt him!' She glanced at the wall and saw that her fist had impacted the forehead of a screaming ebony face, and she laid her palm against it as if easing its pain. 'I'm going to *have* him,' she said mildly. 'Do you like this room?'

'I don't think so,' said Jocundra, enunciating the words with precision, implying a response to both Otille's remarks.

'It takes so much time and energy to keep the place up,' said Otille, blithe and breezy. 'I've let it run down, but I've tried to maintain islands of elegance within it. Would you care to see one?' And before Jocundra could answer, she swirled out of the door, urging her to follow. 'It's just down the hall,' she said. 'My father's old room.'

It was, indeed, elegant. Gobelin tapestries of unicorns and hunts, dozens of original paintings. Klee, Kandinsky, Magritte, Braque, Miró. The black wood of the walls showed between them like veins of coal running through a surreal bedrock. Comfortable sofas and chairs, an antique globe, a magnificent Shiraz carpet. But opposed to this display of good taste, arranged in cabinets and on tables, was a collection of cheap bric-a-brac like that found in airport gift shops and tourist bazaars: mementos of exotic cultures bearing the acultural stamp of sterility most often approved by national chambers of commerce. There were ashtrays, enameled key rings, coin purses, models of famous landmarks, but the bulk of the collection was devoted to mechanical animals. Pandas, monkeys, an elephant which lifted tiny logs, a snake coiling up a plastic palm, on and on. A miniature invasion creeping over the bookshelves and end tables. The collection, said Otille, represented her father's travels on behalf of the Rigaud Foundation and his various charities, and reflected his pack rat's obsession with things bright and trivial.

The room appeared to have calmed Otille. She chatted away as if Jocundra were an old school friend, describing family evenings when her father and she would set all the toy animals in operation and send them bashing into one another. But Jocundra found this wholesale change in mood more alarming than her rage, and in addition, she was beginning to make eerie connections between the generations of Rigauds. Valcours with his anthropomorphic toys, Otille's father's animals, Otille's pets and 'friends.' God only knew what Clothilde had collected. It was easy to see how one could think of the family as a single terrible creature stretching back through time, some genetic flaw or chemical magic binding the spirit to the blood.

'I'm afraid I have a luncheon in New Orleans,' Otille said, ushering Jocundra out. 'Foundation business. But we can talk more another time.' She locked the door behind them and headed down the hall. 'If I see Donnell on my way to the car,' she called back, 'I'll send him along.'

It was said with such unaffected sincerity that for the moment Jocundra did not doubt her.

'An attic's the afterlife of a house,' said Otille, opening the door, 'Or so my mother used to say.'

The air inside was sweetly scented and cool. She stepped aside to let him pass, and as he did, her hip brushed his hand, a silky pass like a cat fitting itself to your palm. She shut the door, and he heard the lock engage. The gable windows were shuttered, the room pitch dark, and when she walked off, he lost sight of her.

'Turn on the light!'

'Why don't you find me like you did Dularde?'

'You might fall.'

She gave a frosty little laugh. Boards creaked.

'Damn it, Otille!'

'Take off your glasses, and I'll turn on the light.'

Christ! He folded the glasses and put them in his pocket. He imagined he could hear her breathing, but realized it was his own breath whining through clogged sinuses.

'What the hell do you want to show me?' he asked.

'You'll have to come to the window,' she said softly.

A rattling to his left made him jump. Metal shutters lifted from the row of gables, strips of silver radiance widening to chutes of dust-hung moonlight spilling into a long, narrow room, so long its far reach was lost in shadow. It must, he thought, run the length of the rear wing. The rattling subsided, and seven windows ranged the darkness, portals opened onto a universe of frozen light. Bales, bundles, and sheet-draped mysteries lined the walls. And then Otille, who had slipped out of her clothing, stepped from the shadows and went to stand by the nearest window. Her reappearance had the quality of illusion, as if she were an image projected by the rays of moonlight. Her skin glowed palely, and the curls of black hair falling onto her shoulder, her pubic triangle, these seemed absent places in her flesh.

'Don't look so dumfounded,' she said, beckoning.

From the window, Donnell saw white flickering lights beyond the conical hills. Welder's arcs, Otille explained. The copper had arrived, and the night shift had begun at once. The peak of the gable cramped them together, and in the course of talking and pointing, her breast nudged his arm. He couldn't help stealing glances at her, at the lapidary fineness of her muscles, the way the moonlight shaded her nipples to lavender, and whenever she looked at him, he felt that something was pouring out of her, that dampers had been withdrawn and her inner core exposed, irradiating him. Though he had steeled himself against her, his body reacted and his thoughts became confused. He wanted to turn and go back downstairs to Jocundra, but he also wanted to touch the curve of Otille's belly and feel the bubble of heat it held. Her black eyes swam with lights, her sulky mouth was drawing him toward her, and he lost track of what she was saying, something about his having validated her beliefs.

'Come along,' she said, taking his hand. 'I'll show you my room. It used to be Clothilde's, but I've had it repaneled and decorated after my own tastes.'

At midpoint of the attic three doors were set into the wall, the central one leading along a short passage to yet another door, and beyond this lay a cavernous room hung with shafts of moonlight. The ceiling was carved to resemble a weave of black branches, leaf sprays, dripping moss; and the light penetrated through the glassed-over interstices. Trunks bulged from the walls, their bark patterns rendered precisely; ebony saplings and bushes – perfect to the detailing of the veins on the leaves – sprouted from the floor, and at the center of the room was a carpeted depression strewn with pillows and having the effect of a still, sable eye at the heart of a whirlpool. A control console was mounted in its side, switches and an intercom, and after pulling him down to sit beside her, Otille flicked one of the switches. Colored filters slid across the rents in the carved canopy, and the beams of moonlight empurpled. Donnell lay back against the pillows, watching her rapt face as she unbuttoned his shirt, and when she bent down to kiss his chest, he shivered. It was as if a pale beast the shape of Otille had dipped her muzzle into him and fed.

Her hips rolled beneath him in practised shudders, her fingers traced the circuits of his nerves, yet her love-making was so adept, so athletic, passion reduced to ornate calisthenics, that the spell she had cast upon him was broken and his interest flagged. Still, like a good pet, he performed, pretending it was Jocundra touching him. And then, because he thought it would be appropriate to the mood, he took his first look at Otille's *gros bon ange*.

If one of her clever movements had not renewed his passionate reflex, he would have thrown himself off her in revulsion. The pile of the carpet resolved into a myriad of silver pinpricks against which her head was silhouetted like a coalsack; but instantly sparks of jeweled light rushed up from the area of her hips, defining the lines of her breasts and ribs as they flowed, and fitting a bestial mask to her face. It was a thing in a constant state of dissolution composed of emerald, azure, gold and ruby glints that coalesced into patches of mineral brilliance, decayed, and melted into new encrusted forms. Black rips for eyes, fangs of gemmy light. It roared silently at him, its mouth twisting open and gnashing shut. Yet each time their hips ground together, the mask wavered, loosing stray sparks downward, as if his thrusts were inducing its animating stuff to join in. He thrust harder, and the entire structure of the mask dissipated for a split second, fiery wax running from a mold. He felt a desolate glee in knowing he could overwhelm this monstrosity, and he turned all his energies to dismantling the mask, battering at Otille, who moaned beneath him. Whenever he let up, the mask's expression grew more feral, but at last it melted away, flowing back into her groin. Looking down to where their bellies merged, he saw an iridescent slick like a film of oil sliding between them.

Afterward he lay quietly, collecting himself, angry at his submission to her, still revolted by the aspect of her *gros bon ange*, her soul, whatever it had been. Finally he began putting on his clothes.

'Stay a while,' she said lazily.

'One bite is all you get, Otille. It won't happen again.'

'It will if I want it to.'

'You don't get the picture,' he said. He started lacing his shoes. 'Out there in the attic it was like the shuffling rube and the scarlet woman. But when it came down to strokes, your little tour of hardcore heaven bored the hell out of me.'

'You bastard!'

'What did you expect?' He unfolded his sunglasses. 'That one of your Blue Plate Special humdingers would make me profess undying love?'

'Love!' Otille spat on the carpet. 'Keep your love for that dimwitted Bobbie Brooks doll you've got downstairs!'

The intercom buzzed, and she smashed down a switch. 'What is it?' she snapped.

'Uh, Otille?' It was Papa.

'Yes.'

'Uh, the hospital called. Dularde didn't make it. I thought I should tell you.'

'Then make the arrangements! You don't need me for that.'

'Well, all right. But I was wonderin' could I come up?'

She cut him off.

'I want you to stay,' she said firmly to Donnell.

'Listen, damn it! We have a deal, and I'll keep my end of it. But if you want hot fun, buy a waterbed and stake yourself out in a cheap motel. I'll write your name in all the men's rooms. For a good time, see Otille. She's mean, she's clean, she can do the Temple Hussy's Contraction!'

She tried to slap him, but he blocked her arm and pushed her away. He stood. The lavender beams of moonlight were as sharp as lasers, and for the first time he recognized the room's similarity to the setting of his stories.

'What is this place?' he asked, his anger eroded by a sudden apprehension. 'I wrote a story about a place like this.'

She appeared dazed, rubbing her forearm where he had blocked it. 'Just a dream I had,' she said. 'Leave me alone.' Her eyes were wide and empty.

'My pleasure,' he said. 'Thanks for the exercise.'

The door at the end of the passage was stuck, no, locked, and the door into Otille's room, which had closed behind him, was also locked. He jiggled the knob. 'Otille!' he shouted. A chill weight gathered in the pit of his stomach.

'Clothilde called this the Replaceable Room.' Her voice came from a speaker over the door. 'It's really more than twenty rooms. Most are stored beneath the house until they're shunted onto the elevator. Every one of them's full of Clothilde's guests.'

The room was hot and stuffy. He wrenched at the doorknob. 'Otille! Can you hear me?'

'Clothilde used to switch the rooms while her lovers slept and challenge them to find the right door. Back then the machinery was as quiet as silk running through your hand.'

'Otille!' He pried at the door with his fingertips.

'But now it's old and creaky,' she said brightly. A grating vibrated the walls, and a whining issued from ducts along the edge of the ceiling. The room was moving downward. 'I'm not sure how long it takes for the pumps to empty the room of air, but it's not very long. I hope there's time.'

'What do you want?' he yelled, kicking at the door. His chest was constricting, he was getting dizzy. The room stopped, jolting sideways.

'You're under the house now,' sang Otille. 'Push the button beside the door. I want you to see something. Hurry!'

Donnell located the button, pushed it, and a section of the wall inched back, revealing a large window opening onto a metal wall set nearly flush with it. He pulled off his shoe and hammered at the glass, but it held and he collapsed, gasping. The metal wall slid back to reveal a window like his own, and behind it, their desiccated limbs posed in conversational attitudes, were a man and a woman. Black sticks of tongues protruding from their mouths, eyelashes like crude stitches sewing their lids fast to their cheeks. Rings hung loosely on their fingers, and they were much shrunken inside antiquated satin rags, the remnants of fancy dress. Donnell sucked at the thinning air, scrabbling back from the window. There was a metallic taste in his throat, his chest weighed a ton, and blackness frittered at the edges of his vision. Otille's voice was booming nonsense about 'Clothilde' and 'parties' and 'guests,' warping the words into mush. The thought of dying was a bubble slowly inflating in his brain, squeezing out the other thoughts, and soon it was going to pop. Very soon. Then he had a sharp sense of Jocundra standing beneath and to the right of him, looking around, walking away. He could feel her, could visualize her depressed walk, as if there were only a thin film between them. God, he thought, what'll happen to her. And that thought was almost as big and important as the one of death. But not quite. Otille's voice had become part of a general roaring, and it seemed the corpses were laughing and pointing at him. Bits of rotten lace flaked from the man's cuff as his hand shook with laughter. The woman's mummified chest heaved like the pulsing of a bat's throat, a thin membrane plumping full of air. The room vibrated with the exact rhythm of the laughter, and the air was glowing bright red.

Then he could breathe.

Sweet, musty air.

He gulped it in, gorging on it. The door to the attic had sprung open. His head spinning, he crawled toward the light of a gable window and slipped; a splinter drove deep into the heel of his palm. He rolled onto his back, applying pressure to the point of entry, almost grateful for the sensation. Blood and gray dust mired on his hand.

'I'm sorry, Donnell,' said Otille's voice from the speaker. 'I couldn't let you leave thinking you'd won. But don't worry. I still want you.'

CHAPTER 16

August 17, 1987

On the morning of Dularde's funeral, Donnell told Jocundra he had slept with Otille. He was contrite; he explained what had happened and why and said it had been awful, and swore there would be no repetition. Jocundra, who had tried to prepare for this turn of events, believed he was truly contrite, that it had been a matter of circumstance allied with Otille's charm, but despite her rational acceptance, she was hurt and angry.

'It's this place,' she said mournfully, staring back at the angelic faces sinking into the black quicksand of their bedroom walls. 'It twists everything.'

'I can't leave ...' he began.

'Why should you? You're the king of Maravillosa! Otille's prince consort!'

'You seem to think everything's fucking normal,' he said. 'That I'm a guy and you're a girl, and we're stuck in this little unpleasantness, but soon we'll be off to some paradisiacal subdivision. Three kids with sunglasses, a green-eyed dog, the *veve* in the back yard next to the barbecue. I'm walking a goddamn tightrope with Otille!'

'Is that what they're calling it now?' she sneered. 'Walking a tightrope? Or is that Otille's erotic specialty?'

'Maybe Edman's right,' he said. 'Maybe you groomed me to be your soulmate. A sappy, morose cripple! Maybe you wanted someone to pity and control, and I'm not pitiable enough anymore.'

'Oh, no?' She laughed. 'Now that you've risen to the status of pet, I'm supposed to be in awe? I watch you swallow every treat she feeds you ...' Tears were starting to come. 'Oh, hell!' she said, and ran out of the door, down the stairs and onto the grounds.

The sunlight leached the wild vegetation of color and acted to parch her tears. She found a flat stone beside the driveway and sat down, watching flies drone in a clump of weeds. The undersides of their leaves were coated with yellow dust. It hadn't rained in a couple of weeks, and everything was shriveling. She felt numb, guilty. He was in enough difficulty; he didn't deserve her insults. A butterfly settled on her knee. *If a butterfly lights on your shoulders, you'll be lucky for a year*, she remembered. Her father had been full of such bayou wisdoms. *Nine leaves on a sprig of lavender brings money luck. Catch a raindrop in your pocket and it'll turn to silver.* As he had grown older, he had stopped quoting the optimistic ones and taken to scribbling darker sayings on scraps of paper. During her last visit home she had seen them scattered about the house like spent fortunes, tucked between the pages of books, crumpled and flung on the floor, and a final one slipped under the door just before she had left. *Those who love laughter pay court to disaster*, it had read. *Prayers said in the dark are said to the Devil.*

Clouds swept overhead, obscuring the sun and passing off so that the light brightened and faded with the rhythm of laboured breathing. Donnell came out of the house and headed toward the graveyard. Jocundra stood and was about to call his name, but a girl, one of the 'friends,' ran down the steps and fell in beside him. *Green eyes in a woman means passion, bitterness in a man*, Jocundra remembered, staring after Donnell's retreating figure. *One who has not seen his mother will be able to cure.*

There were six coffins in the crypt, walled off behind stone and mortar, all containing a portion of Valcours Rigaud's remains; there was space for a seventh, but Otille said it was buried elsewhere on the grounds. She lit a candle and set it into an iron wall mount. The yellow light turned her skin to old ivory, licked up the walls, and illuminated a carved device above each of the burial niches. Donnell recognized the design to be a *veve*, though he had only seen a crude version of it drawn on the back of Jack Richmond's guitar: a stylized three-horned man. The sight of it waked something inside him to a fury. His fists clenched; his mind was flocked with violent urges, shadowy recognitions, images and scenes that flashed past too quickly for recall. He had such a strong sense of being possessed, of being operated by some alienated fragment of his personality. For a long moment he could do nothing but stand and strain against the impulse to tear at the stones with his bare hands, smash the coffins, crush the rags and splinters of Valcours into an unreconstructable dust. At last the sensation left him, and he asked Otille what the design was.

'The *veve* of Mounanchou,' she said. 'Valcours' patron god. And Clothilde's. A nasty sort. The god of gangsters and secret societies.'

'Then why not use *it* on your calling card?' he asked, still angry. 'It seems more appropriate.'

'I've rejected Mounanchou,' said Otille, unflappable. 'Just as I've rejected Clothilde and Valcours. Ogoun Badagris was the patron of ... a family friend. A good man. So I adopted it.' She brushed against him, and her touch had the feel of something roused from the dry air and darkness. 'Why did you look so peculiar when you saw it?'

'I felt the bacteria moving around,' he said. 'It made me a little dizzy.'

Otille went to the door. 'Baron,' she called. 'Would you bring my parasol from my office. I don't want to burn.'

Beyond the door, beyond rows of tombstones tilted at rustic angles, was the raw mound of earth covering Dularde's coffin. A group of 'friends' was in line beside the grave, laughing and chattering; more were straggling toward the line along the path leading from the cabins. Simpkins stood atop the grave, a box of syringes and medicine bottles at his feet. As each of the 'friends' joined him on the mounded earth, he would tie off their arms with a rubber tube and give them an injection. Then they would stagger away, weaving, and collapse among the weeds to vomit and twitch, their arms waving feebly, like poisoned ants crawling from their nest to die. It was, thought Donnell, an ideal representation of the overall process of Maravillosa: these healthy, attractive men and women bumping together in line, playfully smacking one another, being changed into derelicts by the cadaverous Simpkins and his magic fluid. He appeared to be enjoying his work, spanking the newly injected on the rumps to get them moving again, beaming at the next in line and saying, 'This one's on Brother Dularde.' Someone switched on a radio, and a blast of rock and roll static defiled the air.

Donnell stepped out of the crypt, squinting against the sun. Just above his head, surmounting the door, was a whitewashed angel with black tears painted on its cheeks, and he could relate to its languishing expression. Clea, Papa and Downey had not yet arrived, and their absence meant he had to put up with Otille nonstop. He peered down the path, hoping to see them. A man and a woman were walking toward the graveyard, dressed – he assumed at first – in gaudy uniforms of some sort. But as they neared, he realized the uniforms were a satin gown and a brocade jacket, and he saw that their faces were brown and mummified, the faces of the corpses identical to those he had seen in the Replaceable Room. He wheeled about on Otille. She was smiling.

'Just a reminder,' she said.

He looked back at the corpses; they were holding hands, now, skipping along the path, and he wondered if there really had been corpses in the Replaceable Room, or if there had only been these counterfeits. He turned back to Otille.

'I don't need a reminder of what a bitch you are,' he said.

He had expected she would flare up at him, but she drew back in fright as if the sound of his voice had menaced her.

'What's the problem, Otille?' he asked, delighting in her reaction. 'I thought you still wanted me.'

At this, she whirled around and walked hurriedly off toward the house.

'Bitch!' he yelled, venting his rage. 'I'd rather shack up with barnyard animals than make it with you again!'

The people by the grave were staring at him; some were edging back. Still boiling with anger, he gestured at them in disgust and stormed off along one of the paths leading away from the house. He continued to fume as he walked, knocking branches aside, kicking beer cans and bottles out of his way. The thicket was festooned with litter. Charred mattresses, ripped underwear, food wrappers. Scraps of cellophane clung to the twigs, so profuse in places they seemed floral productions of the shrubs. His anger subsided, and he began to worry about his loss of control, not only its possible repercussions, but its relevance to his stability. He had been losing his temper more and more frequently since arriving at Maravillosa, and he did not think it was solely due to Otille's aggravation. Certainly she was not responsible for the feeling of possession. The path jogged to the right, widened, and he saw the sternwheeler between the last of the bushes. Against the glittering water and bright blue sky, it had the unreal look of a superimposed image, a black stage flat propped up from behind. Something snapped in back of him.

'Mornin', brother,' said Simpkins.

Donnell looked around for an escape route, knowing himself in danger, but there was none.

'You just don't understand how to handle Otille,' Simpkins said, advancing on him. 'She's like a fisherman who's been havin' a good day, got herself a string of big cats coolin' in the stream. Every once in a while she hauls one up and thinks about fryin' him. And that's your situation, brother. Just floppin' on the dock.'

Donnell started back up the path, but Simpkins put out a restraining hand.

'You gotta just hang there and let the water flow through your gills,' said Simpkins. 'You struggle too much and you bound to catch her eye.'

'What do you want?' asked Donnell.

'A little talk,' said Simpkins. 'See, brother. Since you arrived, things been goin' downhill for the rest of us, and we'd like to know what it is you got. Maybe we can get some of it for ourselves. And then' – he chucked Donnell under the chin in good buddy fashion – 'once that's done, the one and only Papa Salvatino is goin' to cure your ills.'

Jocundra ran into the Baron on the path to the graveyard. He was standing lost in thought, twirling a yellow parasol. When he saw her, he spat.

'That monkey of yours put on some kind of show at the funeral,' he said. 'Used a trick voice or somethin'. Like to flip Otille out.'

'Where's Donnell now?'

'You ain't seen him?'

'I saw him coming this way about a half hour ago.'

'Ah, damn!' said the Baron. 'Let's head on back up there.'

Bodies were strewn among the tombstones, most unmoving, and most never stirred when the Baron prodded them. Others moaned or frowned groggily. The only person not lying down was a thin-armed, pot-bellied man wearing a bathing suit, who was sitting on top of a tombstone, his stringy brown hair blowing about his face. Static fizzed from a radio on his lap.

'Look like we gonna have to talk to ol' Captain Tomorrow,' said the Baron. 'Dude's been here so long he's fuckin' ossified. The light's on but nobody's home.' He tapped his forehead. 'Let me do the talkin'. He liable to think you an alien or somethin'.'

He sauntered up casually to the tombstone and said, 'Hey, what you know, Captain?'

'What I know,' said the man, staring off at the roof of the main house emerging like a black pyramid above the treeline.

'I say, "What you know, Captain?" ' said the Baron, 'and then you say back, "What I know …" What you mean by that?'

'It's not ordered knowledge,' said Captain Tomorrow. 'It doesn't come in Aristotelian sequence. I'm trying to give it form, but I don't expect you to understand.'

Despite the pomposity of his words, the man's manner was pathetic. His skin showed the effects of bad diet, his eyes were watery and blinking, and when he lifted his hand to scratch his neck, he did not complete the action and left his hand suspended in the air.

'I've been dreaming about flying lately,' he said to Jocundra.

She remembered looking into Magnusson's eyes, feeling sucked in, but looking at this man produced a totally opposite phenomenon. Her gaze skidded away from his, as if his eyes contained polar contradictories to the human senses.

'Probably a result of my work,' he informed her with solemnity. 'I've been translating secret books of the ancient Hindus.' He seemed to be waiting for Jocundra to respond.

'I have a friend who's compiling a Tibetan dictionary,' she said. 'She's working in Nepal.'

'*The Tibetan Book of the Dead*.' He stared at her with renewed intensity. 'Is she translating that?'

'I think it's already been done,' said Jocundra tactfully.

'Not correctly.' He turned away. 'Could you get me a copy of her dictionary?'

'I'll try,' said Jocundra. 'But it'll take a long time to mail it from Nepal. More than a month.'

'Time,' said Captain Tomorrow. He found the concept amusing. 'It's very important I get the dictionary.'

'That green-eyed fella …' the Baron began.

'No, not him.' The Captain hugged himself and hunched his neck and shuddered.

'Naw,' agreed the Baron. 'Naw, he ain't worth a shit wherever he is. Good riddance to him. But whoever's with him is probably pretty scared.'

The Captain smiled; it was a sick, secret-keeping smile.

''Less he's with Simpkins. I don't reckon Simpkins would be scared.'

The radio on the Captain's lap broke into faint song, then lapsed into frying noises.

'Where'd they go, man?'

'Going, going, gone,' said the Captain.

'Jesus!' The Baron spun around and began trying to rouse others of the 'friends,' kicking them, shaking them, asking had they seen Donnell.

'Here,' said Captain Tomorrow; he pulled a plastic baggie from the front of his bathing suit and withdrew a stack of Otille's business cards. He handed one to Jocundra. On the back was a neat, hand-lettered couplet:

Those who cannot cope with the reality of today
Will be literally crushed by the fantasy of tomorrow.

'It's my motto,' he said, slowly reintegrating his gaze with the rooftop.

'Thank you.' Jocundra pocketed the card and was on the verge of joining the Baron, when Captain Tomorrow reached out his hand toward the sun, then brought it back to his lips as if he were swallowing a mouthful of light, accepting communion.

'They're down at the riverboat,' he said to his radio. 'Down, down, down.'

The hold of the sternwheeler had a resiny odor, and the wavelets slapping against the hull were edged with echoes, sounding like the ticking of a thousand clocks. Sunlight showed between the boards where caulking had worn away, and bars of light glowed beneath the hatch cover, dimming when Papa Salvatino lit a battery lamp and positioned it atop a crate. Clea and Downey stood beside him, their faces anxious. Simpkins threw a chokehold around Donnell's neck, wrenched his arms up behind his back, and Papa came toward him, rubbing his hands.

'What's ailin' you tonight, Brother Harrison?' he asked, and laughed.

He placed his hands above Donnell's head, and Donnell had a fuzzy, dislocated feeling. A high-pitched whine switched on inside his ears.

'I can't see what I'm doin' like you, brother,' said Papa. 'I got to work by touch, and sometimes ... sometimes I slip up.'

All the strength suddenly drained from Donnell's body; the weakness was so severe and shocking that his gorge rose, and he would have vomited if Simpkins had not been choking him. Then, as Simpkins released his hold, he sagged to the floor.

'I can make you bleed,' said Papa. 'You won't like it at all.'

'Talk to us, brother,' said Simpkins.

Donnell was silent a moment, and Simpkins kicked him; but Donnell's silence was not due to recalcitrance. He had had and continued to have an impression of Jocundra moving around above him, now standing somewhere near the prow. The impression seemed to be compounded of the smell of her hair, the color of her eyes, her warmth, a thousand different impressions, yet its character was unified, an irreducible distillate of these things. He rubbed his throat and pretended to be straining for air.

'About what?' he gasped. 'Talk about what?'

'Tell us what you did to them birds,' Clea twanged; her voice trembled, and she stood half-hidden behind Downey, who was chewing on his thumbnail. Despite his masterful pose, belly out, thumbs couched behind his lapels, Papa was also exhibiting signs of unease. Even Simpkins' smile looked out of true. Donnell's sunglasses had slipped down onto his nose, and he let them fall, turning away from the lantern so his eyes would show to advantage in the dark.

'Remember, brother,' said Papa. 'You ain't hidin' out behind Otille's skirts no more. You down in dirt alley with the dogs howlin' for your bones.' He drew forth a hunting knife and let light dazzle the blade.

'Just take it from the beginning,' said Simpkins. 'We got all kinds of time.'

Maybe not, thought Donnell; Jocundra was moving again, stopping, moving, stopping, and there was a purposefulness to her actions.

'The beginning's not the place to start,' he said, surprised to hear himself speak because he had been concentrating on Jocundra. Then he realized it had been his alter ego who had spoken, and this time he welcomed it. 'I saw a man die once. He was shot, lying on a restaurant floor. His heart had quit, his blood was everywhere, and yet he still wasn't dead. That's the place to start.'

He told them about the *gros bon ange*, about their specific incarnations of it, about his origins in the laboratories of Tulane, and was satisfied to see Downey and Clea exchange worried glances. The hunting knife hung loose in Papa Salvatino's hand, and his breath was ragged. Simpkins' Adam's apple bobbed. They were already nine-tenths convinced of the supernatural, and his account was serving to confirm their belief. He pitched his voice low and menacing to suit the mood created by the creaking timbers of the boat and began – again, to his surprise – to tell them of the world of Moselantja and the purple sun, the world of the *gros bon ange*. It was, he told them, a world whose every life had its counterpart in this one, joined to each other the way dreams are joined, winds merge and waters flow together; and whose every action also had its counterpart, though these did not always occur simultaneously due to the twisty interface between the worlds. And there were many worlds thus joined. In all of them the Yoalo had made inroads.

'To become Yoalo one must be gifted with the necessary psychic ability to integrate with the suits of black energy,' he said. 'And all here rank high in the cadres, servitors to one or another of the Invisible Ones, the rulers of Moselantja. Legba, Ogoun, Kalfu, Simbi, Damballa, Ghede or Baron Samedi, Erzulie, Aziyan. Men and women grown through much use of power to stand in relation to ordinary men as stone is to clay.'

The story he told did not come to him as invention, but as the memory of a legend ingrained from childhood, and in the manner of Yoalo balladeers – a manner he recalled vividly – he gestured with his right hand to illustrate matters of fact, with his left to embellish and indicate things beyond his knowledge. It was with a left-handed delivery, then, that he had begun to speak of his mission on behalf of the cadre of Ogoun, when Clea broke for the stairs.

'Where you goin,' sister?' Simpkins caught her by the arm.

'I ain't havin' nothin' to do with this,' she said, struggling.

'Me, either,' said Downey, moving toward the hatch.

'What the hell's wrong with you?' said Papa. 'You know he ain't walkin' away from here.'

'He'll come back,' said Clea, her voice rising to a squeak. 'He's already done it once.'

'In the cadre of Ogoun,' said Donnell, wondering with half his mind what Jocundra could be doing behind him, 'there is a song we call "The Song of Returning." Hear me, for it bears upon this moment.'

> 'The sad earth breaks and lets me enter.
> My dust falls like the ashes of a song
> Down the long gray road to heaven.
> Yet as do the souls of the fallen gather
> And take shape from the smoke of battle,
> Casting their frail weights into the fray,
> Influencing by a mortal inch
> The thrust and parry of their ancient foes,
> So will I return to those who wrong me
> And bring grave justice as reward.
> To those who with honor treat me,
> I will return with measured justice,
> No more than is their due.
> And those who have loved me, a few,
> To them as well will I return,
> And all those matters that now lie between us
> Will then be full renewed.'

Cautiously, walking heel-and-toe so as not to be heard below decks, the Baron sneaked away from the hatch and back to Jocundra, who crouched in the prow.

'We need a *di*version,' he said, wiping his brow. 'All four of 'em's down there, and both Simpkins and Papa gon' be packin' knives. That's too much for me.'

He looked around, and Jocundra followed suit. Something pink was sticking out from the door of the pilot house: a rag smeared with black paint. She peeked into the door. There was a box of rags against the wall, other rags scattered on the floor.

'Fire,' she said. 'We could start a fire.'

'I don't know,' said the Baron; he considered it. 'Hell, we ain't got time to think of nothing better. All right. See that far hatch? That goes down to the hold next to theirs. Here.' He gave her his cigarette lighter. 'You tippy-toe down there 'cause them walls is thin, and you pile them rags against the wall they behind. You be able to hear 'em talkin'. Soon as you get 'em goin', you gimme a wave and then yell like your butt was on fire.' He shook his head, dismayed. 'Damn! I don't wanna get killed 'bout no damn green-eyed monkey!'

He took off his jacket and wrapped it around his forearm and pulled a switchblade out of his trousers. 'What you starin' at, woman?' He cast his eyes up to the heavens. 'They gon' stick him 'fore too long. Get your ass in gear!'

She gathered the rags, and carrying an armful of them, made her way to the hatch. The stairs creaked alarmingly. Voices sounded through the wall opposite the stair, some raised in anger, but the words were muffled. As she heaped the rags, something scurried off into the corner and she barely restrained an outcry. Holding her breath, not wanting to give herself away in case of another fright, she touched the lighter to the rags. The cloth smoldered, and some of the paint smears flared. She was about to bend down and fan them when, with a crisp, chuckling noise, a line of fire raced straight up the wall and outlined the design of a three-horned man in yellow-red tips of flame. It danced upon the black boards, exuding a foul chemical stink, seeming to taunt her from the spirit world. Terrified, she backed toward the stairs. Two lines of fire burst from the hands of the three-horned man and sped along the adjoining walls, laying a seam across their midpoints, encircling her, then scooted up the railings of the stairs. More fire spread from the central horn of the figure, washing over the ceiling, delineating a pattern of crosshatches and stickmen, weaving a constellation of flame and blackness over her head. Forgetting all about waving to the Baron, she ran up the stairs, shouting the alarm.

Clea brought her knee up into Simpkins' groin, and he went down squirming, clutching himself. She and Downey clattered up the stairs just as

Jocundra shouted. Donnell saw smoke fuming between the boards behind him. He turned back. Papa Salvatino was coming toward him, swinging his knife in a lazy arc, his head swaying with the movement of the blade. Then the hatch cover was thrown aside, light and a thin boil of smoke poured in, and the huge shadow of the Baron hurtled down the stairs. He dropped into a crouch, his own knife at the ready.

'Get your ass away from him, Papa,' he said.

Simpkins groaned, struggled to rise, and the Baron kicked him in the side.

Papa did not reply, circling, and in the midst of a step he made a clever lunge and sliced the Baron's chest with the tip of his knife, drawing a line of blood across his shirt front.

'Hurry!' shouted Jocundra from the hatch. 'It's spreading!'

Simpkins rolled off the floor, still clutching his groin, and limped up the stairs. Jocundra cried out, but immediately after called again for them to hurry.

Flames began to crackle on the wall behind Donnell, and as he looked, they burst in all directions to trace the image of a woman very like Otille. It might have been a caricature of her, having her serpentine hair, her wry smile: a fiery face floating on the blackness. Donnell got to his feet, weak from Papa's manipulations; too weak, he thought, to engage Papa physically. He searched around for a stick, any sort of weapon, and finding none, he dug into his pocket and pulled out a handful of coins.

'Hey, Papa,' he said, and sailed one of the coins at him. It missed, clinking against the wall. But even the miss caused Papa to lose concentration, and the Baron slashed and touched his hip.

Papa let out a yip and danced away, steadying himself; he cast a vengeful look at Donnell, and as Donnell sailed another coin, he snarled. The Baron nicked his wrist with a second pass and avoided a return swipe.

'You done lost the flow, Papa,' chanted the Baron. 'That iron gettin' heavy in your hand. Your balls is startin' to freeze up. You gon' die, motherfucker!'

Donnell kept throwing the coins, zinging them as hard as he could, and then – as he threw it, his fingers recognized the bulge of Mr Brisbeau's lucky piece – the last coin struck Papa near his eye. He clapped his hand to the spot, and in doing so received a cut high on his knife arm. He backed up the stairs, ducking to keep the Baron in view; he half-turned to run, but something swung down from the open hatch and thunked against his head. He toppled into the hold face downward. A board fell across his legs.

'For God's sake!' Jocundra yelled. 'Hurry!'

As the Baron hustled him up the stairs, Donnell had a final glimpse of the fiery smile floating eerily in the dark, the eyes already absorbed into a wash of flame. Then Jocundra, her face smoke-stained, hauled him toward the rail and onto the dock. The Baron slipped off the mooring line and heaved against the boat with his shoulder, trying to push it out into the current.

'Gimme, a hand, damn it!' he said. 'Else this whole place liable to go up!'

All heaving together, they managed to nudge the boat a couple of feet off the dock, and there it sat, too heavy for the sluggish current to move.

Donnell collapsed against a piling, and Jocundra buried her face in his shoulder, holding him, shaking. His mind whirled with remnant threads of the strange story he had told the pets, and he almost wished he had not been interrupted so he could have learned the ending himself. He had been near to death, he realized, yet he had not been afraid, and he was thankful to the possessive arrogance of his inner self for sparing him fear. But now he reacted to the fear and held to Jocundra, exulting in the jolt of her pulse against his arm.

'That goddamn Clothilde,' said the Baron; he was peeling his shirt away from the cut on his chest. 'Seem like she gon' have her funeral party after all.'

The way the sternwheeler burned was equally beautiful and monstrous. Lines of flame crisscrossed the walls, touching off patterns buried in the paint, repeating the *veve* of Mounanchou and Clothilde's face over and over again, as well as *petro* designs: knives stuck into hearts, hanged men, beheaded goats. Little trains of fire scooted along the railings, illuminating the gingerbread work and support posts. Torches flared at the corners of the roof. Other flames chased each other in and out of passageways with merry abandon, sparking windowframes and hatch covers, until the entire boat was dressed in mystic configurations and fancywork of yellow-red flames, as though for a carnival. Amid a groaning of timbers, the smokestack cannonaded sparks and fell into the bayou, venting a great hiss, and thus lightened, the boat began to turn in a stately clockwise circle, its fiery designs eroding into the general conflagration. The paint of the hull blistered into black wart-like protuberances, the sky above the raging upper deck was distorted by a transparency of flame, and the sound of the fire was the sound of bones splintering in the mouth of a beast. A horrid reek drifted on the breeze.

The boat was about twenty feet off the dock, the prow pointing almost directly toward them, when Papa Salvatino stumbled out of the hatch, coughing, his trousers smoldering. He staggered along the deck, looked up, and they heard him scream as a blazing section of the upper railing fell away and dropped upon him, closing a burning fist around him and bearing him over the side. Charred boards floated off, and in a moment his head reappeared. He raised his arm. It seemed a carefree gesture, a wave to his friends on shore. The boat, continuing to turn, blocked their view of him, turning and turning, a magician's black castle spinning through fire to another dimension, and when it had passed over the spot where he had been, the water was empty of flotsam, undisturbed, reflecting a silken blue like a sheet from which all the wrinkles have been removed by the passage of a hand.

CHAPTER 17

August 18–12 September 1987

'Musta got caught up in the mangrove,' said the Baron when Papa Salvatino's body could not be found. 'Or else,' he said, and grinned, not in the least distressed, 'there's a gator driftin' out there somewhere's with a mean case of the shits.'

Otille, however, was not amused. Screams and the noise of breakage were reported from the attic, and the 'friends' slunk about the downstairs, fleeing to the cabins at the slightest suspicion of her presence. But to Jocundra's knowledge, Otille left her rooms only once between the day of Papa's death and the completion of the *veve* – a period of more than two weeks – and then it was to oversee the punishment of Clea, Simpkins and Downey. She had them tied to the porch railing of the main house and beaten with bamboo canes, the beating applied by a fat, swarthy man apparently imported especially for the occasion. Clea screeched and sobbed, Downey whimpered and begged, Simpkins – to Jocundra's surprise – howled like a dog with every stroke. The 'friends' huddled together in front of the porch, sullen and fearful, and in the manner of an evil plantation queen, Otille stood cold and aloof in the doorway. Her black mourning dress blended so absolutely with the boards that it seemed to Jocundra her porcelain face and hands were disembodied, inset, the antithesis of the ebony faces and limbs inside.

Without Otille's demands to contend with, Donnell relaxed and became less withdrawn, though he still would not talk about his thoughts or his days among the pets. But for a time it was as if they were back at Mr Brisbeau's. They walked and made love and explored the crannies of the house. They were free of pets and 'friends,' of everyone except the Baron, who continued to exercise the role of bodyguard. Yet as the *veve*'s date of completion neared, Donnell grew edgy. 'What if it doesn't work?' he would ask, and she would answer, 'You believe it's going to, don't you?' He would nod, appear confident for a while, but the question always popped up again. 'If it doesn't,' she suggested, 'there's always the project.' He said he would have to think about that.

Jocundra had visited the construction site often, but because of the swarm of workmen and the *veve*'s unfinished state, she had gained no real impression of how it would look. And so, on the night Donnell first used it, when she climbed to the top of the last conical hill and gazed down into the depression where it lay, she was taken aback by its appearance. Three tons of copper, seventy feet long and fifty wide, composed of welded strips and mounted on supports a couple of feet high driven into the ground. Surrounding the clearing was a jungly thickness of oaks, many of them dead and vine-shrouded, towered over by a lone cypress; the spot from which Jocundra, Otille and the Baron were to observe was arched over by two epiphyte-laden branches. Floodlights were hung in the trees, angled downward and rippling up the copper surfaces. Bats, dazed by the lights, skimmed low above the *veve* and thumped into the oak trunks. The ground below it had been bulldozed into a circle of black dirt, and this made the great design seem like a glowing brand poised to sear the earth.

'I certainly hope this works,' said Otille without emotion. She still wore her mourning dress for Papa, and Jocundra believed her grief was real. A cold, ritual grief, but deeply felt all the same. Beside her, the Baron settled a video camera on his shoulder.

'Good luck,' Jocundra whispered, hugging Donnell.

'The worse that can happen is that I fall off,' he said. He tried a smile but it didn't fit. Then he gave her another hug and went down the hill. He looked insignificant against the mass of copper, his jeans and shirt ridiculously modern in conjunction with its archaic pattern. She had the feeling it might suddenly uncoil, revealing itself to have been a copper serpent all along, and swallow him up, and she crossed her fingers behind her back, wishing she could come closer to a prayer than a child's charm, that like her mother she could find comfort at the feet of an idol, or that like Donnell she could shape her faith into the twists and turns of the *veve*.

If even *he* could.

What if it didn't work?

Shortly after he began walking atop the *veve*, a wind kicked up. Jocundra had been expecting it, but Otille became flustered. She darted her head from side to side as if hearing dread whispers, and she picked at the folds of her skirt. She started to say something to Jocundra, but instead took a deep breath and thinned her mouth. The Baron glued his eye to the viewfinder, unmindful of the wind, which now was circling the perimeter of the clearing, moving sluggishly, its passage evident by the lifting of branches and shivering leaves. Each circuit lasted for a slow count of ten. Strands of Otille's hair plastered against her cheek like whip marks every time the wind blew past; she stared open-mouthed, and Jocundra gave her a reassuring smile, then wondered how she could be so reassuring. A burst of static charges crackled along her neck, the hair of her forearms prickled. The air was chilling rapidly, and despite the humidity, her skin felt parched. With every few revolutions, the force of the wind increased appreciably. Hanks of gray moss were ripped from the branches, leaf storms whirled up, and the wind began to pour over the hilltop, its howl oscillating faster and faster, around and around.

Yet through all this Donnell's clothes hung limp, and he had done nothing more than walk.

The Baron staggered and nearly fell, overbalanced by the camera. Otille helped to brace him, but only for a moment. Then she screamed as the top branch of the largest oak tore loose and sailed away. Jocundra scrambled down into the lee of the hill and peered out over the edge. Donnell was standing on a central junction of the *veve*, swaying; his hands waved above his head in languid gestures, the gestures of a pagan priest entreating his god. And she remembered the films she had seen of possession rites, the celebrants' feet rooted, their arms waving in these same ecstatic gestures. Otille came crawling down, clutching at her. But Jocundra drew back in fright. Otille's hair was rising into Medusa coils over her head, twisting and snapping. Out of reflex, Jocundra touched her own hair. It eeled away from her fingers. Her blouse belled, as did her jeans, repelled by the fire accumulating on her skin. Otille pointed toward the *veve*, her face pleading some question. Jocundra followed her point, and this time, as her own scream shattered in her throat unheard, she had no thought of offering reassurance.

Movement, Donnell soon discovered, was the key to operating the *veve*. The magnetic fields of the copper were blurs of opaque white light, clouds of it, hovering, vanishing, fading into view; they drifted away from his hands whenever he tried to manipulate them. He walked along, trying this and that to no avail, and then realized he had been walking the course directed by the movements of the bacteria. He could feel them more discretely than ever, more strongly, a warm trickling inside his head. He continued to walk, following a trail inward, and from every junction of the *veve* but one – and that one, he saw, was to be his destination – a strand of white fire rose, forming into a webwork building up and up around him, a towerlike structure. High above, the milky spectre of the geomagnetic field winked in and out across the sky, and he understood that the complicated flows of the web and his own path were in harmony with it, adapting to its changes. His customary weakness ebbed and he walked faster, causing the structure of the fields to rise higher and become more complex. His new strength acted as a drug, and his thoughts were subsumed by the play of his muscles, the rush of his blood. The fields were singing to him, a reedy insect chorus filling his ears, and he came to know his path as a shaman's dance, an emblem etched upon the floor of the universe by an act both of will and physicality. Then the movements of the bacteria ceased, and he stopped dead center of his predestined junction.

A tower of incendiary wires, intricate as lace, rose around him into the sky, and the geomagnetic field no longer flickered, but was a white road curving from horizon to horizon. Its cold gleam seemed to embody a unity of object and event, being both a destination and a road. Almost tearful, knowing himself unable to reach it yet reaching anyway, like a child trying to touch a star, he lifted his hands to it. The lowest strands of the tower shot toward him and grafted to his fingertips, and at the same time, the geomagnetic field bulged downward, its center fraying into strands that joined with the tower. A flash whitened the sky, and as the light decayed from the outer edges of the flash, it resolved into a latticework of fire, all of its strands flowing inward and pouring down into his outstretched hands.

He had not known his body could encompass such a feeling of power. It was like existing on the boiling edges of a cloud – a place where the borders between the material and immaterial were ceaselessly being redefined – and drawing energy from the transformations. A rapturous strength burned in him. For a moment his eyes were dazzled with whiteness, his consciousness drawn into an involvement of which love and joy, all human emotion, were but fractionated ideals.

Groggy, he blinked and shook his head and looked around.

He might have been standing inside a knot tied in a black rope, gazing up through the interstices at sections of a pale purple ceiling. But directly above him, perhaps a hundred feet distant and visible between coils of black wood, was a castle turret. He recognized it as the turret of Ghazes, the disciplinary post of the Yoalo high in the brambly growth of Moselantja. Characters testifying to the public desire for self-abnegation were carved in the teeth of the battlements.

The apparition of the turret was so unexpected, looming over him like a wave about to crash, that he flung out his right hand in a futile attempt to ward it off. His hand was a negative, featureless black; his fingers shimmered, and gouts of iridescent fire lanced from their tips, merging to a single beam and splashing against the turret, halating it with a rainbow brilliance. He tried to jerk back his hand, but it was locked in position; he wrenched and threw himself in all directions until he sagged from exhaustion, literally hanging by his arm. A few yards away, he made out a fanged door opening into one of the stems, the wall inside furred with lichen that shed a fishbelly phosphorescence. The air stank of ozone, and everything was motionless, soundless.

But then he heard a sound.

At first he thought it was speech of a sort, for it had the rhythm and sonority of words pronounced by a leathery tongue. He stared back over his shoulder and saw something bob up in silhouette against the sky, sink behind a stem and rise again. Something awkward and long-winged, with the bulbous body of a fly. Another creature appeared, another, and another yet. There were at least a dozen, all flapping lazily toward him through the maze of stems.

Once more, this time choking with fear, he tried to wrench himself free. Fire still lanced from his fingertips. The radiance about the turret was pulsing, and the turret itself rippled. Then, berating himself for stupidity, he remembered how to disengage the weapon capacity of the suit. He formed his hand into a claw so that the five beams splashed into each other and slowly brought his fingers together until they met.

The foremost of the beasts cleared the stem beyond his, its face a horror of white-rimmed eyes, an ape's flat nose, needle teeth, tendrils flapping from its lips. It beat its wings, gaining altitude for a dive, and he caught a whiff of fetor and a glimpse of its scabbed underbelly. He crouched down, but a wing buffeted the side of his head and sent him reeling to the edge of the stem. As he teetered, he saw below a puzzle of purple gleam and shadow and interlocking stems. Falling, he clawed at the air and felt a tension on his fingertips.

His fall should have been endless. He should have caromed off the infinity of stems beneath, being battered into shapelessness and blood. But he fell only a couple of feet through a burst of white glory and landed on his side. Dazed, he rolled onto his back. Overhead, slung like a sagging hammock, the crescent moon held sway amid the pinprick stars of a Louisiana night.

The wind shredded Jocundra's scream. From Donnell's fingers a stream of numinous energy, the ghost of a beam, lanced towards the top of the cypress tree. He was struggling as if his arm were gripped by a transparent vise, throwing himself backward, panicked. She started crawling down the hill, but the wind knocked her flat. Crumpled wrappers, tin cans, bottles and twigs skittered along the ground, all shining with coronas; the air was full of stinging grit. Something smacked against her cheek, clung for a second with sticky claws, dropped down into her blouse and walked across her breasts. She rolled over, beating at her chest until a half-crushed cricket fell out and flipped away in the wind, leaving a wet smear on her belly. She looked up just as Donnell toppled off the *veve*, and as the cypress top, surrounded by a halo of ghostly radiance, exploded.

At least it began as an explosion.

There was a blast, flames rayed out, a fireball grew. But when it had reached the limit of its expansion, the fireball did not shrink or dissipate into smoke. Instead, it held its shape; then the flames paled and condensed into a cloud of ruby sparks, which themselves settled into the outlines of a mechanism, one of enigmatic complexity. A piece of jeweled clockwork that folded in upon itself and receded into a previously unnoticed distance: a dark tunnel collapsed through the night sky. The last of the wind went with it, giving out a keening cry that set Jocundra's teeth on edge.

By the time she had crossed the *veve* to the spot where Donnell had fallen, he was sitting up and staring at the blasted cypress. Blood streamed from his nostrils. She jumped down beside him, held his head, and pinched his nostrils to staunch the flow. His eyes showed hardly any green. Thinking it might just be the brightness of the floodlights, she shaded them with her hand. A few flickers, vivid, but only a few.

'I feel good,' he said. 'My heart's not as erratic.' He gazed up at her. 'My eyes?'

She nodded, unable to speak, her own eyes brimming. She put her arms around him and rested her head on the back of his neck.

'You're smothering me,' he mumbled, but held tightly to her waist.

A scream rang out from the hilltop. Jocundra looked back to see Otille struggling in the Baron's grasp. She swung her head back and forth, kicked his legs with her heels. He picked her up and started toward the house; but Otille managed a final scream, and this time it was intelligible. One word.

'Ogoun!'

Donnell stared at the hilltop long after they had gone, and though his features were calm, Jocundra thought she could detect a mixture of hatred and longing in his expression. 'What's wrong with her?' he asked.

'The wind frightened her,' she said. 'And the tree. What did happen with the tree?'

'I don't know,' he muttered. 'An accident. Maybe you can figure it out.' He turned to the cypress. A thin smoke curled from the ruin of its trunk, misting the stars. His voice became resonant, his tone sarcastic, as he said, 'God knows what all this is going to do to Otille.'

Within two days Donnell's eyes were as brilliant as ever, and he went back upon the *veve*, thereafter returning to it at least once a day. There was no danger of him overdoing it. While the treatment did serve to trim the size of the colony, it also appeared to have stimulated their rate of reproduction, and Jocundra doubted he could last much more than two weeks of abstinence. The Baron continued to film Donnell – he had dug a niche into the side of the hill for shelter against the wind – but Otille remained barricaded in her apartments. One experience with Donnell's newly augmented powers had apparently been enough. When asked about her, the Baron would grunt and make offhanded comments.

'Otille just need to sit and watch her forest grow,' he said once. 'She gon' get it back together.' But he didn't seem to be convinced.

Terrified by the wind, which was shredding the jungles of Maravillosa as Donnell's power increased, growing in force and scope, some of the 'friends' left the estate, and those who stayed hid out in the cabins. With the exception of Captain Tomorrow. He was delighted by the wind and had to be shooed away from the *veve*. Whenever he encountered Jocundra, he spoke to her in a scholarly fashion, informing her once that the physics of fantasy was 'on the verge of actuation,' and showing her his design for a thought-powered laser, inspired, he said, by Donnell's 'wind trip.'

As for Jocundra, since the Baron was present to watch over Donnell, she preferred to wait in their room during the treatments. Sometimes she worked on the principles underlying the operation of the *veve*, but she was not often successful in this. The wind unnerved her. Despite her rational understanding of it, charged ions, vacating air masses, she had the feeling it could carry the paper bearing her explanations off to a realm where explanations were no longer relevant. Mostly she thought about Donnell. He was hiding something from her, she believed, and she did not think it could be anything positive. His attitude toward the *veve* puzzled her. He had not been at all distressed to learn of his addiction to it; in fact, he had appeared relieved to learn he could use it frequently.

One evening, eleven days after the completion of the *veve*, while sitting at their window, listening to branches snap, leaves scuttering across the side of the house, Jocundra noticed the corner of a notebook sticking out from beneath their mattress. On first leafing through it, she thought it to be notes for a new story because of the odd nomenclature of towns and people, its references to the purple sun and the Yoalo. But then she realized it was a journal of Donnell's walks upon the *veve*. On the inside foreleaf was a sketch of the *veve*, every junction numbered, and a list of what seemed to be the ranks of the Yoalo. Inductee, Initiate, Medium, Sub-aspect, Aspect, High Aspect. She had a twinge of foreboding, and as she settled back to read the first entry, she tried to tell herself it was only background for a story written in diary form.

Sept. 8. Ended up on Junction 14. The sun edging down, a long pale bulge like a continental margin lifting from the horizon, fringed by a corona of vivid purple. Stars ablaze. No moon. Broken, barren hills to my left, and I thought that Moselantja was somewhere behind them. I was atop a cliff which fell away into a forested valley. Massed empurpled trees locked in shadow, the crooked track of a river cutting through, and two-thirds of the way across the valley, at a forking of the river, was a village laid out in a peculiar pattern, one I could not quite discern because of my angle. I tried to shift my field focus forward; it was harder than usual. Instead of snapping into place, it was as if I were pushing through some barrier heavier than distance. Finally I managed a perspective at eye level of the street. A door opened in one of the houses; a man poked his head out, gave a squeal of fright and ducked inside. How the hell had he seen me? I looked down and saw that I was sheathed in black. Shimmering, unfeatured black. Energy suit. I had been on a clifftop, and now was planted smack in the midst of Rumelya (the name springing unbidden to mind). Memories flooded me, among them information about the suit's capacity for nearly instantaneous travel along line-of-sight distances. The river – the Quinza – was not safe for swimming, though I couldn't recall why, and the name of the forest was the Mothemelle.

Bits of litter, black leaves, were drifting across the dusty street. All the buildings were of weathered black wood, and most were of two stories, the topmost overhanging the lower and supported by carven posts. Every inch of the buildings was carved: lintels evolving into gargoyle's heads, roof peaks into ornate finials. The doorframes flowed with tiny faces intertwined with vines, and stranger faces yet – half flower, half beast – emerged from the walls. The similarity between these embellishments and those of Maravillosa was inescapable. Light issued from shutters pierced by scatters of star-shaped holes so that the appearance was of panels of night sky studded with orange stars. Though many of the details were not of my original invention – the names, for instance – it *was* the village of my story, complete down to the sign above the inn, an odd image I now recognized for a *petro* painting. The evilly tenanted forest looming over the roofs; the tense, secretive atmosphere; the cracked shells and litter blowing on the streets; it was all the same. Voices were raised inside the inn, and I had a strong intuition that some important event was soon to occur there.

As the sun's corona streamed higher above the forest, striking violet glints from the eddies in the river, I noticed an ideograph laid out in black dust centering the crossroads just ahead. The fitful breeze steadied, formed into a whirlwind over the ideograph, and dissipated it into a particulate haze. I had a memory of an old man wearing a dun-colored robe, bending over an orange glow, talking to me. His voice was hoarse and feeble, the creaking of a gate modulated into speech. 'The stars are men's doubles,' he said. 'The wind is a soul without a body.'

Shortly after this, I became afraid I would not be able to leave Rumelya. I had – hadn't I? – moved from my position on the *veve*. I walked back and forth, left and right, attempting to fall off as I had the first time. To no avail. Then, just as had happened beneath the turret of Ghazes, I recalled the necessary function of my suit, that it acted to orient me within the geomagnetic field. I reached up and felt the connections in the air. Again, the mystic experience of transition. It was losing its impact, and I remember thinking during transit that such depersonalized ecstasy might grow boring. I found myself back on Junction 14 waving my arms like a man drowning.

By the time she had finished half the entries, Jocundra's foreboding had matured into disastrous knowledge. Either the immense electromagnetic forces were unhinging him, fueling fantasies with which to form a surrogate past, or – and this she could not fully disbelieve – he was actually traveling somewhere. No matter what the case, and though she was certain he had not told her to protect her from worry, his secrecy was a barrier between them.

The last entry in the journal detailed his arrival in a great hall whose walls were ranked to the ceiling with mirrors. Translucent creatures – 'crystalline imperfections in the air, as quick as hummingbirds' – flew between the mirrors. Images appeared in their wake. One mirror held a view of golden-edged green scales shifting back and forth, as though the coils of an enormous snake enwrapped the hall; a second showed a gem-studded game board, its counters swathed in cobweb; a third depicted a black-suited Yoalo standing atop one of the turrets of Moselantja, spinning around and around, his arms raised overhead, becoming more and more transparent until only a wind whirled in his place, bearing up dust from the turret floor. Each successive mirror image caused him to recall bits and details: the movements of military forces, names, a sequence of letters and numbers which reminded Jocundra of astronomical coordinates. A final mirror offered him the sight of a woman leaning forward, herself looking into a mirror, her face obscured by a fall of dark hair; she then bent her head and lifted her hair up behind her.

> I was overcome with longing. The shade of her hair was identical to Jocundra's, dark brown wound through with gold, and her movements were Jocundra's, the way she held her back perfectly straight while bending. I envisioned the old man once again, his shoulders hunched, holding out something to me: an ivory sphere, one of those conceits carved and hollowed with smaller spheres within. It was cradled in his palm like a pearl in the meat of an oyster. 'If you lose something,' he said, 'you will find it here. And if it truly is yours, it will return to you.' I knew then that this woman, whether Jocundra by name or some other, was bound to me through worlds and time, and that all I had seen within the mirrors were the elements of days to come.

Jocundra set down the journal and went to the window. He was, it appeared, thinking about losing her, and now this same thought infected her. Though it was something she had once taken for granted, the prospect had become terrifying, impossible to accept. The house shuddered. Branches clawed and scuttered against the outer walls. She wished she had a word with which to shout down the wind, an incantation to still it, because it seemed to her a howling prophecy of loss. But growing stronger, it sang in the eaves and shaped groaning, inarticulate words from the open windows, mournful sounds, like sad monsters waking with questions on their minds.

The pale sun, its corona shrunk in a cyanotic rim, showed an arc above the forest of Mothemelle. Donnell stood with an ear pressed in the window of the inn at Rumelya, trying to assure himself that there were no patrons inside.

At last, hearing only a tuneless singing, the clatter of crockery, he pushed in the door. A dumpy serving girl threw up an armload of dishes and ran through a curtained doorway, leaving him alone in the common room. Long gray benches and boards; whitewashed walls, one having a curtained niche; floors of packed sand littered with scraps of gristle, bones, and a striped lizard curled around a table leg; a high ceiling crossed by heavy beams and hung with ladles and pans of black iron. He took a seat near the door and waited. The most peculiar thing about the room was the orange light. It had no apparent source; the room was simply filled with it.

The innkeeper proved to be a chubby young man, his eyes set close together above a squidgy nose and a cherubic mouth. He wore a tunic of coarse cloth, an apron, and carried a tray holding a chipped ceramic mug. 'Brew?' he asked hopefully, his lips aquiver. Donnell nodded, and the innkeeper set down the mug, jerking back his hand. 'Sir,' he said, 'uh, Lord, uh ...' Donnell looked up at him, and he stiffened.

Donnell indicated the curtained niche. 'I will watch from there tonight,' he said, toying with the handle of his mug. Black sparks from his fingers adhered to the ceramic, jittering a second and vanishing.

'Certainly, Lord.' The innkeeper clasped his hands in an attitude of obeisance. 'But, Lord, are you aware that the Aspect comes here of an evening?'

'Yes,' said Donnell, not aware in the least. He picked up the mug – vile-smelling stuff, fermented tree bark – and carried it to the table behind the curtain. 'Where does he usually sit?' he asked. The innkeeper pointed at a spot by the rear wall, and Donnell adjusted the curtain to provide an uninhibited view. He felt no need to urge the innkeeper to be close mouthed about his presence. The man's fear was excessive.

Over the next half hour, seven men filtered into the inn. They might have been cousins, all dark-haired and heavy-boned, ranging from youth to middle age, and all were dressed in fish-hide leggings and loose shirts. Their mood was weary and their talk unenthused, mostly concerned with certain tricky currents which had arisen of late in the river, due, one said, to 'meddling.' Their language, though Donnell had assumed it to be English, was harsh, many words having the sound of a horse munching an apple, and he realized he had been conversing in it quite handily.

Another half hour passed, two men left, three more arrived, and then a wind blew open the door, swirling the sand. A man wearing the black of the Yoalo entered and threw himself down on a bench by the far wall. His face made Donnell wish for a mirror. It was a bestial mask occupying an oval inset in the black stuff. Satiny-looking vermillion cheeks, an ivory forehead figured by stylized lines of rage, golden eyes with slit pupils, a fanged mouth which moved when he spoke. Every one of its features reacted to the musculature beneath. He proceeded to swallow mug after mug of the brew, tossing them off in silence, signaling the serving girl for more. Once he grabbed for her, and as she skipped away, he laughed. 'Trying to tame these country sluts is like trying to cage the wind,' he said loudly. His voice was vibrationless and of startling resonance. All the men laughed and went back to their conversations. Though he was Yoalo, they accorded him only a token respect, and Donnell thought that if he was Aspect here, he would require of them a more rigorous courtesy.

The man drank heavily for a while, apparently depressed; he stared at his feet, scuffing the sand. At length, he hailed the innkeeper and invited him to sit. 'Anyone I ought to know about?' he asked.

'Well,' said the innkeeper, studiously avoiding looking at the niche, 'there was a trickster by last week.' And then, becoming enthusiastic, he added, 'He sent red flames shooting out of the wine bottles.'

'Name?' inquired the Yoalo, then waved off the question. 'Never mind. Probably one of those vagabonds who was camped in the southern crevices. Must have stolen a scrap of power with which to impress the bumpkins.'

The innkeeper looked hurt and bumpkinish. 'I wish I could see Moselantja.'

'Easy enough,' said the Yoalo. 'Volunteer.' He laughed a sneering laugh, and began a boastful account of the wonders of Moselantja, of his various campaigns, of the speeds and distances attained by his 'ourdha,' a word Donnell translated as 'windy soul.'

All at once the door banged open, and a ragged old man, his clothes patched and holed, baskets of various sizes slung about his shoulder, came into the inn. 'Snakes!' he cried. 'Plump full of poison!' He plucked a large banded snake from one of the baskets and held it up for all to see. The village men gave forth with nods and murmurs of admiration, but claimed to be already well supplied with snakes. The old man put on a doleful face, wrinkling so deeply he had the look of a woodcarving. Then he spied the Yoalo and did a little caper toward him, flaunting the snake and whistling.

Furious at this interruption, the Yoalo jumped up and seized the snake. Blood spurted out the sides of his fist, and the severed halves of the snake dropped to the sand, writhing. He aimed a backhand at the old man, who dived onto the floor, and weaved toward the door and into the street. With the exception of the snake-seller – he was bemoaning the loss of his prize catch – the village men remained calm, shrugging, joking about the incident. But upon seeing Donnell emerge from the niche, they knocked over their benches and scrambled to the opposite end of the room.

'Lord!' cried the snake-seller, crawling into Donnell's path. 'My eldest was a tenth-level recruit of your cadre. Hear me!'

'Tenth-level,' said Donnell. 'Then he died upon the turret.'

'But well, Lord. He gave no outcry.'

'I will listen.' Donnell folded his arms, amused by his easy acceptance of rank, but quite prepared to exercise its duties.

'This,' said the old man, picking up the snake's head, 'this is nothing to the abuses we of Rumelya suffer. But to me this is much.'

He began a lengthy tale of its capture, half a day spent among the rocks, tempting it with a gobbet of meat on a forked stick, breaking its teeth with a twist when it struck. He testified to its worth and listed the Yoalo's other abuses. Rape, robbery, assault. His complaint was not the nature of the offences – they were his right – but that they were performed with such vicious erraticism they had the character of a madman's excesses rather than the strictures of a conqueror. He begged for surcease.

The old man's eyes watered; his skin was moley; his forearms were pitted with scarred puckers, places where he had been bitten and had cut away the flesh to prevent the spread of the poison. These imperfections grated on Donnell, but he did not let them affect his judgement.

'It will be considered,' he said. 'But consider this. I have witnessed great disrespect in Rumelya, and perhaps it is due. But had you honored the Aspect properly, he might well have served you better. Should another take his place, your laxity will be counted a factor in determining the measures of governance.' As he left, he heard the village men haranguing the snake-seller for his lack of caution.

The Yoalo's trail – rayed depressions in the sand – turned left, left again, and Donnell saw the river at the end of the street. Above the treeline on the far bank, the sun's corona raised purple auroras into the night sky, and the stars were so large and bright they appeared to be dancing about into new alignments. The street gave out onto a grassy bank where several long canoes were overturned, and sitting upon one of these was the shadowy figure of the Yoalo. In order to get close, Donnell shifted his visual field forward as he had done on his first visit to the village. This time he noticed a shimmering, inconstant feeling in all his flesh as the suit bore him to the rear of a shed some twenty feet along the bank from the Yoalo's canoe. The man was rocking back and forth, chuckling, probably delighting in the incident of the snake. He touched his forehead, the mask wavered and disappeared. But before Donnell could see his face, the man flattened onto his stomach, leaned out above the river and splashed water over himself. Something *ki-yied* deep in the forest, a fierce and solitary cry that might have come from a metal throat. Sputtering, the Yoalo propped himself up on an elbow, staring off in Donnell's direction.

Except for the fact that his eyes were dark, betraying no hint of green, he was the spitting image of Jack Richmond. Skull-featured, thin to the point of emaciation.

All the man's behavior, his fits of violence and depression, his harassment of the serving girl, his obsession with speed, clicked into focus for Donnell. He was about to call to him when the man came up into a crouch, his right hand extended, alerted by something. With his left hand, he reached inside his suit and pulled forth a construction of – it seemed – wires and diamonds, and flicked it open. Its unfolding was a slow organic process, a constant evolution into new alignments like the agitated stars overhead. Drunkenly, the Yoalo stared at it, swaying, then fell on his back; he rolled over and up, and iridescent beams of fire spat from his hand toward a dark object on the bank. It burst into flames, showing itself to be a stack of bales, one of several such stacks dotting the shore.

The Yoalo shook his head at his own foolishness, chuckled, and folded the bright contraption; it shrank to a sparkle of sapphire light as he pocketed it, as if he had collapsed a small galaxy into a single sun. He touched his forehead, and the mask reappeared. Then he went staggering down the bank, his hand extended, firing at the stacked bales, setting every one of them ablaze. With each burst, he shouted, 'Ogoun!' and laughed. His laughter grew in volume, becoming ear-splitting, obviously amplified; it ricocheted off the waterfront buildings. The fires sent dervish shadows leaping up the street, casting gleams over the carved faces on the walls, and illuminated the ebony flow of the river and the thick vegetation of the far bank.

Amid a welter of spear-shaped leaves, Donnell saw the movements of low-slung bodies. But, he thought, the truly dangerous animal wore a suit of negative black and roamed the streets of Rumelya without challenge. A vandal, a coarse outlaw. Yet though he despised the man's abuse of privilege, he was captivated by the drama of the scene. This maniacal warrior with the face of a beast howling his laughter, taunting the lie-abed burghers and fishermen; the rush of dark water; the auroral veils billowing over the deep forest; the slinking animals. It was like a nerve of existence laid bare, a glistening circuit with the impact of a one line poem. He filed the scene away, thinking he might compose the poem during his next period of meditation. Half in salute, honoring the vitality of what he had witnessed, half a warning, he sent a burst of his own fire to scorch the earth at the Yoalo's feet. And then he lifted his hands to engage the fields and returned to Maravillosa.

The sky was graying, coming up dawn. One of the bushes near the *veve* was a blackened skeleton, wisps of smoke curling from the twig ends. He sat down cross-legged on the ground. Within the fields, he thought, he was a far different person than the one who now doubted the validity of the experience. Not that he was capable of real doubt. The whole question was basically uninteresting.

'Hey, monkey!' The Baron waved from the hilltop.

The wind must have been bad. An avenue had been gouged through the undergrowth, and he could see a portion of the house between the hills.

Gables, the top of his bedroom window. Jocundra would be asleep, her long legs drawn up, her hand trailing across his pillow.

'Man,' said the Baron, coming toward him. 'You got to control this shit!' He gestured at the battered foliage.

Donnell shrugged. 'What can I do?'

The Baron sat down on the *veve*. 'I don't know, man,' he said, sounding discouraged. 'Maybe the best thing can happen is for it to all blow away.' He spat. 'You got another nosebleed, man.'

Donnell wiped his upper lip. Blood smeared and settled into the lines of his palm, seeming to form a character, one which had much in common with a tangle of epiphytic stalks and blooms blown beside the *veve*: fleshy leaves, violet florets. More circuitry ripped up from beneath the skin of the world. Every object, the old man had said, is but an interpretation of every other object. There is no sure knowledge, only endless process.

'When you first come here, man,' said the Baron, 'I thought you was sleaze like Papa and them other uglies. But I got to admit you unusual.' He coughed and spat again. 'Things is gettin' pretty loose up in the attic. You and me should have a talk sometime 'bout what's happenin' 'round here.'

'Yeah,' said Donnell, suddenly alert to his weariness, to the fact that he was back in the world. 'Not now, though. I need some sleep.'

But a few days later Otille sent the Baron away on business, and by the time he returned things had gone beyond the talking stage.

CHAPTER 18

September 15–19 September 1987

Ordinarily they would have been asleep at three o'clock in the morning, but for some reason Jocundra's adrenaline was flowing and she just tossed and turned.

'Let's get something to eat,' she suggested, and since Donnell had also been having trouble sleeping, he was agreeable.

It was creepy poking around the house at night, though not seriously so: like sneaking into a funhouse after hours, when all the monsters have been tucked into their niches. These days it was rare to see anyone walking the corridors of Maravillosa. Clea and Downey had moved in together and were busy – said the Baron with a wink – 'lickin' each other's wounds, you unnerstan'?' Simpkins, as always, kept aloof. Only two of the 'friends' remained, a chubby man and, of course, Captain Tomorrow, whom Jocundra had come to think of as a ragged blackbird perched on a volume of Poe stories, pronouncing contemporary 'Nevermores.' And Otille never ventured downstairs. Jocundra imagined her wandering through her ebony shrubs, quoting Ophelia's speeches; and that set her to remembering how, during the early days of the project, Laura Petit had labeled certain of the patients 'Opheliacs' because of their tendency to babble and cry. Jocundra had had one such patient, a thirtyish man with fine, pale red hair, fleshy, an academic suicide. He had licked the maroon stripe of the wallpaper, and at the end, unable to speak coherently, he had tried to proposition her by making woeful faces and exaggerated gestures, reminding her of Quasimodo entreating Esmerelda. She had nearly quit the project after his death.

Moonlight laid jagged patterns of light and shadow over the downstairs corridors, casting images of windows and blinds splintered by the wind. They had considered walking outside, but it started to drizzle and so they stood on the porch instead. The rain had a clean, fragrant smell, and its gentleness, the steady drip from eaves, gave Jocundra the feeling of being a survivor, of emerging from a battered house to inspect the aftermath of a storm. As her eyes adjusted to the dark, she saw something gleaming out along the drive. A car. Long; some pale colour; maybe gray.

'Company,' she said, pointing it out to Donnell.

'No doubt Otille has found solace in a lover's arms,' he said. 'Or else they're delivering a fresh supply of bats to the attic.'

'I wonder who it is, though.'

'Let's go to the kitchen,' he said. 'I'm hungry.'

But on the way to the kitchen, they heard voices from Otille's office.

'I don't want to get involved with her tonight,' said Donnell, trying to steer her away.

'I want to see who it is,' she whispered. 'Come on.'

They eased along the wall toward the office, avoiding the shards of window glass.

'... does seem that the hybrid ameliorates the tendency to violence,' said a man's voice. 'But after seeing him ...'

'It's not his fault he's the way he is,' said Otille. 'It's probably mine.'

'Be that as it may,' said the man patiently. 'We're not ready for live tests. Look. If your family's problems do result from a congenital factor in the DNA, and I'm not convinced they do ...'

Jocundra recognized the voice, though she found it hard to believe that he would be here.

'I'm so sick of being like this,' said Otille.

Jocundra pushed Donnell away, shaping the man's name with her lips, but he resisted.

'Have you been taking your medication?' asked the man.

'It makes me queasy.'

'Evenin', folks,' said Simpkins. He was standing behind Donnell, an apple in one hand, a kitchen knife in the other; he gestured toward the office with the knife.

Donnell hardly reacted to him. 'Ezawa!' he said, and brushed past Jocundra into the office. Simpkins urged her to follow.

Otille was standing against the wall, distraught, her hair in tangles, a black silk robe half open to her waist. Jocundra had not seen her since the night Donnell first used the *veve*, and she was startled by the changes in her. All the hollows of her face had deepened, and her eyes seemed larger, darker, gone black like old collapsed lights. Ezawa was behind the desk, his legs crossed, the image of control. He ran a hand through his shock of white hair and said to Otille, 'This is unfortunate.'

'It was inevitable,' she said. 'Don't worry, Yoshi. I'll take care of it.' She leaned over the desk and pushed a button on the intercom. A man's cultivated voice answered, and Otille said, 'Can you come meet my other guests?'

'Oh?' A rustling noise. 'Certainly. I'll just be a few minutes.'

'Do you need any help?'

'No, no. I'll be fine. I've been looking forward to this.'

'The Rigaud Foundation,' said Donnell suddenly; he had been staring at Ezawa. 'They're funding the project.'

'That's right,' said Ezawa.

'And I've got the family disease. Christ!' He turned to Jocundra. 'The new strain. They dug it out of her damn graveyard. Right?' he asked of Ezawa.

'Half right.' Ezawa peered at Donnell, then settled back, building a church and steeple with his knitted fingers, tapping his thumbs together. The harsh lamplight paled his yellow complexion, making his moles seem as oddly shaped and black as flies, and despite his meticulous appearance, he looked soft, inflated with bad fluids.

'Actually,' he said, 'the entire project is a creation of the Foundation, of Valcours Rigaud specifically. He spent most of his later life trying to create zombies, and amazingly enough achieved a few short-lived reanimations. His method was clumsy, but there was a constant in his formulae – a spoonful of graveyard dirt placed in the corpse's mouth – and so I was led to my own researches.' He sighed. 'You, Mr Harrison, were injected with bacteria bred in Valcours' grave, as were Magnusson and Richmond. But ...'

'That's impossible,' blurted Jocundra. 'Valcours is buried in the crypt. There's no dirt. The bacteria couldn't have bred.'

'His head,' said Otille; she was tying and untying the sash of her robe. 'They buried it down by the pool.'

'As I was saying,' said Ezawa, frowning at Jocundra, then turning his attention back to Donnell. 'You and Magnusson received a hybrid strain. One of the thrusts of the project, you see, has been to isolate a cure for Otille's hereditary disorder, and with that in mind, we interbred Valcours' bacteria with a strain taken from another grave located here on the grounds. The grave of Valcours' magus, his victim. Lucanor Aime.'

'And Aime,' said Donnell coldly, more calmly than Jocundra might have expected. 'His patron deity, that would be Ogoun.'

'Ogoun Badagris,' murmured Otille.

'Astounding, isn't it?' said Ezawa. 'The good magician and the evil apprentice still warring after over a century. Warring inside your head, Mr Harrison. When Otille suggested the hybrid, I ridiculed the idea, but the results have been remarkable. It's enough to make me re-embrace the mysticism of my ancestors.' He gave a snort of self-deprecating laughter. 'The entire experience has been quasi-mystical, even the early days when the lab was full of caged rats and dogs and rabbits and monkeys, all with glowing, green eyes. Pagan science!'

'You're going to die, Ezawa,' said Donnell angrily. 'Just like in the movies, and pretty damn soon. One morning after this breaks, after the papers start howling for your blood, and they will, you can count on it, that old time religion of yours will stir you to wrap a white rag around your head and sit you down facing the sunrise with a fancy knife and a brain full of noble impulse. And the ironic part is that you're going to be swept away by the nobility of it all right up to the time you get a whiff of your bowels and see the tubes squirming out of your stomach.'

He broke off and looked toward the door. Only Simpkins was there, but Jocundra heard dragging footsteps in the hall. 'Who is it?' asked Donnell, whirling on Otille.

'He says he can feel you, too, but from much farther away.' Otille's voice devoid of emotion.

'Our latest success with the new strain,' said Ezawa. 'He's much stronger than you, Mr Harrison. Or he will be. I think we can credit that to his having been a full-fledged psychic, not merely a latent one.'

Donnell leaped toward Otille, furious, but Simpkins intercepted him and threw him onto the floor. Otille never blinked, never flinched.

'Fisticuffs,' said a man at the door. 'Marvelous! Wonderful!'

He wore a black silk bathrobe matching Otille's, carried a cane, and the right side of his puffy face was swathed in bandages; but both his eyes were visible. The irises flickered green.

'Papa!' Jocundra gasped.

He regarded her distantly, puzzled, then inclined his head to Donnell in a sardonic bow. 'Valcours Rigaud at your service, sir,' he said. 'I do hope you're not injured.'

Jocundra took a step toward Ezawa. 'You killed him!' she said. 'You must have!'

'It's questionable he would have lived,' said Ezawa placidly.

'Did you *kill* me, Otille?' Valcours affected a look of hurt disillusionment. 'You only told me I had died.'

It was impossible to think of him as Papa anymore. He was truly Valcours, thought Jocundra, if only a model conjured up by Otille. Death had remolded his face into a sagging, pasty dumpling, reduced all his redneck vitality into the dainty manners of a moldering, middle-aged monster.

'I had to,' said Otille; she walked over to him and took up his hand. 'Or else you wouldn't have come back.'

Valcours drew her into a long, probing kiss, running his free hand across her breasts. He cradled her head against his chest. 'Ah, well,' he said. 'The joys of life are worth a spell of mindlessness and corruption. Don't you agree, Mr Harrison?'

Donnell sat up against the wall, his head lowered. 'What have you got in mind, Otille?'

Valcours answered him. 'There's a world of possibility to explore, Mr Harrison. But as far as you're concerned we'll keep you around until I learn about the *veve*, and as for your beautiful lady ...' Before Jocundra could react, he prodded her breast with the tip of his cane. 'I believe a fate worse than death would be in order.' He laughed, a flighty laugh that tinkled higher and higher, traveling near the verge of hysteria. Tears of mirth streamed from his eyes, and he waved his hand, a foppish gesture that should have been accomplished by a lace handkerchief, signaling his helplessness at the humor of the situation.

'You had your chance,' said Otille bitterly to Donnell. 'I wanted you to help me.'

'Help you rule the universe, like with the evil fairy there?' Donnell said. 'I thought you wanted to be cured, Otille. How could I help you with that? But you don't want a cure. You want zombies and horrors and icky delights. And now' – he cast a disparaging glance at Valcours – 'now your wish has come true.'

'Be still!' said Valcours with a hiss of fury. He raised his cane to strike Donnell, and Jocundra recoiled, bumped against Simpkins, and jumped away from him. In his rage, Valcours possessed a malevolence previously muffled by his effete manner.

'You know, Ezawa,' said Donnell, 'you're in big trouble with all this. Maybe even bigger than you could expect. What if this fruit really is Valcours, what if you've really worked a miracle?'

'What if?' Valcours was once again the dandy, complaining of a gross indignity. 'I'm the very soul of the man! Like the resin left in an opium pipe, the soul leaves its scrapings in the flesh. The essence, the pure narcotic of existence! Whether my dispersed shade had misted up anew, summoned forth by modern alchemies, or whether all is illusory, these are questions for philosophers, and have no moment for men of action.' He giggled, delighting in the flavor of his speech.

'See,' said Donnell to Ezawa. 'It's going to blow up in your face. Fay Wray and the Mummy here will meet the Wolfman, have a group hallucination, and then comes the shitstorm. He's her puppet, and she's out of her fucking mind. Do you honestly believe they can keep it together?'

'Simpkins!' shouted Otille. 'Get them out of here!

Before Simpkins could cross the room, Valcours launched a feeble attack on Donnell, attempting to batter his legs with the cane. But Donnell rolled aside, pulled himself up by the desk and snatched the cane from Valcours. He spun Valcours around, levered the cane under his jaw and started to choke him.

'This bastard's weaker than I am,' he said. 'I bet I could crush his windpipe pretty damn quick.'

Simpkins held his distance, looking to Otille for instruction; but she was again in thrall of the listlessness which had governed her during most of the encounter. Spit bubbled between Valcours' lips and he thrashed in Donnell's grasp.

'Look at her, Ezawa,' said Donnell; he increased pressure on Valcours' throat until his eyes bulged and he hung limp, prying ineffectively at the cane. 'Don't you see what they're hamming up between them? This is her big chance to make it in the Theater of the Real, to go public with her secret third act. A gala of obscenity. Otille and Valcours. Lord and Lady Monster together for the first time. Help us! Help yourself.'

'I can't.' Ezawa had risen and moved around to the side of the deck. 'She'd ruin me.'

'You're already ruined,' said Donnell. 'And it'll be worse if you let it go on. She's so far gone it won't stop until you're scraping dead virgins off the streets of New Orleans. This women thinks evil's a nifty comic book and she's the villainous queen. Maybe she is! Whatever, she's going to do evil, and the word's going to get around. Help us! I'll finish this one, and we'll all jump Simpkins.'

Ezawa's face worked, but his shoulders slumped. 'No,' he said.

'No, huh?' Donnell let Valcours sag to the floor. 'Another time,' he said, prodding him with his foot.

'Hit him,' said Otille in a monotone. 'Don't kill him, but hit him hard.'

Jocundra draped herself around Simpkins' neck as he went for Donnell, but he threw her off and her head struck the desk. White lights seemed to shoot out of her eyes, pain wired through her skull, and someone was holding her wrist. Checking for a pulse, probably. She wanted to tell them she was all right, that she had a pulse, but her mouth wouldn't work. And just before she lost consciousness, she wondered if she did have a pulse after all.

On the fourth day of their confinement Jocundra remembered the trick door in the Baron's room, but for the first three days their position had appeared hopeless. Donnell's jaw was swollen, his eyes rapidly brightening, his skin paling, and he would scarcely say a word. He stared at the bedroom walls as if communicating with the peaceful ebony faces. The wind blew twice a day, not as strongly at first as it had for Donnell, but stronger each time, and they would watch out the window as Otille, invariably clad in her black silk robe, led Valcours back and forth between the *veve* and the house. Their meals were brought by Simpkins and the chubby 'friend,' an innocent-looking sort with close-set eyes and a Cupid's mouth, whose presence seemed to upset Donnell. Simpkins would wait in the hall, picking his teeth, commenting sarcastically, and on the evening of the third day he gave them some bad news.

'Brother Downey has gone the way of all flesh,' he said. 'We hog-tied him and put him on the *veve*, then the late Papa Salvatino started walking around and a pale glow came out of his fingers. Well, when that glow touched Brother Downey, you would have sworn he'd gotten religion. Quakin' and shakin' and yellin'. I was up on the hill and I could hear his bones snap. Looked like he'd been dropped off a skyscraper.' He worried his gums with a toothpick. 'Sister Clea ran off, or I reckon she was next. 'Bout the only reason you alive, brother, is Otille's scared of you. If it was up to me, I'd kill you quick.'

It was then that Jocundra remembered the door. Two iron brads held it in place, but removing them was not the main problem.

'We've got to wire it so we can trip the release,' said Donnell. 'Then we'll lure Simpkins in, try to trap him in the alcove, and hope we can take them one at a time.'

They worked half the night at prying off the molding, both of them breaking fingernails in the process; they disconnected the release mechanism and undid the springs of their bed, straightening and knotting them together to attach to the mechanism; they jiggled loose two bed legs to use as clubs, shoring up the bed with books, and refined their plan.

'You'll be at the table,' said Donnell, 'and I'll be about here.' He took a position halfway between the alcove and the table. 'When the guy sets down the trays, I'll go for him. You drop the door as soon as Simpkins starts to move. Then you hit the other guy. The worst case will be two against two, and even if Simpkins does get through, maybe we can finish the other one off first.'

'I don't know,' she said. 'When I hit Papa on the boat it was all reflexes. Fear. I don't know if I can plan to do it.'

'I think you'll be sufficiently afraid,' he said. 'I know I will.' He hefted his club. 'Afterward, I'll head to the *veve* and see if I can get control of it.'

While the wind was blowing the next morning, they ran a test of the door. Donnell stood on the table beneath it and caught it after it had fallen a couple of inches.

'Let's do it tonight,' he said. 'He's getting stronger all the time, but I still have a physical advantage. You keep away from the *veve* until it's over. Find some car keys, grab some of the videotapes. Maybe we can use them. But keep away from the *veve*.'

Jocundra promised, and while he wound the bedsprings around the leg of the table beside her, she tried to prepare herself for swinging the club. It was carved into whorls on the bottom but the business end was cut square and had an iron bolt sticking out from the side. The thought of what it could do to a face chilled her. She let it lie across her lap for a long time, because when she went to touch it her fingers felt nerveless, and she did not want to drop it and show her fear. Finally she set it against the wall and ran over the exact things she would have to do. Let go the wire, pick up the club, and swing it at the chubby man. The list acquired a singsong, lilting rhythm like a child's rhyme, drowning out her other thoughts, taunting her. *Let go the wire, pick up the club, and swing it at the chubby man.* She saw herself taking a swing, connecting, and him boinging away cartoon style, a goofy grin on his face, red stars and OUCHES and KAPOWS exploding above his head. Then she thought how it really would be, and she just didn't know if she could do it.

Donnell had never been more drawn to her than now, and though he was afraid, his fear was not as strong as his desire to be with her, to ease her fear. She was very nervous. She kept reaching down to check if her club was still leaning against the wall, rubbing her knuckles with the heel of her palm. Tension sharpened her features; her eyes were enormous and dark; she looked breakable. He couldn't think how to take her mind off things, but at last, near twilight, he brought a notebook out from his bureau drawer and handed it to her.

'What's this?' she asked.

'Pictures,' he said; and then, choosing his tense carefully, because his tendency was to think of everything he had planned in the imperfect past, he added, 'I might do something with them one of these days.'

She turned the pages. 'They're all about me!' she said; she smiled. 'They're pretty, but they're so short.'

He knelt down, reading along with her. 'Most are meant to be fragments, short pieces – still they're not finished. Like this one.' He pointed.

> *The gray rain hangs a curtain from the eaves*
> *Behind her, as she tosses*
> *The mildewed flowers to plop in the trash,*
> *Tips the leaf-flocked vase water*
> *Out the window, as she leans*
> *Forward looking at the splash,*
> *As she pours up from the ankle up to slim waist*
> *And white breast and shawl of brown hair,*
> *Every curve seems the process*
> *Of an inexhaustible pouring,*
> *Like the curves of a lotus.*

'Just cleverness,' he said. 'I didn't do what I wanted to do. But all together, and with some work, they might be something.'

She turned another page. 'They're not,' she said, laughing.

'What?'

'My legs.' She quoted: '"… the legs of a ghost woman, elongated by centuries of walking through the walls." They're not that long.' She spanked his hand playfully, then held up a folded piece of paper, one on which he had written down 'The Song of Returning.' He had forgotten about it. 'What's this?' she asked.

'Just some old stuff,' he said.

She read it, refolded the paper, but said nothing.

He rested his head on her forearm and was amazed by the peace that the warmth of her skin seemed to transmit, as if he had plunged his head into the arc of a prayer. He rubbed his cheek along her arm. Her fingers tangled in his hair, and he felt drifty. The lamplight shaded the skin of her arm from gold into pale olive, like delicate brushwork.

'Jocundra?'

'Yes?'

He wanted to tell her something, something that would serve as a goodbye in case things didn't do well; but everything he thought of sounded too final, too certain of disaster.

'Nothing,' he said.

She bent her head close to his and let out a shuddery breath. 'It'll be all right,' she whispered.

Her reassurance reminded him of Shadows, how she had comforted him about the brightness of his eyes, his aches and pains; he felt a rush of anger. It had never been all right, and chances were it never would be. He did not know who to blame. Jocundra had made it bearable, and everyone else was either too weak or too riddled with sickness to be held responsible: it seemed that the whole world had *that* excuse for villainy.

There were footsteps and voices in the hall.

He fumbled with the wire, uncoiled it, thrust it into her hand, making sure she had the grip, and ran to his position near the alcove.

It almost didn't work. She almost waited too long. Simpkins yelled 'Hey!' and came running in, and at first she thought the door had missed him. But then he pitched forward hard, as if someone had picked him up by the feet and slammed him down, and she saw that the door had pinned his ankle. The chubby man looked back at Simpkins just as Donnell swung, and the club glanced off the side of his head and sent him reeling against the wall. Simpkins screamed. The chubby man bounced off the wall and started walking dreamily toward Jocundra, his hands outstretched, a befuddled look on his face. Blood was trickling onto his ear. He heard Donnell behind him, turned, then – just as Jocundra swung – turned back, confused. She caught him flush on the mouth. He staggered away a step and dropped to his knees. He gave a weird, gurgling cry, and his hands fluttered about his mouth, afraid to touch it. A section of his lip was crushed and smeared up beneath his nose, and his gums were a mush of white fragments and blood. Donnell hit him on the neck, and he rolled under the table and lay still.

Simpkins' eyes were dilated, his face ashen, and he had begun to hyperventilate. The door had sunk a couple of inches into his leg above the ankle, and a crescent of his blood stained the wood. Just as they stooped to lift it, a pair of black hands slipped under from the other side and lifted it for them. Jocundra jumped back, Donnell readied his club. The door came up slowly, revealing a pair of brown trousers, a polo shirt, and then the sullen face of the Baron. Simpkins never noticed the door had been raised. His foot flopped at a ridiculous, straw-man angle, and he stared along the nap of the carpet with scrutinous intensity, as if he were reading a tricky green. His nostrils flared.

'You people don't need no damn help,' said the Baron, surveying the carnage. Clea peeped out from behind him, depressed-looking and pale.

'Where's Otille?' asked Donnell.

'Seen her downstairs when we's headin' up,' said the Baron; he kicked Simpkins' leg out of the way and motioned for them to pass on through; then he let the door bang down. 'What the hell is gon' on 'round here? Clea say ...'

'Stay away from the *veve*,' said Donnell, taking Jocundra by the shoulders. 'Understand? Find the tapes.' And then, before she could respond, he said to the Baron, 'Keep her here,' and ran toward the stairs. Clea ran after him.

Despite the warning, Jocundra started to follow, but the Baron blocked her way. 'Do what he say, woman,' he said. 'Way I hear it, ain't nothin' we can do down there 'cept die.'

Dusk had settled over Maravillosa, and a silvery three-quarter moon had risen high above the shattered trees. Scraps of insulation and roofing blown from the cabins glittered among the debris of fronds and branches and vines. The only sound was of Donnell and Clea crunching through the denuded thickets. Because of Valcours' weakness, Otille would be leading him along a circuitous and relatively uncluttered path to the *veve*, so Donnell had made a beeline for it. Clea was breathing hard, squeaking whenever a twig scratched her.

'You should go back,' he said. 'You know what he did to Downey.'

'I promise you,' said Clea, hiccupping. 'If you don't get him, then I'm gonna.'

Donnell glanced back and saw that she was crying.

A dark man-shaped thing floated in the marble pool, and the shadowy forms of Valcours' other anthropomorphic toys were visible among the stripped branches of the shrubbery, leaning, arms outflung, like soldiers fallen in barbed wire while advancing across a no man's land. Towering above them, some twelve or fifteen feet high, was a metal devil's head, lean-skulled and long-eared. Its faceted, moonstruck eyes appeared to be tracking them, and its jaw had fallen open, giving it a dumfounded look. The rivets stitching the plates together resembled tribal tattoos.

As he climbed up the last conical hill, a drop of sweat slid along his ribs and his mouth went dry. There was a terrifying aura of suppressed energy about the clearing. The floodlights were off, but the copper paths of the *veve* rippled with moonlight: a crazy river flowing in every direction at once. He forced himself down the hill and climbed up on it, feeling as though he had just strapped himself into an electric chair. Clea climbed on behind him. He was through warning her; she was her own agent, and he had no time to waste.

He became lost in walking his pattern, in building his fiery tower, so lost that he did not notice Valcours had joined him on the *veve* until the fields began to evolve beyond his control, rising at an incredible rate into the sky. Valcours was walking alone on the opposite end of the *veve*, and from the movements of the bacteria, the height and complexity of the structure above them, from his understanding of the necessities of their patterns, Donnell judged they would reach their terminal junctions simultaneously. The knowledge that they were bound together wrapped him in an exultant rage. No one was going to usurp his place, his authority! He would write his victory poem in the bastard's blood, cage a serpent in his skull. He had a glimpse of Clea trudging toward the man, her mouth opening and closing, and though the whine of the fields drowned out her voice, he knew she must be singing.

Then the white burst of transition, the perfunctory holiness of a spark leaping the gap, and he was once again standing in the purple night and dusty streets of Rumelya.

Somewhere a woman screamed, a guttering, bubbling screech, and as he cast about for the direction of the scream, he realized the town was not Rumelya. The streets were of the same pale sand; the Mothemelle loomed above the hunched rooftops; the buildings were constructed and carved the same, but many were of three and four stories. Looking to the east, he saw a black column. The splinter of Moselantja. This, then, was the high town of the river. Badagris. Where he was Aspect. Normally the streets would be bustling, filled with laughter-loving fools. Fishermen and farmers from upriver; rich men and their women stopping their journey for an evening's festival; the *cultus* playing guitars and singing and writhing as they were possessed by the Invisible Ones. But not tonight. Not until the Election had been won. Then even he might relax his customary reserve, let the dull throng mill around and touch him, squealing at the tingle of his black spark.

He wondered who had been incautious enough to accept candidacy this year. It was no matter. His fires were strong, he was ready and confident.

Too confident.

If his suit had not reacted, urging him to spring into a back somersault, he might have died. As it was, a beam of fire seared his forehead. He came up running from the somersault, never having seen his assailant, half-blind with pain and cursing himself for his carelessness. He cut between buildings, remembering the layout of the town as he ran, its streets designed in accordance with the Aspect's seal. His strength confounded him. Even such a slight wound should have weakened him briefly, overloaded his suit, but he felt more fit than ever, more powerful. At last he slowed to a walk and went padding along, the sand hissing away from his feet. He was at one in stealth and caution with the crouched wooden demons on the roof slants, their vaned wings lifted against the starlight, and it seemed they were peering around the corners for him, scrying, dangers. One day, when he finally lost an Election, his image would join theirs in some high place of the town. But he would not lose this Election.

Turning onto the Street of Beds, he saw a body lying in front of the East Wind Brothel, an evil place offering artificially bred exotics and children. The body was that of a girl. Probably some kitchen drudge who had wanted a glimpse of combat. It happened every year. Beneath the coarse dress, her bones poked in contrary directions. He rolled her over with his foot, and her arm followed her shoulder with a herky-jerky, many-jointed movement. Broken capillaries webbed her face and neck, and blood seeped from the orbits of her eyes. She had not died quickly, and he marked that against the candidate. He ripped down the bodice of her dress and saw the seal of the Aspect tattooed upon her right breast. She was of the *cultus*. Though she had been a fool, he could not withhold the grace of Ogoun. He touched her lips with his forefinger, loosing a black spark to jitter and crawl inside her mouth, and he sang the Psalm of Dissolution.

> *'I am Ogoun, I am the haze on the south wind,*
> *The eddy in the river, the cadence at the heart of light,*
> *The shadow in the mirror and the silence barely broken.*
> *Though you may kill me, I will crawl inside of death*
> *And dwell in the dark next-to-nothingness,*
> *Listening to the tongues of dust tell legends*
> *Until my day of vengeance breaks.'*

Since she was a mere kitchen drudge, he chanted only the one verse.

Lagoon-shaped shadows from the forest crowns spilled onto the street. He shifted forwards, streaming from darkness to darkness, materializing beside walls carved into the faces of forest animals and spirits. What had the old man said? Sorry past and grim future pressing their snouts against the ebony grain of the present. The Aspect poured through the streets, a shadow himself, until finally, near Pointcario's Inn, his favorite spot in the town because of the carved figure of a slender woman emerging from the door, her face half-turned back to someone within, there he found the candidate: a big man with a face half spider, half toad set into his suit. Without hesitation the Aspect attacked, and soon they were locked in combat.

Their beams crossed and deflected, their misfires started blazes on the roofs, and sections of nearby walls were lit by vivid flashes into rows of fanged smiles. The candidate was incredibly strong but clumsy: his patterns of attack and parry were simple, depending on their force to overwhelm the more skillful play of the Aspect's beams. Gradually, their fires intertwined, weaving above and around them into an iridescent rune, a cage of furious energy whose bars flowed back and forth. After having fully tested the candidate's strengths and weaknesses, the Aspect disengaged and shifted toward another district of the town to consider his strategy and rest, though truly he felt no need for rest. Never before had he been so battle ready, his suit so attuned to his reactions, his rage so pure and burning.

He sat down on the porch of Manyanal's Apothecary and stroked the head of the ebony hound rising from the floorboards. The beauty of the night was a vestment to his strength and his rage, fitting to him as sleekly as did his suit. It seemed to move when he moved, the stars dancing to the firings of his nerves. Talons of the purple aurora clawed up half the sky, holding the world in their clutch and shedding violet gleams on the finials and roofpeaks, coursing like violet blood along the wing vanes of a roof demon. The stillness was deep and magical, broken now and then by the hunting cry of an iron-throated lizard prowling the Mothemelle.

A door creaked behind him.

He somersaulted forward, shifting as he did, and landed in the shadows across the street, playing his fires over the front of the doorway. A scream, something slumped on the porch, flames crackling around a dark shape. He shifted back. Beneath the web of broken capillaries was the face of Manyanal, his eyes distended, smoke curling from his stringy brown hair. Had everyone gone mad? One fool was to be expected, but two ... Manyanal was a respected citizen, accorded the reputation of wisdom, a dealer of narcotic herbs who had settled in Badagris years before his own Election. What could have driven him to be so foolhardy? The Aspect had a notion something was wrong, but he pushed it aside. It was time to end the combat before more fools could be exposed. He would harrow the candidate, engage and disengage, diminish his fires and lead him slowly by the nerve-ends down to death. Still vaguely puzzled by the constancy of his strength, he started off along the street, then stopped, thinking to bestow the grace upon Manyanal. But he remembered that the apothecary was not of the *cultus*, and so left him to smoulder on his porch.

Otille came pelting into the house just as Jocundra and the Baron came out of her office, each carrying cans of videotape; she flattened against the wall, staring at them, horrified. Her black silk robe hung open and there was dirt smeared across her stomach and thighs. The wind drove something against the side of the house, and she shrieked, her shriek a grace note to the howling outside. She ran past them, head down and clawing at the air as if fighting off a swarm of bees.

The Baron shouted something that was lost in the wind.

Jocundra signaled that she hadn't heard, and he shook his head to say never mind, gazing after Otille.

Wind battered the house, a gale, perhaps even hurricane force. The walls shuddered, windows exploded, and the wind gushed inside, ripping down blinds, overturning lamps, flipping a coffee table, all with the malevolent energy of a spirit who had waited centuries for the opportunity. A maelstrom of papers swirled out of Otille's office like white birds fluttering down the hall.

'I'm going out!' shouted Jocundra.

The Baron shook his head and tried to grab her. But she eluded him and ran out the door and down the steps. The night thrashed with tormented shadows, the air was filled with debris. Branches and shingles sailed across the ridiculously calm and unclouded moon. Shielding her head, she made for the cover of the underbrush, stumbling, being blown off course. She crouched behind a leafless bush that offered no protection and pricked her with its thorns, but there was no greater protection elsewhere. The fury of the wind blew through her, choking off her thoughts, even her fears, absorbing her into its chaos. The Baron threw himself down beside her. Blood trickled along his jaw, and he was gasping. Then, behind them, a tortured groan split the roar of the wind. She looked back. Slowly, a hinged flap of the roof lifted like a great prehistoric bird hovering over its nest, beat its black wing once and exploded, disintegrating into fragments that showered the bushes around them. In the sharp moonlight, she saw boxes, bundles, and furniture go spiraling up from the attic, and she had the giddy idea that they were being transported to new apartments in the spirit world. The Baron pulled her head down, covering her as a sofa crashed nearby and split in two.

It took forever to reach the *veve*.

A forever of scuttling, crouching, of vines flying out of the night and coiling around them. Once a rotten oak toppled across their path, and as she crawled through its upturned roots, the wind knocked her sideways into its hollow bottom. The moon looked in on her, shining up the filaments of the root hairs. She was groped by claustrophobia, an old man with oaken fingers who wanted to swallow her whole. By the time the Baron hauled her out, she was sobbing with terror, beating at the invisible things crawling beneath her clothes. They went on all fours, cutting their hands on pieces of glass, ducking at shadows. But at last they wriggled up the hill overlooking the *veve*.

Valcours and Donnell stood about a dozen feet apart, and from their fingers flowed streams of the same numinous glow that had destroyed the cypress; the streams twisted and intertwined, joining into a complex design around them, one which constantly changed as they moved their hands in slow, evocative gestures, like Kabuki dancers interpreting a ritual battle. Suddenly Valcours broke off the engagement and limped away along one of the copper paths. The weave of energy dissolved; the pale light bursting from Donnell's hands merged into a single beam and torched a bush below the hill. Maybe, she thought, maybe she could sneak through the wind, get beneath the *veve* and pull Valcours down. She wriggled forward but the Baron dragged her back.

'Look, goddamn it!' he shouted in her ear, pointing to a part of the *veve* far from Valcours and Donnell.

Two bodies lay athwart the struts. One, her dress torn, was Clea, and the other – Jocundra recognized him by the radio clutched in his hand – was Captain Tomorrow. Even at this distance, the deformity of their limbs was apparent. She turned back to see Donnell racing after Valcours. With incredible grace – she could hardly believe he was capable of such – he turned a forward flip, came out of a shoulder roll, and landed on the junction behind Valcours. The bush he had set afire whirled up in a tornado of sparks into the darkness and was gone.

Weakened beyond the possibility of further battle, cornered, the candidate appealed for mercy. He dissolved his mask; his puffy features were strained and anxious. The Aspect was surprised by his age. Usually they sent the youngest, the angriest, but no doubt this man's exceptional strength had qualified him.

'Brother,' said the candidate. 'My soul is not ripe. Grant me two years of meditation, and I will present myself at Ghazes.'

'Your soul will ripen in my fires.' said the Aspect. 'Should it not, then it would never have borne with ripeness.'

'How will it be, brother? I would prepare.'

'Slowly,' said the Aspect. 'Two of my children have died this night.'

He savored the moment of victory. The clarity accessible at these times merited contemplation. He noticed that the glitter of the stars had grown agitated, eager for the death, and in the distance the river chuckled approvingly against the pilings of the wharf. The shadows of the roof demons stretched long across the sand, centering upon the spot where the candidate stood. Everything was stretching toward the moment, adding its strength to his.

'Ogoun will judge me,' said the candidate.

'I am his judgment here in Badagris,' said the Aspect, irked by the man's gross impiety, his needless disruption of the silence. 'And like his mercies, his judgments hold no comfort for the weak.'

He drew his left hand back behind his ear, extended his right, and set an iridescent halo glowing about the candidate. The man began to quiver, and with a series of cracks like a roll of castanets, his fingers fused into crooked knots. A foam of blood fringed his nostrils; the web of capillaries – his new mask of death – faded into view. Another crack, much louder, and the pyramid of a fracture rose at the midpoint of his shoulder. Oh, how he wanted to scream, to retreat into meditation, but he endured. The Aspect silently applauded his endurance and tested it more severely, causing his eyes to pop millimetre by millimetre until the irises were bull's eyes in the midst of veined white globes rimmed with blood. Loud as tree trunks snapping, his thighbones shattered and he fell, his suit changed shape with every subsequent crack. His chest breeched, and something the size of a grapefruit was pushed forward; it dimpled and bulged against the coating of black energy; before long, before the candidate's skull caved inward, it had become still.

After victory, diminution.

The old cadre wisdom was right. He derived no real pleasure from the aftermath of battle. It simply meant he must now live until the next one, and despite his poetry, his meditation, that was never easy. Soon the townspeople would pour out the doors, throw open the shutters and debase the purity of night with their outcries and orange lanterns. Full of praise, they would gather around and ogle the corpse who, having met his death with courage, deserved better. Perhaps he would go to Pointcario's Inn, touch the waist of the ebony girl lost forever in the doorway, pretend some other woman was she. But first there was something to do. The business of the aberrant High Aspect of Mounanchou. He reached up for the circuits of his *ourdha*, concentrated his thoughts into a point of sapphire light, and spun round and round until he arrived at Maravillosa.

The inside of his head was warm, unpleasantly so, as he jumped down, but his muscles were supple, his strength undiminished. He started toward the house, but was brought up short by the sight of the two corpses lying apart from the candidate. From Valcours. Disoriented, he looked around at the moonlit devastation, the gaping roof of the house, and a part of him which had been dormant raised an inner voice to remind him of certain verities. He understood now the meaning of the warmth, the nature of his newfound strength, and as another voice – a more familiar one of late – whispered to him, he also understood how that strength must be put to use.

CHAPTER 19

19 September 1987

Donnell was standing beside the *veve* when Jocundra and the Baron came down from the hill. Hearing their footsteps, he glanced up. His skin was pale and his eyes were terminal, the pupils gone inside radiant green flares. She ran toward him, but he thrust out his hand and boomed '*No!*' with such force that she held up a dozen feet away.

'They're all over,' he said dully. 'All goddamn over!' He slammed his fist against the *veve*, and the copper bulged downward half a foot. He lifted the fist to his eyes, as if inspecting a peculiar root; then, with an inarticulate yell, he struck again and again at the strut, battering the welded strips apart. His hand was bleeding, already swelling.

'Please, Donnell,' she said. 'Get back on it. Maybe ...'

'Too late,' he said, and pointed to a spray of broken blood vessels on his forehead. 'I was dead the second he hit me. It changed them, it ...'

She started toward him again.

'Stay the hell away,' he said. 'I'm not going to end up twitching at your gates, mauling you like some damned animal!' He looked at her, nodding. 'Now I know what all those other poor freaks saw.'

'He ain't got no way to come to you,' said the Baron, pulling at Jocundra's arm. 'Get away from him.'

But everything was balling up inside her chest, and her legs felt weak and watery, as if the beginning of grief was also the beginning of an awful incompetence. She couldn't move.

'They wanted to wallow in life right until the moment their hearts were snatched,' said Donnell. 'And, oh Jesus, it's a temptation to me now!' He turned away.

'God, Donnell!' she said, clapping her hands to her head in frustration. 'Please try!' The Baron put his arm around her, and its weight increased her weakness, dissolved the tightness in her chest into tears.

'Where's Otille?' asked Donnell casually, seeming to notice the Baron for the first time.

The Baron stiffened. 'What you want with her? She crazy gone to hell. She past hurtin' anyone, past takin' care of herself.'

'They can do wonders nowadays,' said Donnell. 'I better make sure.'

The Baron kept silent.

'Where else,' said Donnell. 'She's upstairs.'

'Yeah man!' said the Baron defiantly. 'She upstairs. So what you wanna mess with her for?'

'It needs to be done,' said Donnell, thoughtful.

'What you talkin' 'bout?' The Baron strode forward and swung his fist, but Donnell caught it – as easily as a man catching a rubber ball – and squeezed until it cracked, bringing the Baron to his knees, groaning; he flung out his hand at the Baron, fingers spread. When nothing happened, he appeared surprised.

'What you want to hurt her for?' said the Baron, cradling his hand. 'Hurtin' her ain't 'bout nothin'.'

Donnell ignored him. He opened his mouth to speak to Jocundra, but only jerked his head to the side and laughed.

It was such a corroded laugh, so dead of hope, it twisted into her. She moved close and put her arms around him; and at a distance, curtained off from her voice by numbness, despair, she heard herself asking him to try again. He just stood there, his hands on her waist.

'Maybe,' he said. 'Maybe I …'

'What?' She had a flicker of hope. Nothing concrete; it was unreasonable, all-purpose hope.

His fingers had worked up under her blouse, and he rubbed the ball of his thumb across her stomach. He said something. It started with a peculiar gasp and ended with a noise deep in his throat and it sounded like words in a guttural language: a curse or a fierce blessing. Then he pushed her away. The push spun her around, and by the time she had regained her balance, he was gone. She could hear him crashing through the thickets; but dazedly staring at the place where he had stood, she kept expecting him to reappear.

The dark shell of the house was empty. Splinters of glass glinted on the stairs between the shadows of the shredded blinds. Climbing up to the attic took all his self-control, his training; he wanted to go running back to her, to breathe her in again, to let his life bleed away into hers. Even the knowledge that the way was closed did not diminish his desire to return to the *veve*, to try once more, and only his compulsion to duty drove him onward. He hesitated on the top step; then, angry at his weak-mindedness, he rattled the knob of the attic door. It was locked, but the wood split and the lock came half-out in his hand. He kicked the door open and stepped inside.

Part of the roof was missing, and the moonlight shone on a shambles of burst crates and broken furniture and unrolled bolts of cloth. All Otille's treasures looted and vandalized, their musty perfumes dissipated by the humid smell of the night. It was strange, he thought as he walked toward the three doors, that killing Otille was to be the summary act of his existence, the resolution of his days at Shadows, his life with Jocundra, healing. It seemed inappropriate. Yet it was essential. These aberrations had caused enough trouble in the worlds, and it had been past due that someone be elected to befriend the cadre and eliminate the seam of weakness, disperse the recruits, punish the High Aspect and her officers. He had been an obvious choice; after all, twice before the Aspects at Badagris had dealt with the cadre of Mounanchou. Such purges were becoming a tradition. It might well be time for a restructuring of the cadre's valence, for bringing forth an entirely new aspect from the fires of Ogoun. He was nagged by a moral compunction against the killing, and the frailty of the thought served to remind him how badly he needed a period of meditation. Disdainful of her guessing games, he ripped the central door of the Replaceable Room off its hinges, lowered his shoulder, and charged along the passage. He shattered the second door with ease, but as he came to his feet, he experienced a wave of weakness and dislocation.

The roof of the apartment had been torn off, and the light of moon and stars gave the walls and bushes the look of a real forest. A clearing in a forest. Hanks of moss had been blown into the room and were draped over the branches. An oak had caved in part of the far wall, and through the branch-enlaced gap he could see a tiny orange glow. Probably somebody nightfishing, somebody who didn't know better than to venture near Maravillosa. Otille was standing behind a shrub about twenty feet away; a branch divided her face, a crack forking across her ivory skin. She sprinted for the door, but he cut her off. She caught herself up, flattened against the wall, and began to edge back.

'Come here,' he said.

'Please, Donnell,' she said, groping her way. 'Let me go.' The O sound became a shrinking wail, and then a word. 'Ogoun.' She shivered, blinked, as if waking from a dream. Her silk robe, which hung open, was speckled with leaves and mold, and a large bruise darkened her hip. Her eyes flicked back and forth between Donnell and the door, but her face was frozen in a terrified expression. Black curls matted her cheeks, making it appear her head was gripped within the scrollwork cage of a torturer's restraint. 'Let me go!' she screamed, demanding it.

'Is that what you really want?' He kept his voice insistent and even. 'Do you want to go on hurting yourself, hurting everyone, screwing your sting into people's lives until they curl up in your web and waste?' He eased a step nearer. 'It's time to end this, Otille.'

She edged further away, but not too far. 'I'm afraid,' she said.

'Better to die than go on hurting yourself,' he said, inching forwards, trying to minister her madness, seduce her with the sorry truth. 'Think about the suffering you've caused. You should have seen Valcours die, bleeding from the eyes, his bones crunching like candy. Downey, Clea, Dularde, Simpkins, all your supporters. Gone, dead, vanished. You're alone now. What's there to look forward to but madness and brief periods of clarity when you can see the trail of corpses numbering your days, and feel sorrow and revulsion. Better to die, Otille.'

She raised her hand to her cheek, and the gesture transformed her face into that of a young girl, still frightened but hopeful. 'Ogoun?' she asked.

'I am his judgment,' he said, wondering at the archaic sound of his words, gauging the distance between them.

Otille blinked, alert again, tipped her head to one side and said, 'No, Donnell.' Her left hand, which had been shielded behind her, flashed up and down so quickly that he did not realize she held a knife until he saw the hilt standing out from his chest. A gold hand was carved gripping it. The blade had struck his collarbone dead on, deflected upward, and stuck; she tried to pull it out and stab once more, but her fingers slipped off the hilt as he staggered back.

Angry at his carelessness, he plucked it out and threw it into a far corner. The wound was shallow, seeping blood. 'That was your last chance,' he said. 'And I don't even think you wanted to take it.'

She pressed against the wall, her head drooping onto her shoulder in a half swoon, her eyelids fluttering, helpless; but he could not lift his hand to strike. For the moment she seemed fragile, lovely, a creature deserving a merciful judgment, involved in this tortuous nightmare through no fault of her own. Seeing his hesitation, she hurled herself toward the door; he dove after her, clutching an ankle and dragging her down. He scrambled to his feet, still hesitant. His cold and calculating mood had fled, and he was not sure he could do it. One second she was a monster or a pitiful madwoman, the next a lady frail as alabaster or a little girl, as if she were inhabited by a legion of lost souls not all of whom merited death. And now she stared at him, another soul duly incarnated, this one displaying the sulky pout of adolescence, ignorant and sexual: a black-eyed child with pretty breasts and a dirt-smeared belly. A trickle of sweat crawled into the tuck of skin between her thigh and abdomen. He was bizarrely attracted, then disgusted; he stepped around her and opened the first door of the Replacement Room.

'Go on in,' he said. 'This is the way out.'

Stupefied, she pushed herself up onto an elbow, gazing into the dimly lit passage, her head wobbling.

'You can't hush up what's happened, Otille. Not this time. You're too far gone to deal with it. And you know what they'll do? They'll lock you up somewhere a thousand miles from Maravillosa, in a room with iron bars on the windows and a bed with leather cuffs and leg straps, and a mirror that won't break no matter how hard you hit it, and a blazing light bulb hung so high you can't reach it even if you stand on a chair and jump. And all you'll hear at night will be muffled screams and scurrying footsteps.'

There was no indication that she heard him. She continued to gaze into the room, her head swaying back and forth, lids drooping, as if the sight were making her very, very sleepy.

'And in the day, maybe, if you don't mess the floor or scream too much or spit out your medication, they'll let you into a big sunlit room, the sun shafting down from high windows so bright the light seems to be buzzing inside your ears and melting the glass and glowing in the cracks. And there'll be other women wearing the same starched gray shift as you, and their faces will be the same as yours, dulled and lined and depressed about something they just can't get straight, gnawing their fingers, talking to the cockroaches, shrieking and having to be restrained. Sometimes they'll wander silent as dust around the room, the loony housewives and the mad nuns and the witchy crone who eats cigarette butts and dribbles ash. And there you'll be forever, Otille, because they'll never turn you loose.'

Otille got to her feet, shrinking from the room but unable to tear her eyes off it.

'They'll stuff you with pills that turn the air to shadowy water, put larvae in your food that uncurl and breed in your guts, give you shots to make you crazier. Electroshock. Maybe they'll cut out part of your brain. Why not? No one will be using it, and nobody will care. The doctors and lawyers will grow gray-haired and fat spending your fortune, and you'll just sit there under your light bulb trying to remember what you were thinking. And in the end, Otille, you'll be old. Old and dim and sexless with one sodden black thought flapping around inside your skull like a sick bat.'

Without any fuss Otille took a stroll into the room. She ran her eye along the walls, her attention held briefly by something near the ceiling. The calmness of her inspection was horrifying, as if she were checking a gas chamber for leaks prior to consigning her mortality to it. Then she turned, her slack features firming to a look of fearful comprehension, and darted at him.

The attack caught him off guard. He tripped and landed on his back, and she was all over him. Kneeing, biting, scratching. She had the strength of madness, and he was hard put to throw her off and climb to his feet. As she circled, looking for an opening, it seemed to him a wild animal had become tangled in her robe. Her eyes were holes punched through onto a starless night; her breath was hoarse and creaky. Every nerve in her face was jumping, making it look as though she were shedding her skin. She rushed him again. Wary of her strength, he sidestepped and hit her in the ribs. The bones gave, and she reeled against the wall. He aimed a blow at her head, but she ducked; his fist impacted a carved trunk, and ebony splinters flew. Panting, she backed away. She stroked her broken ribs and hissed, appearing to derive pleasure from the wound. Then she let out a feral scream and threw herself at him. This time he drew her into a bear hug, and she accepted the embrace. Her hands locked in his hair, her legs wrapped around his thigh, and she sank her teeth into his shoulder, tearing at his tendon strings. He yanked her head back by the hair. Blood was smeared over her mouth, and she spat something – something that oozed down his cheek, something he realized was a scrap of his flesh – and tried to shake free. He took a couple of turns of her hair around his wrist, pried a leg loose, walked over to the door of the Replaceable Room and slammed her against the wall. She lay stunned and moaning, her hair splayed out beneath her head like a crushed spider.

'Oh, God. Donnell,' she said weakly. She reached out to him, and he squatted beside her, taking her hand.

He should finish her, he thought; it would be the kindest thing. But she had regained her humanity, her beauty, and he could not. From the angle of her hips, he judged her back was broken; she did not appear to be in pain, though – only disoriented. She whispered, and he bent close. Her lips grazed his ear. He couldn't make out the words; they were a dust of sound, yet they had the ring of a term of endearment, a lover's exhalation. He drew back, not far, and considered her face a few inches below. So delicate, all the ugly tensions withdrawn. He felt at a strange distance from her, as if he were a tiny bird soaring above the face of the universe, a floor of bone and ivory centered by a red plush mouth which lured him down, whirling him in a transparent column of breath. Half-formed phrases flittered through his thoughts, memories of sexual ritual, formal exchanges of energy and grace, and he found himself kissing her. Her lips were salty with his blood, and as if in reflex, her tongue probed feebly. He scrambled to his feet, repelled.

'Donnell,' she said, her voice rough-edged and full of hatred. And then she pushed up onto her arms and began dragging her broken lower half toward him. Dark blood brimmed between her lips.

He stepped back quickly and closed the door.

He went to the carpeted depression at the center of the room, knelt beside the control panel and began flicking the switches two and three at a time. As he engaged a switch on the middle row, her voice burst from the speaker, incoherent. A harsh babble with the rhythm and intensity of an incantation. He switched her off, continuing down the rows, and at last heard the grumble of machinery, the whine of the pumps. He waited beside the panel until the whine had ceased, until whatever was going to die had managed it.

It was very quiet, the sort of blanketing stillness that pours in between the final echo of an explosion and the first cries of its victims. The quietness confused him, lending an air of normalcy to the room, and he was puzzled by his sudden lack of emotion, as if now that he had completed his task, he had been reduced to fundamentals. He stood and almost fell, overwhelmed by the bad news his senses were giving him about death: dizziness, white rips across his vision, his chest thudding with erratic heartbeat.

Done.

Stamp the seal of fate, tie a black cord round the coffin and make a knot only angels can undo.

Both life and duty, done.

Filled with bitterness, he smashed his heel into the control panel, crumpling the metal facing. Smoke fumed from the speaker grille. Then he spun around, sensing Jocundra behind him. No. She was elsewhere, coming toward the house, and she seemed to surround him, every sector of the air holding some intimation. He could taste her, feel her on his skin. He started to the door, thinking there might be time to go back downstairs.

No, not really.

Not according to the twinges at the base of his skull or the dissolute feeling in his chest.

The leaves on the ebony bushes seemed to be stirring, and the dark loom of the forested walls held lifelike gleams of color, a depth of light and foliage showing between the trunks. To the south a road of pale sand plunged off through the trees, and at the bend of the road was a tiny orange glow. He laughed, recalling the light he had seen earlier in the gap made by the toppled oak; but he walked toward it anyway. The place where the road left the clearing was choked with branches, and they scratched him when he crouched to gain an unimpeded view. He must be very near the edge, three floors up, yet all he saw beneath was the starlit dust of the road. He shifted his field of focus toward the glow. The orange light rose from a metal ring, and beside it, sitting with his back against a stump, was a lean, wolfish man. Heavy eyebrows, dark hair flowing over his shoulders. He appeared to be gazing intently at Donnell, and he waved; his mouth opened and closed as if he were calling out.

Someone did call to him, but it was Jocundra, her voice faint and issuing from a different quarter. He forced all thought of her aside. Without access to his *ourdha*, it would be essential to concentrate, to synchronize thought with vision, or else the winds would take him and there would be no hope of return. He pressed forward into the gap, ducking under the branches. Right on the edge, he figured. He shifted his field of focus beyond the wolfish man, who was now waving excitedly, and out to the bend in the road. The forest plummeted into a valley, and below, nestled in a crook of the river, were the scattered orange lights of Badagris. Above the town and forest, the aurora billowed, and higher yet were icy stars thick as gems on a jewel merchant's cloth.

Pain lanced through his chest, an iron spike of it drove up the column of his neck. His vision blurred, and to clear his head he fixed his eyes on the hard glitter of the stars. Something about their pattern was familiar. What was it? Then he remembered. The Short War against Akadja, the Plain of Kadja Bossu. There had been a night skirmish with a company of *dyobolos*, a difficult victory, and afterward he had stood watch on a hummock, the only high ground for miles. The myriad fires of the cadre burning about him, the sable grass hissing with a continental pour of wind. It had seemed to him he was suspended in the night overlooking a plain of stars, its guardian, its ruler, and he had thought of it as a vision of his destiny. Solitary, rigorous, lordly. Yet he had been much younger, barely past induction, and despite the elegance of the vision, the clarity, it had been a comfort to know the war was over for a little while, that the shadows in the grass were friends, and the hours until dawn could be a time of peaceful meditation. The memory was so poignant, so vivid in its emotional detail, that when a branch scraped at the corner of his eye, aggravated by the distraction, he knocked it away with his hand – a black, featureless hand – and thinking to avoid further aggravation, he took another step and shifted forward along the road.

EPILOGUE

15 July 1988

The outcry surrounding the public disclosure of the project had taken only three months to die, this – thought Jocundra – a telling commentary upon the spongelike capacity of the American consciousness to absorb miracles, digest them along with the ordinary whey provided by the media, and reduce them to half-remembered trivia. Coil by coil, the various security agencies encircled the remnants of Ezawa's project and drew them down into some mysterious sub-basement of the bureaucracy. Several people disappeared, evidence was mislaid, an investigative committee foundered in the dull summer heat of the Congress. Ezawa's suicide caused a brief reawakening of interest, but by then the topic had lost vitality for even the off-color jokes of talk show comedians. After her interrogation and release by the CIA, Jocundra submitted a copy of one of the videotapes to a network newswoman and suffered debunking by a professional debunker, a pompous tub of a man, a beard and a belly and a five hundred dollar suit, who claimed any of Donnell's feats could be duplicated by a competent magician. Throughout the winter she was besieged by obscene phone calls and letters, offers from publishers, badgered by the illegitimate press, and when someone painted a pair of devilish green eyes on her apartment door, she packed and moved back to a rented cottage on Bayou Teche.

She used the cottage as a base from which to send out her applications to graduate schools, the idea being – as her psychiatrist had put it – to 'get on with life, find a new direction.' She had agreed to try, though she did not think there was any direction leading away from all that had happened. Not being able to feel the things she had felt with Donnell was intolerable; it was as if she had been given a strength she never knew existed, and once it had been taken from her, her original strength seemed inadequate. And whenever she sought comfort in memory, she was brought up against Otille's conjuration of her fantasy, of Valcours, and the sickly light this shed on her own relationship with Donnell.

'You're underestimating yourself,' the psychiatrist had said. 'You've handled this surprisingly well. Look at some of the others. Petit, for instance. Her incidence of trauma was much less than yours, and I doubt they'll ever put her together. You'll be just fine in a while.'

His pious smile, and everything he said, had come across as an indictment, an unspoken comment that she was an unfeeling bitch and should quit wasting his time. She had flared up, offering an angry apology for not having crumbled into schizophrenia, and walked out. But she had followed his advice. She had been accepted at Berkeley, and if everything went as planned, within a year she would be doing fieldwork in Africa. She had goals, much work to do, yet nothing had changed.

It was all empty without him.

The people of Bayou Teche, those Donnell had cured and others, had raised a stone to him at Mr Brisbeau's. For a month she had avoided visiting it, but then, thinking this avoidance itself might be unhealthy, she drove to the cabin early one morning and – hoping not to rouse Mr Brisbeau – sneaked through the palmettos to the boathouse. It was there the stone had been erected facing the bayou. Her first sight of it appalled her. The stone was ordinary, gray-white marble shot with black veins, TO THE MEMORY OF DONNELL HARRISON incised in neat capitals. But fronting it was a litter of candle stubs, gilt paper angels, satin ribbons, mirrors, rosary beads, and plate after plate of rotting food. Ants and flies crawled everywhere; mites and gnats swarmed the air. Greenish mounds of potato salad, iridescent hunks of meat. The stench made her gag. Dizzy, she sat down on a rickety chair, one of several crowding the boathouse. After a moment she regained her composure. She should have expected it considering how his legend had grown over the year, considering also the cultish nature of religion on the bayous. The chairs, no doubt, had been used in some rite or vigil.

When she looked up again, she paid no attention to the horrid feast and saw only the stone. It glowed under the morning sun, and the glow seemed to be increasing, dazzling her, as if her eyes had suddenly become oversensitized to light. She noticed with peculiar clarity the way the black veins of the marble twisted up through the letters of his name. She had to rest her head on her knees, overcome by emotion. Everything was bright and familiar, yet at the same time it was vacant-feeling, haunted; not by him, but by old husks of moments that flocked to her like ghosts to a newly abandoned castle, wisping up, informing of their sad persistence. God, she never should have come. There was nothing of him here. His body was potions and powders in some government laboratory, and all the stone served to do was punish her.

Someone whistled on the path.

She sat up and wiped her eyes just as Mr Brisbeau appeared around the corner, an empty burlap sack slung over his shoulder.

'Hello,' she said, trying to smile.

'Well,' he said, hunkering by the stone, 'it didn't take you *twelve* years, anyhow. How you doin', girl?'

'I don't know,' she said, incapable of affecting happiness. 'All right, I guess.'

He nodded. 'I jus' come here to pick up the garbage.' He showed her the burlap sack. 'I takes 'em to ol' man Bivalaqua's hogs. Better'n leavin' 'em set.' He opened the sack and dumped one of the plates into it. 'You can't let go,' he said after a bit. 'Ain't that right, girl? It's a hard thing, lettin' go, but there it is.'

'It was so strange at the end,' she said, eager to explain it to someone, someone who would not analyze it. 'So many strange things were happening, and there were things he said and wrote ... I'm just not sure. It sounds foolish, but I can't accept ...' She shook her head, unable to explain it. 'I don't know.'

'You ain't thinkin' he's still alive?'

'No,' she said. 'I saw him fall, I've seen it for a year. I could see his face peering out a break in the wall. It was the only pale spot in all that blackness. And then he jumped. But not down. Forward. As if he were in a hurry to get somewhere. I'm sure he didn't think he was falling, but I don't understand what that means.'

'Girl, you know I believe in the mysteries,' said Mr Brisbeau, continuing to empty plates into the sack. 'In the now and forever, the here and hereafter. I'd be a damn fool, me, if I didn't. Ain't no point in not believin'.' He held up a moldy orange. 'See this here. That Robichaux boy he come 'bout ever' week and leave an orange, and the way that family is, so damn mean to each other and poor, this orange stands for somethin'! Somethin' special. The boy here' – he patted the stone – 'who knows what he could do if he can bring out the soul in Herve Robichaux's boy. Maybe you got reason to hope.' He tossed the orange into the sack.

'It's not hope,' said Jocundra. 'It's just confusion. I know he's dead.'

'Sure it's hope,' said Mr Brisbeau. 'Me, I ain't no genius, but I can tell you 'bout hope. When my boy he's missin' in action, I live wit hope for ten damn years. It's the cruelest thing in the world. If it get a hook in you, maybe it never let you go no matter how hopeless things really is.' He closed up the sack and laughed. 'I remember what my *grand-mère* use to say 'round breakfas' time. My brother John he's always after her to fix pancakes. Firs' ting ever' mornin' he say, "Well, I hope we goin' to have pancakes." And my *grand-mère* she tell him jus' be glad his belly's full, him, and then she say, "You keep your hope for tomorrow, boy, 'cause we got grits for today."' He stood and shouldered the sack. 'Maybe that's all there is to some kinds of hopin'. It makes them grits go down easier.'

He worried the ants with his toe for a few seconds, weighing something, then said, 'You come 'long wit me while I slop ol' man Bivalaqua's hogs, and after that I buy you breakfas' in town. What you say, girl?'

'All right,' she said, thankful for the company. 'I'll be up in a minute.'

As soon as he was out of sight, she opened her purse and took out the folded piece of paper on which Donnell had written 'The Song of Returning.' She went over to the stone and laid the paper on the ground. It fluttered and unfolded in the breeze. An ant ran along the central crease, using it as a bridge between scraps of food, and a stronger breeze sailed it toward the bayou. She started to chase it down, but held back. Even though she remembered the words, she had an idea that if she let it go she would finally be able to let go of Donnell. The paper caught on a myrtle twig beside the boathouse, tattered madly, and then, obeying a shift in the wind, it skittered to rest under the chair where she had been sitting. She waited to see where it would blow next, but the wind had swirled off into the swamp and the paper just lay there. After a while, she picked it up.

THE JAGUAR HUNTER

The Jaguar Hunter	233
The Night of White Bhairab	254
Salvador	282
How the Wind Spoke at Madaket	297
Black Coral	347
The End of Life as We Know It	370
A Traveler's Tale	394
Mengele	434
The Man Who Painted the Dragon Griaule	445
A Spanish Lesson	468
R&R	495
Radiant Green Star	559

For Gullivar

FOREWORD

Seldom do new writers arrive on the scene – whether amid the Scotch and evening-wear ads in *The New Yorker* or in the grainy double columns of *Fantasy and Science Fiction* – with a convincing command of language, a deft display of storytelling techniques, and an authoritative auctorial presence. Attention-grabbing newcomers may write like seraphs in disguise. Or they may expertly set you up for stinger endings that you never once expect. Or (the least likely of these three scenarios) they may show you a hard-won compassion or a with-it worldliness narrowly compensating for their deficiencies as either stylists or spellbinders.

Rarely, though, will you find yourself reading a newcomer whose work manages to combine all three of these virtues. The reason is simple. Except for a few literary prodigies who take to it like termites to timber, writing requires blood, sweat, and tears. It wants not only a developable talent but also a fingers-to-the-nub apprenticeship that may occasionally prove more humbling than uplifting. Because most writers begin to sell their work in their late teens or early twenties, they do part of their apprenticeship in public, keyboarding marginally salable work while struggling to improve their craft and to grow as persons. Little wonder, then, that neophyte writers produce a catch-as-catch-can commodity, now singing exquisite arias, now crudely caterwauling – but even in moments of full-throated triumph betraying more tonsil than tone, more raw power than rigor.

All of which I note by way of introducing, roundabout, Lucius Shepard – who, like Athena stepping magnificently entire from the forehead of Zeus, arrived on the fantasy and science-fiction scene a fully formed talent. (On the other hand, how long did Athena gestate before inflicting her daddy's migraine?) His first stories – 'The Taylorsville Reconstruction' from Terry Carr's *Universe 13* and 'Solitario's Eyes' from *Fantasy and Science Fiction* – appeared in 1983; they showed him to be both an accomplished and a versatile storyteller. In 1984, at least seven more tales (short stories, novelettes, novellas) bearing the Shepard byline cropped up in the field's best magazines and anthologies. These tales displayed a range of experience, and a mature insight into the complexities of human behavior, astonishing in a 'beginner.' In May 1984, his novel *Green Eyes* appeared as the second title in the revived Ace Science Fiction Special series; and in 1985, at the World Science Fiction Convention in Melbourne, Australia, the John W. Campbell Award for Best

New Writer went to Lucius Shepard – with total and therefore gratifying justice.

Okay. Who is this guy? I've never met him, but I *have* read nearly everything he has published to date. Moreover, letters have been exchanged. (I wrote him one, and he wrote me back.) Beyond these glancing run-ins, I've talked to Lucius Shepard twice, long distance, on the telephone; and all my not-quite-close encounters with the man have probably given me the mistaken impression that I know something vital about the person behind the name, when what I chiefly know is really only what you are going to discover when you begin reading this collection of stories – namely, that Lucius Shepard field-marshals the language with the best of them, that he knows not just the tricks but also some of the deeper mysteries of the trade, and that he has lived long enough and intensely enough to have acquired a gut feel for the best ways to use his knowledge of both people and craft to transfigure honest entertainment into unpretentious art. *All* the stories in *The Jaguar Hunter* are fun to read, but several of them – maybe as many as half – rise toward the Keatsian beauty and truth of the long-enduring.

How so? Well, Shepard came somewhat tardily to writing (i.e., in his mid- to late-thirties), after a worldly apprenticeship that included an enforced introduction to the English classics at the hands of his father; a teenage rebellion against institutionalized learning; expatriate sojourns in Europe, the Middle East, India, and Afghanistan, among other exotic places; an intermittent but serious commitment to rock 'n' roll with bands such as The Monsters, Mister Right, Cult Heroes, The Average Joes, Alpha Ratz, and Villain ('We Have Ways of Making You Rock'); occasional trips to Latin America, where he has granted Most Favored Hideaway status to an island off the coast of Honduras; marriage, fatherhood, and divorce; and some stints both employed and unemployed that he may one day decide to narrate in his autobiography but that I know too little about even to mention in passing. Total immersion in the Clarion workshop for budding fantasy and science-fiction writers in the Summer of '80 led him to begin testing his talents, and not too long thereafter his first stories achieved print. In short, Lucius Shepard is so far from a novice – although he may yet qualify as a Young Turk – that even middle-aged professionals with more than a book or two behind them have to acknowledge him as a peer. Indeed, he has already shown signs of outright mastery that both humble and enormously cheer all of us who believe in the power of imaginative fiction to speak to the human heart.

Haunting echoes of the Vietnam conflict reverberate through the distinctive stories 'Salvador' and 'Mengele.' Meanwhile, 'Black Coral,' 'The End of Life as We Know It,' 'A Traveler's Tale,' and 'The Jaguar Hunter' illuminate this same lush Latin American landscape in a fashion vaguely suggestive of Graham Greene, Paul Theroux, and Gabriel Garcia Marquez. Nevertheless,

Shepard's voice remains determinedly his own. In both 'The Night of White Bhairab' and 'How the Wind Spoke at Madaket,' he plays unusual variations on the contemporary horror story. In the latter tale, for instance, he says of the wind, 'It was of nature, not of some netherworld. It was ego without thought, power without morality.' And in the novelette 'A Spanish Lesson,' Shepard dares to conclude his baroque narrative with a practical moral that 'makes the story resonate beyond the measure of the page.' My own favorite in this collection, by the way, is 'The Man Who Painted the Dragon Griaule' – a tale that, in the indirect way of a parable, implies a great deal about both love and creativity. Seldom, though, do you find a parable so vivid or so involvingly sustained.

So pick a story at random, read it, and go helplessly on to all the others at hand. Lucius Shepard has arrived. *The Jaguar Hunter* beautifully announces this fact.

MICHAEL BISHOP

THE JAGUAR HUNTER

It was his wife's debt to Onofrio Esteves, the appliance dealer, that brought Esteban Caax to town for the first time in almost a year. By nature he was a man who enjoyed the sweetness of the countryside above all else; the placid measures of a farmer's day invigorated him, and he took great pleasure in nights spent joking and telling stories around a fire, or lying beside his wife, Encarnación. Puerto Morada, with its fruit company imperatives and sullen dogs and cantinas that blared American music, was a place he avoided like the plague: indeed, from his home atop the mountain whose slopes formed the northernmost enclosure of Bahía Onda, the rusted tin roofs ringing the bay resembled a dried crust of blood such as might appear upon the lips of a dying man.

On this particular morning, however, he had no choice but to visit the town. Encarnación had – without his knowledge – purchased a battery-operated television set on credit from Onofrio, and he was threatening to seize Esteban's three milk cows in lieu of the eight hundred *lempira* that was owed; he refused to accept the return of the television, but had sent word that he was willing to discuss an alternate method of payment. Should Esteban lose the cows, his income would drop below a subsistence level and he would be forced to take up his old occupation, an occupation far more onerous than farming.

As he walked down the mountain, past huts of thatch and brushwood poles identical to his own, following a trail that wound through sun-browned thickets lorded over by banana trees, he was not thinking of Onofrio but of Encarnación. It was in her nature to be frivolous, and he had known this when he had married her; yet the television was emblematic of the differences that had developed between them since their children had reached maturity. She had begun to put on sophisticated airs, to laugh at Esteban's country ways, and she had become the doyenne of a group of older women, mostly widows, all of whom aspired to sophistication. Each night they would huddle around the television and strive to outdo one another in making sagacious comments about the American detective shows they watched; and each night Esteban would sit outside the hut and gloomily ponder the state of his marriage. He believed Encarnación's association with the widows was her manner of telling him that she looked forward to adopting the black skirt and shawl, that – having served his purpose as a father – he was now an impediment to her. Though she was only forty-one, younger by three years than Esteban, she was withdrawing from the life of the senses; they rarely made love anymore, and he was certain that this partially embodied her resentment to the fact that the years had been kind to him. He had the look of one of the Old Patuca – tall, with chiseled features and wide-set eyes; his coppery skin was relatively unlined and his hair jet black. Encarnación's hair was streaked with gray, and the clean beauty of her limbs had dissolved beneath layers of fat. He had not expected her to remain beautiful, and he had tried to assure her that he loved the woman she was and not merely the girl she had been. But that woman was dying, infected by the same disease that had infected Puerto Morada, and perhaps his love for her was dying, too.

The dusty street on which the appliance store was situated ran in back of the movie theater and the Hotel Circo del Mar, and from the inland side of the street Esteban could see the bell towers of Santa Maria del Onda rising above the hotel roof like the horns of a great stone snail. As a young man, obeying his mother's wish that he become a priest, he had spent three years cloistered beneath those towers, preparing for the seminary under the tutelage of old Father Gonsalvo. It was the part of his life he most regretted, because the academic disciplines he had mastered seemed to have stranded him between the world of the Indian and that of contemporary society; in his heart he held to his father's teachings – the principles of magic, the history of the tribe, the lore of nature – and yet he could never escape the feeling that such wisdom was either superstitious or simply unimportant. The shadows of the towers lay upon his soul as surely as they did upon the cobbled square in front of the church, and the sight of them caused him to pick up his pace and lower his eyes.

Farther along the street was the Cantina Atómica, a gathering place for the well-to-do youth of the town, and across from it was the appliance store, a one-story building of yellow stucco with corrugated metal doors that were lowered at night. Its facade was decorated by a mural that supposedly represented the merchandise within: sparkling refrigerators and televisions and washing machines, all given the impression of enormity by the tiny men and women painted below them, their hands upflung in awe. The actual merchandise was much less imposing, consisting mainly of radios and used kitchen equipment. Few people in Puerto Morada could afford more, and those who could generally bought elsewhere. The majority of Onofrio's clientele were poor, hard-pressed to meet his schedule of payments, and to a large degree his wealth derived from selling repossessed appliances over and over.

Raimundo Esteves, a pale young man with puffy cheeks and heavily lidded eyes and a petulant mouth, was leaning against the counter when Esteban entered; Raimundo smirked and let out a piercing whistle, and a few seconds later his father emerged from the back room: a huge slug of a man, even paler than Raimundo. Filaments of gray hair were slicked down across his mottled scalp, and his belly stretched the front of a starched *guayabera*. He beamed and extended a hand.

'How good to see you,' he said. 'Raimundo! Bring us coffee and two chairs.'

Much as he disliked Onofrio, Esteban was in no position to be uncivil: he accepted the handshake. Raimundo spilled coffee in the saucers and clattered the chairs and glowered, angry at being forced to serve an Indian.

'Why will you not let me return the television?' asked Esteban after taking a seat; and then, unable to bite back the words, he added, 'Is it no longer your policy to swindle my people?'

Onofrio sighed, as if it were exhausting to explain things to a fool such as Esteban. 'I do not swindle your people. I go beyond the letter of the contracts in allowing them to make returns rather than pursuing matters through the courts. In your case, however, I have devised a way whereby you can keep the television without any further payments and yet settle the account. Is this a swindle?'

It was pointless to argue with a man whose logic was as facile and self-serving as Onofrio's. 'Tell me what you want,' said Esteban.

Onofrio wetted his lips, which were the color of raw sausage. 'I want you to kill the jaguar of Barrio Carolina.'

'I no longer hunt,' said Esteban.

'The Indian is afraid,' said Raimundo, moving up behind Onofrio's shoulder. 'I told you.'

Onofrio waved him away and said to Esteban, 'That is unreasonable. If I take the cows, you will once again be hunting jaguars. But if you do this, you will have to hunt only one jaguar.'

'One that has killed eight hunters.' Esteban set down his coffee cup and stood. 'It is no ordinary jaguar.'

Raimundo laughed disparagingly, and Esteban skewered him with a stare.

'Ah!' said Onofrio, smiling a flatterer's smile. 'But none of the eight used your method.'

'Your pardon, Don Onofrio,' said Esteban with mock formality. 'I have other business to attend.'

'I will pay you five hundred *lempira* in addition to erasing the debt,' said Onofrio.

'Why?' asked Esteban. 'Forgive me, but I cannot believe it is due to a concern for the public welfare.'

Onofrio's fat throat pulsed, his face darkened.

'Never mind,' said Esteban. 'It is not enough.'

'Very well. A thousand.' Onofrio's casual manner could not conceal the anxiety in his voice.

Intrigued, curious to learn the extent of Onofrio's anxiety, Esteban plucked a figure from the air. 'Ten thousand,' he said. 'And in advance.'

'Ridiculous! I could hire ten hunters for this much! Twenty!'

Esteban shrugged. 'But none with my method.'

For a moment Onofrio sat with hands enlaced, twisting them, as if struggling with some pious conception. 'All right,' he said, the words squeezed out of him. 'Ten thousand!'

The reason for Onofrio's interest in Barrio Carolina suddenly dawned on Esteban, and he understood that the profits involved would make his fee seem pitifully small. But he was possessed by the thought of what ten thousand *lempira* could mean: a herd of cows, a small truck to haul produce, or – and as he thought it, he realized this was the happiest possibility – the little stucco house in Barrio Clarín that Encarnación had set her heart on. Perhaps owning it would soften her toward him. He noticed Raimundo staring at him, his expression a knowing smirk; and even Onofrio, though still outraged by the fee, was beginning to show signs of satisfaction, adjusting the fit of his *guayabera*, slicking down his already-slicked-down hair. Esteban felt debased by their capacity to buy him, and to preserve a last shred of dignity, he turned and walked to the door.

'I will consider it,' he tossed back over his shoulder. 'And I will give you my answer in the morning.'

'Murder Squad of New York,' starring a bald American actor, was the featured attraction on Encarnación's television that night, and the widows sat cross-legged on the floor, filling the hut so completely that the charcoal stove and the sleeping hammock had been moved outside in order to provide good viewing angles for the latecomers. To Esteban, standing in the doorway, it seemed his home had been invaded by a covey of large black birds with cowled heads, who were receiving evil instruction from the core of a flickering gray jewel. Reluctantly, he pushed between them and made his way to the shelves mounted on the wall behind the set; he reached up to the top shelf and pulled down a long bundle wrapped in oil-stained newspapers. Out of the corner of his eye, he saw Encarnación watching him, her lips thinned, curved in a smile, and that cicatrix of a smile branded its mark on Esteban's heart. She knew what he was about, and she was delighted! Not in the least worried! Perhaps she had known of Onofrio's plan to kill the jaguar, perhaps she had schemed with Onofrio to entrap him. Infuriated, he barged through the widows, setting them to gabbling, and walked out into his banana grove and sat on a stone amidst it. The night was cloudy, and only a handful of stars showed between the tattered dark shapes of the leaves; the wind sent the leaves slithering together, and he heard one of his cows snorting and smelled the ripe odor of the corral. It was as if the solidity of his life had been reduced to this isolated perspective, and he bitterly felt the isolation. Though he would admit to fault in the marriage, he could think of nothing he had done that could have bred Encarnación's hateful smile.

After a while, he unwrapped the bundle of newspapers and drew out a thin-bladed machete of the sort used to chop banana stalks, but which he used to kill jaguars. Just holding it renewed his confidence and gave him a feeling of strength. It had been four years since he had hunted, yet he knew he had not lost the skill. Once he had been proclaimed the greatest hunter in the province of Nueva Esperanza, as had his father before him, and he had not retired from hunting because of age or infirmity, but because the jaguars were beautiful, and their beauty had begun to outweigh the reasons he had for killing them. He had no better reason to kill the jaguar of Barrio Carolina. It menaced no one other than those who hunted it, who sought to invade its territory, and its death would profit only a dishonorable man and a shrewish wife, and would spread the contamination of Puerto Morada. And besides, it was a black jaguar.

'Black jaguars,' his father had told him, 'are creatures of the moon. They have other forms and magical purposes with which we must not interfere. Never hunt them!'

His father had not said that the black jaguars lived on the moon, simply that they utilized its power; but as a child, Esteban had dreamed about a moon of ivory forests and silver meadows through which the jaguars flowed as swiftly as black water; and when he had told his father of the dreams, his father had said that such dreams were representations of a truth, and that sooner or later he would discover the truth underlying them. Esteban had never stopped believing in the dreams, not even in face of the rocky, airless place depicted by the science programs on Encarnación's television: that moon, its mystery explained, was merely a less enlightening kind of dream, a statement of fact that reduced reality to the knowable.

But as he thought this, Esteban suddenly realized that killing the jaguar might be the solution to his problems, that by going against his father's teaching, that by killing his dreams, his Indian conception of the world, he might be able to find accord with his wife's; he had been standing halfway between the two conceptions for too long, and it was time for him to choose. And there was no real choice. It was this world he inhabited, not that of the jaguars; if it took the death of a magical creature to permit him to embrace as joys the television and trips to the movies and a stucco house in Barrio Clarín, well, he had faith in this method. He swung the machete, slicing the dark air, and laughed. Encarnación's frivolousness, his skill at hunting, Onofrio's greed, the jaguar, the television ... all these things were neatly woven together like the elements of a spell, one whose products would be a denial of magic and a furthering of the unmagical doctrines that had corrupted Puerto Morada. He laughed again, but a second later he chided himself: it was exactly this sort of thinking he was preparing to root out.

*

Esteban waked Encarnación early the next morning and forced her to accompany him to the appliance store. His machete swung by his side in a leather sheath, and he carried a burlap sack containing food and the herbs he would need for the hunt. Encarnación trotted along beside him, silent, her face hidden by a shawl. When they reached the store, Esteban had Onofrio stamp the bill PAID IN FULL, then he handed the bill and the money to Encarnación.

'If I kill the jaguar or if it kills me,' he said harshly, 'this will be yours. Should I fail to return within a week, you may assume that I will never return.'

She retreated a step, her face registering alarm, as if she had seen him in a new light and understood the consequences of her actions; but she made no move to stop him as he walked out the door.

Across the street, Raimundo Esteves was leaning against the wall of the Cantina Atómica, talking to two girls wearing jeans and frilly blouses; the girls were fluttering their hands and dancing to the music that issued from the cantina, and to Esteban they seemed more alien than the creature he was to hunt. Raimundo spotted him and whispered to the girls; they peeked over their shoulders and laughed. Already angry at Encarnación, Esteban was washed over by a cold fury. He crossed the street to them, rested his hand on the hilt of the machete, and stared at Raimundo; he had never before noticed how soft he was, how empty of presence. A crop of pimples straggled along his jaw, the flesh beneath his eyes was pocked by tiny indentations like those made by a silversmith's hammer, and, unequal to the stare, his eyes darted back and forth between the two girls.

Esteban's anger dissolved into revulsion. 'I am Esteban Caax,' he said. 'I have built my own house, tilled my soil, and brought four children into the world. This day I am going to hunt the jaguar of Barrio Carolina in order to make you and your father even fatter than you are.' He ran his gaze up and down Raimundo's body, and, letting his voice fill with disgust, he asked, 'Who are you?'

Raimundo's puffy face cinched in a knot of hatred, but he offered no response. The girls tittered and skipped through the door of the cantina; Esteban could hear them describing the incident, laughter, and he continued to stare at Raimundo. Several other girls poked their heads out the door, giggling and whispering. After a moment Esteban spun on his heel and walked away. Behind him there was a chorus of unrestrained laughter, and a girl's voice called mockingly, 'Raimundo! Who are you?' Other voices joined in, and it soon became a chant.

Barrio Carolina was not truly a barrio of Puerto Morada; it lay beyond Punta Manabique, the southernmost enclosure of the bay, and was fronted by a palm hammock and the loveliest stretch of beach in all the province, a curving slice of white sand giving way to jade-green shallows. Forty years before, it had been the headquarters of the fruit company's experimental farm, a project of such vast scope that a small town had been built on the site: rows of white frame houses with shingle roofs and screen porches, the kind you might see in a magazine illustration of rural America. The company had touted the project as being the keystone of the country's future and had promised to develop high-yield crops that would banish starvation; but in 1947 a cholera epidemic had ravaged the coast and the town had been abandoned. By the time the cholera scare had died down, the company had become well entrenched in national politics and no longer needed to maintain a benevolent image; the project had been dropped and the property abandoned until – in the same year that Esteban had retired from hunting – developers had bought it, planning to build a major resort. It was then the jaguar had appeared. Though it had not killed any of the workmen, it had terrorized them to the point that they had refused to begin the job. Hunters had been sent, and these the jaguar *had* killed. The last party of hunters had been equipped with automatic rifles, all manner of technological aids; but the jaguar had picked them off one by one, and this project, too, had been abandoned. Rumor had it that the land had recently been resold (now Esteban knew to whom), and that the idea of a resort was once more under consideration.

    The walk from Puerto Morada was hot and tiring, and upon arrival Esteban sat beneath a palm and ate a lunch of cold banana fritters. Combers as white as toothpaste broke on the shore, and there was no human litter, just dead fronds and driftwood and coconuts. All but four of the houses had been swallowed by the jungle, and only sections of those four remained visible, embedded like moldering gates in a blackish-green wall of vegetation. Even under the bright sunlight, they were haunted-looking: their screens ripped, boards weathered gray, vines cascading over their facades. A mango tree had sprouted from one of the porches, and wild parrots were eating its fruit. He had not visited the barrio since childhood: the ruins had frightened him then, but now he found them appealing, testifying to the dominion of natural law. It distressed him that he would help transform it all into a place where the parrots would be chained to perches and the jaguars would be designs on tablecloths, a place of swimming pools and tourists sipping from coconut shells. Nonetheless, after he had finished lunch, he set out to explore the jungle and soon discovered a trail used by the jaguar: a narrow path that wound between the vine-matted shells of the houses for about a half mile and ended at the Rio Dulce. The river was a murkier green than the sea, curving away through the jungle walls; the jaguar's tracks were everywhere along the bank, especially thick upon a tussocky rise some five or six feet above the water. This baffled Esteban. The jaguar could not drink from the rise, and it certainly would not sleep there. He puzzled over it awhile, but eventually shrugged it off, returned to the beach, and, because he planned to keep watch that night, took a nap beneath the palms.

Some hours later, around midafternoon, he was started from his nap by a voice hailing him. A tall, slim, copper-skinned woman was walking toward him, wearing a dress of dark green – almost the exact color of the jungle walls – that exposed the swell of her breasts. As she drew near, he saw that though her features had a Patucan cast, they were of a lapidary fineness uncommon to the tribe; it was as if they had been refined into a lovely mask: cheeks planed into subtle hollows, lips sculpted full, stylized feathers of ebony inlaid for eyebrows, eyes of jet and white onyx, and all this given a human gloss. A sheen of sweat covered her breasts, and a single curl of black hair lay over her collarbone, so artful-seeming it appeared to have been placed there by design. She knelt beside him, gazing at him impassively, and Esteban was flustered by her heated air of sensuality. The sea breeze bore her scent to him, a sweet musk that reminded him of mangoes left ripening in the sun.

'My name is Esteban Caax,' he said, painfully aware of his own sweaty odor.

'I have heard of you,' she said. 'The jaguar hunter. Have you come to kill the jaguar of the barrio?'

'Yes,' he said, and felt shame at admitting it.

She picked up a handful of sand and watched it sift through her fingers.

'What is your name?' he asked.

'If we become friends, I will tell you my name,' she said. 'Why must you kill the jaguar?'

He told her about the television set, and then, to his surprise, he found himself describing his problems with Encarnación, explaining how he intended to adapt to her ways. These were not proper subjects to discuss with a stranger, yet he was lured to intimacy; he thought he sensed an affinity between them, and that prompted him to portray his marriage as more dismal than it was, for though he had never once been unfaithful to Encarnación, he would have welcomed the chance to do so now.

'This is a black jaguar,' she said. 'Surely you know they are not ordinary animals, that they have purposes with which we must not interfere?'

Esteban was startled to hear his father's words from her mouth, but he dismissed it as coincidence and replied, 'Perhaps. But they are not mine.'

'Truly, they are,' she said. 'You have simply chosen to ignore them.' She scooped up another handful of sand. 'How will you do it? You have no gun. Only a machete.'

'I have this as well,' he said, and from his sack he pulled out a small parcel of herbs and handed it to her.

She opened it and sniffed the contents. 'Herbs? Ah! You plan to drug the jaguar.'

'Not the jaguar. Myself.' He took back the parcel. 'The herbs slow the heart and give the body a semblance of death. They induce a trance, but one that can be thrown off at a moment's notice. After I chew them, I will lie down in a place that the jaguar must pass on its nightly hunt. It will think I am dead, but it will not feed unless it is sure that the spirit has left the flesh, and to determine this, it will sit on the body so it can feel the spirit rise up. As soon as it starts to settle, I will throw off the trance and stab it between the ribs. If my hand is steady, it will die instantly.'

'And if your hand is unsteady?'

'I have killed nearly fifty jaguars,' he said. 'I no longer fear unsteadiness. The method comes down through my family from the Old Patuca, and it has never failed, to my knowledge.'

'But a black jaguar ...'

'Black or spotted, it makes no difference. Jaguars are creatures of instinct, and one is like another when it comes to feeding.'

'Well,' she said, 'I cannot wish you luck, but neither do I wish you ill.' She came to her feet, brushing the sand from her dress.

He wanted to ask her to stay, but pride prevented him, and she laughed as if she knew his mind.

'Perhaps we will talk again, Esteban,' she said. 'It would be a pity if we did not, for more lies between us than we have spoken of this day.'

She walked swiftly down the beach, becoming a diminutive black figure that was rippled away by the heat haze.

That evening, needing a place from which to keep watch, Esteban pried open the screen door of one of the houses facing the beach and went onto the porch. Chameleons skittered into the corners, and an iguana slithered off a rusted lawn chair sheathed in spiderweb and vanished through a gap in the floor. The interior of the house was dark and forbidding, except for the bathroom, the roof of which was missing, webbed over by vines that admitted a gray-green infusion of twilight. The cracked toilet was full of rainwater and dead insects. Uneasy, Esteban returned to the porch, cleaned the lawn chair, and sat.

Out on the horizon the sea and sky were blending in a haze of silver and gray; the wind had died, and the palms were as still as sculpture; a string of pelicans flying low above the waves seemed to be spelling a sentence of cryptic black syllables. But the eerie beauty of the scene was lost on him. He could not stop thinking of the woman. The memory of her hips rolling beneath the fabric of her dress as she walked away was repeated over and over in his thoughts, and whenever he tried to turn his attention to the matter at hand, the memory became more compelling. He imagined her naked, the play of muscles rippling her haunches, and this so enflamed him that he started to pace, unmindful of the fact that the creaking boards were signaling his presence. He could not understand her effect upon him. Perhaps, he thought, it was her defense of the jaguar, her calling to mind of all he was putting behind him ... and then a realization settled over him like an icy shroud.

It was commonly held among the Patuca that a man about to suffer a solitary and unexpected death would be visited by an envoy of death, who – standing in for family and friends – would prepare him to face the event; and Esteban was now very sure that the woman had been such an envoy, that her allure had been specifically designed to attract his soul to its imminent fate. He sat back down in the lawn chair, numb with the realization. Her knowledge of his father's words, the odd flavor of her conversation, her intimation that more lay between them: it all accorded perfectly with the traditional wisdom. The moon rose three-quarters full, silvering the sands of the barrio, and still he sat there, rooted to the spot by his fear of death.

He had been watching the jaguar for several seconds before he registered its presence. It seemed at first that a scrap of night sky had fallen onto the sand and was being blown by a fitful breeze; but soon he saw that it was the jaguar, that it was inching along as if stalking some prey. Then it leaped high into the air, twisting and turning, and began to race up and down the beach: a ribbon of black water flowing across the silver sands. He had never before seen a jaguar at play, and this alone was cause for wonder; but most of all, he wondered at the fact that here were his childhood dreams come to life. He might have been peering out onto a silvery meadow of the moon, spying on one of its magical creatures. His fear was eroded by the sight, and like a child he pressed his nose to the screen, trying not to blink, anxious that he might miss a single moment.

At length the jaguar left off its play and came prowling up the beach toward the jungle. By the set of its ears and the purposeful sway of its walk, Esteban recognized that it was hunting. It stopped beneath a palm about twenty feet from the house, lifted its head, and tested the air. Moonlight frayed down through the fronds, applying liquid gleams to its haunches; its eyes, glinting yellow-green, were like peepholes into a lurid dimension of fire. The jaguar's beauty was heart-stopping – the embodiment of a flawless principle – and Esteban, contrasting this beauty with the pallid ugliness of his employer, with the ugly principle that had led to his hiring, doubted that he could ever bring himself to kill it.

All the following day he debated the question. He had hoped the woman would return, because he had rejected the idea that she was death's envoy – that perception, he thought, must have been induced by the mysterious atmosphere of the barrio – and he felt that if she was to argue the jaguar's cause again, he would let himself be persuaded. But she did not put in an appearance, and as he sat upon the beach, watching the evening sun decline through strata of dusky orange and lavender clouds, casting wild glitters over the sea, he understood once more that he had no choice. Whether or not the jaguar was beautiful, whether or not the woman had been on a supernatural errand, he must treat these things as if they had no substance. The point of the hunt had been to deny mysteries of this sort, and he had lost sight of it under the influence of old dreams.

He waited until moonrise to take the herbs, and then lay down beneath the palm tree where the jaguar had paused the previous night. Lizards whispered past in the grasses, sand fleas hopped onto his face: he hardly felt them, sinking deeper into the languor of the herbs. The fronds overhead showed an ashen green in the moonlight, lifting, rustling; and the stars between their feathered edges flickered crazily as if the breeze were fanning their flames. He became immersed in the landscape, savoring the smells of brine and rotting foliage that were blowing across the beach, drifting with them; but when he heard the pad of the jaguar's step, he came alert. Through narrowed eyes he saw it sitting a dozen feet away, a bulky shadow craning its neck toward him, investigating his scent. After a moment it began to circle him, each circle a bit tighter than the one before, and whenever it passed out of view he had to repress a trickle of fear. Then, as it passed close on the seaward side, he caught a whiff of its odor.

A sweet, musky odor that reminded him of mangoes left ripening in the sun.

Fear welled up in him, and he tried to banish it, to tell himself that the odor could not possibly be what he thought. The jaguar snarled, a razor stroke of sound that slit the peaceful mesh of wind and surf, and realizing it had scented his fear, he sprang to his feet, waving his machete. In a whirl of vision he saw the jaguar leap back, then he shouted at it, waved the machete again, and sprinted for the house where he had kept watch. He slipped through the door and went staggering into the front room. There was a crash behind him, and turning, he had a glimpse of a huge black shape struggling to extricate itself from a moonlit tangle of vines and ripped screen. He darted into the bathroom, sat with his back against the toilet bowl, and braced the door shut with his feet.

The sound of the jaguar's struggles subsided, and for a moment he thought it had given up. Sweat left cold trails down his sides, his heart pounded. He held his breath, listening, and it seemed the whole world was holding its breath as well. The noises of wind and surf and insects were a faint seething; moonlight shed a sickly white radiance through the enlaced vines overhead, and a chameleon was frozen among peels of wallpaper beside the door. He let out a sigh and wiped the sweat from his eyes. He swallowed.

Then the top panel of the door exploded, shattered by a black paw. Splinters of rotten wood flew into his face, and he screamed. The sleek wedge of the jaguar's head thrust through the hole, roaring. A gateway of gleaming fangs guarding a plush red throat. Half-paralyzed, Esteban jabbed weakly with the machete. The jaguar withdrew, reached in with its paw, and clawed at his leg. More by accident than design, he managed to slice the jaguar, and the paw, too, was withdrawn. He heard it rumbling in the front room, and then, seconds later, a heavy thump against the wall behind him. The jaguar's head appeared above the edge of the wall; it was hanging by its forepaws, trying to gain a perch from which to leap down into the room. Esteban scrambled to his feet and slashed wildly, severing vines. The jaguar fell back, yowling. For a while it prowled along the wall, fuming to itself. Finally there was silence.

When sunlight began to filter through the vines, Esteban walked out of the house and headed down the beach to Puerto Morada. He went with his head lowered, desolate, thinking of the grim future that awaited him after he returned the money to Onofrio: a life of trying to please an increasingly shrewish Encarnación, of killing lesser jaguars for much less money. He was so mired in depression that he did not notice the woman until she called to him. She was leaning against a palm about thirty feet away, wearing a filmy white dress through which he could see the dark jut of her nipples. He drew his machete and backed off a pace.

'Why do you fear me, Esteban?' she called, walking toward him.

'You tricked me into revealing my method and tried to kill me,' he said. 'Is that not reason for fear?'

'I did not know you or your method in that form. I knew only that you were hunting me. But now the hunt has ended, and we can be as man and woman.'

He kept his machete at point. 'What are you?' he asked.

She smiled. 'My name is Miranda. I am Patuca.'

'Patucas do not have black fur and fangs.'

'I am of the Old Patuca,' she said. 'We have this power.'

'Keep away!' He lifted the machete as if to strike, and she stopped just beyond his reach.

'You can kill me if that is your wish, Esteban.' She spread her arms, and her breasts thrust forward against the fabric of her dress. 'You are stronger than I, now. But listen to me first.'

He did not lower the machete, but his fear and anger were being overridden by a sweeter emotion.

'Long ago,' she said, 'there was a great healer who foresaw that one day the Patuca would lose their place in the world, and so, with the help of the gods, he opened a door into another world where the tribe could flourish. But many of the tribe were afraid and would not follow him. Since then, the door has been left open for those who would come after.' She waved at the ruined houses. 'Barrio Carolina is the site of the door, and the jaguar is its guardian. But soon the fevers of this world will sweep over the barrio, and the door will close forever. For though our hunt has ended, there is no end to hunters or to greed.' She came a step nearer. 'If you listen to the sounding of your heart, you will know this is the truth.'

He half believed her, yet he also believed her words masked a more poignant truth, one that fitted inside the other the way his machete fitted into its sheath.

'What is it?' she asked. 'What troubles you?'

'I think you have come to prepare me for death,' he said, 'and that your door leads only to death.'

'Then why do you not run from me?' She pointed toward Puerto Morada. 'That is death, Esteban. The cries of the gulls are death, and when the hearts of lovers stop at the moment of greatest pleasure, that, too, is death. This world is no more than a thin covering of life drawn over a foundation of death, like a scum of algae upon a rock. Perhaps you are right, perhaps my world lies beyond death. The two ideas are not opposed. But if I am death to you, Esteban, then it is death you love.'

He turned his eyes to the sea, not wanting her to see his face. 'I do not love you,' he said.

'Love awaits us,' she said. 'And someday you will join me in my world.'

He looked back to her, ready with a denial, but was shocked to silence. Her dress had fallen to the sand, and she was smiling. The litheness and purity of the jaguar were reflected in every line of her body; her secret hair was so absolute a black that it seemed an absence in her flesh. She moved close, pushing aside the machete. The tips of her breasts brushed against him, warm through the coarse cloth of his shirt; her hands cupped his face, and he was drowning in her heated scent, weakened by both fear and desire.

'We are of one soul, you and I,' she said. 'One blood and one truth. You cannot reject me.'

Days passed, though Esteban was unclear as to how many. Night and day were unimportant incidences of his relationship with Miranda, serving only to color their lovemaking with a spectral or a sunny mood; and each time they made love, it was as if a thousand new colors were being added to his senses. He had never been so content. Sometimes, gazing at the haunted facades of the barrio, he believed that they might well conceal shadowy avenues leading to another world; however, whenever Miranda tried to convince him to leave with her, he refused: he could not overcome his fear and would never admit – even to himself – that he loved her. He attempted to fix his thoughts on Encarnación, hoping this would undermine his fixation with Miranda and free him to return to Puerto Morada; but he found that he could not picture his wife except as a black bird hunched before a flickering gray jewel. Miranda, however, seemed equally unreal at times. Once as they sat on the bank of the Rio Dulce, watching the reflection of the moon – almost full – floating upon the water, she pointed to it and said, 'My world is that near, Esteban. That touchable. You may think the moon above is real and this is only a reflection, but the thing most real, that most illustrates the real, is the surface that permits the illusion of reflection. Passing through this surface is what you fear, and yet it is so insubstantial, you would scarcely notice the passage.'

'You sound like the old priest who taught me philosophy,' said Esteban. 'His world – his heaven – was also philosophy. Is that what your world is? The idea of a place? Or are there birds and jungles and rivers?'

Her expression was in partial eclipse, half-moonlit, half-shadowed, and her voice revealed nothing of her mood. 'No more than there are here,' she said.

'What does that mean?' he said angrily. 'Why will you not give me a clear answer?'

'If I were to describe my world, you would simply think me a clever liar.' She rested her head on his shoulder. 'Sooner or later you will understand. We did not find each other merely to have the pain of being parted.'

In that moment her beauty – like her words – seemed a kind of evasion, obscuring a dark and frightening beauty beneath; and yet he knew that she was right, that no proof of hers could persuade him contrary to his fear.

One afternoon, an afternoon of such brightness that it was impossible to look at the sea without squinting, they swam out to a sandbar that showed as a thin curving island of white against the green water. Esteban floundered and splashed, but Miranda swam as if born to the element; she darted beneath him, tickling him, pulling at his feet, eeling away before he could catch her. They walked along the sand, turning over starfish with their toes, collecting whelks to boil for their dinner, and then Esteban spotted a dark stain hundreds of yards wide that was moving below the water beyond the bar: a great school of king mackerel.

'It is too bad we have no boat,' he said. 'Mackerel would taste better than whelks.'

'We need no boat,' she said. 'I will show you an old way of catching fish.'

She traced a complicated design in the sand, and when she had done, she led him into the shallows and had him stand facing her a few feet away.

'Look down at the water between us,' she said. 'Do not look up, and keep perfectly still until I tell you.'

She began to sing with a faltering rhythm, a rhythm that put him in mind of the ragged breezes of the season. Most of the words were unfamiliar, but others he recognized as Patuca. After a minute he experienced a wave of dizziness, as if his legs had grown long and spindly, and he was now looking down from a great height, breathing rarefied air. Then a tiny dark stain materialized below the expanse of water between him and Miranda. He remembered his grandfather's stories of the Old Patuca, how – with the help of the gods – they had been able to shrink the world, to bring enemies close and cross vast distances in a matter of moments. But the gods were dead, their powers gone from the world. He wanted to glance back to shore and see if he and Miranda had become coppery giants taller than the palms.

'Now,' she said, breaking off her song, 'you must put your hand into the water on the seaward side of the school and gently wiggle your fingers. Very gently! Be sure not to disturb the surface.'

But when Esteban made to do as he was told, he slipped and caused a splash. Miranda cried out. Looking up, he saw a wall of jade-green water bearing down on them, its face thickly studded with the fleeting dark shapes of the mackerel. Before he could move, the wave swept over the sandbar and carried him under, dragging him along the bottom and finally casting him onto shore. The beach was littered with flopping mackerel; Miranda lay in the shallows, laughing at him. Esteban laughed, too, but only to cover up his rekindled fear of this woman who drew upon the powers of dead gods. He had no wish to hear her explanation; he was certain she would tell him that the gods lived on in her world, and this would only confuse him further.

Later that day as Esteban was cleaning the fish, while Miranda was off picking bananas to cook with them – the sweet little ones that grew along the riverbank – a Land Rover came jouncing up the beach from Puerto Morada, an orange fire of the setting sun dancing on its windshield. It pulled up beside him, and Onofrio climbed out the passenger side. A hectic flush dappled his cheeks, and he was dabbing his sweaty brow with a handkerchief. Raimundo climbed out the driver's side and leaned against the door, staring hatefully at Esteban.

'Nine days and not a word,' said Onofrio gruffly. 'We thought you were dead. How goes the hunt?'

Esteban set down the fish he had been scaling and stood. 'I have failed,' he said. 'I will give you back the money.'

Raimundo chuckled – a dull, cluttered sound – and Onofrio grunted with amusement. 'Impossible,' he said. 'Encarnación has spent the money on a house in Barrio Clarín. You must kill the jaguar.'

'I cannot,' said Esteban. 'I will repay you somehow.'

'The Indian has lost his nerve, Father.' Raimundo spat in the sand. 'Let me and my friends hunt the jaguar.'

The idea of Raimundo and his loutish friends thrashing through the jungle was so ludicrous that Esteban could not restrain a laugh.

'Be careful, Indian!' Raimundo banged the flat of his hand on the roof of the car.

'It is you who should be careful,' said Esteban. 'Most likely the jaguar will be hunting you.' Esteban picked up his machete. 'And whoever hunts this jaguar will answer to me as well.'

Raimundo reached for something in the driver's seat and walked around in front of the hood. In his hand was a silvered automatic. 'I await your answer,' he said.

'Put that away!' Onofrio's tone was that of a man addressing a child whose menace was inconsequential, but the intent surfacing in Raimundo's face was not childish. A tic marred the plump curve of his cheek, the ligature of his neck was cabled, and his lips were drawn back in a joyless grin. It was, thought Esteban – strangely fascinated by the transformation – like watching a demon dissolve its false shape: the true lean features melting up from the illusion of the soft.

'This son of a whore insulted me in front of Julia!' Raimundo's gun hand was shaking.

'Your personal differences can wait,' said Onofrio. 'This is a business matter.' He held out his hand. 'Give me the gun.'

'If he is not going to kill the jaguar, what use is he?' said Raimundo.

'Perhaps we can convince him to change his mind.' Onofrio beamed at Esteban. 'What do you say? Shall I let my son collect his debt of honor, or will you fulfill our contract?'

'Father!' complained Raimundo; his eyes flicked sideways. 'He …'

Esteban broke for the jungle. The gun roared, a white-hot claw swiped at his side, and he went flying. For an instant he did not know where he was; but then, one by one, his impressions began to sort themselves. He was lying on his injured side, and it was throbbing fiercely. Sand crusted his mouth and eyelids. He was curled up around his machete, which was still clutched in his hand. Voices above him, sand fleas hopping on his face. He resisted the urge to brush them off and lay without moving. The throb of his wound and his hatred had the same red force behind them.

'… carry him to the river,' Raimundo was saying, his voice atremble with excitement. 'Everyone will think the jaguar killed him!'

'Fool!' said Onofrio. 'He might have killed the jaguar, and you could have had a sweeter revenge. His wife …'

'This was sweet enough,' said Raimundo.

A shadow fell over Esteban, and he held his breath. He needed no herbs to deceive this pale, flabby jaguar who was bending to him, turning him onto his back.

'Watch out!' cried Onofrio.

Esteban let himself be turned and lashed out with the machete. His contempt for Onofrio and Encarnación, as well as his hatred of Raimundo, was involved in the blow, and the blade lodged deep in Raimundo's side, grating on bone. Raimundo shrieked and would have fallen, but the blade helped to keep him upright; his hands fluttered around the machete as if he wanted to adjust it to a more comfortable position, and his eyes were wide with disbelief. A shudder vibrated the hilt of the machete – it seemed sensual, the spasm of a spent passion – and Raimundo sank to his knees. Blood spilled from his mouth, adding tragic lines to the corners of his lips. He pitched forward, not falling flat but remaining kneeling, his face pressed into the sand: the attitude of an Arab at prayer.

Esteban wrenched the machete free, fearful of an attack by Onofrio, but the appliance dealer was squirming into the Land Rover. The engine caught, the wheels spun, and the car lurched off, turning through the edge of the surf and heading for Puerto Morada. An orange dazzle flared on the rear window, as if the spirit who had lured it to the barrio was now harrying it away.

Unsteadily, Esteban got to his feet. He peeled his shirt back from the bullet wound. There was a lot of blood, but it was only a crease. He avoided looking at Raimundo and walked down to the water and stood gazing out at the waves; his thoughts rolled in with them, less thoughts than tidal sweeps of emotion.

It was twilight by the time Miranda returned, her arms full of bananas and wild figs. She had not heard the shot. He told her what had happened as she dressed his wounds with a poultice of herbs and banana leaves. 'It will mend,' she said of the wound. 'But this' – she gestured at Raimundo – 'this will not. You must come with me, Esteban. The soldiers will kill you.'

'No,' he said. 'They will come, but they are Patuca ... except for the captain, who is a drunkard, a shell of a man. I doubt he will even be notified. They will listen to my story, and we will reach an accommodation. No matter what lies Onofrio tells, his word will not stand against theirs.'

'And then?'

'I may have to go to jail for a while, or I may have to leave the province. But I will not be killed.'

She sat for a minute without speaking, the whites of her eyes glowing in the half-light. Finally she stood and walked off along the beach.

'Where are you going?' he called.

She turned back. 'You speak so casually of losing me ...' she began.

'It is not casual!'

'No!' She laughed bitterly. 'I suppose not. You are so afraid of life, you call it death and would prefer jail or exile to living it. That is hardly casual.' She stared at him, her expression a cypher at that distance. 'I will not lose you, Esteban,' she said. She walked away again, and this time when he called she did not turn.

*

Twilight deepened to dusk, a slow fill of shadow graying the world into negative, and Esteban felt himself graying along with it, his thoughts reduced to echoing the dull wash of the receding tide. The dusk lingered, and he had the idea that night would never fall, that the act of violence had driven a nail through the substance of his irresolute life, pinned him forever to this ashen moment and deserted shore. As a child he had been terrified by the possibility of such magical isolations, but now the prospect seemed a consolation for Miranda's absence, a remembrance of her magic. Despite her parting words, he did not think she would be back – there had been sadness and finality in her voice – and this roused in him feelings of both relief and desolation, feelings that set him to pacing up and down the tidal margin of the shore.

The full moon rose, the sands of the barrio burned silver, and shortly thereafter four soldiers came in a jeep from Puerto Morada. They were gnomish copper-skinned men, and their uniforms were the dark blue of the night sky, bearing no device or decoration. Though they were not close friends, he knew them each by name: Sebastian, Amador, Carlito, and Ramón. In their headlights Raimundo's corpse – startlingly pale, the blood on his face dried into intricate whorls – looked like an exotic creature cast up by the sea, and their inspection of it smacked more of curiosity than of a search for evidence. Amador unearthed Raimundo's gun, sighted along it toward the jungle, and asked Ramón how much he thought it was worth.

'Perhaps Onofrio will give you a good price,' said Ramón, and the others laughed.

They built a fire of driftwood and coconut shells, and sat around it while Esteban told his story; he did not mention either Miranda or her relation to the jaguar, because these men – estranged from the tribe by their government service – had grown conservative in their judgments, and he did not want them to consider him irrational. They listened without comment; the firelight burnished their skins to reddish gold and glinted on their rifle barrels.

'Onofrio will take his charge to the capital if we do nothing,' said Amador after Esteban had finished.

'He may in any case,' said Carlito. 'And then it will go hard with Esteban.'

'And,' said Sebastian, 'if an agent is sent to Puerto Morada and sees how things are with Captain Portales, they will surely replace him and it will go hard with us.'

They stared into the flames, mulling over the problem, and Esteban chose the moment to ask Amador, who lived near him on the mountain, if he had seen Encarnación.

'She will be amazed to learn you are alive,' said Amador. 'I saw her yesterday in the dressmaker's shop. She was admiring the fit of a new black skirt in the mirror.'

It was as if a black swath of Encarnación's skirt had folded around Esteban's thoughts. He lowered his head and carved lines in the sand with the point of his machete.

'I have it,' said Ramón. 'A boycott!'

The others expressed confusion.

'If we do not buy from Onofrio, who will?' said Ramón. 'He will lose his business. Threatened with this, he will not dare involve the government. He will allow Esteban to plead self-defense.'

'But Raimundo was his only son,' said Amador. 'It may be that grief will count more than greed in this instance.'

Again they fell silent. It mattered little to Esteban what was decided. He was coming to understand that without Miranda, his future held nothing but uninteresting choices; he turned his gaze to the sky and noticed that the stars and the fire were flickering with the same rhythm, and he imagined each of them ringed by a group of gnomish copper-skinned men, debating the question of his fate.

'Aha!' said Carlito. 'I know what to do. We will occupy Barrio Carolina – the entire company – and *we* will kill the jaguar. Onofrio's greed cannot withstand this temptation.'

'That you must not do,' said Esteban.

'But why?' asked Amador. 'We may not kill the jaguar, but with so many men we will certainly drive it away.'

Before Esteban could answer, the jaguar roared. It was prowling down the beach toward the fire, like a black flame itself shifting over the glowing sand. Its ears were laid back, and silver drops of moonlight gleamed in its eyes. Amador grabbed his rifle, came to one knee, and fired: the bullet sprayed sand a dozen feet to the left of the jaguar.

'Wait!' cried Esteban, pushing him down.

But the rest had begun to fire, and the jaguar was hit. It leaped high as it had that first night while playing, but this time it landed in a heap, snarling, snapping at its shoulder; it regained its feet and limped toward the jungle, favoring its right foreleg. Excited by their success, the soldiers ran a few paces after it and stopped to fire again. Carlito dropped to one knee, taking careful aim.

'No!' shouted Esteban, and as he hurled his machete at Carlito, desperate to prevent further harm to Miranda, he recognized the trap that had been sprung and the consequences he would face.

The blade sliced across Carlito's thigh, knocking him onto his side. He screamed, and Amador, seeing what had happened, fired wildly at Esteban and called to the others. Esteban ran toward the jungle, making for the jaguar's path. A fusillade of shots rang out behind him, bullets whipped past his ears. Each time his feet slipped in the soft sand, the moonstruck facades of the barrio appeared to lurch sideways as if trying to block his way. And then, as he reached the verge of the jungle, he was hit.

The bullet seemed to throw him forward, to increase his speed, but somehow he managed to keep his feet. He careened along the path, arms waving, breath shrieking in his throat. Palmetto fronds swatted his face, vines tangled his legs. He felt no pain, only a peculiar numbness that pulsed low in his back; he pictured the wound opening and closing like the mouth of an anemone. The soldiers were shouting his name. They would follow, but cautiously, afraid of the jaguar, and he thought he might be able to cross the river before they could catch up. But when he came to the river, he found the jaguar waiting.

It was crouched on the tussocky rise, its neck craned over the water, and below, half a dozen feet from the bank, floated the reflection of the full moon, huge and silvery, an unblemished circle of light. Blood glistened scarlet on the jaguar's shoulder, like a fresh rose pinned in place, and this made it look even more an embodiment of principle: the shape a god might choose, that some universal constant might assume. It gazed calmly at Esteban, growled low in its throat, and dove into the river, cleaving and shattering the moon's reflection, vanishing beneath the surface. The ripples subsided, the image of the moon re-formed. And there, silhouetted against it, Esteban saw the figure of a woman swimming, each stroke causing her to grow smaller and smaller until she seemed no more than a character incised upon a silver plate. It was not only Miranda he saw, but all mystery and beauty receding from him, and he realized how blind he had been not to perceive the truth sheathed inside the truth of death that had been sheathed inside her truth of another world. It was clear to him now. It sang to him from his wound, every syllable a heartbeat. It was written by the dying ripples, it swayed in the banana leaves, it sighed on the wind. It was everywhere, and he had always known it: if you deny mystery – even in the guise of death – then you deny life and you will walk like a ghost through your days, never knowing the secrets of the extremes. The deep sorrows, the absolute joys.

He drew a breath of the rank jungle air, and with it drew a breath of a world no longer his, of the girl Encarnación, of friends and children and country nights ... all his lost sweetness. His chest tightened as with the onset of tears, but the sensation quickly abated, and he understood that the sweetness of the past had been subsumed by a scent of mangoes, that nine magical days – a magical number of days, the number it takes to sing the soul to rest – lay between him and tears. Freed of those associations, he felt as if he were undergoing a subtle refinement of form, a winnowing, and he remembered having felt much the same on the day when he had run out the door of Santa Maria del Onda, putting behind him its dark geometries and cobwebbed catechisms and generations of swallows that had never flown beyond the walls, casting off his acolyte's robe and racing across the square toward the mountain and Encarnación: it had been she who had lured him then, just as his mother had lured him to the church and as Miranda was luring him now, and he laughed at seeing how easily these three women had diverted the flow of his life, how like other men he was in this.

The strange bloom of painlessness in his back was sending out tendrils into his arms and legs, and the cries of the soldiers had grown louder. Miranda was a tiny speck shrinking against a silver immensity. For a moment he hesitated, experiencing a resurgence of fear; then Miranda's face materialized in his mind's eye, and all the emotion he had suppressed for nine days poured through him, washing away the fear. It was a silvery, flawless emotion, and he was giddy with it, light with it; it was like thunder and fire fused into one element and boiling up inside him, and he was overwhelmed by a need to express it, to mold it into a form that would reflect its power and purity. But he was no singer, no poet. There was but a single mode of expression open to him. Hoping he was not too late, that Miranda's door had not shut forever, Esteban dove into the river, cleaving the image of the full moon; and – his eyes still closed from the shock of the splash – with the last of his mortal strength, he swam hard down after her.

THE NIGHT OF WHITE BHAIRAB

Whenever Mr Chatterji went to Delhi on business, twice yearly, he would leave Eliot Blackford in charge of his Katmandu home, and prior to each trip the transfer of keys and instructions would be made at the Hotel Anapurna. Eliot – an angular sharp-featured man in his mid-thirties, with thinning blond hair and a perpetually ardent expression – knew Mr Chatterji for a subtle soul, and he suspected that this subtlety had dictated the choice of meeting place. The Anapurna was the Nepalese equivalent of a Hilton, its bar equipped in vinyl and plastic, with a choirlike arrangement of bottles fronting the mirror. Lights were muted, napkins monogrammed. Mr Chatterji, plump and prosperous in a business suit, would consider it an elegant refutation of Kipling's famous couplet ('East is East,' etc.) that he was at home here, whereas Eliot, wearing a scruffy robe and sandals, was not; he would argue that not only had the twain met, they had actually exchanged places. It was Eliot's own measure of subtlety that restrained him from pointing out what Mr Chatterji could not perceive: that the Anapurna was a skewed version of the American Dream. The carpeting was indoor-outdoor runner; the menu was rife with ludicrous misprints (*Skotch Miss, Screwdiver*); and the lounge act – two turbaned, tuxedoed Indians on electric guitar and traps – was managing to turn 'Evergreen' into a doleful raga.

'There will be one important delivery.' Mr Chatterji hailed the waiter and nudged Eliot's shot glass forward. 'It should have been here days ago, but you know these customs people.' He gave an effeminate shudder to express his distaste for the bureaucracy, and cast an expectant eye on Eliot, who did not disappoint.

'What is it?' he asked, certain that it would be an addition to Mr Chatterji's collection: he enjoyed discussing the collection with Americans; it proved that he had an overview of their culture.

'Something delicious!' said Mr Chatterji. He took the tequila bottle from the waiter and – with a fond look – passed it to Eliot. 'Are you familiar with the Carversville Terror?'

'Yeah, sure.' Eliot knocked back another shot. 'There was a book about it.'

'Indeed,' said Mr Chatterji. 'A bestseller. The Cousineau mansion was once the most notorious haunted house of your New England. It was torn down several months ago, and I've succeeded in acquiring the fireplace, which' – he sipped his drink – 'which was the locus of power. I'm very fortunate to have obtained it.' He fitted his glass into the circle of moisture on the bar and waxed scholarly. 'Aimée Cousineau was a most unusual spirit, capable of a variety of …'

Eliot concentrated on his tequila. These recitals never failed to annoy him, as did – for different reasons – the sleek Western disguise. When Eliot had arrived in Katmandu as a member of the Peace Corps, Mr Chatterji had presented a far less pompous image: a scrawny kid dressed in Levi's that he had wheedled from a tourist. He'd been one of the hangers-on – mostly young Tibetans – who frequented the grubby tearooms on Freak Street, watching the American hippies giggle over their hash yogurt, lusting after their clothes, their women, their entire culture. The hippies had respected the Tibetans: they were a people of legend, symbols of the occultism then in vogue, and the fact that they liked James Bond movies, fast cars, and Jimi Hendrix had increased the hippies' self-esteem. But they had found laughable the fact that Ranjeesh Chatterji – another Westernized Indian – had liked these same things, and they had treated him with mean condescension. Now, thirteen years later, the roles had been reversed; it was Eliot who had become the hanger-on.

He had settled in Katmandu after his tour was up, his idea being to practice meditation, to achieve enlightenment. But it had not gone well. There was an impediment in his mind – he pictured it as a dark stone, a stone compounded of worldly attachments – that no amount of practice could wear down, and his life had fallen into a futile pattern. He would spend ten months of the year living in a small room near the temple of Swayambhunath, meditating, rubbing away at the stone; and then, during March and September, he would occupy Mr Chatterji's house and debauch himself with liquor and sex and drugs. He was aware that Mr Chatterji considered him a burnout, that the position of caretaker was in effect a form of revenge, a means by which his employer could exercise his own brand of condescension; but Eliot minded neither the label nor the attitude. There were worse things to be than a burnout in Nepal. It was beautiful country, it was inexpensive, it was far from Minnesota (Eliot's home). And the concept of personal failure was meaningless here. You lived, died, and were reborn over and over until at last you attained the ultimate success of nonbeing: a terrific consolation for failure.

'… yet in your country,' Mr Chatterji was saying, 'evil has a sultry character. Sexy! It's as if the spirits were adopting vibrant personalities in order to contend with pop groups and movie stars.'

Eliot thought of a comment, but the tequila backed up on him and he belched instead. Everything about Mr Chatterji – teeth, eyes, hair, gold rings – seemed to be gleaming with extraordinary brilliance. He looked as unstable as a soap bubble, a fat little Hindu illusion.

Mr Chatterji clapped a hand to his forehead. 'I nearly forgot. There will be another American staying at the house. A girl. Very shapely!' He shaped an hourglass in the air. 'I'm quite mad for her, but I don't know if she's trustworthy. Please see she doesn't bring in any strays.'

'Right,' said Eliot. 'No problem.'

'I believe I will gamble now,' said Mr Chatterji, standing and gazing toward the lobby. 'Will you join me?'

'No, I think I'll get drunk. I guess I'll see you in October.'

'You're drunk already, Eliot.' Mr Chatterji patted him on the shoulder. 'Hadn't you noticed?'

Early the next morning, hung over, tongue cleaving to the roof of his mouth, Eliot sat himself down for a final bout of trying to visualize the Avalokitesvara Buddha. All the sounds outside – the buzzing of a motor scooter, birdsong, a girl's laughter – seemed to be repeating the mantra, and the gray stone walls of his room looked at once intensely real and yet incredibly fragile, papery, a painted backdrop he could rip with his hands. He began to feel the same fragility, as if he were being immersed in a liquid that was turning him opaque, filling him with clarity. A breath of wind could float him out the window, drift him across the fields, and he would pass through the trees and mountains, all the phantoms of the material world ... but then a trickle of panic welled up from the bottom of his soul, from that dark stone. It was beginning to smolder, to give off poison fumes: a little briquette of anger and lust and fear. Cracks were spreading across the clear substance he had become, and if he didn't move soon, if he didn't break off the meditation, he would shatter.

He toppled out of the lotus position and lay propped on his elbows. His heart raced, his chest heaved, and he felt very much like screaming his frustration. Yeah, that was a temptation. To just say the hell with it and scream, to achieve through chaos what he could not through clarity: to empty himself into the scream. He was trembling, his emotions flowing between self-hate and self-pity. Finally, he struggled up and put on jeans and a cotton shirt. He knew he was close to a breakdown, and he realized that he usually reached this point just before taking up residence at Mr Chatterji's. His life was a frayed thread stretched tight between those two poles of debauchery. One day it would snap.

'The hell with it,' he said. He stuffed the remainder of his clothes into a duffel bag and headed into town.

Walking through Durbar Square – which wasn't really a square but a huge temple complex interspersed with open areas and wound through by cobbled paths – always put Eliot in mind of his brief stint as a tour guide, a career cut short when the agency received complaints about his eccentricity. ('... As you pick your way among the piles of human waste and fruit rinds, I caution you not to breathe too deeply of the divine afflatus; otherwise, it may forever numb you to the scent of Prairie Cove or Petitpoint Gulch or whatever citadel of gracious living it is that you call home ...') It had irked him to have to lecture on the carvings and history of the square, especially to the just-plain-folks who only wanted a Polaroid of Edna or Uncle Jimmy standing next to that weird monkey god on the pedestal. The square was a unique place, and in Eliot's opinion such unenlightened tourism demeaned it.

Pagoda-style temples of red brick and dark wood towered on all sides, their finials rising into brass lightning bolts. They were alien-looking – you half expected the sky above them to be of an otherworldly color and figured by several moons. Their eaves and window screens were ornately carved into the images of gods and demons, and behind a large window screen on the temple of White Bhairab lay the mask of that god. It was almost ten feet high, brass, with a fanciful headdress and long-lobed ears and a mouth full of white fangs; its eyebrows were enameled red, fiercely arched, but the eyes had the goofy quality common to Newari gods – no matter how wrathful they were, there was something essentially friendly about them, and they reminded Eliot of cartoon germs. Once a year – in fact, a little more than a week from now – the screens would be opened, a pipe would be inserted into the god's mouth, and rice beer would jet out into the mouths of the milling crowds; at some point a fish would be slipped into the pipe, and whoever caught it would be deemed the luckiest soul in the Katmandu Valley for the next year. It was one of Eliot's traditions to make a try for the fish, though he knew that it wasn't luck he needed.

Beyond the square, the streets were narrow, running between long brick buildings three and four stories tall, each divided into dozens of separate dwellings. The strip of sky between the roofs was bright, burning blue – a void color – and in the shade the bricks looked purplish. People hung out the windows of the upper stories, talking back and forth: an exotic tenement life. Small shrines – wooden enclosures containing statuary of stucco or brass – were tucked into wall niches and the mouths of alleys. The gods were everywhere in Katmandu, and there was hardly a corner to which their gaze did not penetrate.

On reaching Mr Chatterji's, which occupied half a block-long building, Eliot made for the first of the interior courtyards; a stair led up from it to Mr Chatterji's apartment, and he thought he would check on what had been left to drink. But as he entered the courtyard – a phalanx of jungly plants arranged around a lozenge of cement – he saw the girl and stopped short. She was sitting in a lawn chair, reading, and she was indeed very shapely. She wore loose cotton trousers, a T-shirt, and a long white scarf shot through with golden threads. The scarf and the trousers were the uniform of the young travelers who generally stayed in the expatriate enclave of Temal: it seemed that they all bought them immediately upon arrival in order to identify themselves to each other. Edging closer, peering between the leaves of a rubber plant, Eliot saw that the girl was doe-eyed, with honey-colored skin and shoulder-length brown hair interwoven by lighter strands. Her wide mouth had relaxed into a glum expression. Sensing him, she glanced up, startled; then she waved and set down her book.

'I'm Eliot,' he said, walking over.

'I know. Ranjeesh told me.' She stared at him incuriously.

'And you?' He squatted beside her.

'Michaela.' She fingered the book, as if she were eager to get back to it.

'I can see you're new in town.'

'How's that?'

He told her about the clothes, and she shrugged. 'That's what I am,' she said. 'I'll probably always wear them.' She folded her hands on her stomach: it was a nicely rounded stomach, and Eliot – a connoisseur of women's stomachs – felt the beginnings of arousal.

'Always?' he said. 'You plan on being here that long?'

'I don't know.' She ran a finger along the spine of the book. 'Ranjeesh asked me to marry him, and I said maybe.'

Eliot's infant plan of seduction collapsed beneath this wrecking ball of a statement, and he failed to hide his incredulity. 'You're in love with Ranjeesh?'

'What's that got to do with it?' A wrinkle creased her brow: it was the perfect symptom of her mood, the line a cartoonist might have chosen to express petulant anger.

'Nothing. Not if it doesn't have anything to do with it.' He tried a grin, but to no effect. 'Well,' he said after a pause. 'How do you like Katmandu?'

'I don't get out much,' she said flatly.

She obviously did not want conversation, but Eliot wasn't ready to give up. 'You ought to,' he said. 'The festival of Indra Jatra's about to start. It's pretty wild. Especially on the night of White Bhairab. Buffalo sacrifices, torchlight ...'

'I don't like crowds,' she said.

Strike two.

Eliot strained to think of an enticing topic, but he had the idea it was a lost cause. There was something inert about her, a veneer of listlessness redolent of Thorazine, of hospital routine. 'Have you ever seen the Khaa?' he asked.

'The what?'

'The Khaa. It's a spirit ... though some people will tell you it's partly animal, because over here the animal and spirit worlds overlap. But whatever it is, all the old houses have one, and those that don't are considered unlucky. There's one here.'

'What's it look like?'

'Vaguely anthropomorphic. Black, featureless. Kind of a living shadow. They can stand upright, but they roll instead of walk.'

She laughed. 'No, I haven't seen it. Have you?'

'Maybe,' said Eliot. 'I thought I saw it a couple of times, but I was pretty stoned.'

She sat up straighter and crossed her legs; her breasts jiggled, and Eliot fought to keep his eyes centered on her face. 'Ranjeesh tells me you're a little cracked,' she said.

Good ol' Ranjeesh! He might have known that the son of a bitch would have sandbagged him with his new lady. 'I guess I am,' he said, preparing for the brush-off. 'I do a lot of meditation, and sometimes I teeter on the edge.'

But she appeared more intrigued by this admission than by anything else he had told her; a smile melted up from her carefully composed features. 'Tell me some more about the Khaa,' she said.

Eliot congratulated himself. 'They're quirky sorts,' he said. 'Neither good nor evil. They hide in dark corners, though now and then they're seen in the streets or in the fields out near Jyapu. And the oldest ones, the most powerful ones, live in the temples in Durbar Square. There's a story about the one here that's descriptive of how they operate ... if you're interested.'

'Sure.' Another smile.

'Before Ranjeesh bought this place, it was a guesthouse, and one night a woman with three goiters on her neck came to spend the night. She had two loaves of bread that she was taking home to her family, and she stuck them under her pillow before going to sleep. Around midnight the Khaa rolled into her room and was struck by the sight of her goiters rising and falling as she breathed. He thought they'd make a beautiful necklace, so he took them and put them on his own neck. Then he spotted the loaves sticking out from her pillow. They looked good, so he took them as well and replaced them with two loaves of gold. When the woman woke, she was delighted. She hurried back to her village to tell her family, and on the way she met a friend, a woman, who was going to market. This woman had four goiters. The first woman told her what had happened, and that night the second woman went to the guesthouse and did exactly the same things. Around midnight the Khaa rolled into her room. He'd grown bored with his necklace, and he gave it to the woman. He'd also decided that bread didn't taste very good, but he still had a loaf and he figured he'd give it another chance. So in exchange for the necklace, he took the woman's appetite for bread. When she woke, she had seven goiters, no gold, and she could never eat bread again the rest of her life.'

Eliot had expected a response of mild amusement and had hoped that the story would be the opening gambit in a game with a foregone and pleasurable conclusion; but he had not expected her to stand, to become walled off from him again.

'I've got to go,' she said, and with a distracted wave she made for the front door. She walked with her head down, hands thrust into her pockets as if counting the steps.

'Where are you going?' called Eliot, taken back.

'I don't know. Freak Street, maybe.'

'Want some company?'

She turned back at the door. 'It's not your fault,' she said, 'but I don't really enjoy your company.'

Shot down!

Trailing smoke, spinning, smacking into the hillside, and blowing up into a fireball.

Eliot didn't understand why it had hit him so hard. It had happened before, and it would again. Ordinarily he would have headed for Temal and found himself another long white scarf and pair of cotton trousers, one less morbidly self-involved (that, in retrospect, was how he characterized Michaela), one who would help him refuel for another bout of trying to visualize Avalokitesvara Buddha. He did, in fact, go to Temal; but he merely sat and drank tea and smoked hashish in a restaurant, and watched the young travelers pairing up for the night. Once he caught the bus to Patan and visited a friend, an old hippie pal named Sam Chipley who ran a medical clinic; once he walked out to Swayambhunath, close enough to see the white dome of the stupa, and atop it, the gilt structure on which the all-seeing eyes of Buddha were painted: they seemed squinty and mean-looking, as if taking unfavorable notice of his approach. But mostly over the next week he wandered through Mr Chatterji's house, carrying a bottle, maintaining a buzz, and keeping an eye on Michaela.

The majority of the rooms were unfurnished, but many bore signs of recent habitation: broken hash pipes, ripped sleeping bags, empty packets of incense. Mr Chatterji let travelers – those he fancied sexually, male and female – use the rooms for up to months at a time, and to walk through them was to take a historical tour of the American counterculture. The graffiti spoke of concerns as various as Vietnam, the Sex Pistols, women's lib, and the housing shortage in Great Britain, and also conveyed personal messages: 'Ken Finkel please get in touch with me at Am. Ex. in Bangkok ... love Ruth.' In one of the rooms was a complicated mural depicting Farrah Fawcett sitting on the lap of a Tibetan demon, throttling his barbed phallus with her fingers. It all conjured up the image of a moldering, deranged milieu. Eliot's milieu. At first the tour amused him, but eventually it began to sour him on himself, and he took to spending more and more time on a balcony overlooking the courtyard that was shared with the connecting house, listening to the Newari women sing at their chores and reading books from Mr Chatterji's library. One of the books was titled *The Carversville Terror*.

'Bloodcurdling, chilling ...' said *the New York Times* on the front flap; '... the Terror is unrelenting ...' commented Stephen King; '... riveting, gut-wrenching, mind-bending horror ...' gushed *People* magazine. In neat letters, Eliot appended his own blurb: '... piece of crap ...' The text – written to be read by the marginally literate – was a fictionalized treatment of purportedly real events, dealing with the experiences of the Whitcomb family, who had attempted to renovate the Cousineau mansion during the sixties. Following the usual buildup of apparitions, cold spots, and noisome odors, the family – Papa David, Mama Elaine, young sons Tim and Randy, and teenage Ginny – had met to discuss the situation.

> *... even the kids, thought David, had been aged by the house. Gathered around the dining room table, they looked like a company of the damned – haggard, shadows under their eyes, grim-faced. Even with the windows open and the light streaming in, it seemed there was a pall in the air that no light could dispel. Thank God the damned thing was dormant during the day!*
>
> *'Well,' he said, 'I guess the floor's open for arguments.'*
>
> *'I wanna go home!' Tears sprang from Randy's eyes, and on cue, Tim started crying, too.*
>
> *'It's not that simple,' said David. 'This is home, and I don't know how we'll make it if we do leave. The savings account is just about flat.'*
>
> *'I suppose I could get a job,' said Elaine unenthusiastically.*
>
> *'I'm not leaving!' Ginny jumped to her feet, knocking over her chair. 'Every time I start to make friends, we have to move!'*
>
> *'But Ginny!' Elaine reached out a hand to calm her. 'You were the one ...'*
>
> *'I've changed my mind!' She backed away, as if she had just recognized them all to be mortal enemies. 'You can do what you want, but I'm staying!' And she ran from the room.*
>
> *'Oh, God,' said Elaine wearily. 'What's gotten into her?'*

What had gotten into Ginny, what was in the process of getting into her and was the only interesting part of the book, was the spirit of Aimée Cousineau. Concerned with his daughter's behavior, David Whitcomb had researched the house and learned a great deal about the spirit. Aimée Cousineau, née Vuillemont, had been a native of St Berenice, a Swiss village at the foot of the mountain known as the Eiger (its photograph, as well as one of Aimée – a coldly beautiful woman with black hair and cameo features – was included in the central section of the book). Until the age of fifteen she had been a sweet, unexceptional child; in the summer of 1889, however, while hiking on the slopes of the Eiger, she had become lost in a cave.

The family had all but given up hope when, to their delight – three weeks later – she had turned up on the steps of her father's store. Their delight was short-lived. This Aimée was far different from the one who had entered the cave. Violent, calculating, slatternly.

Over the next two years she succeeded in seducing half the men of the village, including the local priest. According to his testimony, he had been admonishing her that sin was not the path to happiness when she began to undress. 'I'm wed to Happiness,' she told him. 'I've entwined my limbs with the God of Bliss and kissed the scaly thighs of Joy.' Throughout the ensuing affair, she made cryptic comments concerning 'the God below the mountain,' whose soul was now forever joined to hers.

At this point the book reverted to the gruesome adventures of the Whitcomb family, and Eliot, bored, realizing it was noon and that Michaela would be sunbathing, climbed to Mr Chatterji's apartment on the fourth floor. He tossed the book onto a shelf and went out onto the balcony. His continued interest in Michaela puzzled him. It occurred to him that he might be falling in love, and he thought that would be nice. Though it would probably lead nowhere, love would be a good kind of energy to have. But he doubted this was the case. Most likely his interest was founded on some fuming product of the dark stone inside him. Simple lust. He looked over the edge of the balcony. She was lying on a blanket – her bikini top beside her – at the bottom of a well of sunlight: thin, pure sunlight like a refinement of honey spreading down and congealing into the mold of a little gold woman. It seemed that her heat was in the air.

That night Eliot broke one of Mr Chatterji's rules and slept in the master bedroom. It was roofed by a large skylight mounted in a ceiling painted midnight blue. The normal display of stars had not been sufficient for Mr Chatterji, and so he'd had the skylight constructed of faceted glass that multiplied the stars, making it appear that you were at the heart of a galaxy, gazing out between the interstices of its blazing core. The walls consisted of a photomural of the Khumbu Glacier and Chomolungma; and, bathed in the starlight, the mural had acquired the illusion of depth and chill mountain silence. Lying there, Eliot could hear the faint sounds of Indra Jatra: shouts and cymbals, oboes and drums. He was drawn to the sounds; he wanted to run out into the streets, become an element of the drunken crowds, be whirled through torchlight and delirium to the feet of an idol stained with sacrificial blood. But he felt bound to the house, to Michaela. Marooned in the glow of Mr Chatterji's starlight, floating above Chomolungma and listening to the din of the world below, he could almost believe he was a bodhisattva awaiting a call to action, that his watchfulness had some purpose.

The shipment arrived late in the afternoon of the eighth day. Five enormous crates, each requiring the combined energies of Eliot and three Newari workmen to wrangle up to the third-floor room that housed Mr Chatterji's collection. After tipping the men, Eliot – sweaty, panting – sat down against the wall to catch his breath. The room was about twenty-five feet by fifteen, but looked smaller because of the dozens of curious objects standing around the floor and mounted one above the other on the walls. A brass doorknob; a shattered door; a straight-backed chair whose arms were bound with a velvet rope to prevent anyone from sitting; a discolored sink; a mirror streaked by a brown stain; a slashed lampshade. They were all relics of some haunting or possession, some grotesque violence, and there were cards affixed to them testifying to the details and referring those who were interested to materials in Mr Chatterji's library. Sitting amidst these relics, the crates looked innocuous. Bolted shut, chest-high, branded with customs stamps.

When he had recovered, Eliot strolled around the room, amused by the care that Mr Chatterji had squandered on his hobby; the most amusing thing was that no one except Mr Chatterji was impressed by it: it provided travelers with a footnote for their journals. Nothing more.

A wave of dizziness swept over him – he had stood too soon – and he leaned against one of the crates for support. Jesus, he was in lousy shape! And then, as he blinked away the tangles of opaque cells drifting across his field of vision, the crate shifted. Just a little shift, as if something inside had twitched in its sleep. But palpable, real. He flung himself toward the door, backing away. A chill mapped every knob and articulation of his spine, and his sweat had evaporated, leaving clammy patches on his skin. The crate was motionless. But he was afraid to take his eyes off it, certain that if he did, it would release its pent-up fury. 'Hi,' said Michaela from the doorway.

Her voice electrified Eliot. He let out a squawk and wheeled around, his hands outheld to ward off attack.

'I didn't mean to startle you,' she said. 'I'm sorry.'

'Goddamn!' he said. 'Don't sneak up like that!' He remembered the crate and glanced back at it. 'Listen, I was just locking ...'

'I'm sorry,' she repeated, and walked past him into the room. 'Ranjeesh is such an idiot about all this,' she said, running her hand over the top of the crate. 'Don't you think?'

Her familiarity with the crate eased Eliot's apprehension. Maybe he had been the one who had twitched: a spasm of overstrained muscles. 'Yeah, I guess.'

She walked over to the straight-backed chair, slipped off the velvet rope, and sat down. She was wearing a pale brown skirt and a plaid blouse that made her look schoolgirlish. 'I want to apologize about the other day,' she said; she bowed her head, and the fall of her hair swung forward to obscure her face. 'I've been having a bad time lately. I have trouble relating to people. To anything. But since we're living here together, I'd like to be friends.' She stood and spread the folds of her skirt. 'See? I even put on different clothes. I could tell the others offended you.'

The innocent sexuality of the pose caused Eliot to have a rush of desire. 'Looks nice,' he said with forced casualness. 'Why've you been having a bad time?'

She wandered to the door and gazed out. 'Do you really want to hear about it?'

'Not if it's painful for you.'

'It doesn't matter,' she said, leaning against the doorframe. 'I was in a band back in the States, and we were doing okay. Cutting an album, talking to record labels. I was living with the guitarist, in love with him. But then I had an affair. Not even an affair. It was stupid. Meaningless. I still don't know why I did it. The heat of the moment, I guess. That's what rock 'n' roll's all about, and maybe I was just acting out the myth. One of the other musicians told my boyfriend. That's the way bands are – you're friends with everyone, but never at the same time. See, I told this guy about the affair. We'd always confided. But one day he got mad at me over something. Something else stupid and meaningless.' Her chin was struggling to stay firm; the breeze from the courtyard drifted fine strands of hair across her face. 'My boyfriend went crazy and beat up my …' She gave a dismal laugh. 'I don't know what to call him. My lover. Whatever. My boyfriend killed him. It was an accident, but he tried to run, and the police shot him.'

Eliot wanted to stop her; she was obviously seeing it all again, seeing blood and police flashers and cold white morgue lights. But she was riding a wave of memory, borne along by its energy, and he knew that she had to crest with it, crash with it.

'I was out of it for a while. Dreamy. Nothing touched me. Not the funerals, the angry parents. I went away for months, to the mountains, and I started to feel better. But when I came home, I found that the musician who'd told my boyfriend had written a song about it. The affair, the killings. He'd cut a record. People were buying it, singing the hook when they walked down the street or took a shower. Dancing to it! They were dancing on blood and bones, humming grief, shelling out $5.98 for a jingle about suffering. Looking back, I realize I was crazy, but at the time everything I did seemed normal. More than normal. Directed, inspired. I bought a gun. A ladies' model, the salesman said. I remember thinking how strange it was that there were male and female guns, just like with electric razors. I felt enormous carrying it. I had to be meek and polite or else I was sure people would notice how large and purposeful I was. It wasn't hard to track down Ronnie – that's the guy who wrote the song. He was in Germany, cutting a second album. I couldn't believe it, I wasn't going to be able to kill him! I was so frustrated that one night I went down to a park and started shooting. I missed everything. Out of all the bums and joggers and squirrels, I hit leaves and air. They locked me up after that. A hospital. I think it helped, but …' She blinked, waking from a trance. 'But I still feel so disconnected, you know?'

Eliot carefully lifted away the strands of hair that had blown across her face and laid them back in place. Her smile flickered. 'I know,' he said. 'I feel that way sometimes.'

She nodded thoughtfully, as if to verify that she had recognized this quality in him.

They ate dinner in a Tibetan place in Temal; it had no name and was a dump with flyspecked tables and rickety chairs, specializing in water buffalo and barley soup. But it was away from the city center, which meant they could avoid the worst of the festival crowds. The waiter was a young Tibetan wearing jeans and a T-shirt that bore the legend MAGIC IS THE ANSWER; the earphones of a personal stereo dangled about his neck. The walls – visible through a haze of smoke – were covered with snapshots, most featuring the waiter in the company of various tourists, but a few showing an older Tibetan in blue robes and turquoise jewelry, carrying an automatic rifle; this was the owner, one of the Khampa tribesmen who had fought a guerrilla war against the Chinese. He rarely put in an appearance at the restaurant, and when he did, his glowering presence tended to dampen conversation.

Over dinner, Eliot tried to steer clear of topics that might unsettle Michaela. He told her about Sam Chipley's clinic, the time the Dalai Lama had come to Katmandu, the musicians at Swayambhunath. Cheerful, exotic topics. Her listlessness was such an inessential part of her that Eliot was led to chip away at it, curious to learn what lay beneath; and the more he chipped away, the more animated her gestures, the more luminous her smile became. This was a different sort of smile than she had displayed on their first meeting. It came so suddenly over her face, it seemed an autonomic reaction, like the opening of a sunflower, as if she were facing not you but the principle of light upon which you were grounded. It was aware of you, of course, but it chose to see past the imperfections of the flesh and know the perfected thing you truly were. It boosted your sense of worth to realize that you were its target, and Eliot – whose sense of worth was at low ebb – would have done pratfalls to sustain it. Even when he told his own story, he told it as a joke, a metaphor for American misconceptions of oriental pursuits.

'Why don't you quit it?' she asked. 'The meditation, I mean. If it's not working out, why keep on with it?'

'My life's in perfect suspension,' he said. 'I'm afraid that if I quit practicing, if I change anything, I'll either sink to the bottom or fly off.' He tapped his spoon against his cup, signaling for more tea. 'You're not really going to marry Ranjeesh, are you?' he asked, and was surprised at the concern he felt that she actually might.

'Probably not.' The waiter poured their tea, whispery drumbeats issuing from his earphones. 'I was just feeling lost. You see, my parents sued Ronnie over the song, and I ended up with a lot of money – which made me feel even worse …'

'Let's not talk about it,' he said.

'It's all right.' She touched his wrist, reassuring, and the skin remained warm after her fingers had withdrawn. 'Anyway,' she went on, 'I decided to travel, and all the strangeness … I don't know. I was starting to slip away. Ranjeesh was a kind of sanctuary.'

Eliot was vastly relieved.

Outside, the streets were thronged with festivalgoers, and Michaela took Eliot's arm and let him guide her through the crowds. Newars wearing Nehru hats and white trousers that bagged at the hips and wrapped tightly around the calves; groups of tourists, shouting and waving bottles of rice beer; Indians in white robes and saris. The air was spiced with incense, and the strip of empurpled sky above was so regularly patterned with stars that it looked like a banner draped between the roofs. Near the house, a wild-eyed man in a blue satin robe rushed past, bumping into them, and he was followed by two boys dragging a goat, its forehead smeared with crimson powder: a sacrifice.

'This is crazy!' Michaela laughed.

'It's nothing. Wait'll tomorrow night.'

'What happens then?'

'The night of White Bhairab.' Eliot put on a grimace. 'You'll have to watch yourself. Bhairab's a lusty, wrathful sort.'

She laughed again and gave his arm an affectionate squeeze.

Inside the house, the moon – past full, blank and golden – floated dead center on the square of night sky admitted by the roof. They stood close together in the courtyard, silent, suddenly awkward.

'I enjoyed tonight,' said Michaela; she leaned forward and brushed his cheek with her lips. 'Thank you,' she whispered.

Eliot caught her as she drew back, tipped her chin, and kissed her mouth. Her lips parted, her tongue darted out. Then she pushed him away. 'I'm tired,' she said, her face tightened with anxiety. She walked off a few steps, but stopped and turned back. 'If you want to … to be with me, maybe it'll be all right. We could try.'

Eliot went to her and took her hands. 'I want to make love with you,' he said, no longer trying to hide his urgency. And that *was* what he wanted: to make love. Not to ball or bang or screw or any other inelegant version of the act.

But it was not love they made.

Under the starlit blaze of Mr Chatterji's ceiling, she was very beautiful, and at first she was very loving, moving with a genuine involvement; then abruptly, she quit moving altogether and turned her face to the pillow. Her eyes were glistening. Left alone atop her, listening to the animal sound of his breathing, the impact of his flesh against hers, Eliot knew he should stop and comfort her. But the months of abstinence, the eight days of wanting her, all this fused into a bright flare in the small of his back, a reactor core of lust that irradiated his conscience, and he continued to plunge into her, hurrying to completion. She let out a gasp when he withdrew, and curled up, facing away from him.

'God, I'm so sorry,' she said, her voice cracking.

Eliot shut his eyes. He felt sickened, reduced to the bestial. It had been like two mental patients doing nasty on the sly, two fragments of people who together didn't form a whole. He understood now why Mr Chatterji wanted to marry her: he planned to add her to his collection, to enshrine her with the other splinters of violence. And each night he would complete his revenge, substantiate his cultural overview, by making something less than love with this sad, inert girl, this American ghost. Her shoulders shook with muffled sobs. She needed someone to console her, to help her find her own strength and capacity for love. Eliot reached out to her, willing to do his best. But he knew it shouldn't be him.

Several hours later, after she had fallen asleep, unconsolable, Eliot sat in the courtyard, thoughtless, dejected, staring at a rubber plant. It was mired in shadow, its leaves hanging limp. He had been staring for a couple of minutes when he noticed that a shadow in back of the plant was swaying ever so slightly; he tried to make it out, and the swaying subsided. He stood. The chair scraped on the concrete, sounding unnaturally loud. His neck prickled, and he glanced behind him. Nothing. Ye Olde Mental Fatigue, he thought. Ye Olde Emotional Strain. He laughed, and the clarity of the laugh – echoing up through the empty well – alarmed him; it seemed to stir little flickers of motion everywhere in the darkness. What he needed was a drink! The problem was how to get into the bedroom without waking Michaela. Hell, maybe he should wake her. Maybe they should talk more before what had happened hardened into a set of unbreakable attitudes.

He turned toward the stairs ... and then, yelling out in panic, entangling his feet with the lawn chairs as he leaped backward midstep, he fell onto his side. A shadow – roughly man-shaped and man-sized – was standing a yard away; it was undulating the way a strand of kelp undulates in a gentle tide.

The patch of air around it was rippling, as if the entire image had been badly edited into reality. Eliot scrambled away, coming to his knees. The shadow melted downward, puddling on the concrete; it bunched in the middle like a caterpillar, folded over itself, and flowed after him: a rolling sort of motion. Then it reared up, again assuming its manlike shape, looming over him.

Eliot got to his feet, still frightened, but less so. If he had previously been asked to testify as to the existence of the Khaa, he would have rejected the evidence of his bleared senses and come down on the side of hallucination, folktale. But now, though he was tempted to draw that same conclusion, there was too much evidence to the contrary. Staring at the featureless black cowl of the Khaa's head, he had a sense of something staring back. More than a sense. A distinct impression of personality. It was as if the Khaa's undulations were producing a breeze that bore its psychic odor through the air. Eliot began to picture it as a loony, shy old uncle who liked to sit under the basement steps and eat flies and cackle to himself, but who could tell when the first frost was due and knew how to fix the tail on your kite. Weird, yet harmless. The Khaa stretched out an arm: the arm just peeled away from its torso, its hand a thumbless black mitten. Eliot edged back. He wasn't quite prepared to believe it was harmless. But the arm stretched farther than he had thought possible and enveloped his wrist. It was soft, ticklish, a river of furry moths crawling over his skin.

In the instant before he jumped away, Eliot heard a whining note inside his skull, and that whining – seeming to flow through his brain with the same suppleness that the Khaa's arm had displayed – was translated into a wordless plea. From it he understood that the Khaa was afraid. Terribly afraid. Suddenly it melted downward and went rolling, bunching, flowing up the stairs; it stopped on the first landing, rolled halfway down, then up again, repeating the process over and over. It came clear to Eliot (*Oh, Jesus! This is nuts!*) that it was trying to convince him to follow. Just like Lassie or some other ridiculous TV animal, it was trying to tell him something, to lead him to where the wounded forest ranger had fallen, where the nest of baby ducks was being threatened by the brush fire. He should walk over, rumple its head, and say, 'What's the matter, girl? Those squirrels been teasing you?' This time his laughter had a sobering effect, acting to settle his thoughts. One likelihood was that his experience with Michaela had been sufficient to snap his frayed connection with consensus reality; but there was no point in buying that. Even if that were the case, he might as well go with it. He crossed to the stairs, and climbed toward the rippling shadow on the landing.

'Okay, Bongo,' he said. 'Let's see what's got you so excited.'

On the third floor the Khaa turned down a hallway, moving fast, and Eliot didn't see it again until he was approaching the room that housed Mr

Chatterji's collection. It was standing beside the door, flapping its arms, apparently indicating that he should enter. Eliot remembered the crate.

'No, thanks,' he said. A drop of sweat slid down his rib cage, and he realized that it was unusually warm next to the door.

The Khaa's hand flowed over the doorknob, enveloping it, and when the hand pulled back, it was bulging, oddly deformed, and there was a hole through the wood where the lock mechanism had been. The door swung open a couple of inches. Darkness leaked out of the room, adding an oily essence to the air. Eliot took a backward step. The Khaa dropped the lock mechanism – it materialized from beneath the black formless hand and clattered to the floor – and latched onto Eliot's arm. Once again he heard the whining, the plea for help, and since he did not jump away, he had a clearer understanding of the process of translation. He could feel the whining as a cold fluid coursing through his brain, and as the whining died, the message simply appeared – the way an image might appear in a crystal ball. There was an undertone of reassurance to the Khaa's fear, and though Eliot knew this was the mistake people in horror movies were always making, he reached inside the room and fumbled for the wall switch, half-expecting to be snatched up and savaged. He flicked on the light and pushed the door open with his foot.

And wished that he hadn't.

The crates had exploded. Splinters and shards of wood were scattered everywhere, and the bricks had been heaped at the center of the room. They were dark red, friable bricks like crumbling cakes of dried blood, and each was marked with black letters and numbers that signified its original position in the fireplace. But none were in their proper position now, though they were quite artfully arranged. They had been piled into the shape of a mountain, one that – despite the crudity of its building blocks – duplicated the sheer faces and chimneys and gentle slopes of a real mountain. Eliot recognized it from its photograph. The Eiger. It towered to the ceiling, and under the glare of the lights, it gave off a radiation of ugliness and barbarity. It seemed alive, a fang of dark red meat, and the charred smell of the bricks was like a hum in Eliot's nostrils.

Ignoring the Khaa, who was again flapping its arms, Eliot broke for the landing; there he paused, and after a brief struggle between fear and conscience, he sprinted up the stairs to the bedroom, taking them three at a time. Michaela was gone! He stared at the starlit billows of the sheets. Where the hell ... her room! He hurtled down the stairs and fell sprawling on the second-floor landing. Pain lanced through his kneecap, but he came to his feet running, certain that something was behind him.

A seam of reddish orange light – not lamplight – edged the bottom of Michaela's door, and he heard a crispy chuckling noise like a fire crackling in a hearth. The wood was warm to the touch. Eliot's hand hovered over the doorknob. His heart seemed to have swelled to the size of a basketball and was doing a fancy dribble against his chest wall. The sensible thing to do would be to get out quick, because whatever lay beyond the door was bound to be too much for him to handle. But instead he did the stupid thing and burst into the room.

His first impression was that the room was burning, but then he saw that though the fire looked real, it did not spread; the flames clung to the outlines of things that were themselves unreal, that had no substance of their own and were made of the ghostly fire: belted drapes, an overstuffed chair and sofa, a carved mantelpiece, all of antique design. The actual furniture – production-line junk – was undamaged. Intense reddish orange light glowed around the bed, and at its heart lay Michaela. Naked, her back arched. Lengths of her hair lifted into the air and tangled, floating in an invisible current; the muscles of her legs and abdomen were coiling, bunching, as if she were shedding her skin. The crackling grew louder, and the light began to rise from the bed, to form into a column of even brighter light; it narrowed at the midpoint, bulged in an approximation of hips and breasts, gradually assuming the shape of a burning woman. She was faceless, a fiery silhouette. Her flickering gown shifted as with the movements of walking, and flames leaped out behind her head like windblown hair.

Eliot was pumped full of terror, too afraid to scream or run. Her aura of heat and power wrapped around him. Though she was within arm's length, she seemed a long way off, inset into a great distance and walking toward him down a tunnel that conformed exactly to her shape. She stretched out a hand, brushing his cheek with a finger. The touch brought more pain than he had ever known. It was luminous, lighting every circuit of his body. He could feel his skin crisping, cracking, fluids leaking forth and sizzling. He heard himself moan: a gush of rotten sound like something trapped in a drain.

Then she jerked back her hand, as if *he* had burned *her*.

Dazed, his nerves screaming, Eliot slumped to the floor and – through blurred eyes – caught sight of a blackness rippling by the door. The Khaa. The burning woman stood facing it a few feet away. It was such an uncanny scene, this confrontation of fire and darkness, of two supernatural systems, that Eliot was shocked to alertness. He had the idea that neither of them knew what to do. Surrounded by its patch of disturbed air, the Khaa undulated; the burning woman crackled and flickered, embedded in her eerie distance. Tentatively, she lifted her hand; but before she could complete the gesture, the Khaa reached with blinding swiftness and its hand enveloped hers.

A shriek like tortured metal issued from them, as if some iron-clad principle had been breached. Dark tendrils wound through the burning woman's arm, seams of fire striped the Khaa, and there was a high-pitched humming, a vibration that jarred Eliot's teeth. For a moment he was afraid that spiritual versions of antimatter and matter had been brought into conjunction, that the room would explode. But the hum was sheared off as the Khaa snatched back its hand: a scrap of reddish orange flame glimmered within it. The Khaa melted downward and went rolling out the door. The burning woman – and every bit of flame in the room – shrank to an incandescent point and vanished.

Still dazed, Eliot touched his face. It felt burned, but there was no apparent damage. He hauled himself to his feet, staggered to the bed, and collapsed next to Michaela. She was breathing deeply, unconscious. 'Michaela!' He shook her. She moaned, her head rolled from side to side. He heaved her over his shoulder in a fireman's lift and crept out into the hall. Moving stealthily, he eased along the hall to the balcony overlooking the courtyard and peered over the edge ... and bit his lip to stifle a cry. Clearly visible in the electric blue air of the predawn darkness, standing in the middle of the courtyard, was a tall, pale woman wearing a white nightgown. Her black hair fanned across her back. She snapped her head around to stare at him, her cameo features twisted by a gloating smile, and that smile told Eliot everything he had wanted to know about the possibility of escape. Just try to leave, Aimée Cousineau was saying. Go ahead and try. I'd like that. A shadow sprang erect about a dozen feet away from her, and she turned to it. Suddenly there was a wind in the courtyard: a violent whirling wind of which she was the calm center. Plants went flapping up into the well like leathery birds; pots shattered, and the shards flew toward the Khaa. Slowed by Michaela's weight, wanting to get as far as he could from the battle, Eliot headed up the stairs toward Mr Chatterji's bedroom.

It was an hour later, an hour of peeking down into the courtyard, watching the game of hide-and-seek that the Khaa was playing with Aimée Cousineau, realizing that the Khaa was protecting them by keeping her busy ... it was then that Eliot remembered the book. He retrieved it from the shelf and began to skim through it, hoping to learn something helpful. There was nothing else to do. He picked up at the point of Aimée's rap about her marriage to Happiness, passed over the transformation of Ginny Whitcomb into a teenage monster, and found a second section dealing with Aimée.

In 1895 a wealthy Swiss-American named Armand Cousineau had returned to St Berenice – his birthplace – for a visit. He was smitten with Aimée Vuillemont, and her family, seizing the opportunity to be rid of her, allowed Cousineau to marry Aimée and sail her off to his home in Carversville, New Hampshire. Aimée's taste for seduction had not been curbed by the move. Lawyers, deacons, merchants, farmers: they were all grist for her mill. But in the winter of 1905, she fell in love – obsessively, passionately in love – with a young schoolmaster. She believed that the schoolmaster had saved her from her unholy marriage, and her gratitude knew no bounds. Unfortunately, when the schoolmaster fell in love with another woman, neither did her fury. One night while passing the Cousineau mansion, the town doctor spotted a woman walking the grounds: '... a woman of flame, not burning but composed of flame, her every particular a fiery construct ...' Smoke was curling from a window; the doctor rushed inside and discovered the schoolmaster wrapped in chains, burning like a log in the vast fireplace. He put out the small blaze spreading from the hearth, and on going back onto the grounds, he stumbled over Aimée's charred corpse.

It was not clear whether Aimée's death had been accidental, a stray spark catching on her nightgown, or the result of suicide; but it *was* clear that thereafter the mansion had been haunted by a spirit who delighted in possessing women and driving them to kill their men. The spirit's supernatural powers were limited by the flesh but were augmented by immense physical strength. Ginny Whitcomb, for example, had killed her brother Tim by twisting off his arm, and then had gone after her other brother and her father, a harrowing chase that had lasted a day and a night: while in possession of a body, the spirit was not limited to nocturnal activity ...

Christ!

The light coming through the skylight was gray.

They were safe!

Eliot went to the bed and began shaking Michaela. She moaned, her eyes blinked open. 'Wake up!' he said. 'We've got to get out!'

'What?' She batted at his hands. 'What are you talking about?'

'Don't you remember?'

'Remember what?' She swung her legs onto the floor, sitting with her head down, stunned by wakefulness; she stood, swayed, and said, 'God, what did you do to me? I feel ...' A dull, suspicious expression washed over her face.

'We have to leave.' He walked around the bed to her. 'Ranjeesh hit the jackpot. Those crates of his had an honest-to-God spirit packed in with the bricks. Last night it tried to possess you.' He saw her disbelief. 'You must have blanked out. Here.' He offered the book. 'This'll explain ...'

'Oh, God!' she shouted. 'What did you do? I'm all raw inside!' She backed away, eyes wide with fright.

'I didn't do anything.' He held out his palms as if to prove he had no weapons.

'You raped me! While I was asleep!' She looked left, right, in a panic.

'That's ridiculous!'

'You must have drugged me or something! Oh, God! Go away!'

'I won't argue,' he said. 'We have to get out. After that you can turn me in for rape or whatever. But we're leaving, even if I have to drag you.'

Some of her desperation evaporated, her shoulders sagged.

'Look,' he said, moving closer. 'I didn't rape you. What you're feeling is something that goddamn spirit did to you. It was ...'

She brought her knee up into his groin.

As he writhed on the floor, curled up around the pain, Eliot heard the door open and her footsteps receding. He caught at the edge of the bed, hauled himself to his knees, and vomited all over the sheets. He fell back and lay there for several minutes until the pain had dwindled to a powerful throbbing, a throbbing that jolted his heart into the same rhythm; then, gingerly, he stood and shuffled out into the hall. Leaning on the railing, he eased down the stairs to Michaela's room and lowered himself into a sitting position. He let out a shuddering sigh. Actinic flashes burst in front of his eyes.

'Michaela,' he said. 'Listen to me.' His voice sounded feeble: the voice of an old, old man.

'I've got a knife,' she said from just behind the door. 'I'll use it if you try to break in.'

'I wouldn't worry about that,' he said. 'And I sure as hell wouldn't worry about being raped. Now will you listen?'

No response.

He told her everything, and when he was done, she said, 'You're insane. You raped me.'

'I wouldn't hurt you. I ...' He had been on the verge of telling her he loved her, but decided it probably wasn't true. He probably just wished that he had a good, clean truth like love. The pain was making him nauseated again, as if the blackish purple stain of his bruises were seeping up into his stomach and filling him with bad gases. He struggled to his feet and leaned against the wall. There was no point in arguing, and there was not much hope that she would leave the house on her own, not if she reacted to Aimée like Ginny Whitcomb. The only solution was to go to the police, accuse her of some crime. Assault. She would accuse him of rape, but with luck they would both be held overnight. And he would have time to wire Mr Chatterji ... who would believe him. Mr Chatterji was by nature a believer: it simply hadn't fit his notion of sophistication to give credence to his native spirits. He'd be on the first flight from Delhi, eager to document the Terror.

Himself eager to get it over, Eliot negotiated the stairs and hobbled across the courtyard; but the Khaa was waiting, flapping its arms in the shadowed alcove that led to the street. Whether it was an effect of the light or of its battle with Aimée, or, specifically, of the pale scrap of fire visible within its hand, the Khaa looked less substantial. Its blackness was somewhat opaque, and the air around it was blurred, smeary, like waves washing over a lens: it was as if the Khaa were being submerged more deeply in its own medium. Eliot felt no compunction about allowing it to touch him; he was grateful to it, and his relaxed attitude seemed to intensify the communication. He began to see images in his mind's eye: Michaela's face, Aimée's, and then the two faces were superimposed. He was shown this over and over, and he understood from it that the Khaa wanted the possession to take place. But he didn't understand why. More images. Himself running, Michaela running, Durbar Square, the mask of White Bhairab, the Khaa. Lots of Khaa. Like black hieroglyphs. These images were repeated, too, and after each sequence the Khaa would hold its hand up to his face and display the glimmering scrap of Aimée's fire. Eliot thought he understood, but whenever he tried to convey that he wasn't sure, the Khaa merely repeated the images.

At last, realizing that the Khaa had reached the limits of its ability to communicate, Eliot headed for the street. The Khaa melted down, reared up in the doorway to block his path, and flapped its arms desperately. Once again Eliot had a sense of its weird-old-manness. It went against logic to put his trust in such an erratic creature, especially in such a dangerous plan; but logic had little hold on him, and this was a permanent solution. If it worked. If he hadn't misread it. He laughed. The hell with it!

'Take it easy, Bongo,' he said. 'I'll be back as soon as I get my shootin' iron fixed.'

The waiting room of Sam Chipley's clinic was crowded with Newari mothers and children, who giggled as Eliot did a bow-legged shuffle through their midst. Sam's wife led him into the examination room, where Sam – a burly, bearded man, his long hair tied in a ponytail – helped him onto a surgical table.

'Holy shit!' he said after inspecting the injury. 'What you been into, man?' He began rubbing ointment into the bruises.

'Accident,' gritted Eliot, trying not to cry out.

'Yeah, I bet,' said Sam. 'Maybe a sexy little accident who had a change of heart when it come down to strokes. You know, not gettin' it steady might tend to make you a tad intense for some ladies, man. Ever think about that?'

'That's not how it was. Am I all right?'

'Yeah, but you ain't gonna be superstud for a while.' Sam went to the sink and washed his hands. 'Don't gimme that innocent bullshit. You were tryin' to slip it to Chatterji's new squeeze, right?'

'You know her?'

'He brought her over one day, showin' her off. She's a head case, man. You should know better.'

'Will I be able to run?'

Sam laughed. 'Not hardly.'

'Listen, Sam.' Eliot sat up, winced. 'Chatterji's lady. She's in bad trouble, and I'm the only one who can help her. I have to be able to run, and I need something to keep me awake. I haven't slept for a couple of days.'

'I ain't givin' you pills, Eliot. You can stagger through your doper phase without my help.' Sam finished drying his hands and went to sit on a stool beside the window; beyond the window was a brick wall, and atop it a string of prayer flags snapped in the breeze.

'I'm not after a supply, damn it! Just enough to keep me going tonight. This is important, Sam!'

Sam scratched his neck. 'What kind of trouble she in?'

'I can't tell you now,' said Eliot, knowing that Sam would laugh at the idea of something as metaphysically suspect as the Khaa. 'But I will tomorrow. It's not illegal. Come on, man! There's got to be something you can give me.'

'Oh, I can fix you up. I can make you feel like King Shit on Coronation Day.' Sam mulled it over. 'Okay, Eliot. But you get your ass back here tomorrow and tell me what's happenin'.' He gave a snort of amusement. 'All I can say is, it must be some strange damn trouble for you to be the only one who can save her.'

After wiring Mr Chatterji, urging him to come home at once, Eliot returned to the house and unscrewed the hinges of the front door. He was not certain that Aimée would be able to control the house, to slam doors and make windows stick as she had with her house in New Hampshire, but he didn't want to take any chances. As he lifted the door and set it against the wall of the alcove, he was amazed by its lightness; he felt possessed of a giddy strength, capable of heaving the door up through the well of the courtyard and over the roofs. The cocktail of painkillers and speed was working wonders. His groin ached, but the ache was distant, far removed form the center of his consciousness, which was a fount of well-being. When he had finished with the door, he grabbed some fruit juice from the kitchen and went back to the alcove to wait.

In midafternoon Michaela came downstairs. Eliot tried to talk to her, to convince her to leave, but she warned him to keep away and scuttled back to her room. Then, around five o'clock, the burning woman appeared, floating a few feet above the courtyard floor. The sun had withdrawn to the upper third of the well, and her fiery silhouette was inset into slate-blue shadow, the flames of her hair dancing about her head. Eliot, who had been hitting the painkillers heavily, was dazzled by her: had she been a hallucination, she would have made his All-Time Top Ten. But even realizing that she was not, he was too drugged to relate to her as a threat. He snickered and shied a piece of broken pot at her. She shrank to an incandescent point, vanished, and that brought home to him his foolhardiness. He took more speed to counteract his euphoria, and did stretching exercises to loosen the kinks and to rid himself of the cramped sensation in his chest.

Twilight blended the shadows in the courtyard, celebrants passed in the street, and he could hear distant drums and cymbals. He felt cut off from the city, the festival. Afraid. Not even the presence of the Khaa, half-merged with the shadows along the wall, served to comfort him. Near dusk, Aimée Cousineau walked into the courtyard and stopped about twenty feet away, staring at him. He had no desire to laugh or throw things. At this distance he could see that her eyes had no whites or pupils or irises. They were dead black. One moment they seemed to be the bulging heads of black screws threaded into her skull; the next they seemed to recede into blackness, into a cave beneath a mountain where something waited to teach the joys of hell to whoever wandered in. Eliot sidled closer to the door. But she turned, climbed the stairs to the second landing, and walked down Michaela's hallway.

Eliot's waiting began in earnest.

An hour passed. He paced between the door and the courtyard. His mouth was cottony; his joints felt brittle, held together by frail wires of speed and adrenaline. This was insane! All he had done was to put them in worse danger. Finally he heard a door close upstairs. He backed into the street, bumping into two Newari girls, who giggled and skipped away. Crowds of people were moving toward Durbar Square.

'Eliot!'

Michaela's voice. He'd expected a hoarse demon voice, and when she walked into the alcove, her white scarf glowing palely against the dark air, he was surprised to see that she was unchanged. Her features held no trace of anything other than her usual listlessness.

'I'm sorry I hurt you,' she said, walking toward him. 'I know you didn't do anything. I was just upset about last night.'

Eliot continued to back away.

'What's wrong?' She stopped in the doorway.

It might have been his imagination, the drugs, but Eliot could have sworn that her eyes were much darker than normal. He trotted off a dozen yards or so and stood looking at her.

'Eliot!'

It was a scream of rage and frustration, and he could scarcely believe the speed with which she darted toward him. He ran full tilt at first, leaping sideways to avoid collisions, veering past alarmed dark-skinned faces; but after a couple of blocks he found a more efficient rhythm and began to anticipate obstacles, to glide in and out of the crowd. Angry shouts were raised behind him. He glanced back. Michaela was closing the distance, beelining for him, knocking people sprawling with what seemed effortless blows. He ran harder. The crowd grew thicker, and he kept near the walls of the houses, where it was thinnest; but even there it was hard to maintain a good pace. Torches were waved in his face; young men – singing, their arms linked – posed barriers that slowed him further. He could no longer see Michaela, but he could see the wake of her passage. Fists shaking, heads jerking. The entire scene was starting to lose cohesiveness to Eliot. There were screams of torchlight, bright shards of deranged shouts, jostling waves of incense and ordure. He felt like the only solid chunk in a glittering soup that was being poured through a stone trough.

At the edge of Durbar Square he had a brief glimpse of a shadow standing by the massive gilt doors of Degutale Temple. It was larger and a more anthracitic black than Mr Chatterji's Khaa: one of the old ones, the powerful ones. The sight buoyed his confidence and restored his equilibrium. He had not misread the plan. But he knew that this was the most dangerous part. He had lost track of Michaela, and the crowd was sweeping him along; if she caught up to him now, he would not be able to run. Fighting for elbow room, struggling to keep his feet, he was borne into the temple complex. The pagoda roofs sloped up into darkness like strangely carved mountains, their peaks hidden by a moonless night; the cobbled paths were narrow, barely ten feet across, and the crowd was being squeezed along them, a lava flow of humanity. Torches bobbed everywhere, sending wild licks of shadow and orange light up the walls, revealing scowling faces on the eaves. Atop its pedestal, the gilt statue of Hanuman – the monkey god – looked to be swaying. Clashing cymbals and arrhythmic drumming scattered Eliot's heartbeat; the sinewy wail of oboes seemed to be graphing the fluctuations of his nerves.

As he swept past Hanuman Dhoka Temple, he caught sight of the brass mask of White Bhairab shining over the heads of the crowd like the face of an evil clown. It was less than a hundred feet away, set in a huge niche in a temple wall and illuminated by light bulbs that hung down among strings of prayer flags. The crowd surged faster, knocking him this way and that; but he managed to spot two more Khaa in the doorway of Hanuman Dhoka. Both melted downward, vanishing, and Eliot's hopes soared. They must have located Michaela, they must be attacking! By the time he had been carried to within a few yards of the mask, he was sure that he was safe. They must have finished her exorcism by now. The only problem left was to find her. That, he realized, had been the weak link in the plan. He'd been an idiot not to have foreseen it. Who knows what might happen if she were to fall in the midst of the crowd. Suddenly he was beneath the pipe that stuck out of the god's mouth; the stream of rice beer arching from it looked translucent under the lights, and as it splashed his face (no fish), its coldness acted to wash away his veneer of chemical strength. He was dizzy, his groin throbbed. The great face, with its fierce fangs and goofy, startled eyes, appeared to be swelling and rocking back and forth. He took a deep breath. The thing to do would be to find a place next to a wall where he could wedge himself against the flow of the crowd, wait until it had thinned, and then search for her. He was about to do that very thing when two powerful hands gripped his elbows from behind.

Unable to turn, he craned his neck and peered over his shoulder. Michaela smiled at him: a gloating 'gotcha!' smile. Her eyes were dead-black ovals. She shaped his name with her mouth, her voice inaudible above the music and shouting, and she began to push him ahead of her, using him as a battering ram to forge a path through the crowd. To anyone watching, it might have appeared that he was running interference for her, but his feet were dangling just off the ground. Angry Newars yelled at him as he knocked them aside. He yelled, too. No one noticed. Within seconds they had got clear into a side street, threading between groups of drunkards. People laughed at Eliot's cries for help, and one guy imitated the awkward loose-limbed way he was running.

Michaela turned into a doorway, carrying him down a dirt-floored corridor whose walls were carved into ornate screens; the dusky orange lamplight shining through the screens cast a lacework of shadow on the dirt. The corridor widened to a small courtyard, the age-darkened wood of its walls and doors inlaid with intricate mosaics of ivory. Michaela stopped and slammed him against a wall. He was stunned, but he recognized the place to be one of the old Buddhist temples that surrounded the square. Except for a life-sized statue of a golden cow, the courtyard was empty.

'Eliot.' The way she said it, it was more of a curse than a name.

He opened his mouth to scream, but she drew him into an embrace; her grip on his right elbow tightened, and her other hand squeezed the back of his neck, pinching off the scream.

'Don't be afraid,' she said. 'I only want to kiss you.'

Her breasts crushed into his chest, her pelvis ground against him in a mockery of passion, and inch by inch she forced his face down to hers. Her lips parted, and – *oh, Christ Jesus*! – Eliot writhed in her grasp, enlivened by a new horror. The inside of her mouth was as black as her eyes. She wanted him to kiss that blackness, to taste the evil she had kissed beneath the Eiger. He kicked and clawed with his free hand, but she was irresistible, her hands like iron. His elbow cracked, and brilliant pain shot through his arm. Something else was cracking in his neck. Yet none of that compared to what he felt as her tongue – a burning black poker – pushed between his lips. His chest was bursting with the need to scream, and everything was going dark. Thinking this was death, he experienced a peevish resentment that death was not – as he'd been led to believe – an end to pain, that it merely added a tickling sensation to all his other pain. Then the searing heat in his mouth diminished, and he thought that death must just have been a bit slower than usual.

Several seconds passed before he realized that he was lying on the ground, several more before he noticed Michaela lying beside him, and – because darkness was tattering the edges of his vision – it was considerably longer before he distinguished the six undulating darknesses that had ringed Aimée Cousineau. They towered over her; their blackness gleamed like thick fur, and the air around them was awash with vibration. In her fluted white nightgown, her cameo face composed in an expression of calm, Aimée looked the antithesis of the vaguely male giants that were menacing her, delicate and finely worked in contrast to their crudity. Her eyes appeared to mirror their negative color. After a moment, a little wind kicked up, swirling about her. The undulations of the Khaa increased, becoming rhythmic, the movements of boneless dancers, and the wind subsided. Puzzled, she darted between two of them and took a defensive stance next to the golden cow; she lowered her head and stared up through her brows at the Khaa. They melted downward, rolled forward, sprang erect, and hemmed her in against the statue. But the stare was doing its damage. Pieces of ivory and wood were splintering, flying off the walls toward the Khaa, and one of them was fading, a mist of black particles accumulating around its body; then, with a shrill noise that reminded Eliot of a jet passing overhead, it misted away.

Five Khaa remained in the courtyard. Aimée smiled and turned her stare on another. Before the stare could take effect, however, the Khaa moved close, blocking Eliot's view of her; and when they pulled back, it was Aimée who showed signs of damage. Rills of blackness were leaking from her eyes, webbing her cheeks, making it look as if her face were cracking. Her nightgown caught fire, her hair began to leap. Flames danced on her fingertips, spread to her arms, her breast, and she assumed the form of the burning woman.

As soon as the transformation was complete, she tried to shrink, to dwindle to her vanishing point; but, acting in unison, the Khaa extended their hands and touched her. There was that shriek of tortured metal, lapsing to a high-pitched hum, and to Eliot's amazement, the Khaa were sucked inside her. It was a rapid process. The Khaa faded to a haze, to nothing, and veins of black marbled the burning woman's fire; the blackness coalesced, forming into five tiny stick figures, a hieroglyphic design patterning her gown. With a fuming sound she expanded again, regaining her normal dimensions, and the Khaa flowed back out, surrounding her. For an instant she stood motionless, dwarfed: a schoolgirl helpless amidst a circle of bullies. Then she clawed at the nearest of them. Though she had no features with which to express emotion, it seemed to Eliot there was desperation in her gesture, in the agitated leaping of her fiery hair. Unperturbed, the Khaa stretched out their enormous mitten hands, hands that spread like oil and enveloped her.

The destruction of the burning woman, of Aimée Cousineau, lasted only a matter of seconds; but to Eliot it occurred within a bubble of slow time, a time during which he achieved a speculative distance. He wondered if – as the Khaa stole portions of her fire and secreted it within their bodies – they were removing disparate elements of her soul, if she consisted of psychologically distinct fragments: the girl who had wandered into the cave, the girl who had returned from it, the betrayed lover. Did she embody gradations of innocence and sinfulness, or was she a contaminated essence, an unfractionated evil? While still involved in this speculation, half a reaction to pain, half to the metallic shriek of her losing battle, he lost consciousness, and when he reopened his eyes, the courtyard was deserted. He could hear music and shouting from Durbar Square. The golden cow stared contentedly into nowhere.

He had the idea that if he moved, he would further break all the broken things inside him; but he inched his left hand across the dirt and rested it on Michaela's breast. It was rising and falling with a steady rhythm. That made him happy, and he kept his hand there, exulting in the hits of her life against his palm. Something shadowy above him. He strained to see it. One of the Khaa … No! It was Mr Chatterji's Khaa. Opaquely black, scrap of fire glimmering in its hand. Compared to its big brothers, it had the look of a skinny, sorry mutt. Eliot felt camaraderie toward it.

'Hey, Bongo,' he said weakly. 'We won.'

A tickling at the top of his head, a whining note, and he had an impression not of gratitude – as he might have expected – but of intense curiosity. The tickling stopped, and Eliot suddenly felt clear in his mind. Strange. He was passing out once again, his consciousness whirling, darkening, and yet he was calm and unafraid. A roar came from the direction of the square. Somebody – the luckiest somebody in the Katmandu Valley – had caught the fish. But as Eliot's eyelids fluttered shut, as he had a last glimpse of the Khaa looming above them and felt the warm measure of Michaela's heartbeat, he thought maybe that the crowd was cheering the wrong man.

Three weeks after the night of White Bhairab, Ranjeesh Chatterji divested himself of all worldly possessions (including the gift of a year's free rent at his house to Eliot) and took up residence at Swayambhunath where – according to Sam Chipley, who visited Eliot in the hospital – he was attempting to visualize the Avalokitesvara Buddha. It was then that Eliot understood the nature of his newfound clarity. Just as it had done long ago with the woman's goiters, the Khaa had tried his habituation to meditation on for size, had not cared for it, and sloughed it off in a handy repository: Ranjeesh Chatterji.

It was such a delicious irony that Eliot had to restrain himself from telling Michaela when she visited that same afternoon; she had no memory of the Khaa, and news of it tended to unsettle her. But otherwise she had been healing right along with Eliot. All her listlessness had eroded over the weeks, her capacity for love was returning and was focused solely on Eliot. 'I guess I needed someone to show me that I was worth an effort,' she told him. 'I'll never stop trying to repay you.' She kissed him. 'I can hardly wait till you come home.' She brought him books and candy and flowers; she sat with him each day until the nurses shooed her away. Yet being the center of her devotion disturbed him. He was still uncertain whether or not he loved her. Clarity, it seemed, made a man dangerously versatile, his conscience flexible, and instituted a cautious approach to commitment. At least this was the substance of Eliot's clarity. He didn't want to rush into anything.

When at last he did come home, he and Michaela made love beneath the starlight glory of Mr Chatterji's skylight. Because of Eliot's neck brace and cast, they had to manage the act with extreme care, but despite that, despite the ambivalence of his feelings, this time it *was* love they made. Afterward, lying with his good arm around her, he edged nearer to commitment. Whether or not he loved her, there was no way this part of things could be improved by any increment of emotion. Maybe he'd give it a try with her. If it didn't work out, well, he was not going to be responsible for her mental health. She would have to learn to live without him.

'Happy?' he asked, caressing her shoulder.

She nodded and cuddled closer and whispered something that was partially drowned out by the crinkling of the pillow. He was sure he had misheard her, but the mere thought that he hadn't was enough to lodge a nugget of chill between his shoulder blades.

'What did you say?' he asked.

She turned to him and propped herself on an elbow, silhouetted by the starlight, her features obscured. But when she spoke, he realized that Mr Chatterji's Khaa had been true to its erratic traditions of barter on the night of White Bhairab; and he knew that if she were to tip back her head ever so slightly and let the light shine into her eyes, he would be able to resolve all his speculations about the composition of Aimée Cousineau's soul.

'I'm wed to Happiness,' she said.

SALVADOR

Three weeks before they wasted Tecolutla, Dantzler had his baptism of fire. The platoon was crossing a meadow at the foot of an emerald-green volcano, and being a dreamy sort, he was idling along, swatting tall grasses with his rifle barrel and thinking how it might have been a first-grader with crayons who had devised this elementary landscape of a perfect cone rising into a cloudless sky, when cap-pistol noises sounded on the slope. Someone screamed for the medic, and Dantzler dove into the grass, fumbling for his ampules. He slipped one from the dispenser and popped it under his nose, inhaling frantically; then, to be on the safe side, he popped another – 'A double helpin' of martial arts,' as DT would say – and lay with his head down until the drugs had worked their magic. There was dirt in his mouth, and he was very afraid.

Gradually his arms and legs lost their heaviness, and his heart rate slowed. His vision sharpened to the point that he could see not only the pinpricks of fire blooming on the slope, but also the figures behind them, half-obscured by brush. A bubble of grim anger welled up in his brain, hardened to a fierce resolve, and he started moving toward the volcano. By the time he reached the base of the cone, he was all rage and reflexes. He spent the next forty minutes spinning acrobatically through the thickets, spraying shadows with bursts of his M-18; yet part of his mind remained distant from the action, marveling at his efficiency, at the comic-strip enthusiasm he felt for the task of killing. He shouted at the men he shot, and he shot them many more times than was necessary, like a child playing soldier.

'Playin' my ass!' DT would say. 'You just actin' natural.'

DT was a firm believer in the ampules; though the official line was that they contained tailored RNA compounds and pseudoendorphins modified to an inhalant form, he held the opinion that they opened a man up to his inner nature. He was big, black, with heavily muscled arms and crudely stamped features, and he had come to the Special Forces direct from prison, where he had done a stretch for attempted murder; the palms of his hands were covered by jail tattoos – a pentagram and a horned monster. The words DIE HIGH were painted on his helmet. This was his second tour in Salvador, and Moody – who was Dantzler's buddy – said the drugs had addled DT's brains, that he was crazy and gone to hell.

'He collects trophies,' Moody had said. 'And not just ears like they done in 'Nam.'

When Dantzler had finally gotten a glimpse of the trophies, he had been appalled. They were kept in a tin box in DT's pack and were nearly unrecognizable; they looked like withered brown orchids. But despite his revulsion, despite the fact that he was afraid of DT, he admired the man's capacity for survival and had taken to heart his advice to rely on the drugs.

On the way back down the slope they discovered a live casualty, an Indian kid about Dantzler's age, nineteen or twenty. Black hair, adobe skin, and heavy-lidded brown eyes. Dantzler, whose father was an anthropologist and had done fieldwork in Salvador, figured him for a Santa Ana tribesman; before leaving the States, Dantzler had pored over his father's notes, hoping this would give him an edge, and had learned to identify the various regional types. The kid had a minor leg wound and was wearing fatigue pants and a faded COKE ADDS LIFE T-shirt. This T-shirt irritated DT no end.

'What the hell you know 'bout Coke?' he asked the kid as they headed for the chopper that was to carry them deeper into Morazán Province. 'You think it's funny or somethin'?' He whacked the kid in the back with his rifle butt, and when they reached the chopper, he slung him inside and had him sit by the door. He sat beside him, tapped out a joint from a pack of Kools, and asked, 'Where's Infante?'

'Dead,' said the medic.

'Shit!' DT licked the joint so it would burn evenly. 'Goddamn beaner ain't no use 'cept somebody else know Spanish.'

'I know a little,' Dantzler volunteered.

Staring at Dantzler, DT's eyes went empty and unfocused. 'Naw,' he said. 'You don't know no Spanish.'

Dantzler ducked his head to avoid DT's stare and said nothing; he thought he understood what DT meant, but he ducked away from the understanding as well. The chopper bore them aloft, and DT lit the joint. He let the smoke out his nostrils and passed the joint to the kid, who accepted gratefully.

'*Qué sabor!*' he said, exhaling a billow; he smiled and nodded, wanting to be friends.

Dantzler turned his gaze to the open door. They were flying low between the hills, and looking at the deep bays of shadow in their folds acted to drain away the residue of the drugs, leaving him weary and frazzled. Sunlight poured in, dazzling the oil-smeared floor.

'Hey, Dantzler!' DT had to shout over the noise of the rotors. 'Ask him whass his name!'

The kid's eyelids were drooping from the joint, but on hearing Spanish he perked up; he shook his head, though, refusing to answer. Dantzler smiled and told him not to be afraid.

'Ricardo Quu,' said the kid.

'Kool!' said DT with false heartiness. 'Thass my brand!' He offered his pack to the kid.

'*Gracias, no.*' The kid waved the joint and grinned.

'Dude's named for a goddamn cigarette,' said DT disparagingly, as if this were the height of insanity.

Dantzler asked the kid if there were more soldiers nearby, and once again received no reply; but, apparently sensing in Dantzler a kindred soul, the kid leaned forward and spoke rapidly, saying that his village was Santander Jimenez, that his father was – he hesitated – a man of power. He asked where they were taking him. Dantzler returned a stony glare. He found it easy to reject the kid, and he realized later this was because he had already given up on him.

Latching his hands behind his head, DT began to sing – a wordless melody. His voice was discordant, barely audible above the rotors; but the tune had a familiar ring and Dantzler soon placed it. The theme from 'Star Trek.' It brought back memories of watching TV with his sister, laughing at the low-budget aliens and Scotty's Actors' Equity accent. He gazed out the door again. The sun was behind the hills, and the hillsides were unfeatured blurs of dark green smoke. Oh, God, he wanted to be home, to be anywhere but Salvador! A couple of the guys joined in the singing at DT's urging, and as the volume swelled, Dantzler's emotion peaked. He was on the verge of tears, remembering tastes and sights, the way his girl Jeanine had smelled, so clean and fresh, not reeking of sweat and perfume like the whores around Ilopango – finding all this substance in the banal touchstone of his culture and the illusions of the hillsides rushing past. Then Moody tensed beside him, and he glanced up to learn the reason why.

In the gloom of the chopper's belly, DT was as unfeatured as the hills – a black presence ruling them, more the leader of a coven than a platoon. The other two guys were singing their lungs out, and even the kid was getting into the spirit of things. '*Música!*' he said at one point, smiling at everybody, trying to fan the flame of good feeling. He swayed to the rhythm and essayed a 'la-la' now and again. But no one else was responding.

The singing stopped, and Dantzler saw that the whole platoon was staring at the kid, their expressions slack and dispirited.

'Space!' shouted DT, giving the kid a little shove. 'The final frontier!'

The smile had not yet left the kid's face when he toppled out the door. DT peered after him; a few seconds later he smacked his hand against the floor and sat back, grinning. Dantzler felt like screaming, the stupid horror of the joke was so at odds with the languor of his homesickness. He looked to the others for reaction. They were sitting with their heads down, fiddling with trigger guards and pack straps, studying their bootlaces, and seeing this, he quickly imitated them.

Morazán Province was spook country. Santa Ana spooks. Flights of birds had been reported to attack patrols; animals appeared at the perimeters of campsites and vanished when you shot at them; dreams afflicted everyone who ventured there. Dantzler could not testify to the birds and animals, but he did have a recurring dream. In it the kid DT had killed was pinwheeling down through a golden fog, his T-shirt visible against the roiling backdrop, and sometimes a voice would boom out of the fog, saying, 'You are killing my son.' No, no, Dantzler would reply, it wasn't me, and besides, he's already dead. Then he would wake covered with sweat, groping for his rifle, his heart racing.

But the dream was not an important terror, and he assigned it no significance. The land was far more terrifying. Pine-forested ridges that stood out against the sky like fringes of electrified hair; little trails winding off into thickets and petering out, as if what they led to had been magicked away; gray rock faces along which they were forced to walk, hopelessly exposed to ambush. There were innumerable booby traps set by the guerrillas, and they lost several men to rockfalls. It was the emptiest place of Dantzler's experience. No people, no animals, just a few hawks circling the solitudes between the ridges. Once in a while they found tunnels, and these they blew with the new gas grenades; the gas ignited the rich concentrations of hydrocarbons and sent flame sweeping through the entire system. DT would praise whoever had discovered the tunnel and would estimate in a loud voice how many beaners they had 'refried.' But Dantzler knew they were traversing pure emptiness and burning empty holes. Days, under debilitating heat, they humped the mountains, traveling seven, eight, even ten klicks up trails so steep that frequently the feet of the guy ahead of you would be on a level with your face; nights, it was cold, the darkness absolute, the silence so profound that Dantzler imagined he could hear the great humming vibration of the earth. They might have been anywhere or nowhere. Their fear was nourished by the isolation, and the only remedy was 'martial arts.'

Dantzler took to popping the pills without the excuse of combat. Moody cautioned him against abusing the drugs, citing rumors of bad side effects and DT's madness; but even he was using them more and more often. During basic training, Dantzler's D.I. had told the boots that the drugs were available only to the Special Forces, that their use was optional; but there had been too many instances of lackluster battlefield performance in the last war, and this was to prevent a reoccurrence.

'The chickenshit infantry should take 'em,' the D.I. had said. 'You bastards are brave already. You're born killers, right?'

'Right, sir!' they had shouted.

'What are you?'

'Born killers, sir!'

But Dantzler was not a born killer; he was not even clear as to how he had been drafted, less clear as to how he had been manipulated into the Special Forces, and he had learned that nothing was optional in Salvador, with the possible exception of life itself.

The platoon's mission was reconnaissance and mop-up. Along with other Special Forces platoons, they were to secure Morazán prior to the invasion of Nicaragua; specifically, they were to proceed to the village of Tecolutla, where a Sandinista patrol had recently been spotted, and following that they were to join up with the First Infantry and take part in the offensive against León, a provincial capital just across the Nicaraguan border. As Dantzler and Moody walked together, they frequently talked about the offensive, how it would be good to get down into flat country; occasionally they talked about the possibility of reporting DT, and once, after he had led them on a forced night march, they toyed with the idea of killing him. But most often they discussed the ways of the Indians and the land, since this was what had caused them to become buddies.

Moody was slightly built, freckled, and red-haired; his eyes had the 'thousand-yard stare' that came from too much war. Dantzler had seen winos with such vacant, lusterless stares. Moody's father had been in 'Nam, and Moody said it had been worse than Salvador because there had been no real commitment to win; but he thought Nicaragua and Guatemala might be the worst of all, especially if the Cubans sent in troops as they had threatened. He was adept at locating tunnels and detecting booby traps, and it was for this reason Dantzler had cultivated his friendship. Essentially a loner, Moody had resisted all advances until learning of Dantzler's father; thereafter he had buddied up, eager to hear about the field notes, believing they might give him an edge.

'They think the land has animal traits,' said Dantzler one day as they climbed along a ridgetop. 'Just like some kinds of fish look like plants or sea bottom, parts of the land look like plain ground, jungle ... whatever. But when you enter them, you find you've entered the spirit world, the world of *Sukias*.'

'What's *Sukias*?' asked Moody.

'Magicians.' A twig snapped behind Dantzler, and he spun around, twitching off the safety of his rifle. It was only Hodge – a lanky kid with the beginnings of a beer gut. He stared hollow-eyed at Dantzler and popped an ampule.

Moody made a noise of disbelief. 'If they got magicians, why ain't they winnin'? Why ain't they zappin' us off the cliffs?'

'It's not their business,' said Dantzler. 'They don't believe in messing with worldly affairs unless it concerns them directly. Anyway, these places – the ones that look like normal land but aren't – they're called …' He drew a blank on the name. 'A*ya*-something. I can't remember. But they have different laws. They're where your spirit goes to die after your body dies.'

'Don't they got no Heaven?'

'Nope. It just takes longer for your spirit to die, and so it goes to one of these places that's between everything and nothing.'

'Nothin',' said Moody disconsolately, as if all his hopes for an afterlife had been dashed. 'Don't make no sense to have spirits and not have no Heaven.'

'Hey,' said Dantzler, tensing as wind rustled the pine boughs. 'They're just a bunch of damn primitives. You know what their sacred drink is? Hot chocolate! My old man was a guest at one of their funerals, and he said they carried cups of hot chocolate balanced on these little red towers and acted like drinking it was going to wake them to the secrets of the universe.' He laughed, and the laughter sounded tinny and psychotic to his own ears. 'So you're going to worry about fools who think hot chocolate's holy water?'

'Maybe they just like it,' said Moody. 'Maybe somebody dyin' just give 'em an excuse to drink it.'

But Dantzler was no longer listening. A moment before, as they emerged from pine cover onto the highest point of the ridge, a stony scarp open to the winds and providing a view of rumpled mountains and valleys extending to the horizon, he had popped an ampule. He felt so strong, so full of righteous purpose and controlled fury, it seemed only the sky was around him, that he was still ascending, preparing to do battle with the gods themselves.

Tecolutla was a village of whitewashed stone tucked into a notch between two hills. From above, the houses – with their shadow-blackened windows and doorways – looked like an unlucky throw of dice. The streets ran uphill and down, diverging around boulders. Bougainvilleas and hibiscuses speckled the hillsides, and there were tilled fields on the gentler slopes. It was a sweet, peaceful place when they arrived, and after they had gone it was once again peaceful; but its sweetness had been permanently banished. The reports of Sandinistas had proved accurate, and though they were casualties left behind to recuperate, DT had decided their presence called for extreme measures. Fu gas, frag grenades, and such. He had fired an M-60 until the barrel melted down, and then had manned the flamethrower. Afterward, as they rested atop the next ridge, exhausted and begrimed, having radioed in a chopper for resupply, he could not get over how one of the houses he had torched had come to resemble a toasted marshmallow.

'Ain't that how it was, man?' he asked, striding up and down the line. He did not care if they agreed about the house; it was a deeper question he was asking, one concerning the ethics of their actions.

'Yeah,' said Dantzler, forcing a smile. 'Sure did.'

DT grunted with laughter. 'You *know* I'm right, don'tcha man?'

The sun hung directly behind his head, a golden corona rimming a black oval, and Dantzler could not turn his eyes away. He felt weak and weakening, as if threads of himself were being spun loose and sucked into the blackness. He had popped three ampules prior to the firefight, and his experience of Tecolutla had been a kind of mad whirling dance through the streets, spraying erratic bursts that appeared to be writing weird names on the walls. The leader of the Sandinistas had worn a mask – a gray face with a surprised hole of a mouth and pink circles around the eyes. A ghost face. Dantzler had been afraid of the mask and had poured round after round into it. Then, leaving the village, he had seen a small girl standing beside the shell of the last house, watching them, her colorless rag of a dress tattering in the breeze. She had been a victim of that malnutrition disease, the one that paled your skin and whitened your hair and left you retarded. He could not recall the name of the disease – things like names were slipping away from him – nor could he believe anyone had survived, and for a moment he had thought the spirit of the village had come out to mark their trail.

That was all he could remember of Tecolutla, all he wanted to remember. But he knew he had been brave.

Four days later, they headed up into a cloud forest. It was the dry season, but dry season or not, blackish gray clouds always shrouded these peaks. They were shot through by ugly glimmers of lightning, making it seem that malfunctioning neon signs were hidden beneath them, advertisements for evil. Everyone was jittery, and Jerry LeDoux – a slim dark-haired Cajun kid – flat-out refused to go.

'It ain't reasonable,' he said. 'Be easier to go through the passes.'

'We're on recon, man! You think the beaners be waitin' in the passes, wavin' their white flags?' DT whipped his rifle into firing position and pointed it at LeDoux. 'C'mon, Louisiana man. Pop a few, and you feel different.'

As LeDoux popped the ampules, DT talked to him.

'Look at it this way, man. This is your big adventure. Up there it be like all them animal shows on the tube. The savage kingdom, the unknown. Could be like Mars or somethin'. Monsters and shit, with big red eyes and tentacles. You wanna miss that, man? You wanna miss bein' the first grunt on Mars?'

Soon LeDoux was raring to go, giggling at DT's rap.

Moody kept his mouth shut, but he fingered the safety of his rifle and glared at DT's back. When DT turned to him, however, he relaxed. Since Tecolutla he had grown taciturn, and there seemed to be a shifting of lights and darks in his eyes, as if something were scurrying back and forth behind them. He had taken to wearing banana leaves on his head, arranging them under his helmet so the frayed ends stuck out the sides like strange green hair. He said this was camouflage, but Dantzler was certain it bespoke some secretive irrational purpose. Of course DT had noticed Moody's spiritual erosion, and as they prepared to move out, he called Dantzler aside.

'He done found someplace inside his head that feel good to him,' said DT. 'He's tryin' to curl up into it, and once he do that he ain't gon' be responsible. Keep an eye on him.'

Dantzler mumbled his assent, but was not enthused.

'I know he your fren', man, but that don't mean shit. Not the way things are. Now me, I don't give a damn 'bout you personally. But I'm your brother-in-arms, and thass somethin' you can count on ... y'understand.'

To Dantzler's shame, he did understand.

They had planned on negotiating the cloud forest by nightfall, but they had underestimated the difficulty. The vegetation beneath the clouds was lush – thick, juicy leaves that mashed underfoot, tangles of vines, trees with slick, pale bark and waxy leaves – and the visibility was only about fifteen feet. They were gray wraiths passing through grayness. The vague shapes of the foliage reminded Dantzler of fancifully engraved letters, and for a while he entertained himself with the notion that they were walking among the half-formed phrases of a constitution not yet manifest in the land. They barged off the trail, losing it completely, becoming veiled in spiderwebs and drenched by spills of water; their voices were oddly muffled, the tag ends of words swallowed up. After seven hours of this, DT reluctantly gave the order to pitch camp. They set electric lamps around the perimeter so they could see to string the jungle hammocks; the beam of light illuminated the moisture in the air, piercing the murk with jeweled blades. They talked in hushed tones, alarmed by the eerie atmosphere. When they had done with the hammocks, DT posted four sentries – Moody, LeDoux, Dantzler, and himself. Then they switched off the lamps.

It grew pitch-dark, and the darkness was picked out by plips and plops, the entire spectrum of dripping sounds. To Dantzler's ears they blended into a gabbling speech. He imagined tiny Santa Ana demons talking about him, and to stave off paranoia he popped two ampules. He continued to pop them, trying to limit himself to one every half hour; but he was uneasy, unsure where to train his rifle in the dark, and he exceeded his limit. Soon it began to grow light again, and he assumed that more time had passed than he had thought. That often happened with the ampules – it was easy to lose yourself in being alert, in the wealth of perceptual detail available to your sharpened senses. Yet on checking his watch, he saw it was only a few minutes after two o'clock. His system was too inundated with the drugs to allow panic, but he twitched his head from side to side in tight little arcs to determine the source of the brightness. There did not appear to be a single source; it was simply that filaments of the cloud were gleaming, casting a diffuse golden glow, as if they were elements of a nervous system coming to life. He started to call out, then held back. The others must have seen the light, and they had given no cry; they probably had a good reason for their silence. He scrunched down flat, pointing his rifle out from the campsite.

Bathed in the golden mist, the forest had acquired an alchemic beauty. Beads of water glittered with gemmy brilliance; the leaves and vines and bark were gilded. Every surface shimmered with light ... everything except a fleck of blackness hovering between two of the trunks, its size gradually increasing. As it swelled in his vision, he saw it had the shape of a bird, its wings beating, flying toward him from an inconceivable distance – inconceivable, because the dense vegetation did not permit you to see very far in a straight line, and yet the bird was growing larger with such slowness that it must have been coming from a long way off. It was not really flying, he realized; rather, it was as if the forest were painted on a piece of paper, as if someone were holding a lit match behind it and burning a hole, a hole that maintained the shape of a bird as it spread. He was transfixed, unable to react. Even when it had blotted out half the light, when he lay before it no bigger than a mote in relation to its huge span, he could not move or squeeze the trigger. And then the blackness swept over him. He had the sensation of being borne along at incredible speed, and he could no longer hear the dripping of the forest.

'Moody!' he shouted. 'DT!'

But the voice that answered belonged to neither of them. It was hoarse, issuing from every part of the surrounding blackness, and he recognized it as the voice of his recurring dream.

'You are killing my son,' it said. 'I have led you here, to this *ayahuamaco*, so he may judge you.'

Dantzler knew to his bones the voice was that of the *Sukia* of the village of Santander Jimenez. He wanted to offer a denial, to explain his innocence, but all he could manage was, 'No.' He said it tearfully, hopelessly, his forehead resting on his rifle barrel. Then his mind gave a savage twist, and his soldiery self regained control. He ejected an ampule from his dispenser and popped it.

The voice laughed – malefic, damning laughter whose vibrations shuddered Dantzler. He opened up with the rifle, spraying fire in all directions. Filigrees of golden holes appeared in the blackness, tendrils of mist coiled through them. He kept on firing until the blackness shattered and fell in jagged sections toward him. Slowly. Like shards of black glass dropping through water. He emptied the rifle and flung himself flat, shielding his head with his arms, expecting to be sliced into bits; but nothing touched him. At last he peeked between his arms; then – amazed, because the forest was now a uniform lustrous yellow – he rose to his knees. He scraped his hand on one of the crushed leaves beneath him, and blood welled from the cut. The broken fibers of the leaf were as stiff as wires. He stood, a giddy trickle of hysteria leaking up from the bottom of his soul. It was no forest, but a building of solid gold worked to resemble a forest – the sort of conceit that might have been fabricated for the child of an emperor. Canopied by golden leaves, columned by slender golden trunks, carpeted by golden grasses. The water beads were diamonds. All the gleam and glitter soothed his apprehension; here was something out of a myth, a habitat for princesses and wizards and dragons. Almost gleeful, he turned to the campsite to see how the others were reacting.

Once, when he was nine years old, he had sneaked into the attic to rummage through the boxes and trunks, and he had run across an old morocco-bound copy of *Gulliver's Travels*. He had been taught to treasure old books, and so he had opened it eagerly to look at the illustrations, only to find that the centers of the pages had been eaten away, and there, right in the heart of the fiction, was a nest of larvae. Pulpy, horrid things. It had been an awful sight, but one unique in his experience, and he might have studied those crawling scraps of life for a very long time if his father had not interrupted. Such a sight was now before him, and he was numb with it.

They were all dead. He should have guessed they would be; he had given no thought to them while firing his rifle. They had been struggling out of their hammocks when the bullets hit, and as a result they were hanging half-in, half-out, their limbs dangling, blood pooled beneath them. The veils of golden mist made them look dark and mysterious and malformed, like monsters killed as they emerged from their cocoons. Dantzler could not stop staring, but he was shrinking inside himself. It was not his fault. That thought kept swooping in and out of a flock of less acceptable thoughts; he wanted it to stay put, to be true, to alleviate the sick horror he was beginning to feel.

'What's your name?' asked a girl's voice behind him.

She was sitting on a stone about twenty feet away. Her hair was a tawny shade of gold, her skin a half-tone lighter, and her dress was cunningly formed out of the mist. Only her eyes were real. Brown heavy-lidded eyes – they were at variance with the rest of her face, which had the fresh, unaffected beauty of an American teenager.

'Don't be afraid,' she said, and patted the ground, inviting him to sit beside her.

He recognized the eyes, but it was no matter. He badly needed the consolation she could offer; he walked over and sat down. She let him lean his head against her thigh.

'What's your name?' she repeated.

'Dantzler,' he said. 'John Dantzler.' And then he added, 'I'm from Boston. My father's ...' It would be too difficult to explain about anthropology. 'He's a teacher.'

'Are there many soldiers in Boston?' She stroked his cheek with a golden finger.

The caress made Dantzler happy. 'Oh, no,' he said. 'They hardly know there's a war going on.'

'This is true?' she said, incredulous.

'Well, they *do* know about it, but it's just news on the TV to them. They've got more pressing problems. Their jobs, families.'

'Will you let them know about the war when you return home?' she asked. 'Will you do that for me?'

Dantzler had given up hope of returning home, of surviving, and her assumption that he would do both acted to awaken his gratitude. 'Yes,' he said fervently. 'I will.'

'You must hurry,' she said. 'If you stay in the *ayahuamaco* too long, you will never leave. You must find the way out. It is a way not of directions or trails, but of events.'

'Where is this place?' he asked, suddenly aware of how much he had taken it for granted.

She shifted her leg away, and if he had not caught himself on the stone, he would have fallen. When he looked up, she had vanished. He was surprised that her disappearance did not alarm him; in reflex he slipped out a couple of ampules, but after a moment's reflection he decided not to use them. It was impossible to slip them back into the dispenser, so he tucked them into the interior webbing of his helmet for later. He doubted he would need them, though. He felt strong, competent, and unafraid.

Dantzler stepped carefully between the hammocks, not wanting to brush against them; it might have been his imagination, but they seemed to be bulging down lower than before, as if death had weighed out heavier than life. That heaviness was in the air, pressuring him. Mist rose like golden steam from the corpses, but the sight no longer affected him – perhaps because the mist gave the illusion of being their souls. He picked up a rifle with a full magazine and headed off into the forest.

The tips of the golden leaves were sharp, and he had to ease past them to avoid being cut; but he was at the top of his form, moving gracefully, and the obstacles barely slowed his pace. He was not even anxious about the girl's warning to hurry; he was certain the way out would soon present itself. After a minute or so he heard voices, and after another few seconds he came to a clearing divided by a stream, one so perfectly reflecting that its banks appeared to enclose a wedge of golden mist. Moody was squatting to the left of the stream, staring at the blade of his survival knife and singing under his breath – a wordless melody that had the erratic rhythm of a trapped fly. Beside him lay Jerry LeDoux, his throat slashed from ear to ear. DT was sitting on the other side of the stream; he had been shot just above the knee, and though he had ripped up his shirt for bandages and tied off the leg with a tourniquet, he was not in good shape. He was sweating, and a gray chalky pallor infused his skin. The entire scene had the weird vitality of something that had materialized in a magic mirror, a bubble of reality enclosed within a gilt frame.

DT heard Dantzler's footfalls and glanced up. 'Waste him!' he shouted, pointing to Moody.

Moody did not turn from contemplation of the knife. 'No,' he said, as if speaking to someone whose image was held in the blade.

'Waste him, man!' screamed DT. 'He killed LeDoux!'

'Please,' said Moody to the knife. 'I don't want to.'

There was blood clotted on his face, more blood on the banana leaves sticking out of his helmet.

'Did you kill Jerry?' asked Dantzler; while he addressed the question to Moody, he did not relate to him as an individual, only as part of a design whose message he had to unravel.

'Jesus Christ! Waste him!' DT smashed his fist against the ground in frustration.

'Okay,' said Moody. With an apologetic look, he sprang to his feet and charged Dantzler, swinging the knife.

Emotionless, Dantzler stitched a line of fire across Moody's chest; he went sideways into the bushes and down.

'What the hell was you waitin' for!' DT tried to rise, but winced and fell back. 'Damn! Don't know if I can walk.'

'Pop a few,' Dantzler suggested mildly.

'Yeah. Good thinkin', man.' DT fumbled for his dispenser.

Dantzler peered into the bushes to see where Moody had fallen. He felt nothing, and this pleased him. He was weary of feeling.

DT popped an ampule with a flourish, as if making a toast, and inhaled. 'Ain't you gon' to do some, man?'

'I don't need them,' said Dantzler. 'I'm fine.'

The stream interested him; it did not reflect the mist, as he had supposed, but was itself a seam of the mist.

'How many you think they was?' asked DT.

'How many what?'

'Beaners, man! I wasted three or four after they hit us, but I couldn't tell how many they was.'

Dantzler considered this in light of his own interpretation of events and Moody's conversation with the knife. It made sense. A Santa Ana kind of sense.

'Beats me,' he said. 'But I guess there's less than there used to be.'

DT snorted. 'You got *that* right!' He heaved to his feet and limped to the edge of the stream. 'Gimme a hand across.'

Dantzler reached out to him, but instead of taking his hand, he grabbed his wrist and pulled him off-balance. DT teetered on his good leg, then toppled and vanished beneath the mist. Dantzler had expected him to fall, but he surfaced instantly, mist clinging to his skin. Of course, thought Dantzler; his body would have to die before his spirit would fall.

'What you doin', man?' DT was more disbelieving than enraged.

Dantzler planted a foot in the middle of his back and pushed him down until his head was submerged. DT bucked and clawed at the foot and managed to come to his hands and knees. Mist slithered from his eyes, his nose, and he choked out the words '... kill you ...' Dantzler pushed him down again; he got into pushing him down and letting him up, over and over. Not so as to torture him. Not really. It was because he had suddenly understood the nature of the *ayahuamaco's* laws, that they were approximations of normal laws, and he further understood that his actions had to approximate those of someone jiggling a key in a lock. DT was the key to the way out, and Dantzler was jiggling him, making sure all the tumblers were engaged.

Some of the vessels in DT's eyes had burst, and the whites were occluded by films of blood. When he tried to speak, mist curled from his mouth. Gradually his struggles subsided; he clawed runnels in the gleaming yellow dirt of the bank and shuddered. His shoulders were knobs of black land foundering in a mystic sea.

For a long time after DT sank from view, Dantzler stood beside the stream, uncertain of what was left to do and unable to remember a lesson he had been taught. Finally he shouldered his rifle and walked away from the clearing. Morning had broken, the mist had thinned, and the forest had regained its usual coloration. But he scarcely noticed these changes, still troubled by his faulty memory. Eventually, he let it slide – it would all come clear sooner or later. He was just happy to be alive. After a while he began to kick the stones as he went, and to swing his rifle in a carefree fashion against the weeds.

When the First Infantry poured across the Nicaraguan border and wasted León, Dantzler was having a quiet time at the VA hospital in Ann Arbor, Michigan; and at the precise moment the bulletin was flashed nationwide, he was sitting in the lounge, watching the American League playoffs between Detroit and Texas. Some of the patients ranted at the interruption, while others shouted them down, wanting to hear the details. Dantzler expressed no reaction whatsoever. He was solely concerned with being a model patient; however, noticing that one of the staff was giving him a clinical stare, he added his weight on the side of the baseball fans. He did not want to appear too controlled. The doctors were as suspicious of that sort of behavior as they were of its contrary. But the funny thing was – at least it was funny to Dantzler – that his feigned annoyance at the bulletin was an exemplary proof of his control, his expertise at moving through life the way he had moved through the golden leaves of the cloud forest. Cautiously, gracefully, efficiently. Touching nothing, and being touched by nothing. That was the lesson he had learned – to be as perfect a counterfeit of a man as the *ayahuamaco* had been of the land; to adopt the various stances of a man, and yet, by virtue of his distance from things human, to be all the more prepared for the onset of crisis or a call to action. He saw nothing aberrant in this; even the doctors would admit that men were little more than organized pretense. If he was different from other men, it was only that he had a deeper awareness of the principles on which his personality was founded.

When the battle of Managua was joined, Dantzler was living at home. His parents had urged him to go easy in readjusting to civilian life, but he had immediately gotten a job as a management trainee in a bank. Each morning he would drive to work and spend a controlled, quiet eight hours; each night he would watch TV with his mother, and before going to bed, he would climb to the attic and inspect the trunk containing his souvenirs of war – helmet, fatigues, knife, boots. The doctors had insisted he face his experiences, and this ritual was his way of following their instructions. All in all, he was quite pleased with his progress, but he still had problems. He had not been able to force himself to venture out at night, remembering too well the darkness in the cloud forest, and he had rejected his friends, refusing to see them or answer their calls – he was not secure with the idea of friendship. Further, despite his methodical approach to life, he was prone to a nagging restlessness, the feeling of a chore left undone.

One night his mother came into his room and told him that an old friend, Phil Curry, was on the phone. 'Please talk to him, Johnny,' she said. 'He's been drafted, and I think he's a little scared.'

The word *drafted* struck a responsive chord in Dantzler's soul, and after brief deliberation he went downstairs and picked up the receiver.

'Hey,' said Phil. 'What's the story, man? Three months, and you don't even give me a call.'

'I'm sorry,' said Dantzler. 'I haven't been feeling so hot.'

'Yeah, I understand.' Phil was silent a moment. 'Listen, man. I'm leaving,' y'know, and we're having a big send-off at Sparky's. It's goin' on right now. Why don't you come down?'

'I don't know.'

'Jeanine's here, man. Y'know, she's still crazy 'bout you, talks 'bout you alla time. She don't go out with nobody.'

Dantzler was unable to think of anything to say.

'Look,' said Phil, 'I'm pretty weirded out by this soldier shit. I hear it's pretty bad down there. If you got anything you can tell me 'bout what it's like, man, I'd 'preciate it.'

Dantzler could relate to Phil's concern, his desire for an edge, and besides, it felt right to go. Very right. He would take some precautions against the darkness.

'I'll be there,' he said.

It was a foul night, spitting snow, but Sparky's parking lot was jammed. Dantzler's mind was flurried like the snow, crowded like the lot – thoughts whirling in, jockeying for position, melting away. He hoped his mother would not wait up, he wondered if Jeanine still wore her hair long, he was worried because the palms of his hands were unnaturally warm. Even with the car windows rolled up, he could hear loud music coming from inside the club. Above the door the words SPARKY'S ROCK CITY were being spelled out a letter at a time in red neon, and when the spelling was complete, the letters flashed off and on and a golden neon explosion bloomed around them. After the explosion, the entire sign went dark for a split second, and the big ramshackle building seemed to grow large and merge with the black sky. He had an idea it was watching him, and he shuddered – one of those sudden lurches downward of the kind that take you just before you fall asleep. He knew the people inside did not intend him any harm, but he also knew that places have a way of changing people's intent, and he did not want to be caught off guard. Sparky's might be such a place, might be a huge black presence camouflaged by neon, its true substance one with the abyss of the sky, the phosphorescent snowflakes jittering in his headlights, the wind keening through the side vent. He would have liked very much to drive home and forget about his promise to Phil; however, he felt a responsibility to explain about the war. More than a responsibility, an evangelistic urge. He would tell them about the kid falling out of the chopper, the white-haired girl in Tecolutla, the emptiness. God, yes! How you went down chock-full of ordinary American thoughts and dreams, memories of smoking weed and chasing tail and hanging out and freeway flying with a case of something cold, and how you smuggled back a human-shaped container of pure Salvadorian emptiness. Primo grade. Smuggled it back to the land of silk and money, of mindfuck video games and topless tennis matches and fast-food solutions to the nutritional problem. Just a taste of Salvador would banish all those trivial obsessions. Just a taste. It would be easy to explain.

Of course, some things beggared explanation.

He bent down and adjusted the survival knife in his boot so the hilt would not rub against his calf. From his coat pocket he withdrew the two ampules he had secreted in his helmet that long-ago night in the cloud forest. As the neon explosion flashed once more, glimmers of gold coursed along their shiny surfaces. He did not think he would need them; his hand was steady, and his purpose was clear. But to be on the safe side, he popped them both.

HOW THE WIND SPOKE AT MADAKET

I

Softly at dawn, rustling dead leaves in the roof gutters, ticking the wires of the television antenna against the shingled wall, seething through the beach grasses, shifting the bare twigs of a hawthorn to claw at the toolshed door, playfully flipping a peg off the clothesline, snuffling the garbage and tattering the plastic bags, creating a thousand nervous flutters, a thousand more shivery whispers, then building, keening in the window cracks and rattling the panes, smacking down a sheet of ply-board that has been leaning against the woodpile, swelling to a pour off the open sea, its howl articulated by throats of narrow streets and teeth of vacant houses, until you begin to imagine a huge invisible animal throwing back its head and roaring, and the cottage is creaking like the timbers of an old ship ...

II

Waking at first light, Peter Ramey lay abed awhile and listened to the wind; then, steeling himself against the cold, he threw off the covers, hurriedly pulled on jeans, tennis shoes, and a flannel shirt, and went into the front room to kindle a fire in the wood stove. Outside, the trees were silhouetted by a backdrop of slate clouds, but the sky wasn't yet bright enough to cast the shadow of the window frame across the picnic-style table beneath it; the other furniture – three chewed-up wicker chairs and a sofa bunk – hunched in their dark corners. The tinder caught, and soon the fire was snapping inside the stove. Still cold, Peter beat his arms against his shoulders and hopped from one foot to another, setting dishes and drawers to rattling. He was a pale, heavyset man of thirty-three, with ragged black hair and beard, so tall that he had to duck through the doors of the cottage; and because of his size he had never really settled into the place: he felt like a tramp who had appropriated a child's abandoned treehouse in which to spend the winter.

The kitchen was an alcove off the front room, and after easing the chill, his face stinging with heat, he lit the gas stove and started breakfast. He cut a hole in a slice of bread, laid it in the frying pan, then cracked an egg and poured it into the hole (usually he just opened cans and cereal boxes or heated frozen food, but Sara Tappinger, his current lover, had taught him to fix eggs this way, and it made him feel like a competent bachelor to keep up the practice). He shoveled down the egg and bread standing at the kitchen window, watching the gray-shingled houses across the street melt from the darkness, shadowy clumps resolving into thickets of bayberry and sheep laurel, a picket line of Japanese pines beyond them. The wind had dropped and it looked as if the clouds were going to hang around, which was fine by Peter. Since renting the cottage in Madaket eight months before, he had learned that he thrived on bleakness, that the blustery, overcast days nourished his imagination. He had finished one novel here, and he planned to stay until the second was done. And maybe a third. What the hell? There wasn't much point in returning to California. He turned on the water to do the dishes, but the thought of LA had soured him on being competent. Screw it! Let the roaches breed. He pulled on a sweater, stuffed a notebook in his pocket, and stepped out into the cold.

As if it had been waiting for him, a blast of wind came swerving around the corner of the cottage and numbed his face. He tucked his chin onto his chest and set out walking, turning left on Tennessee Avenue and heading toward Smith Point, past more gray-shingled houses with quarterboards bearing cutesy names above their doors: names like Sea Shanty and Tooth Acres (the vacation home of a New Jersey dentist). When he had arrived on Nantucket he'd been amused by the fact that almost every structure on the island, even the Sears, Roebuck store, had gray shingles, and he had written his ex-wife a long humorous let's-be-friends letter telling about the shingles, about all the odd characters and quirkiness of the place. His ex-wife had not answered, and Peter couldn't blame her, not after what he had done. Solitude was the reason he gave for having moved to Madaket, but while this was superficially true, it would have been more accurate to say that he had been fleeing the ruins of his life. He had been idling along, content with his marriage, churning out scripts for a PBS children's show, when he had fallen obsessively in love with another woman, herself married. Plans and promises had been made, as a result of which he had left his wife; but then, in a sudden reversal of form, the woman – who had never expressed any sentiment other than boredom and resentment concerning her husband – had decided to honor her vows, leaving Peter alone and feeling both a damned fool and a villain. Desperate, he had fought for her, failed, tried to hate her, failed, and finally, hoping a change of geography would provoke a change of heart – hers or his – he had come to Madaket. That had been in September, directly after the exodus of the summer tourists; it was now May, and though the cold weather still lingered, the tourists were beginning to filter back. But no hearts had changed.

Twenty minutes of brisk walking brought him to the top of a dune overlooking Smith Point, a jut of sand extending a hundred yards or so into the water, with three small islands strung out beyond it; the nearest of these had been separated from the Point during a hurricane, and had the island still been attached, it – in conjunction with Eel Point, some three-quarters of a mile distant – would have given the western end of the land mass the shape of a crab's claw. Far out at sea a ray of sunlight pierced the overcast and dazzled the water beneath to such brilliance that it looked like a laving of fresh white paint. Sea gulls made curving flights overhead, hovered and dropped scallops onto the gravelly shingle to break the shells, then swooped down to pluck the meat. Sad-voweled gusts of wind sprayed a fine grit through the air.

Peter sat in the lee of a dune, choosing a spot from which he could see the ocean between stalks of the pale green beach grass, and opened his notebook. The words HOW THE WIND SPOKE AT MADAKET were printed on the inside cover. He had no illusions that the publishers would keep the title; they would change it to *The Keening* or *The Huffing and Puffing*, package it with a garish cover, and stick it next to *Love's Tormenting Itch* by Wanda LaFontaine on the grocery store racks. But none of that mattered as long as the words were good, and they were, though it hadn't gone well at first, not until he had started walking each morning to Smith Point and writing longhand. Then everything had snapped into focus. He had realized that it was *his* story he wanted to tell – the woman, his loneliness, his psychic flashes, the resolution of his character – all wrapped in the eerie metaphor of the wind; the writing had flowed so easily that it seemed the wind was collaborating on the book, whispering in his ear and guiding his hand across the page. He flipped the pages and noticed a paragraph that was a bit too formal, that he should break up and seed throughout the story:

Sadler had spent much of his life in Los Angeles, where the sounds of nature were obscured, and to his mind the constancy of the wind was Nantucket's most remarkable feature. Morning, noon, and night it flowed across the island, giving him a sense of being a bottom-dweller in an ocean of air, buffeted by currents that sprang from exotic quarters of the globe. He was a lonely soul, and the wind served to articulate his loneliness, to point up the immensity of the world in which he had become isolated; over the months he had come to feel an affinity with it, to consider it a fellow-traveler through emptiness and time. He half believed its vague speechlike utterances to be exactly that – an oracular voice whose powers of speech were not yet fully developed – and from listening to them he derived an impression of impending strangeness. He did not discount the impression, because as far back as he could recall he had received similar ones, and most had been borne out by reality. It was no great prophetic gift, no foreshadowings of earthquakes or assassinations; rather, it was a low-grade psychic ability: flashes of vision often accompanied by queasiness and headaches. Sometimes he could touch an object and know something about its owner, sometimes he would glimpse the shape of an upcoming event. But these premonitions were never clear enough to do him any good, to prevent broken arms or – as he had lately discovered – emotional disaster. Still, he hearkened to them. And now he thought the wind might actually be trying to tell him something of his future, of a new factor about to complicate his existence, for whenever he staked himself out on the dune at Smith Point he would feel …

Gooseflesh pebbling his skin, nausea, an eddying sensation behind his forehead as if his thoughts were spinning out of control. Peter rested his head on his knees and took deep breaths until the spell had abated. It was happening more and more often, and while it was most likely a product of suggestibility, a side effect of writing such a personal story, he couldn't shake the notion that he had become involved in some Twilight Zone irony, that the story was coming true as he wrote it. He hoped not: it wasn't going to be a very pleasant story. When the last of his nausea had passed, he took out a blue felt-tip, turned to a clean page, and began to detail the unpleasantness.

Two hours and fifteen pages later, hands stiff with cold, he heard a voice hailing him. Sara Tappinger was struggling up the side of the dune from the blacktop, slipping in the soft sand. She was, he thought with a degree of self-satisfaction, a damned pretty woman. Thirtyish; long auburn hair and nice cheekbones; endowed with what one of Peter's islander acquaintances called 'big chest problems.' That same acquaintance had congratulated him for having scored with Sara, saying that she'd blue-balled half the men on the island after her divorce, and wasn't he the lucky son of a bitch. Peter supposed he *was*: Sara was witty, bright, independent (she ran the local Montessori school), and they were compatible in every way. Yet it was not a towering passion. It was friendly, comfortable, and this Peter found alarming. Although being with her only glossed over his loneliness, he had come to depend on the relationship, and he was concerned that this signaled an overall reduction of his expectations, and that this in turn signaled the onset of middle age, a state for which he was unprepared.

'Hi,' she said, flinging herself down beside him and planting a kiss on his cheek. 'Wanna play?'

'Why aren't you in school?'

'It's Friday. I told you, remember? Parent-teacher conferences.' She took his hand. 'You're cold as ice! How long have you been here?'

'Couple of hours.'

'You're insane.' She laughed, delighted by his insanity. 'I was watching you for a bit before I called. With your hair flying about, you looked like a mad Bolshevik hatching a plot.'

'Actually,' he said, adopting a Russian accent, 'I come here to make contact with our submarines.'

'Oh? What's up? An invasion?'

'Not exactly. You see, in Russia we have many shortages. Grain, high technology, blue jeans. But the Russian soul can fly above such hardships. There is, however, a shortage of one commodity that we must solve immediately, and this is why I have lured you here.'

She pretended bewilderment. 'You need school administrators?'

'No, no. It is more serious. I believe the American word for it is …' He caught her by the shoulders and pushed her down on the sand, pinning her beneath him. 'Poontang. We cannot do without.'

Her smile faltered, then faded to a look of rapt anticipation. He kissed her. Through her coat he felt the softness of her breasts. The wind ruffled his hair, and he had the idea that it was leaning over his shoulder, spying on them; he broke off the kiss. He was queasy again. Dizzy.

'You're sweating,' she said, dabbing at his brow with a gloved hand. 'Is this one of those spells?'

He nodded and lay back against the dune.

'What do you see?' She continued to pat his brow dry, a concerned frown etching delicate lines at the corners of her mouth.

'Nothing,' he said.

But he did see something. Something glinting behind a cloudy surface. Something that attracted him yet frightened him at the same time. Something he knew would soon fall to his hand.

Though nobody realized it at the time, the first sign of trouble was the disappearance of Ellen Borchard, age thirteen, on the evening of Tuesday, May 19 – an event Peter had written into his book just prior to Sara's visit on Friday morning; but it didn't really begin for him until Friday night while drinking at the Atlantic Cafe in the village of Nantucket. He had gone there with Sara for dinner, and since the restaurant section was filled to capacity, they had opted for drinks and sandwiches at the bar. They had hardly settled on their stools when Jerry Highsmith – a blond young man who conducted bicycle tours of the island ('… the self-proclaimed Hunk of Hunks,' was Sara's description of him) – latched onto Peter; he was a regular at the cafe and an aspiring writer, and he took every opportunity to get Peter's advice. As always, Peter offered encouragement, but he secretly felt that anyone who liked to do their drinking at the Atlantic could have little to say to the reading public: it was a typical New England tourist trap, decorated with brass barometers and old life preservers, and it catered to the young summer crowd, many of whom – evident by their Bahama tans – were packed around the bar. Soon Jerry moved off in pursuit of a redhead with a honeysuckle drawl, a member of his latest tour group, and his stool was taken by Mills Lindstrom, a retired fisherman and a neighbor of Peter's.

'Damn wind out there's sharp enough to carve bone,' said Mills by way of a greeting, and ordered a whiskey. He was a big red-faced man stuffed into overalls and a Levi's jacket; white curls spilled from under his cap, and a lacing of broken blood vessels webbed his cheeks. The lacing was more prominent than usual, because Mills had a load on.

'What are you doing here?' Peter was surprised that Mills would set foot in the cafe; it was his conviction that tourism was a deadly pollution, and places like the Atlantic were its mutant growths.

'Took the boat out today. First time in two months.' Mills knocked back half his whiskey. 'Thought I might set a few lines, but then I run into that thing off Smith Point. Didn't feel like fishin' anymore.' He emptied his glass and signaled for a refill. 'Carl Keating told me it was formin' out there a while back. Guess it slipped my mind.'

'What thing?' asked Peter.

Mills sipped at his second whiskey. 'Offshore pollution aggregate,' he said grimly. 'That's the fancy name, but basically it's a garbage dump. Must be pretty near a kilometer square of water covered in garbage. Oil slick, plastic bottles, driftwood. They collect at slack points in the tides, but not usually so close to land. This one ain't more'n fifteen miles off the Point.'

Peter was intrigued. 'You're talking about something like the Sargasso Sea, right?'

''Spose so. 'Cept these ain't so big and there ain't no seaweed.'

'Are they permanent?'

'This one's new, the one off Smith Point. But there's one about thirty miles off the Vineyard that's been there for some years. Big storm'll break it up, but it'll always come back.' Mills patted his pockets, trying unsuccessfully to find his pipe. 'Ocean's gettin' like a stagnant pond. Gettin' to where a man throws in a line and more'n likely he'll come up with an ol' boot 'stead of a fish. I 'member twenty years ago when the mackerel was runnin', there'd be so many fish the water would look black for miles. Now you spot a patch of dark water and you know some damn tanker's taken a shit!'

Sara, who had been talking to a friend, put her arm around Peter's shoulder and asked what was up; after Peter had explained, she gave a dramatic shudder and said, 'It sounds spooky to me.' She affected a sepulchral tone. 'Strange magnetic zones that lure sailors to their dooms.'

'Spooky!' Mills scoffed. 'You got better sense than that, Sara. Spooky!' The more he considered the comment, the madder he became. He stood and made a flailing gesture that spilled the drink of a tanned college-age kid behind him; he ignored the kid's complaint and glared at Sara. 'Maybe you think this place is spooky. It's the same damn thing! A garbage dump! 'Cept here the garbage walks and talks' – he turned his glare on the kid – 'and thinks it owns the goddamn world!'

'Shit,' said Peter, watching Mills shoulder his way through the crowd. 'I was going to ask him to take me to see it.'

'Ask him tomorrow,' said Sara. 'Though I don't know why you'd want to see it.' She grinned and held up her hands to ward off his explanation. 'Sorry. I should realize that anyone who'll spend all day staring at sea gulls would find a square kilometer of garbage downright erotic.'

He made a grab for her breasts. 'I'll show you erotic!'

She laughed and caught his hand and – her mood suddenly altered – brushed the knuckles against her lips. 'Show me later,' she said.

They had a few more drinks, talked about Peter's work, about Sara's, and discussed the idea of taking a weekend together in New York. Peter began to acquire a glow. It was partly the drinks, yet he realized that Sara, too, was responsible. Though there had been other women since he had left his wife, he had scarcely noticed them; he had tried to be honest with them, had explained that he was in love with someone else, but he had learned that this was simply a sly form of dishonesty, that when you went to bed with someone – no matter how frank you had been as to your emotional state – they would refuse to believe there was any impediment to commitment that their love could not overcome; and so, in effect, he had used those women. But he did notice Sara, he did appreciate her, and he had not told her about the woman back in LA: once he had thought this a lie, but now he was beginning to suspect it was a sign that the passion was over. He had been in love for such a long time with a woman absent from him that perhaps he had grown to believe absence was a precondition for intensity, and perhaps it was causing him to overlook the birth of a far more realistic yet equally intense passion closer at hand. He studied Sara's face as she rambled on about New York. Beautiful. The kind of beauty that sneaks up on you, that you assumed was mere prettiness. But then, noticing her mouth was a bit too full, you decided that she was interestingly pretty; and then, noticing the energy of the face, how her eyes widened when she talked, how expressive her mouth was, you were led feature by feature to a perception of her beauty. Oh, he noticed her all right. The trouble was that during those months of loneliness (*Months? Christ, it had been over a year!*) he had become distanced from his emotions; he had set up surveillance systems inside his soul, and every time he started to twitch one way or the other, instead of completing the action he analyzed it and thus aborted it. He doubted he would ever be able to lose himself again.

Sara glanced questioningly at someone behind him. Hugh Weldon, the chief of police. He nodded at them and settled onto the stool. 'Sara,' he said. 'Mr Ramey. Glad I caught you.'

Weldon always struck Peter as the archetypal New Englander. Gaunt; weatherbeaten; dour. His basic expression was so bleak you assumed his gray crewcut to have been an act of penance. He was in his fifties but had a habit of sucking at his teeth that made him seem ten years older. Usually Peter found him amusing; however, on this occasion he experienced nausea and a sense of unease, feelings he recognized as the onset of a premonitory spell.

After exchanging pleasantries with Sara, Weldon turned to Peter. 'Don't want you to go takin' this wrong, Mr Ramey. But I got to ask where you were last Tuesday evenin' 'round six o'clock.'

The feelings were growing stronger, evolving into a sluggish panic that roiled inside Peter like the effects of a bad drug. 'Tuesday,' he said. 'That's when the Borchard girl disappeared.'

'My God, Hugh,' said Sara testily. 'What is this? Roust out the bearded stranger every time somebody's kid runs away? You know damn well that's what Ellen did. I'd run away myself if Ethan Borchard was my father.'

'Mebbe.' Weldon favored Peter with a neutral stare. 'Did you happen to see Ellen last Tuesday, Mr Ramey?'

'I was home,' said Peter, barely able to speak. Sweat was popping out on his forehead, all over his body, and he knew he must look as guilty as hell; but that didn't matter, because he could almost see what was going to happen. He was sitting somewhere, and just out of reach below him something glinted.

'Then you musta seen her,' said Weldon. ''Cordin' to witnesses she was mopin' 'round your woodpile for pretty near an hour. Wearin' bright yellow. Be hard to miss that.'

'No,' said Peter. He was reaching for that glint, and he knew it was going to be bad in any case, very bad, but it would be even worse if he touched it and he couldn't stop himself.

'Now that don't make sense,' said Weldon from a long way off. 'That cottage of yours is so small, it 'pears to me a man would just naturally catch sight of somethin' like a girl standin' by his woodpile while he was movin' 'round. Six o'clock's dinnertime for most folks, and you got a nice view of the woodpile out your kitchen window.'

'I didn't see her.' The spell was starting to fade, and Peter was terribly dizzy.

'Don't see how that's possible.' Weldon sucked at his teeth, and the glutinous sound caused Peter's stomach to do a slow flip-flop.

'You ever stop to think, Hugh,' said Sara angrily, 'that maybe he was otherwise occupied?'

'You know somethin', Sara, why don't you say it plain?'

'I was with him last Tuesday. He was moving around, all right, but he wasn't looking out any window. Is that plain enough?'

Weldon sucked at his teeth again. 'I 'spect it is. You sure 'bout this?'

Sara gave a sarcastic laugh. 'Wanna see my hickey?'

'No reason to be snitty, Sara. I ain't doin' this for pleasure.' Weldon heaved to his feet and gazed down at Peter. 'You lookin' a bit peaked, Mr Ramey.

Hope it ain't somethin' you ate.' He held the stare a moment longer, then pushed off through the crowd.

'God, Peter!' Sara cupped his face in her hands. 'You look awful!'

'Dizzy,' he said, fumbling for his wallet; he tossed some bills on the counter. 'C'mon, I need some air.'

With Sara guiding him, he made it through the front door and leaned on the hood of a parked car, head down, gulping in the cold air. Her arm around his shoulders was a good weight that helped steady him, and after a few seconds he began to feel stronger, able to lift his head. The street – with its cobblestones and newly budded trees and old-fashioned lampposts and tiny shops – looked like a prop for a model railroad. Wind prowled the sidewalks, spinning paper cups and fluttering awnings. A strong gust shivered him and brought a flashback of dizziness and vision. Once more he was reaching down toward that glint, only this time it was very close, so close that its energies were tingling his fingertips, pulling at him, and if he could just stretch out his hand another inch or two ... Dizziness overwhelmed him. He caught himself on the hood of the car; his arm gave way, and he slumped forward, feeling the cold metal against his cheek. Sara was calling to someone, asking for help, and he wanted to reassure her, to say he'd be all right in a minute, but the words clogged in his throat and he continued lying there, watching the world tip and spin, until someone with arms stronger than Sara's lifted him and said, 'Hey, man! You better stop hittin' the sauce, or I might be tempted to snake your ol' lady.'

Streetlight angled a rectangle of yellow glare across the foot of Sara's bed, illuminating her stockinged legs and half of Peter's bulk beneath the covers. She lit a cigarette, then – exasperated at having given into the habit again – she stubbed it out, turned on her side, and lay watching the rise and fall of Peter's chest. Dead to the world. Why, she wondered, was she such a sucker for the damaged ones? She laughed at herself; she knew the answer. She wanted to be the one to make them forget whatever had hurt them, usually another woman. A combination Florence Nightingale and sex therapist, that was her, and she could never resist a new challenge. Though Peter had not talked about it, she could tell some LA ghost owned half his heart. He had all the symptoms. Sudden silences, distracted stares, the way he jumped for the mailbox as soon as the postman came and yet was always disappointed by what he had received. She believed that she owned the other half of his heart, but whenever he started to go with it, to forget the past and immerse himself in the here and now, the ghost would rear up and he'd create a little distance. His approach to lovemaking, for instance. He'd come on soft and gentle, and then, just as they were on the verge of a new level of intimacy, he'd draw back, crack a joke, or do something rough – like tackling her on the beach that morning – and she would feel cheap and sluttish. Sometimes she thought that the thing to do would be to tell him to get the hell out of her life, to come back and see her when his head was clear. But she knew she wouldn't. He owned more than half her heart.

She eased off the bed, careful not to wake him, and slipped out of her clothes. A branch scraped the window, startling her, and she held her blouse up to cover her breasts. Oh, right! A Peeping Tom at a third-floor window. In New York, maybe, but not in Nantucket. She tossed the blouse into the laundry hamper and caught sight of herself in the full-length mirror affixed to the closet door. In the dim light the reflection looked elongated and unfamiliar, and she had a feeling that Peter's ghost woman was watching her from across the continent, from another mirror. She could almost make her out. Tall, long-legged, a mournful expression. Sara didn't need to see her to know the woman had been sad: it was the sad ones who were the real heartbreakers, and the men whose hearts they had broken were like fossil records of what the women were. They offered their sadness to be cured, yet it wasn't a cure they wanted, only another reason for sadness, a spicy bit to mix in with the stew they had been stirring all their lives. Sara moved closer to the mirror, and the illusion of the other woman was replaced by the conformation of her own body. 'That's what I'm going to do to you, lady,' she whispered. 'Blot you out.' The words sounded empty.

She turned back the bedspread and slid in beside Peter. He made a muffled noise, and she saw gleams of the streetlights in his eyes. 'Sorry about earlier,' he said.

'No problem,' she said brightly. 'I got Bob Frazier and Jerry Highsmith to help bring you home. Do you remember?'

'Vaguely. I'm surprised Jerry could tear himself away from his redhead. Him and his sweet Ginger!' He lifted his arm so Sara could burrow in against his shoulder. 'I guess your reputation's ruined.'

'I don't know about that, but it's certainly getting more exotic all the time.'

He laughed.

'Peter?' she said.

'Yeah?'

'I'm worried about these spells of yours. That's what this was, wasn't it?'

'Yeah.' He was silent a moment. 'I'm worried, too. I've been having them two and three times a day, and that's never happened before. But there's nothing I can do except try not to think about them.'

'Can you see what's going to happen?'

'Not really, and there's no point in trying to figure it out. I can't ever use what I see. It just happens, whatever's going to, and then I understand that *that* was what the premonition was about. It's a pretty worthless gift.'

Sara snuggled closer, throwing her leg across his hip. 'Why don't we go over to the Cape tomorrow?'

'I was going to check out Mills' garbage dump.'

'Okay. We can do that in the morning and still catch the three o'clock boat. It might be good for you to get off the island for a day or so.'

'All right. Maybe that's not such a bad idea.'

Sara shifted her leg and realized that he was erect. She eased her hand beneath the covers to touch him, and he turned so as to allow her better access. His breath quickened and he kissed her – gentle, treasuring kisses on her lips, her throat, her eyes – and his hips moved in counterpoint to the rhythm of her hand, slowly at first, becoming insistent, convulsive, until he was prodding against her thigh and she had to take her hand away and let him slip between her legs, opening her. Her thoughts were dissolving into a medium of urgency, her consciousness being reduced to an awareness of heat and shadows. But when he lifted himself above her, that brief separation broke the spell, and she could suddenly hear the fretful sounds of the wind, could see the particulars of his face and the light fixture on the ceiling behind him. His features seemed to sharpen, to grow alert, and he opened his mouth to speak. She put a finger to his lips. *Please, Peter! No jokes. This is serious.* She beamed the thoughts at him, and maybe they sank in. His face slackened, and as she guided him into place he moaned, a despairing sound such as a ghost might make at the end of its earthly term; and then she was clawing at him, driving him deeper inside, and talking to him, not words, just breathy noises, sighs and whispers, but having meanings that he would understand.

III

That same night while Peter and Sara were asleep, Sally McColl was driving her jeep along the blacktop that led to Smith Point. She was drunk and not giving a good goddamn where she wandered, steering in a never-ending S, sending the headlights veering across low gorsey hills and gnarled hawthorns. With one hand she kept a choke hold on a pint of cherry brandy, her third of the evening. 'Sconset Sally, they called her. Crazy Sally. Seventy-four years old and still able to shell scallops and row better than most men on the island. Wrapped in a couple of Salvation Army dresses, two moth-eaten sweaters, a tweed jacket gone at the elbows, and generally looking like a bag lady from hell. Brambles of white hair sticking out from under a battered fisherman's hat. Static fizzled on the radio, and Sally accompanied it with mutters, curses, and fitful bursts of song, all things that echoed the jumble of her thoughts. She parked near the spot where the blacktop gave out, staggered from the jeep and stumped through the soft sand to the top of a dune. There she swayed for a moment, dizzied by the pour of wind and the sweep of darkness broken only by a few stars on the horizon. 'Whoo-ooh!' she screeched; the wind sucked up her yell and added it to its sound. She lurched forward, slipped, and went rolling down the face of the dune. Sand adhering to her tongue, spitting, she sat up and found that somehow she'd managed to hold on to the bottle, that the cap was still on even though she hadn't screwed it tight. A flicker of paranoia set her to jerking her head from side to side. She didn't want anybody spying on her, spreading more stories about old drunk Sally. The ones they told were bad enough. Half were lies, and the rest were slanted to make her seem loopy ... like the one about how she'd bought herself a mail-order husband and he'd run off after two weeks, stowed away on a boat, scared to death of her, and she had come riding on horseback through Nantucket, hoping to bring him home. A swarthy little bump of a man, Eye-talian, no English, and he hadn't known shit from shortcake in bed. Better to do yourself than fool with a pimple like him. All she'd wanted had been the goddamn trousers she'd dressed him in, and the tale-tellers had cast her as a desperate woman. Bastards! Buncha goddamn ...

Sally's train of thought pulled into a tunnel, and she sat staring blankly at the dark. Damn cold, it was, and windy a bit as well. She took a swig of brandy; when it hit bottom she felt ten degrees warmer. Another swig put her legs under her, and she started walking along the beach away from the Point, searching for a nice lonesome spot where nobody was likely to happen by. That was what she wanted. Just to sit and spit and feel the night on her skin. You couldn't hardly find such a place nowadays, what with all the summer trash floating in from the mainland, the Gucci-Pucci sissies and the little swish-tailed chick-women eager to bend over and butter their behinds for the first five-hundred-dollar suit that showed interest, probably some fat-boy junior executive who couldn't get it up and would marry 'em just for the privilege of being humiliated every night ... That train of thought went spiraling off, and Sally spiraled after it. She sat down with a thump. She gave out with a cackle, liked the sound of it, and cackled louder. She sipped at the brandy, wishing that she had brought another bottle, letting her thoughts subside into a crackle of half-formed images and memories that seemed to have been urged upon her by the thrashings and skitterings of the wind. As her eyes adjusted, she made out a couple of houses lumped against the lesser blackness of the sky. Vacant summer places. No, wait! Those were them whatchamacallems. Condominiums. What had that Ramey boy said about 'em? Iniums with a condom slipped over each. Prophylactic lives. He was a good boy, that Peter. The first person she'd met with the gift for dog's years, and it was strong in him, stronger than her gift, which wasn't good for much except for guessing the weather, and she was so old now that her bones could do that just as well. He'd told her how some people in California had blown up condominiums to protect the beauty of their coastline, and it had struck her as a fine idea. The thought of condominiums ringing the island caused her to tear up, and with a burst of drunken nostalgia she remembered what a wonder the sea had been when she was a girl. Clean, pure, rife with spirits. She'd been able to sense those spirits ...

Battering and crunching from somewhere off in the dunes. She staggered to her feet, cocking an ear. More sounds of breakage. She headed toward them, toward the condominiums. Might be some kids vandalizing the place. If so, she'd cheer 'em on. But as she climbed to the top of the nearest dune, the sounds died away. Then the wind picked up, not howling or roaring, but with a weird ululation, almost a melody, as if it were pouring through the holes of an enormous flute.

The back of Sally's neck prickled, and a cold slimy worm of fear wriggled the length of her spine. She was close enough to the condominiums to see their rooflines against the sky, but she could see nothing else. There was only the eerie music of the wind, repeating the same passage of five notes over and over. Then it, too, died. Sally took a slug of brandy, screwed up her courage, and started walking again; the beach grass swayed and tickled her hands, and the tickling spread gooseflesh up her arms. About twenty feet from the first condominium she stopped, her heartbeat ragged. Fear was turning the brandy to a sour mess in her stomach. What was there to be afraid of, she asked herself. The wind? Shit! She had another slug of brandy and went forward. It was so dark she had to grope her way along the wall, and she was startled to find a hole smack in the middle of it. Bigger than a damn door, it was. Edged by broken boards and ripped shingles. Like a giant fist had smashed it through. Her mouth was cottony, but she stepped inside. She rummaged in her pockets, dug out a box of kitchen matches, lit one and cupped it with her hands until it burned steadily. The room was unfurnished, just carpeting and telephone fixtures and paint-spattered newspapers and rags. Sliding glass doors were inset into the opposite wall, but most of the glass had been blown out, crunching under her feet; as she drew near, an icicle-shaped piece hanging from the frame caught the glow of the match and for a second was etched on the dark like a fiery tooth. The match scorched her fingers. She dropped it and lit another and moved into the next room. More holes and a heaviness in the air, as if the house were holding its breath. Nerves, she thought. Goddamn old-woman nerves. Maybe it *had* been kids, drunk and ramming a car into the walls. A breeze eeled from somewhere and puffed out the match. She lit a third one. The breeze extinguished it, too, and she realized that kids hadn't been responsible for the damage, because the breeze didn't blow away this time: it fluttered around her, lifting her dress, her hair, twining about her legs, patting and frisking her all over, and in the breeze was a feeling, a knowledge, that turned her bones to splinters of black ice. Something had come from the sea, some evil thing with the wind for a body had smashed holes in the walls to play its foul, spine-chilling music, and it was surrounding her, toying with her, getting ready to whirl her off to hell and gone. It had a clammy, bitter smell, and that smell clung to her skin everywhere it touched.

Sally backed into the first room, wanting to scream but only able to manage a feeble squawk. The wind flowed after her, lifting the newspapers and flapping them at her like crinkly white bats, matting them against her face and chest. Then she screamed. She dove for the hole in the wall and flung herself into a frenzied heart-busting run, stumbling, falling, scrambling to her feet, and waving her arms and yelling. Behind her, the wind gushed from the house, roaring, and she imagined it shaping itself into a towering figure, a black demon who was laughing at her, letting her think she might make it before swooping down and tearing her apart. She rolled down the face of the last dune, and, her breath sobbing, clawed at the door handle of the jeep; she jiggled the key in the ignition, prayed until the engine turned over, and then, gears grinding, swerved off along the Nantucket road.

She was halfway to 'Sconset before she grew calm enough to think what to do, and the first thing she decided was to drive straight to Nantucket and tell Hugh Weldon. Though God only knew what *he'd* do. Or what he'd say. That scrawny flint of a man! Like as not he'd laugh in her face and be off to share the latest 'Sconset Sally story with his cronies. No, she told herself. There weren't going to be any more stories about ol' Sally drunk as the moon and seeing ghosts and raving about the wind. They wouldn't believe her, so let 'em think kids had done it. A little sun of gleeful viciousness rose in her thoughts, burning away the shadows of her fear and heating her blood even quicker than would a jolt of cherry brandy. Let it happen, whatever was going to happen, and *then* she'd tell her story, *then* she'd say I would have told you sooner, but you would have called me crazy. Oh, no! She wouldn't be the butt of their jokes this time. Let 'em find out for themselves that some new devil had come from the sea.

IV

Mills Lindstrom's boat was a Boston whaler, about twenty feet of blue squarish hull with a couple of bucket seats, a control pylon, and a fifty-five-horsepower outboard racketing behind. Sara had to sit on Peter's lap, and while he wouldn't have minded that in any case, in this case he appreciated the extra warmth. Though it was calm, the sea rolling in long swells, heavy clouds and a cold front had settled over the island; farther out the sun was breaking through, but all around them crumbling banks of whitish mist hung close to the water. The gloom couldn't dampen Peter's mood, however; he was anticipating a pleasant weekend with Sara and gave hardly a thought to their destination, carrying on a steady stream of chatter. Mills, on the other hand, was brooding and taciturn, and when they came in sight of the offshore pollution aggregate, a dirty brown stain spreading for hundreds of yards across the water, he pulled his pipe from beneath his rain gear and set to chomping the stem, as if to restrain impassioned speech.

Peter borrowed Mills' binoculars and peered ahead. The surface of the aggregate was pocked by thousands of white objects; at this distance they looked like bones sticking up from thin soil. Streamers of mist were woven across it, and the edge was shifting sluggishly, an obscene cap sliding over the dome of a swell. It was a no-man's-land, an ugly blot, and as they drew near, its ugliness increased. The most common of the white objects were Clorox bottles such as fishermen used to mark the spread of their nets; there were also a great many fluorescent tubes, other plastic debris, torn pieces of netting, and driftwood, all mired in a pale brown jelly of decayed oil products. It was a Golgotha of the inorganic world, a plain of ultimate spiritual malaise, of entropy triumphant, and perhaps, thought Peter, the entire earth would one day come to resemble it. The briny, bitter stench made his skin crawl.

'God,' said Sara as they began cruising along the edge; she opened her mouth to say more but couldn't find the words.

'I see why you felt like drinking last night,' said Peter to Mills, who just shook his head and grunted.

'Can we go into it?' asked Sara.

'All them torn nets'll foul the propeller.' Mills stared at her askance. 'Ain't it bad enough from out here?'

'We can tip up the motor and row in,' Peter suggested. 'Come on, Mills. It'll be like landing on the moon.'

And, indeed, as they rowed into the aggregate, cutting through the pale brown stuff, Peter felt that they had crossed some intangible border into uncharted territory. The air seemed heavier, full of suppressed energy, and the silence seemed deeper; the only sound was the slosh of the oars. Mills had told Peter that the thing would have roughly a spiral shape, due to the actions of opposing currents, and that intensified his feeling of having entered the unknown; he pictured them as characters in a fantasy novel, creeping across a great device inlaid on the floor of an abandoned temple. Debris bobbed against the hull. The brown glop had the consistency of Jell-O that hadn't set properly, and when Peter dipped his hands into it, beads accumulated on his fingers. Some of the textures on the surface had a horrid, almost organic, beauty: bleached, wormlike tendrils of netting mired in the slick, reminding Peter of some animal's diseased spoor; larval chips of wood matted on a bed of glistening cellophane; a blue plastic lid bearing a girl's sunbonneted face embedded in a spaghetti of Styrofoam strips. They would point out such oddities to each other, but nobody was eager to talk. The desolation of the aggregate was oppressive, and not even a ray of sunlight fingering the boat, as if a searchlight were keeping track of them from the real world, not even that could dispel the gloom. Then, about two hundred yards in, Peter saw something shiny inside an opaque plastic container, reached down and picked it up.

The instant he brought it on board he realized that this was the object about which he had experienced the premonition, and he had the urge to throw it back; but he felt such a powerful attraction to it that instead he removed the lid and lifted out a pair of silver combs, the sort Spanish women wear in their hair. Touching them, he had a vivid mental image of a young woman's face: a pale, drawn face that might have been beautiful but was starved-thin and worn by sorrows. Gabriela. The name seeped into his consciousness the way a paw track frozen in the ground melts up from beneath the snow during a thaw. Gabriela Pa ... Pasco ... Pascual. His finger traced the design etched on the combs, and every curlicue conveyed a sense of her personality. Sadness, loneliness, and – most of all – terror. She'd been afraid for a very long time. Sara asked to see the combs, took them, and his ghostly impression of Gabriela Pascual's life flew apart like a creature of foam, leaving him disoriented.

'They're beautiful,' said Sara. 'And they must be really old.'

'Looks like Mexican work,' said Mills. 'Hmph. What we got here?' He stretched out his oar, trying to snag something; he hauled the oar back in and Sara lifted the thing from the blade: a rag showing yellow streaks through its coating of slick.

'It's a blouse.' Sara turned it in her hands, her nose wrinkling at having to touch the slick; she stopped turning it and stared at Peter. 'Oh, God! It's Ellen Borchard's.'

Peter took it from her. Beneath the manufacturer's label was Ellen Borchard's name tag. He closed his eyes, hoping to read some impression as he had with the silver combs. Nothing. His gift had deserted him. But he had a bad feeling that he knew exactly what had happened to the girl.

'Better take that to Hugh Weldon,' said Mills. 'Might ...' He broke off and stared out over the aggregate.

At first Peter didn't see what had caught Mills' eyes; then he noticed that a wind had sprung up. A most peculiar wind. It was moving slowly around the boat about fifty feet away, its path evident by the agitation of the debris over which it passed; it whispered and sighed, and with a sucking noise a couple of Clorox bottles popped out of the slick and spun into the air. Each time the wind made a complete circuit of the boat, it seemed to have grown a little stronger.

'What the hell!' Mills' face was drained of color, the web of broken blood vessels on his cheeks showing like a bright red tattoo.

Sara's nails bit into Peter's arm, and he was overwhelmed by the knowledge that this wind was what he had been warned against. Panicked, he shook Sara off, scrambled to the back of the boat, and tipped down the outboard motor.

'The nets ...' Mills began.

'Fuck the nets! Let's get out of here!'

The wind was keening, and the entire surface of the aggregate was starting to heave. Crouched in the stern, Peter was again struck by its resemblance to a graveyard with bones sticking out of the earth, only now all the bones were wiggling, working themselves loose. Some of the Clorox bottles were rolling sluggishly along, bouncing high when they hit an obstruction. The sight froze him for a moment, but as Mills fired the engine, he crawled back to his seat and pulled Sara down with him. Mills turned the boat toward Madaket. The slick glubbed and smacked against the hull, and brown flecks splashed onto the windshield and oozed sideways. With each passing second the wind grew stronger and louder, building to a howl that drowned out the motor. A fluorescent tube went twirling up beside them like a cheerleader's baton; bottles and cellophane and splatters of oil slick flew at them from every direction. Sara ducked her face into Peter's shoulder, and he held her tight, praying that the propeller wouldn't foul. Mills swerved the boat to avoid a piece of driftwood that sailed past the bow, and then they were into clear water, out of the wind – though they could still hear it raging – and running down the long slope of a swell.

Relieved, Peter stroked Sara's hair and let out a shuddering breath; but when he glanced behind them all his relief went glimmering. Thousands upon thousands of Clorox bottles and fluorescent tubes and other debris were spinning in midair above the aggregate – an insane mobile posed against the gray sky – and just beyond the edge narrow tracks of water were being lashed up, as if a windy knife were slicing back and forth across it, undecided whether or not to follow them home.

Hugh Weldon had been out in Madaket investigating the vandalism of the condominiums, and after receiving the radio call it had only taken him a few minutes to get to Peter's cottage. He sat beside Mills at the picnic table, listening to their story, and from the perspective of the sofa bunk, where Peter was sitting, his arms around Sara, the chief presented an angular mantislike silhouette against the gray light from the window; the squabbling of the police radio outside seemed part of his persona, a radiation emanating from him. When they had finished he stood, walked to the wood stove, lifted the lid, and spat inside it; the stove crackled and spat back a spark.

'If it was just you two,' he said to Peter and Sara, 'I'd run you in and find out what you been smokin'. But Mills here don't have the imagination for this kind of foolishness, so I guess I got to believe you.' He set down the lid with a clank and squinted at Peter. 'You said you wrote somethin' 'bout Ellen Borchard in your book. What?'

Peter leaned forward, resting his elbows on his knees. 'She was down at Smith Point just after dark. She was angry at her parents, and she wanted to scare them. So she took off her blouse – she had extra clothes with her, because she was planning to run away – and was about to rip it up, to make them think she'd been murdered, when the wind killed her.'

'Now how'd it do that?' asked Weldon.

'In the book the wind was a sort of elemental. Cruel, capricious. It played with her. Knocked her down, rolled her along the shingle. Then it would let her up and knock her down again. She was bleeding all over from the shell-cuts, and screaming. Finally it whirled her up and out to sea.' Peter stared down at his hands; the inside of his head felt heavy, solid, as if his brains were made of mercury.

'Jesus Christ!' said Weldon. 'What you got to say 'bout that, Mills?'

'It wasn't no normal wind,' said Mills. 'That's all I know.'

'Jesus Christ!' repeated Weldon; he rubbed the back of his neck and peered at Peter. 'I been twenty years at this job, and I've heard some tall tales. But this ... what did you say it was? An elemental?'

'Yeah, but I don't really know for sure. Maybe if I could handle those combs again. I could learn more about it.'

'Peter.' Sara put her hand on his arm; her brow was furrowed. 'Why don't we let Hugh deal with it?'

Weldon was amused. 'Naw, Sara. You let Mr Ramey see what he can do.' He chuckled. 'Maybe he can tell me how the Red Sox are gonna do this year. Me and Mills can have another look at that mess off the Point.'

Mills' neck seemed to retract into his shoulders. 'I ain't goin' back out there, Hugh. And if you want my opinion, you better keep clear of it yourself.'

'Damn it, Mills.' Weldon smacked his hand against his hip. 'I ain't gonna beg, but you sure as hell could save me some trouble. It'll take me an hour to get the Coast Guard boys off their duffs. Wait a minute!' He turned to Peter. 'Maybe you people were seein' things. There musta been all kinds of bad chemicals fumin' up from that mess. Could be you breathed somethin' in.' Brakes squealed, a car door slammed, and seconds later the bedraggled figure of Sally McColl strode past the window and knocked on the door.

'What in God's name does she want?' said Weldon.

Peter opened the door, and Sally gave him a gap-toothed grin. 'Mornin', Peter,' she said. She was wearing a stained raincoat over her usual assortment of dresses and sweaters, and a gaily colored man's necktie for a scarf. 'Is that skinny ol' fart Hugh Weldon inside?'

'I ain't got time for your crap today, Sally,' called Weldon.

Sally pushed past Peter. 'Mornin', Sara. Mills.'

'Hear one of your dogs just had a litter,' said Mills.

'Yep. Six snarly little bastards.' Sally wiped her nose with the back of her hand and checked it to see what had rubbed off. 'You in the market?'

'I might drop 'round and take a look,' said Mills. 'Dobermans or Shepherds?'

'Dobermans. Gonna be fierce.'

'What's on your mind, Sally?' said Weldon, stepping between them.

'Got a confession to make.'

Weldon chuckled. 'What'd you do now? You sure as hell didn't burglarize no dress shop.'

A frown etched the wrinkles deeper on Sally's face. 'You stupid son of a bitch,' she said flatly. 'I swear, God musta been runnin' short of everything but horseshit when He made you.'

'Listen, you ol' ...'

'Musta ground up your balls and used 'em for brains,' Sally went on. 'Musta ...'

'Sally!' Peter pushed them apart and took the old woman by the shoulders. A glaze faded from her eyes as she looked at him. At last she shrugged free of his grasp and patted down her hair: a peculiarly feminine gesture for someone so shapeless and careworn.

'I shoulda told you sooner,' she said to Weldon. 'But I was sick of you laughin' at me. Then I decided it might be important and I'd have to risk listenin' to your jackass bray. So I'm tellin' you.' She looked out the window. 'I know what done them condominiums. It was the wind.' She snapped a hateful glance at Weldon. 'And I ain't crazy, neither!'

Peter felt weak in the knees. They were surrounded by trouble; it was in the air as it had been off Smith Point, yet stronger, as if he were becoming sensitized to the feeling.

'The wind,' said Weldon, acting dazed.

'That's right,' said Sally defiantly. 'It punched holes in them damn buildin's and was whistlin' through 'em like it was playin' music.' She glared at him. 'Don't you believe me?'

'He believes you,' said Peter. 'We think the wind killed Ellen Borchard.'

'Now don't be spreadin' that around! We ain't sure!' Weldon said it desperately, clinging to disbelief.

Sally crossed the room to Peter. 'It's true 'bout the Borchard girl, ain't it?'

'I think so,' he said.

'And that thing what killed her, it's here in Madaket. You feel it, don'tcha?'

He nodded. 'Yeah.'

Sally headed for the door.

'Where you goin'?' asked Weldon. She mumbled and went outside; Peter saw her pacing back and forth in the yard. 'Crazy ol' bat,' said Weldon.

'Mebbe she is,' said Mills. 'But you ought not to be treatin' her so harsh after all she's done.'

'What's she done?' asked Peter.

'Sally used to live up in Madaket,' said Mills. 'And whenever a ship would run up on Dry Shoals or one of the others, she'd make for the wreck in that ol' lobster boat of hers. Most times she'd beat the Coast Guard to 'em. Musta saved fifty or sixty souls over the years, sailin' out in the worst kind of weather.'

'Mills!' said Weldon emphatically. 'Run me out to that garbage dump of yours.'

Mills stood and hitched up his pants. 'Ain't you been listenin', Hugh? Peter and Sally say that thing's 'round here somewhere.'

Weldon was a frustrated man. He sucked at his teeth, and his face worked. He picked up the container holding the combs, glanced at Peter, then set the container down.

'You want me to see what I can learn from those?' asked Peter.

Weldon shrugged. 'Can't hurt nothin', I guess.' He stared out the window as if unconcerned with the issue.

Peter took the container and sat down next to Sara. 'Wait,' she said. 'I don't understand. If this thing is nearby, shouldn't we get away from here?' Nobody answered.

The plastic container was cold, and when Peter pried off the lid, the cold welled out at him. Intense, aching cold, as if he had opened the door to a meat locker.

Sally burst into the room and pointed at the container. 'What's that?'

'Some old combs,' said Peter. 'They didn't feel like this when I found them. Not as strong.'

'Feel like what?' asked Weldon; every new mystery seemed to be unnerving him further, and Peter suspected that if the mysteries weren't cleared up soon, the chief would start disbelieving them on purely practical grounds.

Sally came over to Peter and looked into the container. 'Gimme one,' she said, extending a grimy hand. Weldon and Mills moved up behind her, like two old soldiers flanking their mad queen.

Reluctantly, Peter picked up one of the combs. Its coldness flowed into his arm, his head, and for a moment he was in the midst of a storm-tossed sea, terrified, waves crashing over the bows of a fishing boat and the wind singing around him. He dropped the comb. His hands were trembling, and his heart was doing a jig against his chest wall.

'Oh, shit,' he said to no one in particular. 'I don't know if I want to do this.'

*

Sara gave Sally her seat beside Peter, and as they handled the combs, setting them down every minute or so to report what they had learned, she chewed her nails and fretted. She could relate to Hugh Weldon's frustration; it was awful just to sit and watch. Each time Peter and Sally handled the combs their respiration grew shallow and their eyes rolled back, and when they laid them aside they appeared drained and frightened.

'Gabriela Pascual was from Miami,' said Peter. 'I can't tell exactly when all this happened, but it was years ago ... because in my image of her, her clothes look a little old-fashioned. Maybe ten or fifteen years back. Something like that. Anyway, there was trouble for her onshore, some emotional entanglement, and her brother didn't want to leave her alone, so he took her along on a fishing voyage. He was a commercial fisherman.'

'She had the gift,' Sally chimed in. 'That's why there's so much of her in the combs. That, and because she killed herself and died holdin' 'em.'

'Why'd she kill herself?' asked Weldon.

'Fear,' said Peter. 'Loneliness. Crazy as it sounds, the wind was holding her prisoner. I think she cracked up from being alone on a drifting boat with only this thing – the elemental – for company.'

'Alone?' said Weldon. 'What happened to her brother?'

'He died.' Sally's voice was shaky. 'The wind came down and killed 'em all 'cept this Gabriela. It wanted her.'

As the story unfolded, gusts of wind began to shudder the cottage and Sara tried to remain unconcerned as to whether or not they were natural phenomena. She turned her eyes from the window, away from the heaving trees and bushes, and concentrated on what was being said; but that in itself was so eerie that she couldn't keep from jumping whenever the panes rattled. Gabriela Pascual, said Peter, had been frequently seasick during the cruise; she had been frightened of the crew, most of whom considered her bad luck, and possessed by a feeling of imminent disaster. And, Sally added, that premonition had been borne out. One cloudless calm day the elemental had swept down and killed everyone. Everyone except Gabriela. It had whirled the crew and her brother into the air, smashed them against bulkheads, dropped them onto the decks. She had expected to die as well, but it had seemed interested in her. It had caressed her and played with her, knocking her down and rolling her about; and at night it had poured through the passageways and broken windows, making a chilling music that – as the days passed and the ship drifted north – she came to half-understand.

'She didn't think of it as a spirit,' said Peter. 'There wasn't anything mystical about it to her mind. It struck her as being kind of a ...'

'An animal,' interrupted Sally. 'A big, stupid animal. Vicious, it was. But not evil. 'Least it didn't feel evil to her.'

Gabriela, Peter went on, had never been sure what it wanted of her – perhaps her presence had been all. Most of the time it had left her alone. Then, suddenly, it would spring up out of a calm to juggle splinters of glass or chase her about. Once the ship had drifted near to shore, and when she had attempted to jump over the side, the elemental had battered her and driven her below-decks. Though at first it had controlled the drift of the ship, gradually it lost interest in her and on several occasions the ship almost foundered. Finally, no longer caring to prolong the inevitable, she had cut her wrists and died clutching the container holding her most valued possessions, her grandmother's silver combs, with the wind howling in her ears.

Peter leaned back against the wall, his eyes shut, and Sally sighed and patted her breast. For a long moment no one spoke.

'Wonder why it's hangin' 'round that garbage out there,' said Mills.

'Maybe no reason,' said Peter dully. 'Or maybe it's attracted to slack points in the tides, to some condition of the air.'

'I don't get it,' said Weldon. 'What the hell is it? It can't be no animal.'

'Why not?' Peter stood, swayed, then righted himself. 'What's wind, anyway? Charged ions, vacating air masses. Who's to say that some stable form of ions couldn't approximate a life? Could be there's one of these at the heart of every storm, and they've always been mistaken for spirits, given an anthropomorphic character. Like Ariel.' He laughed disconsolately. 'It's no sprite, that's for sure.'

Sally's eyes looked unnaturally bright, like watery jewels lodged in her weathered face. 'The sea breeds 'em,' she said firmly, as if that were explanation enough of anything strange.

'Peter's book was right,' said Sara. 'It's an elemental. That's what you're describing, anyway. A violent, inhuman creature, part spirit and part animal.' She laughed, and the laugh edged a bit high, bordering on the hysteric. 'It's hard to believe.'

'Right!' said Weldon. 'Damned hard! I got an ol' crazy woman and a man I don't know from Adam tellin' me …'

'Listen!' said Mills; he walked to the door and swung it open.

It took Sara a second to fix on the sound, but then she realized that the wind had died, had gone from heavy gusts to trifling breezes in an instant, and farther away, coming from the sea, or nearer, maybe as close as Tennessee Avenue, she heard a roaring.

V

A few moments earlier Jerry Highsmith had been both earning his living and looking forward to a night of exotic pleasures in the arms of Ginger McCurdy. He was standing in front of one of the houses on Tennessee Avenue, its quarterboard reading AHAB-ITAT, and a collection of old harpoons and whalebones mounted on either side of the door; his bicycle leaned against a rail fence behind him, and ranged around him, straddling their bikes, dolled up in pastel-hued jogging suits and sweat clothes, were twenty-six members of the Peach State Ramblers Bicycle Club. Ten men, sixteen women. The women were all in good shape, but most were in their thirties, a bit long in the tooth for Jerry's taste. Ginger, on the other hand, was prime. Twenty-three or twenty-four, with red hair down to her ass and a body that wouldn't quit. She had peeled off her sweats and was blooming out a halter and shorts cut so high that each time she dismounted you could see right up to the Pearly Gates. And she knew what she was doing: every jiggle of those twin jaloobies was aimed at his crotch. She had pressed to the front of the group and was attending to his spiel about the bullshit whaling days. Oh, yeah! Ginger was ready. A couple of lobsters, a little wine, a stroll along the waterfront, and then by God he'd pump her so full of the Nantucket Experience that she'd breach like a snow-white hill.

Thar she fuckin' blows!

'Now, y'all ...' he began.

They tittered; they liked him mocking their accent.

He grinned abashedly as if he hadn't known what he was doing. 'Must be catchin',' he said. 'Now you people probably haven't had a chance to visit the Whaling Museum, have you?'

A chorus of Nos.

'Well then, I'll give you a course in harpoonin'.' He pointed at the wall of the AHAB-ITAT. 'That top one with the single barb stickin' off the side, that's the kind most commonly used during the whalin' era. The shaft's of ash. That was the preferred wood. It stands up to the weather' – he stared pointedly at Ginger – 'and it won't bend under pressure.' Ginger tried to constrain a smile. 'Now that one,' he continued, keeping an eye on her, 'the one with the arrow point and no barbs, that was favored by some whalers. They said it allowed for deeper penetration.'

'What about the one with two barbs?' asked someone.

Jerry peered over heads and saw that the questioner was his second choice. Ms Selena Persons. A nice thirtyish brunette, flat-chested, but with killer legs. Despite the fact that he was obviously after Ginger, she hadn't lost interest. Who knows? A double-header might be a possibility.

'That was used toward the end of the whalin' era,' he said. 'But generally two-barbed harpoons weren't considered as effective as single-barbed ones. I don't know why, exactly. Might have just been stubbornness on the whalers' part. Resistance to change. They knew the ol' single-barb could give satisfaction.'

Ms. Persons met his gaze with the glimmer of a smile.

''Course,' Jerry continued, addressing all the Ramblers, 'now the shaft's tipped with a charge that explodes inside the whale.' He winked at Ginger and added *sotto voce*, 'Must be a rush.'

She covered her mouth with her hand.

'Okay, folks!' Jerry swung his bike away from the fence. 'Mount up, and we'll be off to the next thrillin' attraction.'

Laughing and chattering, the Ramblers started to mount, but just then a powerful gust of wind swept down Tennessee Avenue, causing squeals and blowing away hats. Several of the riders overbalanced and fell, and several more nearly did. Ginger stumbled forward and clung to Jerry, giving him chest-to-chest massage. 'Nice catch,' she said, doing a little writhe as she stepped away.

'Nice toss,' he replied.

She smiled, but the smile faded and was replaced by a bewildered look. 'What's that?'

Jerry turned. About twenty yards away a column of whirling leaves had formed above the blacktop; it was slender, only a few feet high, and though he had never seen anything similar, it alarmed him no more than had the freakish gust of wind. Within seconds, however, the column had grown to a height of fifteen feet; twigs and gravel and branches were being sucked into it, and it sounded like a miniature tornado. Someone screamed. Ginger clung to him in genuine fright. There was a rank smell in the air, and a pressure was building in Jerry's ears. He couldn't be sure, because the column was spinning so rapidly, but it seemed to be assuming a roughly human shape, a dark green figure made of plant litter and stones. His mouth had gone dry, and he restrained an urge to throw Ginger aside and run.

'Come on!' he shouted.

A couple of the Ramblers managed to mount their bicycles, but the wind had grown stronger, roaring, and it sent them wobbling and crashing into the weeds. The rest huddled together, their hair whipping about, and stared at the great Druid thing that was taking shape and swaying above them, as tall as the treetops. Shingles were popping off the sides of the houses, sailing up and being absorbed by the figure; and as Jerry tried to outvoice the wind, yelling at the Ramblers to lie flat, he saw the whalebones and harpoons ripped from the wall of the AHAB-ITAT. The windows of the house exploded outward. One man clutched the bloody flap of his cheek, which had been sliced open by a shard of glass; a woman grabbed the back of her knee and crumpled. Jerry shouted a final warning and pulled Ginger down with him into the roadside ditch. She squirmed and struggled, in a panic, but he forced her head down and held tight. The figure had risen much higher than the trees, and though it was still swaying, its form had stabilized somewhat. It had a face now: a graveyard smile of gray shingles and two circular patches of stones for eyes: a terrible blank gaze that seemed responsible for the increasing air pressure. Jerry's heart boomed in his inner ear, and his blood felt like sludge. The figure kept swelling, up and up; the roar was resolving into an oscillating hum that shivered the ground. Stones and leaves were beginning to spray out of it. Jerry knew, *knew*, what was going to happen, and he couldn't keep from watching. Amid a flurry of leaves he saw one of the harpoons flit through the air, impaling a woman who had been trying to stand. The force of the blow drove her out of Jerry's field of vision. Then the great figure exploded. Jerry squeezed his eyes shut. Twigs and balls of dirt and gravel stung him. Ginger leaped sideways and collapsed atop him, clawing at his hip. He waited for something worse to happen, but nothing did. 'You okay?' he asked, pushing Ginger away by the shoulders.

She wasn't okay.

A splintered inch of whalebone stuck out from the center of her forehead. Shrieking with revulsion, Jerry wriggled from beneath her and came to his hands and knees. A moan. One of the men was crawling toward him, his face a mask of blood, a ragged hole where his right eye had been; his good eye looked glazed like a doll's. Horrified, not knowing what to do, Jerry scrambled to his feet and backed away. All the harpoons, he saw, had found targets. Most of the Ramblers lay unmoving, their blood smeared over the blacktop; the rest were sitting up, dazed and bleeding. Jerry's heel struck something, and he spun about. The quarterboard of the AHAB-ITAT had nailed Ms Selena Persons vampire-style to the roadside dirt; the board had been driven so deep into the ground that only the letter *A* was showing above the mired ruin of her jogging suit, as if she were an exhibit. Jerry began to tremble, and tears started from his eyes.

A breeze ruffled his hair.

Somebody wailed, shocking him from his daze. He should call the hospital, the police. But where was a phone? Most of the houses were empty, waiting for summer tenants, and the phones wouldn't be working. Somebody must have seen what had happened, though. He should just do what he could until help arrived. Gathering himself, he walked toward the man whose eye was missing; but before he had gone more than a few paces a fierce gust of wind struck him in the back and knocked him flat.

This time the roaring was all around him, the pressure so intense that it seemed a white-hot needle had pierced him from ear to ear. He shut his eyes and clamped both hands to his ears, trying to smother the pain. Then he felt himself lifted. He couldn't believe it at first. Even when he opened his eyes and saw that he was being borne aloft, revolving in a slow circle, it made no sense. He couldn't hear, and the quiet added to his sense of unreality; further adding to it, a riderless bicycle pedaled past. The air was full of sticks and leaves and pebbles, a threadbare curtain between him and the world, and he imagined himself rising in the gorge of that hideous dark figure. Ginger

McCurdy was flying about twenty feet overhead, her red hair streaming, arms floating languidly as if in a dance. She was revolving faster than he, and he realized that his rate of spin was increasing as he rose. He saw what was going to happen: you went higher and higher, faster and faster, until you were spewed out, shot out over the village. His mind rebelled at the prospect of death, and he tried to swim back down the wind, flailing, kicking, bursting with fear. But as he whirled higher, twisting and turning, it became hard to breathe, to think, and he was too dizzy to be afraid any longer. Another woman sailed by a few feet away. Her mouth was open, her face contorted; blood dripped from her scalp. She clawed at him, and he reached out to her, not knowing why he bothered. Their hands just missed touching. Thoughts were coming one at a time. Maybe he'd land in the water. MIRACULOUS SURVIVOR OF FREAK TORNADO. Maybe he'd fly across the island and settle gently in a Nantucket treetop. A broken leg, a bruise or two. They'd set up drinks for him in the Atlantic Cafe. Maybe Connie Keating would finally come across, would finally recognize the miraculous potential of Jerry Highsmith. Maybe. He was tumbling now, limbs jerking about, and he gave up thinking. Flash glimpses of the gapped houses below, of the other dancers on the wind, moving with spasmodic abandon. Suddenly, as he was bent backward by a violent updraft, there was a wrenching pain inside him, a grating, then a vital dislocation that delivered him from pain. Oh, Christ Jesus! Oh, God! Dazzles exploded behind his eyes. Something bright blue flipped past him, and he died.

VI

After the column of leaves and branches looming up from Tennessee Avenue had vanished, after the roaring had died, Hugh Weldon sprinted for his squad car with Peter and Sara at his heels. He frowned as they piled in but made no objection, and this, Peter thought, was probably a sign that he had stopped trying to rationalize events, that he accepted the wind as a force to which normal procedures did not apply. He switched on the siren, and they sped off. But less than fifty yards from the cottage he slammed on the brakes. A woman was hanging in a hawthorn tree beside the road, an old-fashioned harpoon plunged through her chest. There was no point in checking to see if she was alive. All her major bones were quite obviously broken, and she was painted with blood head to foot, making her look like a horrid African doll set out as a warning to trespassers.

Weldon got on the radio. 'Body out in Madaket,' he said. 'Send a wagon.'

'You might need more than one,' said Sara; she pointed to three dabs of color farther up the road. She was very pale, and she squeezed Peter's hand so hard that she left white imprints on his skin.

Over the next twenty-five minutes they found eighteen bodies: broken, mutilated, several pierced by harpoons or fragments of bone. Peter would not have believed that the human form could be reduced to such grotesque statements, and though he was horrified, nauseated, he became increasingly numbed by what he saw. Odd thoughts flocked to his brain, most persistent among them being that the violence had been done partly for his benefit. It was a sick, nasty idea, and he tried to dismiss it; but after a while he began to consider it in light of other thoughts that had lately been striking him out of the blue. The manuscript of *How the Wind Spoke at Madaket*, for instance. As improbable as it sounded, it was hard to escape the conclusion that the wind had been seeding all this in his brain. He didn't want to believe it, yet there it was, as believable as anything else that had happened. And given that, was his latest thought any less believable? He was beginning to understand the progression of events, to understand it with the same sudden clarity that had helped him solve the problems of his book, and he wished very much that he could have obeyed his premonition and not touched the combs. Until then the elemental had not been sure of him; it had been nosing around him like – as Sally had described it – a big, stupid animal, sensing something familiar about him but unable to remember what. And when he had found the combs, when he had opened the container, there must have been some kind of circuit closed, a flash point sparked between his power and Gabriela Pascual's, and the elemental had made the connection. He recalled how excited it had seemed, darting back and forth beyond the borders of the aggregate.

As they turned back onto Tennessee Avenue, where a small group of townsfolk were covering bodies with blankets, Weldon got on the radio again, interrupting Peter's chain of logic. 'Where the hell are them ambulances?' he snapped.

'Sent 'em a half hour ago,' came the reply. 'Shoulda been there by now.'

Weldon cast a grim look at Peter and Sara. 'Try 'em on the radio,' he told the operator.

A few minutes later the report came that none of the ambulances were answering their radios. Weldon told his people to stay put, that he'd check it out himself. As they turned off Tennessee Avenue onto the Nantucket road, the sun broke through the overcast, flooding the landscape in a thin yellow light and warming the interior of the car. The light seemed to be illuminating Peter's weaknesses, making him realize how tense he was, how his muscles ached with the poisons of adrenaline and fatigue. Sara leaned against him, her eyes closed, and the pressure of her body acted to shore him up, to give him a burst of vitality.

Weldon kept the speed at thirty, glancing left and right, but nothing was out of the ordinary. Deserted streets, houses with blank-looking windows. Many of the homes in Madaket were vacant, and the occupants of many of the rest were away at work or off on errands. About two miles out of town, as they crested a low rise just beyond the dump, they spotted the ambulances. Weldon pulled onto the shoulder, letting the engine idle, and stared at the sight. Four ambulances were strewn across the blacktop, forming an effective roadblock a hundred feet away. One had been flipped over on its roof like a dead white bug; another had crashed into a light pole and was swathed in electrical lines whose broken ends were sticking in through the driver's window, humping and writhing and sparking. The other two had been smashed together and were burning; transparent licks of flame warped the air above their blackened husks. But the wrecked ambulances were not the reason that Weldon had stopped so far away, why they sat silent and hopeless. To the right of the road was a field of bleached weeds and grasses, an Andrew Wyeth field glowing yellow in the pale sun, figured by a few stunted oaks and extending to a hill overlooking the sea, where three gray houses were posed against a faded blue sky. Though only fitful breezes played about the squad car, the field was registering the passage of heavy winds; the grasses were rippling, eddying, bending, and swaying in contrary directions, as if thousands of low-slung animals were scampering through them to and fro, and this rippling was so constant, so furious, it seemed that the shadows of the clouds passing overhead were standing still and the land was flowing away. The sound of the wind was a mournful whistling rush. Peter was entranced. The scene had a fey power that weighed upon him, and he had trouble catching his breath.

'Let's go,' said Sara tremulously. 'Let's …' She stared past Peter, a look of fearful comprehension forming on her face.

The wind had begun to roar. Less than thirty feet away a patch of grass had been flattened, and a man wearing an orderly's uniform was being lifted into the air, revolving slowly. His head flopped at a ridiculous straw-man angle, and the front of his tunic was drenched with blood. The car shuddered in the turbulence.

Sara shrieked and clutched at Peter. Weldon tried to jam the gearshift into reverse, missed, and the car stalled. He twisted the key in the ignition. The engine sputtered, dieseled, and went dead. The orderly continued to rise, assuming a vertical position. He spun faster and faster, blurring like an ice skater doing a fancy finish, and at the same time drifted closer to the car. Sara was screaming, and Peter wished he could scream, could do something to release the tightness in his chest. The engine caught. But before Weldon could put the car in gear, the wind subsided and the orderly fell onto the hood. Drops of blood sprinkled the windshield. He lay spread-eagled for a moment, his dead eyes staring at them. Then, with the obscene sluggishness of a snail retracting its foot, he slumped down onto the road, leaving a red smear across the white metal.

Weldon rested his head on the wheel, taking deep breaths. Peter cradled

Sara in his arms. After a second Weldon leaned back, picked up the radio mike, and thumbed the switch open. 'Jack,' he said. 'This is Hugh. You copy?'

'Loud and clear, Chief.'

'We got us a problem out in Madaket.' Weldon swallowed hard and gave a little twitch of his head. 'I want you to set up a roadblock 'bout five miles from town. No closer. And don't let nobody through, y'understand?'

'What's happenin' out there, Chief? Alice Cuddy called in and said somethin' 'bout a freak wind, but the phone went dead and I couldn't get her back.'

'Yeah, we had us some wind.' Weldon exchanged a glance with Peter. 'But the main problem's a chemical spill. It's under control for now, but you keep everybody away. Madaket's in quarantine.'

'You need some help?'

'I need you to do what I told you! Get on the horn and call everyone livin' 'tween the roadblock and Madaket. Tell 'em to head for Nantucket as quick as they can. Put the word on the radio, too.'

'What 'bout folks comin' from Madaket? Do I let 'em through?'

'Won't be nobody comin' that way,' said Weldon.

Silence. 'Chief, you okay?'

'Hell, yes!' Weldon switched off.

'Why didn't you tell them?' asked Peter.

'Don't want 'em thinkin' I'm crazy and comin' out to check on me,' said Weldon. 'Ain't no point in them dyin', too.' He shifted into reverse. 'I'm gonna tell everyone to get in their cellars and wait this damn thing out. Maybe we can figure out somethin' to do. But first I'll take you home and let Sara get some rest.'

'I'm all right,' she said, lifting her head from Peter's chest.

'You'll feel better after a rest,' he said, forcing her head back down: it was an act of tenderness, but also he did not want her to catch sight of the field. Dappled with cloud shadow; glowing palely; some quality of light different from that which shone upon the squad car; it seemed at a strange distance from the road, a view into an alternate universe where things were familiar yet not quite the same. The grasses were rippling more furiously than ever, and every so often a column of yellow stalks would whirl high into the air and scatter, as if an enormous child were running through the field, ripping up handfuls of them to celebrate his exuberance.

'I'm not sleepy,' Sara complained; she still hadn't regained her color, and one of her eyelids had developed a tic.

Peter sat beside her on the bed. 'There's nothing you can do, so why not rest?'

'What are you going to do?'

'I thought I'd have another go at the combs.'

The idea distressed her. He started to explain why he had to, but instead bent and kissed her on the forehead. 'I love you,' he said. The words slipped out so easily that he was amazed. It had been a very long time since he had spoken them to anyone other than a memory.

'You don't have to tell me that just because things look bad,' she said, frowning.

'Maybe that's why I'm telling you now,' he said. 'But I don't believe it's a lie.'

She gave a dispirited laugh. 'You don't sound very confident.'

He thought it over. 'I was in love with someone once,' he said, 'and that relationship colored my view of love. I guess I believed that it always had to happen the same way. A nuclear strike. But I'm beginning to understand it can be different, that you can build toward the sound and the fury.'

'It's nice to hear,' she said, and then, after a pause, 'but you're still in love with her, aren't you?'

'I still think about her, but …' He shook his head. 'I'm trying to put it behind me, and maybe I'm succeeding. I had a dream about her this morning.'

She arched an eyebrow. 'Oh?'

'It wasn't a sweet dream,' he said. 'She was telling me how she'd cemented over her feelings for me. "All that's left," she said, "is this little hard place on my breast." And she told me that sometimes it moved around, twitched, and she showed me. I could see the damn thing jumping underneath her blouse, and when I touched it – she wanted me to – it was unbelievably hard. Like a pebble lodged beneath her skin. A heart stone. That was all that was left of us. Just this piece of hardness. It pissed me off so much that I threw her on the floor. Then I woke up.' He scratched his beard, embarrassed by confession. 'It was the first time I've ever had a violent thought about her.'

Sara stared at him, expressionless.

'I don't know if it's meaningful,' he said lamely. 'But it seemed so.'

She remained silent. Her stare made him feel guilty for having had the dream, sorry that he had mentioned it.

'I don't dream about her very much,' he said.

'It's not important,' she said.

'Well.' He stood. 'Try and get some sleep, okay?'

She reached for his hand. 'Peter?'

'Yeah?'

'I love you. But you knew that, right?'

It hurt him to see how hesitantly she said it, because he knew that he was to blame for her hesitancy. He bent down and kissed her again. 'Sleep,' he said. 'We'll talk about it later.'

He closed the door behind him gently. Mills was sitting at the table, gazing out at 'Sconset Sally, who was pacing the yard, her lips moving, waving her arms, as if arguing with an invisible playmate. 'That ol' gal sure's gone down these last years,' said Mills. 'Used to be sharp as a tack, but she's actin' pretty crazy now.'

'Can't blame her,' said Peter, sitting down across from Mills. 'I'm feeling pretty crazy myself.'

'So.' Mills tamped tobacco into the bowl of his pipe. 'You got a line on what this thing is?'

'Maybe it's the Devil.' Peter leaned against the wall. 'I don't really know, but I'm starting to think that Gabriela Pascual was right about it being an animal.'

Mills chomped on the stem of his pipe and fished in his pocket for a lighter. 'How's that?'

'Like I said, I don't really know for sure, but I've been getting more and more sensitized to it ever since I found the combs. At least it seems that way. As if the connection between us were growing stronger.' Peter spotted a book of matches tucked under his sugar bowl and slid them across to Mills. 'I'm beginning to have some insights into it. When we were out on the road just now, I felt that it was exhibiting an animal trait. Staking out territory. Protecting it from invaders. Look who it's attacked. Ambulances, bicyclists. People who were entering its territory. It attacked us when we visited the aggregate.'

'But it didn't kill us,' said Mills.

The logical response to Mills' statement surfaced from Peter's thoughts, but he didn't want to admit to it and shunted it aside. 'Maybe I'm wrong,' he said.

'Well, if it is an animal, then it can take a hook. All we got to do is find its mouth.' Mills grunted laughter, lit his pipe, and puffed bluish smoke. 'After you been out on the water a coupla weeks, you can feel when something strange is hard by ... even if you can't see it. I ain't no psychic, but seems to me I brushed past this thing once or twice.'

Peter glanced up at him. Though Mills was a typical barroom creature, an old salt with a supply of exotic tales, every now and then Peter could sense about him the sort of specific gravity that accrues to those who have spent time in the solitudes. 'You don't seem afraid,' he said.

'Oh, don't I?' Mills chuckled. 'I'm afraid. I'm just too old to be runnin' 'round in circles 'bout it.'

The door flew open, and Sally came in. 'Hot in here,' she said; she went to the stove and laid a finger against it. 'Hmph! Must be all this shit I'm wearin'.' She plumped herself down beside Mills, squirmed into a comfortable position, and squinted at Peter. 'Goddamn wind won't have me,' she said. 'It wants you.'

Peter was startled. 'What do you mean?'

Sally pursed her lips as if she had tasted something sour. 'It would take me if you wasn't here, but you're too strong. I can't figure a way 'round that.'

'Leave the boy alone,' said Mills.

'Can't.' Sally glowered at him. 'He's got to do it.'

'You know what she's talkin' 'bout?' asked Mills.

'Hell, yes! He knows! And if he don't, all he's got to do is go talk to it. You understand me, boy. It wants *you*.'

An icy fluid squirted down Peter's spine. 'Like Gabriela,' he said. 'Is that what you mean?'

'Go on,' said Sally. 'Talk to it.' She pointed a bony finger at the door. 'Just take a stand out there, and it'll come to you.'

Behind the cottage, walled off by the spread of two Japanese pines and a toolshed, was a field that the previous tenant had used for a garden. Peter had let it go to seed, and the entire plot was choked with weeds and litter: gas cans, rusty nails, a plastic toy truck, the decaying hide of a softball, cardboard scraps, this and more resting upon a matte of desiccated vines. It reminded him of the aggregate, and thus seemed an appropriate place to stand and commune with the wind … if such a communion weren't the product of 'Sconset Sally's imagination. Which Peter hoped it was. The afternoon was waning, and it had grown colder. Silver blares of wintery sunlight edged the blackish-gray clouds scudding overhead, and the wind was a steady pour off the sea. He could detect no presence in it, and he was beginning to feel foolish, thinking about going back inside, when a bitter-smelling breeze rippled across his face. He stiffened. Again he felt it: it was acting independent of the offshore wind, touching delicate fingers to his lips, his eyes, fondling him the way a blind man would in trying to know your shape in his brain. It feathered his hair and pried under the pocket flaps of his army jacket like a pet mouse searching for cheese; it frittered with his shoelaces and stroked him between the legs, shriveling his groin and sending a chill washing through his body.

He did not quite understand how the wind spoke to him, yet he had an image of the process as being similar to how a cat will rub against your hand and transmit a static charge. The charge was actual, a mild stinging and popping. Somehow it was translated into knowledge, doubtless by means of his gift. The knowledge was personified, and he was aware that his conceptions were human renderings of inhuman impulses; but at the same time he was certain that they were basically accurate. Most of all it was lonely. It was the only one of its kind, or, if there were others, it had never encountered them. Peter felt no sympathy for its loneliness, because it felt no sympathy for him. It wanted him not as a friend or companion but as a witness to its power. It would enjoy preening for him, showing off, rubbing against his sensitivity to it and deriving some unfathomable pleasure. It was very powerful. Though its touch was light, its vitality was undeniable, and it was even stronger over water. The land weakened it, and it was eager to return to the sea with Peter in tow. Gliding together through the wild canyons of the waves, into a chaos of booming darkness and salt spray, traveling the most profound of all deserts – the sky above the sea – and testing its strength against the lesser powers of the storms, seizing flying fish and juggling them like silver blades, gathering nests of floating treasures and playing for weeks with the bodies of the drowned. Always at play. Or perhaps 'play' was not the right word. Always employed in expressing the capricious violence that was its essential quality. Gabriela Pascual might not have been exact in calling it an animal, but what else could you call it? It was of nature, not of some netherworld. It was ego without thought, power without morality, and it looked upon Peter as a man might look upon a clever toy: something to be cherished for a while, then neglected, then forgotten.

Then lost.

Sara waked at twilight from a dream of suffocation. She sat bolt upright, covered with sweat, her chest heaving. After a moment she calmed herself and swung her legs onto the floor and sat staring into space. In the half-light the dark grain of the boards looked like a pattern of animal faces emerging from the wall; out the window she could see shivering bushes and banks of running clouds. Still feeling sluggish, she went into the front room, intending to wash her face; but the bathroom door was locked and 'Sconset Sally cawed at her from inside. Mills was snoozing on the sofa bunk, and Hugh Weldon was sitting at the table, sipping a cup of coffee; a cigarette smoldered in the saucer, and that struck her as funny: she had known Hugh all her life and had never seen him smoke.

'Where's Peter?' she asked.

'Out back,' he said moodily. 'Buncha damn foolishness, if you ask me.'

'What is?'

He gave a snort of laughter. 'Sally says he's talkin' to the goddamn wind.'

Sara felt as if her heart had constricted. 'What do you mean?'

'Beats the hell outta me,' said Weldon. 'Just more of Sally's nonsense.' But when their eyes met she could sense his hopelessness and fear.

She broke for the door. Weldon grabbed at her arm, but she shook free and headed for the Japanese pines back of the cottage. She brushed aside the branches and stopped short, suddenly afraid. The bending and swaying of the weeds revealed a slow circular passage of wind, as if the belly of a great beast were dragging across them, and at the center of the field stood Peter. His eyes were closed, his mouth open, and strands of hair were floating above his head like the hair of a drowned man. The sight stabbed into her, and forgetting her fear, she ran toward him, calling his name. She had covered half the distance between them when a blast of wind smashed her to the ground.

Stunned and disoriented, she tried to get to her feet, but the wind smacked her flat again, pressing her into the damp earth. As had happened out on the aggregate, garbage was rising from the weeds. Scraps of plastic, rusty nails, a yellowed newspaper, rags, and directly overhead, a large chunk of kindling. She was still dazed, yet she saw with peculiar clarity how the bottom of the chunk was splintered and flecked with whitish mold. It was quivering, as if the hand that held it were barely able to restrain its fury. And then, as she realized it was about to plunge down, to jab out her eyes and pulp her skull, Peter dived on top of her. His weight knocked the breath out of her, but she heard the piece of kindling *thunk* against the back of his head; she sucked in air and pushed at him, rolling him away, and came to her knees. He was dead-pale.

'Is he all right?'

It was Mills, lumbering across the field. Behind him, Weldon had hold of 'Sconset Sally, who was struggling to escape. Mills had come perhaps a third of the way when the garbage, which had fallen back into the weeds, once more was lifted into the air, swirling, jiggling, and – as the wind produced one of its powerful gusts – hurtling toward him. For a second he was surrounded by a storm of cardboard and plastic; then this fell away, and he took a staggering step forward. A number of dark dots speckled his face. Sara thought at first they were clots of dirt. Then blood seeped out around them. They were rusty nailheads. Piercing his brow, his cheeks, pinning his upper lip to his gum. He gave no cry. His eyes bulged, his knees buckled, he did an ungainly pirouette and pitched into the weeds.

Sara watched dully as the wind fluttered about Hugh Weldon and Sally, belling their clothes; it passed beyond them, lashing the pine boughs and vanishing. She spotted the hump of Mills' belly through the weeds. A tear seemed to be carving a cold groove in her cheek. She hiccuped, and thought what a pathetic reaction to death that was. Another hiccup, and another. She couldn't stop. Each successive spasm made her weaker, more unsteady, as if she were spitting up tiny fragments of her soul.

VII

As darkness fell, the wind poured through the streets of the village, playing its tricks with the living, the inanimate, and the dead. It was indiscriminate, the ultimate free spirit doing its thing, and yet one might have ascribed a touch of frustration to its actions. Over Warren's Landing it crumpled a sea gull into a bloody rag, and near the mouth of Hither Creek it scattered field mice into the air. It sent a spare tire rolling down the middle of Tennessee Avenue and skied shingles from the roof of the AHAB-ITAT. For a while it flowed about aimlessly; then, increasing to tornado-force, it uprooted a

Japanese pine, just yanked it from the ground, dangling huge black root balls, and chucked it like a spear through the side of a house across the street. It repeated the process with two oaks and a hawthorn. Finally it began to blast holes in the walls of the houses and snatch the wriggling creatures inside. It blew off old Julia Stackpole's cellar door and sailed it down into the shelves full of preserves behind which she was hiding; it gathered the broken glass into a hurricane of knives that slashed her arms, her face, and – most pertinently – her throat. It found even older George Coffin (who wasn't about to hide, because in his opinion Hugh Weldon was a damned fool) standing in his kitchen, having just stepped back in after lighting his barbecue; it swept up the coals and hurled them at him with uncanny accuracy. Over the space of a half hour it killed twenty-one people and flung their bodies onto their lawns, leaving them to bleed pale in the accumulating dusk. Its fury apparently abated, it dissipated to a breeze and – zipping through shrubs and pine boughs – it fled back to the cottage, where something it now wanted was waiting in the yard.

VIII

'Sconset Sally sat on the woodpile, sucking at a bottle of beer that she'd taken from Peter's refrigerator. She was as mad as a wet hen because she had a plan – a good plan – and that brainless wonder Hugh Weldon wouldn't hear it, wouldn't listen to a damn word she said. Stuck on being a hero, he was.

The sky had deepened to indigo, and a big lopsided silver moon was leering at her from over the roof of the cottage. She didn't like its eye on her, and she spat toward it. The elemental caught the gob of spit and spun it around high in the air, making it glisten oysterlike. Fool thing! Half monster, half a walloping, invisible dog. It reminded her of that outsized old male of hers, Rommel. One second he'd be going for the mailman's throat, and the next he'd be on his back and waggling his paws, begging for a treat. She screwed her bottle into the grass so it wouldn't spill and picked up a stick of kindling. 'Here,' she said, and shied the stick. 'Fetch.' The elemental caught the stick and juggled it for a few seconds, then let it fall at her feet. Sally chuckled. 'Me'n you might get along,' she told the air. ''Cause neither one of us gives a shit!' The beer bottle lifted from the grass. She made a grab for it and missed. 'Goddamn it!' she yelled. 'Bring that back!' The bottle sailed to a height of about twenty feet and tipped over; the beer spilled out, collected in half a dozen large drops that – one by one – exploded into spray, showering her. Sputtering, she jumped to her feet and started to wipe her face; but the elemental knocked her back down. A trickle of fear welled up inside her. The bottle still hovered above her; after a second it plopped into the grass, and the elemental curled around her, fidgeting with her hair, her collar, slithering inside her raincoat; then, abruptly, as if something else had attracted its attention, it was gone. She saw the grass flatten as it passed over, moving toward the street. She propped herself against the woodpile and finished wiping her face; she spotted Hugh Weldon through the window, pacing, and her anger was rekindled. Thought he was so goddamn masterful, did he? He didn't know piss about the elemental, and there he was, laughing at her plan.

Well, screw him!

He'd find out soon enough that his plan wouldn't work, that hers was the reasonable one, the surefire one.

A little scary, maybe, but surefire all the same.

IX

It had come full dark by the time Peter regained consciousness. He moved his head, and the throbbing nearly caused him to black out. He lay still, getting his bearings. Moonlight spilled through the bedroom window, and Sara was leaning beside it, her blouse glowing a phosphorescent white. From the tilt of her head he judged that she was listening to something, and he soon distinguished an unusual pattern to the wind: five notes followed by a glissando, which led to a repetition of the passage. It was heavy, angry music, an ominous hook that might have been intended to signal the approach of a villain. Shortly thereafter the pattern broke into a thousand skirling notes, as if the wind were being forced through the open stops of a chorus of flutes. Then another passage, this of seven notes, more rapid but equally ominous. A chill, helpless feeling stole over Peter, like the drawing of a morgue sheet. That breathy music was being played for him. It was swelling in volume, as if – and he was certain this was the case – the elemental was heralding his awakening, was once again sure of his presence. It was impatient, and it would not wait for him much longer. Each note drilled that message home. The thought of being alone with it on the open sea terrified him. Yet he had no choice. There was no way to fight it, and it would simply keep on killing until he obeyed. If it weren't for the others he would refuse to go; he would rather die here than submit to that harrowing unnatural relationship. Or was it unnatural? It occurred to him that the history of the wind and Gabriela Pascual had a great deal in common with the histories of many human relationships. Desiring; obtaining; neglecting; forgetting. It might be that the elemental was some sort of core existence, that at the heart of every relationship lay a howling emptiness, a chaotic music.

'Sara,' he said, wanting to deny it.

The moonlight seemed to wrap around her as she turned. She came to sit beside him. 'How are you feeling?'

'Woozy.' He gestured toward the window. 'How long's that been going on?'

'It just started,' she said. 'It's punched holes in a lot of houses. Hugh and Sally were out a while ago. More people are dead.' She brushed a lock of hair from his forehead. 'But ...'

'But what?'

'We have a plan.'

The wind was playing eerie triplets, an agitated whistling that set Peter's teeth on edge. 'It better be a doozy,' he said.

'Actually, it's Hugh's plan,' she said. 'He noticed something out in the field. The instant you touched me, the wind withdrew from us. If it hadn't, if it had hurled that piece of wood at you instead of letting it drop, you would have died. And it didn't want that ... at least that's what Sally says.'

'She's right. Did she tell you what it does want?'

'Yes.' She looked away, and her eyes caught the moonlight; they were teary. 'Anyway, we think it was confused, that when we're close together it can't tell us apart. And since it doesn't want to hurt you or Sally, Hugh and I are safe as long as we maintain proximity. If Mills had just stayed where he was ...'

'Mills?'

She told him.

After a moment, still seeing Mills' nail-studded face in his mind's eye, he asked, 'What's the plan?'

'I'm going to ride in the jeep with Sally, and you're going with Hugh. We'll drive toward Nantucket, and when we reach the dump ... you know that dirt road there that leads off into the moors?'

'The one that leads to Altar Rock? Yeah.'

'At that point you'll jump into the jeep with us, and we'll head for Altar Rock. Hugh will keep going toward Nantucket. Since it seems to be trying to isolate this end of the island, he figures it'll come after him and we might be able to get beyond its range, and with both of us heading in different directions, we might be able to confuse it enough so that it won't react quickly, and he'll be able to escape, too.' She said all this in a rush that reminded Peter of the way a teenager would try to convince her parents to let her stay out late, blurting out the good reasons before they had time to raise any objections.

'You might be right about it not being able to tell us apart when we're close to each other,' he said. 'God knows how it senses things, and that seems plausible. But the rest is stupid. We don't know whether its territoriality is limited to this end of the island. And what if it does lose track of me and Sally? What's it going to do then? Just blow away? Somehow I doubt it. It might head for Nantucket and do what it's done here.'

'Sally says she has a backup plan.'

'Christ, Sara!' Gingerly, he eased up into a sitting position. 'Sally's nuts. She doesn't have a clue.'

'Well, what choice do we have?' Her voice broke. 'You can't go with it.'

'You think I want to? Jesus!'

The bedroom door opened, and Weldon appeared silhouetted in a blur of orange light that hurt Peter's eyes. 'Ready to travel?' said Weldon. 'Sconset Sally was at his rear, muttering, humming, producing a human static.

Peter swung his legs off the bed. 'This is nuts, Weldon.' He stood and steadied himself on Sara's shoulder. 'You're just going to get killed.' He gestured toward the window and the constant music of the wind. 'Do you think you can outrun that in a squad car?'

'Mebbe this plan ain't worth a shit ...' Weldon began.

'You got that right!' said Peter. 'If you want to confuse the elemental, why not split me and Sally up? One goes with you, the other with Sara. That way at least there's some logic to this.'

'Way I figure it,' said Weldon, hitching up his pants, 'it ain't your job to be riskin' yourself. It's mine. If Sally, say, goes with me, you're right, that'd confuse it. But so might this. Seems to me it's as eager to keep us normal people in line as it is to run off with freaks like you 'n Sally.'

'What ...'

'Shut up!' Weldon eased a step closer. 'Now if my way don't work, you try it yours. And if *that* don't do it, then you can go for a cruise with the damn thing. But we don't have no guarantees it's gonna let anybody live, no matter what you do.'

'No, but ...'

'No buts about it! This is my bailiwick, and we're gonna do what I say. If it don't work, well, then you can do what you have to. But 'til that happens ...'

'"Til that happens you're going to keep on making an ass of yourself,' said Peter. 'Right? Man, all day you've been looking for a way to assert your fucking authority! You don't have any authority in this situation. Don't you understand?'

Weldon went jaw to jaw with him. 'Okay,' he said. 'You go on out there, Mr Ramey. Go ahead. Just march on out there. You can use Mills' boat, or if you want something bigger, how 'bout Sally's.' He snapped a glance back at Sally. 'That okay with you, Sally?' She continued muttering, humming, and nodded her head. 'See!' Weldon turned to Peter. 'She don't mind. So you go ahead. You draw that son of a bitch away from us if you can.' He hitched up his pants and exhaled; his breath smelled like a coffee cup full of cigarette butts. 'But if it was me, I'd be 'bout ready to try anything else.'

Peter's legs felt rooted to the floor. He realized that he had been using anger to muffle fear, and he did not know if he could muster up the courage to take a walk out into the wind, to sail away into the terror and nothingness that Gabriela Pascual had faced.

Sara slipped her hand through his arm. 'Please, Peter,' she said. 'It can't hurt to try.'

Weldon backed off a step. 'Nobody's blamin' you for bein' scared, Mr Ramey,' he said. 'I'm scared myself. But this is the only way I can figure to do my job.'

'You're going to die.' Peter had trouble swallowing. 'I can't let you do that.'

'You ain't got nothin' to say 'bout it,' said Weldon. ' 'Cause you got no more authority than me. 'Less you can tell that thing to leave us be. Can you?'

Sara's fingers tightened on Peter's arm, but relaxed when he said, 'No.'

'Then we'll do 'er my way.' Weldon rubbed his hands together in what seemed to Peter hearty anticipation. 'Got your keys, Sally?'

'Yeah,' she said, exasperated; she moved close to Peter and put a bird-claw hand on his wrist. 'Don't worry, Peter. This don't work, I got somethin' up my sleeve. We'll pull a fast one on that devil.' She cackled and gave a little whistle, like a parrot chortling over a piece of fruit.

As they drove slowly along the streets of Madaket, the wind sang through the ruined houses, playing passages that sounded mournful and questioning, as if it were puzzled by the movements of the jeep and the squad car. The light of a three-quarter moon illuminated the destruction: gaping holes in the walls, denuded bushes, toppled trees. One of the houses had been given a surprised look, an O of a mouth where the door had been, flanked by two shattered windows. Litter covered the lawns. Flapping paperbacks, clothing, furniture, food, toys. And bodies. In the silvery light their flesh was as pale as Swiss cheese, the wounds dark. They didn't seem real; they might have been a part of a gruesome environment created by an avant-garde sculptor. A carving knife skittered along the blacktop, and for a moment Peter thought it would jump into the air and hurtle toward him. He glanced over at Weldon to see how he was taking it all. Wooden Indian profile, eyes on the road. Peter envied him his pose of duty; he wished he had such a role to play, something that would brace him up, because every shift in the wind made him feel frail and rattled.

They turned onto the Nantucket road, and Weldon straightened in his seat. He checked the rearview mirror, keeping an eye on Sally and Sara, and held the speed at twenty-five. 'Okay,' he said as they neared the dump and the road to Altar Rock. 'I ain't gonna come to a full stop, so when I give the word you move it.'

'All right,' said Peter; he took hold of the door handle and let out a calming breath. 'Good luck.'

'Yeah.' Weldon sucked at his teeth. 'Same to you.'

The speed indicator dropped to fifteen, to ten, to five, and the moonlit landscape inched past.

'Go!' shouted Weldon.

Peter went. He heard the squad car squeal off as he sprinted toward the jeep; Sara helped haul him into the back, and then they were veering onto the dirt road. Peter grabbed the frame of Sara's seat, bouncing up and down. The thickets that covered the moors grew close to the road, and branches whipped the sides of the jeep. Sally was hunched over the wheel, driving like a maniac; she sent them skipping over potholes, swerving around tight corners, grinding up the little hills. There was no time to think, only to hold on and be afraid, to await the inevitable appearance of the elemental. Fear was a metallic taste in Peter's mouth; it was in the white gleam of Sara's eyes as she glanced back at him and the smears of moonlight that coursed along the hood; it was in every breath he took, every trembling shadow he saw. But by the time they reached Altar Rock, after fifteen minutes or so, he had begun to hope, to half-believe, that Weldon's plan had worked.

The rock was almost dead-center of the island, its highest point. It was a barren hill atop which stood a stone where the Indians had once conducted human sacrifices – a bit of history that did no good whatsoever for Peter's nerves. From the crest you could see for miles over the moors, and the rumpled pattern of depressions and small hills had the look of a sea that had been magically transformed to leaves during a moment of fury. The thickets – bayberry and such – were dusted to a silvery-green by the moonlight, and the wind blew steadily, giving no evidence of unnatural forces.

Sara and Peter climbed from the jeep, followed after a second by Sally. Peter's legs were shaky and he leaned against the hood; Sara leaned back beside him, her hip touching his. He caught the scent of her hair. Sally peered toward Madaket. She was still muttering, and Peter made out some of the words.

'Stupid ... never would listen to me ... never would ... son of a bitch ... keep it to my goddamn self ...'

Sara nudged him. 'What do you think?'

'All we can do is wait,' he said.

'We're going to be all right,' she said firmly; she rubbed the heel of her right hand against the knuckles of her left. It seemed the kind of childish gesture intended to insure good luck, and it inspired him to tenderness. He pulled her into an embrace. Standing there, gazing past her head over the moors, he had an image of them as being the standard lovers on the cover of a paperback, clinging together on a lonely hill, with all probability spread out around them. A corny way of looking at things, yet he felt the truth of it, the dizzying immersion that a paperback lover was supposed to feel. It was not as clear a feeling as he had once had, but perhaps clarity was no longer possible for him. Perhaps all his past clarity had simply been an instance of faulty perception, a flash of immaturity, an adolescent misunderstanding of what was possible. But whether or not that was the case, self-analysis would not solve his confusion. That sort of thinking blinded you to the world, made you disinclined to take risks. It was similar to what happened to academics, how they became so committed to their theories that they began to reject facts to the contrary, to grow conservative in their judgments and deny the inexplicable, the magical. If there was magic in the world – and he knew there was – you could only approach it by abandoning the constraints of logic and lessons learned. For more than a year he had forgotten this and had constructed defenses against magic; now in a single night they had been blasted away, and at a terrible cost he had been made capable of risking himself again, of hoping.

Then he noticed something that wasted hope.

Another voice had been added to the natural flow of wind from the ocean, and in every direction, as far as the eye could see, the moon-silvered thickets were rippling, betraying the presence of far more wind than was evident atop the hill. He pushed Sara away. She followed his gaze and put a hand to her mouth. The immensity of the elemental stunned Peter. They might have been standing on a crag in the midst of a troubled sea, one that receded into an interstellar dark. For the first time, despite his fear, he had an apprehension of the elemental's beauty, of the precision and intricacy of its power. One moment it could be a tendril of breeze, capable of delicate manipulations, and the next it could become an entity the size of a city. Leaves and branches – like flecks of black space – were streaming up from the thickets, forming into columns. Six of them, at regular intervals about Altar Rock, maybe a hundred yards away. The sound of the wind evolved into a roar as they thickened and grew higher. And they grew swiftly. Within seconds the tops of the columns were lost in darkness. They did not have the squat, conical shapes of tornadoes, nor did they twist and jab down their tails; they merely swayed, slender and graceful and menacing. In the moonlight their whirling was almost undetectable and they looked to be made of shining ebony, like six enormous savages poised to attack. They began moving toward the hill. Splintered bushes exploded upward from their bases, and the roaring swelled into a dissonant chord: the sound of a hundred harmonicas being blown at once. Only much, much louder.

The sight of 'Sconset Sally scuttling for the jeep waked Peter from his daze; he pushed Sara into the rear seat and climbed in beside Sally. Though the engine was running, it was drowned out by the wind. Sally drove even less cautiously than before; the island was crisscrossed by narrow dirt roads, and it seemed to Peter that they almost crashed on every one of them. Skidding sideways through a flurry of bushes, flying over the crests of hills, diving down steep slopes. The thickets grew too high in most places for him to see much, but the fury of the wind was all around them, and once, as they passed a place where the bushes had been burned off, he caught a glimpse of an ebony column about fifty yards away. It was traveling alongside them, he realized. Harrowing them, running them to and fro. Peter lost track of where they were, and he could not believe that Sally had any better idea. She was trying to do the impossible, to drive out the wind, which was everywhere, and her lips were drawn back in a grimace of fear. Suddenly – they had just turned east – she slammed on the brakes. Sara flew halfway into the front seat, and if Peter had not been braced he might have gone through the windshield. Farther along the road one of the columns had taken a stand, blocking their path. It looked like God, he thought. An ebony tower reaching from the earth to the sky, spraying clouds of dust and plant litter from its bottom. And it was moving toward them. Slowly. A few feet per second. But definitely on the move. The jeep was shaking, and the roar seemed to be coming from the ground beneath them, from the air, from Peter's body, as if the atoms of things were all grinding together. Frozen-faced, Sally wrangled with the gearshift. Sara screamed, and Peter, too, screamed as the windshield was sucked out of its frame and whirled off. He braced himself against the dash, but his arms were weak and with a rush of shame he felt his bladder go. The column was less than a hundred feet away, a great spinning pillar of darkness. He could see how the material inside it aligned itself into tightly packed rings like the segments of a worm. The air was syrupy, hard to breathe. And then, miraculously, they were swerving away from it, away from the roaring, backing along the road. They turned a corner, and Sally got the jeep going forward; she sent them grinding up a largish hill … and braked. And let her head drop onto the steering wheel in an attitude of despair. They were once again at Altar Rock.

And Hugh Weldon was waiting for them.

He was sitting with his head propped against the boulder that gave the place its name. His eyes were filled with shadows. His mouth was open, and his chest rose and fell. Labored breathing, as if he had just run a long way. There was no sign of the squad car. Peter tried to call to him, but his tongue was stuck to his palate and all that came out was a strangled grunt. He tried again.

'Weldon!'

Sara started to sob, and Sally gasped. Peter didn't know what had frightened them and didn't care; for him the process of thought had been thinned down to following one track at a time. He climbed from the jeep and went over to the chief. 'Weldon,' he said again.

Weldon sighed.

'What happened?' Peter knelt beside him and put a hand on his shoulder; he heard a hiss and felt a tremor pass through the body.

Weldon's right eye began to bulge. Peter lost his balance and sat back hard. Then the eye popped out and dropped into the dust. With a high-pitched whistling, wind and blood sprayed from the empty socket. Peter fell backward, scrabbling at the dirt in an effort to put distance between himself and

Weldon. The corpse toppled onto its side, its head vibrating as the wind continued to pour out, boiling up dust beneath the socket. There was a dark smear marking the spot on the boulder where the head had rested.

Until his heart rate slowed, Peter lay staring at the moon, as bright and distant as a wish. He heard the roaring of the wind from all sides and realized that it was growing louder, but he didn't want to admit to it. Finally, though, he got to his feet and gazed out across the moors.

It was as if he were standing at the center of an unimaginably large temple, one forested with dozens upon dozens of shiny black pillars rising from a dark green floor. The nearest of them were about a hundred yards away, and those were unmoving; but as Peter watched, others farther off began to slew back and forth, gliding in and out of the stationary ones, like dancing cobras. There was a fever in the air, a pulse of heat and energy, and this as much as the alienness of the sight was what transfixed him and held him immobile. He found that he had gone beyond fear. You could no more hide from the elemental than you could from God. It would lead him on to the sea to die, and its power was so compelling that he almost acknowledged its right to do this. He climbed into the jeep. Sara looked beaten. Sally touched his leg with a palsied hand.

'You can use my boat,' she said.

On the way back to Madaket, Sara sat with her hands clasped in her lap, outwardly calm but inwardly turbulent. Thoughts fired across her brain so quickly that they left only partial impressions, and those were seared away by lightning strokes of terror. She wanted to say something to Peter, but words seemed inadequate to all she was feeling. At one point she decided to go with him, but the decision sparked a sudden resentment. He didn't love her! Why should she sacrifice herself for him? Then, realizing that he was sacrificing himself for her, that he did love her or that at least this was an act of love, she decided that if she went it would make his act meaningless. That decision caused her to question whether or not she was using his sacrifice to obscure her true reason for staying behind: her fear. And what about the quality of her feelings for him? Were they so uncertain that fear could undermine them? In a blaze of irrationality she saw that he was pressuring her to go with him, to prove her love, something she had never asked him to do. What right did he have? With half her mind she understood the unreasonableness of these thoughts, yet she couldn't stop thinking them. She felt all her emotions winnowing, leaving her hollow ... like Hugh Weldon, with only the wind inside him, propping him up, giving him the semblance of life. The grotesqueness of the image caused her to shrink further inside herself, and she just sat there, growing dim and empty, saying nothing.

'Buck up,' said Sally out of the blue, and patted Peter's leg. 'We got one thing left to try.' And then, with what seemed to Sara an irrational good cheer, she added: 'But if that don't work, the boat's got fishin' tackle and a coupla cases of cherry brandy on board. I was too damn drunk to unload 'em yesterday. Cherry brandy be better'n water for where you're headed.'

Peter gave no reply.

As they entered the village, the elemental chased beside them, whirling up debris, scattering leaves, tossing things high into the air. Playing, thought Sara. It was playing. Frisking along like a happy pup, like a petulant child who'd gotten his way and now was all smiles. She was overwhelmed with hatred for it, and she dug her nails into the seat cushion, wishing she had a way to hurt it. Then, as they passed Julia Stackpole's house, the corpse of Julia Stackpole sat up. Its bloody head hung down, its frail arms flapping. The entire body appeared to be vibrating, and with a horrid disjointed motion, amid a swirling of papers and trash, it went rolling over and over and came to rest against a broken chair. Sara shrank back into a corner of the seat, her breath ragged and shallow. A thin cloud swept free of the moon, and the light measurably brightened, making the gray of the houses seem gauzy and immaterial; the holes in their sides looked real enough – black, cavernous – as if the walls and doors and windows had only been a facade concealing emptiness.

Sally parked next to a boathouse a couple of hundred yards north of Smith Point: a rickety wooden structure the size of a garage. Beyond it a stretch of calm black water was figured by a blaze of moonlight. 'You gonna have to row out to the boat,' Sally told Peter. 'Oars are in here.' She unlocked the door and flicked on a light. The inside of the place was as dilapidated as Sally herself. Raw boards; spiderwebs spanning between paint cans and busted lobster traps; a jumble of two-by-fours. Sally went stumping around, mumbling and kicking things, searching for the oars; her footsteps set the light bulb dangling from the roof to swaying, and the light slopped back and forth over the walls like dirty yellow water. Sara's legs were leaden. It was hard to move, and she thought maybe this was because there weren't any moves left. Peter took a few steps toward the center of the boathouse and stopped, looking lost. His hands twitched at his sides. She had the idea that his expression mirrored her own: slack, spiritless, with bruised crescents under his eyes. She moved, then. The dam that had been holding back her emotions burst, and her arms were around him, and she was telling him that she couldn't let him go alone, telling him half-sentences, phrases that didn't connect. 'Sara,' he said, 'Jesus.' He held her very tightly. The next second, though, she heard a dull *thonk* and he sagged against her, almost knocking her down, and slumped to the floor. Brandishing a two-by-four, Sally bent to him and struck again.

'What are you doing?' Sara screamed it and began to wrestle with Sally. Their arms locked, they waltzed around and around for a matter of seconds, the light bulb jiggling madly. Sally sputtered and fumed; spittle glistened on her lips. Finally, with a snarl, she shoved Sara away. Sara staggered back, tripped over Peter, and fell sprawling beside him.

'Listen!' Sally cocked her head and pointed to the roof with the two-by-four. 'Goddamn it! It's workin'!'

Sara came warily to her feet. 'What are you talking about?'

Sally picked up her fisherman's hat, which had fallen off during the struggle, and squashed it down onto her head. 'The wind, goddamn it! I told that stupid son of a bitch Hugh Weldon, but oh, no! He never listened to nobody.'

The wind was rising and fading in volume, doing so with such a regular rhythm that Sara had the impression of a creature made of wind running frantically back and forth. Something splintered in the distance.

'I don't understand,' said Sara.

'Unconscious is like dead to it,' said Sally; she gestured at Peter with the board. 'I knew it was so, 'cause after it did for Mills it came for me. It touched me up all over, and I could tell it'd have me, then. But that stupid bastard wouldn't listen. Had to do things his goddamn way!'

'It would have you?' Sara glanced down at Peter, who was unstirring, bleeding from the scalp. 'You mean instead of Peter?'

''Course that's what I mean.' Sally frowned. 'Don't make no sense him goin'. Young man with all his future ahead. Now me ...' She yanked at the lapel of her raincoat as if intending to throw herself away. 'What I got to lose? A coupla years of bein' alone. I ain't eager for it, y'understand. But it don't make sense any other way. Tried to tell Hugh that, but he was stuck on bein' a goddamn hero.'

Her bird-bright eyes glittered in the webbed flesh, and Sara had a perception of her that she had not had since childhood: the zany old spirit, half-mad but with one eye fixed on some corner of creation that nobody else could see. She remembered all the stories. Sally trying to signal the moon with a hurricane lamp; Sally rowing through a nor'easter to pluck six sailors off Whale Shoals; Sally passing out dead-drunk at the ceremony the Coast Guard had given in her honor; Sally loosing her dogs on the then-junior senator from Massachusetts when he had come to present her a medal. Crazy Sally. She suddenly seemed valuable to Sara.

'You can't ...' she began, but broke off and stared at Peter.

'Can't not,' said Sally, and clucked her tongue. 'You see somebody looks after my dogs.'

Sara nodded.

'And you better check on Peter,' said Sally. 'See if I hit him too hard.'

Sara started to comply but was struck by a thought. 'Won't it know better this time? Peter was knocked out before. Won't it have learned?'

'I suppose it can learn,' said Sally. 'But it's real stupid, and I don't think it's figured this out.' She gestured at Peter. 'Go ahead. See if he's all right.'

The hairs on Sara's neck prickled as she knelt beside Peter, and she was later to reflect that in the back of her mind she had known what was about to happen. But even so she was startled by the blow.

X

It wasn't until late the next afternoon that the doctors allowed Peter to have visitors other than the police. He was still suffering from dizziness and blurred vision, and mentally speaking, he alternated between periods of relief and depression. Seeing in his mind's eye the mutilated bodies, the whirling black pillars. Tensing as the wind prowled along the hospital walls. In general he felt walled off from emotion, but when Sara came into the room those walls crumbled. He drew her down beside him and buried his face in her hair. They lay for a long time without speaking, and it was Sara who finally broke the silence.

'Do they believe you?' she asked. 'I don't think they believe me.'

'They don't have much choice,' he said. 'I just think they don't want to believe it.'

After a moment she said, 'Are you going away?'

He pulled back from her. She had never looked more beautiful. Her eyes were wide, her mouth drawn thin, and the strain of all that had happened to them seemed to have carved an unnecessary ounce of fullness from her face. 'That depends on whether or not you'll go with me,' he said. 'I don't want to stay. Whenever the wind changes pitch, every nerve in my body signals an air raid. But I won't leave you. I want to marry you.'

Her reaction was not what he had expected. She closed her eyes and kissed him on the forehead – a motherly, understanding kiss; then she settled back on the pillow, gazing calmly at him.

'That was a proposal,' he said. 'Didn't you catch it?'

'Marriage?' She seemed perplexed by the idea.

'Why not? We're qualified.' He grinned. 'We both have concussions.'

'I don't know,' she said. 'I love you, Peter, but ...'

'But you don't trust me?'

'Maybe that's part of it,' she said, annoyed. 'I don't know.'

'Look.' He smoothed down her hair. 'Do you know what really happened in the boathouse last night?'

'I'm not sure what you mean.'

'I'll tell you. What happened was that an old woman gave her life so you and I could have a chance at something.' She started to speak, but he cut her off. 'That's the bones of it. I admit the reality's a bit more murky. God knows why Sally did what she did. Maybe saving lives was a reflex of her madness, maybe she was tired of living. Maybe it just seemed a good idea at the time.

And as for us, we haven't exactly been Romeo and Juliet. I've been confused, and I've confused you. And aside from whatever problems we might have as a couple, we have a lot to forget. Until you came in I was feeling shell-shocked, and that's a feeling that's probably going to last for a while. But like I said, the heart of the matter is that Sally died to give us a chance. No matter what her motives, what our circumstance, that's what happened. And we'd be fools to let that chance slip away.' He traced the line of her cheekbone with a finger. 'I love you. I've loved you for a long time and tried to deny it, to hold on to a dead issue. But that's all over.'

'We can't make this sort of decision now,' she murmured.

'Why not?'

'You said it yourself. You're shell-shocked. So am I. And I don't know how I feel about ... everything.'

'Everything? You mean me?'

She made a noncommittal noise, closed her eyes, and after a moment she said, 'I need time to think.'

In Peter's experience when women said they needed time to think, nothing good ever came of it. 'Jesus!' he said angrily. 'Is this how it has to be between people? One approaches, the other avoids, and then they switch roles. Like insects whose mating instincts have been screwed up by pollution.' He registered what he had said and had a flash-feeling of horror. 'Come on, Sara! We're past that kind of dance, aren't we? It doesn't have to be marriage, but let's commit to something. Maybe we'll make a mess of it, maybe we'll end up boring each other. But let's try. It might not be any effort at all.' He put his arms around her, brought her tight against him, and was immersed in a cocoon of heat and weakness. He loved her, he realized, with an intensity that he had not believed he could recapture. His mouth had been smarter than his brain for once – either that or he had talked himself into it. The reasons didn't matter.

'For Christ's sake, Sara!' he said. 'Marry me. Live with me. Do something with me!'

She was silent; her left hand moved gently over his hair. Light, distracted touches. Tucking a curl behind his ear, toying with his beard, smoothing his mustache. As if she were making him presentable. He remembered how that other long-ago woman had become increasingly silent and distracted and gentle in the days before she had dumped him.

'Damn it!' he said with a growing sense of helplessness. 'Answer me!'

XI

On the second night out 'Sconset Sally caught sight of a winking red light off her port bow. Some ship's riding light. It brought a tear to her eye, making her think of home. But she wiped the tear away with the back of her hand and had another slug of cherry brandy. The cramped wheelhouse of the lobster boat was cozy and relatively warm; beyond, the moonlit plain of the sea was rising in light swells. Even if you didn't have nowhere good to go, she thought, wheels and keels and wings gave a boost to your spirit. She laughed. Especially if you had a supply of cherry brandy. She had another slug. A breeze curled around her arm and tugged at the neck of the bottle. 'Goddamn it!' she squawked. 'Get away!' She batted at the air as if she could shoo away the elemental, and hugged the bottle to her breast. Wind uncoiled a length of rope on the deck behind her, and then she could hear it moaning about the hull. She staggered to the wheelhouse door. 'Whoo-oo-ooh!' she sang, mocking it. 'Don't be making your godawful noises at me, you sorry bastard! Go kill another goddamn fish if you want somethin' to do. Just leave me alone to my drinkin'.'

Waves surged up on the port side. Big ones, like black teeth. Sally almost dropped the bottle in her surprise. Then she saw they weren't really waves but shapes of water made by the elemental. 'You're losin' your touch, asshole!' she shouted. 'I seen better'n that in the movies!' She slumped down beside the door, clutching the bottle. The word *movies* conjured flashes of old films she'd seen, and she started singing songs from them. She did 'Singin' in the Rain' and 'Blue Moon' and 'Love Me Tender.' She knocked back swallows of brandy in between the verses, and when she felt primed enough she launched into her favorite. 'The sound that you hear,' she bawled, 'is the sound of Sally! A joy to be heard for a thousand years.' She belched. 'The hills are alive with the sound of Sally ...' She couldn't recall the next line, and that ended the concert.

The wind built to a howl around her, and her thoughts sank into a place where there were only dim urges and nerves fizzling and blood whining in her ears. Gradually she surfaced from it and found that her mood had become one of regret. Not about anything specific. Just general regrets. General Regrets. She pictured him as an old fogey with a white walrus mustache and a Gilbert-and-Sullivan uniform. Epaulets the size of skateboards. She couldn't get the picture out of her head, and she wondered if it stood for something important. If it did, she couldn't make it come clear. Like that line of her favorite song, it had leaked out through one of her cracks. Life had leaked out the same way, and all she could remember of it was a muddle of lonely nights and sick dogs and scallop shells and half-drowned sailors. Nothing important sticking up from the muddle. No monument to accomplishment or romance. Hah! She'd never met the man who could do what men said they could. The most reasonable men she'd known were those shipwrecked sailors, and their eyes big and dark as if they'd seen into some terrible bottomland that had sheared away their pride and stupidity. Her mind began to whirl, trying to get a fix on life, to pin it down like a dead butterfly and know its patterns, and soon she realized that she was literally whirling. Slowly, but getting faster and faster. She hauled herself up and clung to the wheelhouse door and peered over the side. The lobster boat was spinning around and around on the lip of a bowl of black water several hundred yards across. A whirlpool. Moonlight struck a glaze down its slopes but didn't reach the bottom. Its roaring, heart-stopping power scared her, made her giddy and faint. But after a moment she banished fear. So this was death. It just opened up and swallowed you whole. All right. That was fine by her. She slumped against the wheelhouse and drank deeply of the cherry brandy, listening to the wind and the singing of her blood as she went down not giving a damn. It sure beat puking up life a gob at a time in some hospital room. She kept slurping away at the brandy, guzzling it, wanting to be as looped as possible when the time came. But the time didn't come, and before too long she noticed that the boat had stopped spinning. The wind had quieted and the sea was calm.

A breeze coiled about her neck, slithered down her breast, and began curling around her legs, flipping the hem of her dress. 'You bastard,' she said soddenly, too drunk to move. The elemental swirled around her knees, belling the dress, and touched her between the legs. It tickled, and she swatted at it ineffectually, as if it were one of the dogs snooting at her. But a second later it prodded her there again, a little harder than before, rubbing back and forth, and she felt a quiver of arousal. It startled her so that she went rolling across the deck, somehow keeping her bottle upright. That quiver stuck with her, though, and for an instant a red craving dominated the broken mosaic of her thoughts. Cackling and scratching herself, she staggered to her feet and leaned on the rail. The elemental was about fifty yards off the port bow, shaping itself a waterspout, a moonstruck column of blackness, from the placid surface of the sea.

'Hey!' she shouted, wobbling along the rail. 'You come on back here! *I'll teach you a new trick!*'

The waterspout grew higher, a glistening black serpent that *whooshed* and sucked the boat toward it; but it didn't bother Sally. A devilish joy was in her, and her mind crackled with lightnings of pure craziness. She thought she had figured out something. Maybe nobody had ever taken a real interest in the elemental, and maybe that was why it eventually lost interest in them. Wellsir! She had an interest in it. Damn thing couldn't be any more stupid than some of her Dobermans. Snooted like one, for sure. She'd teach it to roll over and beg and who knows what else. Fetch me that fish, she'd tell it. Blow me over to Hyannis and smash the liquor-store window and bring me six bottles of brandy. She'd show it who was boss. And could be one day she'd sail into the harbor at Nantucket with the thing on a leash. 'Sconset Sally and her pet storm, Scourge of the Seven Seas.

The boat was beginning to tip and slew sideways in the pull of the waterspout, but Sally scarcely noticed. 'Hey!' she shouted again, and chuckled. 'Maybe we can work things out! Maybe we're meant for each other!' She tripped over a warp in the planking, and the arm holding the bottle flailed above her head. Moonlight seemed to stream down into the bottle, igniting the brandy so that it glowed like a magic elixir, a dark red ruby flashing from her hand. Her maniacal laugh went sky-high.

'You come on back here!' she screeched at the elemental, exulting in the wild frequencies of her life, at the thought of herself in league with this idiot god, and unmindful of her true circumstance, of the thundering around her and the tiny boat slipping toward the foaming base of the waterspout. 'Come back here, damn it! We're two of a kind! We're birds of a feather! I'll sing you to sleep each night! You'll serve me my supper! I'll be your old cracked bride, and we'll have a hell of a honeymoon while it lasts!'

BLACK CORAL

The bearded young man who didn't give a damn about anyone (or so he'd just shouted – whereupon the bartender had grabbed his scaling knife and said, 'Dat bein' de way of it, you can do your drinkin' elsewhere!') came staggering out of the bar and shielded his eyes against the afternoon glare. Violet afterimages flared and fizzled under his lids. He eased down the rickety stair, holding on to the rail, and stepped into the street, still blinking. And then, as he adjusted to the brightness, a ragged man with freckled cocoa-colored skin and a prophet's beard swung into view, blocking out the sun.

'Hot enough de sun duppy be writhin' in de street, ain't it, Mr Prince?'

Prince choked. Christ! That damned St Cecilia rum was eating holes in his stomach! He reeled. The rum backed up into his throat and the sun blinded him again, but he squinted and made out old Spurgeon James, grinning, rotten teeth angled like untended tombstones, holding an empty Coke bottle whose mouth was crusted with flies.

'Gotta go,' said Prince, lurching off.

'You got work for me, Mr Prince?'

Prince kept walking.

Old Spurgeon would lean on his shovel all day, reminisce about 'de back time,' and offer advice ('Dat might go easier with de barrow, now') while Prince sweated like a donkey and lifted concrete blocks. Work! Still, for entertainment's sake alone he'd be worth more than most of the black trash on the island. And the ladinos! ('De dommed Sponnish!') They'd work until they had enough to get drunk, play sick, then vanish with your best tools. Prince spotted a rooster pecking at a mango rind by the roadside, elected him representative of the island's work force, and kicked; but the rooster flapped up, squabbling, lit on an overturned dinghy, and gave an assertive cluck.

'Wait dere a moment, Mr Prince!'

Prince quickened his pace. If Spurgeon latched on, he'd never let loose. And today, January 18, marked the tenth anniversary of his departure from Vietnam. He didn't want any company.

The yellow dirt road rippled in a heat haze that made the houses – rows of weathered shanties set on pilings against the storm tides – appear to be dancing on thin rubbery legs. Their tin roofs were buckled, pitched at every angle, showing patches of rust like scabs. That one – teetering on splayed pilings over a dirt front yard, the shutter hung by a single hinge, gray flour-sack curtain belling inward – it always reminded him of a cranky old hen on her roost trying grimly to hatch a nonexistent egg. He'd seen a photograph of it taken seventy years before, and it had looked equally dejected and bedraggled then. Well, almost. There *had* been a sapodilla tree overspreading the roof.

'Givin' out a warnin', Mr Prince! Best you listen!'

Spurgeon, rags tattering in the breeze, stumbled toward him and nearly fell. He waved his arms to regain his balance, like a drunken ant, toppled sideways, and fetched up against a palm trunk, hugging it for support. Prince, in dizzy sympathy with the sight, tottered backward and caught himself on some shanty steps, for a second going eye to eye with Spurgeon. The old man's mouth worked, and a strand of spittle eeled out onto his beard.

Prince pushed off from the steps. Stupidity! That was why nothing changed for the better on Guanoja Menor (derived from the Spanish *guano* and *hoja*, a fair translation being Lesser Leaf-shaped Piece of Bird Shit), why unemployable drunks hounded you in the street, why the rum poisoned you, why the shanties crashed from their perches in the least of storms. Unwavering stupidity! The islanders built outhouses on piers over the shallows where they bathed and fished the banks with no thought for conservation, then wondered why they stank and went hungry. They cut off their fingers to win bets that they wouldn't; they smoked black coral and inhaled gasoline fumes for escape; they fought with conch shells, wrapping their hands around the inner volute of the shell so it fit like a spiky boxing glove. And when the nearly as stupid ladinos had come from the Honduran mainland, they'd been able to steal and swindle half the land on the island.

Prince had learned from their example.

'Mr Prince!'

Spurgeon again, weaving after him, his palm outstretched. Angrily, Prince dug out a coin and threw it at his feet.

'Dass so nice, dass so kind of you!' Spurgeon spat on the coin. But he stooped for it and, in stooping, lost his balance and fell, smashing his Coke bottle on a stone. There went fifty centavos. There went two glasses of rum. The old man rolled in the street, too drunk to stand, smearing himself with yellow dirt. 'Even de sick dog gots teeth,' he croaked. 'Just you remember dat, Mr Prince!'

Prince couldn't keep from laughing.

Meachem's Landing, the town ('a quaint seaport, steeped in pirate legend,' prattled the guidebook), lay along the curve of a bay inset between two scrub-thatched hills and served as the island capital. At midpoint of the bay stood the government office, a low white stucco building with sliding glass doors like a cheap motel. Three prosperous-looking Spanish men were sitting on oil drums in its shade, talking to a soldier wearing blue fatigues. As Prince passed, an offshore breeze kicked up and blew scents of rotted coconut, papaya, and creosote in from the customs dock, a concrete strip stretching one hundred yards or so into the glittering cobalt reach of the water.

There was a vacancy about the scene, a lethargy uniformly affecting its every element. Cocals twitched the ends of their fronds, leaning in over the tin roofs; a pariah dog sniffed at a dried lobster claw in the dust; ghost crabs scuttered under the shanties. It seemed to Prince that the tide of event had withdrawn, leaving the bottom dwellers exposed, creating a lull before some culminative action. And he remembered how it had been the same on bright afternoons in Saigon when passersby stopped and listened to the whine of an incoming rocket, how the plastic flags on the Hondas parked in front of the bars snapped in the wind, how a prostitute's monkey had screamed in its cage on hearing the distant *crump* and everyone had laughed with relief. He felt less irritable, remembering, more at rights with the commemorative nature of the day.

Beyond the government office, past the tiny public square and its dusty-leaved acacia, propped against the cement wall of the general store, clinging to it like a gaudy barnacle, was a shanty whose walls and trim had been painted crimson and bright blue and pink and quarantine yellow. Itchy-sounding reggae leaked from the closed shutter. Ghetto Liquors. He tramped heavily on the stair, letting them know within that the drunkest mother on the island, Neal His Bloody Majesty Prince, was about to integrate their little rainbow paradise, and pushed into the hot, dark room.

'Service!' he said, kicking the counter.

'What you want?'

Rudy Welcomes stirred behind the bar. A slash of light from a split seam in the roof jiggled on his shaved skull.

'Saint Cecilia!' Prince leaned on the bar, reconnoitering. Two men sat at a rear table, their hair in spiky dreadlocks, wraiths materializing from the dark. The darkness was picked out by the purplish glow of black lights illuminating four Jimi Hendrix posters. Though of island stock, Rudy was American-born and, like Prince, a child of the sixties and a veteran. He said that the lights and posters put him in mind of a brothel on Tu Do Street, where he had won the money with which to establish Ghetto Liquors; and Prince, recalling similar brothels, found that the lights provided an excellent frame of reference for the thoughtful, reminiscent stages of his drunk. The eerie purple radiance escaping the slender black canisters seemed the crystallized expression of war, and he fancied the color emblematic of evil energies and sluggish tropical demons.

'So this your big day for drinkin'.' Rudy slid a pint bottle along the bar and resettled on his stool. 'Don't you be startin' that war-buddy crap with me, now. I ain't in the mood.'

'Shucks, Rudy!' Prince adopted a Southern accent. 'You know I ain't war buddies with no nigger.'

Rudy stiffened but let it pass; he gave a disaffected grunt. 'Don't know why not, man. You could pass *yourself*. Way your hair's gotten all crispy and your skin's gone dark. See here?'

He laid his hand on Prince's to compare the color, but Prince knocked it aside and stared, challenging.

'Damn! Seem like Clint Eastwood done wandered into town!' Rudy shook his head in disgust and moved off along the bar to change the record. The two men at the rear drifted across the room and whispered with him, casting sly looks at Prince.

Prince basked in the tension. It further fleshed out his frame of reference. Confident that he'd established dominance, he took a table beside the shutter, relaxed, and sipped his rum. Through a gap in the boards he saw a girl stringing up colored lights on the shanty opposite the bar. His private holiday had this year coincided with Independence Day, always celebrated upon the third Friday in January. Stalls would sprout in the public square, offering strips of roast turtle and games of chance. Contending music would blare from the bars – reggae and salsa. Prince enjoyed watching street dancers lose their way in the mishmash of rhythms. It emphasized the fact that neither the Spanish nor the islanders could cope with the other's presence and further emphasized that they were celebrating two different events – on the day that Queen Victoria had granted the islands their freedom, the Honduran military had sailed in and established governance.

More stupidity.

The rum was sitting easier on his stomach. Prince mellowed and went with the purple lights, seeing twisted black branches in them, seeing the twilit jungle in Lang Biang, and he heard the hiss of the walkie-talkie and León's stagy whisper, 'Hey, Prince! I got a funny shadow in that bombax tree ...' He had turned his scope on the tree, following the course of the serpentine limbs through the grainy empurpling air. And then the stutter of automatic fire, and he could hear León's screams in the air *and* carrying over the radio ...

'Got somethin' for help you celebrate, Mr Prince.'

A thin hawk-faced man wearing frayed shorts dropped into the chair next to him, his dreadlocks wriggling. George Ebanks.

Prince gripped the rum bottle, angry, ready to strike, but George thrust out a bristling something – a branch of black coral.

'Dis de upful stuff, Mr Prince,' he said. 'Rife with de island's secret.' He pulled out a knife and whittled at the branch. Curly black shavings fell onto the table. 'You just scrapes de color off and dass what you smokes.'

The branch intrigued Prince; it was dead black, unshining, hard to tell where each stalk ended and the room's darkness began. He'd heard the stories. Old Spurgeon said it drove you crazy. And even older John Anderson McCrae had said, 'De coral so black dat when you smokes it de color will rush into your eyes and allow you vision of de spirit world. And will allow dem sight of you.'

'What's it do?' he asked, tempted.

'It make you more a part of things. Dass all, Mr Prince. Don't fret. We goin' to smoke it with you.'

Rudy and the third man – wiry, short Jubert Cox – sidled up behind George's shoulder, and Rudy winked at Prince. George loaded the knife blade with black shavings and tamped them into a hash pipe, then lit it, drawing hard until the hollows of his cheeks reflected the violet-red coal. He handed the pipe across, a wisp of smoke curling from his tight-lipped smile, and watched Prince toke it down.

The smoke tasted vile. It had a mustiness he associated with the thousands of dead polyps (was it thousands per lungful or merely hundreds?) he'd just inhaled, but it was so cool that he did not concern himself with taste and noticed only the coolness.

Cold black stone lined his throat.

The coolness spread to his arms and legs, weighting them down, and he imagined it questing with black tendrils through veins and arteries, finding out secret passages unknown even to his blood. Drifty stuff ... and dizzying. He wasn't sure if he was sweating or not, but he *was* a little nauseous. And he didn't seem to be inhaling anymore. Not really. The smoke seemed to be issuing of its own volition from the pipestem, a silken rope, a cold strangler's cord tying a labyrinthine knot throughout his body ...

'Take but a trifle, don't it, Mr Prince?' Jubert giggled.

Rudy lifted the pipe from his numbed fingers.

... and involving the fissures of his brain in an intricate design, binding his thoughts into a coralline structure. The bright gaps in the shutter planking dwindled, receded, until they were golden straws adrift in the blackness, then golden pinpricks, then gone. And though he was initially fascinated by this production of the drug, as it progressed Prince became worried that he was going blind.

'Wuh ...' His tongue wouldn't work. His flesh was choked with black dust, distant from him, and the coolness had deepened to a penetrating chill. And as a faint radiance suffused the dark, he imagined that the process of the drug had been reversed, that now he was flowing up the pipestem into the heart of the violet-red coal.

'Oh, dis de upful stuff all right, Mr Prince,' said George, from afar. 'Dat what grows down to de root of de island.'

Rippling kelp beds faded in from the blackness, illuminated by a violet glow, and Prince saw that he was passing above them toward a dim wall (the reef?) at whose base thousands upon thousands of witchy fires burned, flickering, ranging in color from indigo to violet-white, all clinging (he saw, drawing near) to the stalks and branches of black coral – a bristling jungle of coral, stalks twenty and thirty feet high, and more. The fires were smaller than candle flames and did not seem as much presences as they did peepholes into a cold furnace behind the reef. Maybe they were some sort of copepod, bioluminescent and half-alive. He descended among the stalks, moving along the channels between them. Barracuda, sleek triggerfish … There! A grouper – four hundred pounds if it was an ounce – angelfish and rays … bones showed in negative through their luminous flesh. Schools of smaller fish darted as one, stopped, darted again, into and out of the black branches. The place had a strange kinetic geometry, as if it were the innards of an organic machine whose creatures performed its functions by maneuvering in precise patterns through its interstices, and in which the violet fires served as the insane, empowering thoughts within an inky skull. Beautiful! Thomas De Quincey Land. A jeweled shade, an occulted paradise. Then, rising into the murk above him, an *immense* stalk – a shadowy, sinister Christmas tree poxed with flickering decorations. Sharks circled its upper reaches, cast in silhouette by the glow. Several of the fires detached from a branch and drifted toward him, eddying like slow moths.

'Dey just markin' you, Mr Prince. Don't be troubled.'

Where was George's voice coming from? It sounded right inside his ear. Oh, well … He wasn't troubled. The fires were weird, lovely. One drifted to within a foot of his eyes, hovering there, its violet-tipped edges shifting, not with the randomness of flame but with a flowing, patterned movement, a complex pulse; its center was an iridescent white. Must not be copepods.

It drifted closer.

Very lovely. A wash of violet spread from its edges in and was absorbed by the whiteness.

It brushed against his left eye.

Prince's vision went haywire, spinning. He had a glimpse of the sentinel sharks, a blurred impression of the latticework of shadow on the reef wall, then darkness. The cold touch, brief as it had been, a split second, had burned him, chilled him, as if a hypodermic had ever so slightly pricked the humor and flooded him with an icy serum, leaving him shuddering.

'Dey bound him!' George?

'Be watchful down dere, Mr Prince.' Jubert.

The shutter banged open, and bright, sweet, warming sunlight poured in. He realized he had fallen. His legs were entangled in an unyielding something that must be the chair.

'You just had a little fit, man. Happens sometimes the first time. You gonna be fine.'

They pulled him up and helped him out onto the landing and down the stair. He tripped and fell the last three steps, weak and drunk, still shivering, fuddled by the sunlight.

Rudy pressed the rum bottle into his hands. 'Keep in the sun for a while, man. Get your strength back.'

'Oh, Mr Prince!' A skinny black arm waved from the window of the gaudy box on stilts, and he heard smothered giggles. 'You got work for me, Mr Prince?'

Severe physical punishment was called for! Nobody was going to get away with bad-tripping him!

Prince drank, warmed himself, and plotted his revenge on the steps of the dilapidated Hotel Captain Henry. (The hotel was named for Henry Meachem, the pirate whose crews had interbred with Carib and Jamaican women, thereby populating the island, and whose treasure was the focal point of many tall tales.) A scrawny, just-delivered bitch growled at him from the doorway. Between growls she worried her inflamed teats, a nasty sucking that turned Prince's saliva thick and ropy. He gave old Mike, the hotel flunky, twenty-five centavos to chase her off, but afterward old Mike wanted more.

'I be a bitch, mon! I strip de shadow from your back!' He danced around Prince, flicking puny left jabs. Filthy, wearing colorless rags and a grease-stained baseball cap, flecks of egg yolk clotting his iron-gray whiskers.

Prince flipped him another coin and watched as he ran off to bury it. The stories said that Mike had been a miser, had gone mad when he'd discovered all his money eaten by mice and insects. But Roblie Meachem, owner of the hotel, said, 'He just come home to us one mornin'. Didn't have no recollection of his name, so we call him Mike after my cousin in Miami.' Still, the stories persisted. It was the island way. ('Say de thing long enough and it be so.') And perhaps the stories had done some good for old Mike, effecting a primitive psychotherapy and giving him a legend to inhabit. Mike returned from his hiding place and sat beside the steps, drawing circles in the dust with his finger and rubbing them out, mumbling, as if he couldn't get them right.

Prince flung his empty bottle over a shanty roof, caring not where it fell. The clarity of his thoughts annoyed him; the coral had sobered him somewhat, and he needed to regain his lost momentum. If Rita Steedly wasn't home, well, he'd be within a half mile of his own bar, the Sea Breeze; but if she was ... Her husband, an ecologist working for the government, would be off island until evening, and Prince felt certain that a go-round with Rita would reorient him and reinstitute the mean drunken process which the coral had interrupted.

Vultures perched on the pilings of Rita Steedly's dock, making them look like carved ebony posts. Not an uncommon sight on the island, but one Prince considered appropriate as to the owner's nature, more so when the largest of them flapped up and landed with a crunch in a palm top overlooking the sun deck where she lay. The house was blue stucco on concrete pilings standing in a palm grove. Between the trunks, the enclosed waters of the reef glittered in bands and swirls of aquamarine, lavender, and green according to the varying depth and bottom. Sea grape grew close by the house, and the point of land beyond it gave out into mangrove radicle.

As he topped the stairs, Rita propped herself on her elbows, pushed back her sunglasses, and weakly murmured, 'Neal,' as if summoning her lover to a deathbed embrace. Then she collapsed again upon the blanket, the exhausted motion of a pale dead frond. Her body glistened with oils and sweat, and her bikini top was unhooked and had slipped partway off.

Prince mixed a rum and papaya juice from the serving cart by the stair. 'Just smoked some black coral with the boys down at Ghetto Liquors.' He looked back at her over his shoulder and grinned. 'De spirits tol' me dat I must purify myself wit de body of a woman fore de moon is high.'

'I *thought* your eyes were very yellow today. You should know better.' She sat up; the bikini top dropped down onto her arms. She lifted a coil of hair which had stuck to her breast, patting it into place behind her ear. 'There ain't anything on this island that's healthy anymore. Even the fruit's poisoned! Did I tell you about the fruit?'

She had. Her little girl's voice grated on Prince, but he found her earnestness amusing, attractive for its perversity. Her obsession with health seemed no less a product of trauma than did his own violent disposition.

'It was just purple lights and mild discomfort,' he said, sitting beside her. 'But a headache and a drowsy sensation would be a good buzz to those black hicks. They tried to mess with my mind, but ...' He leaned over and kissed her. 'I made good my escape and came straightaway.'

'Jerry said he saw purple lights, too.' A grackle holding a cigarette butt in its beak hopped up on the railing, and Rita shooed it off.

'*He* smoked it?'

'He smokes it all the time. He wanted me to try it, but I'm not poisoning myself any more than I have to with this ... this garbage heap.' She checked his eyes. 'They're getting as bad as everyone else's. Still, they aren't as bad as the people's in Arkansas. They were so yellow they almost glowed in the dark. Like phosphorescent urine!' She shuddered dramatically, sighed, and stared glumly up into the palms. 'God! I hate this place!'

Prince dragged her down to face him. 'You're a twitch,' he said.

'I'm not!' she said angrily, but fingered loose the buttons of his shirt as she talked. 'Everything's polluted down here. Dying. And it's worse in the States.

You can see the wasting in people's faces if you know how to look for it. I've tried to talk Jerry into leaving, but he says he's committed. Maybe I'll leave him. Maybe I'll go to Peru. I've heard good things about Peru.'

'You'll see the wasting in *their* faces,' said Prince.

Her arms slid around his back, and her eyes opened and closed, opened and closed, the eyes of a doll whose head you manipulated. Barely seeing him, seeing something else in his place, some bad sign or ugly rumor.

As his own eyes closed, as he stopped thinking, he gazed out past her head to the glowing, many-colored sea and saw in the pale sky along the horizon a flash of the way it had been after a burn-off: the full-bore immensity and silence of the light; the clear, innocent air over paddies and palms blackened like matchsticks; and how they'd moved through the dead land, crunching the scorched, brittle stalks underfoot, unafraid, because every snake within miles was now just a shadow in the cinders.

Drunk, blind, old John Anderson McCrae was telling stories at the Sea Breeze, and Prince wandered out onto the beach for some peace and quiet. The wind brought fragments of the creaky voice. '... dat cross were studded with emeralds ... and sapphires ...' The story about Meachem's gold cross (supposedly buried off the west end of the island) was John's masterpiece, told only at great expense to the listener. He told how Meachem's ghost appeared each time his treasure was threatened, huge, a constellation made of the island stars. '... and de round end of his peg leg were de moon shine down ...' Of course, Meachem had had two sound legs, but the knowledge didn't trouble John. 'A mon's ghost may suffer injury every bit as de mon,' he'd say; and then, to any further challenge, 'Well, de truth may be lackin' in it, but it capture de spirit of de truth.' And he'd laugh, spray his rummy breath in the tourists' faces, and repeat his commonplace pun. And they would pay him more because they thought he was cute, colorful, and beneath them.

White cumulus swelled from the horizon, and the stars blazed overhead so bright and jittery they seemed to have a pulse in common with the rattle of the Sea Breeze's generator. The reef crashed and hissed. Prince screwed his glass into the sand and settled back against a palm trunk, angled so he could see the deck of the bar. Benches and tables were built around coconut palms that grew up through the deck; orange lights in the form of plastic palms were mounted on the trunks. Not an unpleasant place to sit and watch the sea.

But the interior of the Sea Breeze bordered on the monstrous: lamps made of transparent-skinned blowfish with bulbs in their stomachs; treasure maps and T-shirts for sale; a giant jukebox glowing red and purple like the crown jewels in a protective cage of two-by-fours; garish pirate murals on the walls; and skull-and-crossbones pennants hanging from the thatched roof. The bar had been built and painted to simulate a treasure chest with its lid ajar. Three Carib skulls sat on shelves over the bottles, with red bulbs in their jaws that winked on and off for birthdays and other celebrations. It was his temple to the stupidity of Guanoja Menor; and, being his first acquisition, memorialized a commitment he had made to the grotesque heart of acquisition itself.

A burst of laughter, shouts of 'Watch out!' and 'Good luck!' and old John appeared at the railing, groping his way along until he found the stair and stumbled down onto the beach. He weaved back and forth, poking the air with his cane, and sprawled in the sand at Prince's feet. A withered brown dummy stuffed into rags and flung overboard. He sat up, cocking his head. 'Who's dere?' The lights from the Sea Breeze reflected off his cataracts; they looked like raw silver nuggets embedded in his skull.

'Me, John.'

'Is dat you, Mr Prince? Well, God bless you!' John patted the sand, feeling for his cane, then clutched it and pointed out to sea. 'Look, Mr Prince. Dere where de *Miss Faye* go turtlin' off to de Chinchorro Bank.'

Prince saw the riding lights moving toward the horizon, the indigo light rocking on the masthead, then wondered how in the hell … The indigo light swooped at him, darting across miles of wind and water in an instant, into his eyes. His vision went purple, normalized, purpled again, as if the thing were a police flasher going around and around in his head.

And it was cold.

Searing, immobilizing cold.

'Ain't dis a fine night, Mr Prince? No matter how blind a mon gets, he can recognize a fine night!'

With a tremendous effort Prince clawed at the sand, but old John continued talking.

'Dey say de island take hold of a mon. Now dat hold be gentle 'cause de island bear no ill against dem dat dwell upon it in de lawful way. But dose dat lords it over de island, comes a night dere rule is done.'

Prince wanted badly to scream because that might release the cold trapped inside him; but he could not even strain. The cold possessed him. He yearned after John's words, not listening but stretching out toward them with his wish. They issued from the soft tropic air like the ends of warm brown ropes dangling just beyond his frozen grasp.

'Dis island poor! And de people fools! But I know you hear de sayin' dat even de sick dog gots teeth. Well, dis island gots teeth dat grows down to de center of things. De Carib say dat dere's a spirit from before de back time locked into de island's root, and de Baptist say dat de island be a fountainhead of de Holy Spirit. But no matter what de truth, de people have each been granted a portion of dat spirit. And dat spirit legion now!'

The light behind Prince's eyes whirled so fast he could no longer distinguish periods of normal vision, and everything he saw had a purplish cast. He heard his entire agony as a tiny, scratchy sound deep in his throat. He toppled on his side and saw out over the bumpy sand, out to a point of land where wild palms, in silhouette against a vivid purple sky, shook their fronds like plumed African dancers, writhing up, ecstatic.

'Dat spirit have drove off de English! And one day it will drive de Sponnish home! It slow, but it certain. And dat is why we celebrate dis night ... 'Cause on dis very night all dose not of de spirit and de law must come to judgment.'

John's shoes scraped on the sand.

'Well, I'll be along now, Mr Prince. God bless you.'

Even when his head had cleared and the cold dissipated, Prince couldn't work it out. If Jerry Steedly smoked this stuff all the time, then *he* must be having an abnormal reaction. A flashback. The thing to do would be to overpower the drug with depressants. But how could old John have seen the turtling boat? Maybe it never happened? Maybe the coral simply twitched reality a bit, and everything since Ghetto Liquors had been a real-life fantasy of amazing exactitude. He finished his drink, had another, steadied himself, and then hailed the jitney when it passed on its way to town, on *his* way to see Rudy and Jubert and George.

Vengeance would be the best antidote of all for this black sediment within him.

Independence Day.

The shanties dripped with colored lights, and the dirt road glowed orange, crisscrossed by dancers and drunks who collided and fell. Skinny black casualties lay underneath the shanties, striped by light shining down through the floorboards. Young women danced in the bar windows; older, fatter women, their hair in turbans, glowering, stood beside tubs of lobster salad and tables laden with coconut bread and pastries. The night was raucous, blaring, hooting, shouting. All the dogs were in hiding.

Prince stuffed himself on the rich food, drank, and then went from bar to bar asking questions of men who pawed his shirt, rolled their eyes, and passed out for an answer. He could find no trace of Rudy or George, but he tracked Jubert down in a shanty bar whose sole designation as a bar was a cardboard sign, tacked on a palm tree beside it, which read FRENLY CLUB No RIOT. Prince lured him outside with the promise of marijuana, and Jubert, stupidly drunk, followed to a clearing behind the bar where dirt trails crossed, a patch of ground bounded by two other shanties and banana trees. Prince smiled a smile of good fellowship, kicked him in the groin and the stomach, and broke Jubert's jaw with the heel of his hand.

'Short cut draw blood,' said Prince. 'Ain't dat right. You don't trick with de mighty.'

He nudged Jubert's jaw with his toe.

Jubert groaned; blood welled from his mouth, puddling black in the moonlight.

'Come back at me and I'll kill you,' said Prince.

He sat cross-legged beside Jubert. Moonlight saturated the clearing, and the tattered banana leaves seemed made of gray-green silk. Their trunks showed bone white. A plastic curtain in a shanty window glowed with mystic roses, lit by the oil lamp inside. Jukebox reggae chip-chipped at the soft night, distant laughter ...

He let the clearing come together around him. The moon brightened as though a film had washed from its face; the light tingled his shoulders. Everything – shanties, palms, banana trees, and bushes – sharpened, loomed, grew more encircling. He felt a measure of hilarity on seeing himself as he'd been in the jungle of Lang Biang, freakishly alert. It conjured up clichéd movie images. Prince, the veteran maddened by memory and distanced by trauma, compelled to relive his nightmares and hunt down these measly offenders in the derelict town. The violent American legend. The war-torn Prince of the cinema. He chuckled. His life, he knew, was devoid of such thematic material.

He was free of compulsion.

Thousands of tiny shake-hands lizards were slithering under the banana trees, running over the sandy soil on their hind legs. He could see the disturbance in the weeds. A hibiscus blossom nodded from behind a shanty, an exotic lure dangling out of the darkness, and the shadows beneath the palms were deep and restless ... not like the shadows in Lang Biang, still and green, high in the vaulted trees. Spirits had lived in those trees, so the stories said, demon-things with iron beaks who'd chew your soul into rags. Once he had shot one. It had been (they told him) only a large fruit bat, deranged, probably by some chemical poison, driven to fly at him in broad daylight. But *he* had seen a demon with an iron beak sail from a green shadow and fired. Nearly every round must have hit, because all they'd found had been scraps of bloody, leathery wing. Afterward they called him Deadeye and described how he'd bounced the bat along through the air with bursts of unbelievable accuracy.

He wasn't afraid of spirits.

'How you doin', Jube?' Prince asked.

Jubert was staring at him, wide-eyed.

Clouds swept across the moon, and the clearing went dark, then brightened.

'Dere's big vultures up dere, Jubert, flyin' cross de moon and screamin' your name.'

Prince was a little afraid of the drug, but less afraid of the islanders – nowhere near as afraid as Jubert was of him right now. Prince had been much more afraid, had cried and soiled himself; but he'd always emptied his gun into the shadows and stayed stoned and alert for eleven months. Fear, he'd learned, had its own continuum of right actions. He could handle it.

Jubert made a gurgling noise.

'Got a question, Jube?' Prince leaned over, solicitous.

A sudden gust of wind sent a dead frond crashing down, and the sound scared Jubert. He tried to lift his head and passed out from the pain.

Somebody shouted, 'Listen to dat boy sing! Oh, he slick, mon!' and turned up the jukebox. The tinny music broke Prince's mood. Everything looked scattered. The moonlight showed the grime and slovenliness of the place, the sprinkles of chicken droppings and the empty crab shells. He'd lost most of his enthusiasm for hunting down Rudy and George, and he decided to head for Maud Price's place, the Golden Dream. Sooner or later everyone stopped in at the Dream. It was the island's gambling center, and because it was an anomaly among the shanties, with their two stucco rooms lit by naked light bulbs, drinking there conferred a certain prestige.

He thought about telling them in the bar about Jubert, but decided no and left him for someone else to rob.

Rudy and George hadn't been in, said Maud, smacking down a bottle on the counter. Bar flies buzzed up from the spills and orbited her like haywire electrons. Then she went back to chopping fish heads, scaling and filleting them. Monstrously fat and jet black, bloody smears on her white dress. The record player at her elbow ground out warped Freddy Fender tunes.

Prince spotted Jerry Steedly (who didn't seem glad to see Prince) sitting at a table along the wall, joined him, and told him about the black coral.

'Everybody sees the same things,' said Steedly, uninterested. 'The reef, the fires …'

'What about flashbacks? Is that typical?'

'It happens. I wouldn't worry about it.' Steedly checked his watch. He was in his forties, fifteen years older than Rita, a gangly Arkansas hick whose brush-cut red hair was going gray.

'I'm not worried,' said Prince. 'It was fine except for the fires or whatever they were. I thought they were copepods at first, but I guess they were just part of the trip.'

'The islanders think they're spirits.' Steedly glanced toward the door, nervous, then looked at Prince, dead serious, as if he were considering a deep question. He kicked back in his chair and leaned against the wall, decided, half smiling. 'Know what I think they are? Aliens.'

Prince made a show of staring goggle-eyed, gave a dumb laugh, and drank.

'No kiddin', Neal. Parasites. Actually, copepods might not be so far off. They're not intelligent. They're reef dwellers from the next continuum over.

The coral opens the perceptual gates or lets them see the gates that are already there, and ... Wham! They latch right on. They induce a low-grade telepathy in human hosts. Among other things.'

Steedly scraped back his chair and pointed at the adjoining room where people thronged, waving cards and money, shouting, losers threatening winners. 'I gotta go lose some money, Neal. You take it easy.'

'Are you trying to mess me around?' Prince asked with mild incredulity.

'Nope. It's just a theory of mine. They exhibit colonial behavior like a lot of small crustaceans. But they *may* be spirits. Maybe spirits aren't anything more than vague animal things slopping over from another world and setting their hooks in your soul, infecting you, dwelling in you. Who knows? I wouldn't worry about it, though.'

He walked away.

'Say hi to Rita for me,' Prince called.

Steedly turned, struggling with himself, but he smiled.

'Hey, Neal,' he said. 'It's not over.'

Prince nursed his rum, cocked an eye toward the door whenever anyone entered (the place was rapidly filling), and watched Maud gutting fish. A light-bulb sun dangled inches over her head, and he imagined her with a necklace of skeletons, reaching down into a bucketful of little silver-scaled men. The thunk of her knife punctuated the babble around him. He drowsed. Idly, he began listening to the conversation of three men at the next table, resting his head against the wall. If he nodded out, Maud would wake him.

'De mon ain't got good sense, always spittin' and fumin'!'

'He harsh, mon! Dere's no denyin".'

'Harsh? De mon worse den dat. Now de way Arlie tell it ...'

Arlie? He wondered if they meant Arlie Brooks, who tended bar at the Sea Breeze.

'... dat Mary Ebanks bled to death ...'

'Dey say dat de stain where she bled still shine at night on de floor of de Sea Breeze!'

Maybe it was Arlie.

'Dat be fool duppy talk, mon!'

'Well, never mind dat! *He* never shot her. Dat was Eusebio Conejo from over at Sandy Bar. But de mon might have saved her with his knowledge of wounds if he had not run off at de gunshot!'

'Ain't he de one dat stole dat gold cross from old Byrum Waters?'

'Correct! Told him dat de gold have gone bad and dass why it so black. And Byrum, not mindful of de ways of gold, didn't know dat was only tarnish!'

'Dat was de treasure lost by old Meachem? Am I right?'

'Correct! De Carib watched him bury it, and when he gone dey move it to de hills. And den when Byrum found it he told his American friend. Hah! And dat friend become a wealthy mon and old Byrum go to de ground wrapped in a blanket!'

That was *his* cross! That was *him* they were talking about! Outraged, Prince came up out of his stupor and opened his eyes.

Then he sat very still.

The music, the shouts from the back room, the conversations had died, been sheared away without the least whisper or cough remaining, and the room had gone black ... except the ceiling. And it brimmed, seethed with purple fire: swirls of indigo and royal purple and violet-white, a pattern similar to the enclosed waters of the reef, as if it, too, signaled varying depths and bottoms; incandescent-looking, though, a rectangle of violent, shifting light, like a corpse's first glimpse of sky when his coffin is opened up in hell ... and cold.

Prince ducked, expecting they would swoop at him, pin him against the freezing darkness. But they did not. One by one the fires separated from the blazing ceiling and flowed down over the walls, settling on the creases and edges of things, outlining them in points of flickering radiance. Their procession seemed almost ordered, stately, and Prince thought of a congregation filing into their allotted pews preparatory to some great function. They illuminated the rumples in ragged shirts (and the ragged ends, as well) and the wrinkles in faces. They traced the shapes of glasses, bottles, tables, spiderwebs, the electric fan, light bulbs and their cords. They glowed nebular in the liquor, they became the smoldering ends of cigarettes, they mapped the spills on the counter and turned them into miniature phosphorescent seas. And when they had all taken their places, their design complete, Prince sat dumbstruck in the midst of an incredibly detailed constellation, one composed of ghostly purple stars against an ebony sky – the constellation of a tropic barroom, of Maud Price's Golden Dream.

He laughed, a venturing laugh; it sounded forced even to his own ears. There was no door, he noticed, no window outlined in purple fire. He touched the wall behind him for reassurance and jerked his hand away: it was freezing. Nothing moved other than the flickering, no sound. The blackness held him fast to his chair as though it were a swamp sucking him under.

'I hurt bad, mon! It hurt inside my head!' A bleary and distressed voice. Jubert's voice!

'Mon, I hurt you bad myself and you slip me de black coral!'

'Dass de truth!'

'De mon had de right to take action!'

Other voices tumbled forth in argument, most of them drunken, sodden, and seeming to issue from starry brooms and chairs and glassware. Many of them took his side in the matter of Jubert's beating – *that*, he realized, was the topic under discussion. And he was winning! But still other voices blurted out, accusing him.

'He took dat fat Yankee tourist down to print old Mrs Ebanks with her camera, and Mrs Ebanks shamed by it!'

'No, mon! I not dat shamed! Let not dat be against him!'

'He pay me for de three barracuda and take de five!'

'He knock me down when I tell him how he favor dat cousin of mine dat live in Ceiba!'

'He beat me ...'

'He cheat me ...'

'He curse me ...'

The voices argued points of accuracy, mitigating circumstances, and accused each other of exaggeration. Their logic was faulty and stupidly conceived. It had the feel of malicious, drunken gossip, as if a group of islanders were loitering on some dusty street and disputing the truth of a tall tale. But in this case it was *his* tale they disputed; for though Prince did not recognize all the voices, he did recognize his crimes, his prideful excesses, his slurs and petty slights. Had it not been so cold, he might have been amused, because the general consensus appeared to be that he was no worse or better than any of his accusers and therefore merited no outrageous judgment.

But then a wheezy voice, the expression of a dulled, ancient sensibility, said, 'I found dat gold cross in a cave up on Hermit's Ridge ...'

Prince panicked, sprang for the door, forgetting there was none, scrabbled at the stony surface, fell, and crawled along, probing for an exit. Byrum's voice harrowed him.

'And I come to him and say, "Mr Prince, I got dis terrible pain in de chest. Can't you give me money? I know dat your money come from meltin' down de gold cross." And he say, "Byrum, I don't give jack-shit about your chest!" And den he show me de door!'

Prince collapsed in a corner, eyes fixed on the starry record player from which the old man's voice came. No one argued against Byrum. When he had finished there was a silence.

'The bastard's been sleeping with my wife,' said a twangy American voice.

'Jerry!' Prince yelled. 'Where are you?'

A constellate bottle of rum was the source of the voice. 'Right here, you son ...'

'Dere's to be no talkin' with de mon before judgment!'

'Dass right! De spirits make dat clear!'

'These damn things aren't spirits ...'

'If dey ain't, den why Byrum Waters in de Dream tonight?'

'De mon can't hear de voices of de spirits 'cause he not *of* de island hisself!'

'Byrum's not here! I've told you people so many times I'm sick of it! These things induce telepathy in humans. That means you can hear each others' minds, that your thoughts resonate and amplify each others', maybe even tap into some kind of collective unconscious. That's how ...'

'I believe somebody done pelt a rock at de mon's head! He crazy!'

The matter of the purple fires was tabled, and the voices discussed Prince's affair with Rita Steedly ('Dere's no proof de mon been messin' with your wife!'), reaching a majority opinion of guilty on what seemed to Prince shaky evidence indeed. The chill in the room had begun to affect him, and though he noticed that unfamiliar voices had joined the dialogue – British voices whose speech was laden with archaisms, guttural Carib voices – he did not wonder at them. He was far more concerned by the trembling of his muscles and the slow, flabby rhythm of his heart; he hugged his knees and buried his head in them for warmth. And so he hardly registered the verdict announced in Byrum Waters' cracked whisper ('De island never cast you out, Mr Prince') nor did he even hear the resultant argument ('Dat all you goin' to tell him?' 'De mon have a right to hear his fate!') except as a stupid hypnotic round that dazed him further and increased the chill, then turned into ghostly laughter. And he did not notice for quite a while that the chill had lessened, that the light filtering through his lids was yellow, and that the laughter was not voiced by spectral fires but by ragged drunks packed closely around him, sweating, howling, and slopping their drinks on his feet. Their gap-toothed mouths opened wider and wider in his dimming sight, as if he were falling into the jaws of ancient animals who had waited in their jungle centuries for such as he. Fat moths danced around them in the air.

Prince pushed feebly at the floor, trying to stand. They laughed louder, and he felt his own lips twitch in a smile, an involuntary reaction to all the good humor in the room.

'Oh, damn!' Maud slammed the flat of her hand down on the counter, starting up the bar flies and hiccuping Freddy Fender's wail. Her smile was fierce and malefic. 'How you like dat, Mr Prince? You one of us now!'

He must've passed out. They must've dumped him in the street like a sack of manure! His head swam as he pulled himself up by the window ledge; his hip pocket clinked on the stucco wall ... rum bottle. He fumbled it out, swallowed, gagged, but felt it strengthen him. The town was dead, lightless, and winded. He reeled against the doorway of the Dream and saw the moldering shanties swing down beneath running banks of moonlit cloud. Peaked and eerie, witches' hats, the sharp jut of folded black wings. He couldn't think.

Dizzy, he staggered between the shanties and fell on all fours in the shallows, then soaked his head in the wavelets lapping the shingle. There were slippery things under his hands. No telling what ... hog guts, kelp. He sat on a piling and let the wind shiver him and straighten him out. Home. Better than fighting off the rabid dog at the Hotel Captain Henry, better than passing out again right here. Two and a half miles across island, no more than an hour even in his condition. But watch out for the purple fires! He laughed. The silence gulped it up. If this were just the drug doing tricks ... God! You could make a fortune selling it in the States.

'You scrapes off de color and dass what you smokes,' he sang, calypso style. 'De black coral takes, boom-boom, just one toke.'

He giggled. But what the hell *were* those purple fires?

Duppies? Aliens? How 'bout the purple souls of the niggers? The niggers' stinging purple souls!

He took another drink. 'Better ration it, pilgrim,' he said to the dark road in his best John Wayne. 'Or you'll never reach the fort alive!'

And like John Wayne, he'd be back, he'd chew out the bullet with his teeth and brand himself clean with a red-hot knife and blow holes in the bad guys.

Oh, yeah!

But suppose they were spirits? Aliens? Not hallucinations?

So what!

'I one of dem, now!' he shouted.

He breezed the first two miles. The road wound through the brush-covered hills at an easy grade. Stars shone in the west, but the moon had gone behind the clouds and the darkness was as thick as mud. He wished he'd brought his flashlight ... That had been the first thing that had attracted him to the island: how the people carried flashlights to show their paths in the hills, along the beaches, in the towns after the generators had been shut down. And when an ignorant, flashlightless stranger came by, they'd shine a path from your feet to theirs and ask, 'How de night?'

'Beautiful,' he'd replied; or, 'Fine, just fine.' And it *had* been. He'd loved everything about the island – the stories, the musical cadences of island speech, the sea-grape trees with their funny round leathery leaves, and the glowing, many-colored sea. He'd seen that the island operated along an ingenious and flexible principle, one capable of accommodating any contrary and eventually absorbing it through a process of calm acceptance. He'd envied the islanders their peaceful, unhurried lives. But that had been before Vietnam. During the war something inside him had gone irreversibly stone-cold sober, screwed up his natural high, and when he returned their idyllic lives had seemed despicable, listless, a bacterial culture shifting on its slide.

Every now and then he saw the peak of a thatched roof in silhouette against the stars, strands of barbed wire hemming in a few acres of scrub and bananas. He stayed dead center in the road, away from the deepest shadow, sang old Stones and Dylan, and fueled himself with hits of rum. It had been a good decision to head back, because a norther was definitely brewing. The wind rushed cold in his face, spitting rain. Storms blew up quickly at this time of year, but he could make it home and secure his house before the worst of the rains.

Something crashed in the brush. Prince jumped away from the sound, looking wildly about for the danger. The tufted hillock on his right suddenly sprouted horns against the starlight and charged at him, bellowing, passing so raw and close that he could hear the breath articulated in the huge red throat. Christ! It had sounded more like a demon's bellow than a cow's, which it was. Prince lost his balance and sprawled in the dirt, shaking. The damned thing lowed again, crunching off through a thicket. He started to get up. But the rum, the adrenaline, all the poisons of his day-long exertions roiled around in him, and his stomach emptied, spewing out liquor and lobster salad and coconut bread. Afterward he felt better – weaker, yet not on the verge of as great a weakness as before. He tore off his fouled shirt and slung it into a bush.

The bush was a blaze of purple fires.

They hung on twig ends and leaf tips and marked the twisting course of branches, outlining them as they had done at Maud's. But at the center of this tracery the fires clustered together in a globe – a wicked violet-white sun extruding spidery filaments and generating forked, leafy electricities.

Prince backed away. The fires flickered in the bush, unmoving. Maybe the drug had finished its run, maybe now that he'd burned most of it out the fires could no longer affect him as they had previously. But then a cold, cold prickle shifted along his spine and he knew – oh, God! – he knew for a certainty there were fires on his back, playing hide-and-seek where he could never find them. He beat at his shoulderblades, like a man putting out flames, and the cold stuck to his fingertips. He held them up before his eyes. They flickered, pulsing from indigo to violet-white. He shook them so hard that his joints cracked, but the fires spread over his hands, encasing his forearms in a lurid glare.

In blind panic Prince staggered off the road, fell, scrambled up, and ran, holding his glowing arms stiff out in front of him. He tumbled down an embankment and came to his feet, running. He saw that the fires had spread above his elbows and felt the chill margin inching upward. His arms lit the brush around him, as if they were the wavering beams of tinted flashlights. Vines whipped out of the dark, the lengths of a black serpent coiled everywhere, lashed into a frenzy by the purple light. Dead fronds clawed his face with sharp papery fingers. He was so afraid, so empty of everything but fear, that when a palm trunk loomed ahead he ran straight into it, embracing it with his shining arms.

There were hard fragments in his mouth, blood, more blood flowing into his eyes. He spat and probed his mouth, wincing as he touched the torn gums.

Three teeth missing, maybe four. He hugged the palm trunk and hauled himself up. This was the grove near his house! He could see the lights of St Mark's Key between the trunks, white seas driving in over the reef. Leaning on the palms as he went, he made his way to the water's edge. The wind-driven rain slashed at his split forehead. Christ! It was swollen big as an onion! The wet sand sucked off one of his tennis shoes, but he left it.

He washed his mouth and forehead in the stinging saltwater, then slogged toward the house, fumbling for his key. Damn! It had been in his shirt. But it was all right. He'd built the house Hawaiian style, with wooden slats on every side to admit the breeze; it would be easy to break in. He could barely see the roof peak against the toiling darkness of the palms and the hills behind, and he banged his shins on the porch. Distant lightning flashed, and he found the stair and spotted the conch shell lying on the top step. He wrapped his hand inside it, punched a head-sized hole in the door slats, and leaned on the door, exhausted by the effort. He was just about to reach in for the latch when the darkness within – visible against the lesser darkness of night as a coil of dead, unshining emptiness – squeezed from the hole like black toothpaste and tried to encircle him.

Prince tottered backward off the porch and landed on his side; he dragged himself away a few feet, stopped, and looked up at the house. The blackness was growing out into the night, encysting him in a thicket of coral branches so dense that he could see between them only glints of the lightning bolts striking down beyond the reef. 'Please,' he said, lifting his hand in supplication. And something broke in him, some grimly held thing whose residue was tears. The wind's howl and the booming reef came as a single ominous vowel, roaring, rising in pitch.

The house seemed to inhale the blackness, to suck it slithering back inside, and for a moment Prince thought it was over. But then violet beams lanced from the open slats, as if the fuming heart of a reactor had been uncovered within. The beach bloomed in livid daylight – a no-man's-land littered with dead fish, half-buried conchs, rusted cans, and driftwood logs like the broken, corroded limbs of iron statues. Inky palms thrashed and shivered. Rotting coconuts cast shadows on the sand. And then the light swarmed up from the house, scattering into a myriad of fiery splinters and settling on palm tops, on the prows of dinghies, on the reef, on tin roofs set among the palms, and on sea grape and cashew trees, where they burned. The ghosts of candles illuminating a sacred shore, haunting the dark interior of a church whose anthem was wind, whose litany was thunder, and upon whose walls feathered shadows leapt and lightnings crawled.

Prince got to his knees, watching, waiting, not really afraid any longer, but gone into fear. Like a sparrow in a serpent's gaze, he saw everything of his devourer, knew with great clarity that these *were* the island people, all of them who had ever lived, and that they *were* possessed of some otherworldly vitality – though whether spirit or alien or both, he could not determine – and that they had taken their accustomed places, their ritual stands. Byrum Waters hovering in the cashew tree he had planted as a boy; John Anderson McCrae flitting above the reef where he and his father had swung lanterns to lure ships in onto the rocks; Maud Price ghosting over the grave of her infant child hidden in the weeds behind a shanty. But then he doubted his knowledge and wondered if they were not telling him this, advising him of the island's consensus, for he heard the mutter of a vast conversation becoming distinct, outvoicing the wind.

He stood, searching for an avenue of escape, not in the least hopeful of finding one, but choosing to exercise a final option. Everywhere he turned the world pitched and tossed as if troubled by his sight, and only the flickering purple fires held constant. 'Oh, my God!' he screamed, almost singing it in an ecstasy of fear, realizing that the precise moment for which they'd gathered had arrived.

As one, from every corner of the shore, they darted into his eyes.

Before the cold overcame him, Prince heard island voices in his head. They ranted ('Lessee how you rank with de spirit, now! Boog man!'). They instructed ('Best you not struggle against de spirit. Be more merciful dat way.'). They insulted, rambled, and construed illogics. For a few seconds he tried to follow the thread of their discourse, thinking if he could understand and comply, then they might stop. But when he could not understand he clawed his face in frustration. The voices rose to a chorus, to a mob howling separately for his attention, then swelled into a roar greater than the wind's but equally single-minded and bent on his annihilation. He dropped onto his hands and knees, sensing the beginning of a terrifying dissolution, as if he were being poured out into a shimmering violet-red bowl. And he saw the film of fire coating his chest and arms, saw his own horrid glare reflected on the broken seashells and mucky sand, shifting from violet-red into violet-white and brightening, growing whiter and whiter until it became a white darkness in which he lost all track of being.

The bearded old man wandered into Meachem's Landing early Sunday morning after the storm. He stopped for a while beside the stone bench in the public square where the sentry, a man even older than himself, was leaning on his deer rifle, asleep. When the voices bubbled up in his thoughts – he pictured his thoughts as a soup with bubbles boiling up and popping, and the voices coming from the pops – and yammered at him ('No, no! Dat ain't de mon!' 'Keep walkin', old fool!'). It was a chorus, a clamor that caused his head to throb; he continued on. The street was littered with palm husks and fronds and broken bottles buried in the mud that showed only their glittering edges.

The voices warned him these were sharp and would cut him ('Make it hurtful like dem gashes on your face'), and he stepped around them. He wanted to do what they told him because ... it just seemed the way of things.

The glint of a rain-filled pothole caught his eye, and he knelt by it, looking at his reflection. Bits of seaweed clung to his crispy gray hair, and he picked them out, laying them carefully in the mud. The pattern in which they lay seemed familiar. He drew a rectangle around them with his finger and it seemed even more familiar, but the voices told him to forget about it and keep going. One voice advised him to wash his cuts in the pothole. The water smelled bad, however, and other voices warned him away. They grew in number and volume, driving him along the street until he followed their instructions and sat down on the steps of a shanty painted all the colors of the rainbow. Footsteps sounded inside the shanty, and a black bald-headed man wearing shorts came out and stretched himself on the landing.

'Damn!' he said. 'Just look what come home to us this mornin'. Hey, Lizabeth!'

A pretty woman joined him, yawning, and stopped mid-yawn when she saw the old man.

'Oh, Lord! Dat poor creature!'

She went back inside and reappeared shortly carrying a towel and a basin, squatted beside him, and began dabbing at his wounds. It seemed such a kind, a human thing to be so treated, and the old man kissed her soapy fingers.

'De mon a caution!' Lizabeth gave him a playful smack. 'I know dass why he in such a state. See de way de skin's all tore on his forehead dere? Must be he been fightin' with de conchs over some other mon's woman.'

'Could be,' said the bald man. 'How 'bout that? You a fool for the ladies?'

The old man nodded. He heard a chorus of affirming voices. ('Oh, dass it!' 'De mon cootin' and cootin' until he half-crazy, den he coot with de *wrong* woman!' 'Must have been grazed with de conch and left for dead.')

'Lord, yes!' said Lizabeth. 'Dis mon goin' to trouble all de ladies, goin' to be kissin' after dem and huggin' dem ...'

'Can't you talk?' asked the bald man.

He thought he could, but there were so many voices, so many words to choose from ... maybe later. No.

'Well, I guess we'd better get you a name. How 'bout Bill? I got a good friend up in Boston's named Bill.'

That suited the old man fine. He liked being associated with the bald man's good friend.

'Tell you what, Bill.' The bald man reached inside the door and handed him a broom. 'You sweep off the steps and pick up what you see needs pickin', and we'll pass you out some beans and bread after a while. How's that sound?'

It sounded *good*, and Bill began sweeping at once, taking meticulous care with each step. The voices died to a murmurous purr in his thoughts. He beat the broom against the pilings, and dust fell onto it from the floorboards; he beat it until no more would fall. He was happy to be among people again because ... ('Don't be thinkin' 'bout the back time, mon! Dat all gone.' 'You just get on with your clean dere, Bill. Everything goin' to work out in de end.' 'Dass it, mon! You goin' to clean dis whole town before you through!' 'Don't vex with de mon! He doin' his work!') And he was! He picked up everything within fifty feet of the shanty and chased off a ghost crab, smoothing over the delicate slashes its legs made in the sand.

By the time Bill had cleaned for a half hour he felt so at home, so content and enwrapped in his place and purpose, that when the old woman next door came out to toss her slops into the street, he scampered up her stairs, threw his arms around her, and kissed her full on the mouth. Then he stood grinning, at attention with his broom.

Startled at first, the woman put her hands on her hips and looked him up and down, shaking her head in dismay.

'My God,' she said sorrowfully. 'Dis de best we can do for dis poor mon? Dis de best thing de island can make of itself?'

Bill didn't understand. The voices chattered, irritated; they didn't seem angry at him, though, and he kept on smiling. Once again the woman shook her head and sighed, but after a few seconds Bill's smile encouraged her to smile in return.

'I guess if dis de worst of it,' she said, 'den better must come.' She patted Bill on the shoulder and turned to the door. 'Everybody!' she called. 'Quickly now! Come see dis lovin' soul dat de storm have let fall on Rudy Welcomes' door!'

THE END OF LIFE AS WE KNOW IT

What Lisa hated most about Mexico was the flies, and Richard said Yeah, the flies were bad, but it was the lousy attitude of the people that did him in, you know, the way the waiters ignored you and the taxi drivers sneered, the sour expressions of desk clerks – as if they were doing you a big favor by letting you stay in their fleabag hotels. All that. Lisa replied that she couldn't blame the people, because they were probably irritated by the flies; this set Richard to laughing, and though Lisa had not meant it to be funny, after a moment she joined in. They needed laughter. They had come to Mexico to Save Their Marriage, and things were not going well ... except in bed, where things had always gone well. Lisa had never been less than ardent with Richard, even during her affair.

They were an attractive couple in their thirties, the sort to whom a healthy sex life seems an essential of style, a trendy accessory to pleasure like a Jacuzzi or a French food processor. She was a tall, fey-looking brunette with fair skin, an aerobically nurtured slimness, and a face that managed to express both sensuality and intelligence ('hooker eyes and Vassar bones,' Richard had told her); he was lean from handball and weights, with an executive touch of gray in his black hair and the bland, firm-jawed handsomeness of a youthful anchorman. Once they had held to the illusion that they kept fit and beautiful for one another, but all their illusions had been tarnished and they no longer understood their reasons for maintaining them.

For a while they made a game of hating Mexico, pretending it was a new bond between them, striving to outdo each other in pointing out instances of filth and native insensitivity; finally they realized that what they hated most about the country was their own perceptions of it, and they headed south to Guatemala where – they had been informed – the atmosphere was conducive to romance. They were leery about the reports of guerrilla activity, but their informant had assured them that the dangers were overstated. He was a seasoned traveler, an elderly Englishman who had spent his last twelve winters in Central America; Richard thought he was colorful, a Graham Greene character, whereas Lisa described him in her journal as 'a deracinated old fag.'

'You mustn't miss Lake Atitlán,' he'd told them. 'It's absolutely breathtaking. Revolution there is an aesthetic impossibility.'

Before boarding the plane Richard bought the latest *Miami Herald*, and he entertained himself during the flight by bemoaning the decline of Western civilization. It was his conviction that the United States was becoming part of the Third World and that their grandchildren would inhabit a mildly poisoned earth and endure lives of back-breaking drudgery under an increasingly Orwellian government. Though this conviction was hardly startling, it being evident from the newspaper that such a world was close upon them, Lisa accorded his viewpoint the status of wisdom; in fact, she had relegated wisdom in general to be his preserve, staking claim herself to the traditional feminine precincts of soulfulness and caring. Sometimes back in Connecticut, while teaching her art class at the Y or manning the telephones for PBS or Greenpeace or whatever cause had enlisted her soulfulness, looking around at the other women, all – like her – expensively kept and hopeless and with an eye cocked for the least glimmer of excitement, then she would see how marriage had decreased her wattage; and yet, though she had fallen in love with another man, she had clung to the marriage for almost a year thereafter, unable to escape the fear that this was the best she could hope for, that no matter what steps she took to change her situation, her life would always be ruled by a canon of mediocrity. That she had recently stopped clinging did not signal a slackening of fear, only that her fingers were slipping, her energy no longer sufficient to maintain a good grip.

As the plane came down into Guatemala City, passing over rumpled green hills dotted with shacks whose colors looked deceptively bright and cheerful from a height, Richard began talking about his various investments, saying he was glad he'd bought this and that, because things were getting worse every day. 'The shitstorm's a-comin', babe,' he said, patting her knee. 'But we're gonna be awright.' It annoyed Lisa no end that whenever he was feeling particularly accomplished his language became countrified, and she only shrugged in response.

After clearing customs they rented a car and drove to Panajachel, a village on the shores of Lake Atitlán. There was a fancy hotel on the shore, but in the spirit of 'roughing it' Richard insisted they stay at a cheaper place on the edge of town – an old green stucco building with red trim and an arched entranceway and a courtyard choked with ferns; it catered to what he called 'the bleeding-ear set,' a reference to the loud rock 'n' roll that blasted from the windows. The other guests were mostly college-age vacationers, a mixture of French and Scandinavians and Americans, and as soon as they had unpacked, Lisa changed into jeans and a work shirt so she would fit in among them. They ate dinner in the hotel dining room, which was cramped and furnished with red wooden tables and chairs and had the menu painted on the wall in English and Spanish. Richard appeared to be enjoying himself; he was relaxed, and his speech was peppered with slang that he hadn't used in almost a decade. Lisa liked listening to the glib chatter around them, talk of dope and how the people treat you in Huehuetenango and watch out if you're goin'

to Bogotá, man, 'cause they got packs of street kids will pick you clean ...'
These conversations reminded her of the world in which she had traveled at Vassar before Richard had snatched her up during her junior year. He had been just back from Vietnam, a medic, full of anguish at the horrors he had seen, yet strong for having seen them; he had seemed to her a source of strength, a shining knight, a rescuer. After the wedding, though, she had not been able to recall why she had wanted to be rescued; she thought now that she had derived some cheap thrill from his aura of recent violence and had applied it to herself out of a romantic need to feel imperiled.

They lingered over dinner, watching the younger guests drift off into the evening and being watched themselves – at least in Lisa's case – by a fortyish Guatemalan man with a pencil-line mustache, a dark suit, and patent-leather hair. He stared at her as he chewed, ducking his eyes each time he speared a fresh bite, then resuming his stare. Ordinarily Lisa would have been irritated, but she found the man's conspicuous anonymity appealing and she adopted a flirtatious air, laughing too loudly and fluttering her hands, in hopes that she was frustrating him.

'His name's Raoul,' said Richard. 'He's a white slaver in the employ of the Generalisimo, and he's been commissioned to bring in a new *gringa* for the harem.'

'He's somebody's uncle,' said Lisa. 'Here to settle a family dispute. He's married to a dumpy Indian woman, has seven kids, and he's wearing his only suit to impress the Americans.'

'God, you're a romantic!' Richard sipped his coffee, made a face, and set it down.

Lisa bit back a sarcastic reply. 'I think he's very romantic. Let's say he's staring at me because he wants me. If that's true, right now he's probably thinking how to do you in, or maybe wondering if he could trade you his truck, his means of livelihood, for a night with me. That's real romance. Passionate stupidity and bloody consequences.'

'I guess,' said Richard, unhappy with the definition; he took another sip of coffee and changed the subject.

At sunset they walked down to the lake. The village was charming enough – the streets cobbled, the houses whitewashed and roofed with tile; but the rows of tourist shops and the American voices acted to dispel the charm. The lake, however, was beautiful. Ringed by three volcanoes, bordered by palms, Indians poling canoes toward scatters of light on the far shore. The water was lacquered with vivid crimson and yellow reflection, and silhouetted against an equally vivid sky, the palms and volcanic cones gave the place the look of a prehistoric landscape. As they stood at the end of a wooden pier, Richard drew her into a kiss and she felt again the explosive dizziness of their first kisses; yet she knew it was a sham, a false magic born of geography and their own contrivance. They could keep traveling, keep filling their days with exotic sights, lacquering their lives with reflection, but when they stopped they would discover that they had merely been preserving the forms of the marriage. There was no remedy for their dissolution.

Roosters crowing waked her to gray dawn light. She remembered a dream about a faceless lover, and she stretched and rolled onto her side. Richard was sitting at the window, wearing jeans and a T-shirt; he glanced at her, then turned his gaze to the window, to the sight of a pale green volcano wreathed in mist. 'It's not working,' he said, and when she failed to respond, still half-asleep, he buried his face in his hands, muffling his voice. 'I can't make it without you, babe.'

She had dreaded this moment, but there was no reason to put it off. 'That's the problem,' she said. 'You used to be able to.' She plumped the pillows and leaned back against them.

He looked up, baffled. 'What do you mean?'

'Why should *I* have to explain it? You know it as well as I do. We weaken each other, we exhaust each other, we depress each other.' She lowered her eyes, not wanting to see his face. 'Maybe it's not even us. Sometimes I think marriage is this big pasty spell of cakes and veils that shrivels everything it touches.'

'Lisa, you know there isn't anything I wouldn't …'

'What? What'll you do?' Angrily, she wadded the sheet. 'I don't understand how we've managed to hurt each other so much. If I did, I'd try to fix it. But there's nothing left to do. Not together, anyway.'

He let out a long sigh – the sigh of a man who has just finished defusing a bomb and can allow himself to breathe again. 'It's him, right? You still want to be with him.'

It angered her that he would never say the name, as if the name were what counted. 'No,' she said stiffly. 'It's not *him*.'

'But you still love him.'

'That's not the point! I still love you, but love …' She drew up her legs and rested her forehead on her knees. 'Christ, Richard. I don't know what more to tell you. I've said it all a hundred times.'

'Maybe,' he said softly, 'maybe this discussion is premature.'

'Oh, Richard!'

'No, really. Let's go on with the trip.'

'Where, next? The Mountains of the Moon? Brazil? It won't change anything.'

'You can't be sure of that!' He came toward the bed, his face knitted into lines of despair. 'We'll just stay a few more days. We'll visit the villages on the other side of the lake, where they do the weaving.'

'Why, Richard? God, I don't even understand why you still want me ...'

'Please, Lisa. Please. After eleven years you can try for a few more days.'

'All right,' she said, weary of hurting him. 'A few days.'

'And you'll try?'

I've always tried, she wanted to say; but then, wondering if it were true, as true as it should be, she merely said, 'Yes.'

The motor launch that ran back and forth across the lake between Panajachel and San Augustin had seating room for fifteen, and nine of those places were occupied by Germans, apparently members of a family – kids, two sets of parents, and a pair of portly red-cheeked grandparents. They reeked of crudity and good health, and made Lisa feel refined by comparison. The young men snapped their wives' bra straps – grandpa almost choked with laughter each time this happened; the kids whined; the women were heavy and hairy-legged. They spent the entire trip taking pictures of one another. They must have understood English, because when Richard cracked a joke about them, they frowned and whispered and became standoffish. Lisa and Richard moved to the stern, a superficial union imposed, and watched the shore glide past. Though it was still early, the sun reflected a dynamited white glare on the water; in the daylight the volcanoes looked depressingly real, their slopes covered by patchy grass and scrub and stunted palms.

San Augustin was situated at the base of the largest volcano, and was probably like what Panajachel had been before tourism. Weeds grew between the cobblestones, the whitewash was flaked away in places, and grimy, naked toddlers sat in the doorways, chewing sugarcane and drooling. Inside the houses it was the fourteenth century. Packed dirt floors, iron cauldrons suspended over fires, chickens pecking and pigs asleep. Gnomish old Indian women worked at handlooms, turning out strange tapestries – as for example a design of black cranelike birds against a backdrop of purple sky and green trees, the image repeated over and over – and bolts of dress material, fabric that on first impression seemed to be of a hundred colors, all in perfect harmony. Lisa wanted to be sad for the women, to sympathize with their poverty and particular female plight, and to some extent she managed it; but the women were uncomplaining and appeared reasonably content and their weaving was better work than she had ever done, even when she had been serious about art. She bought several yards of the material, tried to strike up a conversation with one of the women, who spoke neither English nor Spanish, and then they returned to the dock, to the village's only bar-restaurant – a place right out of a spaghetti western, with a hitching rail in front and skinned sapling trunks propping up the porch roof and a handful of young long-haired American men standing along the bar, having an early-morning beer. 'Holy marijuana!' said Richard, winking. 'Hippies! I wondered where they'd gone.' They took a table by the rear window so they could see the slopes of the volcano. The scarred varnish of the table was dazzled by sunlight; flies buzzed against the heated panes.

'So what do you think?' Richard squinted against the glare.

'I thought we were going to give it a few days,' she said testily.

'Jesus, Lisa! I meant what do you think about the weaving.' He adopted a pained expression.

'I'm sorry.' She touched his hand, and he shook his head ruefully. 'It's beautiful ... I mean the weaving's beautiful. Oh God, Richard. I don't intend to be so awkward.'

'Forget it.' He stared out the window, deadpan, as if he were giving serious consideration to climbing the volcano, sizing up the problems involved. 'What did you think of it?'

'It was beautiful,' she said flatly. The buzzing of the flies intensified, and she had the notion that they were telling her to try harder. 'I know it's corny to say, but watching her work ... What was her name?'

'Expectatión.'

'Oh, right. Well, watching her I got the feeling I was watching something magical, something that went on and on ...' She trailed off, feeling foolish at having to legitimize with conversation what had been a momentary whimsy; but she could think of nothing else to say. 'Something that went on forever,' she continued. 'With different hands, of course, but always that something the same. And the weavers, while they had their own lives and problems, that was less important than what they were doing. You know, like the generations of weavers were weaving something through time as well as space. A long, woven magic.' She laughed, embarrassed.

'It's not corny. I know what you're talking about.' He pushed back his chair and grinned. 'How about I get us a couple of beers?'

'Okay,' she said brightly, and smiled until his back was turned. He thought he had her now. That was his plan – to get her a little drunk, not drunk enough for a midday hangover, just enough to get her happy and energized, and then that afternoon they'd go for a ride to the next village, the next exotic attraction, and more drinks and dinner and a new hotel. He'd keep her whirling, an endless date, an infinitely prolonged seduction. She pictured the two of them as a pair of silhouetted dancers tangoing across the borders of map colored countries. Whirling and whirling, and the thing was, the very sad thing was, that sooner or later, if he kept her whirling, she would lose her own momentum and be sucked into the spin, into that loving-the-spin-I'm-in-old-black-magic routine. Then final rinse. Final spin. Then the machine would stop and she'd be plastered to the side of the marriage like a wet blouse, needing a hand to lift her out. She should do what had to be done right now. Right this moment. Cause a scene, hit him. Whatever it took. Because if she didn't … He *thunked* down a bottle of beer in front of her, and her smile twitched by reflex into place.

'Thanks,' she said.

'*Por nada.*' He delivered a gallant bow and sat down. 'Listen …'

There was a clatter from outside, and through the door she saw a skinny bearded man tying a donkey to the hitching rail. He strode on in, dusting off his jeans cowboy-style, and ordered a beer. Richard turned to look and chuckled. The man was worth a chuckle. He might have been the Spirit of the Sixties, the Wild Hippie King. His hair was a ratty brown thatch hanging to his shoulders, and braided into it were long gray feathers that dangled still lower; his jeans were festooned with painted symbols, and there were streaks of what appeared to be green dye in his thicket of a beard. He noticed them staring, waved, and came toward them.

'Mind if I join you folks?' Before they could answer, he dropped into a chair. 'I'm Dowdy. Believe it or not, that's a name, not a self-description.' He smiled, and his blue eyes crinkled up. His features were sharp, thin to the point of being wizened. It was hard to tell his age because of the beard, but Lisa figured him for around thirty-five. Her first reaction had been to ask him to leave; the instant he had started talking, though, she had sensed a cheerful kind of sanity about him that intrigued her. 'I live up yonder,' he went on, gesturing at the volcano. 'Been there goin' on four years.'

'Inside the volcano?' Lisa meant it for a joke.

'Yep! Got me a little shack back in under the lip. Hot in the summer, freezin' in the winter, and none of the comforts of home. I got to bust my tail on Secretariat there' – he waved at the donkey – 'just to haul water and supplies.' In waving he must have caught a whiff of his underarm – he gave it an ostentatious sniff. '*And* to get me a bath. Hope I ain't too ripe for you folks.' He chugged down a third of his beer. 'So! How you like Guatemala?'

'Fine,' said Richard. 'Why do you live in a volcano?'

'Kinda peculiar, ain't it,' said Dowdy by way of response; he turned to Lisa. 'And how you like it here?'

'We haven't seen much,' she said. 'Just the lake.'

'Oh, yeah? Well, it ain't so bad 'round here. They keep it nice for the tourists. But the rest of the country … whooeee! Violent?' Dowdy made a show of awed disbelief. 'You got your death squads, your guerrillas, your secret police, not to mention your basic crazed killers. Hell, they even got a political party called the Party of Organized Violence. Bad dudes. They like to twist people's arms off. It ain't that they're evil, though. It's just the land's so full of blood and brimstone and Mayan weirdness, it fumes up and freaks 'em out. That's how come we got volcanoes. Safety valves to blow off the excess poison. But things are on the improve.'

'Really?' said Richard, amused.

'Yes, indeed!' Dowdy tipped back in his chair, propping the beer bottle on his stomach; he had a little potbelly like that of a cartoon elf. 'The whole world's changing. I s'pose y'all have noticed the way things are goin' to hell back in the States?'

Lisa could tell that the question had mined Richard's core of political pessimism, and he started to frame an answer, but Dowdy talked through him.

'That's part of the change,' he said. 'All them scientists say they figured out reasons for the violence and pollution and economic failure, but what them things really are is just the sound of consensus reality scrapin' contrary to the flow of the change. They ain't nothin' but symptoms of the real change, of everything comin' to an end.'

Richard made silent speech with his eyes, indicating that it was time to leave.

'Now, now,' said Dowdy, who had caught the signal. 'Don't get me wrong. I ain't talkin' Apocalypse, here. And I for sure ain't no Bible basher like them Mormons you see walkin' 'round the villages. Huh! Them suckers is so scared of life they travel in pairs so's they can keep each other from bein' corrupted. "Watch it there, Billy! You're steppin' in some sin!"' Dowdy rolled his eyes to the ceiling in a parody of prayer. '"Sweet Jesus, gimme the strength to scrape this sin off my shoe!" Then off they go, purified, a couple of All-American haircuts with souls stuffed fulla white-bread gospel and crosses 'round their necks to keep off the vampire women. Shit!' He leaned forward, resting his elbows on the table. 'But I digress. I got me a religion, all right. Not Jesus, though. I'll tell you 'bout it if you want, but I ain't gonna force it down your throat.'

'Well,' Richard began, but Lisa interrupted.

'We've got an hour until the boat,' she said. 'Does your religion have anything to do with your living in the volcano?'

'Sure does.' Dowdy pulled a hand-rolled cigar from his shirt pocket, lit it, and blew out a plume of smoke that boiled into a bluish cloud against the windowpanes. 'I used to smoke, drink' – he flourished his beer – 'and I was a bear for the ladies. Praise God, religion ain't changed that none!' He laughed, and Lisa smiled at him. Whatever it was that had put Dowdy in such good spirits seemed to be contagious. 'Actually,' he said, 'I wasn't a hell-raiser at all. I was a painfully shy little fella, come from backwoods Tennessee. Like my daddy'd say, town so small you could spit between the city-limits signs. Anyway, I was shy but I was smart, and with that combination it was a natural for me to end up in computers. Gave me someone I could feel comfortable talkin' to. After college I took a job designin' software out in Silicon Valley, and seven years later there I was … Livin' in an apartment tract with no real friends, no pictures on the walls, and a buncha terminals. A real computer nerd. Wellsir! Somehow I got it in mind to take a vacation. I'd never had one.

Guess I figured I'd just end up somewhere weird, sittin' in a room and thinkin' 'bout computers, so what was the point? But I was determined to do it this time, and I came to Panajachel. First few days I did what you folks probably been doin'. Wanderin', not meetin' anyone, buyin' a few geegaws. Then I caught the launch across the lake and ran into ol' Murciélago.' He clucked his tongue against his teeth. 'Man, I didn't know what to make of him at first. He was the oldest human bein' I'd ever seen. Looked centuries old. All hunched up, white-haired, as wrinkled as a walnut shell. He couldn't speak no English, just Cakchiquel, but he had this mestizo fella with him who did his interpretin', and it was through him I learned that Murciélago was a *brujo*.'

'A wizard,' said Lisa, who had read Castaneda, to Richard, who hadn't.

'Yep,' said Dowdy. ''Course I didn't believe it. Thought it was some kinda hustle. But he interested me, and I kept hangin' 'round just to see what he was up to. Well, one night he says to me – through the mestizo fella – "I like you," he says. "Ain't nothin' wrong with you that a little magic wouldn't cure. I'd be glad to make you a gift if you got no objections." I said to myself, "Oh-oh, here it comes." But I reckoned it couldn't do me no harm to let him play his hand, and I told him to go ahead. So he does some singin' and rubs powder on my mouth and mutters and touches me, and that was it. "You gonna be fine now," he tells me. I felt sorta strange, but no finer than I had. Still, there wasn't any hustle, and that same night I realized that his magic was doin' its stuff. Confused the hell out of me, and the only thing I could think to do was to hike on up to the volcano, where he lived, and ask him about it. Murciélago was waitin' for me. The mestizo had gone, but he'd left a note explainin' the situation. Seems he'd learned all he could from Murciélago and had taken up his own post, and it was time the ol' man had a new apprentice. He told me how to cook for him, wished me luck, and said he'd be seein' me around.' Dowdy twirled his cigar and watched smoke rings float up. 'Been there ever since and ain't regretted it a day.'

Richard was incredulous. 'You gave up a job in Silicon Valley to become a sorcerer's apprentice?'

'That's right.' Dowdy pulled at one of the feathers in his hair. 'But I didn't give up nothin' real, Richard.'

'How do you know my name?'

'People grow into their names, and if you know how to look for it, it's written everywhere on 'em. 'Bout half of magic is bein' able to see clear.'

Richard snorted. 'You read our names off the passenger manifest for the launch.'

'I don't blame you for thinkin' that,' said Dowdy. 'It's hard to accept the existence of magic. But that ain't how it happened.' He drained the dregs of his beer. 'You were easy to read, but Lisa here was sorta hard 'cause she never liked her name. Ain't that so?'

Lisa nodded, surprised.

'Yeah, see when a person don't like their name it muddies up the writin', so to speak, and you gotta scour away a lotta half-formed names to see down to the actual one.' Dowdy heaved a sigh and stood. 'Time I'm takin' care of business, but tell you what! I'll bring ol' Murciélago down to the bar around seven o'clock, and you can check him out. You can catch the nine o'clock boat back. I know he'd like to meet you.'

'*How* do you know?' asked Richard.

'It ain't my place to explain. Look here, Rich. I ain't gonna twist your arm, but if you go back to Panajachel you're just gonna wander 'round and maybe buy some garbage. If you stay, well, whether or not you believe Murciélago's a *brujo*, you'll be doin' somethin' out of the ordinary. Could be he'll give you a gift.'

'What gift did he give you?' asked Lisa.

'The gift of gab,' said Dowdy. 'Surprised you ain't deduced that for yourself, Lisa, 'cause I can tell you're a perceptive soul. 'Course that was just part of the gift. The gift wrappin', as it were. It's like Murciélago says, a real gift ain't known by its name.' He winked at her. 'But it took pretty damn good, didn't it?'

As soon as Dowdy had gone, Richard asked Lisa if she wanted a last look at the weaving before heading back, but she told him she would like to meet Murciélago. He argued briefly, then acquiesced. She knew what he was thinking. He had no interest in the *brujo*, but he would humor her; it would be an Experience, a Shared Memory, another increment of momentum added to the spin of their marriage. To pass the time she bought a notebook from a tiny store, whose entire inventory would have fit in her suitcases, and sat outside the bar sketching the volcanoes, the people, the houses. Richard *oohed* and *ahhed* over the sketches, but in her judgment they were lifeless – accurate, yet dull and uninspired. She kept at it, though; it beat her other options.

Toward four o'clock dark thunderheads muscled up from behind the volcano, drops of cold rain spattered down, and they retreated into the bar. Lisa did not intend to get drunk, but she found herself drinking to Richard's rhythm. He would nurse each beer for a while, shearing away the label with his thumbnail; once the label had been removed he would empty the bottle in a few swallows and bring them a couple more. After four bottles she was tipsy, and after six walking to the bathroom became an adventure in vertigo. Once she stumbled against the only other customer, a long-haired guy left over from the morning crowd, and caused him to spill his drink. 'My pleasure,' he said when she apologized, leering, running his hands along her hips as he pushed her gently away. She wanted to pose a vicious comeback, but was too fuddled. The bathroom served to make her drunker. It was a chamber of horrors, a hole in the middle of the floor with a ridged footprint on either side, scraps of brown paper strewn about, dark stains everywhere, reeking. There was a narrow window that – if she stood on tiptoe – offered a view of two volcanoes and the lake. The water mirrored the grayish-black of the sky. She stared through the smeared glass, watching waves pile in toward shore, and soon she realized that she was staring at the scene with something like longing, as if the storm held a promise of resolution. By the time she returned to the bar, the bartender had lit three kerosene lamps; they added a shabby glory to the place, casting rich gleams along the countertop and gemmy orange reflections in the windowpanes. Richard had brought her a fresh beer.

'They might not come, what with the rain,' he said.

'Maybe not.' She downed a swallow of beer, beginning to like its sour taste.

'Probably for the best,' he said. 'I've been thinking, and I'm sure he was setting us up for a robbery.'

'You're paranoid. If he were going to rob us, he'd pick a spot where there weren't any soldiers.'

'Well, he's got something in mind ... though I have to admit that was a clever story he told. All that stuff about his own doubts tended to sandbag any notion that he was hustling us.'

'I don't believe he was hustling us. Maybe he's deluded, but he's not a criminal.'

'How the hell could you tell that?' He picked at a stubborn fleck of beer label. 'Feminine intuition? God, he was only here a few minutes.'

'You know,' she said angrily, 'I deserve that. I've been buying that whole feminine intuition chump ever since we were married. I've let you play the intelligent one, while I' – she affected a Southern accent and a breathy voice – 'I just get these little flashes. I swear I don't know where they come from, but they turn out right so often I must be psychic or somethin'. Jesus!'

'Lisa, please.'

He looked utterly defeated, but she was drunk and sick of all the futile effort and she couldn't stop. 'Any idiot could've seen that Dowdy was just a nice, weird little guy. Not a threat! But you had to turn him into a threat so you could feel you were protecting me from dangers I was too naïve to see. What's that do for you? Does it wipe out the fact that I've been unfaithful, that I've walked all over your self-respect? Does it restore your masculine pride?'

His face worked, and she hoped he would hit her, punctuate the murkiness of their lives with a single instance of shock and clarity. But she knew he wouldn't. He relied on his sadness to defeat her. 'You must hate me,' he said.

She bowed her head, her anger emptying into the hollow created by his dead voice. 'I don't hate you. I'm just tired.'

'Let's go home. Let's get it over with.'

She glanced up, startled. His lips were thinned, a muscle clenching in his jaw.

'We can catch a flight tomorrow. If not tomorrow, the next day. I won't try to hold you anymore.'

She was amazed by the panic she felt; she couldn't tell if it resulted from surprise, the kind you feel when you haven't shut the car door properly and suddenly there you are, hanging out the side, unprepared for the sight of the pavement flowing past; or if it was that she had never really wanted freedom, that all her protest had been a means of killing boredom. Maybe, she thought, this was a new tactic on his part, and then she realized that everything between them had become tactical. They played each other without conscious effort, and their games bordered on the absurd. To her further amazement she heard herself say in a tremulous voice, 'Is that what *you* want?'

'Hell, no!' He smacked his palm against the table, rattling the bottles. 'I want you! I want children, eternal love ... all those dumb bullshit things we wanted in the beginning! But you don't want them anymore, do you?'

She saw how willingly she had given him an opening in which to assert his masculinity, his moral position, combining them into a terrific left hook to the heart. *Oh Jesus, they were pathetic!* Tears started from her eyes, and she had a dizzying sense of location, as if she were looking up from a well-bottom through the strata of her various conditions. Drunk, in a filthy bar, in Guatemala, shadowed by volcanoes, under a stormy sky, and – spanning it all, binding it all together – the strange webs of their relationship.

'Do you?' He frowned at her, demanding that she finish the game, speak her line, admit to the one verity that prevented them from ever truly finishing – her uncertainty.

'I don't know,' she answered; she tried to say it in a neutral tone, but it came out hopeless.

The storm's darkness passed, and true darkness slipped in under cover of the final clouds. Stars pricked out above the rim of the volcano. The food in the bar was greasy – fried fish, beans, and a salad that she was afraid to eat (stains on the lettuce) – but eating steadied her, and she managed to start a conversation about their recent meals. Remember the weird Chinese place in Mérida, hot sauce in the Lobster Cantonese? Or what had passed for crepes at their hotel in Zihuatanejo? Things like that. The bartender hauled out a portable record player and put on an album of romantic ballads sung by a man with a sexy voice and a gaspy female chorus; the needle kept skipping, and finally, with an apologetic smile and a shrug, the bartender switched it off. It came to be seven-thirty, and they talked about Dowdy not showing, about catching the eight o'clock boat. Then there he was. Standing in the door next to a tiny, shrunken old man, who was leaning on a cane. He was deeply wrinkled, skin the color of weathered mahogany, wearing grungy white trousers and a gray blanket draped around his shoulders. All his vitality seemed to have collected in an astounding shock of thick white hair that – to Lisa's drunken eyes – looked like a white flame licking up from his skull.

It took the old man almost a minute to hobble the length of the room, and a considerable time thereafter to lower himself, wheezing and shaking, into a chair. Dowdy hauled up another chair beside him; he had washed the dye from his beard, and his hair was clean, free of feathers. His manner, too, had changed. He was no longer breezy, but subdued and serious, and even his grammar had improved.

'Now listen,' he said. 'I don't know what Murciélago will say to you, but he's a man who speaks his mind and sometimes he tells people things they don't like to hear. Just remember he bears you no ill will and don't be upset. All right?'

Lisa gave the old man a reassuring smile, not wanting him to think that they were going to laugh; but upon meeting his eyes all thought of reassuring him vanished. They were ordinary eyes. Dark; wet-looking under the lamplight. And yet they were compelling – like an animal's eyes, they radiated strangeness and pulled you in. They made the rest of his ruined face seem irrelevant. He muttered to Dowdy.

'He wants to know if you have any questions,' said Dowdy.

Richard was apparently as fascinated by the old man as was Lisa; she had expected him to be glib and sardonic, but instead he cleared his throat and said gravely, 'I'd like to hear about how the world's changing.'

Dowdy repeated the question in Cakchiquel, and Murciélago began to speak, staring at Richard, his voice a gravelly whisper. At last he made a slashing gesture, signaling that he was finished, and Dowdy turned to them. 'It's like this,' he said. 'The world is not one but many. Thousands upon thousands of worlds. Even those who do not have the power of clear sight can perceive this if they consider the myriad realities of the world they do see. It's easiest to imagine the thousands of worlds as different-colored lights all focused on a single point, having varying degrees of effectiveness as to how much part they play in determinin' the character of that point. What's happenin' now is that the strongest light – the one most responsible for determinin' this character – is startin' to fade and another is startin' to shine bright and dominate. When it has gained dominance, the old age will end and the new begin.'

Richard smirked, and Lisa realized that he had been putting the old man on. 'If that's the case,' he said snottily, 'then …'

Murciélago broke in with a burst of harsh, angry syllables.

'He doesn't care if you believe him,' said Dowdy. 'Only that you understand his words. Do you?'

'Yes.' Richard mulled it over. 'Ask him what the character of the new age will be.'

Again, the process of interpretation.

'It'll be the first age of magic,' said Dowdy. 'You see, all the old tales of wizards and great beasts and warriors and undyin' kings, they aren't fantasy or even fragments of a distant past. They're visions, the first unclear glimpses seen long ago of a future that's now dawnin'. This place, Lake Atitlán, is one of those where the dawn has come early, where the light of the new age shines the strongest and its forms are visible to those who can see.' The old man spoke again, and Dowdy arched an eyebrow. 'Hmm! He says that because he's tellin' you this, and for reasons not yet clear to him, you will be more a part of the new age than the old.'

Richard gave Lisa a nudge under the table, but she chose to ignore it. 'Why hasn't someone noticed this change?' he asked.

Dowdy translated and in a moment had a response. 'Murciélago says he has noticed it, and asks if you have not noticed it yourself. For instance, have you not noticed the increased interest in magic and other occult matters in your own land? And surely you must have noticed the breakdown in systems, economies, governments. This is due to the fact that the light that empowered them is fadin', not to any other cause. The change comes slowly. The dawn will take centuries to brighten into day, and then the sorrows of this age will be gone from the memories of all but those few who have the ability to draw upon the dawnin' power and live long in their mortal bodies. Most will die and be reborn. The change comes subtly, as does twilight change to dusk, an almost imperceptible merging of light into dark. It will be noticed and it will be recorded. Then, just as the last age, it will be forgotten.'

'I don't mean to be impertinent,' said Richard, giving Lisa another nudge, 'but Murciélago looks pretty frail. He can't have much of a role to play in all this.'

The old man rapped the floor with his cane for emphasis as he answered, and Dowdy's tone was peeved. 'Murciélago is involved in great struggles against enemies whose nature he's only beginnin' to discern. He has no time to waste with fools. But because you're not a total fool, because you need instruction, he will answer. Day by day his power grows, and at night the volcano is barely able to contain his force. Soon he will shed this frailty and flow between the forms of his spirit. He will answer no more of your questions.' Dowdy looked at Lisa. 'Do you have a question?'

Murciélago's stare burned into her, and she felt disoriented, as insubstantial as one of the gleams slipping across his eyes. 'I don't know,' she said. 'Yes. What does he think about us?'

'This is a good question,' said Dowdy after consulting with Murciélago, 'because it concerns self-knowledge, and all important answers relate to the self. I will not tell you what you are. You know that, and you have shame in the knowledge. What you will be is manifest, and soon you will know that. Therefore I will answer the question you have not asked, the one that most troubles you. You and the man will part and come together, part and come together. Many times. For though you are lovers, you are not true companions and you both must follow your own ways. I will help you in this. I will free the hooks that tear at you and give you back your natures. And when this is done, you and the man may share each other, may part and come together without sadness or weakness.'

Murciélago fumbled for something under his blanket, and Dowdy glanced back and forth between Richard and Lisa. 'He wants to make you a gift,' he said.

'What kind of gift?' asked Richard.

'A gift is not known by its name,' Dowdy reminded him. 'But it won't be a mystery for long.'

The old man muttered again and stretched out a trembling hand to Richard; in his palm were four black seeds.

'You must swallow them one at a time,' said Dowdy. 'And as you do, he will channel his power through them.'

Richard's face tightened with suspicion. 'It's some sort of drug, right? Take four, and I won't care what happens.'

Dowdy reverted to his ungrammatical self. 'Life is a drug, man. You think me and the ol' boy are gonna get you high and boost your traveler's checks. Shit! You ain't thinkin' clear.'

'Maybe that's exactly what you're going to do,' said Richard stonily. 'And I'm not falling for it.'

Lisa slipped her hand into his. 'They're not going to hurt us. Why don't you try it?'

'You believe this old fraud, don't you?' He disengaged his hand, looking betrayed. 'You believe what he said about us?'

'I'd like to believe it,' she said. 'It would be better than what we have, wouldn't it?'

The lamplight flickered, and a shadow veered across his face. Then the light steadied, and so it seemed did he. It was as if the orange glow were burning away eleven years of wrong-thinking, and the old unparanoid sure-of-himself Richard was shining through. Christ, she wanted to say, you're really in there!

'Aw, hell! He who steals my purse steals only forty cents on the dollar, right?' He plucked the seeds from Murciélago's hand, picked one up, and held it to his mouth. 'Anytime.'

Before letting Richard swallow the seeds, Murciélago sang for a while. The song made Lisa think of a comic fight in a movie, the guy carrying on a conversation in between ducking and throwing punches, packing his words into short, rushed phrases. Murciélago built it to a fierce rhythm, signaled Richard, and grunted each time a seed went down, putting – Lisa thought – some magical English on it.

'God!' said Richard afterward, eyes wide with mock awe. 'I had no idea! The colors, the infinite harmony! If only ...' He broke it off and blinked, as if suddenly waking to an unaccustomed thought.

Murciélago smiled and gave out with a growly humming noise that Lisa assumed was a sign of satisfaction. 'Where are mine?' she asked.

'It's different for you,' said Dowdy. 'He has to anoint you, touch you.'

At this juncture Richard would normally have cracked a joke about dirty old men, but he was gazing out the window at shadowy figures on the street. She asked if he were okay, and he patted her hand. 'Yeah, don't worry. I'm just thinking.'

Murciélago had pulled out a bottle of iodine-colored liquid and was dipping his fingers into it, wetting the tips. He began to sing again – a softer, less hurried song with the rhythm of fading echoes – and Dowdy had Lisa lean forward so the old man wouldn't have to strain to reach her. The song seemed to be all around her, turning her thoughts slow and drifty. Callused brown fingers trembled in front of her face; the calluses were split, and the splits crusted with grime. She shut her eyes. The fingers left wet, cool tracks on her skin, and she could feel the shape he was tracing. A mask. Widening her eyes, giving her a smile, drawing curlicues on her cheeks and forehead. She had the idea that he was tracing the conformation of her real face, doing what the lamplight had done for Richard. Then his fingers brushed her eyelids. There was a stinging sensation, and dazzles exploded behind her eyes.

'Keep 'em shut,' advised Dowdy. 'It'll pass.'

When at last she opened them, Dowdy was helping Murciélago to his feet. The old man nodded but did not smile at her as he had with Richard; from the thinned set of his mouth she took it that he was either measuring her or judging his work.

'That's all, folks!' said Dowdy, grinning. 'See? No dirty tricks, nothin' up his sleeve. Just good ol' newfangled stick-to-your-soul magic.' He waved his arms high like an evangelist. 'Can you feel it, brothers and sisters? Feel it wormin' its way through your bones?'

Richard mumbled affirmatively. He seemed lost in himself, studying the pattern of rips his thumb had scraped on the label of the beer bottle, and Lisa was beginning to feel a bit lost herself. 'Do we pay him anything?' she asked Dowdy; her voice sounded small and metallic, like a recorded message.

'There'll come a day when the answer's Yes,' said Dowdy. 'But not now.' The old man hobbled toward the door, Dowdy guiding him by the arm.

'Goodbye,' called Lisa, alarmed by their abrupt exit.

'Yeah,' said Dowdy over his shoulder, paying more attention to assisting Murciélago. 'See ya.'

They were mostly silent while waiting for the launch, limiting their conversation to asking how the other was doing and receiving distracted answers; and later, aboard the launch, the black water shining under the stars and the motor racketing, their silence deepened. They sat with their hips pressed together, and Lisa felt close to Richard; yet she also felt that the closeness wasn't important; or if it was, it was of memorial importance, a tribute to past closeness, because things were changing between them. That, too, she could feel. Old postures were being redefined, webs were tearing loose, shadowy corners of their souls were coming to light. She knew this was happening to Richard as well as to herself, and she wondered how she knew, whether it was her gift to know these things. But the first real inkling she had of her gift was when she noticed that the stars were shining different colors – red, yellow, blue, and white – and there were pale gassy shapes passing across them. Clouds, she realized. Very high clouds that she would not ordinarily have seen. The sight frightened her, but a calm presence inside her would not admit to fright; and this presence, she further realized, had been there all along. Just like the true colors of the stars. It was her fearful self that was relatively new, an obscuring factor, and it – like the clouds – was passing. She considered telling Richard, but decided that he would be busy deciphering his gift. She concentrated on her own, and as they walked from the pier to the hotel, she saw halos around leaves, gleams coursing along electrical wires, and opaque films shifting over people's faces.

They went straight up to their room and lay without talking in the dark. But the room wasn't dark for Lisa. Pointillistic fires bloomed and faded in midair, seams of molten light spread along the cracks in the wall, and once a vague human shape – she identified it as a ghostly man wearing robes – crossed from the door to the window and vanished. Every piece of furniture began to glow golden around the edges, brighter and brighter, until it seemed they each had a more ornate shape superimposed. There came to be so much light that it disconcerted her, and though she was unafraid, she wished she could have a moment's normalcy just to get her bearings. And her wish was granted. In a wink the room had reverted to dim bulky shadows and a rectangle of streetlight slanting onto the floor from the window. She sat bolt upright, astonished that it could be controlled with such ease. Richard pulled her back down beside him and asked, 'What is it?' She told him some of what she had seen, and he said, 'It sounds like hallucinations.'

'No, that's not how it feels,' she said. 'How about you?'

'I'm not hallucinating, anyway. I feel restless, penned in, and I keep thinking that I'm going somewhere. I mean, I have this sense of motion, of speed, and I can almost tell where I am and who's with me. I'm full of energy; it's like I'm sixteen again or something.' He paused. 'And I'm having these thoughts that ought to scare me but don't.'

'What, for instance?'

'For instance' – he laughed – 'and this really is the most important "for instance," I'll be thinking about us and I'll understand that what the old guy said about us parting is true, and I don't want to accept it. But I can't help accepting it. I know it's true, for the best. All that. And then I'll have that feeling of motion again. It's like I'm sensing the shape of an event or …' He shook his head, befuddled. 'Maybe they did drug us, Lisa. We sound like a couple of acidheads out of the sixties.'

'I don't think so,' she said; and then, after a silence, she asked, 'Do you want to make love?'

He trailed his fingers along the curve of her stomach. 'No offense, but I'm not sure I could concentrate on it just now.'

'All right. But …'

He rolled onto his side and pressed against her, his breath warm on her cheeks. 'You think we might not have another chance?'

Embarrassed, she turned her face into his chest. 'I'm just horny, is all.'

'God, Lisa. You pick the weirdest times to get aroused.'

'You've picked some pretty weird times yourself.'

'I've always been absolutely correct in my behavior toward you, madam,' he said in an English accent.

'Really? What about the time in Jim and Karen's bathroom?'

'I was drunk.'

'Well? I'm nervous now. You know how that affects me.'

'A common glandular condition, Fräulein.' German accent this time. 'Correctable by simple surgery.' He laughed and dropped the accent. 'I wonder what Karen and Jim would be doing in our shoes.'

For a while they told stories about what their various friends might do, and afterward they lay quietly, arms around each other. Richard's heart jolted against Lisa's breast, and she thought back to the first time they had been together this way. How protected she had felt, yet how fragile the strength of his heartbeat had made him seem. She'd had the idea that she could reach into his chest and touch his heart. And she could have. You had that much power over your lover; his heart was in your care, and at moments like this it was easy to believe that you would always be caring. But the moments failed you. They were peaks, and from them you slid into a mire where caring dissolved into mistrust and selfishness, where you saw that your feeling of being protected was illusory, and the moments were few and far between. Marriage sought to institutionalize those moments, by law, to butter them over a ridiculous number of years; but all it did was lessen their intensity and open you up to a new potential for failure. Everyone talked about 'good marriages,' ones that evolved into hallowed friendships, an emeritus passion of the spirit. Maybe they did exist. Maybe there were – as Murciélago had implied – true companions. But most of the old marrieds Lisa had known were simply exhausted, weary of struggling, and had reached an accommodation with their mates based upon mutual despair. If Murciélago was right, if the world was changing, possibly the condition of marriage would change. Lisa doubted it, though. Hearts would have to be changed as well, and not even magic could affect their basic nature. Like with seashells, you could put your ear to one and hear the sad truth of an ocean breaking on a deserted shore. They were always empty, always unfulfilled. *Deeds fill them*, said an almost-voice inside her head, and she almost knew whose voice it had been; she pushed the knowledge aside, wanting to hold on to the moment.

Somebody shrieked in the courtyard. Not unusual. Groups of people frequently hung around the courtyard at night, smoking dope and exchanging bits of travel lore; the previous night two French girls and an American boy had been fighting with water pistols, and the girls had shrieked whenever they were hit. But this time the shriek was followed by shouts in Spanish and, in broken English, a scream of pure terror, then silence. Richard sprang to his feet and cracked the door. Lisa moved up behind him. Another shout in Spanish – she recognized the word *doctor*. Richard put a finger to his lips and slipped out into the hall. Together they edged along the wall and peeked down into the courtyard. About a dozen guests were standing against the rear wall, some with their hands in the air; facing them, carrying automatic rifles, were three young men and a girl. Teenagers. Wearing jeans and polo shirts. A fourth man lay on the ground, his hands and head swathed in bandages. The guests were very pale – at this distance their eyes looked like raisins in uncooked dough – and a couple of the women were sobbing. One of the gunmen was wounded, a patch of blood staining his side; he was having to lean on the girl's shoulder, and his rifle barrel was wavering back and forth. With all the ferns sprouting around them, the pots of flowers hanging from the green stucco wall, the scene had an air of mythic significance – a chance meeting between good and evil in the Garden of Eden.

'Sssst!' A hiss behind Lisa's shoulder. It was the Guatemalan man who had watched her during dinner the night before; he had a machine pistol in one hand, and in the other he was flapping a leather card case. ID. He beckoned, and they moved after him down the hall. '*Policía!*' he whispered, displaying the ID; in the photograph he was younger, his mustache so black it appeared to have been painted on for a joke. His nervous eyes and baggy suit and five o'clock shadow reminded Lisa of 1940s movie heavies, the evil flunky out to kill George Sanders or Humphrey Bogart; but the way his breath whined through his nostrils, the oily smell of the gun, his radiation of callous stupidity, all that reduced her romantic impression. '*Malos!*' he said, pointing to the courtyard. '*Comunistas! Guerrillas!*' He patted the gun barrel.

'Okay,' said Richard, holding up both hands to show his neutrality, his noninvolvement. But as the man crept toward the courtyard, toward the balcony railing, Richard locked his hands together and brought them down on the back of the man's neck, then fell atop him, kneeing and pummeling him. Lisa was frozen by the attack, half-disbelieving that Richard was capable of such decisive action. He scrambled to his feet, breathing hard, and tossed the machine pistol down into the courtyard. '*Amigos!*' he shouted, and turned to Lisa, his mouth still open from the shout.

Their eyes met, and that stare was a divorce, an acknowledgment that something was happening to separate them, happening right now, and though they weren't exactly sure what, they were willing to accept the fact and allow it to happen. 'I couldn't let him shoot,' said Richard. 'I didn't have a choice.' He sounded amazed, as if he hadn't known until this moment why he had acted.

Lisa wanted to console him, to tell him he'd done the right thing, but her emotions were locked away, under restraint, and she sensed a gulf between them that nothing could bridge – all their intimate connections were withdrawing, receding. Hooks, Murciélago had called them.

One of the guerrillas, the girl, was sneaking up the stairs, gun at the ready. She was pretty but on the chubby side, with shiny wings of black hair falling over her shoulders. She motioned for them to move back and nudged the unconscious man with her toe. He moaned, his hand twitched. 'You?' she said, pointing at Richard and then to the man.

'He was going to shoot,' said Richard hollowly.

From the girl's blank expression Lisa could tell that she hadn't understood. She rummaged in the man's jacket, pulled out the ID case, and shouted in rapid-fire Spanish. '*Vámonos!*' she said to them, indicating that they should precede her down the stairs. As Lisa started down, there was a short burst of automatic fire from the hall; startled, she turned to see the girl lifting the barrel of her rifle from the man's head, a stippling of red droplets on the green stucco. The girl frowned and trained the rifle on her, and Lisa hurried after Richard, horrified. But before her emotional reaction could mature into fear, her vision began to erode.

Glowing white flickers were edging every figure in the room, with the exception of the bandaged man, and as they grew clearer, she realized that they were phantom human shapes; they were like the afterimages of movement you see on Benzedrine, yet sharper and slower to fade, and the movements were different from those of their originals – an arm flailing, a half-formed figure falling or running off. Each time one vanished another would take its place. She tried to banish them, to will them away, but was unsuccessful, and she found that watching them distracted her from thinking about the body upstairs.

The tallest of the guerrillas – a gangly kid with a skull face and huge dark eyes and a skimpy mustache – entered into conversation with the girl, and Richard dropped to his knees beside the bandaged man. Blood had seeped through the layers of wrapping, producing a grotesque striping around the man's head. The gangly kid scowled and prodded Richard with his rifle.

'I'm a medic,' Richard told him. '*Como un doctor*.' Gingerly he peeled back some layers of bandage and looked away, his face twisted in disgust. 'Jesus Christ!'

'The soldiers torture him.' The kid spat into the ferns. 'They think he is *guerrillero* because he's my cousin.'

'And is he?' Richard was probing for a pulse under the bandaged man's jaw.

'No.' The kid leaned over Richard's shoulder. 'He studies at San Carlos University. But because we have killed the soldiers, now he will have to fight.' Richard sighed, and the kid faltered. 'It is good you are here. We think a friend is here, a doctor. But he's gone.' He made a gesture toward the street. '*Pasado*.'

Richard stood and cleaned his fingers on his jeans. 'He's dead.'

One of the women who had been sobbing let out a wail, and the kid snapped his rifle into firing position and shouted, '*Cáyete, gringa!*' His face was stony, the vein in his temple throbbed. A balding, bearded man wearing an embroidered native shirt embraced the woman, muting her sobs, and glared fiercely at the kid; one of his afterimages raised a fist. The rest of the imprisoned guests were terrified, their Adam's apples working, eyes darting about; and the girl was arguing with the kid, pushing his rifle down. He kept shaking her off. Lisa felt detached from the tension, out of phase with existence, as if she were gazing down from a higher plane.

With what seemed foolhardy bravado, the bearded guy called out to Richard. 'Hey, you! The American! You with these people or somethin'?'

Richard had squatted beside the wounded guerrilla – a boy barely old enough to shave – and was probing his side. 'Or something,' he said without glancing up. The boy winced and gritted his teeth and leaned on his friend, a boy not much older.

'You gonna let 'em kill us?' said the bearded guy. 'That's what's happenin', y'know. The girl's sayin' to let us go, but the dude's tellin' her he wants to make a statement.' Panic seeped into his voice. 'Y'understand that, man? The dude's lookin' to waste us so he can make a statement.'

'Take it easy,' Richard got to his feet. 'The bullet needs to come out,' he said to the gangly kid. 'I ...'

The kid swiped at Richard's head with the rifle barrel, and Richard staggered back, clutching his brow; when he straightened up, Lisa saw blood welling from his hairline. 'Your friend's going to die,' he said stubbornly. 'The bullet needs to come out.' The kid jammed the muzzle of the rifle into Richard's throat, forcing him to tip back his head.

With a tremendous effort of will Lisa shook off the fog that had enveloped her. The afterimages vanished. 'He's trying to help you,' she said, going toward the kid. 'Don't you understand?' The girl pushed her back and aimed her rifle at Lisa's stomach. Looking into her eyes, Lisa had an intimation of the depth of her seriousness, the ferocity of her commitment. 'He's trying to help,' Lisa repeated. The girl studied her, and after a moment she called over her shoulder to the kid. Some of the hostility drained from the kid's face and was replaced by suspicion.

'Why?' the kid asked Richard. 'Why you help us?'

Richard seemed confused, and then he started to laugh; he wiped his forehead with the back of his hand, smearing the blood and sweat, and laughed some more. The kid was puzzled at first, but a few seconds later he smiled and nodded as if he and Richard were sharing a secret male joke. 'Okay,' he said. 'Okay. You help him. But here is danger. We go now.'

'Yeah,' said Richard, absorbing this. 'Yeah, okay.' He stepped over to Lisa and drew her into a smothering hug. She gripped his shoulders hard, and she thought her emotions were going to break free; but when he stepped back, appearing stunned, she sensed again that distance between them ... He put his arm around the wounded boy and helped him through the entrance; the others were already peering out the door. Lisa followed. The rows of tourist shops and restaurants looked unreal – a deserted stage set – and the colors seemed streaky and too bright. Parked under a streetlight near the entrance, gleaming toylike in the yellow glare, was a Suzuki mini-truck, the kind with a canvas-draped frame over the rear. Beyond it the road wound away into darkened hills. The girl vaulted the tailgate and hauled the wounded boy after her; the other two climbed into the cab and fired the engine. Only Richard was left standing on the cobblestones.

'*Dése prisa!*' The girl banged on the tailgate.

As Richard hesitated, there was a volley of shots. The noise sent Lisa scuttling away from the entrance toward the lake. Three policemen were behind a parked car on the opposite side of the street. More shots. The girl returned the fire, blowing out the windshield of the car, and they ducked out of sight. Another shot. Sparks and stone chips were kicked up near Richard's feet. Still he hesitated.

'Richard!' Lisa had intended the shout as a caution, but the name floated out of her, not desperate-sounding at all – it had the ring of an assurance. He dove for the tailgate. The girl helped him scramble inside, and the truck sped off over the first rise. The policemen ran after it, firing; then, like Keystone Cops, they put on the brakes and ran in the opposite direction.

Lisa had a flash feeling of anguish that almost instantly began to subside, as if it had been the freakish firing of a nerve. Dazedly, she moved farther away from the hotel entrance. A jeep stuffed with policemen came swerving past, but she hardly noticed. The world was dissolving in golden light, every source of light intensifying and crumbling the outlines of things. Streetlights burned like novas, sunbursts shone from windows, and even the cracks in the sidewalk glowed; misty shapes were fading into view, overlaying the familiar with tall peak-roofed houses and carved wagons and people dressed in robes. All rippling, illusory. It was as if a fantastic illustration were coming to life, and she was the only real-life character left in the story, a contemporary Alice with designer jeans and turquoise earrings, who had been set to wander through a golden fairy tale. She was entranced, and yet at the same time she resented the fact that the display was cheating her of the right to sadness. She needed to sort herself out, and she continued toward the lake, toward the pier where she and Richard had kissed. By the time she reached it, the lake itself had been transformed into a scintillating body of light, and out on the water the ghost of a sleek sailboat, its canvas belling, glided past for an instant and was gone.

She sat at the end of the pier, dangling her feet over the edge. The cool roughness of the planks was a comfort, a proof against the strangeness of the world ... or was it *worlds?* The forms of the new age. Was that what she saw? Weary of seeing it, she willed the light away and before she could register whether or not she had been successful, she shut her eyes and tried to think about Richard. And, as if thought were a vehicle for sight, she saw him. A ragged-edged patch of vision appeared against the darkness of her closed eyes, like a hole punched through black boards. He was sitting on the oil-smeared floor of the truck, cradling the wounded boy's head in his lap; the girl was bending over the boy, mopping his forehead, holding on to Richard's shoulder so the bouncing of the truck wouldn't throw her off-balance. Lisa felt a pang of jealousy, but she kept watching for a very long time. She didn't wonder how she saw them. It all meant something, and she knew that meaning would come clear.

When she opened her eyes, she found it had grown pitch-dark. She couldn't see her hand in front of her face, and she panicked, thinking she had gone blind; but accompanying the panic was a gradual brightening, and she realized that she must have willed away all light. Soon the world had returned to normal. Almost. Though the slopes of the volcanoes were unlighted – shadows bulking against the stars – above each of their cones blazed a nimbus of ruby glow, flickering with an inconstant rhythm. The glow above Murciélago's volcano was the brightest – at least it was for a few seconds. Then it faded, and in its place a fan of rippling white radiance sprayed from the cone, penetrating high into the dark. It was such an eerie sight, she panicked.

Christ, what was she doing just sitting here and watching pretty lights? And what was she going to do? Insecurity and isolation combined into an electricity that jolted her to her feet. Maybe there was an antidote for this, maybe the thing to do would be to go see Murciélago ... And she remembered Dowdy's story. How he'd been afraid and had gone to Murciélago, only to find that the old apprentice had taken up his own post, leaving a vacancy. She looked back at the other two volcanoes, still pulsing with their ruby glow. Dowdy and the mestizo? It had to be. The white light was Murciélago's vacancy sign. The longer she stared at it, the more certain knowledge became.

Stunned by the prospect of setting out on such an eccentric course, by the realization that everything she knew was dissolving in light or fleeing into darkness, she walked away from the pier, following the shoreline. She wanted to hold on to Richard, to sadness – her old familiar and their common woe – but with each step her mood brightened, and she couldn't even feel guilty about not being sad. Four or five hours would take her to the far side of the lake. A long walk, alone, in the dark, hallucinations lurking behind every bush. She could handle it, though. It would give her time to work at controlling her vision, to understand some of what she saw, and when she had climbed the volcano she'd find a rickety cabin back in under the lip, a place as quirky as Dowdy himself. She saw it the same way she had seen Richard and the girl. Tilting walls; ferns growing from the roof; a door made from the side of a packing crate, with the legend THIS END UP upside down. Tacked to the door was a piece of paper, probably Dowdy's note explaining the care and feeding of wizards. And inside, the thousandfold forms of his spirit compacted into a gnarled shape, a nugget of power (she experienced an upwelling of sadness, and then she felt that power surging through her, nourishing her own strength, making her aware of the thousands of bodies of light she was, all focused upon this moment in her flesh), there Murciélago would be waiting to teach her power's usage and her purpose in the world.

Oh God, Richard, goodbye.

A TRAVELER'S TALE

All this happened several years ago on the island of Guanoja Menor, most of it to a young American named Ray Milliken. I doubt you will have heard of him, not unless you have been blessed with an exceptional memory and chanced to read the sketchy article about his colony printed by one of the national tabloids; but in these parts his name remains something to conjure with.

'Who were dat Yankee,' a drunkard will say (the average Guanojan conversation incorporates at least one), 'de one who lease de Buryin' Ground and say he goin' to bring down de space duppies?'

'Dat were Ray Milliken,' will be the reply, and this invariably will initiate a round of stories revolving about the theme of Yankee foolishness, as if Ray's experiences were the central expression of such a history – which they well may be.

Most Americans one meets abroad seem to fall into types. I ascribe this to the fact that when we encounter a fellow countryman, we tend to exaggerate ourselves, to adopt categorizable modes of behavior, to advertise our classifiable eccentricities and political views, anything that may later prove a bone of contention, all so we may be more readily recognizable to the other. This tendency, I believe, bears upon our reputation for being people to whom time is a precious commodity; we do not want to waste a moment of our vacations or, as in the case of expatriates like myself, our retirements, by pursuing relationships based on a mistaken affinity. My type is of a grand tradition. Fifty-eight years old, with a paunch and a salt-and-pepper beard; retired from a government accounting job to this island off the coast of Honduras; once-divorced; now sharing my days with a daughter of the island, a twenty-year-old black girl named Elizabeth, whose cooking is indifferent but whose amatory performance never lacks enthusiasm. When I tally up these truths, I feel that my life has been triangulated by the works of Maugham, Green, and Conrad. The Ex-Civil Servant Gone To Seed In A Squalid Tropic. And I look forward to evolving into a further type, a gray eminence, the sort of degenerate emeritus figure called upon to settle disputes over some trifling point of island lore.

'Better now you ask ol' Franklin Winship 'bout dat,' they'll say. 'De mon been here since de big storm in 'seventy-eight.'

Ray's type, however, was of a more contemporary variety; he was one of those child-men who are to be found wandering the sunstruck ends of the earth, always seeming to be headed toward some rumored paradise, a beach said to be unspoiled, where they hope to achieve ... something, the realization of a half-formed ambition whose criteria of peace and purity are so high as to guarantee failure. Travelers, they call themselves, and in truth, travel is their only area of expertise. They know the cheapest restaurant in Belize City, how to sleep for free on Buttermilk Key, the best sandalmaker in Panajachel; they have languished in Mexican jails, contracted dysentery while hiking through the wilds of Olancho, and been run out of various towns for drug abuse or lack of funds. But despite their knowledge and experience, they are curiously empty young men, methodical and unexcitable, possessing personalities that have been carefully edited to give the least effrontery to the widest spectrum of the populace. As they enter their thirties – and this was Ray's age when I met him – they will often settle for long periods in a favorite spot, and societies of even younger travelers will accrete around them. During these periods a subtype may emerge – crypto-Charles Mansons who use their self-assurance to wield influence over the currencies of sex and drugs. But Ray was not of this mold. It seemed to me that his wanderings had robbed him of guile, of all predilection for power-tripping, and had left him a worldly innocent. He was of medium stature, tanned, with ragged sun-streaked hair and brown eyes set in a handsome but unremarkable face; he had the look of a castaway frat boy. Faint, fine lines radiated from the corners of his eyes, like scratches in sandstone. He usually dressed in shorts and a flour-sack shirt, one of several he owned that were decorated with a line drawing of a polar bear above the name of the mill and the words HARINA BLANCA.

'That's me,' he would say, pointing to the words and smiling. 'White bread.'

I first saw him in the town square of Meachem's Landing, sitting on a stone bench beneath the square's single tree – a blighted acacia – and tying trick knots for the amusement of a clutch of spidery black children. He grinned at me as I passed, and, surprised, being used to the hostile stares with which many young Americans generally favor their elders, I grinned back and stopped to watch. I had just arrived on the island and was snarled in red tape over the leasing of land, aggravated by dealing with a lawyer who insisted on practicing his broken English when explaining things, driven to distraction by the incompetent drunks who were building my house, transforming my neat blueprints into the reality of a Cubist nightmare. I welcomed Ray's companionship as a respite. Over a span of four months we met two or three times a week for drinks at the Salón de Carmín – a ramshackle bar collapsing on its pilings above the polluted shallows of the harbor. To avoid the noise and frequent brawls, we would sit out back on the walkway from which the proprietress tossed her slops.

We did not dig into each other's souls, Ray and I; we told stories. Mine described the vicissitudes of Washington life, while his were exotic accounts of chicleros and cursed Mayan jade; how he had sailed to Guayaquil on a rock star's yacht or paddled alone up the Rio de la Pasión to the unexcavated ruin of Yaxchilán; a meeting with guerrillas in Salvador. Quite simply, he was the finest storyteller I have ever known. A real spellbinder. Each of his stories had obviously been worked and reworked until the emotional valence of their events had been woven into clear, colorful prose; yet they maintained a casual edge, and when listening to him it was easy to believe that they had sprung full-blown from his imagination. They were, he told me, his stock-in-trade. Whenever times were lean, he would find a rich American and manage to weasel a few dollars by sharing his past.

Knowing he considered me rich, I glanced at him suspiciously; but he laughed and reminded me that he had bought the last two rounds.

Though he was always the protagonist of his stories, I realized that some of them must have been secondhand, otherwise he would have been a much older, much unhealthier man; but despite this I came to understand that secondhand or not, they *were* his, that they had become part of his substance in the way a poster glued to a wall eventually merges with the surface beneath through a process of the weather. In between the stories I learned that he had grown up in Sacramento and had briefly attended Cal Tech, majoring in astronomy; but thereafter the thread of his life story unraveled into a welter of anecdote. From various sources I heard that he had rented a shanty near Punta Palmetto, sharing it with a Danish girl named Rigmor and several others, and that the police had been nosing around in response to reports of nudity and drugs; yet I never impinged on this area of his life. We were drinking companions, nothing more, and only once did I catch a glimpse of the soul buried beneath his placid exterior.

We were sitting as usual with our feet propped on the walkway railing, taking shelter in the night from the discordant reggae band inside and gazing out at the heat lightning that flashed orange above the Honduran coast. Moths batted at the necklace of light bulbs strung over the door, and the black water was lacquered with reflection. On either side, rows of yellow-lit windows marked the shanties that followed the sweep of the harbor. We had been discussing women – in particular a local woman whose husband appeared to be more concerned with holding on to her than curbing her infidelities.

'Being cuckolded seems the official penalty for marriage down here,' I said. 'It's as if they're paying the man back for being fool enough to marry them.'

'Women are funny,' said Ray; he laughed, realizing the inadequacy of the cliché. 'They're into sacrifice,' he said. 'They'll break your heart and mean well by it.' He made a gesture of frustration, unable to express what he intended, and stared gloomily down at his hands.

I had never before seen such an intense expression on his face; it was clear that he was not talking about women in the abstract. 'Having trouble with Rigmor?' I asked.

'Rigmor?' He looked confused, then laughed again. 'No, that's just fun and games.' He went back to staring at his hands.

I was curious; I had a feeling that I had glimpsed beneath his surface, that the puzzle he presented – a bright young man wasting himself in endless wandering – might have a simple solution. I phrased my next words carefully, hoping to draw him out.

'I suppose most men have a woman in their past,' I said, 'one who failed to recognize the mutuality of a relationship.'

Ray glanced at me sharply, but made no comment.

'Sometimes,' I continued, 'we use those women as justifications for our success or failure, and I guess they do deserve partial credit or blame. After all, they do sink their claws in us ... but we let them.'

He opened his mouth, and I believe he was about to tell me a story, the one story of real moment in his life; but just then old Spurgeon James, drunk, clad in tattered shirt and shorts, the tangle of his once-white beard stained a motley color by nicotine and rum, staggered out of the bar and began to urinate into the shallows. 'Oh, mon!' he said. 'Dis night wild!' He reeled against the wall, half-turning, the arc of his urine glistening in the yellow light and splashing near Ray's feet. When he had finished, he tried to extort money from us by relating the story that had gained him notoriety the week before – he claimed to have seen flying saucers hanging over Flowers' Bay. Anxious to hear Ray's story, I thrust a *lempira* note at Spurgeon to get rid of him; but by the time he had gone back in, Ray had lost the impulse to talk about his past and was off instead on the subject of Spurgeon's UFOs.

'You don't believe him, do you?' I said. 'Once Spurgeon gets a load on, he's liable to see the Pope driving a dune buggy.'

'No,' said Ray. 'But I wish I could believe him. Back at Cal Tech I'd planned on joining one of the projects that were searching for extraterrestrial life.'

'Well then,' I said, fumbling out my wallet, 'you'd probably be interested to know that there's been a more reliable sighting on the island. That is, if you consider a pirate reliable. Henry Meachem saw a UFO back in the 1700s – 1793, I think.' I pulled out a folded square of paper and handed it to Ray. 'It's an excerpt from the old boy's journal. I had the clerk at the Historical Society run me off a Xerox. My youngest girl reads science fiction and I thought she might get a laugh out of it.'

Ray unfolded the paper and read the excerpt, which I reproduce below.

7 May 1793. I had just gone below to my Cabin after negotiating the Reef, when I heard divers Cries of astonishment and panic echoing down the

Companion-way. I return'd to the Fore-Deck and there found most of the Crew gather'd along the Port-Rail, many of them pointing to the Heavens. Almost directly overhead and at an unguessable Distance, I espi'd an Object of supernal red brilliance, round, no larger than a Ha'penny. The brightness of the Object was most curious, and perhaps brightness is not the proper Term to describe its Effect. While it was, indeed, bright, it was not sufficiently so to cause me to shield my Eyes; and yet whenever I attempt'd to direct my Gaze upon it, I experienc'd a sensation of Vertigo and so was forc'd to view it obliquely. I call'd for my Glass, but before it could be bro't there was a Windy Noise – yet not a whit more Wind – and the Object began to expand, all the while maintaining its circular Forme. Initially, I thought it to be falling towards us, as did the Crew, and several Men flung themselves into the Sea to escape immolation. However, I soon realis'd that it was merely growing larger, as tho' a Hole were being burned thro' the Sky to reveal the flamelash'd Sky of Hell behind. Suddenly a Beam of Light, so distinct as to appear a reddish-gold Wire strung between Sky and Sea, lanc'd down from the Thing and struck the Waters inside the Reef. There was no Splash, but a great hissing and venting of Steam, and after this had subsided, the Windy Noise also began to subside, and the fiery Circle above dwindled to a point and vanish'd. I consider'd putting forth a Long-Boat to discover what had fall'n, but I was loathe to waste the Southerly Wind. I mark'd the position of the Fall – a scant 3 miles from our Camp at Sandy Bay – and upon our Return there will be ample Opportunity to explore the Phenomenon ...

As I recall, Ray was impressed by the excerpt, saying that he had never read of a sighting quite like this one. Our conversation meandered over the topics of space colonies, quasars, and UFO nuts – whom he deprecated as having given extraterrestrial research a bad name – and though I tried to resurrect the topic of women, I never succeeded.

At the time I was frantically busy with supervising the building of my house, maneuvering along the path of bribery and collusion that would lead to my obtaining final residence papers, and I took for granted these meetings at the Salón de Carmín. If I had been asked my opinion of Ray in those days, I would have said that he was a pleasant-enough sort but rather shallow. I never considered him my friend; in fact, I looked on our relationship as being free from the responsibilities of friendship, as a safe harbor from the storms of social convention – new friends, new neighbors, new woman – that were blowing around me. And so, when he finally left the island after four months of such conversations, I was surprised to find that I missed him.

Islands are places of mystery. Washed by the greater mysteries of wind and sea, swept over by tides of human event, they accumulate eerie magnetisms that attract the lawless, the eccentric, and – it is said – the supernatural; they shelter oddments of civilization that evolve into involute societies, and their histories are less likely to reflect orderly patterns of culture than mosaics of bizarre circumstance. Guanoja's embodiment of the mystery had fascinated me from the beginning. It had originally been home to Caribe Indians, who had moved on when Henry Meachem's crews and their slaves established their colonies – their black descendants still spoke an English dotted with eighteenth- and nineteenth-century colloquialisms. Rum-running, gun-smuggling, and revolution had all had their moment in the island's tradition; but the largest part of this tradition involved the spirit world. Duppies (a word used to cover a variety of unusual manifestations, but generally referring to ghosts, both human and animal); the mystical rumors associated with the smoking of black coral; and then there was the idea that some of the spirits dwelling there were not the shades of dead men and women, but ancient and magical creatures, demigods left over from the days of the Caribe. John Anderson McCrae, the patriarch of the island's storytellers, once put it to me this way:

'Dis island may look like a chewed-up bone some dog have dropped in a puddle, and de soil may be no good for plantains, no good for corn. But when it come to de breedin' of spirits, dere ain't no soil better.'

It was, as John Anderson McCrae pointed out, no tropic paradise. Though the barrier reef was lovely and nourished a half-dozen diving resorts, the interior consisted of low scrub-thatched hills and much of the coast was given over to mangrove. A dirt road ran partway around the island, connecting the shantytowns of Meachem's Landing, Spanish Harbor, and West End, and a second road crossed from Meachem's Landing to Sandy Bay on the northern coast – a curving stretch of beach that at one moment seemed beautiful, and the next abysmally ugly. That was the charm of the island, that you could be walking along a filthy beach, slapping at flies, stepping carefully to avoid dead fish and pig droppings; and then, as if a different filter had slid across the sun, you suddenly noticed the hummingbirds flitting in the sea grape, the hammocks of coco palms, the reef water glowing in bands of jade and turquoise and aquamarine. Sprinkled among the palms at Sandy Bay were a few dozen shanties set on pilings, their tin roofs scabbed by rust; jetties with gap-boarded outhouses at their seaward ends extended out over the shallows, looking like charcoal sketches by Picasso. It had no special point of attraction, but because Elizabeth's family lived nearby, I had built my house – three rooms of concrete block and a wooden porch – about a hundred yards from the terminus of the cross-island road.

A half-mile down the beach stood The Chicken Shack, and its presence had been a further inducement to build in Sandy Bay. Not that the food or decor was in the least appealing; the sole item on the menu was fried chicken, mostly bone and gristle, and the shanty was hardly larger than a chicken coop itself, containing three picnic tables and a kitchen. Mounted opposite each other on the walls was a pair of plates upon which a transient artist had painted crude likenesses of the proprietor, John James, and his wife; and these two black faces, their smiles so poorly rendered as to appear ferocious, always seemed to me to be locked in a magical duel, one whose stray energies caused the food to be overdone. If your taste was for a good meal, you would have done better elsewhere; but if you had an appetite for gossip, The Chicken Shack was unsurpassed in this regard; and it was there one night, after a hiatus of almost two years, that I next had word of Ray Milliken.

I had been out of circulation for a couple of weeks, repairing damage done to my house by the last norther, and since Elizabeth was grouchy with her monthlies, I decided to waste a few hours watching Hatfield Brooks tell fortunes at the Shack. He did so each Wednesday without fail. On arriving, I found him sitting at the table nearest the door – a thin young man who affected natty dreads but none of the hostility usually attendant to the hairstyle. Compared to most of the islanders, he was a saintly sort. Hardworking; charitable; a nondrinker; faithful to his wife. In front of him was what looked to be a bowling ball of marbled red plastic, but was actually a Zodiac Ball – a child's toy containing a second ball inside, and between the inner and outer shells, a film of water. There was a small window at the top, and if you shook the ball, either the word *Yes* or *No* would appear in the window, answering your question. Sitting beside Hatfield, scrunched into the corner, was his cousin Jimmy Mullins, a diminutive wiry man of thirty-five. He had fierce black eyes that glittered under the harsh light; the skin around them was puckered as if they had been surgically removed and later reembedded. He was shirtless, his genitals partly exposed by a hole in his shorts. John James, portly and white-haired, waved to me from behind the counter, and Hatfield asked, 'How de night goin', Mr Winship?'

'So-so,' I replied, and ordered a bottle of Superior from John. 'Not much business,' I remarked to Hatfield, pressing the cold bottle against my forehead.

'Oh, dere's a trickle now and den,' he said.

All this time Mullins had said not a word. He was apparently angry at something, glowering at Hatfield, shifting uncomfortably on the bench, the tip of his tongue darting in and out.

'Been hunting lately?' I asked him, taking a seat at the table by the counter.

I could tell he did not want to answer, to shift his focus from whatever had upset him; but he was a wheedler, a borrower, and he did not want to offend a potential source of small loans. In any case, hunting was his passion. He did his hunting by night, hypnotizing the island deer with beams from his flashlight; nonetheless he considered himself a great sportsman, and not even his bad mood could prevent him from boasting.

'Shot me a nice little buck Friday mornin',' he mumbled; and then, becoming animated, he said, 'De minute I see he eye, podner, I know he got to crumble.'

There was a clatter on the stairs, and a teenage girl wearing a man's undershirt and a print skirt pushed in through the door. Junie Elkins. She had been causing the gossip mills to run overtime due to a romance she was having with a boy from Spanish Harbor, something of which her parents disapproved. She exchanged greetings, handed a coin to Hatfield, and sat across from him. Then she looked back at me, embarrassed. I pretended to be reading the label of my beer bottle.

'What you after knowin', darlin'?' asked Hatfield.

Junie leaned over the table and whispered. Hatfield nodded, made a series of mystic passes, shook the ball, and Junie peered intently at the window in its top.

'Dere,' said Hatfield. 'Everything goin' to work out in de end.'

Other Americans have used Hatfield's method of fortune-telling to exemplify the islanders' gullibility and ignorance, and even Hatfield would admit to an element of hoax. He did not think he had power over the ball; he had worked off-island on the steamship lines and had gained a measure of sophistication. Still he credited the ball with having some magical potential. 'De thing made to tell fortunes even if it just a toy,' he said to me once. He did not deny that it gave wrong answers, but suggested these might be blamed on changing conditions and imperfect manufacture. The way he explained it was so sweetly reasonable that I almost believed him; and I did believe that if the ball was going to work anywhere, it would be on this island, a place where the rudimentary underpinnings of culture there were still in evidence, where simpler laws obtained.

After Junie had gone, Mullins' hostility again dominated the room and we sat in silence. John set about cleaning the kitchen, and the clatter of dishes accentuated the tension. Suddenly Mullins brought his fist down on the table.

'Damn it, mon!' he said to Hatfield. 'Gimme my money!'

'Ain't your money,' said Hatfield gently.

'De mon has got to pay *me* for *my* land!'

'Ain't your land.'

'I got testimony dat it's mine!' Again Mullins pounded the table.

John moved up to the counter. 'Dere's goin' to be no riot in dis place tonight,' he said sternly.

Land disputes – as this appeared to be – were common on the island and often led to duels with conch shells or machetes. The pirates had not troubled with legal documents, and after taking over the island, the Hondurans had managed to swindle the best of the land from the blacks; though the old families had retained much of the acreage in the vicinity of Sandy Bay. But, since most of the blacks were at least marginally related, matters of ownership proved cloudy.

'What's the problem?' I asked.

Hatfield shrugged, and Mullins refused to answer; anger seemed visible above his head like heat ripples rising from a tin roof.

'Some damn fool have leased de Buryin' Ground,' said John. 'Now dese two feudin''

'Who'd want that pesthole?'

'A true damn fool, dat's who,' said John. 'Ray Milliken.'

I was startled to hear Ray's name – I had not expected to hear it again – and also by the fact that he or anyone would spend good money on the Burying Ground. It was a large acreage three miles west of Sandy Bar near Punta Palmetto, mostly mangrove swamp, and notable for its population of snakes and insects.

'It ain't de Garden of Eden, dat's true,' said Hatfield. 'I been over de other day watchin' dem clear stumps, and every time de blade dig down it churn up three or four snakes. *Coralitos*, yellowjaws.'

'Snakes don't bother dis negro,' said Mullins pompously.

His referral to himself as 'dis negro' was a sure sign that he was drunk, and I realized now that he had scrunched into the corner to preserve his balance. His gestures were sluggish, and his eyes were bloodshot and rolling.

'Dat's right,' he went on. 'Everybody know dat if de yellowjaw bite, den you just bites de pizen back in he neck.'

John made a noise of disgust.

'What's Milliken want the place for?' I asked.

'He goin' to start up a town,' said Hatfield. ' 'Least dat's what he hopin'. De lawyer say we best hold up de paperwork 'til we find out what de government think 'bout de idea.'

'De fools dat goin' to live in de town already on de island,' said John. 'Dey stayin' over in Meachem's Landin'. Must be forty or fifty of dem. Dey go 'round smilin' all de time, sayin', "Ain't dis nice," and "Ain't dat pretty." Dey of a cult or somethin'.'

'All I know,' said Hatfield, 'is dat de mon come to me and say, "Hatfield, I got three thousand *lemps*, fifteen hundred dollars gold, if you give me ninety-nine years on de Buryin' Ground." And I say, "What for you want dat piece of perdition? My cousin Arlie he lease you a nice section of beachfront." And den he tell me 'bout how de Caribe live dere 'cause dat's where dey get together with de space duppies …'

'Aliens,' said John disparagingly.

'Correct! Aliens.' Hatfield stroked the Zodiac Ball. 'He say de aliens talk to de Caribe 'cause de Caribe's lives is upful and just naturally 'tracts de aliens. I tell him, "Mon, de Caribe fierce! Dey warriors!" And he say, "Maybe so, but dey must have been doin' somethin' right or de aliens won't be comin' 'round." And den he tell me dat dey plan to live like de Caribe and bring de aliens back to Guanoja.'

'Gimme a Superior, John,' said Mullins bossily.

'You got de money?' asked John, his arms folded, knowing the answer.

'No, I ain't got de money!' shouted Mullins. 'Dis boog clot got my money!' He threw himself at Hatfield and tried to wrestle him to the floor; but Hatfield, being younger, stronger, and sober, caught his wrists and shoved him back into the corner. Mullins' head struck the wall with a *thwack*, and he grabbed the injured area with both hands.

'Look,' I said. 'Even if the government permits the town, which isn't likely, do you really believe a town can survive on the Burying Ground? Hell, they'll be straggling back to Meachem's Landing before the end of the first night.'

'Dat's de gospel,' said John, who had come out from back of the counter to prevent further riot.

'Has any money changed hands?' I asked.

'He give me two hundred *lemps* as security,' said Hatfield. 'But I 'spect he want dat back if de government disallow de town.'

'Well,' I said, 'if there's no town, there's no argument. Why not ask the ball if there's going to be a town on the Burying Ground?'

'Sound reasonable to me,' said John; he gave the ball no credence, but was willing to suspend disbelief in order to make peace.

'Lemme do it!' Mullins snatched the ball up, staring crosseyed into the red plastic. 'Is dere goin' to be a town on de Buryin' Ground?' he asked solemnly; then he turned it over twice and set it down. I stood and leaned forward to see the little window.

No, it read.

'Let's have beers all around,' I said to John. 'And a soda for Hatfield. We'll toast the solution of a problem.'

But the problem was not solved – it was only in the first stages of inception – and though the Zodiac Ball's answer eventually proved accurate, we had not asked it the right question.

This was in October, a time for every sort of inclement weather, and it rained steadily over the next few days. Fog banks moved in, transforming the sea into a mystic gray dimension, muffling the crash of waves on the reef so they sounded like bones being crunched in an enormous mouth. Not good weather for visiting the Burying Ground. But finally a sunny day dawned, and I set out to find Ray Milliken. I must admit I had been hurt by his lack of interest in renewing our acquaintance, but I had too many questions to let this stop me from hunting him up. Something about a colony built to attract aliens struck me as sinister rather than foolhardy – this being how it struck most people. I could not conceive of a person like Ray falling prey to such a crackpot notion; nor could I support the idea, one broached by Elizabeth, that he was involved in a swindle. She had heard that he had sold memberships in the colony and raised upwards of a hundred thousand dollars. The report was correct, but I doubt that Ray's original motives have much importance.

There was no road inland, only a snake-infested track, and so I borrowed a neighbor's dory and rowed along inside the reef. The tide was low, and iron-black coral heads lifted from the sea like the crenellated parapets of a drowned castle; beyond, the water was banded with sun-spattered streaks of slate and lavender. I could not help being nervous. People steered clear of the Burying Ground – it was rumored to harbor duppies ... but then so was every other part of the island, and I suspect the actual reason for its desertion was that it had no worth to anyone, except perhaps to a herpetologist. The name of the place had come down from the Caribe; this was a puzzling fact, since all their grave sites were located high in the hills. Pottery and tools had been found in the area, but no solid evidence of burials. Two graves did exist, those belonging to Ezekiel Brooks, the son of William, a mate on Henry Meachem's privateer, and to Ezekiel's son Carl. They had lived most of their lives on the land as hermits, and it was their solitary endurance that had ratified the Brooks family's claim to ownership.

On arriving, I tied the dory to a mangrove root and immediately became lost in a stand of scrub palmetto. I had sweated off my repellent, and mosquitoes swarmed over me; I stepped cautiously, probing the weeds with my machete to stir up any lurking snakes. After a short walk I came to a clearing about fifty yards square; it had been scraped down to the raw dirt. On the far side stood a bulldozer, and next to it was a thatched shelter beneath which a group of men were sitting. The primary colors and simple shapes – yellow bulldozer, red dirt, dark green walls of brush – made the clearing look like a test for motor skills that might be given to a gigantic child. As I crossed to the shelter, one of the men jumped up and walked toward me. It was Ray. He was shirtless, wearing boots and faded jeans, and a rosy sheen of new sunburn overlaid his tan.

'Frank,' he said, pumping my hand.

I was taken aback by the religious affirmation in his voice – it was as if my name were something he had long treasured.

'I was planning to drop around in a few days,' he said. 'After we got set up. How are you?'

'Old and tormented,' I said, slapping at a mosquito.

'Here.' He gestured at the shelter. 'Let's get into the shade.'

'How are *you*?' I asked as we walked.

'Great, Frank,' he replied. 'Really great.' His smile seemed the product of an absolute knowledge that things, indeed, were really great.

He introduced me to the others; I cannot recall their names, a typical sampling of Jims and Daves and Toms. They all had Ray's Krishna-conscious smile, his ultrasincerity, and they delighted in sharing with me their lunch of banana fritters and coconut. 'Isn't this food beautiful?' said one. There was so much beatitude around me that I, grumpy from the heat and mosquitoes, felt like a heathen among them. Ray kept staring at me, smiling, and this was the main cause of my discomfort. I had the impression that something was shining too brightly behind his eyes, a kind of manic brilliance flaring in him the way an old light bulb flares just before it goes dark for good. He began to tell me of the improvements they were planning – wells, electronic mosquito traps, generators, schools with computers, a medical clinic for the islanders, on and on. His friends chimed in with additions to the list, and I had the feeling that I was listening to a well-rehearsed litany.

'I thought you were going to live off the land like the Caribe,' I said.

'Oh, no,' said Ray. 'There are some things they did that we're going to do, but we'll do them better.'

'Suppose the government denies your permits?'

I was targeted by a congregation of imperturbable smiles. 'They came through two days ago,' said Ray. 'We're going to call the colony Port Ezekiel.'

After lunch, Ray led me through the brush to a smaller clearing where half-a-dozen shelters were erected; hammocks were strung beneath each one. His had a fringe of snakeskins tacked to the roofpoles, at least thirty of them; they were crusted with flies, shifting horribly in the breeze. They were mostly yellowjaws – the local name for the fer-de-lance – and he said they killed ten or twelve a day. He sat cross-legged on the ground and invited me to take the hammock.

'Want to hear what I've been up to?' he asked.

'I've heard some of it.'

'I bet you have.' He laughed. 'They think we're looney.' He started as the bulldozer roared to life in the clearing behind us. 'Do you remember showing me old Meachem's journal?'

'Yes.'

'In a way you're responsible for all this.' He waved at the dirt and the shelters. 'That was my first real clue.' He clasped his hands between his legs. 'When I left here, I went back to the States. To school. I guess I was tired of traveling, or maybe I realized what a waste of space I'd been. I took up astronomy again. I wasn't very interested in it, but I wasn't more interested in anything else. Then one day I was going over a star chart, and I noticed something amazing. You see, while I was here I'd gotten into the Caribe culture. I used to wander around the Burying Ground looking for pottery. Found some pretty good pieces. And I'd hike up into the hills and make maps of the villages, where they'd stationed their lookouts and set their signal fires. I still had those maps, and what I'd noticed was that the pattern of the Caribe signal fires corresponded exactly to the constellation Cassiopeia. It was incredible! The size of the fires even corresponded to the magnitudes of the specific stars. I dropped out of school and headed back to the island.' He gave me an apologetic look. 'I tried to see you, but you were on the mainland.'

'That must have been when Elizabeth's old boyfriend was giving us some trouble,' I said. 'We had to lie low for a while.'

'I guess so.' Ray reached for a pack that was propped against the wall and extracted a sheaf of 8' by 11" photographs; they appeared to consist chiefly of smudges and crooked lines. 'I began digging through the old sites, especially here – this is the only place I found pottery with these particular designs ...'

From this point on I had difficulty keeping a straight face. Have you ever had a friend tell you something unbelievable, something they believed in so strongly that for you to discredit it would cause them pain? Perhaps it was a story about a transcendent drug experience or their conversion to Christianity. And did they stare at you earnestly as they spoke, watching your reactions? I mumbled affirmatively and nodded and avoided Ray's eyes. Compared to Ray's thesis, Erich von Däniken's ravings were a model of academic discipline. From the coincidental pattern of the signal fires, the incident of Meachem's UFO and some drunken tales he had solicited, from these smudges and lines that – if you exerted your imagination – bore a vague resemblance to bipeds wearing fishbowls on their heads, Ray had concocted an intricate scenario of alien visitation. It was essentially the same story as von Däniken's – the ancient star-seeding race. But where Ray's account differed was in his insistence that the aliens had had a special relationship with the Caribe, that the Caribe could call them down by lighting their fires. The landing Meachem had witnessed had been one of the last, because with the arrival of the English the Caribe had gradually retreated from the island, and the aliens no longer had a reason for visiting. Ray meant to lure them back by means of a laser display that would cast a brighter image of Cassiopeia than the Caribe could have managed; and when the aliens returned, he would entreat them to save our foundering civilization.

He had sold the idea of the colony by organizing a society to study the possibility of extraterrestrial life; he had presented slides and lectured on the Guanojan Outer Space Connection. I did not doubt his ability to make such a presentation, but I was amazed that educated people had swallowed it. He told me that his group included a doctor, an engineer, and sundry Ph.D.s, and that they all had some college background. And yet perhaps it was not so amazing. Even today there must be in America, as there were when I left it, a great many aimless and exhausted people like Ray and his friends, people damaged by some powerful trouble in their past and searching for an acceptable madness.

When Ray had finished, he looked at me soberly and said, 'You think we're nuts, don't you?'

'No,' I said; but I did not meet his eyes.

'We're not,' he said.

'It's not important.' I tried to pass it off as a joke. 'Not down here, anyway.'

'It's not just the evidence that convinced me,' he said. 'I knew it the first time I came to the Burying Ground. I could feel it.'

'Do you remember what else we talked about the night I showed you Meachem's journal?' I am not sure why I wanted to challenge him; perhaps it was simply curiosity, a desire to know how fragile his calm mask really was.

'No,' he said, and smiled. 'We talked about a lot of things.'

'We were talking about women, and then Spurgeon James interrupted us. But I think you were on the verge of telling me about a woman who had hurt you. Badly. Is all that behind you now?'

His smile dissolved, and the expression that flared briefly in its place was terrible to see – grieving, and baffled by the grief. This time it was *his* eyes that drifted away from mine. 'You're wrong about me, Frank,' he said. 'Port Ezekiel is going to be something very special.'

Shortly thereafter I made my excuses, and he walked me down to the dory. I invited him to visit me and have a meal, but I knew he would not come. I had threatened his beliefs, the beliefs he thought would shore him up, save him, and there was now a tangible barrier between us.

'Come back anytime,' he called as I rowed away.

He stood watching me, not moving at all, an insignificant figure being merged by distance into the dark green gnarl of the mangrove; even when I could barely see him, he continued to stand there, as ritually attendant as his mythical Caribe hosts might have been while watching the departure of their alien guests.

Over five weeks passed before I again gave much thought to Ray and Port Ezekiel. (Port Ezekiel! That name as much as anything had persuaded me of Ray's insanity, smacking as it did of Biblical smugness, a common shelter for the deluded.) This was a studied lack of concern on my part. I felt he was lost and wanted no involvement with his tragedy. And besides, though the colony remained newsworthy, other events came to supersede it. The shrimp fleet struck against its parent American company, and riots broke out in the streets of Spanish Harbor. The old talk of independence was revived in the bars – idle talk, but it stirred the coals of anti-Americanism. Normally smiling faces frowned at me, the prices went up when I shopped in town, and once a child yelled at me, 'Get off de island!' Small things, but they shook me. And since the establishment of Port Ezekiel had been prelude to these events, I could not help feeling that Ray was somehow to blame for this peculiarly American darkness now shadowing my home.

Despite my attempt to ignore Ray's presence, I did have news of him. I heard that he had paid Hatfield in full and that Jimmy Mullins was on the warpath. Three thousand *lempira* must have seemed a king's ransom to him; he lived in a tiny shanty with his wife Hettie and two underfed children, and he had not worked for over a year. I also heard that the shipments of modern conveniences intended for Port Ezekiel had been waylaid by customs – someone overlooked in the chain of bribery, no doubt – and that the colonists had moved into the Burying Ground and were living in brushwood shacks. And then, over a span of a couple of weeks, I learned that they were deserting the colony. Groups of them turned up daily in Meachem's Landing, complaining that Ray had misled them. Two came to our door one evening, a young man and woman, both delirious, sick with dysentery and covered with infected mosquito bites. They were too wasted to tell us much, but after we had bedded them down I asked the woman what was happening at the colony.

'It was awful,' she said, twisting her hand in the blanket and shivering. 'Bugs and snakes … and …' Her eyes squeezed shut. 'He just sits there with the snakes.'

'You mean Ray?'

'I don't know,' she said, her voice cracking into hysteria. 'I don't know.'

Then, one night as Elizabeth and I were sitting on the porch, I saw a flashlight beam weaving toward us along the beach. By the way the light wavered, swooping up to illuminate the palm crowns, down to shine upon a stoved-in dory, I could tell the bearer was very drunk. Elizabeth leaned forward, peering into the dark. 'Oh, Lord,' she said, holding her bathrobe closed. 'It dat damn Jimmy Mullins.' She rose and went into the house, pausing at the door to add, 'If he after foolin' with me, you tell him I'm goin' to speak with my uncle 'bout him.'

Mullins stopped at the margin of the porch light to urinate, then he staggered up onto the steps; he dropped his flashlight, and it rolled over beside my machete, which was propped by the door. He was wearing his town clothes – a white rayon shirt with the silk-screened photo of a soccer star on the back, and brown slacks spattered with urine. Threads of saliva hung from his chin.

'Mr Frank, sir,' he said with great effort. His eyes rolled up, and for a moment I thought he was going to pass out; but he pulled himself together, shook his head to clear the fog, and said, 'De mon have got to pay me.'

I wanted no part of his feud with Hatfield. 'Why don't I give you a ride home?' I said. 'Hettie'll be worried.'

Blearily, he focused on me, clinging to a support post. 'Dat boog Yankee clot have cheated me,' he said. 'You talk to him, Mr Frank. You tell him he got to pay.'

'Ray Milliken? He doesn't owe you anything.'

'Somebody owe me!' Mullins flailed his arm at the night. 'And I ain't got de force to war with Hatfield.' He adopted a clownish expression of sadness. 'I born in de summer and never get no bigger den what you seein' now.'

So, sucked along by the feeble tide of anti-Americanism, Mullins had given up on Hatfield and shifted his aim to a more vulnerable target. I told him that Ray was crazy and would likely not respond to either threats or logic; but Mullins insisted that Ray should have checked Hatfield's claim before paying him. Finally I agreed to speak to Ray on his behalf and – somewhat mollified – he grew silent. He clung to the post, pouting; I settled back in my chair. It was a beautiful night, the phosphorescent manes of the breakers tossing high above the reef, and I wished he would leave us alone to the view.

'Damn boog Yankee!' He reeled away from the post and careened against the doorframe; his hand fell upon my machete. Before I could react, he picked it up and slashed at the air. 'I cut dat bastard down to de deck!' he shouted, glaring at me.

The moment seemed endless, as if the flow of time had snagged on the point of the machete. Drunk, he might do anything. I felt weak and helpless, my stomach knotted by a chill. The blade looked to have the same drunken glitter as his eyes. God knows what might have happened, but at that moment Elizabeth – her robe belling open, eyes gleaming crazily – sneaked up behind him and smacked him on the neck with an ax handle. Her first blow sent him tottering forward, the machete still raised in a parody of attack; and the second drove him off the porch to sprawl facedown in the sand.

Later, after John James and Hettie had dragged Mullins home, as Elizabeth and I lay in bed, I confessed that I had been too afraid to move during the confrontation. 'Don't vex yourself, Frank,' she said. 'Dere's enough trouble on de island dat sooner or later you be takin' care of some of mine.' And after we had made love, she curled against me, tucked under my arm, and told me of a dream that had frightened her the previous night. I knew what she was doing – nothing about her was mysterious – and yet, as with every woman I have known, I could not escape the feeling that a stranger lay beside me, someone whose soul had been molded by a stronger gravity and under a hotter star.

I spent the next morning patching things up with Mullins, making him a gift of vegetable seeds and listening to his complaints, and I did not leave for the Burying Ground until midafternoon. It had rained earlier, and gray clouds were still passing overhead, hazy fans of sunlight breaking through now and again. The chop of the water pulled against me, and it was getting on toward sunset by the time I arrived – out on the horizon the sea and sky were blending in lines of blackish squalls. I hurried through the brush, intending to convey my warning as quickly as possible and be home before the winds; but when I reached the first clearing, I stopped short.

The thatch and poles of the brushwood huts were strewn over the dirt, torn apart, mixed in with charred tin cans, food wrappers, the craters of old cooking fires, broken tools, mildewed paperbacks, and dozens of conch shells, each with their whorled tops sliced off – that must have been a staple of their diet. I called Ray's name, and the only answer was an intensification in the buzzing of the flies. It was like the aftermath of a measly war, stinking and silent. I picked my way across the litter to the second clearing and again was brought up short. An identical mess carpeted the dirt and Ray's shelter remained intact, the fringe of rotting snakeskins still hanging from the roofpoles – but that was not what had drawn my attention.

A trench had been dug in front of the shelter and covered with a sheet of wire mesh; large rocks held the wire in place. Within the trench were forty or fifty snakes. *Coralitos*, yellowjaws, Tom Goffs, cottonmouths. Their slithering, their noses scraping against the wire as they tried to escape, created a sibilance that tuned my nerves a notch higher. As I stepped over the trench and into the shelter, several of them struck at me; patches of the mesh glistened with their venom. Ray's hammock was balled up in a corner, and the ground over which it had swung had been excavated; the hole was nearly full of murky water – groundwater by the briny smell. I poked a stick into it and encountered something hard at a depth of about three feet. A boulder, probably. Aside from Ray's pack, the only other sign of habitation was a circular area of dirt that had been patted smooth; dozens of bits of oyster shell were scattered across it, all worked into geometric shapes – stars, hexagons, squares, and so forth. A primitive gameboard. I did not know what exactly to make of these things, but I knew they were the trappings of madness. There was an air of savagery about them, of a mind as tattered as its surroundings, shriveled to the simplest of considerations; and I did not believe that the man who lived here would understand any warning I might convey. Suddenly afraid, I turned to leave and was given such a shock that I nearly fell back into the water-filled pit.

Ray was standing an arm's length away, watching me. His hair was ragged, shoulder-length, and bound by a cottonmouth-skin band; his shorts were holed and filth-encrusted. The dirt smeared on his cheeks and forehead made his eyes appear round and staring. Mosquito bites speckled his chest – though not as many as had afflicted the colonists I had treated. In his right hand he carried a long stick with a twine noose at one end, and in his left hand was a burlap sack whose bottom humped and writhed.

'Ray,' I said, sidling away from him.

I expected a croak or a scream of rage for an answer, but when he spoke it was in his usual voice. 'I'm glad you're here,' he said. He dropped the sack – it was tied at the top – beside the trench and leaned his stick against the wall of the shelter.

Still afraid, but encouraged by the normalcy of his actions, I said, 'What's going on here?'

He gave me an appraising stare. 'You better see her for yourself, Frank. You wouldn't believe me if I told you.' He sat cross-legged beside the patch of smoothed dirt and began picking up the shell-bits. The way he picked them up fascinated me – so rapidly, pinching them up between thumb and forefinger, and funneling them back into his palm with the other three fingers, displaying an expert facility. And, I noticed, he was only picking up the hexagons.

'Sit down,' he said. 'We've got an hour or so to kill.'

I squatted on the opposite side of the gameboard. 'You can't stay here, Ray.'

He finished with the hexagons, set them aside, and started on the squares. 'Why not?'

I told him about Mullins, but as I had presumed he was unconcerned. All his money, he said, was tied up in investment funds; he would find a way to deal with Mullins. He was calm in the face of my arguments, and though this calm seemed to reflect a more deep-seated confidence than had been evident on my first visit, I did not trust it. To my mind the barrier between us had hardened, become as tricky to navigate as the reef around the island. I gave up arguing and sat quietly, watching him play with the shells. Night was falling, banks of dark clouds were rushing overhead, and gusts of wind shredded the thatch. Heavy seas would soon be washing over the reef, and it would be beyond my strength to row against them. But I did not want to abandon him. Under the dreary storm-light, the wreckage of Port Ezekiel looked leached of color and vitality, and I had an image of the two of us being survivors of a great disaster, stalemated in debate over the worth of restarting civilization.

'It's almost time,' he said, breaking the silence. He gazed out to the swaying tops of the bushes that bounded the clearing. 'This is so wild, Frank. Sometimes I can't believe it myself.'

The soft astonishment in his voice brought the pathos of his situation home to me. 'Jesus, Ray,' I said. 'Come back with me. There's nothing here.'

'Tell me that when you've seen her.' He stood and walked over to the water-filled pit. 'You were right, Frank. I was crazy, and maybe I still am. But I was right, too. Just not in the way I expected.'

'Right about what?'

He smiled. 'Cassiopeia.' He hunkered down by the pit. 'I've got to get in the water. There has to be physical contact or else the exchange can't occur. I'll be unconscious for a while, but don't worry about it. All right?'

Without waiting for my approval, he lowered himself into the water. He seemed to be groping for something, and he shifted about until he had found a suitable position. His shoulders just cleared the surface. Then he bowed his head so that I could no longer see his face.

My thoughts were in turmoil. His references to 'her,' his self-baptism, and now the sight of his disembodied head and tendrils of hair floating on the water, all this had rekindled my fear. I decided that the best thing I could do for him, for both of us, would be to knock him out, to haul him back to Sandy Bay for treatment. But as I looked around for a club, I noticed something that rooted me in my tracks. The snakes had grown frantic in their efforts to escape; they were massed at the far side of the trench, pushing at the mesh with such desperation that the rocks holding it down were wobbling. And then, an instant later, I began to sense another presence in the clearing.

How did I sense this? It was similar to the feeling you have when you are alone for the first time with a woman to whom you are attracted, how it seems you could close your eyes and stopper your ears and still be aware of her every shift in position, registering these changes as thrills running along your nerves and muscles. And I knew beyond a shadow of a doubt that this presence was female. I whirled around, certain that someone was behind me. Nothing. I turned back to Ray. Tremors were passing through his shoulders, and his breath came in hoarse shudders as if he had been removed from his natural element and were having trouble with the air. Scenes from old horror movies flashed through my brain. The stranger lured to an open grave by an odd noise; the ghoul rising from the swamp, black water dripping from his talons; the maniac with the split-personality, smiling, hiding a bloody knife under his coat. And then I saw, or imagined I saw, movement on the surface of the water; it was bulging – not bubbling, but the entire surface bulging upward as if some force below were building to an explosion. Terrified, I took a backward step, and as my foot nudged the wire screen over the trench, as the snakes struck madly at the mesh, terrified themselves, I broke and ran.

I went crashing through the brush, certain that Ray was after me, possessed by some demon dredged up from his psyche ... or by worse. I did not stop to untie the dory, but grabbed the machete from beneath the seat, hacked the rope in two, and pulled hard out into the water. Waves slopped over the bow, the dory bucked and plunged, and the noise from the reef was deafening. But even had a hurricane been raging, I would not have put back into the Burying Ground. I strained at the oars, gulping down breaths that were half salt spray, and I did not feel secure until I had passed beyond Punta Palmetto and was hidden from the view of whatever was now wandering that malarial shore.

After a night's sleep, after dosing my fears with the comforts of home, all my rational structures were re-erected. I was ashamed at having run, at having left Ray to endure his solitary hell, and I assigned everything I had seen and felt to a case of nerves or – and I did not think this impossible – to poltergeistlike powers brought on by his madness. Something had to be done for him. As soon as I had finished breakfast, I drove over to Meachem's Landing and asked the militia for their help. I explained the situation to one Sergeant Colmenares, who thanked me for my good citizenship but said he could do nothing unless the poor man had committed a crime. If I had been clearheaded, I would have invented a crime, anything to return Ray to civilization; instead, I railed at the sergeant, stumped out of the office, and drove back to Sandy Bay.

Elizabeth had asked me to buy some cooking oil, and so I stopped off at Sarah's Store, a green-painted shanty the size of a horse stall not far from The Chicken Shack. Inside, there was room for three people to stand at the counter, and behind it Sarah was enthroned on her stool. An old woman, almost ninety, with a frizzy crown of white hair and coal-black skin that took on bluish highlights under the sun. It was impossible to do business with her and not hear the latest gossip, and during our conversation she mentioned that Ray had stopped in the night before.

'He after havin' a strife wit dat Jimmy Mullins,' she said. 'Now Jimmy he have followed dis tourist fella down from de Sea Breeze where dey been drinkin', and he settin' up to beg de mon fah somet'ing. You know how he gets wit his lies.' She did her Jimmy Mullins imitation, puffing out her chest and frowning. '"I been in Vietnam," he say, and show de mon dat scar from when he shot himself in de leg. "I bleed fah Oncle Sam, and now Oncle Sam goin' to take care of dis negro." Den in walk Ray Milliken. He did not look left or right but jus' stare at de cans of fruit juice and ax how much dey was. Talkin' wit dat duppy voice. Lord! De duppy force crawlin' all over him. Now dis tourist fella have gone 'cause de sight of Ray wit his wild look and his scrapes have made de fella leery. But Jimmy jus' stand dere, watchful. And when Ray pay fah de juice, Jimmy say, "Gimme dat money." Ray make no reply. He drink de juice down and den he amble out de door. Jimmy follow him and he screamin'. "You scorn me like dat!" he say. "You scorn me like dat!" It take no wisdom to know dere's blood in de air, so I set a Superior on de counter and call out, "Jimmy, you come here 'fore yo' beer lose de chill." And dat lure him back.'

I asked Sarah what she meant by 'duppy voice,' but she would only say, 'Dat's what it were – de duppy voice.' I paid for my oil, and as I went out the door, she called, 'God bless America!' She always said it as a farewell to her American customers; most thought she was putting them on, but knowing Sarah's compassion for waifs and strays, her conviction that material wealth was the greatest curse one could have, I believe it was heartfelt.

*

Sarah's story had convinced me of the need for action, and that afternoon I returned to the Burying Ground. I did not confront Ray; I stationed myself behind some bushes twenty feet to the right of the shelter. I planned to do as I should have done before – hit him and drag him back to Sandy Bay. I had with me Elizabeth's ax handle and an ample supply of bug repellent.

Ray was not at the clearing when I arrived, and he did not put in an appearance until after five o'clock. This time he was carrying a guitar, probably gleaned from the debris. He sat beside the trench and began chording, singing in a sour, puny voice that sent a chill through me despite the heat; it seemed he was giving tongue to the stink of the rotting snakeskins, amplifying the whine of the insects. The sun reflected an orange fire on the panels of the guitar.

'Cas-si-o-pee-ee-ya,' he sang, country-western style, 'I'll be yours tonight.' He laughed – cracked, high-pitched laughter – and rocked back and forth on his haunches. 'Cas-si-o-pee-ee-ya, why don't you treat me right.'

Either he was bored or else that was the whole song. He set down the guitar and for the next hour he hardly moved, scratching, looking up to the sun as if checking its decline. Sunset faded, and the evening star climbed above Alps of purple cumulus. Finally, stretching and shaking out the kinks, he stood and walked to the pit and lowered himself into the water. It was at this point that I had intended to hit him, but my curiosity got the best of me and I decided to observe him instead; I told myself that I would be better able to debunk his fantasies if I had some personal experience of them. I would hit him after he had fallen asleep.

It was over an hour before he emerged from the water, and when he did I was very glad to be hidden. Icy stars outlined the massed clouds, and the moon had risen three-quarters full, transforming the clearing into a landscape of black and silvery-gray. Everything had a shadow, even the tattered fronds lying on the ground. There was just enough wind to make the shadows tremble, and the only noise apart from the wind was the pattering of lizards across the desiccated leaves. From my vantage I could not see if the water was bulging upward, but soon the snakes began their hissing, their pushing at the mesh, and I felt again that female presence.

Then Ray leaped from the pit.

It was the most fluid entrance I have ever seen – like a dancer mounting onto stage from a sunken level. He came straight up in a shower of silver droplets and landed with his legs straddling the pit, snapping his head from side to side. He stepped out of the shelter, pacing back and forth along the trench, and as the light struck him full, I stopped thinking of him as *he*.

Even now, at a remove from the events, I have difficulty thinking of Ray as a man; the impression of femininity was so powerful that it obliterated all my previous impressions of him. Though not in the least dainty or swishy, every one of his movements had a casual female sensuality, and his walk was potently feminine in the way of a lioness. His face was leaner, sleeker of line. Aside from these changes was the force of that presence pouring over me. I had the feeling that I was involved in a scene out of prehistory – the hominid warrior with his club spying on an unknown female, scenting her, knowing her sex along the circuits of his nerves. When he ... when she had done pacing, she squatted beside the trench, removed one of the rocks, and lifted the edge of the screen. With incredible speed, she reached in and snatched out a wriggling yellowjaw. I heard a sickening mushy crack as she crushed its head between her thumb and forefinger. She skinned it with her teeth, worrying a rip, tearing loose long peels until the blood-rilled meat gleamed in the moonlight. All this in a matter of seconds. Watching her eat, I found I was gripping the ax handle so tightly that my hand ached. She tossed the remains of the snake into the bushes, then she stood – again, that marvelous fluidity – and turned toward the spot where I was hiding.

'Frank,' she said; she barely pronounced the *a* and trilled the *r*, so that the word came out as 'Frrenn-kuh.'

It was like hearing one's name spoken by an idol. The ax handle slipped from my hand. I stood, weak-kneed. If her speed afoot was equal to her speed of hand, I had no chance of escape.

'I won't kill you,' she said, her accent slurring the words into the rhythm of a musical phrase. She went back under the shelter and sat beside the patch of smoothed dirt.

The phrasing of her assurance did nothing to ease my fears, yet I came forward. I told myself that this was Ray, that he had created this demoness from his sick needs and imaginings; but I could not believe it. With each step I became more immersed in her, as if her soul were too large for the body and I was passing through its outer fringes. She motioned me to sit, and as I did, her strangeness lapped over me like heat from an open fire.

My throat was constricted, but I managed to say, 'Cassiopeia?'

Her lips thinned and drew back from her teeth in a feral smile. 'That's what Ray calls me. He can't pronounce my name. My home ...' She glanced at the sky. 'The clouds obscure it.'

I gawped at her; I had so many questions, I could not frame even one. Finally I said, 'Meachem's UFO. Was that your ship?'

'The ship was destroyed far from here. What Meachem saw was a ghost, or rather the opening and closing of a road traveled by one.' She gestured at the pit. 'It lies there, beneath the water.'

I remembered the hard something I had poked with a stick; it had not felt in the least ectoplasmic, and I pointed this out.

'"Ghost" is a translation of the word for it in my language,' she said. 'You touched the energy fields of a ... a machine. It was equipped with a homing capacity, but its fields were disrupted by the accident that befell my ship. It can no longer open the roads between the worlds.'

'Roads?' I said.

'I don't understand the roads, and if I could explain them it would translate as metaphysics. The islanders would probably accept the explanation, but I doubt you would.' She traced a line in the dirt with her forefinger. 'To enter the superluminal universe the body must die and be reanimated at journey's end. The other components of the life travel with the machine. All I know of the roads is that though journeys often last for years, they appear to be direct. When Meachem saw flame in the sky, it was because I came from flame, from the destruction of my ship.'

'The machine ...' I began.

'It's an engineered life form,' she said. 'You see, any life consists of a system of energy fields unified in the flesh. The machine is a partial simulation of that system, a kind of phantom life that's designed to sustain the most crucial of those fields – what you'd call the *anima*, the soul – until the body can be reanimated ... or, if the body has been destroyed, until an artificial host has been supplied. Of course there was no such host here. So the machine attracted those whose souls were impaired, those with whom a temporary exchange could be made. Without embodiment I would have gone mad.' She scooped up a handful of shell-bits. 'I suppose I've gone mad in spite of it. I've rubbed souls with too many madmen.'

She tossed out the shell-bits. A haphazard toss, I thought; but then I noticed that they had fallen into neat rows.

'The differences between us are too great for the exchange to be other than temporary,' she went on. 'If I didn't reenter the machine each morning, both I and my host – and the machine – would die.'

Despite the evidence of my senses, this talk of souls and energy fields – reminding me of the occult claptrap of the sixties – had renewed my doubts. 'People have been digging up the Burying Ground for years,' I said. 'Why hasn't someone found this machine?'

'It's a very clever machine,' she said, smiling again. 'It hides from those who aren't meant to find it.'

'Why would it choose only impaired hosts?'

'To choose an unimpaired one would run contrary to the machine's morality. And to mine.'

'How does it attract them?'

'My understanding of the machine is limited, but I assume there's a process of conditioning involved. Each time I wake in a new host, it's always the same. A clearing, a shelter, the snakes.'

I started to ask another question, but she waved me off.

'You act as though I must prove something,' she said. 'I have no wish to prove anything. Even if I did, I'm not sure I could. Most of my memories were stripped from me at the death of my body, and those that remain are those that have stained the soul. In a sense I'm as much Ray as I am myself. Each night I inherit his memories, his abilities. It's like living in a closet filled with someone else's belongings.'

I continued to ask questions, with part of my mind playing the psychiatrist, eliciting answers in order to catalog Ray's insanity; yet my doubts were fading. She could not recall the purpose of her journey or even of her life, but she said that her original body had been similar to the human form – her people, too, had a myth of an ancient star-seeding race – though it had been larger, stronger, with superior organs of perception. Her world was a place of thick jungles, and her remote ancestors had been nocturnal predators. An old Caribe man had been her first host on the island; he had wandered onto the Burying Ground six months after her arrival, maddened by pain from a cancer that riddled his stomach. His wife had been convinced that a goddess had possessed him, and she had brought the tribal elders to bear witness.

'They were afraid of me,' she said. 'And I was equally afraid of them. Little devil-men with ruddy skins and necklaces of jaguar teeth. They built fires around me, hemming me in, and they'd dance and screech and thrust their spears at me through the flames. It was nightmarish. I knew they might lose control of their fear at any second and try to kill me. I might have defended myself, but life was sacred to me then. They were whole, vital beings. To harm them would have been to mock what remained of me.'

She had cultivated them, and they had responded by providing her with new hosts, by arranging their fires to depict the constellation Cassiopeia, hoping to call down other gods to keep her company. It had been a fruitless hope, and there were other signals that would have been more recognizable to her people, but she had been touched by their concern and had not told them.

I will not pretend that I recall exactly everything she said, yet I believe what follows captures the gist of her tale. At first I was disconcerted by its fluency and humanity; but I soon realized that not only had she had two centuries in which to practice her humanity, not only was she taking advantage of Ray's gift for storytelling, but also that she had told much of it before.

For twenty-two years [she said] I inhabited Caribe bodies, most of them terribly damaged. Cripples, people with degenerative diseases, and once a young girl with a huge dent in her skull, an injury gotten during a raid. Though my energies increased the efficiency of their muscles, I endured all their agonies. But as the Caribe retreated from the island in face of the English, even this tortured existence was denied to me. I spent four years within the machine, despairing of ever leaving it again. Then, in 1819, Ezekiel Brooks stumbled onto the Burying Ground. He was a retarded boy of seventeen and had become lost in the mangrove. When his father, William, came in search of him, he found me instead. He remembered the fiery object that had fallen from the sky and was delighted to have solved a puzzle that had baffled his captain for so many years. Thereafter he visited every week and dragged old Henry Meachem along.

Meachem was in his seventies then, fat, with a doughy, wrinkled face and long gray hair done up into ringlets; he affected foppish clothes and a lordly manner. He had the gout and had to be carried through the mangrove by his slaves. They brought with them a teakwood chair, its grips carved into lions' heads, and there he'd sit, wheezing, bellowing at the slaves to keep busy with their fly whisks, plying me with questions. He did not believe my story, and on his second visit, a night much like this one, moonstruck and lightly winded, he was accompanied by a Spanish woman, a scrawny old hag enveloped in a black shawl and skirt, who he told me was a witch.

'Sit you down with Tía Claudia,' he said, prodding her forward with his cane, 'and she'll have the truth of you. She'll unravel your thoughts like a ball of twine.'

The old woman sat cross-legged beside the pit, pulled a lump of clouded crystal from her skirt, and set it on the ground before her. Beneath the shawl her shadowed wrinkles had the look of a pattern in tree bark, and despite her apparent frailty I could feel her presence as a chill pressure on my skin. Uneasy, I sat down on the opposite side of the pit. Her eyelids drooped, her breath grew shallow and irregular, and the force of her life flooded me, intensifying in the exercise of her power. The fracture planes inside the crystal appeared to be gleaming with more than refracted moonlight, and as I stared at them, a drowsy sensation stole over me ... but then I was distracted by a faint rushing noise from the pit.

Hatchings of fine lines were etching the surface of the water, sending up sprays of mist. The patterns they formed resembled the fracture planes of the crystal. I glanced up at Tía Claudia. She was trembling, a horror-stricken expression on her face, and the rushing noise was issuing from her parted lips as though she had been invaded by a ghostly wind. The ligature of her neck was cabled, her hands were clawed. I looked back to the pit. Beneath the surface, shrinking and expanding in a faltering rhythm, was a point of crimson light. Tía Claudia's power, I realized, was somehow akin to that of the machine. She was healing it, restoring its homing capacity, and it was opening a road! Hope blazed in me. I eased into the pit, and the fields gripped me, stronger than ever. But as the old woman let out a shriek and slumped to the ground, they weakened; the point of light shrank to nothing, gone glimmering like my hope. It had only been a momentary restoration, a product of her mind joined to the machine's.

Two of Meachem's slaves helped Tía Claudia to her feet, but she shook them off and backed out of the shelter, her eyes fixed on the pit. She leaned against Meachem's chair for support.

'Well?' he said.

'Kill him!' she said. 'He's too dangerous, too powerful.'

'Him?' Meachem laughed.

Tía Claudia said that I was who I claimed to be and argued that I was a threat to him. I understood that she was really concerned with my threat to her influence over Meachem, but I was so distressed by the lapsing of the machine's power that I didn't care what they did to me. Bathed in the silvery light, stars shining around their heads, they seemed emblematic of something – perhaps of all humanity – this ludicrous old pirate in his ruffled shirt, and, shaking her knobbly finger at him, the manipulative witch who wanted to be his master.

After that night, Meachem took me under his wing. I learned that he was an exile, outlawed by the English and obsessed with the idea of returning home, and I think he was happy to have met someone even more displaced than he. Occasionally he'd invite me to his house, a gabled building of pitch-coated boards that clung to a strip of iron shore east of Sandy Bay. He'd sit me down in his study and read to me for hours from his journals; he thought that – being a member of an advanced civilization – I'd have the wit to appreciate his intellect. The study was a room that reflected his obsession with England, its walls covered with Union Jacks, a riot of scarlet and blue. Sometimes, watching the flies crusting the lip of his pewter mug, his sagging face looming above them, the colors on the wall appearing to drip in the unsteady glare of the oil lamp ... sometimes it seemed a more nightmarish environment than the Caribe's circle of fires. He'd pore over the pages, now and again saying, 'Ah, here's one you'll like,' and would quote the passage.

'"Wars,"' he read to me once, '"are the solstices of the human spirit, ushering in winter to a young man's thought and rekindling the spring of an old man's anger."'

Every page was filled with aphorisms like that – high-sounding, yet empty of meaning except as regarded his own nature. He was the cruelest man I've ever known. A wife-beater, a tyrant to his slaves and children. Some nights he would have himself borne down to the beach, order torches lit, and watch as those who had offended him were flogged – often to the death – with stalks of withe. After witnessing one of the floggings, I considered killing him, even though such an act would have been in violation of everything I believed.

Then one night he brought another woman to the Burying Ground, a young mulatto girl named Nora Mullins.

'She be weak-minded like Ezekiel,' said Meachem. 'She'll make you a perfect wife.'

She would have run, but his slaves herded her forward. Her eyes darted left and right, her hands fidgeted with the folds of her skirt.

'I don't need a wife,' I said.

'Don't you now? Here's a chance to create your own lineage, to escape that infernal contraption of yours. Nora'll bear you a child, and if blood holds true, it'll be as witless as its parents. After Ezekiel's gone, you can take up residence in your heir.' His laugh disintegrated into a hacking cough.

The idea had logic behind it, but the thought of being intimate with a member of another species, especially one whose sex might be said to approximate my own, repelled me. Further, I didn't trust his motives. 'Why are you doing this?' I asked.

'I'm dyin'.' The old monster worked up a tear over the prospect. 'Nora's my legacy to you. I've always thought it a vast irony that a high-flyin' soul such as yourself should have been brought so low. It'll please me to think of you marooned among generations of idiots while I'm wingin' off to my reward.'

'This island is your reward,' I said. 'Even the soul dies.'

'You know that for a fact?' He was worried.

'No,' I said, relenting. 'No one knows that.'

'Well, then I'll come back to haunt you.'

But he never did.

I had intended to send Nora away after he left, but Ezekiel – though too timid to approach her sexually – found her attractive, and I didn't want to deprive him of her companionship. In addition, I began to realize how lonely I had been myself. The idea of keeping her with me and fathering a child seemed more and more appealing, and a week later, using Ezekiel's memories to rouse lust, I set out to become a family man.

What a strange union that was! The moon sailing overhead, chased by ragged blue clouds; the wind and insects and frogs combining into a primitive music. Nora was terrified. She whimpered and rolled her eyes and halfheartedly tried to fight me off. I don't believe she was clear as to what was happening, but eventually her instincts took control. It would be hard to imagine two more inept virgins. I had a logical understanding of the act, at least one superior to Nora's; but this was counterbalanced by her sluggish coordination and my revulsion. Somehow we managed. I think it was mainly due to the fact that she sensed I was like her, female in a way that transcended anatomy, and this helped us to employ tenderness with one another. Over the succeeding nights an honest affection developed between us; though her speech was limited to strangled cries, we learned to communicate after a fashion, and our lovemaking grew more expert, more genuine.

Fourteen years we were together. She bore me three children, two stillborn, but the third a slow-witted boy whom we named Carl – it was a name that Nora could almost pronounce. By day she and Ezekiel were brother and sister, and by night she and I were husband and wife. Carl needed things the land couldn't provide, milk, vegetables, and these were given us by William Brooks; but when he died several years after Carl's birth, taking with him the secret of my identity, Nora began going into Sandy Bay to beg – or so I thought until I was visited by her brother Robert. I knew something must be wrong. We were the shame of the family; they had never acknowledged us in any way.

'Nora she dead,' he told me. 'Murdered.'

He explained that two of her customers had been fighting over her, and that when she had tried to leave, one – a man named Halsey Brooks – had slit her throat. I didn't understand. Customers? Nothing Mullins said made sense.

'Don't you know she been whorin'?' he said. 'Mon, you a worse fool dan I think. She been whorin' dese six, seven years.'

'Carl,' I said. 'Where is he?'

'My woman takin' charge of him,' he said. 'I come for to bring you to dis Brooks. If you ain't mon enough, den I handle it myself. Family's family, no matter how crooked de tie.'

What I felt then was purely human – loss, rage, guilt over the fact that Nora had been driven to such straits. 'Show him to me,' I said.

Hearing the murderousness in my voice, Robert Mullins smiled.

Halsey Brooks was drinking in a shanty bar, a single room lit by oil lamps whose glass tops were so sooty that the light penetrated them as baleful orange gleams. The rickety tables looked like black spiders standing at attention. Brooks was sitting against the rear wall, a big slack-bellied man with skin the color of sunbaked mud, wearing a shirt and trousers of sailcloth. Mullins stationed himself out of sight at the door, his machete at the ready in case I failed, and I went inside.

Catching sight of me, Brooks grinned and drew a knife from his boot. 'Dat little squirt of yours be missin' you down in hell,' he said, and threw the knife.

I twisted aside, and the knife struck the wall. Brooks' eyes widened. He got to his feet, wary; the other customers headed for the door, knocking over chairs in their haste.

'You a quick little nigger,' said Brooks, advancing on me. 'But quick won't help you now.'

He would have been no match for me; but confronted by the actual task of shedding blood, I found that I couldn't go through with it. I was nauseated by the thought that I had even considered it. I backed away, tripped over a chair, and went sprawling in the corner.

'Dat de best you got to offer?' said Brooks, chuckling.

As he reached for me, Mullins slipped up behind and slashed him across the neck and back. Brooks screamed – an incredibly girlish sound for a man so large – and sank to his knees beside me, trying to pinch together the lips of his wounds. He held a hand to his face, seemingly amazed by the redness. Then he pitched forward on top of me. The reek of his blood and sweat, just the feel of him in my hands as I started to push him away, all that drove me into a fury. One of his eyes was an inch from mine, half-closed and clouding over. He was dying, but I wanted to dig the last flicker of life out of him. I tore at his cheek with my teeth. The eye snapped open, I heard the beginning of his scream, and I remember nothing more until I threw him aside. His face was flayed to the muscle-strings, his nose was pulped, and there were brimming dark-red craters where his eyes had been.

'My God!' said Mullins, staring at the ruin of Brooks' head; he turned to me. 'Go home! De thing more dan settled.'

All my rage had drained and been replaced by self-loathing. Home! I *was* home. The island had eroded my spirit, transformed me into one of its violent creatures.

'Don't come 'round no more,' said Mullins, wiping his blade on Brooks' trousers; he gave me a final look of disgust. 'Get back to de damn Buryin' Ground where you belong.'

Cassiopeia sprang to her feet and stepped out into the clearing. Her expression was grim, and I was worried that she might have worked herself into a rage by rehashing the killing. But she only walked a few paces away. Silvered by the moonlight, she looked unnaturally slim, and it seemed more than ever that I was seeing an approximation of her original form. The snakes had grown dead-still in the trench.

'You didn't really kill him,' I said.

'I would have,' she said. 'But never again.' She kicked at a pile of conch shells and sent them clattering down.

'What happened then?'

She did not answer for a moment, gazing out toward the sound of the reef. 'I was sickened by the changes I'd undergone,' she said. 'I became a hermit, and after Ezekiel died I continued my hermitage in Carl's body. That poor soul!' She walked a little farther away. 'I taught him to hide whenever men visited the Burying Ground. He lived like a wild animal, grubbing for roots, fishing with his bare hands. At the time it seemed the kindest thing I could do. I wanted to cleanse him of the taint of humanity. Of course that proved impossible ... for both of us.'

'You know,' I said, 'with all the technological advances these days, you might be able to contact ...'

'Don't you think I've considered my prospects!' she said angrily; and then, in a quieter tone, 'I used to hope that human science would permit me to return home someday, but I'm not sure I want to anymore. I've been perverted by this culture. I'd be as repulsive to my people as Ezekiel was to Robert Mullins, and I doubt that I'd be comfortable among them myself.'

I should have understood the finality of her loneliness – she had been detailing it in her story. But I understood now. She was a mixture of human and alien, spiritually a half-breed, gone native over a span of two centuries. She had no people, no place except this patch of sand and mangrove, no tradition except the clearing and the snakes and a game made of broken shells. 'I'm sorry,' I said.

'It's not your fault, Frank,' she said, and smiled. 'It's your American heritage that makes you tend to enshrine the obvious.'

'Ray and I aren't a fair sample,' I said defensively.

'I've known other Americans,' she said. 'They've all had that tendency. Everyone down here thought they were fools when they first came. They seemed totally unaware of the way things worked, and no one understood that their tremendous energy and capacity for deceit would compensate. But they were worse than either the pirates or the Spanish.'

Without another word, she turned and walked toward the brush.

'Wait!' I said. I was eager to hear about her experiences with Americans.

'You can come back tomorrow, Frank,' she said. 'Though maybe you shouldn't.'

'Why not?' Then, thinking that she might have some personal reason for distrusting Americans, I said, 'I won't hurt you. I don't believe I'm physically capable of it.'

'What a misleading way to measure security,' she said. 'In terms of hurt. You avoid using the word "kill," and yet you kill so readily. It's as though you're all pretending it's a secret.'

She slipped into the brush, moving soundlessly, somehow avoiding the dry branches, the papery fronds.

I drove all over the island the next day, trying to find a tape recorder, eventually borrowing one from a tourist in Meachem's Landing. Half-baked delusions of grandeur had been roused in me. I would be the Schliemann of extraterrestrial research, uncovering the ruin of an alien beneath the waste of a human being. There would be bestsellers, talk shows, exclamations of academic awe. Of course there was no real proof. A psychiatrist would point out how conveniently pat the story was – the machine that hid itself, the loss of memory, the alien woman conjured up by a man whose disorder stemmed from a disappointment in love. He would say it was the masterwork of a gifted tale-spinner, complete with special effects. Yet I thought that whoever heard it would hear – as I had – the commonplace perfection of truth underlying its exotic detail.

I had forgotten my original purpose for visiting the Burying Ground, but that afternoon Jimmy Mullins turned up at my door, eager to learn if I had news for him. He was only moderately drunk and had his wife Hettie in tow – a slender, mahogany-skinned woman wearing a dirty blue dress. She was careworn, but still prettier than Mullins deserved. I was busy and put him off, telling him that I was exploring something with Ray that could lead to money. And, I realized, I was. Knowing his character, I had assumed Mullins was attempting to swindle Hatfield; but Nora Mullins' common-law marriage to Ezekiel Brooks gave credence to his claim. I should have explained it to him. As it was, he knew I was just getting rid of him, and Hettie had to pull him down from the porch to cut short his arguments. My news must have given him some heart, though, because a few minutes later Hatfield knocked at the door.

'What you tellin' Jimmy?' he asked. 'He braggin' dat you got proof de Buryin' Ground his.'

I denied the charge and told him what I had learned, but not how I had learned it.

'I never mean to cheat Jimmy,' he said, scratching his head. 'I just want to make sure he not cheatin' me. If he got a case ... well, miserable as he is, he blood.'

After he left, I had problems. I found I needed new batteries for the recorder and had to drive into Meachem's Landing; and when I returned home I had an argument with Elizabeth that lasted well past sunset. As a result, I did not start out for the Burying Ground until almost ten o'clock, and while I was stowing my pack in the dory, I saw Cassiopeia walking toward me along the beach.

It was a clear night, the shadows of the palms sharp on the sand, and each time she passed through a shadow, it seemed I was seeing Ray; but then, as she emerged into the light, I would undergo a peculiar dislocation and realize that it was not Ray at all.

'I was on my way out to you,' I said. 'You didn't have to come into town.'

'I gave up being a hermit long ago, Frank,' she said. 'I like coming here. Sometimes it jogs my memory to be around so many others, though there's nothing really familiar about them.'

'What do you remember?'

'Not much. Flashes of scenery, conversations. But once I did remember something concrete. I think it had to do with my work, my profession. I'll show you.'

She squatted, smoothed a patch of sand, and began tracing a design. As with all her actions, this one was quick and complicated; she used three fingers of each hand, moving them in contrary directions, adding a squiggle here, a straight line there, until the design looked like a cross between a mandala and a printed circuit. Watching it evolve, I was overcome by a feeling of peace, not the drowsiness of hypnotism, but a powerful, enlivening sensation that alerted me to the peacefulness around me. The soughing of the palms, the lapping of the water, the stillness of the reef – it was low tide. This feeling was as potent as the effect of a strong drug, and yet it had none of the fuzziness that I associate with drugs. By the time she had finished, I was so wrapped in contentment that all my curiosity had abated – I was not even curious about the design – and I put aside for the moment the idea of recording her. We strolled eastward along the beach without talking, past Sarah's Store and The Chicken Shack, taking in the sights. The tin roofs of the shanties gleamed under the moonlight, and, their imperfections hidden by the darkness, the shanties themselves looked quaint and cozy. Shadows were dancing behind the curtains, soft reggae drifted on the breeze. Peace. When I finally broke the silence, it was not out of curiosity but in the spirit of that peace, of friendship.

'What about Ray?' I asked. 'He was in pretty rough shape when I visited him the other afternoon.'

'He's better off than he would be elsewhere,' she said. 'Calmer, steadier.'

'But he can't be happy.'

'Maybe not,' she said. 'But in a way I'm what he was always seeking, even before he began to deteriorate. He actually thinks of me in romantic terms.' She laughed – a trilling note. 'I'm very happy with him myself. I've never had a host with so few defects.'

We were drawing near the New Byzantine Church of the Archangel, a small white-frame building set back from the shore. This being Friday, it had been turned into a movie theater. The light above the door illuminated a gaudy poster that had been inserted into the glass case normally displaying the subject of the sermon; the poster showed two bloodstained Chinese men fighting with curved knives. Several teenagers were silhouetted by the light, practicing martial-art kicks beside the steps – like stick figures come to life – and a group of men was watching them, passing a bottle. One of the men detached himself from the group and headed toward us. Jimmy Mullins.

'Mr Milliken!' he shouted. 'Dis de owner of de Buryin' Ground wantin' to speak with you!'

Cassiopeia spun on her heel and went wading out into the water. Infuriated, Mullins ran after her, and – myself infuriated at the interruption, this breach of peace – I stuck out a foot and tripped him. I threw myself on top of him, trying for a pin, but he was stronger than I had supposed. He wrenched an arm loose, stunned me with a blow to the head, and wriggled free. I clamped my arms around his leg, and he dragged me along, yelling at Cassiopeia.

'Pay me my money, bastard!'

'I'll pay you!' I said out of desperation.

It might have been a magic spell that I had pronounced. He quit dragging me; I clung to his leg with one hand, and with the other I wiped a crust of mucky sand from my mouth.

'You goin' to pay me three thousand *lemps?*' he said in a tone of disbelief.

It occurred to me that he had not expected the entire amount, that he had only been hoping for a nuisance payment. But I was committed. Fifteen hundred dollars was no trifle to me, but I might be able to recoup it from Ray, and if not, well, I could make it up by foregoing my Christmas trip to the States. I pulled out my wallet and handed Mullins all the bills, about fifty or sixty *lempira*.

'That's all I've got now,' I said, 'but I'll get the rest in the morning. Just leave Milliken alone.'

Mullins stared at the money in his hand, his little snappish eyes blinking rapidly, speechless. I stared out to sea, searching for a sign of Cassiopeia, but found none. Not at first. Then I spotted her, a slim, pale figure standing atop a coral head about fifteen yards from shore. Without taking a running start, she leaped – at that distance she looked like a white splinter being blown through the night – and landed upon another coral head some twenty, twenty-five feet away. Before I could absorb the improbability of the leap, she dived and vanished into the water beyond the reef.

'I be at your house nine o'clock sharp,' said Mullins joyfully. 'And we go to de bank together. You not goin' to be havin' no more strife with dis negro!'

But Mullins did not show up the next morning, not at nine o'clock or ten or eleven. I asked around and heard that he had been drinking in Spanish Harbor; he had probably forgotten the appointment and passed out beneath some shanty. I drove to the bank, withdrew the money, and returned home. Still no Mullins. I wandered the beach, hoping to find him, and around three o'clock I ran into Hettie at Sarah's Store.

'Jimmy he never home of a Saturday,' she told me ruefully.

I considered giving her the money, but I suspected that she would not tell Mullins, would use it for the children, and though this would be an admirable use, I doubted that it would please Mullins. Twilight fell, and my patience was exhausted. I left a message for Mullins with Elizabeth, stashed the money in a trunk, and headed for the Burying Ground.

After mooring the dory, I switched on the recorder and secreted it in my pack. My investigative zeal of the previous day had been reborn, and not even the desolation of Port Ezekiel could dim my spirits. I had solved the ultimate problem of the retiree; I had come up with a project that was not only time-consuming but perhaps had some importance. And now that Mullins had been taken care of, nothing would interfere.

Cassiopeia was sitting beneath the shelter when I reached the clearing, a silvery star of moonlight shifting across her face from a ragged hole in the thatch. She pointed to my pack and asked, 'What's that?'

'The pack?' I said innocently.

'Inside it.'

I knew she meant the recorder. I showed it to her and said, 'I want to document your story.'

She snatched it from me and slung it into the bushes.

'You're a stupid man, Frank,' she said. 'What do you suppose would happen if you played a recording of me for someone? They'd say it was an interesting form of insanity, and if they could profit, or if they were driven by misguided compassion, they'd send me away for treatment. And that would be that.'

For a long while afterward she would not talk to me. Clouds were passing across the moon, gradually thinning, so that each time the light brightened it was brighter than the time before, as if the clearing were being dipped repeatedly into a stream and washed free of a grimy film. Cassiopeia sat brooding over her gameboard. Having grown somewhat accustomed to her, to that strong female presence, I was beginning to be able to detect her changes in mood. And they were rapid changes, fluctuating every few seconds between hostility and sadness. I recalled her telling me that she was probably mad; I had taken the statement to be an expression of gloom, but now I wondered if any creature whose moods shifted with such rapidity could be judged sane. Nonetheless, I was about to ask her to continue her story when I heard an outboard motor, and, moments after it had been shut off, a man's voice shouting, 'Mr Milliken!'

It was Jimmy Mullins.

A woman's voice shrilled, unintelligible, and there was a crash as if someone had fallen; a second later Mullins pushed into the clearing. Hettie was clinging to his arm, restraining him; but on seeing us, he cuffed her to the ground and staggered forward. His town clothes were matted with filth and damp. Two other men crowded up behind Hettie. They were both younger than Mullins, slouching, dressed in rags and sporting natty dreads. One held a rum bottle, and the second, the taller, carried a machete.

'You owe me three thousand *lemps!*' said Mullins to Cassiopeia; his head lolled back, and silver dots of moonlight flared in his eyes.

'Sick of dis Yankee domination,' said the taller men; he giggled. 'Ain't dat right, Jimmy?'

'Jimmy,' I said. 'We had a bargain.'

Mullins said nothing, his face a mask of sodden fury; he teetered on the edge of the trench, unaware of the snakes.

'Tired of dis exploitation,' said the man, and his friend, who had been taking a pull from the bottle, elbowed him gleefully and said, 'Dat pretty slick, mon! Listen up.' He snapped his fingers in a reggae tempo and sang in a sweet, tremulous voice:

'Sick of dis Yankee domination.
Oh yea – aa-ay,
Tired of dis exploitation ...'

The scenario was clear – these two had encountered the drunken Mullins in a bar, listened to the story of his windfall, and, thinking that he was being had, hoping to gain by it, they had egged him into this confrontation.

'Dis my land, and you ain't legal on it,' said Mullins.

'What about our bargain Jimmy?' I asked. 'The money's back at the house.'

He was tempted, but drunkenness and politics had infected his pride. 'I ain't no beggar,' he said. 'I wants what's mine, and *dis* mon's money mine.' He bent down and picked up one of the conch shells that were lying about; he curled his fingers around the inner curve of the shell – it fit over his hand like the spiked glove of a gladiator. He took a vicious swipe in our direction, and it *whooshed* through the air.

Cassiopeia let out a hissing breath.

It was very tense in the clearing. The two men were watching Mullins with new respect, new alertness, no longer joking. Even in the hands of a fool, conch shells were serious business; they had a ritual potency. Cassiopeia was deadpan, measuring Mullins. Her anger washed over me – I gauged it to be less anger than a cold disapproval, the caliber of emotion one experiences in reaction to a nasty child. But I was ready to intervene if her mood should escalate. Mullins was a coward at heart, and I thought that he would go to the brink but no further. I edged forward, halfway between them. My mouth was dry.

'I goin' to bash you simple, and you not pay me,' said Mullins, crossing over the trench.

'Listen, Jimmy ...' I said, raising the voice of reason.

Cassiopeia lunged for him. I threw my arms around her, and Mullins, panicked, seeing her disadvantage, swung the shell. She heaved me aside with a shrug and tried to slip the punch. But I had hampered her just enough. The shell glanced off her shoulder. She gave a cawing guttural screech that scraped a nail down the slate of my spine, and clutched at the wound.

'See dere,' said Mullins to his friends, triumphant. 'Dis negro take care of he own.' He went reeling back over the trench, nearly tripping, and in righting himself, he caught sight of the snakes. It would have been impossible not to see them – they were thrusting frenziedly at the wire. Mullins' jaw fell, and he backed away. One of the rocks was dislodged from the screen. The snakes began to slither out, writing rippling black figures on the dirt and vanishing into the litter, rustling the dead fronds.

'Oh, Jimmy!' Hettie held out a hand to him. 'Have a care!

Cassiopeia gave another of those chilling screeches and lowered into a crouch. Her torso swaying, her hands hooked. The flesh of her left shoulder was torn, and blood webbed her arm, dripping from her fingertips, giving them the look of claws. She stepped across the trench after Mullins. Without warning, the taller of the two men sprinted toward her, his machete raised. Cassiopeia caught his wrist and flipped him one-handed into the trench as easily as she might have tossed away an empty bottle.

There were still snakes in the trench.

They struck at his arms, his legs, and he thrashed about wildly, crying out; but one must have hit a vein, for the cry was sheared off. His limbs beat a tattoo against the dirt, his eyes rolled up. Slivers of iris peeped beneath the lids. A tiny *coralito* hung like a tassel from his cheek, and a yellowjaw was coiling around his throat; its flat head poked from the spikes of his hair. I heard a squawk, a sharp crack, and looked to the center of the clearing. The second man was crumpled at Cassiopeia's feet, his neck broken. Dark blood poured from his mouth, puddling under his jaw.

'Mr Milliken,' said Mullins, backing, his bravado gone. 'I goin' to make things right. Hettie she fix dat little scrape …'

He stumbled, and as he flung out an arm for balance, Cassiopeia leaped toward him, going impossibly high. It was a gorgeous movement, as smooth as the arc of a diver but more complex. She maintained a crouch in midair, and passing close to Mullins, she plucked the conch shell from his waving hand, fitted it to her own, and spun round to face him – all before she had landed.

Hettie began to scream. Short, piercing shrieks, as if she were being stabbed over and over.

Mullins ran for the brush, but Cassiopeia darted ahead of him and blocked his path. She was smiling. Again Mullins ran, and again she cut him off, keeping low, flowing across the ground. Again and again she let him run, offering him hope and dashing it, harrying him this way and that. The wind had increased, and clouds were racing overhead, strobing the moonlight; the clearing seemed to be spinning, a carousel of glare and shadow, and Hettie's screams were keeping time with the spin. Mullins' legs grew rubbery, he weaved back and forth, his arms windmilling, and at last he collapsed in a heap of fronds. Almost instantly he scrambled to his knees, yelling and tearing loose a snake that had been hanging from his wrist.

A *coralito*, I think.

'Ah!' he said. 'Ah … ah!'

His stare lanced into my eyes, freezing me with its hopelessness; a slant of light grazed his forehead, shining his sweat to silver beads.

Cassiopeia walked over and grabbed a handful of his shirt-front, hoisting him up until his feet were dangling. He kicked feebly and made a piteous bubbling noise. Then she drove the conch shell into his face. Once. Twice. Three times. Each blow splintered bone and sent a spray of blood flying. Hettie's scream became a wail. After the final blow, a spasm passed through Mullins' body – it looked too inconsequential to be death.

I was dimly aware that Hettie had stopped screaming, that the outboard motor had been started, but I was transfixed. Cassiopeia was still holding Mullins aloft, as if admiring her handiwork. His head glistened black in the moonlight, featureless and oddly misshapen. At least a minute went by before she dropped him. The thump of the body broke the spell that the scene had cast. I eased toward the brush.

'You can leave, Frank,' she said. 'I won't kill you.'

I was giddy with fear, and I almost laughed. She did not turn but cocked an eye at me over her shoulder – a menacing posture. I was afraid that if I tried to leave she would hunt me through the brush.

'I won't kill you,' she said again. She lowered her head, and I could feel her despair, her shame; it acted to lessen my fear.

'The soldiers will be coming,' I said.

She was silent, motionless.

'You should make the exchange with Ray.'

I was horrified by what she had done, but I wanted her to live. Insane or not, she was too rare to lose – a voice of mystery in all this ordinary matter.

'No more.' She said it in a grim whisper. 'I know it's much to ask, Frank, but will you keep me company?'

'What are you going to do?'

'Nothing. Wait for the soldiers.' She inspected her wound; the blood had quit flowing. 'And if they don't come before dawn, I'll watch the sunrise. I've always been curious about it.'

She scarcely said a word the rest of the night. We went down to the shore and sat beside a tangle of mangrove. I tried to convince her to survive, but she warded off every argument with a slashing gesture. Toward dawn, as the first gray appeared in the east, she had a convulsion, a brief flailing of the limbs that stretched her out flat. Dawn comes swiftly on the water, and by the time she had regained consciousness, pink streaks were infiltrating the gray.

'Make the exchange,' I urged her. 'It's not too late, is it?'

She ignored me. Her eyes were fixed on the horizon, where the rim of the solar disc was edging up; the sea reflected a rippling path of crimson and purple leading away from it, and the bottoms of the clouds were dyed these same colors.

Ten minutes later she had a more severe convulsion. This one left a froth of bloody bubbles rimming her nostrils. She groped for my hand, and as she squeezed it, I felt my bones grinding together. My emotions were grinding together as well; my situation – like Henry Meachem's – was so similar to hers. Aliens and strangers, all of us, unable to come to grips with this melancholy island.

Shortly after her third convulsion, I heard an outboard motor. A dory was cutting toward us from the reef wall; it was not a large enough craft to be the militia, and as it drew near, I recognized Hatfield Brooks by his silhouette hunched over the tiller, his natty dreads. He switched off the motor and let the dory drift until he was about fifty feet away; then he dropped the anchor and picked up a rifle that had been leaning against the front seat. He set the stock to his shoulder.

'Keep clear of dere, Mr Winship!' he called. 'I can't vouch for de steadiness of my aim.'

Behind him, shafts of light were spearing up through balconies of cloud – a cathedral of a sky.

'Don't, Hatfield!' I stepped in front of Cassiopeia, waving my arms. 'She's ... he's dying! There's no need for it!'

'Keep clear!' he shouted. 'De mon have killed Jimmy, and I come for him!'

'Just let him die!'

'He don't just let Jimmy die! Hettie been sayin' how dat crazy mon batter him!' He braced himself in the stern and took aim.

With a hoarse sigh, Cassiopeia climbed to her feet. I caught her wrist. Her skin was burning hot, her pulse drummed. Nerves twitched at the corners of her eyes, and one of the pupils was twice the size of the other. It was Ray's face I was seeing in that dawn light – hollow-cheeked, dirt-smeared, haggard; but even then I saw a sleeker shape beneath. She peeled my fingers off her wrist.

'Goodbye, Frank,' she said; she pushed me away and ran toward Hatfield. Ran!

The water was waist-deep all the way to the reef, yet she knifed through it as if it were nothing, ploughing a wake like the hull of a speedboat. It was a more disturbing sight than her destruction of Mullins had been. Thoroughly inhuman. Hatfield's first shot struck her in the chest and barely slowed her. She was twenty feet from the dory when the second shot hit, and that knocked her sideways, clawing at her stomach. The third drilled a jet of blood from her shoulder, driving her back; but she came forward again. One plodding step after another, shaking her head with pain. Four, five, six. Hatfield kept squeezing off the rounds, and I was screaming for him to finish her – each shot was a hammerblow that shivered loose a new scream. An arm's length from the dory, she sank to her knees and grabbed the keel, rocking it violently. Hatfield bounced side to side, unable to bring the rifle to bear. It discharged twice. Wild misses aimed at the sky, the trees.

And then, her head thrown back, arms upflung, Cassiopeia leaped out of the water.

Out of the world.

I am not sure whether she meant to kill Hatfield or if this was just a last expression of physicality – whatever her intent, she went so high that it was more a flight than a leap. Surrounded by a halo of fiery drops, twisting above the dory, her chest striped with blood, she seemed a creation of some visionary's imagination, bursting from a jeweled egg and being drawn gracefully into the heavens. But at the peak of the leap, she came all disjointed and fell, disappearing in a splash. Moments later, she floated up – face downward – and began to drift away. The sound of the reef faded in a steady, soothing hiss. The body spun slowly on the tide; the patch of water around it was stained gold and purple, as if the wounds were leaking the colors of sunrise.

Hatfield and I stared at each other across the distance. He did not lower the rifle. Strangely enough, I was not afraid. I had come to the same conclusion as Cassiopeia, the knowledge that the years could only decline from this point onward. I felt ready to die. The soft crush of waves building louder and louder on the reef, the body drifting leisurely toward shore, the black snaky-haired figure bobbing in his little boat against the enormous flag of the sunburst – it was a perfect medium for death. The whole world was steeped in it. But Hatfield laid the rifle down. He half raised his hand to me – an aborted salute or farewell – and held the pose a second or two; he must have recognized the futility of any gesture, for he ducked his head then and fired up the motor, leaving me to take charge of the dead.

The authorities were unable to contact Ray's family. It may be that he had none; he had never spoken of them. The local cemetery refused his remains – too many Brookses and Mullinses under the soil; and so, as was appropriate, he was laid to rest beside Ezekiel and Carl on the Burying Ground. Hatfield fled off-island and worked his passage to Miami; though he is still considered something of a hero, the tide of anti-Americanism ebbed – it was as if Ray had been a surrogate for the mercenaries and development bankers who had raped the island over the years. Once more there were friendly greetings, smiling faces, and contented shrimp-workers. As for me, I married Elizabeth. I have no illusions about the relationship; in retrospect, it seems a self-destructive move. But I was shaken, haunted. If I had not committed my stupidity with the recorder, if I had not thrown my arms around Cassiopeia, would she have been able to control her anger? Would she merely have disarmed Mullins? I needed the bitter enchantment of a marriage to ground myself in the world again, to obscure the answers to these questions, to blur the meaning of these events.

And what was their meaning?

Was this a traveler's tale like none other, a weaving together of starships and pirates, madmen and ghosts, into the history of an alien being and a sorry plot of mangrove? Or was it simply an extraordinary instance of psychosis, a labyrinthine justification for a young man's lack of inner strength?

I have no proof that would be measurable by any scientific rule, though I can offer one that is purely Guanojan and therefore open to interpretation – what was seen might have been an actual event or the shade of such an event, or it might have been the relic of a wish powerful enough to outlast the brain that conceived it. Witness the testimony of Donald Ebanks, a fisherman, who put in at night to the Burying Ground for repairs several months after Cassiopeia's death. I heard him tell the story at The Chicken Shack, and since it was only the third retelling, since he had only downed two rums, it had not changed character much from the original.

'I tinkerin' wit de fuel line,' he said, 'when of a sudden dere's de sound of wind, and yet dere ain't no wind to feel. I 'ware dat dis de duppy sign, but I ain't fearful 'cause my mother she take me to Escuilpas as a child and have de Black Virgin bless me. After dat no duppy can do me harm. Still, I wary. I turn and dere dey is. Two of dem, bot' shinin' pale white wit dat duppy glow dat don't 'low you to see dere trut'ful colors. One were Ray Milliken, and de other ... God! I fall back in de boat to see it. De face ain't not'ing but teeth and eyes, and dere's a fringe 'round de head like de fringe of de anemone – snappin' and twistin'. And tall! Dis duppy mus' be two foot taller dan Ray. Skinny-tall. Wearin' somet'ing dat fit tight to it frame neck-to-toe, and shine even brighter dan de glow 'round dere bodies. Now Ray he smile and come a step to me, but dis other cotch he arm and 'pear to be scoldin' him. It point behind dem, and dere, right where it pointin', some of de glow clear a spot, and de spot growin' wider and wider to a circle, and t'rough de circle I'm seein' creepers, trees ... solid jungle like dey gots in Miskitia. Ray have a fretful look on he face, but he shrug and dey walks off into de circle. Not walkin' proper, you understand. Dey dwindlin', and de wind dwindlin' wit dem. See, dey not travelin' over de Buryin' Ground but 'pon duppy roads dat draws dem quick from de world, and dey jus' dwindlin' and dwindlin' 'til dey's not'ing but a speck of gleam and a whisper of wind. Den dey gone. Gone for good was de feelin' I got. But where, I cannot tell you.'

MENGELE

During the Vietnam War I served as an aerial scout, piloting a single-engine Cessna low above the jungles, spotting targets for the F-16s. It was not nearly so dangerous as it sounds; the VC preferred to risk the slim chance of being spotted rather than giving away their positions by shooting me down, and most of my flights were made in an atmosphere of relative peace and quiet. I had always been a loner, perhaps even a bit of a misanthrope, and after my tour was up, after returning to the States, I found these attitudes had hardened. War had either colored my perceptions or dropped the scales from my eyes, for everywhere I went I noticed a great dissolution. In the combat zones and shooting galleries, in the bombed-looking districts of urban decay, in the violent music and the cities teeming with derelicts and burned-out children, I saw reflected the energies that had created Vietnam; and it occurred to me that in our culture war and peace had virtually the same effects. The West, it seemed, was truly in decline. I was less in sympathy with those who preached social reform than with the wild-eyed street evangelists who proclaimed the last days and the triumph of evil. Yet evil struck me then as too emotional and unsophisticated a term, redolent of swarming demons and medieval plagues, and I preferred to think of it as a spiritual malaise. No matter what label was given to the affliction, though, I wanted no part of it. I came to think of my wartime experiences, the clean minimalism of my solo flights, as an idyll, and thus I entered into the business of ferrying small planes (Phelan's Air Pherry I called it, until I smartened up).

My disposition to the business was similar to that of someone who is faced with the prospect of crossing a puddle too large to leap; he must plot a course between the shallow spots and then skip on tiptoe from point to point, landing as lightly as possible in order to avoid a contaminating splash. It was my intent to soar above decay, to touch down only in those places as yet unspoiled. Some of the planes I ferried carried cargos, which I did not rigorously inspect; others I delivered to their owners, however far away their homes. The farther away the better, to my mind. By my reckoning I have spent fifteen months in propeller-driven aircraft over water, a good portion of this over the North Atlantic; and so, when I was offered a substantial fee to pilot a twin-engine Beechcraft from Miami to Asunción, the capital of Paraguay, it hardly posed a challenge.

From the outset, though, the flight proved to be anything but unchallenging:

the Beechcraft was a lemon. The right wing shimmied, the inside of the cabin rattled like an old jalopy, and the radio was constantly on the fritz, giving up the ghost once and for all as I crossed into Paraguayan airspace. I had to set down in Guayaquil for repairs to the electrical system, and then, as I was passing over the Gran Chaco – the great forest that sprawls across western Paraguay, a wilderness of rumpled, dark green hills – the engines died.

In those first seconds of pure silence before the weight of the world dragged me down and the wind began ripping past, I experienced an exhilaration, an irrational confidence that God had chosen to make an exception of me and had repealed the law of gravity, that I would float the rest of the way to Asunción. But as the nose of the plane tipped earthward and a chill fanned out from my groin, I shook off this notion and started fighting for my life. A river – the Pilcomayo – was glinting silver among the hills several miles to my left; I banked into a glide and headed toward it. Under ordinary conditions I would have had time to pick an optimal stretch of water, but the Beechcraft was an even worse glider than airplane, and I had to settle for the nearest likely spot: a fairly straight section enclosed by steep piney slopes. As I flashed between the slopes, I caught sight of black-roofed cottages along the shore, a much larger house looming on the crest. Then I smacked down, skipping like a stone for at least a hundred yards. I felt the tail lift, and everything became a sickening whirl of dark green and glare, and the hard silver light of the river came up to shatter the windshield.

I must have regained consciousness shortly after the crash, for I recall a face peering in at me. There was something malformed about the face, some wrongness of hue and shape, but I was too dizzy to see clearly. I tried to speak, managed a croak, and just this slight effort caused me to lose consciousness again. The next thing I recall is waking in a high-ceilinged room whose size led me to believe that I was inside the large house I had noticed atop the slope. My head ached fiercely, and when I put a hand to my brow I found it to be bandaged. As soon as the aching had diminished, I sat up and looked around. The decor of the room had a rectitude that would have been appropriate to a mausoleum. The walls and floors were of gray marble inscribed by veins of deeper gray; the door – a featureless rectangle of ebony – was flanked by two black wooden chairs; the bed itself was spread with a black silk coverlet. I assumed the drapes overhanging the window to be black also, but on closer inspection I discovered that they were woven of a cloth that under various intensities of light displayed many colors of darkness. These were the only furnishings. Carefully, because I was still dizzy, I walked to the window and pulled back the drapes. Scattered among the pines below were a dozen or so black roofs – tile, they were – and a handful of people were visible on the paths between them. There was a terrible, slow awkwardness to their movements that brought to mind the malformed face

I had seen earlier, and a nervous thrill ran across the muscles of my shoulders. Farther down the slope the pines grew more thickly, obscuring the wreckage of the plane, though patches of shining water showed through the boughs.

I heard a click behind me, and turning I saw an old man in the doorway. He was leaning on a cane, wearing a loose gray shirt that buttoned high about his throat, and dark trousers – apparently of the same material as the drapes; he was so hunched that it was only with great difficulty he was able to lift his eyes from the floor (an infirmity, he told me later, that had led to his acquiring an interest in entomology). He was bald, his scalp mottled like a bird's egg, and when he spoke the creakiness of his voice could not disguise a thick German accent.

'I'm pleased to see you up and about, Mr Phelan,' he said, indicating by a gesture that I should sit on the bed.

'I take it I have you to thank for this,' I said, pointing to my bandage. 'I'm very grateful, Mr ...?'

'You may call me Dr Mengele.' He shuffled toward me at a snail's pace. 'I have of course learned your name from your papers. They will be returned to you.'

The name Mengele, which had the sound of a dull bell ringing, was familiar; but I was neither Jewish nor a student of history, and it was not until after he had examined me, pronouncing me fit, that I began to put together the name and the facts of his age, his accent, and his presence in this remote Paraguayan village. Then I remembered a photograph I had seen as a child: a fleshy, smiling man with dark hair cut high above his ears was standing beside a surgical table, where lay a young woman, her torso draped by a sheet; her legs were exposed, and from the calves down all the flesh had been removed, leaving the skeleton protruding from the bloody casings of her knees. *Josef Mengele in his surgery at Auschwitz* had read the caption. That photograph had had quite an effect on me, because of its horrific detail and also because I had not understood what scientific purpose could have been served by this sort of mutilation. I stared at the old man, trying to match his face with the smiling, fleshy one, trying to feel the emanation of evil; but he was withered and shrunken to the point of anonymity, and the only impression I received from him was of an enormous vitality, a forceful physical glow such as might have accrued to a healthy young man.

'Mengele,' I said. 'Not ...'

'Yes, yes!' he said impatiently. '*That* Mengele. The mad doctor of the Third Reich. The monster, the sadist.'

I was repelled, and yet I did not feel outrage as I might have, had I been Jewish. I had been born in 1948, and the terrors of World War II, the concentration camps, Mengele's hideous pseudoscientific experiments, they had the reality of vampire movies for me. I was curious, intensely so, in the way a child becomes fascinated with a crawling thing he has turned up from beneath a stone: he is inclined to crush it, but more likely to watch it ooze along.

'Come with me,' said Mengele, shuffling toward the door. 'I can offer you dinner, but afterward I'm afraid you must leave. We have but one law here, and that is that no stranger may pass the night within our borders.' I had not observed any roads leading away from the village, and when I asked if I might have use of a radio, he laughed. 'We have no communication with the outside world. We are self-sufficient here. None of the villagers ever leave, and rarely do we have visitors. You will have to make your way as best you can.'

'Are you saying I'll have to walk?' I asked.

'You have no choice. If you head south along the river, some twenty or twenty-five kilometers, you will reach another village and there you will find a radio.'

The prospect of being thrown out into the Gran Chaco made me even less eager for his company, but if I was going on a twenty-five-kilometer hike I needed food. His pace was so slow that our walk to the dining room effectively constituted a tour of the house. He talked as we went, telling me – surprisingly enough – of his conversion to Nazism (National Socialism, he termed it) and his work at the camps. Whenever I asked a question he would pause, his expression would go blank, and after a moment he would pose a complicated answer. I had the idea that his answers were prerehearsed, that he had long ago anticipated every possible question and during those pauses he was rummaging through a file. In truth I only half listened to him, being disconcerted by the house. It seemed less a house than a bleak mental landscape, and though I was accompanied by the man whose mind it no doubt reflected, I felt imperiled, out of my element. We passed room after room of gray marble and black furnishings identical to those I have already noted, but with an occasional variant: a pedestal supporting nothing but an obsidian surface; a bookshelf containing rows of black volumes; a carpet of so lusterless and deep a black that it looked to be an opening into some negative dimension. The silence added to my sense of endangerment, and as we entered the dining room, a huge marble cell distinguished from the other rooms by a long ebony table and an iron chandelier, I forced myself to pay attention to him, hoping the sound of his voice would steady my nerves. He had been telling me, I realized, about his flight from Germany.

'It hardly felt like an escape,' he said. 'It had more the air of a vacation. Packing, hurried goodbyes, and as soon as I reached Italy and met my Vatican contact, it all became quite relaxing. Good dinners, fine wines, and at last a leisurely sea voyage.' He seated himself at one end of the table and rang a small black bell: it had been muffled in some way and barely produced a note. 'It will be several minutes before you are served, I fear,' he went on. 'I did not know when you would be sufficiently recovered to eat.'

I took a seat at the opposite end of the table. The strangeness of the environment, meeting Mengele, and now his reminiscences, all coming on the heels of my crash ... it had left me fuddled. I felt as if I were phasing in and out of existence; at one moment I would be alert, intent upon his words, and the next I would be wrapped in vagueness and staring at the walls. The veins of the marble appeared to be writhing, spelling out messages in an archaic script.

'This house,' I said suddenly, interrupting him. 'Why is it like it is? It doesn't seem a place in which a man – even one with your history – would choose to live.'

Again, that momentary blankness. 'I believe you may well be a kindred spirit, Mr Phelan,' he said, and smiled. 'Only one other has asked that particular question, and though he did not understand my answer at first, he came to understand it as you may someday.' He cleared his throat. 'You see, several years after I had settled in Paraguay I underwent a crisis of conscience. Not that I had regrets concerning my actions during the war. Oh, I had nightmares now and again, but no more than such as come to every man. No, I had faith in my work, despite the fact that it had been countenanced as evil, and as it turned out, that work proved to be the foundation of consequential discoveries. But perhaps, I thought, it *was* evil. If this were the case, I freely admitted to it ... and yet I had never seen myself as an evil man. Only a committed one. And now the focus of my commitment – National Socialism – had failed. It was inconceivable to me, though, that the principles underlying it had failed, and I came to the conclusion that the failure could probably be laid to a misapprehension of those principles. Things had happened too fast for us. We had always been in a hurry, overborne by the needs of the country; we had been too pressured to act coherently, and the movement had become less a religion than a church. Empty, pompous ritual had taken the place of contemplated action. But now I had no pressure and all the time in the world, and I set out to understand the nature of evil.'

He sighed and drummed his fingers on the table. 'It was a slow process. Years of study, reading philosophy and natural history and cabalistic works, anything that might have a bearing on the subject. And when finally I did understand, I was amazed that I had not done so sooner. It was obvious! Evil was not – as it had been depicted for centuries – the tool of chaos. Creation was the chaotic force. Why, you can see this truth in every mechanism of the natural world, in the clouds of pollen, the swarms of flies, the migrations of birds. There is precision in those events, but they are nonetheless chaotic. Their precision is one born of overabundance, a million pellets shot and several dozen hitting the mark. No, evil was not chaotic. It was simplicity, it was system, it was the severing stroke of a knife. And most of all, it was inevitable. The entropic resolution of good, the utter simplification of the creative. Hitler had always known this, and National Socialism had always embodied it. What were the blitzkrieg and the concentration camps if not tactical expressions of that simplicity? What is this house if not its esthetic employment?' Mengele smiled, apparently amused by something he saw written on my face. 'This understanding of mine may not strike you as revelatory, yet once I did understand everything I had been doing, all my researches began to succeed whereas previously they had failed. By understanding, of course, I do not mean that I merely acknowledged the principle. I absorbed it, I dissolved in it, I let it rule me like magic. I *understood!*'

I am not sure what I might have said – I was revolted by the depth of his madness, his iniquity – but at that moment he turned to the door and said, 'Ah! Your dinner.' A man dressed in the same manner as Mengele was shuffling across the room, carrying a tray. I barely glanced at him, intent upon my host. The man moved behind my chair and, leaning in over my shoulder, began to lay down plates and silverware. Then I noticed his hand. The skin was ashen gray, the fingers knobbly and unnaturally long – the fingers of a demon – and the nails were figured by half-moons of dead white. Startled, I looked up at him.

He had almost finished setting my place, and I doubt I stared at him for more than a few seconds, but those seconds passed as slowly as drops of water welling from a leaky tap. His face had a horrid simplicity that echoed the decor of the house. His mouth was a lipless slit, his eyes narrow black ovals, his nose a slight swelling perforated by two neat holes; he was bald, his skull elongated, and each time he inclined his head I could see a ridge of bone bisecting the scalp like the sagittal crest of a lizard. All his movements had that awful slowness I had observed in the people of the village. I wanted to fling myself away from the table, but I maintained control and waited until he had gone before I spoke.

'My God!' I said. 'What's wrong with him?'

Mengele pursed his lips in disapproval. 'The deformed are ever with us, Mr Phelan. Surely you have seen worse in your time.'

'Yes, but …'

'Tell me of an instance.' He leaned forward, eager to hear.

I was nonplused, but I told him how one night in New York City – my home – I had been walking in the East Village when a man had come toward me from the opposite corner; his collar had been turned up, his chin tucked in, so that most of his face was obscured; yet as he had passed, the flare of the streetlight had revealed a grimacing mouth set vertically just beneath his cheekbone, complete with tiny teeth. I had not been able to tell if he had in addition a normal mouth, and over the years I had grown uncertain as to whether or not it had been a hallucination. Mengele was delighted and asked me to supply more descriptive details, as if he planned to add the event to his file.

'But your servant,' I asked. 'What of him?'

'Merely a decoration,' he said. 'A creature of my design. The village and the woods abound with them. No doubt you will encounter a fair sampling on your walk along the Pilcomayo.'

'Your design!' I was enraged. 'You made him that way?'

'You cannot have expected my work to have an angelic character.' Mengele paused, thoughtful. 'You must understand that what you see here, the villagers, the house, everything, is a memorial to my work. It has the reality of one of those glass baubles that contain wintry rural scenes and when shaken produce whirling snowstorms. The same actions are repeated over and over, the same effects produced. There is nothing for you to be upset about. The people here are content to serve me in this fashion. They understand.' He pointed to the plates in front of me. 'Eat, Mr Phelan. Time is pressing.'

I looked down at the plates. They were black ceramic. One held a green salad, and the other slices of roast beef swimming in blood. I have always enjoyed rare beef, but in that place it seemed an obscenity. Nonetheless, I was hungry, and I ate. And while I did, while Mengele told me of his work in genetics – work that had created monstrosities such as his servant – I determined to kill him. We were natural enemies, he and I. For though I had no personal score to settle, he exulted in the dissolution that I had spent most of my postwar life in avoiding. It was time, I thought, to do more than avoid it. I decided to take the knife with which I cut my beef and slash his throat. Perhaps he would appreciate the simplicity.

'Naturally,' he said, 'the creation of grotesques was not the pinnacle of my achievements. That pinnacle I reached nine years ago when I discovered a means of chemically affecting the mechanisms that underlie gene regulation, specifically those that control cell breakdown and rebuilding.'

Being no scientist, I was not sure what he meant. 'Cell breakdown?' I said. 'Are you …'

'Simply stated,' he said, 'I learned to reverse the process of aging. It may be that I have discovered the secret of immortality, though it is not yet clear how many treatments the body will accept.'

'If that's true, why haven't you treated yourself?'

'Indeed,' he said with a chuckle. 'Why not?'

There was no doubt in my mind that he was lying about his great triumph, and this lie – which put into an even darker perspective the malignancy of his work, showing it to be purposeless, serving no end other than to further the vileness of his ego – this lie firmed my resolve to kill him. I gripped the knife and started to push back my chair; but then a disturbing thought crossed my mind. 'Why have you revealed yourself to me?' I asked. 'Surely you know that I'm liable to mention this to someone.'

'First, Mr Phelan, you may never have a chance to mention it; a twenty-five-kilometer walk along the Pilcomayo is no Sunday stroll. Second, whom would you tell? The officialdom of this country are my associates.'

'What about the Israelis? If they knew of this place, they'd be swarming all over you.'

'The Israelis!' Mengele made a noise of disgust. 'They would not find me here. Tell them if you wish. I will give you proof.' He opened a drawer in the end of the table and from it removed an ink bottle and a sheet of paper; he poured a few drops of ink onto the paper, and after a moment pressed his thumb down to make a print; then he blew on the paper and slid it toward me. 'Show that to the Israelis and tell them I am not afraid of their reprisals. My work will go on.'

I picked up the paper. 'I suppose you've altered your prints, and this will only prove to the Israelis that I'm a madman.'

'These fingerprints have not been altered.'

'Good.' I folded the paper and stuck it into my shirt pocket. Knife in hand, I stood and walked along the table toward him. I am certain he knew my intention, yet his bemused expression did not falter; and when I reached his side he looked me in the eyes. I wanted to say something, pronounce a curse that would harrow him to hell; his calm stare, however, unnerved me. I put my left hand behind his neck to steady him and prepared to draw the blade across his jugular. But as I did, he seized my wrist in a powerful grip, holding me immobile. I clubbed him on the brow with my left hand, and his head scarcely wobbled. Terrified, I tried to wrench free and managed to stagger a few paces away, pulling him after me. He did not attack; he only laughed and maintained his grip. I battered him again and again, I clawed at his face, his neck, and in so doing I tore the buttons from his shirt. The two halves fell open, and I screamed at what I saw.

He flung me to the floor and shrugged off the torn shirt. I was transfixed. Though he was still hunched, his torso was smooth-skinned and powerfully muscled, the torso of a young man from which a withered neck had sprouted; his arms, too, bulged with muscle and evolved into gnarled, liver-spotted hands. There was no trace of surgical scarring; the skin flowed from youth to old age in the way a tributary changes color upon merging with the mainstream. 'Why not?' he had answered when I asked why he did not avail himself of his treatments. Of course he had, and – in keeping with his warped sensibilities – he had transformed himself into a monster. The sight of that shrunken face perched atop a youthful body was enough to shred the last of my rationality. Ablaze with fear, I scrambled to my feet and ran from the room, bursting through the main doors and down the piney slope, with Mengele's laughter echoing behind.

Night had fallen, a three-quarter moon rode high, and as I plunged along the path toward the river, in the slants of silvery light piercing the boughs I saw the villagers standing by the doors of their cottages. Some moved after me, stretching out their arms ... whether in supplication or aggression, I was unable to tell. I did not stop to take note of their particular deformities, but glimpsed oblate heads, strangely configured hands, great bruised-looking eyes that seemed patches of velvet woven into their skins rather than organs with humors and capillaries. Breath shrieked in my throat as I zigzagged among them, eluding their sluggish attempts to touch me. And then I was splashing through the shallows, past the wreckage of my plane, past those godforsaken slopes, panicked, falling, crawling, sending up silvery sprays of water that were like shouts, pure expressions of my fear.

Twenty-five kilometers along the Río Pilcomayo. Fifteen miles. Twelve hours. No measure could encompass the terrors of that walk. Mengele's creatures did, indeed, abound. Once, while pausing to catch my breath, I spotted an owl on a branch that overhung the water. A jet-black owl, its eyes glowing faintly orange. Once a vast bulk heaved up from midstream, just the back of the thing, an expanse of smooth dark skin: it may have been thirty feet long. Once, at a point where the Pilcomayo fell into a gorge and I was forced to go overland, something heavy pursued me through the brush, and at last, fearing it more than the rapids, I dove into the river; as the current bore me off, I saw its huge misshapen head leaning over the cliff, silhouetted against the stars. All around I heard cries that I did not believe could issue from an earthly throat. Bubbling screeches, grinding roars, eerie whistles that reminded me of the keening made by incoming artillery rounds. By the time I reached the village of which Mengele had spoken, I was incoherent and I remember little of the flight that carried me to Asunción.

The authorities questioned me about my accident. I told them my compass had malfunctioned, that I had no idea where I had crashed. I was afraid to mention Mengele. These men were his accomplices, and besides, if his creatures flourished along the Pilcomayo, could not some of them be here? What had he said? 'The deformed are ever with us, Mr Phelan.' True enough, but since my experiences in his house it seemed I had become sensitized to their presence. I picked them out of crowds, I encountered them on street corners, I saw the potential for deformity in every normal face. Even after returning to New York, every subway ride, every walk, every meal out, brought me into contact with men and women who hid their faces – all having the gray city pallor – yet who could not quite disguise some grotesque disfigurement. I suffered nightmares; I imagined I was being watched. Finally, in hopes of exorcising these fears, I went to see an old Jewish man, a colleague of Simon Wiesenthal, the famous Nazi hunter.

His office in the East Seventies was a picture of clutter, with stacks of papers and folios teetering on his desk, overflowing file cabinets. He was as old a man as Mengele had appeared, his forehead tiered by wrinkles, cadaverous cheeks, weepy brown eyes. I took a seat at the desk and handed him the paper on which Mengele had made his thumbprint. 'I'd like this identified,' I said. 'I believe it belongs to Josef Mengele.'

He stared at it a moment, then hobbled over to a cabinet and began shuffling through papers. After several minutes he clicked his tongue against his teeth and came back to the desk. 'Where did you get this?' he asked with a degree of urgency.

'Does it match?'

He hesitated. 'Yes, it matches. Now where did you get it?'

As I told my story, he leaned back and closed his eyes and nodded thoughtfully, interrupting me to ask an occasional question. 'Well,' I said when I had finished. 'What are you going to do?'

'I don't know. There may be nothing I can do.'

'What do you mean?' I said, dumbfounded. 'I can give you the exact position of the village. Hell, I can take you there myself!'

He let out a weary sigh. 'This' – he tapped the paper – 'this is not Mengele's thumbprint.'

'He must have altered it,' I said, desperate to prove my case. 'He *is* there! I swear it! If you would just ...' And then I realized something. 'You said it matched?'

The old man's face seemed to have sagged further into decay. 'Six years ago a man came to the office and told me almost verbatim the story you have told. I thought he was insane and threw him out, but before he left he thrust a paper at me, one that bore a thumbprint. That print matches yours. But it does not belong to Mengele.'

'Then it is proof!' I said excitedly. 'Don't you see? He may have altered it, but this proves that he exists, and the existence of the village where he lives.'

'Does he live there?' he asked. 'I'm afraid there is another possibility.'

I was not sure what he meant at first; then I remembered Mengele's description of the village. '... what you see here, the villagers, the house, everything, is a memorial to my work. It has the reality of one of those glass baubles that contain wintry rural scenes and when shaken produce whirling snowstorms.' The key word was 'everything.' I had likened the way he had paused before giving answers to rummaging through a file, but it was probably more accurate to say he had been recalling a memorized biography. It had been a stand-in I had met, a young man made old or the reverse. Mengele was many years gone from the village, gone God knows where and in God knows what disguise, doing his work. Perhaps he was once again the fleshy, smiling man whose photograph I had seen as a child.

The old man and I had little else to say to one another. He was anxious to be rid of me; I had, after all, shed a wan light on his forty years of vengeful labor. I asked if he had an address for the other man who had told him of the village; I thought he alone might be able to offer me solace. The old man gave it to me – an address in the West Twenties – and promised to initiate an investigation of the village; but I think we both knew that Mengele had won, that *his* principle, not ours, was in accord with the times. I felt hopeless, stunned, and on stepping outside I became aware of Mengele's victory in an even more poignant way.

It was a gray, blustery afternoon, a few snowflakes whirling between the drab facades of the buildings; the windows were glinting blackly, reflecting opaque diagonals of the sky. Garbage was piled in the gutters, spilling onto the sidewalks, and wedges of grimy crusted snow clung to the bumpers of the cars. Hunched against the wind, holding their coat collars closed over their faces, pedestrians struggled past. What I could see of their expressions was either hateful or angry or worried. It was a perfect Mengelian day, all underpinnings visible, everything pared down to ordinary bone; and as I walked along, I wondered for how much of it he was directly responsible. Oh, he was somewhere turning out grotesques, working scientific charms, but I doubted his efforts were essential to that gray principle underlying the factory air, the principle he worshiped, whose high priest he was. He had been right. Good *was* eroding into evil, bright into dark, abundance into uniformity. Everywhere I went I saw that truth reflected. In the simple shapes and primary colors of the cars, in the mad eyes of the bag ladies, in the featureless sky, in the single-minded stares of businessmen. We were all suffering a reduction to simpler forms, a draining of spirit and vitality.

I walked aimlessly, but I was not surprised to find myself some time later standing before an apartment building in the West Twenties; nor was I any more surprised when shortly thereafter a particularly gray-looking man came down the steps, his face muffled by a scarf and a wool hat pulled low over his brow. He shuffled across the street toward me, unwrapping the scarf. I knew I would be horrified by his deformity, yet I was willing to accept him, to listen, to hear what comforts deformity bestowed; because, though I did not understand Mengele's principle, though I had not dissolved in it or let it rule me, I had acknowledged it and sensed its inevitability. I could almost detect its slow vibrations ringing the changes of the world with – like the syllables of Mengele's name – the sullen, unmusical timbre of a deadened bell.

THE MAN WHO PAINTED
THE DRAGON GRIAULE

Other than the Sichi Collection, Cattanay's only surviving works are to be found in the Municipal Gallery at Regensburg, a group of eight oils-on-canvas, most notable among them being Woman With Oranges. *These paintings constitute his portion of a student exhibition hung some weeks after he had left the city of his birth and traveled south to Teocinte, there to present his proposal to the city fathers; it is unlikely he ever learned of the disposition of his work, and even more unlikely that he was aware of the general critical indifference with which it was received. Perhaps the most interesting of the group to modern scholars, the most indicative as to Cattanay's later preoccupations, is the Self-Portrait, painted at the age of twenty-eight, a year before his departure.*

The majority of the canvas is a richly varnished black in which the vague shapes of floorboards are presented, barely visible. Two irregular slashes of gold cross the blackness, and within these we can see a section of the artist's thin features and the shoulder panel of his shirt. The perspective given is that we are looking down at the artist, perhaps through a tear in the roof, and that he is looking up at us, squinting into the light, his mouth distorted by a grimace born of intense concentration. On first viewing the painting, I was struck by the atmosphere of tension that radiated from it. It seemed I was spying upon a man imprisoned within a shadow having two golden bars, tormented by the possibilities of light beyond the walls. And though this may be the reaction of the art historian, not the less knowledgeable and therefore more trustworthy response of the gallery-goer, it also seemed that this imprisonment was self-imposed, that he could have easily escaped his confine; but that he had realized a feeling of stricture was an essential fuel to his ambition, and so had chained himself to this arduous and thoroughly unreasonable chore of perception ...

– FROM *MERIC CATTANAY:*
THE POLITICS OF CONCEPTION
BY READE HOLLAND, PH. D

I

In 1853, in a country far to the south, in a world separated from this one by the thinnest margin of possibility, a dragon named Griaule dominated the region of the Carbonales Valley, a fertile area centering upon the town of

Teocinte and renowned for its production of silver, mahogany, and indigo. There were other dragons in those days, most dwelling on the rocky islands west of Patagonia – tiny, irascible creatures, the largest of them no bigger than a swallow. But Griaule was one of the great Beasts who had ruled an age. Over the centuries he had grown to stand 750 feet high at the midback, and from the tip of his tail to his nose he was six thousand feet long. (It should be noted here that the growth of dragons was due not to caloric intake, but to the absorption of energy derived from the passage of time.) Had it not been for a miscast spell, Griaule would have died millennia before. The wizard entrusted with the task of slaying him – knowing his own life would be forfeited as a result of the magical backwash – had experienced a last-second twinge of fear, and, diminished by this ounce of courage, the spell had flown a mortal inch awry. Though the wizard's whereabouts was unknown, Griaule had remained alive. His heart had stopped, his breath stilled, but his mind continued to seethe, to send forth the gloomy vibrations that enslaved all who stayed for long within range of his influence.

This dominance of Griaule's was an elusive thing. The people of the valley attributed their dour character to years of living under his mental shadow, yet there were other regional populations who maintained a harsh face to the world and had no dragon on which to blame the condition; they also attributed their frequent raids against the neighboring states to Griaule's effect, claiming to be a peaceful folk at heart – but again, was this not human nature? Perhaps the most certifiable proof of Griaule's primacy was the fact that despite a standing offer of a fortune in silver to anyone who could kill him, no one had succeeded. Hundreds of plans had been put forward, and all had failed, either through inanition or impracticality. The archives of Teocinte were filled with schematics for enormous steam-powered swords and other such improbable devices, and the architects of these plans had every one stayed too long in the valley and become part of the disgruntled populace. And so they went on with their lives, coming and going, always returning, bound to the valley, until one spring day in 1853, Meric Cattanay arrived and proposed that the dragon be painted.

He was a lanky young man with a shock of black hair and a pinched look to his cheeks; he affected the loose trousers and shirt of a peasant, and waved his arms to make a point. His eyes grew wide when listening, as if his brain were bursting with illumination, and at times he talked incoherently about 'the conceptual statement of death by art.' And though the city fathers could not be sure, though they allowed for the possibility that he simply had an unfortunate manner, it seemed he was mocking them. All in all, he was not the sort they were inclined to trust. But, because he had come armed with such a wealth of diagrams and charts, they were forced to give him serious consideration.

'I don't believe Griaule will be able to perceive the menace in a process as subtle as art,' Meric told them. 'We'll proceed as if we were going to illustrate him, grace his side with a work of true vision, and all the while we'll be poisoning him with the paint.'

The city fathers voiced their incredulity, and Meric waited impatiently until they quieted. He did not enjoy dealing with these worthies. Seated at their long table, sour-faced, a huge smudge of soot on the wall above their heads like an ugly thought they were sharing, they reminded him of the Wine Merchants Association in Regensburg, the time they had rejected his group portrait.

'Paint can be deadly stuff,' he said after their muttering had died down. 'Take Vert Veronese, for example. It's derived from oxide of chrome and barium. Just a whiff would make you keel over. But we have to go about it seriously, create a real piece of art. If we just slap paint on his side, he might see through us.'

The first step in the process, he told them, would be to build a tower of scaffolding, complete with hoists and ladders, that would brace against the supraorbital plates above the dragon's eye; this would provide a direct route to a seven-hundred-foot-square loading platform and base station behind the eye. He estimated it would take eight-one-thousand board feet of lumber, and a crew of ninety men should be able to finish construction within five months. Ground crews accompanied by chemists and geologists would search out limestone deposits (useful in priming the scales) and sources of pigments, whether organic or minerals such as azurite and hematite. Other teams would be set to scraping the dragon's side clean of algae, peeled skin, any decayed material, and afterward would laminate the surface with resins.

'It would be easier to bleach him with quicklime,' he said. 'But that way we lose the discolorations and ridges generated by growth and age, and I think what we'll paint will be defined by those shapes. Anything else would look like a damn tattoo!'

There would be storage vats and mills: edge-runner mills to separate pigments from crude ores, ball mills to powder the pigments, pug mills to mix them with oil. There would be boiling vats and calciners – fifteen-foot-high furnaces used to produce caustic lime for sealant solutions.

'We'll build most of them atop the dragon's head for purposes of access,' he said. 'On the frontoparietal plate.' He checked some figures. 'By my reckoning, the plate's about 350 feet wide. Does that sound accurate?'

Most of the city fathers were stunned by the prospect, but one managed a nod, and another asked, 'How long will it take for him to die?'

'Hard to say,' came the answer. 'Who knows how much poison he's capable of absorbing? It might just take a few years. But in the worst instance, within forty or fifty years, enough chemicals will have seeped through the scales to have weakened the skeleton and he'll fall in like an old barn.'

'Forty years!' exclaimed someone. 'Preposterous!'

'Or fifty.' Meric smiled. 'That way we'll have time to finish the painting.' He turned and walked to the window and stood gazing out at the white stone houses of Teocinte. This was going to be the sticky part, but if he read them right, they would not believe in the plan if it seemed too easy. They needed to feel they were making a sacrifice, that they were nobly bound to a great labor. 'If it does take forty or fifty years,' he went on, 'the project will drain your resources. Timber, animal life, minerals. Everything will be used up by the work. Your lives will be totally changed. But I guarantee you'll be rid of him.'

The city fathers broke into an outraged babble.

'Do you really want to kill him?' cried Meric, stalking over to them and planting his fists on the table. 'You've been waiting centuries for someone to come along and chop off his head or send him up in a puff of smoke. That's not going to happen! There is no easy solution. But there is a practical one, an elegant one. To use the stuff of the land he dominates to destroy him. It will *not* be easy, but you *will* be rid of him. And that's what you want, isn't it?'

They were silent, exchanging glances, and he saw that they now believed he could do what he proposed and were wondering if the cost was too high.

'I'll need five hundred ounces of silver to hire engineers and artisans,' said Meric. 'Think it over. I'll take a few days and go see this dragon of yours ... inspect the scales and so forth. When I return, you can give me your answer.'

The city fathers grumbled and scratched their heads, but at last they agreed to put the question before the body politic. They asked for a week in which to decide and appointed Jarcke, who was the mayoress of Hangtown, to guide Meric to Griaule.

The valley extended seventy miles from north to south, and was enclosed by jungled hills whose folded sides and spiny backs gave rise to the idea that beasts were sleeping beneath them. The valley floor was cultivated into fields of bananas and cane and melons, and where it was not cultivated, there were stands of thistle palms and berry thickets and the occasional giant fig brooding sentinel over the rest. Jarcke and Meric tethered their horses a half-hour's ride from town and began to ascend a gentle incline that rose into the notch between two hills. Sweaty and short of breath, Meric stopped a third of the way up; but Jarcke kept plodding along, unaware he was no longer following. She was by nature as blunt as her name – a stump beer keg of a woman with a brown weathered face. Though she appeared to be ten years older then Meric, she was nearly the same age. She wore a gray robe belted at the waist with a leather band that held four throwing knives, and a coil of rope was slung over her shoulder.

'How much farther?' called Meric.

She turned and frowned. 'You're standin' on his tail. Rest of him's around back of the hill.'

A pinprick of chill bloomed in Meric's abdomen, and he stared down at the grass, expecting it to dissolve and reveal a mass of glittering scales.

'Why don't we take the horses?' he asked.

'Horses don't like it up here.' She grunted with amusement. 'Neither do most people, for that matter.' She trudged off.

Another twenty minutes brought them to the other side of the hill high above the valley floor. The land continued to slope upward, but more gently than before. Gnarled, stunted oaks pushed up from thickets of chokecherry, and insects sizzled in the weeds. They might have been walking on a natural shelf several hundred feet across; but ahead of them, where the ground rose abruptly, a number of thick greenish-black columns broke from the earth. Leathery folds hung between them, and these were encrusted with clumps of earth and brocaded with mold. They had the look of a collapsed palisade and the ghosted feel of ancient ruins.

'Them's the wings,' said Jarcke. 'Mostly they's covered, but you can catch sight of 'em off the edge, and up near Hangtown there's places where you can walk in under 'em ... but I wouldn't advise it.'

'I'd like to take a look off the edge,' said Meric, unable to tear his eyes away from the wings; though the surfaces of the leaves gleamed in the strong sun, the wings seemed to absorb the light, as if their age and strangeness were proof against reflection.

Jarcke led him to a glade in which tree ferns and oaks crowded together and cast a green gloom, and where the earth sloped sharply downward. She lashed her rope to an oak and tied the other end around Meric's waist. 'Give a yank when you want to stop, and another when you want to be hauled up,' she said, and began paying out the rope, letting him walk backward against her pull.

Ferns tickled Meric's neck as he pushed through the brush, and the oak leaves pricked his cheeks. Suddenly he emerged into bright sunlight. On looking down, he found his feet were braced against a fold of the dragon's wing, and on looking up, he saw that the wing vanished beneath a mantle of earth and vegetation. He let Jarcke lower him a dozen feet more, yanked, and gazed off northward along the enormous swell of Griaule's side.

The scales were hexagonals thirty feet across and half that distance high; their basic color was a pale greenish gold, but some were whitish, draped with peels of dead skin, and others were overgrown by viridian moss, and the rest were scrolled with patterns of lichen and algae that resembled the characters of a serpentine alphabet. Birds had nested in the cracks, and ferns plumed from the interstices, thousands of them lifting in the breeze. It was a great hanging garden whose scope took Meric's breath away – like looking around the curve of a fossil moon. The sense of all the centuries accreted in the scales made him dizzy, and he found he could not turn his head, but could only stare at the panorama, his soul shriveling with a comprehension of the timelessness and bulk of this creature to which he clung like a fly. He lost perspective on the scene – Griaule's side was bigger than the sky, possessing its own potent gravity, and it seemed completely reasonable that he should be able to walk out along it and suffer no fall. He started to do so, and Jarcke, mistaking the strain on the rope for a signal, hauled him up, dragging him across the wing, through the dirt and ferns, and back into the glade. He lay speechless and gasping at her feet.

'Big 'un, ain't he,' she said, and grinned.

After Meric had gotten his legs under him, they set off toward Hangtown; but they had not gone a hundred yards, following a trail that wound through the thickets, before Jarcke whipped out a knife and hurled it at a raccoon-sized creature that leaped out in front of them.

'Skizzer,' she said, kneeling beside it and pulling the knife from its neck. 'Calls 'em that 'cause they hisses when they runs. They eats snakes, but they'll go after children what ain't careful.'

Meric dropped down next to her. The skizzer's body was covered with short black fur, but its head was hairless, corpse-pale, the skin wrinkled as if it had been immersed too long in water. Its face was squinty-eyed, flat-nosed, with a disproportionately large jaw that hinged open to expose a nasty set of teeth.

'They's the dragon's critters,' said Jarcke. 'Used to live in his bunghole.' She pressed one of its paws, and claws curved like hooks slid forth. 'They'd hang around the lip and drop on other critters what wandered in. And if nothin' wandered in ...' She pried out the tongue with her knife – its surface was studded with jagged points like the blade of a rasp. 'Then they'd lick Griaule clean for their supper.'

Back in Teocinte, the dragon had seemed to Meric a simple thing, a big lizard with a tick of life left inside, the residue of a dim sensibility; but he was beginning to suspect that this tick of life was more complex than any he had encountered.

'My gram used to say,' Jarcke went on, 'that the old dragons could fling themselves up to the sun in a blink and travel back to their own world, and when they come back, they'd bring the skizzers and all the rest with 'em. They was immortal, she said. Only the young ones came here 'cause later on they grew too big to fly on Earth.' She made a sour face. 'Don't know as I believe it.'

'Then you're a fool,' said Meric.

Jarcke glanced up at him, her hand twitching toward her belt.

'How can you live here and *not* believe it!' he said, surprised to hear himself so fervently defending a myth. 'God! This …' He broke off, noticing the flicker of a smile on her face.

She clucked her tongue, apparently satisfied by something. 'Come on,' she said. 'I want to be at the eye before sunset.'

The peaks of Griaule's folded wings, completely overgrown by grass and shrubs and dwarfish trees, formed two spiny hills that cast a shadow over Hangtown and the narrow lake around which it sprawled. Jarcke said the lake was a stream flowing off the hill behind the dragon, and that it drained away through the membranes of his wing and down onto his shoulder. It was beautiful beneath the wing, she told him. Ferns and waterfalls. But it was reckoned an evil place. From a distance the town looked picturesque – rustic cabins, smoking chimneys. As they approached, however, the cabins resolved into dilapidated shanties with missing boards and broken windows; suds and garbage and offal floated in the shallows of the lake. Aside from a few men idling on the stoops, who squinted at Meric and nodded glumly at Jarcke, no one was about. The grass-blades stirred in the breeze, spiders scuttled under the shanties, and there was an air of torpor and dissolution.

Jarcke seemed embarrassed by the town. She made no attempt at introductions, stopping only long enough to fetch another coil of rope from one of the shanties, and as they walked between the wings, down through the neck spines – a forest of greenish gold spikes burnished by the lowering sun – she explained how the townsfolk grubbed a livelihood from Griaule. Herbs gathered on his back were valued as medicine and charms, as were the peels of dead skin; the artifacts left by previous Hangtown generations were of some worth to various collectors.

'Then there's scale hunters,' she said with disgust. 'Henry Sichi from Port Chantay'll pay good money for pieces of scale, and though it's bad luck to do it, some'll have a go at chippin' off the loose 'uns,' She walked a few paces in silence. 'But there's others who've got better reasons for livin' here.'

The frontal spike above Griaule's eyes was whorled at the base like a narwhal's horn and curved back toward the wings. Jarcke attached the ropes to eyebolts drilled into the spike, tied one about her waist, the other about Meric's; she cautioned him to wait, and rappelled off the side. In a moment she called for him to come down. Once again he grew dizzy as he descended; he glimpsed a clawed foot far below, mossy fangs jutting from an impossibly long jaw; and then he began to spin and bash against the scales. Jarcke gathered him in and helped him sit on the lip of the socket.

'Damn!' she said, stamping her foot.

A three-foot-long section of the adjoining scale shifted slowly away. Peering close, Meric saw that while in texture and hue it was indistinguishable from the scale, there was a hairline division between it and the surface.

Jarcke, her face twisted in disgust, continued to harry the thing until it moved out of reach.

'Call 'em flakes,' she said when he asked what it was. 'Some kind of insect. Got a long tube that they pokes down between the scales and sucks the blood. See there?' She pointed off to where a flock of birds was wheeling close to Griaule's side; a chip of pale gold broke loose and went tumbling down to the valley. 'Birds pry 'em off, let 'em bust open, and eats the innards.' She hunkered down beside him and after a moment asked, 'You really think you can do it?'

'What? You mean kill the dragon?'

She nodded.

'Certainly,' he said, and then added, lying, 'I've spent years devising the method.'

'If all the paint's goin' to be atop his head, how're you goin' to get it to where the paintin's done?'

'That's no problem. We'll pipe it to wherever it's needed.'

She nodded again. 'You're a clever fellow,' she said; and when Meric, pleased, made as if to thank her for the compliment, she cut in and said, 'Don't mean nothin' by it. Bein' clever ain't an accomplishment. It's just somethin' you come by, like bein' tall.' She turned away, ending the conversation.

Meric was weary of being awestruck, but even so he could not help marveling at the eye. By his estimate it was seventy feet long and fifty feet high, and it was shuttered by an opaque membrane that was unusually clear of algae and lichen, glistening, with vague glints of color visible behind it. As the westering sun reddened and sank between two distant hills, the membrane began to quiver and then split open down the center. With the ponderous slowness of a theater curtain opening, the halves slid apart to reveal the glowing humor. Terrified by the idea that Griaule could see him, Meric sprang to his feet, but Jarcke restrained him.

'Stay still and watch,' she said.

He had no choice – the eye was mesmerizing. The pupil was slit and featureless black, but the humor … he had never seen such fiery blues and crimsons and golds. What had looked to be vague glints, odd refractions of the sunset, he now realized were photic reactions of some sort. Fairy rings of light developed deep within the eye, expanded into spoked shapes, flooded the humor, and faded – only to be replaced by another and another. He felt the pressure of Griaule's vision, his ancient mind, pouring through him, and as if in response to this pressure, memories bubbled up in his thoughts. Particularly sharp ones. The way a bowlful of brush water had looked after freezing over during a winter's night – a delicate, fractured flower of murky yellow. An archipelago of orange peels that his girl had left strewn across the floor of the studio. Sketching atop Jokenam Hill one sunrise, the snow-capped roofs of Regensburg below pitched at all angles like broken paving stones, and silver shafts of the sun striking down through a leaden overcast. It was as if these things were being drawn forth for his inspection. Then they were washed away by what also seemed a memory, though at the same time it was wholly unfamiliar. Essentially it was a landscape of light, and he was plunging through it, up and up. Prisms and lattices of iridescent fire bloomed around him, and everything was a roaring fall into brightness, and finally he was clear into its white furnace heart, his own heart swelling with the joy of his strength and dominion.

It was dusk before Meric realized the eye had closed. His mouth hung open, his eyes ached from straining to see, and his tongue was glued to his palate. Jarcke sat motionless, buried in shadow.

'Th ...' He had to swallow to clear his throat of mucus. 'This is the reason you live here, isn't it?'

'Part of the reason,' she said. 'I can see things comin' way up here. Things to watch out for, things to study on.'

She stood and walked to the lip of the socket and spat off the edge; the valley stretched out gray and unreal behind her, the folds of the hills barely visible in the gathering dusk.

'I seen you comin',' she said.

A week later, after much exploration, much talk, they went down into Teocinte. The town was a shambles – shattered windows, slogans painted on the walls, glass and torn banners and spoiled food littering the streets – as if there had been both a celebration and a battle. Which there had. The city fathers met with Meric in the town hall and informed him that his plan had been approved. They presented him a chest containing five hundred ounces of silver and said that the entire resources of the community were at his disposal. They offered a wagon and a team to transport him and the chest to Regensburg and asked if any of the preliminary work could be begun during his absence.

Meric hefted one of the silver bars. In its cold gleam he saw the object of his desire – two, perhaps three years of freedom, of doing the work he wanted and not having to accept commissions. But all that had been confused. He glanced at Jarcke; she was staring out the window, leaving it to him. He set the bar back in the chest and shut the lid.

'You'll have to send someone else,' he said. And then, as the city fathers looked at each other askance, he laughed and laughed at how easily he had discarded all his dreams and expectations.

It had been eleven years since I had been to the valley, twelve since work had begun on the painting, and I was appalled by the changes that had taken place.

Many of the hills were scraped brown and treeless, and there was a general dearth of wildlife. Griaule, of course, was most changed. Scaffolding hung from his back; artisans, suspended by webworks of ropes, crawled over his side; and all the scales to be worked had either been painted or primed. The tower rising to his eye was swarmed by laborers, and at night the calciners and vats atop his head belched flame into the sky, making it seem there was a mill town in the heavens. At his feet was a brawling shantytown populated by prostitutes, workers, gamblers, ne'er-do-wells of every sort, and soldiers: the burdensome cost of the project had encouraged the city fathers of Teocinte to form a regular militia, which regularly plundered the adjoining states and had posted occupation forces to some areas. Herds of frightened animals milled in the slaughtering pens, waiting to be rendered into oils and pigments. Wagons filled with ores and vegetable products rattled in the streets. I myself had brought a cargo of madder roots from which a rose tint would be derived.

It was not easy to arrange a meeting with Cattanay. While he did none of the actual painting, he was always busy in his office consulting with engineers and artisans, or involved in some other part of the logistical process. When at last I did meet with him, I found he had changed as drastically as Griaule. His hair had gone gray, deep lines scored his features, and his right shoulder had a peculiar bulge at its midpoint – the product of a fall. He was amused by the fact that I wanted to buy the painting, to collect the scales after Griaule's death, and I do not believe he took me at all seriously. But the woman Jarcke, his constant companion, informed him that I was a responsible businessman, that I had already bought the bones, the teeth, even the dirt beneath Griaule's belly (this I eventually sold as having magical properties).

'Well,' said Cattanay, 'I suppose someone has to own them.'

He led me outside, and we stood looking at the painting.

'You'll keep them together?' he asked.

I said, 'Yes.'

'If you'll put that in writing,' he said, 'then they're yours.'

Having expected to haggle long and hard over the price, I was flabbergasted; but I was even more flabbergasted by what he said next.

'Do you think it's any good?' he asked.

Cattanay did not consider the painting to be the work of his imagination; he felt he was simply illuminating the shapes that appeared on Griaule's side and was convinced that once the paint was applied, new shapes were produced beneath it, causing him to make constant changes. He saw himself as an artisan more than a creative artist. But to put his question into perspective, people were beginning to flock from all over the world and marvel at the painting. Some claimed they saw intimations of the future in its gleaming surface; others underwent transfiguring experiences; still others – artists themselves – attempted to capture something of the work on canvas, hopeful of establishing reputations merely by being competent copyists of Cattanay's art. The painting was nonrepresentational in character, essentially a wash of pale gold spread across the dragon's side; but buried beneath the laminated surface were a myriad tints of iridescent color that, as the sun passed through the heavens and the light bloomed and faded, solidified into innumerable forms and figures that seemed to flow back and forth. I will not try to categorize these forms, because there was no end to them; they were as varied as the conditions under which they were viewed. But I will say that on the morning I met with Cattanay, I – who was the soul of the practical man, without a visionary bone in my body – felt as though I were being whirled away into the painting, up through geometries of light, latticeworks of rainbow color that built the way the edges of a cloud build, past orbs, sprials, wheels of flame …

– FROM THIS BUSINESS OF GRIAULE
BY HENRY SICHI

II

There had been several women in Meric's life since he arrived in the valley; most had been attracted by his growing fame and his association with the mystery of the dragon, and most had left for the same reasons, feeling daunted and unappreciated. But Lise was different in two respects. First, because she loved Meric truly and well; and second, because she was married – albeit unhappily – to a man named Pardiel, the foreman of the calciner crew. She did not love him as she did Meric, yet she respected him and felt obliged to consider carefully before ending the relationship. Meric had never known such an introspective soul. She was twelve years younger than he, tall and lovely, with sun-streaked hair and brown eyes that went dark and seemed to turn inward whenever she was pensive. She was in the habit of analyzing everything that affected her, drawing back from her emotions and inspecting them as if they were a clutch of strange insects she had discovered crawling on her skirt. Though her penchant for self-examination kept her from him, Meric viewed it as a kind of baffling virtue. He had the classic malady and could find no fault with her. For almost a year they were as happy as could be expected; they talked long hours and walked together on those occasions when Pardiel worked double shifts and was forced to bed down by his furnaces, they spent the nights making love in the cavernous spaces beneath the dragon's wing.

It was still reckoned an evil place. Something far worse than skizzers or flakes was rumored to live there, and the ravages of this creature were blamed for every disappearance, even that of the most malcontented laborer. But Meric did not give credence to the rumors. He half believed Griaule had chosen him to be his executioner and that the dragon would never let him be harmed; and besides, it was the only place where they could be assured of privacy.

A crude stair led under the wing, handholds and steps hacked from the scales – doubtless the work of scale hunters. It was a treacherous passage, six hundred feet above the valley floor; but Lise and Meric were secured by ropes, and over the months, driven by the urgency of passion, they adapted to it. Their favorite spot lay fifty feet in (Lise would go no farther; she was afraid even if he was not), near a waterfall that trickled over the leathery folds, causing them to glisten with a mineral brilliance. It was eerily beautiful, a haunted gallery. Peels of dead skin hung down from the shadows like torn veils of ectoplasm; ferns sprouted from the vanes, which were thicker than cathedral columns; swallows curved through the black air. Sometimes, lying with her hidden by a tuck of the wing, Meric would think the beating of their hearts was what really animated the place, that the instant they left, the water ceased flowing and the swallows vanished. He had an unshakable faith in the transforming power of their affections, and one morning as they dressed, preparing to return to Hangtown, he asked her to leave with him.

'To another part of the valley?' She laughed sadly. 'What good would that do? Pardiel would follow us.'

'No,' he said. 'To another country. Anywhere far from here.'

'We can't,' she said, kicking at the wing. 'Not until Griaule dies. Have you forgotten?'

'We haven't tried.'

'Others have.'

'But we'd be strong enough. I know it!'

'You're a romantic,' she said gloomily, and stared out over the slope of Griaule's back at the valley. Sunrise had washed the hills to crimson, and even the tips of the wings were glowing a dull red.

'Of course I'm a romantic!' He stood, angry. 'What the hell's wrong with that?'

She sighed with exasperation. 'You wouldn't leave your work,' she said. 'And if we did leave, what work would you do? Would ...'

'Why must everything be a problem in advance!' he shouted. 'I'll tattoo elephants! I'll paint murals on the chests of giants, I'll illuminate whales! Who else is better qualified?'

She smiled, and his anger evaporated.

'I didn't mean it that way,' she said. 'I just wondered if you could be satisfied with anything else.'

She reached out her hand to be pulled up, and he drew her into an embrace. As he held her, inhaling the scent of vanilla water from her hair, he saw a diminutive figure silhouetted against the backdrop of the valley. It did not seem real – a black homunculus – and even when it began to come forward, growing larger and larger, it looked less a man than a magical keyhole opening in a crimson-set hillside. But Meric knew from the man's rolling walk and the hulking set of his shoulders that it was Pardiel; he was carrying a long-handled hook, one of those used by artisans to maneuver along the scales.

Meric tensed, and Lise looked back to see what had alarmed him. 'Oh, my God!' she said, moving out of the embrace.

Pardiel stopped a dozen feet away. He said nothing. His face was in shadow, and the hook swung lazily from his hand. Lise took a step toward him, then stepped back and stood in front of Meric as if to shield him. Seeing this, Pardiel let out an inarticulate yell and charged, slashing with the hook. Meric pushed Lise aside and ducked. He caught a brimstone whiff of the calciners as Pardiel rushed past and went sprawling, tripped by some irregularity in the scale. Deathly afraid, knowing he was no match for the foreman, Meric seized Lise's hand and ran deeper under the wing. He hoped Pardiel would be too frightened to follow, leery of the creature that was rumored to live there; but he was not. He came after them at a measured pace, tapping the hook against his leg.

Higher on Griaule's back, the wing was dimpled downward by hundreds of bulges, and this created a maze of small chambers and tunnels so low that they had to crouch to pass along them. The sound of their breathing and the scrape of their feet were amplified by the enclosed spaces, and Meric could no longer hear Pardiel. He had never been this deep before. He had thought it would be pitch-dark; but the lichen and algae adhering to the wing were luminescent and patterned every surface, even the scales beneath them, with whorls of blue and green fire that shed a sickly radiance. It was as if they were giants crawling through a universe whose starry matter had not yet congealed into galaxies and nebulas. In the wan light, Lise's face – turned back to him now and again – was teary and frantic; and then, as she straightened, passing into still another chamber, she drew in breath with a shriek.

At first Meric thought Pardiel had somehow managed to get ahead of them; but on entering he saw that the cause of her fright was a man propped in a sitting position against the far wall. He looked mummified. Wisps of brittle hair poked up from his scalp, the shapes of his bones were visible through his skin, and his eyes were empty holes. Between his legs was a scatter of dust where his genitals had been. Meric pushed Lise toward the next tunnel, but she resisted and pointed at the man.

'His eyes,' she said, horror-struck.

Though the eyes were mostly a negative black, Meric now realized they were shot through by opalescent flickers. He felt compelled to kneel beside the man – it was a sudden, motiveless urge that gripped him, bent him to its will, and released him a second later. As he rested his hand on the scale, he brushed a massive ring that was lying beneath the shrunken fingers. Its stone was black, shot through by flickers identical to those within the eyes, and incised with the letter S. He found his gaze was deflected away from both the stone and the eyes, as if they contained charges repellent to the senses. He touched the man's withered arm; the flesh was rock-hard, petrified. But alive. From that brief touch he gained an impression of the man's life, of gazing for centuries at the same patch of unearthly fire, of a mind gone beyond mere madness into a perverse rapture, a meditation upon some foul principle. He snatched back his hand in revulsion.

There was a noise behind them, and Meric jumped up, pushing Lise into the next tunnel. 'Go right,' he whispered. 'We'll circle back toward the stair.' But Pardiel was too close to confuse with such tactics, and their flight became a wild chase, scrambling, falling, catching glimpses of Pardiel's smoke-stained face, until finally – as Meric came to a large chamber – he felt the hook bite into his thigh. He went down, clutching at the wound, pulling the hook loose. The next moment Pardiel was atop him; Lise appeared over his shoulder, but he knocked her away and locked his fingers in Meric's hair and smashed his head against the scale. Lise screamed, and white lights fired through Meric's skull. Again his head was smashed down. And again. Dimly, he saw Lise struggling with Pardiel, saw her shoved away, saw the hook raised high and the foreman's mouth distorted by a grimace. Then the grimace vanished. His jaw dropped open, and he reached behind him as if to scratch his shoulder blade. A line of dark blood eeled from his mouth and he collapsed, smothering Meric beneath his chest. Meric heard voices. He tried to dislodge the body, and the effects drained the last of his strength. He whirled down through a blackness that seemed as negative and inexhaustible as the petrified man's eyes.

Someone had propped his head on their lap and was bathing his brow with a damp cloth. He assumed it was Lise, but when he asked what had happened, it was Jarcke who answered, saying, 'Had to kill him.' His head throbbed, his leg throbbed even worse, and his eyes would not focus. The peels of dead skin hanging overhead appeared to be writhing. He realized they were out near the edge of the wing.

'Where's Lise?'

'Don't worry,' said Jarcke. 'You'll see her again.' She made it sound like an indictment.

'Where is she?'

'Sent her back to Hangtown. Won't do you two bein' seen hand in hand the same day Pardiel's missin'.'

'She wouldn't have left ...' He blinked, trying to see her face; the lines around her mouth were etched deep and reminded him of the patterns of lichen on the dragon's scale. 'What did you do?'

'Convinced her it was best,' said Jarcke. 'Don't you know she's just foolin' with you?'

'I've got to talk to her.' He was full of remorse, and it was unthinkable that Lise should be bearing her grief alone; but when he struggled to rise, pain lanced through his leg.

'You wouldn't get ten feet,' she said. 'Soon as your head's clear, I'll help you with the stairs.'

He closed his eyes, resolving to find Lise the instant he got back to Hangtown – together they would decide what to do. The scale beneath him was cool, and that coolness was transmitted to his skin, his flesh, as if he were merging with it, becoming one of its ridges.

'What was the wizard's name?' he asked after a while, recalling the petrified man, the ring and its incised letter. 'The one who tried to kill Griaule ...'

'Don't know as I ever heard it,' said Jarcke. 'But I reckon it's him back there.'

'You saw him?'

'I was chasin' a scale hunter once what stole some rope, and I found him instead. Pretty miserable sort, whoever he is.'

Her fingers trailed over his shoulder – a gentle, treasuring touch. He did not understand what it signaled, being too concerned with Lise, with the terrifying potentials of all that had happened; but years later, after things had passed beyond remedy, he cursed himself for not having understood.

At length Jarcke helped him to his feet, and they climbed up to Hangtown, to bitter realizations and regrets, leaving Pardiel to the birds or the weather or worse.

It seems it is considered irreligious for a woman in love to hesitate or examine the situation, to do anything other than blindly follow the impulse of her emotions. I felt the brunt of such an attitude – people judged it my fault for not having acted quickly and decisively one way or another. Perhaps I was overcautious. I do not claim to be free of blame, only innocent of sacrilege. I believe I might have eventually left Pardiel – there was not enough in the relationship to sustain happiness for either of us. But I had good reason for cautious examination. My husband was not an evil man, and there were matters of loyalty between us.

I could not face Meric after Pardiel's death, and I moved to another part of the valley. He tried to see me on many occasions, but I always refused. Though I was greatly tempted, my guilt was greater. Four years later, after Jarcke died – crushed by a runaway wagon – one of her associates wrote and told me Jarcke had been in love with Meric, that it had been she who had informed Pardiel of the affair, and that she may well have staged the murder. The letter acted somewhat to expiate my guilt, and I weighed the possibility of seeing Meric again. But too much time had passed, and we had both assumed other lives. I decided against it. Six years later, when Griaule's influence had weakened sufficiently to allow emigration, I moved to Port Chantay. I did not hear from Meric for almost twenty years after that, and then one day I received a letter, which I will reproduce in part:

'... My old friend from Regensburg, Louis Dardano, has been living here for the past few years, engaged in writing my biography. The narrative has a breezy feel, like a tale being told in a tavern, which – if you recall my telling you how this all began – is quite appropriate. But on reading it, I am amazed my life has had such a simple shape. One task, one passion. God, Lise! Seventy years old, and I still dream of you. And I still think of what happened that morning under the wing. Strange, that it has taken me all this time to realize it was not Jarcke, not you or I who was culpable, but Griaule. How obvious it seems now. I was leaving, and he needed me to complete the expression on his side, his dream of flying, of escape, to grant him the death of his desire. I am certain you will think I have leaped to this assumption, but I remind you that it has been a leap of forty years' duration. I know Griaule, know his monstrous subtlety. I can see it at work in every action that has taken place in the valley since my arrival. I was a fool not to understand that his powers were at the heart of our sad conclusion.

'The army now runs everything here, as no doubt you are aware. It is rumored they are planning a winter campaign against Regensburg. Can you believe it! Their fathers were ignorant, but this generation is brutally stupid. Otherwise, the work goes well and things are as usual with me. My shoulder aches, children stare at me on the street, and it is whispered I am mad ...'

– FROM *UNDER GRIAULE'S WING*
BY LISE CLAVERIE

III

Acne-scarred, lean, arrogant, Major Hauk was a very young major with a limp. When Meric had entered, the major had been practicing his signature – it was a thing of elegant loops and flourishes, obviously intended to have a place in posterity. As he strode back and forth during their conversation, he paused frequently to admire himself in the window glass, settling the hang of his red jacket or running his fingers along the crease of his white trousers. It was the new style of uniform, the first Meric had seen at close range, and he noted with amusement the dragons embossed on the epaulets. He wondered if Griaule was capable of such an irony, if his influence was sufficiently discreet to have planted the idea for this comic-opera apparel in the brain of some general's wife.

'... not a question of manpower,' the major was saying, 'but of ...' He broke off, and after a moment cleared his throat.

Meric, who had been studying the blotches on the backs of his hands, glanced up; the cane that had been resting against his knee slipped and clattered to the floor.

'A question of matériel,' said the major firmly. 'The price of antimony, for example ...'

'Hardly use it anymore,' said Meric. 'I'm almost done with the mineral reds.'

A look of impatience crossed the major's face. 'Very well,' he said; he stooped to his desk and shuffled through some papers. 'Ah! Here's a bill for a shipment of cuttlefish from which you derive ...' He shuffled more papers.

'Syrian brown,' said Meric gruffly. 'I'm done with that, too. Golds and violets are all I need anymore. A little blue and rose.' He wished the man would stop badgering him; he wanted to be at the eye before sunset.

As the major continued his accounting, Meric's gaze wandered out the window. The shantytown surrounding Griaule had swelled into a city and now sprawled across the hills. Most of the buildings were permanent, wood and stone, and the cant of the roofs, the smoke from the factories around the perimeter, put him in mind of Regensburg. All the natural beauty of the land had been drained into the painting. Blackish gray rain clouds were muscling up from the east, but the afternoon sun shone clear and shed a heavy gold radiance on Griaule's side. It looked as if the sunlight were an extension of the gleaming resins, as if the thickness of the paint were becoming infinite. He let the major's voice recede to a buzz and followed the scatter and dazzle of the images; and then, with a start, he realized the major was sounding him out about stopping the work.

The idea panicked him at first. He tried to interrupt, to raise objections; but the major talked through him, and as Meric thought it over, he grew less and less opposed. The painting would never be finished, and he was tired. Perhaps it was time to have done with it, to accept a university post somewhere and enjoy life for a while.

'We've been thinking about a temporary stoppage,' said Major Hauk. 'Then if the winter campaign goes well ...' He smiled. 'If we're not visited by plague and pestilence, we'll assume things are in hand. Of course we'd like your opinion.'

Meric felt a surge of anger toward this smug little monster. 'In my opinion, you people are idiots,' he said. 'You wear Griaule's image on your shoulders, weave him on your flags, and yet you don't have the least comprehension of what that means. You think it's just a useful symbol ...'

'Excuse me,' said the major stiffly.

'The hell I will!' Meric groped for his cane and heaved up to his feet. 'You see yourselves as conquerors. Shapers of destiny. But all your rapes and slaughters are Griaule's expressions. *His* will. You're every bit as much his parasites as the skizzers.'

The major sat, picked up a pen, and began to write.

'It astounds me,' Meric went on, 'that you can live next to a miracle, a source of mystery, and treat him as if he were an oddly shaped rock.'

The major kept writing.

'What are you doing?' asked Meric.

'My recommendation,' said the major without looking up.

'Which is?'

'That we initiate stoppage at once.'

They exchanged hostile stares, and Meric turned to leave; but as he took hold of the doorknob, the major spoke again.

'We owe you so much,' he said; he wore an expression of mingled pity and respect that further irritated Meric.

'How many men have you killed, Major?' he asked, opening the door.

'I'm not sure. I was in the artillery. We were never able to be sure.'

'Well, I'm sure of my tally,' said Meric. 'It's taken me forty years to amass it. Fifteen hundred and ninety-three men and women. Poisoned, scalded, broken by falls, savaged by animals. Murdered. Why don't we – you and I – just call it even.'

Though it was a sultry afternoon, he felt cold as he walked toward the tower – an internal cold that left him light-headed and weak. He tried to think what he would do. The idea of a university post seemed less appealing away from the major's office; he would soon grow weary of worshipful students and in-depth dissections of his work by jealous academics. A man hailed him as he turned into the market. Meric waved but did not stop, and heard another man say, '*That's* Cattanay?' (That ragged old ruin?)

The colors of the market were too bright, the smells of charcoal cookery too cloying, the crowds too thick, and he made for the side streets, hobbling past one-room stucco houses and tiny stores where they sold cooking oil by the ounce and cut cigars in half if you could not afford a whole one. Garbage, tornadoes of dust and flies, drunks with bloody mouths. Somebody had tied wires around a pariah dog – a bitch with slack teats; the wires had sliced into her flesh, and she lay panting in an alley mouth, gaunt ribs flecked with pink lather, gazing into nowhere. She, thought Meric, and not Griaule, should be the symbol of their flag.

As he rode the hoist up the side of the tower, he fell into his old habit of jotting down notes for the next day. *What's that cord of wood doing on level five? Slow leak of chrome yellow from pipes on level twelve.* Only when he saw a man dismantling some scaffolding did he recall Major Hauk's recommendation and understand that the order must already have been given. The loss of his work struck home to him then, and he leaned against the railing, his chest constricted and his eyes brimming. He straightened, ashamed of himself. The sun hung in a haze of iron-colored light low above the western hills, looking red and bloated and vile as a vulture's ruff. That polluted sky was his creation as much as was the painting, and it would be good to leave it behind. Once away from the valley, from all the influences of the place, he would be able to consider the future.

A young girl was sitting on the twentieth level just beneath the eye. Years before, the ritual of viewing the eye had grown to cultish proportions; there had been group chanting and praying and discussions of the experience. But these were more practical times, and no doubt the young men and women who had congregated here were now manning administrative desks somewhere in the burgeoning empire. They were the ones about whom Dardano should write; they, and all the eccentric characters who had played roles in this slow pageant. The gypsy woman who had danced every night by the eye, hoping to charm Griaule into killing her faithless lover – she had gone away satisfied. The man who had tried to extract one of the fangs – nobody knew what had become of him. The scale hunters, the artisans. A history of Hangtown would be a volume in itself.

The walk had left Meric weak and breathless; he sat down clumsily beside the girl, who smiled. He could not remember her name, but she came often to the eye. Small and dark, with an inner reserve that reminded him of Lise. He laughed inwardly – most women reminded him of Lise in some way.

'Are you all right?' she asked, her brow wrinkled with concern.

'Oh, yes,' he said; he felt a need for conversation to take his mind off things, but he could think of nothing more to say. She was so young! All freshness and gleam and nerves.

'This will be my last time,' she said. 'At least for a while. I'll miss it.' And then, before he could ask why, she added, 'I'm getting married tomorrow, and we're moving away.'

He offered congratulations and asked her who was the lucky fellow.

'Just a boy.' She tossed her hair, as if to dismiss the boy's importance; she gazed up at the shuttered membrane. 'What's it like for you when the eye opens?' she asked.

'Like everyone else,' he said. 'I remember ... memories of my life. Other lives, too.' He did not tell her about Griaule's memory of flight; he had never told anyone except Lise about that.

'All those bits of souls trapped in there,' she said, gesturing at the eye. 'What do they mean to him? Why does he show them to us?'

'I imagine he has his purposes, but I can't explain them.'

'Once I remembered being with you,' said the girl, peeking at him shyly through a dark curl. 'We were under the wing.'

He glanced at her sharply. 'Tell me.'

'We were ... together,' she said, blushing. 'Intimate, you know. I was very afraid of the place, of the sounds and shadows. But I loved you so much, it didn't matter. We made love all night, and I was surprised because I thought that kind of passion was just in stories, something people had invented to make up for how ordinary it really was. And in the morning even that dreadful place had become beautiful, with the wing tips glowing red and the waterfall echoing …' She lowered her eyes. 'Ever since I had that memory, I've been a little in love with you.'

'Lise,' he said, feeling helpless before her.

'Was that her name?'

He nodded and put a hand to his brow, trying to pinch back the emotions that flooded him.

'I'm sorry.' Her lips grazed his cheek, and just that slight touch seemed to weaken him further. 'I wanted to tell you how she felt in case she hadn't told you herself. She was very troubled by something, and I wasn't sure she had.'

She shifted away from him, made uncomfortable by the intensity of his reaction, and they sat without speaking. Meric became lost in watching how the sun glazed the scales to reddish gold, how the light was channeled along the ridges in molten streams that paled as the day wound down. He was startled when the girl jumped to her feet and backed toward the hoist.

'He's dead,' she said wonderingly.

Meric looked at her, uncomprehending.

'See?' She pointed at the sun, which showed a crimson silver above the hill. 'He's dead,' she repeated, and the expression on her face flowed between fear and exultation.

The idea of Griaule's death was too large for Meric's mind to encompass, and he turned to the eye to find a counter proof – no glints of color flickered beneath the membrane. He heard the hoist creak as the girl headed down, but he continued to wait. Perhaps only the dragon's vision had failed. No. It was likely not a coincidence that work had been officially terminated today. Stunned, he sat staring at the lifeless membrane until the sun sank below the hills; then he stood and went over to the hoist. Before he could throw the switch, the cables thrummed – somebody heading up. Of course. The girl would have spread the news, and all the Major Hauks and their underlings would be hurrying to test Griaule's reflexes. He did not want to be there when they arrived, to watch them pose with their trophy like successful fishermen.

It was hard work climbing up to the frontoparietal plate. The ladder swayed, the wind buffeted him, and by the time he clambered onto the plate he was giddy, his chest full of twinges. He hobbled forward and leaned against the rust-caked side of a boiling vat. Shadowy in the twilight, the great furnaces and vats towered around him, and it seemed this system of fiery devices reeking of cooked flesh and minerals was the actual machinery of Griaule's thought materialized above his skull. Energyless, abandoned. They had been replaced by more efficient equipment down below, and it had been – what was it? – almost five years since they were last used. Cobwebs veiled a pyramid of firewood; the stairs leading to the rims of the vats were crumbling. The plate itself was scarred and coated with sludge.

'Cattanay!'

Someone shouted from below, and the top of the ladder trembled. God, they were coming after him! Bubbling over with congratulations and plans for testimonial dinners, memorial plaques, specially struck medals. They would have him draped in bunting and bronzed and covered with pigeon shit before they were done. All these years he had been among them, both their slave and their master, yet he had never felt at home. Leaning heavily on his cane, he made his way past the frontal spike – blackened by years of oily smoke – and down between the wings to Hangtown. It was a ghost town, now. Weeds overgrowing the collapsed shanties; the lake a stinking pit, drained after some children had drowned in the summer of '91. Where Jarcke's home had stood was a huge pile of animal bones, taking a pale shine from the half-light. Wind keened through the tattered shrubs.

'Meric!'

'Cattanay.'

The voices were closer.

Well, there was one place where they would not follow.

The leaves of the thickets were speckled with mold and brittle, flaking away as he brushed them. He hesitated at the top of the scale hunters' stair. He had no rope. Though he had done the climb unaided many times, it had been quite a few years. The gusts of wind, the shouts, the sweep of the valley and the lights scattered across it like diamonds on gray velvet – it all seemed a single inconstant medium. He heard the brush crunch behind him, more voices. To hell with it! Gritting his teeth against a twinge of pain in his shoulder, hooking his cane over his belt, he inched onto the stair and locked his fingers in the handholds. The wind whipped his clothes and threatened to pry him loose and send him pinwheeling off. Once he slipped; once he froze, unable to move backward or forward. But at last he reached the bottom and edged upslope until he found a spot flat enough to stand.

The mystery of the place suddenly bore in upon him, and he was afraid. He half turned to the stair, thinking he would go back to Hangtown and accept the hurly-burly. But a moment later he realized how foolish a thought that was. Waves of weakness poured through him, his heart hammered, and white dazzles flared in his vision. His chest felt heavy as iron. Rattled, he went a few steps forward, the cane pocking the silence. It was too dark to see more than outlines, but up ahead was the fold of wing where he and Lise had sheltered. He walked toward it, intent on revisiting it; then he remembered the girl beneath the eye and understood that he had already said that goodbye. And it *was* goodbye – that he understood vividly. He kept walking. Blackness looked to be welling from the wing joint, from the entrances to the maze of luminous tunnels where they had stumbled onto the petrified man. Had it really been the old wizard, doomed by magical justice to molder and live on and on? It made sense. At least it accorded with what happened to wizards who slew their dragons.

'Griaule?' he whispered to the darkness, and cocked his head, half-expecting an answer. The sound of his voice pointed up the immensity of the great gallery under the wing, the emptiness, and he recalled how vital a habitat it had once been. Flakes shifting over the surface, skizzers, peculiar insects fuming in the thickets, the glum populace of Hangtown, waterfalls. He had never been able to picture Griaule fully alive – that kind of vitality was beyond the powers of the imagination. Yet he wondered if by some miracle the dragon were alive now, flying up through his golden night to the sun's core. Or had that merely been a dream, a bit of tissue glittering deep in the cold tons of his brain? He laughed. Ask the stars for their first names, and you'd be more likely to receive a reply.

He decided not to walk any farther – it was really no decision. Pain was spreading through his shoulder, so intense he imagined it must be glowing inside. Carefully, carefully, he lowered himself and lay propped on an elbow, hanging on to the cane. Good, magical wood. Cut from a hawthorn atop Griaule's haunch. A man had once offered him a small fortune for it. Who would claim it now? Probably old Henry Sichi would snatch it for his museum, stick it in a glass case next to his boots. What a joke! He decided to lie flat on his stomach, resting his chin on an arm – the stony coolness beneath acted to muffle the pain. Amusing, how the range of one's decision dwindled. You decided to paint a dragon, to send hundreds of men searching for malachite and cochineal beetles, to love a woman, to heighten an undertone here and there, and finally to position your body a certain way. He seemed to have reached the end of the process. What next? He tried to regulate his breathing, to ease the pressure on his chest. Then, as something rustled out near the wing joint, he turned on his side. He thought he detected movement, a gleaming blackness flowing toward him ... or else it was only the haphazard firing of his nerves playing tricks with his vision. More surprised than afraid, wanting to see, he peered into the darkness and felt his heart beating erratically against the dragon's scale.

> *It's foolish to draw simple conclusions from complex events, but I suppose there must be both moral and truth to this life, these events. I'll leave that to the gadflies. The historians, the social scientists, the expert apologists for reality. All I know is that he had a fight with his girlfriend over money and*

walked out. He sent her a letter saying he had gone south and would be back in a few months with more money than she could ever spend. I had no idea what he'd done. The whole thing about Griaule had just been a bunch of us sitting around the Red Bear, drinking up my pay – I'd sold an article – and somebody said, 'Wouldn't it be great if Dardano didn't have to write articles, if we didn't have to paint pictures that color-coordinated with people's furniture or slave at getting the gooey smiles of little nieces and nephews just right?' All sorts of improbable moneymaking schemes were put forward. Robberies, kidnappings. Then the idea of swindling the city fathers of Teocinte came up, and the entire plan was fleshed out in minutes. Scribbled on napkins, scrawled on sketchpads. A group effort. I keep trying to remember if anyone got a glassy look in their eye, if I felt a cold tendril of Griaule's thought stirring my brains. But I can't. It was a half-hour's sensation, nothing more. A drunken whimsy, an art-school metaphor. Shortly thereafter, we ran out of money and staggered into the streets. It was snowing – big wet flakes that melted down our collars. God, we were drunk! Laughing, balancing on the icy railing of the University Bridge. Making faces at the bundled-up burghers and their fat ladies who huffed and puffed past, spouting steam and never giving us a glance, and none of us – not even the burghers – knowing that we were living our happy ending in advance ...

– FROM THE MAN WHO PAINTED
THE DRAGON GRIAULE
BY LOUIS DARDANO

A SPANISH LESSON

That winter of '64, when I was seventeen and prone to obey the impulses of my heart as if they were illuminations produced by years of contemplative study, I dropped out of college and sailed to Europe, landing in Belfast, hitchhiking across Britain, down through France and Spain, and winding up on the Costa del Sol – to be specific, in a village near Málaga by the name of Pedregalejo – where one night I was to learn something of importance. What had attracted me to the village was not its quaintness, its vista of the placid Mediterranean and neat white stucco houses and little bandy-legged fishermen mending nets; rather, it was the fact that the houses along the shore were occupied by a group of expatriates, mostly Americans, who posed for me a bohemian ideal.

The youngest of them was seven years older than I, the eldest three times my age, and among them they had amassed a wealth of experience that caused me envy and made me want to become like them: bearded, be-earringed, and travel-wise. There was, for example, Leonard Somstaad, a Swedish poet with the poetic malady of a weak heart and a fondness for *marjoun* (hashish candy); there was Art Shapiro, a wanderer who had for ten years migrated between Pedregalejo and Istanbul; there was Don Washington, a black ex-GI and blues singer, whose Danish girlfriend – much to the delight of the locals – was given to nude sunbathing; there was Robert Braehme, a New York actor who, in the best theatrical tradition, attempted halfheartedly to kill several of the others, suffered a nervous breakdown, and had to be returned to the States under restraint.

And then there was Richard Shockley, a tanned, hook-nosed man in his late twenties, who was the celebrity of the group. A part-time smuggler (mainly of marijuana) and a writer of some accomplishment. His first novel, *The Celebrant*, had created a minor critical stir. Being a fledgling writer myself, it was he whom I most envied. In appearance and manner he suited my notion of what a writer should be. For a while he took an interest in me, teaching me smuggling tricks and lecturing on the moral imperatives of art; but shortly thereafter he became preoccupied with his own affairs and our relationship deteriorated.

In retrospect I can see that these people were unremarkable; but at the time they seemed impossibly wise, and in order to align myself with them I rented a small beach house, bought a supply of notebooks, and began to fill them with page after page of attempted poetry.

Though I had insinuated myself into the group, I was not immediately accepted. My adolescence showed plainly against the backdrop of their experience. I had no store of anecdotes, no expertise with flute or guitar, and my conversation was lacking in hip savoir faire. In their eyes I was a kid, a baby, a clever puppy who had learned how to beg, and I was often the object of ridicule. Three factors saved me from worse ridicule: my size (six foot three, one-ninety), my erratic temper, and my ability to consume enormous quantities of drugs. This last was my great trick, my means of gaining respect. I would perform feats of ingestion that would leave Don Washington, a consummate doper, shaking his head in awe. Pills, powders, herbs – I was indiscriminate, and I initiated several dangerous dependencies in hopes of achieving equal status.

Six weeks after moving to the beach, I raised myself a notch in the general esteem by acquiring a girlfriend, a fey California blonde named Anne Fisher. It amuses me to recall the event that led Anne to my bed, because it smacked of the worst of cinema verité, an existential moment opening onto a bitter sweet romance. We were walking on the beach, a rainy day, sea and sky blending in a slate fog toward Africa, both of us stoned near to the point of catatonia, when we happened upon a drowned kitten. Had I been unaccompanied, I might have inspected the corpse for bugs and passed on; but as it was, being under Anne's scrutiny, I babbled some nonsense about 'this inconstant image of the world,' half of which I was parroting from a Eugenio Montale poem, and proceeded to give the kitten decent burial beneath a flat rock.

After completing this nasty chore, I stood and discovered Anne staring at me wetly, her maidenly nature overborne by my unexpected sensitivity. No words were needed. We were alone on the beach, with Nina Simone's bluesy whisper issuing from a window of one of the houses, gray waves slopping at our feet. As if pressed together by the vast emptiness around us, we kissed. Anne clawed my back and ground herself against me: you might have thought she had been thirsting for me all her nineteen years, but I came to understand that her desperation was born of philosophical bias and not sexual compulsion. She was deep into sadness as a motif for passion, and she liked thinking of us as two worthless strangers united by a sudden perception of life's pathetic fragility. Fits of weeping and malaise alternating with furious bouts of lovemaking were her idea of romantic counterpoint.

By the time she left me some months later, I had grown thoroughly sick of her; but she had – I believed – served her purpose in establishing me as a full-fledged expatriate.

Wrong. I soon found that I was still the kid, the baby, and I realized that I would remain so until someone of even lesser status moved to the beach, thereby nudging me closer to the mainstream. This didn't seem likely, and in truth I no longer cared; I had lost respect for the group: had I not, at seventeen, become as hiply expatriated as they, and wouldn't I, when I reached their age, be off to brighter horizons? Then, as is often the case with reality, presenting us with what we desire at the moment desire begins to flag, two suitably substandard people rented the house next to mine.

Their names were Tom and Alise, and they were twins a couple of years older than I, uncannily alike in appearance, and hailing from – if you were to believe their story – Canada. Yet they had no knowledge of things Canadian, and their accent was definitely northern European. Not an auspicious entrée into a society as picky as Pedregalejo's. Everyone was put off by them, especially Richard Shockley, who saw them as a threat. 'Those kind of people make trouble for everyone else,' he said to me at once. 'They're just too damn weird.' (It has always astounded me that those who pride themselves on eccentricity are so quick to deride this quality in strangers.) Others as well testified to the twins' weirdness: they were secretive, hostile; they had been seen making strange passes in the air on the beach, and that led some to believe they were religious nuts; they set lanterns in their windows at night and left them burning until dawn. Their most disturbing aspect, however, was their appearance. Both were scarcely five feet tall, emaciated, pale, with black hair and squinty dark eyes and an elfin cleverness of feature that Shockley described as 'prettily ugly, like Munchkins.' He suggested that this look might be a product of inbreeding, and I thought he might be right: the twins had the sort of dulled presence that one associates with the retarded or the severely tranquilized. The fishermen treated them as if they were the devil's spawn, crossing themselves and spitting at the sight of them, and the expatriates were concerned that the fishermen's enmity would focus the attention of the Guardia Civil upon the beach.

The Guardia – with their comic-opera uniforms, their machine guns, their funny patent-leather hats that from a distance looked like Mickey Mouse ears – were a legitimate menace. They had a long-standing reputation for murder and corruption, and were particularly fond of harassing foreigners. Therefore I was not surprised when a committee led by Shockley asked me to keep an eye on my new neighbors, the idea being that we should close ranks against them, even to the point of reporting any illegalities. Despite knowing that refusal would consolidate my status as a young nothing, I told Shockley and his pals to screw off. I'm not able to take pride in this – had they been friendlier to me in the past, I might have gone along with the scheme; but as it was, I was happy to reject them. And further, in the spirit of revenge, I went next door to warn Tom and Alise.

My knock roused a stirring inside the house, whispers, and at last the door was cracked and an eye peeped forth. 'Yes?' said Alise.

'Uh,' I said, taken aback by this suspicious response. 'My name's Lucius.

From next door. I've got something to tell you about the people around here.' Silence. 'They're afraid of you,' I went on. 'They're nervous because they've got dope and stuff, and they think you're going to bring the cops down on them.'

Alise glanced behind her, more whispers, and then she said, 'Why would we do that?'

'It's not that you'd do it on purpose,' I said. 'It's just that you're ... different. You're attracting a lot of attention, and everyone's afraid that the cops will investigate you and then decide to bust the whole beach.'

'Oh.' Another conference, and finally she said, 'Would you please come in?'

The door swung open, creaking like a coffin lid centuries closed, and I crossed the threshold. Tom was behind the door, and after shutting it, Alise ranged herself beside him. Her chest was so flat, their features so alike, it was only the length of her hair that allowed me to tell them apart. She gestured at a table-and-chairs set in the far corner, and, feeling a prickle of nervousness, I took a seat there. The room was similar to the living room of my house: whitewashed walls, unadorned and flaking; cheap production-line furniture (the signal difference being that they had two beds instead of one); a gas stove in a niche to the left of the door. Mounted just above the light switch was a plastic crucifix; a frayed cord ran up behind the cross to the fixture on the ceiling, giving the impression that Christ had some role to play in the transmission of the current. They had kept the place scrupulously neat; the one sign of occupancy was a pile of notebooks and a sketchpad lying on the table. The pad was open to what appeared to be a rendering of complex circuitry. Before I could get a better look at it, Tom picked up the pad and tossed it onto the stove. Then they sat across from me, hands in their laps, as meek and quiet as two white mice. It was dark in the room, knife-edges of golden sunlight slanting through gaps in the shutter boards, and the twins' eyes were like dirty smudges on their pale skins.

'I don't know what more to tell you,' I said. 'And I don't have any idea what you should do. But I'd watch myself.' They did not exchange glances or in any way visibly communicate, yet there was a peculiar tension to their silence, and I had the notion that they were again conferring: this increased my nervousness.

'We realize we're different,' said Tom at length; his voice had the exact pitch and timbre of Alise's, soft and faintly blurred. 'We don't want to cause harm, but there's something we have to do here. It's dangerous, but we have to do it. We can't leave until it's done.'

'We think you're a good boy,' chimed in Alise, rankling me with this characterization. 'We wonder if you would help us?'

I was perplexed. 'What can I do?'

'The problem is one of appearances,' said Tom. 'We can't change the way we look, but perhaps we can change the way others perceive us. If we were to become more a part of the community, we might not be so noticeable.'

'They won't have anything to do with you,' I told him. 'They're too ...'

'We have an idea,' Alise cut in.

'Yes,' said Tom. 'We thought if there was the appearance of a romantic involvement between you and Alise, people might take us more for granted. We hoped you would be agreeable to having Alise move in with you.'

'Now wait!' I said, startled. 'I don't mind helping you, but I ...'

'It would only be for appearance's sake,' said Alise, deadpan. 'There'd be no need for physical contact, and I would try not to be an imposition. I could clean for you and do the shopping.'

Perhaps it was something in Alise's voice or a subtle shift in attitude, but for whatever reason, it was then that I sensed their desperation. They were very, very afraid ... of what, I had no inkling. But fear was palpable, a thready pulse in the air. It was a symptom of my youth that I did not associate their fear with any potential threat to myself; I was merely made the more curious. 'What sort of danger are you in?' I asked.

Once again there was that peculiar nervy silence, at the end of which Tom said, 'We ask that you treat this as a confidence.'

'Sure,' I said casually. 'Who am I gonna tell?'

The story Tom told was plausible; in fact, considering my own history – a repressive, intellectual father who considered me a major disappointment, who had characterized my dropping out as 'the irresponsible actions of a glandular case' – it seemed programmed to enlist my sympathy. He said that they were not Canadian but German, and had been raised by a dictatorial stepfather after their mother's death. They had been beaten, locked in closets, and fed so poorly that their growth had been affected. Several months before, after almost twenty years of virtual confinement, they had managed to escape, and since then they had kept one step ahead of detectives hired by the stepfather. Now, penniless, they were trying to sell some antiquities that they had stolen from their home; and once they succeeded in this, they planned to travel east, perhaps to India, where they would be beyond detection. But they were afraid that they would be caught while waiting for the sale to go through; they had had too little practice with the world to be able to pass as ordinary citizens.

'Well,' I said when he had finished. 'If you want to move in' – I nodded at Alise – 'I guess it's all right. I'll do what I can to help you. But first thing you should do is quit leaving lanterns in your window all night. That's what really weirds the fishermen out. They think you're doing some kind of magic or something.' I glanced back and forth between them. 'What are you doing?'

'It's just a habit,' said Alise. 'Our stepfather made us sleep with the lights on.'

'You'd better stop it,' I said firmly; I suddenly saw myself playing Anne

Sullivan to their Helen Keller, paving their way to a full and happy life, and this noble self-image caused me to wax enthusiastic. 'Don't worry,' I told them. 'Before I'm through, you people are going to pass for genu-*wine* All-American freaks. I guarantee it!'

If I had expected thanks, I would have been disappointed. Alise stood, saying that she'd be right back, she was going to pack her things, and Tom stared at me with an expression that – had I not been so pleased with myself – I might have recognized for pained distaste.

The beach at Pedregalejo inscribed a grayish white crescent for about a hundred yards along the Mediterranean, bounded on the west by a rocky point and on the east by a condominium under construction, among the first of many that were gradually to obliterate the beauty of the coast. Beyond the beachfront houses occupied by the expatriates were several dusty streets lined with similar houses, and beyond them rose a cliff of ocher rock surmounted by a number of villas, one of which had been rented by an English actor who was in the area shooting a bullfighting movie: I had been earning my living of late as an extra on the film, receiving the equivalent of five dollars a day and lunch (also an equivalent value, consisting of a greasy sandwich and soda pop).

My house was at the extreme eastern end of the beach and differed from the rest in that it had a stucco porch that extended into the water. Inside, as mentioned, it was almost identical to the twins' house; but despite this likeness, when Alise entered, clutching an airline bag to her chest, she acted as if she had walked into an alien spacecraft. At first, ignoring my invitation to sit, she stood stiffly in the corner, flinching every time I passed; then, keeping as close to the walls as a cat exploring new territory, she inspected my possessions, peeking into my backpack, touching the strings of my guitar, studying the crude watercolors with which I had covered up flaking spots in the whitewash. Finally she sat at the table, knees pressed tightly together and staring at her hands. I tried to draw her into a conversation but received mumbles in reply, and eventually, near sunset, I took a notebook and a bagful of dope, and went out onto the porch to write.

When I was even younger than I was in 1964, a boy, I'd assumed that all seas were wild storm-tossed enormities, rife with monsters and mysteries; and so, at first sight, the relatively tame waters of the Mediterranean had proved a disappointment. However, as time had passed, I'd come to appreciate the Mediterranean's subtle shifts in mood. On that particular afternoon the sea near to shore lay in a rippled sheet stained reddish-orange by the dying light; farther out, a golden haze obscured the horizon and made the skeletal riggings of the returning fishing boats seem like the crawling of huge insects in a cloud of pollen. It was the kind of antique weather from which you might expect the glowing figure of Agamemnon, say, or of some martial Roman soul to emerge with ghostly news concerning the sack of Troy or Masada.

I smoked several pipefuls of dope – it was Moroccan kef, a fine grade of marijuana salted with flecks of white opium – and was busy recording the moment in overwrought poetry when Alise came up beside me and, again reminding me of a white mouse, sniffed the air. 'What's that?' she asked, pointing at the pipe. I explained and offered a toke. 'Oh, no,' she said, but continued peering at the dope and after a second added, 'My stepfather used to give us drugs. Pills that made us sleepy.'

'This might do the same thing,' I said airily, and went back to my scribbling.

'Well,' she said a short while later. 'Perhaps I'll try a little.'

I doubt that she had ever smoked before. She coughed and hacked, and her eyes grew red-veined and weepy, but she denied that the kef was having any effect. Gradually, though, she lapsed into silence and sat staring at the water; then, perhaps five minutes after finishing her last pipe, she ran into the house and returned with a sketchpad. 'This is wonderful,' she said. 'Wonderful! Usually it's so hard to see.' And began sketching with a charcoal pencil.

I giggled, taking perverse delight in having gotten her high, and asked, 'What's wonderful?' She merely shook her head, intent on her work. I would have pursued the question, but at that moment I noticed a group of expatriates strolling toward us along the beach. 'Here's your chance to act normal,' I said, too stoned to recognize the cruelty of my words.

She glanced up. 'What do you mean?'

I nodded in the direction of the proto-hippies. They appeared to be as ripped as we were: one of the women was doing a clumsy skipping dance along the tidal margin, and the others were staggering, laughing, shouting encouragement. Silhouetted against the violent colors of sunset, with their floppy hats and jerky movements, they had the look of shadow actors in a medieval mystery play. 'Kiss me,' I suggested to Alise. 'Or act affectionate. Reports of your normalcy will be all over the beach before dark.'

Alise's eyes widened, but she set down her pad. She hesitated briefly, then edged her chair closer; she leaned forward, hesitated again, waiting until the group had come within good viewing range, and pressed her lips to mine.

Though I was not in the least attracted to Alise, kissing her was a powerful sexual experience. It was a chaste kiss. Her lips trembled but did not part, and it lasted only a matter of seconds; yet for its duration, as if her mouth had been coated with some psychochemical, my senses sharpened to embrace the moment in microscopic detail. Kissing had always struck me as a blurred pleasure, a smashing together of pulpy flesh accompanied by a flurry of groping. But with Alise I could feel the exact conformation of our lips, the minuscule changes in pressure as they settled into place, the rough material of her blouse grazing my arm, the erratic measures of her breath (which was surprisingly sweet). The delicacy of the act aroused me as no other kiss had before, and when I drew back I half expected her to have been transformed into a beautiful princess. Not so. She was as ever small and pale. Prettily ugly.

Stunned, I turned toward the beach. The expatriates were gawping at us, and their astonishment reoriented me. I gave them a cheery wave, put my arm around Alise, and inclining my head to hers in a pretense of young love, I led her into the house.

That night I went to sleep while she was off visiting Tom. I tried to station myself on the extreme edge of the bed, leaving her enough room to be comfortable; but by the time she returned I had rolled onto the center of the mattress, and when she slipped in beside me, turning on her side, her thin buttocks cupped spoon-style by my groin, I came drowsily awake and realized that my erection was butting between her legs. Once again physical contact with her caused a sharpening of my senses, and due to the intimacy of the contact my desire, too, was sharpened. I could no more have stopped myself than I could have stopped breathing. Gently, as gently as though she were the truest of trueloves – and, indeed, I felt that sort of tenderness toward her – I began moving against her, thrusting more and more forcefully until I had eased partway inside. All this time she had made no sound, no comment, but now she cocked her leg back over my hip, wriggled closer, and let me penetrate her fully.

It had been a month since Anne had left, and I was undeniably horny; but not even this could explain the fervor of my performance that night. I lost track of how many times we made love. And yet we never exchanged endearments, never spoke or in any way acknowledged one another as lovers. Though Alise's breath quickened, her face remained set in that characteristic deadpan, and I wasn't sure if she was deriving pleasure from the act or simply providing a service, paying rent. It didn't matter. I was having enough fun for both of us. The last thing I recall is that she had mounted me, female superior, her skin glowing ghost-pale in the dawn light, single-scoop breasts barely jiggling; her charcoal eyes were fixed on the wall, as if she saw there an important destination toward which she was galloping me posthaste.

My romance with Alise – this, and the fact that she and Tom had taken to smoking vast amounts of kef and wandering the beach glassy-eyed, thus emulating the behavior of the other expatriates – had more or less the desired effect upon everyone ... everyone except Richard Shockley. He accosted me on my way to work one morning and told me in no uncertain terms that if I knew what was good for me, I should break all ties with the twins. I had about three inches and thirty pounds on him, and – for reasons I will shortly explain – I was in an irascible mood; I gave him a push and asked him to keep out of my business or suffer the consequences.

'You stupid punk!' he said, but backed away.

'Punk?' I laughed – laughter has always been for me a spark to fuel rage – and followed him. 'Come on, Rich. You can work up a better insult than that. A verbal guy like you. Come on! Give me a reason to get really crazy.'

We were standing in one of the dusty streets back of the beach, not far from a bakery, a little shop with dozens of loaves of bread laid neatly in the window, and at that moment a member of the Guardia Civil poked his head out the door. He was munching a sweet roll, watching us with casual interest: a short, swarthy man, wearing an olive green uniform with fancy epaulets, an automatic rifle slung over his shoulder, and sporting one of those goofy patent-leather hats. Shockley blanched at the sight, wheeled around, and walked away. I was about to walk away myself, but the guardsman beckoned. With a sinking feeling in the pit of my stomach, I went over to him.

'*Cobarde*,' he said, gesturing at Shockley.

My Spanish was poor, but I knew that word: coward. 'Yeah,' I said. 'In *inglés, cobarde* means chickenshit.'

'Cheek-sheet,' he said; then, more forcefully: 'Cheek-sheet!'

He asked me to teach him some more English; he wanted to know all the curse words. His name was Francisco, he had fierce bad breath, and he seemed genuinely friendly. But I knew damn well that he was most likely trying to recruit me as an informant. He talked about his family in Seville, his girlfriend, how beautiful it was in Spain. I smiled, kept repeating. '*Sí, sí*,' and was very relieved when he had to go off on his rounds.

Despite Shockley's attitude, the rest of the expatriates began to accept the twins, lumping us together as weirdos of the most perverted sort, yet explicable in our weirdness. From Don Washington I learned that Tom, Alise, and I were thought to be involved in a ménage à trois, and when I attempted to deny this, he said it was no big thing. He did ask, however, what I saw in Alise; I gave some high-school reply about it all being the same in the dark, but in truth I had no answer to his question. Since Alise had moved in, my life had assumed a distinct pattern. Each morning I would hurry off to Málaga to work on the movie set; each night I would return home and enter into brainless rut with Alise. I found this confusing. Separated from Alise, I felt only mild pity for her, yet her proximity would drive me into a lustful frenzy. I lost interest in writing, in Spain, in everything except Alise's undernourished body. I slept hardly at all, my temper worsened, and I began to wonder if she were a witch and had ensorcelled me. Often I would come home to discover her and Tom sitting stoned on my porch, the floor littered with sketches of those circuitlike designs (actually they less resembled circuits than a kind of mechanistic vegetation). I asked once what they were. 'A game,' replied Alise, and distracted me with a caress.

Two weeks after she moved in, I shouted at the assistant director of the movie (he had been instructing me on how to throw a wineskin with the proper degree of adulation as the English actor-matador paraded in triumph around the bullring) and was fired. After being hustled off the set, I vowed to get rid of Alise, whom I blamed for all my troubles. But when I arrived home, she was nowhere to be seen. I stumped over to Tom's house and pounded on the door. It swung open, and I peeked inside. Empty. Half a dozen notebooks were scattered on the floor. Curiosity overrode my anger. I stepped in and picked up a notebook.

The front cover was decorated with a hand-drawn swastika, and while it is not uncommon to find swastikas on notebook covers – they make for entertaining doodling – the sight of this one gave me a chill. I leafed through the pages, noticing that though the entries were in English, there were occasional words and phrases in German, these having question marks beside them; then I went back and read the first entry.

> *The Führer had been dead three days, and still no one had ventured into the office where he had been exposed to the poisoned blooms, although a servant had crawled along the ledge to the window and returned with the news that the corpse was stiffened in its leather tunic, its cheeks bristling with a dead man's growth, and strings of desiccated blood were hanging from its chin. But as we well remembered his habit of reviving the dead for a final bout of torture, we were afraid that he might have set an igniter in his cells to ensure rebirth, and so we waited while the wine in his goblet turned to vinegar and then to a murky gas that hid him from our view. Nothing had changed. The garden of hydrophobic roses fertilized with his blood continued to lash and slather, and the hieroglyphs of his shadow selves could be seen patrolling the streets ...*

The entry went on in like fashion for several pages, depicting a magical-seeming Third Reich, ruled by a dead or moribund Hitler, policed by shadow men known collectively as The Disciples, and populated by a terrified citizenry. All the entries were similar in character, but in the margins were brief notations, most having to do with either Tom's or Alise's physical state, and one passage in particular caught my eye:

> *Alise's control of her endocrine system continues to outpace mine. Could this simply be a product of male and female differences? It seems likely, since we have all else in common.*

Endocrine? Didn't that have something to do with glands and secretions? And if so, couldn't this be a clue to Alise's seductive powers? I wished that old

Mrs Adkins (General Science, fifth period) had been more persevering with me. I picked up another notebook. No swastika on the cover, but on the foreleaf was written: 'Tom and Alise, "born" 12 March 1944.' The entire notebook contained a single entry, apparently autobiographical, and after checking out the window to see if the twins were in sight, I sat down to read it.

Five pages later I had become convinced that Tom was either seriously crazy or that he and Alise were the subjects of an insane Nazi experiment ... or both. The word *clone* was not then in my vocabulary, but this was exactly what Tom claimed that he and Alise were. They, he said, along with eighteen others, had been grown from a single cell (donor unknown), part of an attempt to speed up development of a true Master Race. A successful attempt, according to him, for not only were the twenty possessed of supernormal physical and mental abilities, but they were stronger and more handsome than the run of humanity: this seemed to me wish fulfillment, pure and simple, and other elements of the story – for example, the continuation of an exotic Third Reich past 1945 – seemed delusion. But upon reading further, learning that they had been sequestered in a cave for almost twenty years, being educated by scientific personnel, I realized that Tom and Alise could have been told these things and have assumed their truth. One could easily make a case for some portion of the Reich having survived the war.

I was about to put down the notebook when I noticed several loose sheets of paper stuck in the rear; I pulled them out and unfolded them. The first appeared to be a map of part of a city, with a large central square labeled 'Citadel,' and the rest were covered in a neat script that – after reading a paragraph or two – I deduced to be Alise's.

> Tom says that since I'm the only one ever to leave the caves (before we all finally left them, that is), I should set down my experiences. He seems to think that having even a horrid past is preferable to having none, and insists that we should document it as well as we can. For myself, I would like to forget the past, but I'll write down what I remember to satisfy his compulsiveness.
>
> When we were first experimenting with the tunnel, we knew nothing more about it than that it was a metaphysical construct of some sort. Our control of it was poor, and we had no idea how far it reached or through what medium it penetrated. Nor had we explored it to any great extent. It was terrifying. The only constant was that it was always dark, with fuzzy different-colored lights shining at what seemed tremendous distances away. Often you would feel disembodied, and sometimes your body was painfully real, subject to odd twinges and shocks. Sometimes it was hard to move – like walking through black glue, and other times it was as if the darkness were a frictionless substance that squeezed you along faster than you wanted to go.

Horrible afterimages materialized and vanished on all sides – monsters, animals, things to which I couldn't put a name. We were almost as frightened of the tunnel as we were of our masters. Almost.

One night after the guards had taken some of the girls into their quarters, we opened the tunnel and three of us entered it. I was in the lead when our control slipped and the tunnel began to constrict. I started to turn back, and the next I knew I was standing under the sky, surrounded by windowless buildings. Warehouses, I think. The street was deserted, and I had no idea where I was. In a panic, I ran down the street and soon I heard the sounds of traffic. I turned a corner and stopped short. A broad avenue lined with gray buildings – all decorated with carved eagles – led away from where I stood and terminated in front of an enormous building of black stone. I recognized it at once from pictures we had been shown – Hitler's Citadel.

Though I was still very afraid, perhaps even more so, I realized that I had learned two things of importance. First, that no matter through what otherworldly medium it stretched, the tunnel also negotiated a worldly distance. Second, I understood that the portrait painted of the world by our masters was more or less accurate. We had never been sure of this, despite having been visited by Disciples and other of Hitler's creatures, their purpose being to frighten us into compliance.

I only stood a few minutes in that place, yet I'll never be able to forget it. No description could convey its air of menace, its oppressiveness. The avenue was thronged with people, all – like our guards – shorter and less attractive than I and my siblings, all standing stock-still, silent, and gazing at the Citadel. A procession of electric cars was passing through their midst, blowing horns, apparently to celebrate a triumph, because no one was obstructing their path. Several Disciples were prowling the fringes of the crowd, and overhead a huge winged shape was flying. It was no aircraft; its wings beat, and it swooped and soared like a live thing. Yet it must have been forty or fifty feet long. I couldn't make out what it was; it kept close to the sun, and therefore was always partly in silhouette. (I should mention that although the sun was at meridian, the sky was a deep blue such as I have come to associate with the late-afternoon skies of this world, and the sun itself was tinged with red, its globe well defined – I think it may have been farther along the path to dwarfism than the sun of this world.) All these elements contributed to the menace of the scene, but the dominant force was the Citadel. Unlike the other buildings, no carvings adorned it. No screaming eagles, no symbols of terror and war. It was a construct of simple curves and straight lines; but that simplicity implied an animal sleekness, communicated a sense of great power under restraint, and I had the feeling that at any moment the building might come alive and devour everyone within its reach. It seemed to give its darkness to the air.

I approached a man standing nearby and asked what was going on. He looked at me askance, then checked around to see if anyone was watching us. 'Haven't you heard?' he said.

'I've been away,' I told him.

This, I could see, struck him as peculiar, but he accepted the fact and said, 'They thought he was coming back to life, but it was a false alarm. Now they're offering sacrifices.'

The procession of cars had reached the steps of the Citadel, and from them emerged a number of people with their hands bound behind their backs, and a lesser number of very large men, who began shoving them up the steps toward the main doors. Those doors swung open, and from the depths of the Citadel issued a kind of growling music overlaid with fanfares of trumpets. A reddish glow – feeble at first, then brightening to a blaze – shone from within. The light and the music set my heart racing. I backed away, and as I did, I thought I saw a face forming in the midst of that red glow. Hitler's face, I believe. But I didn't wait to validate this. I ran, ran as hard as I could back to the street behind the warehouses, and there, to my relief, I discovered that the tunnel had once again been opened.

I leaned back, trying to compare what I had read with my knowledge of the twins. Those instances of silent communication. Telepathy? Alise's endocrinal control. Their habit of turning lamps on to burn away the night – could this be some residual behavior left over from cave life? Tom had mentioned that the lights had never been completely extinguished, merely dimmed. Was this all an elaborate fantasy he had concocted to obscure their pitiful reality? I was certain this was the case with Alise's testimony; but whatever, I found that I was no longer angry at the twins, that they had been elevated in my thoughts from nuisance to mystery. Looking back, I can see that my new attitude was every bit as discriminatory as my previous one. I felt for them an adolescent avidity such as I might have exhibited toward a strange pet. They were neat, weird, with the freakish appeal of Venus' flytraps and sea monkeys. Nobody else had one like them, and having them to myself made me feel superior. I would discover what sort of tricks they could perform, take notes on their peculiarities, and then, eventually growing bored, I'd move along to a more consuming interest. Though I was intelligent enough to understand that this attitude was – in its indulgence and lack of concern for others – typically ugly-American, I saw no harm in adopting it. Why, they might even benefit from my attention.

At that moment I heard voices outside. I skimmed the notebook toward the others on the floor and affected nonchalance. The door opened; they entered and froze upon seeing me. 'Hi,' I said. 'Door was open, so I waited for you here. What you been up to?'

Tom's eyes flicked to the notebooks, and Alise said, 'We've been walking.'

'Yeah?' I said this with great good cheer, as if pleased that they had been taking exercise. 'Too bad I didn't get back earlier. I could have gone with you.'

'Why *are* you back?' asked Tom, gathering the notebooks.

I didn't want to let on about the loss of my job, thinking that the subterfuge would give me a means of keeping track of them. 'Some screw-up on the set,' I told him. 'They had to put off filming. What say we go into town?'

From that point on, no question I asked them was casual; I was always testing, probing, trying to ferret out some of their truth.

'Oh, I don't know,' said Tom. 'I thought I'd have a swim.'

I took a mental note: why do subjects exhibit avoidance of town? For an instant I had an unpleasant vision of myself, a teenage monster gloating over his two gifted white mice, but this was overborne by my delight in the puzzle they presented. 'Yeah,' I said breezily. 'A swim would be nice.'

That night making love with Alise was a whole new experience. I wasn't merely screwing; I was exploring the unknown, penetrating mystery. Watching her pale, passionless face, I imagined the brain behind it to be a strange glowing jewel, with facets instead of convolutions. *National Enquirer* headlines flashed through my head. NAZI MUTANTS ALIVE IN SPAIN. AMERICAN TEEN UNCOVERS HITLER'S SECRET PLOT. Of course there would be no such publicity. Even if Tom's story was true – and I was far from certain that it was – I had no intention of betraying them. I wasn't that big a jerk.

For the next month I maintained the illusion that I was still employed by the film company and left home each morning at dawn; but rather than catching the bus into Malaga, I would hide between the houses, and as soon as Tom and Alise went off on one of their walks (they always walked west along the beach, vanishing behind a rocky point), I would sneak into Tom's house and continue investigating the notebooks. The more I read, the more firmly I believed the story. There was a flatness to the narrative tone that reminded me of a man I had heard speaking about the concentration camps, dully recounting atrocities, staring into space, as if the things he said were putting him into a trance. For example:

> *... It was on July 2nd that they came for Urduja and Klaus. For the past few months they had been making us sleep together in a room lit by harsh fluorescents. There were no mattresses, no pillows, and they took our clothes so we could not use them as covering. It was like day under those trays of white light, and we lay curled around each other for warmth. They gassed us before they entered, but we had long since learned how to neutralize the gas, and so we were all awake, linked, pretending to be asleep. Three of them*

came into the room, and three more stood at the door with guns. At first it seemed that this would be just another instance of rape. The three men violated Urduja, one after the other. She kept up her pretense of unconsciousness, but she felt everything. We tried to comfort her, sending out our love and encouragement. But I could sense her hysteria, her pain. They were rough with her, and when they had finished, her thighs were bloody. She was very brave and gave no cry; she was determined not to give us away. Finally they picked her and Klaus up and carried them off. An hour later we felt them die. It was horrible, as if part of my mind had short-circuited, a corner of it left forever dim.

We were angry and confused. Why would they kill what they had worked so hard to create? Some of us, Uwe and Peter foremost among them, wanted to give up the tunnel and revenge ourselves as best we could; but the rest of us managed to calm things down. Was it revenge we wanted, we asked, or was it freedom? If freedom was to be our choice, then the tunnel was our best hope. Would I – I wonder – have lobbied so hard for the tunnel if I had known that only Alise and I would survive it?

The story ended shortly before the escape attempt was to be made; the remainder of the notebooks contained further depictions of that fantastic Third Reich – genetically created giants who served as executioners, fountains of blood in the squares of Berlin, dogs that spoke with human voices and spied for the government – and also marginalia concerning the twins' abilities, among them being the control of certain forms of energy: these particular powers had apparently been used to create the tunnel. All this fanciful detail unsettled me, as did several elements of the story. Tom had stated that the usual avenues of escape had been closed to the twenty clones, but what was a tunnel if not a usual avenue of escape? Once he had mentioned that the tunnel was 'unstable.' What did that mean? And he seemed to imply that the escape had not yet been effected.

By the time I had digested the notebooks, I had begun to notice the regular pattern of the twins' walks; they would disappear around the point that bounded the western end of the beach, and then, a half hour later, they would return, looking worn-out. Perhaps, I thought, they were doing something there that would shed light on my confusion, and so one morning I decided to follow them.

The point was a spine of blackish rock shaped like a lizard's tail that extended about fifty feet out into the water. Tom and Alise would always wade around it. I, however, scrambled up the side and lay flat like a sniper atop it. From my vantage I overlooked a narrow stretch of gravelly shingle, a little trough scooped out between the point and low brown hills that rolled away inland. Tom and Alise were sitting ten or twelve feet below, passing a kef pipe, coughing, exhaling billows of smoke.

That puzzled me. Why would they come here just to get high? I scrunched into a more comfortable position. It was a bright, breezy day; the sea was heaving with a light chop, but the waves slopping onto the shingle were ripples. A few fishing boats were herding a freighter along the horizon. I turned my attention back to the twins. They were standing, making peculiar gestures that reminded me of T'ai Chi, though these were more labored. Then I noticed that the air above the tidal margin had become distorted as with a heat haze … yet it was not hot in the least. I stared at the patch of distorted air – it was growing larger and larger – and I began to see odd translucent shapes eddying within it: they were similar to the shapes that the twins were always sketching. There was a funny pressure in my ears; a drop of sweat slid down the hollow of my throat, leaving a cold track.

Suddenly the twins broke off gesturing and leaned against each other; the patch of distorted air misted away. Both were breathing heavily, obviously exhausted. They sat down a couple of feet from the water's edge, and after a long silence Tom said, 'We should try again to be certain.'

'Why don't we finish it now?' said Alise. 'I'm so tired of this place.'

'It's too dangerous in the daylight.' Tom shied a pebble out over the water. 'If they're waiting at the other end, we might have to run. We'll need the darkness for cover.'

'What about tonight?'

'I'd rather wait until tomorrow night. There's supposed to be a storm front coming, and nobody will be outside.'

Alise sighed.

'What's wrong?' Tom asked. 'Is it Lucius?'

I listened with even more intent.

'No,' she said. 'I just want it to be over.'

Tom nodded and gazed out to sea. The freighter appeared to have moved a couple of inches eastward; gulls were flying under the sun, becoming invisible as they passed across its glaring face, and then swooping away like bits of winged matter blown from its core. Tom picked up the kef pipe. 'Let's try it again,' he said.

At that instant someone shouted, 'Hey!' Richard Shockley came striding down out of the hills behind the shingle. Tom and Alise got to their feet. 'I can't believe you people are so fucking uncool,' said Shockley, walking up to them; his face was dark with anger, and the breeze was lashing his hair as if it, too, were enraged. 'What the hell are you trying to do? Get everyone busted?'

'We're not doing anything,' said Alise.

'Naw!' sneered Shockley. 'You're just breaking the law in plain view. Plain fucking view!' His fists clenched, and I thought for a moment he was going to hit them. They were so much smaller than he that they looked like children facing an irate parent.

'You won't have to be concerned with us much longer,' said Tom. 'We're leaving soon.'

'Good,' said Shockley. 'That's real good. But lemme tell you something, man. I catch you smoking out here again, and you might be leaving quicker than you think.'

'What do you mean?' asked Alise.

'Don't you worry about what I fucking mean,' said Shockley. 'You just watch your behavior. We had a good scene going here until you people showed up, and I'll be damned if I'm going to let you blow it.' He snatched the pipe from Tom's hand and slung it out to sea. He shook his finger in Tom's face. 'I swear, man! One more fuckup, and I'll be on you like white on rice!' Then he stalked off around the point.

As soon as he was out of sight, without a word exchanged between them, Tom and Alise waded into the water and began groping beneath the surface, searching for the pipe. To my amazement, because the shallows were murky and full of floating litter, they found it almost instantly.

I was angry at Shockley, both for his treatment of the twins and for his invasion of what I considered my private preserve, and I headed toward his house to tell him to lay off. When I entered I was greeted by a skinny, sandy-haired guy – Skipper by name – who was sprawled on pillows in the front room; from the refuse of candy wrappers, crumpled cigarette packs, and empty pop bottles surrounding him, I judged him to have been in this position for quite some time. He was so opiated that he spoke in mumbles and could scarcely open his eyes, but from him I learned the reason for Shockley's outburst. 'You don't wanna see him now, man,' said Skipper, and flicked out his tongue to retrieve a runner of drool that had leaked from the corner of his mouth. 'Dude's on a rampage, y'know?'

'Yeah,' I said. 'I know.'

'Fucker's paranoid,' said Skipper. 'Be paranoid myself if I was holding a key of smack.'

'Heroin?'

'King H,' said Skipper with immense satisfaction, as if pronouncing the name of his favorite restaurant, remembering past culinary treats. 'He's gonna run it up to Copenhagen soon as—'

'Shut the hell up!' It was Shockley, standing in the front door. 'Get out,' he said to me.

'Be a pleasure.' I strolled over to him. 'The twins are leaving tomorrow night. Stay off their case.'

He squared his shoulders, trying to be taller. 'Or what?'

'Gee, Rich,' I said. 'I'd hate to see anything get in the way of your mission to Denmark.'

Though in most areas of experience I was a neophyte compared to Shockley, he was just a beginner compared to me as regarded fighting. I could tell a punch was coming from the slight widening of his eyes, the tensing of his shoulders. It was a silly school-girlish punch. I stepped inside it, forced him against the wall, and jammed my forearm under his chin. 'Listen, Rich,' I said mildly. 'Nobody wants trouble with the Guardia, right?' My hold prevented him from speaking, but he nodded. Spit bubbled between his teeth. 'Then there's no problem. You leave the twins alone, and I'll forget about the dope. Okay?' Again he nodded. I let him go, and he slumped to the floor, holding his throat. 'See how easy things go when you just sit down and talk about them?' I said, and grinned. He glared at me. I gave him a cheerful wink and walked off along the beach.

I see now that I credited Shockley with too much wisdom; I assumed that he was an expert smuggler and would maintain a professional calm. I underestimated his paranoia and gave no thought to his reasons for dealing with a substance as volatile as heroin: they must have involved a measure of desperation, because he was not a man prone to taking whimsical risks. But I wasn't thinking about the consequences of my actions. After what I had seen earlier beyond the point, I believed that I had figured out what Tom and Alise were up to. It seemed implausible, yet equally inescapable. And if I was right, this was my chance to witness something extraordinary. I wanted nothing to interfere.

Gray clouds blew in the next morning from the east, and a steady downpour hung a silver beaded curtain from the eaves of my porch. I spent the day pretending to write and watching Alise out of the corner of my eye. She went about her routines, washing the dishes, straightening up, sketching – the sketching was done with a bit more intensity than usual. Finally, late that afternoon, having concluded that she was not going to tell me she was leaving, I sat down beside her at the table and initiated a conversation. 'You ever read science fiction?' I asked.

'No,' she said, and continued sketching.

'Interesting stuff. Lots of weird ideas. Time travel, aliens ...' I jiggled the table, causing her to look up, and fixed her with a stare. 'Alternate worlds.'

She tensed but said nothing.

'I've read your notebooks,' I told her.

'Tom thought you might have.' She closed the sketchpad.

'And I saw you trying to open the tunnel yesterday. I know that you're leaving.'

She fingered the edge of the pad. I couldn't tell if she was nervous or merely thinking.

I kept after her. 'What I can't figure out is *why* you're leaving. No matter who's chasing you, this world can't be as bad as the one described in the notebooks. At least we don't have anything like The Disciples.'

'You've got it wrong,' she said after a silence. 'The Disciples are of my world.'

I had more or less deduced what she was admitting to, but I hadn't really been prepared to accept that it was true, and for a moment I retrenched, believing again that she was crazy, that she had tricked me into swallowing her craziness as fact. She must have seen this in my face or read my thoughts, because she said then, 'It's the truth.'

'I don't understand,' I said. 'Why are you going back?'

'We're not; we're going to collapse the tunnel, and to do that we have to activate it. It took all of us to manage it before; Tom and I wouldn't have been able to see the configurations clearly enough if it hadn't been for your drugs. We owe you a great deal.' A worry line creased her brow. 'You mustn't spy on us tonight. It could be dangerous.'

'Because someone might be waiting,' I said. 'The Disciples?'

She nodded. 'We think one followed us into the tunnel and was trapped. It apparently can't control the fields involved in the tunnel, but if it's nearby when we activate the opening ...' She shrugged.

'What'll you do if it is?'

'Lead it away from the beach,' she said.

She seemed assured in this, and I let the topic drop. 'What are they, anyway?' I asked.

'Hitler once gave a speech in which he told us they were magical reproductions of his soul. Who knows? They're horrid enough for that to be true.'

'If you collapse the tunnel, then you'll be safe from pursuit. Right?'

'Yes.'

'Then why leave Pedregalejo?'

'We don't fit in,' she said, and let the words hang in the air a few seconds. 'Look at me. Can you believe that in my world I'm considered beautiful?'

An awkward silence ensued. Then she smiled. I'd never seen her smile before. I can't say it made her beautiful – her skin looked dead-pale in the dreary light, her features asexual – but in the smile I could detect the passive confidence with which beauty encounters the world. It was the first time I had perceived her as a person and not as a hobby, a project.

'But that's not the point,' she went on. 'There's somewhere we want to go.'

'Where?'

She reached into her airline bag, which was beside the chair, and pulled out a dog-eared copy of *The Tibetan Book of the Dead*. 'To find the people who understand this.'

I scoffed. 'You believe that crap?'

'What would you know?' she snapped. 'It's chaos inside the tunnel. It's ...'

She waved her hand in disgust, as if it weren't worth explaining anything to such an idiot.

'Tell me about it,' I said. Her anger had eroded some of my skepticism.

'If you've read the notebooks, you've seen my best attempt at telling about it. Ordinary referents don't often apply inside the tunnel. But it appears to pass by places described in this book. You catch glimpses of lights, and you're drawn to them. You seem to have an innate understanding that the lights are the entrances to worlds, and you sense that they're fearsome. But you're afraid that if you don't stop at one of them, you'll be killed. The others let themselves be drawn. Tom and I kept going. This light, this world, felt less fearsome than the rest.' She gave a doleful laugh. 'Now I'm not so sure.'

'In one of the notebooks,' I said, 'Tom wrote that the others didn't survive.'

'He doesn't really know,' she said. 'Perhaps he wrote that to make himself feel better about having wound up here. That would be like him.'

We continued talking until dark. It was the longest time I had spent in her company without making love, and yet – because of this abstinence – we were more lovers then than we had ever been before. I listened to her not with an eye toward collecting data, but with genuine interest, and though everything she told me about her world smacked of insanity, I believed her. There were, she said, rivers that sprang from enormous crystals, birds with teeth, bats as large as eagles, cave cities, wizards, winged men who inhabited the thin Andean air. It was a place of evil grandeur, and at its heart, its ruler, was the dead Hitler, his body uncorrupting, his death a matter of conjecture, his terrible rule maintained by a myriad of servants in hopes of his rebirth.

At the time Alise's world seemed wholly alien to me, as distinct from our own as Jupiter or Venus. But now I wonder if – at least in the manner of its rule – it is not much the same: are we not also governed by the dead, by the uncorrupting laws they have made, laws whose outmoded concepts enforce a logical tyranny upon a populace that no longer meets their standards of morality? And I wonder further if each alternate world (Alise told me they were infinite in number) is but a distillation of the one adjoining, and if somewhere at the heart of this complex lies a compacted essence of a world, a blazing point of pure principle that plays cosmic Hitler to its shadow selves.

The storm that blew in just after dark was – like the Mediterranean – an age-worn elemental. Distant thunder, a few strokes of lightning, spreading glowing cracks down the sky, a blustery wind. Alise cautioned me again against following her and told me she'd be back to say goodbye. I told her I'd wait, but as soon as she and Tom had left, I set out toward the point. I would no more have missed their performance than I would have turned down, say, a free ticket to see the Rolling Stones. A few drops of rain were falling, but a foggy moon was visible through high clouds inland. Shadows were moving in the lighted windows of the houses; shards of atonal jazz alternated with mournful gusts of wind. Once Tom and Alise glanced back, and I dropped down on the mucky sand, lying flat until they had waded around the point. By the time I reached the top of the rocks, the rain had stopped. Directly below me were two shadows and the glowing coal of the kef pipe. I was exhilarated. I wished my father were there so I could say to him, 'All your crap about "slow and steady wins the race," all your rationalist bullshit, it doesn't mean anything in the face of this. There's mystery in the world, and if I'd stayed in school, I'd never have known it.'

I was so caught up in thinking about my father's reactions that I lost track of Tom and Alise. When I looked down again, I found that they had taken a stand by the shore and were performing those odd, graceful gestures. Just beyond them, its lowest edge level with the water, was a patch of darkness blacker than night, roughly circular, and approximately the size of a circus ring. Lightning was still striking down out to sea, but the moon had sailed clear of the clouds, staining silver the surrounding hilltops, bringing them close, and in that light I could see that the patch of darkness had depth ... depth, and agitated motion. Staring into it was like staring into a fire while hallucinating, watching the flames adopt the forms of monsters; only in this case there were no flames but the vague impressions of monstrous faces melting up from the tunnel walls, showing a shinier black, then fading. I was at an angle to the tunnel, and while I could see inside it, I could also see that it had no exterior walls, that it was a hole hanging in midair, leading to an unearthly distance. Every muscle in my body was tensed, pressure was building in my ears, and I heard a static hiss overriding the grumble of thunder and the mash of the waves against the point.

My opinion of the twins had gone up another notch. Anyone who would enter that fuming nothingness was worthy of respect. They looked the image of courage: two pale children daring the darkness to swallow them. They kept on with their gestures until the depths of the tunnel began to pulse like a black gulping throat. The static hiss grew louder, oscillating in pitch, and the twins tipped their heads to the side, admiring their handiwork.

Then a shout in Spanish, a beam of light probing at the twins from the seaward reach of the point.

Seconds later Richard Shockley splashed through the shallows and onto shore; he was holding a flashlight, and the wind was whipping his hair. Behind him came a short dark-skinned man carrying an automatic rifle, wearing the hat and uniform of the Guardia Civil. As he drew near I recognized him to be Francisco, the guardsman who had tried to cozy up to me. He had a Band-Aid on his chin, which – despite his weapon and traditions – made him seem an innocent. The two men's attention was fixed on the twins, and they didn't notice the tunnel, though they passed close to its edge. Francisco began to harangue the twins in Spanish, menacing them with his gun. I crept nearer and heard the word *heroína*. Heroin. I managed to hear enough to realize what had happened. Shockley, either for the sake of vengeance or – more likely – panicked by what he considered a threat to his security, had planted heroin in Tom's house and informed on him, hoping perhaps to divert suspicion and ingratiate himself with the Guardia. Alise was denying the charges, but Francisco was shouting her down.

And then he caught sight of the tunnel. His mouth fell open, and he backed against the rocks directly beneath me. Shockley spotted it, too. He shined his flashlight into the tunnel, and the beam was sheared off where it entered the blackness, as if it had been bitten in half. For a moment they were frozen in a tableau. Only the moonlight seemed in motion, coursing along Francisco's patent-leather hat.

What got into me then was not bravery or any analogue thereof, but a sudden violent impulse such as had often landed me in trouble. I jumped feetfirst onto Francisco's back. I heard a grunt as we hit the ground, a snapping noise, and the next I knew I was scrambling off him, reaching for his gun, which had flown a couple of yards away. I had no clue of how to operate the safety or even of where it was located. But Shockley wasn't aware of that. His eyes were popped, and he sidled along the rocks toward the water, his head twitching from side to side, searching for a way out.

Hefting the cold, slick weight of the gun gave me a sense of power – a feeling tinged with hilarity – and as I came to my feet, aiming at Shockley's chest, I let out a purposefully demented laugh. 'Tell me, Rich,' I said. 'Do you believe in God?'

He held out a hand palm-up and said, 'Don't,' in a choked voice.

'Remember that garbage you used to feed me about the moral force of poetry?' I said. 'How you figure that jibes with setting up these two?' I waved the rifle barrel at the twins; they were staring into the tunnel, unmindful of me and Shockley.

'You don't understand,' said Shockley.

'Sure I do, Rich.' I essayed another deranged-teenage-killer laugh. 'You're not a nice guy.'

In the moonlight his face looked glossy with sweat. 'Wait a minute,' he said. 'I'll ...'

Then Alise screamed, and I never did learn what Shockley had in mind. I spun around and was so shocked that I nearly dropped the gun. The tunnel was still pulsing, its depths shrinking and expanding like the gullet of a black worm, and in front of it stood a ... my first impulse is to say 'a shadow,' but that description would not do justice to the Disciple. To picture it you must imagine the mold of an androgynous human body constructed from a material of such translucency that you couldn't see it under any condition of light;

then you must further imagine that the mold contains a black substance (negatively black) that shares the properties of both gas and fluid, which is slipping around inside, never filling the mold completely – at one moment presenting to you a knife-edge, the next a frontal silhouette, and at other times displaying all the other possible angles of attitude, shifting among them. Watching it made me dizzy. Tom and Alise cowered from it, and when it turned full face to me, I, too, cowered. Red glowing pinpricks appeared in the places where its eyes should have been; the pinpricks swelled, developing into real eyes. The pupils were black planets eclipsing bloody suns.

I wanted to run, but those eyes held me. Insanity was like a heat in them. They radiated fury, loathing, hatred, and I wonder now if anything human, even some perverted fraction of mad Hitler's soul, could have achieved such an alien resolve. My blood felt as thick as syrup, my scrotum tightened. Then something splashed behind me, and though I couldn't look away from the eyes, I knew that Shockley had run. The Disciple moved after him. And how it moved! It was as if it were turning sideways and vanishing, repeating the process over and over, and doing this so rapidly that it seemed to be strobing, winking in and out of existence, each wink transporting it several feet farther along. Shockley never had a chance. It was too dark out near the end of the point for me to tell what really happened, but I saw two shadows merge and heard a bubbling scream.

A moment later the Disciple came whirling back toward the shore. Instinctively I clawed the trigger of Francisco's gun – the safety had not been on. Bullets stitched across the Disciple's torso, throwing up geysers of blackness that almost instantly were reabsorbed into its body, as if by force of gravity. Otherwise they had no effect. The Disciple stopped just beyond arm's reach, nailing me with its burning gaze, flickering with the rhythm of a shadow cast by a fire. Only its eyes were constant, harrowing me.

Someone shouted – I think it was Tom, but I'm not sure; I had shrunk so far within myself that every element of the scene except the glowing red eyes had a dim value. Abruptly the Disciple moved away. Tom was standing at the mouth of the tunnel. When the Disciple had come half the distance toward him, he took a step forward and – like a man walking into a black mirror – disappeared. The Disciple sped into the tunnel after him. For a time I could see their shapes melting up and fading among the other, more monstrous shapes.

A couple of minutes after they had entered it, the tunnel collapsed. Accompanied by a keening hiss, the interior walls constricted utterly and flecks of ebony space flew up from the mouth. Night flowed in to take its place. Alise remained standing by the shore, staring at the spot where the tunnel had been. In a daze, I walked over and put an arm around her shoulder, wanting to comfort her. But she shook me off and went a few steps into the water, as if to say that she would rather drown than accept my consolation.

My thoughts were in chaos, and needing something to focus them, I knelt beside Francisco, who was still lying facedown. I rolled him onto his back, and his head turned with a horrid grating sound. Blood and sand crusted his mouth. He was dead, his neck broken. For a long while I sat there, noticing the particulars of death, absorbed by them: how the blood within him had begun to settle to one side, discoloring his cheek; how his eyes, though glazed, had maintained a bewildered look. The Band-Aid on his chin had come unstuck, revealing a shaving nick. I might have sat there forever, hypnotized by the sight; but then a bank of clouds overswept the moon, and the pitch-darkness shocked me, alerted me to the possible consequences of what I had done.

From that point on I was operating in a panic, inspired by fear to acts of survival. I dragged Francisco's body into the hills; I waded into the water and found Shockley's body floating in the shallows. Every inch of his skin was horribly charred, and as I hauled him to his resting place beside Francisco, black flakes came away on my fingers. After I had covered the bodies with brush, I led Alise – by then unresisting – back to the house, packed for us both, and hailed a taxi for the airport. There I had a moment of hysteria, realizing that she would not have a passport. But she did. A Canadian one, forged in Málaga. We boarded the midnight flight to Casablanca, and the next day – because I was still fearful of pursuit – we began hitchhiking east across the desert.

Our travels were arduous. I had only three hundred dollars, and Alise had none. Tom's story about their having valuables to sell had been more or less true, but in our haste we had left them behind. In Cairo, partly due to our lack of funds and partly to medical expenses incurred by Alise's illness (amoebic dysentery), I was forced to take a job. I worked for a perfume merchant in the Khan el-Khalili Bazaar, steering tourists to his shop, where they could buy rare essences and drugs and change money at the black market rates. In order to save enough to pay our passage east, I began to cheat my employer, servicing some of his clients myself, and when he found me out I had to flee with Alise, who had not yet shaken her illness.

I felt responsible for her, guilty about my role in the proceedings. I'd come to terms with Francisco's death. Naturally I regretted it, and sometimes I would see that dark, surprised face in my dreams. But acts of violence did not trouble my heart then as they do now. I had grown up violent in a violent culture, and I was able to rationalize the death as an accident. And, too, it had been no saint I had killed. I could not, however, rationalize my guilt concerning Alise, and this confounded me. Hadn't I tried to save her and Tom? I realized that my actions had essentially been an expression of adolescent fury, yet they had been somewhat on the twins' behalf. And no one could have stood against the Disciple. What more could I have done? Nothing, I told myself. But this answer failed to satisfy me.

In Afghanistan, Alise suffered a severe recurrence of her dysentery. This time I had sufficient funds (money earned by smuggling, thanks to Shockley's lessons) to avoid having to work, and we rented a house on the outskirts of Kabul. We lived there three months until she had regained her health. I fed her yogurt, red meat, vegetables; I bought her books and a tape recorder and music to play on it; I brought people in whom I thought she might be interested to visit her. I wish I could report that we grew to be friends, but she had withdrawn into herself and thus remained a mystery to me, something curious and inexplicable. She would lie in her room – a cubicle of whitewashed stone – with the sunlight slanting in across her bed, paling her further, transforming her into a piece of ivory sculpture, and would gaze out the window for hours, seeing, I believe, not the exotic traffic on the street – robed horsemen from the north, ox-drawn carts, and Chinese-made trucks – but some otherworldly vista. Often I wanted to ask her more about her world, about the tunnel and Tom and a hundred other things. But while I could not institute a new relationship with her, I did not care to reinstitute our previous one. And so my questions went unasked. And so certain threads of this narrative must be left untied, reflecting the messiness of reality as opposed to the neatness of fiction.

Though this story is true, I do not ask that you believe it. To my mind it is true enough, and if you have read it to the end, then you have sufficiently extended your belief. In any case, it is a verity that the truth becomes a lie when it is written down, and it is the art of writing to wring as much truth as possible from its own dishonest fabric. I have but a single truth to offer, one that came home to me on the last day I saw Alise, one that stands outside both the story and the act of writing it.

We had reached the object of our months-long journey, the gates of a Tibetan nunnery on a hill beneath Dhaulagiri in Nepal, a high blue day with a chill wind blowing. It was here that Alise planned to stay. Why? She never told me more than she had in our conversation shortly before she and Tom set out to collapse the tunnel. The gates – huge wooden barriers carved with the faces of gods – swung open, and the female lamas began to applaud, their way of frightening off demons who might try to enter. They formed a crowd of yellow robes and tanned, smiling faces that seemed to me another kind of barrier, a deceptively plain facade masking some rarefied contentment. Alise and I had said a perfunctory goodbye, but as she walked inside, I thought – I hoped – that she would turn back and give vent to emotion.

She did not. The gates swung shut, and she was gone into the only haven that might accept her as commonplace.

Gone, and I had never really known her.

I sat down outside the gates, alone for the first time in many months, with no urgent destination or commanding purpose, and took stock. High above, the snowy fang of Dhaulagiri reared against a cloudless sky; its sheer faces deepened to gentler slopes seamed with the ice-blue tongues of glaciers, and those slopes eroded into barren brown hills such as the one upon which the nunnery was situated. That was half the world. The other half, the half I faced, was steep green hills terraced into barley fields, and winding through them a river, looking as unfeatured as a shiny aluminum ribbon. Hawks were circling the middle distance, and somewhere, perhaps from the monastery that I knew to be off among the hills, a horn sounded a great bass note like a distant dragon signaling its hunger or its rage.

I sat at the center of these events and things, at the dividing line of these half-worlds that seemed to me less in opposition than equally empty, and I felt that emptiness pouring into me. I was so empty, I thought that if the wind were to strike me at the correct angle, I might chime like a bell ... and perhaps it did, perhaps the clarity of the Himalayan weather and this sudden increment of emptiness acted to produce a tone, an illumination, for I saw myself then as Tom and Alise must have seen me. Brawling, loutish, indulgent. The two most notable facts of my life were negatives: I had killed a man, and I had encountered the unknown and let it elude me. I tried once again to think what more I could have done, and this time, rather than arriving at the usual conclusion, I started to understand what lesson I had been taught on the beach at Pedregalejo.

Some years ago a friend of mine, a writer and a teacher of writing, told me that my stories had a tendency to run on past the climax, and that I frequently ended them with a moral, a technique he considered outmoded. He was, in the main, correct. But it occurs to me that sometimes a moral – whether or not clearly stated by the prose – is what provides us with the real climax, the good weight that makes the story resonate beyond the measure of the page. So, in this instance, I will go contrary to my friend's advice and tell you what I learned, because it strikes me as being particularly applicable to the American consciousness, which is insulated from much painful reality, and further because it relates to a process of indifference that puts us all at risk.

When the tragedies of others become for us diversions, sad stories with which to enthrall our friends, interesting bits of data to toss out at cocktail parties, a means of presenting a pose of political concern, or whatever ... when this happens we commit the gravest of sins, condemn ourselves to ignominy, and consign the world to a dangerous course. We begin to justify our casual overview of pain and suffering by portraying ourselves as do-gooders incapacitated by the inexorable forces of poverty, famine, and war. 'What can I do?' we say. 'I'm only one person, and these things are beyond my control. I care about the world's trouble, but there are no solutions.'

Yet no matter how accurate this assessment, most of us are relying on it to be true, using it to mask our indulgence, our deep-seated lack of concern, our pathological self-involvement. In adopting this attitude we delimit the possibilities for action by letting events progress to a point at which, indeed, action becomes impossible, at which we can righteously say that nothing can be done. And so we are born, we breed, we are happy, we are sad, we deal with consequential problems of our own, we have cancer or a car crash, and in the end our actions prove insignificant. Some will tell you that to feel guilt or remorse over the vast inaction of our society is utter foolishness; life, they insist, is patently unfair, and all anyone can do is to look out for his own interest. Perhaps they are right; perhaps we are so mired in our self-conceptions that we can change nothing. Perhaps this is the way of the world. But, for the sake of my soul and because I no longer wish to hide my sins behind a guise of mortal incapacity, I tell you it is not.

R&R

I

One of the new Sikorsky gunships, an element of the First Air Cavalry with the words *Whispering Death* painted on its side, gave Mingolla and Gilbey and Baylor a lift from the Ant Farm to San Francisco de Juticlan, a small town located inside the green zone, which on the latest maps was designated Free Occupied Guatemala. To the east of this green zone lay an undesignated band of yellow that crossed the country from the Mexican border to the Caribbean. The Ant Farm was a firebase on the eastern edge of the yellow band, and it was from there that Mingolla – an artillery specialist not yet twenty-one years old – lobbed shells into an area that the maps depicted in black-and-white terrain markings. And thus it was that he often thought of myself as engaged in a struggle to keep the world safe for primary colors.

Mingolla and his buddies could have taken their R&R in Rio or Caracas, but they had noticed that the men who visited these cities had a tendency to grow careless upon their return; they understood from this that the more exuberant your R&R, the more likely you were to wind up a casualty, and so they always opted for the lesser distractions of the Guatemalan towns. They were not really friends: they had little in common, and under different circumstances they might well have been enemies. But taking their R&R together had come to be a ritual of survival, and once they had reached the town of their choice, they would go their separate ways and perform further rituals. Because the three had survived so much already, they believed that if they continued to perform these same rituals they would complete their tours unscathed. They had never acknowledged their belief to one another, speaking of it only obliquely – that, too, was part of the ritual – and had this belief been challenged they would have admitted its irrationality; yet they would also have pointed out that the strange character of the war acted to enforce it.

The gunship set down at an airbase a mile west of town, a concrete strip penned in on three sides by barracks and offices, with the jungle rising behind them. At the center of the strip another Sikorsky was practicing take-offs and landings – a drunken, camouflage-colored dragonfly – and two others were hovering overhead like anxious parents. As Mingolla jumped out, a hot breeze fluttered his shirt. He was wearing civvies for the first time in weeks, and they felt flimsy compared to his combat gear; he glanced around nervously, half-expecting an unseen enemy to take advantage of his exposure. Some mechanics were lounging in the shade of a chopper whose cockpit had been destroyed, leaving fanglike shards of plastic curving from the charred metal. Dusty jeeps trundled back and forth between the buildings; a brace of crisply starched lieutenants were making a brisk beeline toward a forklift stacked high with aluminum coffins. Afternoon sunlight fired dazzles on the seams and handles of the coffins, and through the heat haze the distant line of barracks shifted like waves in a troubled olive-drab sea. The incongruity of the scene – its What's-Wrong-With-This-Picture mix of the horrid and the commonplace – wrenched at Mingolla. His left hand trembled, and the light seemed to grow brighter, making him weak and vague. He leaned against the Sikorsky's rocket pod to steady himself. Far above, contrails were fraying in the deep blue range of the sky: XL-16s off to blow holes in Nicaragua. He stared after them with something akin to longing, listening for their engines, but heard only the spacy whisper of the Sikorskys.

Gilbey hopped down from the hatch that led to the computer deck behind the cockpit; he brushed imaginary dirt from his jeans, sauntered over to Mingolla, and stood with hands on hips: a short muscular kid whose blond crew cut and petulant mouth gave him the look of a grumpy child. Baylor stuck his head out of the hatch and worriedly scanned the horizon. Then he, too, hopped down. He was tall and rawboned, a couple of years older than Mingolla, with lank black hair and pimply olive skin and features so sharp that they appeared to have been hatcheted into shape. He rested a hand on the side of the Sikorsky, but almost instantly, noticing that he was touching the flaming letter W in *Whispering Death*, he jerked the hand away as if he'd been scorched. Three days before there had been an all-out assault on the Ant Farm, and Baylor had not recovered from it. Neither had Mingolla. It was hard to tell whether or not Gilbey had been affected.

One of the Sikorsky's pilots cracked the cockpit door. 'Y'all can catch a ride into 'Frisco at the PX,' he said, his voice muffled by the black bubble of his visor. The sun shined a white blaze on the visor, making it seem that the helmet contained night and a single star.

'Where's the PX?' asked Gilbey.

The pilot said something too muffled to be understood.

'What?' said Gilbey.

Again the pilot's response was muffled, and Gilbey became angry. 'Take that damn thing off!' he said.

'This?' The pilot pointed to his visor. 'What for?'

'So I can hear what the hell you sayin'.'

'You can hear now, can'tcha?'

'Okay,' said Gilbey, his voice tight. 'Where's the goddamn PX?'

The pilot's reply was unintelligible; his faceless mask regarded Gilbey with inscrutable intent.

Gilbey balled up his fists. 'Take that son of a bitch off!'

'Can't do it, soldier,' said the second pilot, leaning over so that the two black bubbles were nearly side by side. 'These here doobies' – he tapped his visor – 'they got microcircuits that beams shit into our eyes. 'Fects the optic nerve. Makes it so we can see the beaners even when they undercover. Longer we wear 'em, the better we see.'

Baylor laughed edgily, and Gilbey said, 'Bullshit!' Mingolla naturally assumed that the pilots were putting Gilbey on, or else their reluctance to remove the helmets stemmed from a superstition, perhaps from a deluded belief, that the visors actually did bestow special powers. But given a war in which combat drugs were issued and psychics predicted enemy movements, anything was possible, even microcircuits that enhanced vision.

'You don't wanna see us, nohow,' said the first pilot. 'The beams fuck up our faces. We're deformed-lookin' mothers.'

''Course you might not notice the changes,' said the second pilot. 'Lotsa people don't. But if you did, it'd mess you up.'

Imagining the pilots' deformities sent a sick chill mounting from Mingolla's stomach. Gilbey, however, wasn't buying it. 'You think I'm stupid?' he shouted, his neck reddening.

'Naw,' said the first pilot. 'We can *see* you ain't stupid. We can see lotsa shit other people can't, 'cause of the beams.'

'All kindsa weird stuff,' chipped in the second pilot. 'Like souls.'

'Ghosts.'

'Even the future.'

'The future's our best thing,' said the first pilot. 'You guys wanna know what's ahead, we'll tell you.'

They nodded in unison, the blaze of sunlight sliding across both visors: two evil robots responding to the same program.

Gilbey lunged for the cockpit door. The first pilot slammed it shut, and Gilbey pounded on the plastic, screaming curses. The second pilot flipped a switch on the control console, and a moment later his amplified voice boomed out: 'Make straight past that forklift 'til you hit the barracks. You'll run right into the PX.'

It took both Mingolla and Baylor to drag Gilbey away from the Sikorsky, and he didn't stop shouting until they drew near the forklift with its load of coffins: a giant's treasure of enormous silver ingots. Then he grew silent and lowered his eyes. They wangled a ride with an MP corporal outside the PX, and as the jeep hummed across the concrete, Mingolla glanced over at the Sikorsky that had transported them. The two pilots had spread a canvas on the ground, had stripped to shorts and were sunning themselves. But they had not removed their helmets. The weird juxtaposition of tanned bodies and shiny black heads disturbed Mingolla, reminding him of an old movie in which a guy had gone through a matter transmitter along with a fly and had ended up with the fly's head on his shoulders. Maybe, he thought, the helmets were like that, impossible to remove. Maybe the war had gotten that strange.

The MP corporal noticed him watching the pilots and let out a barking laugh. 'Those guys,' he said, with the flat emphatic tone of a man who knew whereof he spoke, 'are fuckin' nuts!'

Six years before, San Francisco de Juticlan had been a scatter of thatched huts and concrete block structures deployed among palms and banana leaves on the east bank of the Río Dulce, at the junction of the river and a gravel road that connected with the Pan American Highway; but it had since grown to occupy substantial sections of both banks, increased by dozens of bars and brothels: stucco cubes painted all the colors of the rainbow, with a fantastic bestiary of neon signs mounted atop their tin roofs. Dragons; unicorns; fiery birds; centaurs. The MP corporal told Mingolla that the signs were not advertisements but coded symbols of pride; for example, from the representation of a winged red tiger crouched amidst green lilies and blue crosses, you could deduce that the owner was wealthy, a member of a Catholic secret society, and ambivalent toward government policies. Old signs were constantly being dismantled, and larger, more ornate ones erected in their stead as testament to improved profits, and this warfare of light and image was appropriate to the time and place because San Francisco de Juticlan was less a town than a symptom of war. Though by night the sky above it was radiant, at ground level it was mean and squalid. Pariah dogs foraged in piles of garbage, hard-bitten whores spat from the windows, and according to the corporal, it was not unusual to stumble across a corpse, likely a victim of the gangs of abandoned children who lived in the fringes of the jungle. Narrow streets of tawny dirt cut between the bars, carpeted with a litter of flattened cans and feces and broken glass; refugees begged at every corner, displaying burns and bullet wounds. Many of the buildings had been thrown up with such haste that their walls were tilted, their roofs canted, and this made the shadows they cast appear exaggerated in their jaggedness, like shadows in the work of a psychotic artist, giving visual expression to a pervasive undercurrent of tension. Yet as Mingolla moved along, he felt at ease, almost happy. His mood was due in part to his hunch that it was going to be one hell of an R&R (he had learned to trust his hunches); but it mainly spoke to the fact that towns like this had become for him a kind of afterlife, a reward for having endured a harsh term of existence.

The corporal dropped them off at a drugstore, where Mingolla bought a box of stationery, and then they stopped for a drink at the Club Demonio: a tiny place whose whitewashed walls were shined to faint phosphorescence by the glare of purple light bulbs dangling from the ceiling like radioactive fruit. The club was packed with soldiers and whores, most sitting at tables around a dance floor not much bigger than a king-size mattress. Two couples were swaying to a ballad that welled from a jukebox encaged in chicken wire and two-by-fours; veils of cigarette smoke drifted with underwater slowness above their heads. Some of the soldiers were mauling their whores, and one whore was trying to steal the wallet of a soldier who was on the verge of passing out; her hand worked between his legs, encouraging him to thrust his hips forward, and when he did this, she pried with her other hand at the wallet stuck in the back pocket of his tight-fitting jeans. But all the action seemed listless, halfhearted, as if the dimness and syrupy music had thickened the air and were hampering movement. Mingolla took a seat at the bar. The bartender glanced at him inquiringly, his pupils becoming cored with purple reflections, and Mingolla said, 'Beer.'

'Hey, check that out!' Gilbey slid onto an adjoining stool and jerked his thumb toward a whore at the end of the bar. Her skirt was hiked to midthigh, and her breasts, judging by their fullness and lack of sag, were likely the product of elective surgery.

'Nice,' said Mingolla, disinterested. The bartender set a bottle of beer in front of him, and he had a swig; it tasted sour, watery, like a distillation of the stale air.

Baylor slumped onto the stool next to Gilbey and buried his face in his hands. Gilbey said something to him that Mingolla didn't catch, and Baylor lifted his head. 'I ain't goin' back,' he said.

'Aw, Jesus!' said Gilbey. 'Don't start that crap.'

In the half-dark Baylor's eye sockets were clotted with shadows. His stare locked onto Mingolla. 'They'll get us next time,' he said. 'We should head downriver. They got boats in Livingston that'll take you to Panama.'

'Panama!' sneered Gilbey. 'Nothin' there 'cept more beaners.'

'We'll be okay at the Farm,' offered Mingolla. 'Things get too heavy, they'll pull us back.'

'"Too heavy"?' A vein throbbed in Baylor's temple. 'What the fuck you call "too heavy"?'

'Screw this!' Gilbey heaved up from his stool. 'You deal with him, man,' he said to Mingolla; he gestured at the big-breasted whore. 'I'm' gonna climb Mount Silicon.'

'Nine o'clock,' said Mingolla. 'The PX. Okay?'

Gilbey said, 'Yeah,' and moved off. Baylor took over his stool and leaned close to Mingolla. 'You know I'm right,' he said in an urgent whisper. 'They almost got us this time.'

'Air Cav'll handle 'em,' said Mingolla, affecting nonchalance. He opened the box of stationery and unclipped a pen from his shirt pocket.

'You *know* I'm right,' Baylor repeated.

Mingolla tapped the pen against his lips, pretending to be distracted.

'Air Cav!' said Baylor with a despairing laugh. 'Air Cav ain't gonna do squat!'

'Why don't you put on some decent tunes?' Mingolla suggested. 'See if they got any Prowler on the box.'

'Dammit!' Baylor grabbed his wrist. 'Don't you understand, man? This shit ain't workin' no more!'

Mingolla shook him off. 'Maybe you need some change,' he said coldly; he dug out a handful of coins and tossed them on the counter. 'There! There's some change.'

'I'm tellin' you …'

'I don't wanna hear it!' snapped Mingolla.

'You don't wanna hear it?' said Baylor, incredulous. He was on the verge of losing control. His dark face slick with sweat, one eyelid fluttering. He pounded the countertop for emphasis. 'Man, you better hear it! Cause we don't pull somethin' together soon, *real* soon, we're gonna fuckin' die! You hear that, don'tcha?'

Mingolla caught him by the shirtfront. 'Shut up!'

'I ain't shuttin' up!' Baylor shrilled. 'You and Gilbey, man, you think you can save your ass by stickin' your head in the sand. But I'm gonna make you listen.' He threw back his head, his voice rose to a shout. 'We're gonna die!'

The way he shouted it – almost gleefully, like a kid yelling a dirty word to spite his parents – pissed Mingolla off. He was sick of Baylor's scenes. Without planning it, he hit him, pulling the punch at the last instant. Kept a hold of his shirt and clipped him on the jaw, just enough to rock back his head. Baylor blinked at him, stunned, his mouth open. Blood seeped from his gums. At the opposite end of the counter, the bartender was leaning beside a choirlike arrangement of liquor bottles, watching Mingolla and Baylor, and some of the soldiers were watching, too: they looked pleased, as if they had been hoping for a spot of violence to liven things up. Mingolla felt debased by their attentiveness, ashamed of his bullying. 'Hey, I'm sorry, man,' he said. 'I …'

'I don't give a shit 'bout you're sorry,' said Baylor, rubbing his mouth. 'Don't give a shit 'bout nothin' 'cept gettin' the hell outta here.'

'Leave it alone, all right?'

But Baylor wouldn't leave it alone. He continued to argue, adopting the long-suffering tone of someone carrying on bravely in the face of great injustice. Mingolla tried to ignore him by studying the label on his beer bottle: a red and black graphic portraying a Guatemalan soldier, his rifle upheld in victory. It was an attractive design, putting him in mind of the poster work he had done before being drafted; but considering the unreliability of Guatemalan troops, he perceived the heroic pose as a bad joke. Mingolla gouged a trench through the center of the label with his thumbnail.

At last Baylor gave it up and sat staring down at the warped veneer of the counter. Mingolla let him sit a minute; then, without shifting his gaze from the bottle, he said, 'Why don't you put on some decent tunes?'

Baylor tucked his chin onto his chest, maintaining a stubborn silence.

'It's your only option, man,' Mingolla went on. 'What else you gonna do?'

'You're crazy,' said Baylor; he flicked his eyes toward Mingolla and hissed it like a curse. 'Crazy!'

'You gonna take off for Panama by yourself? Un-unh. You know the three of us got something going. We come this far together, and if you just hang tough, we'll go home together.'

'I don't know,' said Baylor. 'I don't know anymore.'

'Look at it this way,' said Mingolla. 'Maybe we're all three of us right. Maybe Panama *is* the answer, but the time just isn't ripe. If that's true, me and Gilbey will see it sooner or later.'

With a heavy sigh, Baylor got to his feet. 'You ain't never gonna see it, man,' he said dejectedly.

Mingolla had a swallow of beer. 'Check if they got any Prowler on the box. I could relate to some Prowler.'

Baylor stood for a moment, indecisive. He started for the jukebox, then veered toward the door. Mingolla tensed, preparing to run after him. But Baylor stopped and walked back over to the bar. Lines of strain were etched deep in his forehead. 'Okay,' he said, a catch in his voice. 'Okay. What time tomorrow? Nine o'clock?'

'Right,' said Mingolla, turning away. 'The PX.'

Out of the corner of his eye he saw Baylor cross the room and bend over the jukebox to inspect the selections. He felt relieved. This was the way all their R&Rs had begun, with Gilbey chasing a whore and Baylor feeding the jukebox while he wrote a letter home. On their first R&R he had written his parents about the war and its bizarre forms of attrition; then, realizing that the letter would alarm his mother, he had torn it up and written another, saying merely that he was fine. He would tear this letter up as well, but he wondered how his father would react if he were to read it. Most likely with anger. His father was a firm believer in God and country, and though Mingolla understood the futility of adhering to any moral code in light of the insanity around him, he had found that something of his father's tenets had been ingrained in him: he would never be able to desert as Baylor kept insisting. He knew it wasn't that simple, that other factors, too, were responsible for his devotion to duty; but since his father would have been happy to accept the responsibility, Mingolla tended to blame it on him. He tried to picture what his parents were doing at that moment – father watching the Mets on TV, mother puttering in the garden – and then, holding those images in mind, he began to write.

Dear Mom and Dad,

In your last letter you asked if I thought we were winning the war. Down here you'd get a lot of blank stares in response to that question, because most people have a perspective on the war to which the overall result isn't relevant. Like there's a guy I know who has this rap about how the war is a magical operation of immense proportions, how the movements of the planes and troops are inscribing a mystical sign on the surface of reality, and to survive you have to figure out your location within the design and move accordingly. I'm sure that sounds crazy to you, but down here everyone's crazy the same way (some shrink's actually done a study on the incidence of superstition among the occupation forces). They're looking for a magic that will ensure their survival. You may find it hard to believe that I subscribe to this sort of thing, but I do. I carve my initials on the shell casings, wear parrot feathers inside my helmet ... and a lot more.

To get back to your question, I'll try to do better than a blank stare, but I can't give you a simple Yes or No. The matter can't be summed up that neatly. But I can illustrate the situation by telling you a story and let you draw your own conclusions. There are hundreds of stories that would do, but the one that comes to mind now concerns the Lost Patrol ...

A Prowler tune blasted from the jukebox, and Mingolla broke off writing to listen: it was a furious, jittery music, fueled – it seemed – by the same aggressive paranoia that had generated the war. People shoved back chairs, overturned tables, and began dancing in the vacated spaces; they were crammed together, able to do no more than shuffle in rhythm, but their tread set the light bulbs jiggling at the end of their cords, the purple glare slopping over the walls. A slim acne-scarred whore came to dance in front of Mingolla, shaking her breasts, holding out her arms to him. Her face was corpse-pale in the unsteady light, her smile a dead leer. Trickling from one eye like some exquisite secretion of death, was a black tear of sweat and mascara. Mingolla couldn't be sure he was seeing her right. His left hand started trembling, and for a couple of seconds the entire scene lost its cohesiveness. Everything looked scattered, unrecognizable, embedded in a separate context from everything else: a welter of meaningless objects bobbing up and down on a tide of deranged music. Then somebody opened the door, admitting a wedge of sunlight, and the room settled back to normal. Scowling, the whore danced away. Mingolla breathed easier. The tremors in his hand subsided. He spotted Baylor near the door talking to a scruffy Guatemalan guy ... probably a coke connection. Coke was Baylor's panacea, his remedy for fear and desperation. He always returned from R&R bleary-eyed and prone to nosebleeds, boasting about the great dope he'd scored. Pleased that he was following routine, Mingolla went back to his letter.

> ... Remember me telling you that the Green Berets took drugs to make them better fighters? Most everyone calls the drugs 'Sammy,' which is short for 'samurai.' They come in ampule form, and when you pop them under your nose, for the next thirty minutes or so you feel like a cross between a Medal of Honor winner and Superman. The trouble is that a lot of Berets overdo them and flip out. They sell them on the black market, too, and some guys use them for sport. They take the ampules and fight each other in pits ... like human cockfights.
> Anyway, about two years ago a patrol of Berets went on patrol up in Fire Zone Emerald, not far from my base, and they didn't come back. They were listed MIA. A month or so after they'd disappeared, somebody started ripping off ampules from various dispensaries. At first the crimes were chalked up to guerrillas, but then a doctor caught sight of the robbers and said they were Americans. They were wearing rotted fatigues, acting nuts. An artist did a sketch of their leader according to the doctor's description, and it turned out to be a dead ringer for the sergeant of that missing patrol. After that they were sighted all over the place. Some of the sightings were obviously false, but others sounded like the real thing. They were said to have shot down a couple of our choppers and to have knocked over a supply column near Zacapa.
> I'd never put much stock in the story, to tell you the truth, but about four months ago this infantryman came walking out of the jungle and reported to the firebase. He claimed he'd been captured by the Lost Patrol, and when I heard his story, I believed him. He said they had told him that they weren't Americans anymore but citizens of the jungle. They lived like animals, sleeping under palm fronds, popping the ampules night and day. They were crazy, but they'd become geniuses at survival. They knew everything about the jungle. When the weather was going to change, what animals were near. And they had this weird religion based on the beams of light that would shine down through the canopy. They'd sit under those beams, like saints being blessed by God, and rave about the purity of the light, the joys of killing, and the new world they were going to build.
> So that's what occurs to me when you ask your question, Mom and Dad. The Lost Patrol. I'm not attempting to be circumspect in order to make a point about the horrors of war. Not at all. When I think about the Lost Patrol I'm not thinking about how sad and crazy they are. I'm wondering what it is they see in that light, wondering if it might be of help to me. And maybe therein lies your answer ...

It was nearly sunset by the time Mingolla left the bar to begin the second part of his ritual, to wander innocent as a tourist through the native quarter, partaking of whatever fell to hand, maybe having dinner with a Guatemalan family, or buddying up with a soldier from another outfit and going to church, or hanging out with some young guys who'd ask him about America. He had done each of these things on previous R&Rs, and his pretense of innocence always amused him. If he were to follow his inner directives, he would burn out the horrors of the firebase with whores and drugs; but on that first R&R – stunned by the experience of combat and needing solitude – a protracted walk had been his course of action, and he was committed not only to repeating it but also to recapturing his dazed mental set: it would not do to half-ass the ritual. In this instance, given recent events at the Ant Farm, he did not have to work very hard to achieve confusion.

The Rio Dulce was a wide blue river, heaving with a light chop. Thick jungle hedged its banks, and yellowish reed beds grew out from both shores. At the spot where the gravel road ended was a concrete pier, and moored to it a barge that served as a ferry; it was already loaded with its full complement of vehicles – two trucks – and carried about thirty pedestrians. Mingolla boarded and stood in the stern beside three infantrymen who were still wearing their combat suits and helmets, holding double-barreled rifles that were connected by flexible tubing to backpack computers; through their smoked faceplates he could see green reflections from the readouts on their visor displays. They made him uneasy, reminding him of the two pilots, and he felt better after they had removed their helmets and proved to have normal human faces. Spanning a third of the way across the river was a sweeping curve of white concrete supported by slender columns, like a piece fallen out of a Dali landscape: a bridge upon which construction had been halted. Mingolla had noticed it from the air just before landing and hadn't thought much about it; but now the sight took him by storm. It seemed less an unfinished bridge than a monument to some exalted ideal, more beautiful than any finished bridge could be. And as he stood rapt, with the ferry's oily smoke farting out around him, he sensed there was an analogue of that beautiful curving shape inside him; that he, too, was a road ending in midair. It gave him confidence to associate himself with such loftiness and purity, and for a moment he let himself believe that he also might have – as the upward-angled terminus of the bridge implied – a point of completion lying far beyond the one anticipated by the architects of his fate.

On the west bank past the town the gravel road was lined with stalls: skeletal frameworks of brushwood poles roofed with palm thatch. Children chased in and out among them, pretending to aim and fire at each other with stalks of sugarcane. But hardly any soldiers were in evidence. The crowds that moved along the road were composed mostly of Indians: young couples too shy to hold hands; old men who looked lost and poked litter with their canes; dumpy matrons who made outraged faces at the high prices; shoeless farmers who kept their backs ramrod-straight and wore grave expressions and carried their money knotted in handkerchiefs. At one of the stalls Mingolla bought a fish sandwich and a Coca-Cola. He sat on a stool and ate contentedly, relishing the hot bread and the spicy meat cooked inside it, watching the passing parade. Gray clouds were bulking up and moving in from the south, from the Caribbean; now and then a flight of XL-16s would arrow northward toward the oil fields beyond Lake Izabal, where the fighting was very bad. Twilight fell. The lights of town began to be picked out sharply against the empurpling air. Guitars were plucked, hoarse voices sang, the crowds thinned. Mingolla ordered another sandwich and Coke. He leaned back, sipped and chewed, steeping himself in the good magic of the land, the sweetness of the moment. Beside the sandwich stall, four old women were squatting by a cooking fire, preparing chicken stew and corn fritters; scraps of black ash drifted up from the flames, and as twilight deepened, it seemed these scraps were the pieces of a jigsaw puzzle that were fitting together overhead into the image of a starless night.

Darkness closed in, the crowds thickened again, and Mingolla continued his walk, strolling past stalls with necklaces of light bulbs strung along their frames, wires leading off them to generators whose rattle drowned out the chirring of frogs and crickets. Stalls selling plastic rosaries, Chinese switchblades, tin lanterns; others selling embroidered Indian shirts, flour-sack trousers, wooden masks; others yet where old men in shabby suit coats sat cross-legged behind pyramids of tomatoes and melons and green peppers, each with a candle cemented in melted wax atop them, like primitive altars. Laughter, shrieks, vendors shouting. Mingolla breathed in perfume, charcoal smoke, the scents of rotting fruit. He began to idle from stall to stall, buying a few souvenirs for friends back in New York, feeling part of the hustle, the noise, the shining black air, and eventually he came to a stall around which forty or fifty people had gathered, blocking all but its thatched roof from view. A woman's amplified voice cried out, *'LA MARIPOSA!'* Excited squeals from the crowd. Again the woman cried out, *'EL CUCHILLO!'* The two words she had called – the butterfly and the knife – intrigued Mingolla, and he peered over heads.

Framed by the thatch and rickety poles, a dusky-skinned young woman was turning a handle that spun a wire cage: it was filled with white plastic cubes, bolted to a plank counter. Her black hair was pulled back from her face, tied behind her neck, and she wore a red sundress that left her shoulders bare. She stopped cranking, reached into the cage, and without looking plucked one of the cubes; she examined it, picked up a microphone and cried, *'LA LUNA!'* A bearded man pushed forward and handed her a card.

She checked the card, comparing it with some cubes that were lined up on the counter; then she gave the man a few bills in Guatemalan currency.

The composition of the game appealed to Mingolla. The dark woman; her red dress and cryptic words; the runelike shadow of the wire cage – all this seemed magical, an image out of an occult dream. Part of the crowd moved off, accompanying the winner, and Mingolla let himself be forced closer by new arrivals pressing in from behind. He secured a position at the corner of the stall, fought to maintain it against the eddying of the crowd, and on glancing up, he saw the woman smiling at him from a couple of feet away, holding out a card and a pencil stub. 'Only ten cents Guatemalan,' she said in American-sounding English.

The people flanking Mingolla urged him to play, grinning and clapping him on the back. But he didn't need urging. He knew he was going to win: it was the clearest premonition he had ever had, and it was signaled mostly by the woman herself. He felt a powerful attraction to her. It was as if she were a source of heat … not of heat alone but also of vitality, sensuality, and now that he was within range, that heat was washing over him, making him aware of a sexual tension developing between them, bringing with it the knowledge that he would win. The strength of the attraction surprised him, because his first impression had been that she was exotic-looking but not beautiful. Though slim, she was a little wide-hipped, and her breasts, mounded high and served up in separate scoops by her tight bodice, were quite small. Her face, like her coloring, had an East Indian cast, its features too large and voluptuous to suit the delicate bone structure; yet they were so expressive, so finely cut, that their disproportion came to seem a virtue. Except that it was thinner, her face resembled one of those handmaidens featured on Hindu religious posters, kneeling beneath Krishna's throne. Very sexy, very serene. That serenity, Mingolla decided, wasn't just a veneer. It ran deep. But at the moment he was more interested in her breasts. They looked nice pushed up like that, gleaming with a sheen of sweat. Two helpings of shaky pudding.

The woman waggled the card, and he took it: a simplified Bingo card with symbols instead of letters and numbers. 'Good luck,' she said, and laughed, as if in reaction to some private irony. Then she began to spin the cage.

Mingolla didn't recognize many of the words she called, but an old man cozied up to him and pointed to the appropriate square whenever he got a match. Soon several rows were almost complete. '*LA MANZANA!*' cried the woman, and the old man tugged at Mingolla's sleeve, shouting, '*Se ganó!*'

As the woman checked his card, Mingolla thought about the mystery she presented. Her calmness, her unaccented English and the upper class background it implied, made her seem out of place here. Could be she was a student, her education interrupted by the war … though she might be a bit too old for that. He figured her to be twenty-two or twenty-three. Graduate school, maybe. But there was an air of worldliness about her that didn't support that theory. He watched her eyes dart back and forth between the card and the plastic cubes. Large heavy-lidded eyes. The whites stood in such sharp contrast to her dusky skin that they looked fake: milky stones with black centers.

'You see?' she said, handing him his winnings – about three dollars – and another card.

'See what?' Mingolla asked, perplexed.

But she had already begun to spin the cage again.

He won three of the next seven cards. People congratulated him, shaking their heads in amazement; the old man cozied up further, suggesting in sign language that he was the agency responsible for Mingolla's good fortune. Mingolla, however, was nervous. His ritual was founded on a principle of small miracles, and though he was certain the woman was cheating on his behalf (that, he assumed, had been the meaning of her laughter, her 'You see?'), though his luck was not really luck, its excessiveness menaced that principle. He lost three cards in a row, but thereafter won two of four and grew even more nervous. He considered leaving. But what if it was luck? Leaving might run him afoul of a higher principle, interfere with some cosmic process and draw down misfortune. It was a ridiculous idea, but he couldn't bring himself to risk the faint chance that it might be true.

He continued to win. The people who had congratulated him became disgruntled and drifted off, and when there were only a handful of players left, the woman closed down the game. A grimy street kid materialized from the shadows and began dismantling the equipment. Unbolting the wire cage, unplugging the microphone, boxing up the plastic cubes, stuffing it all into a burlap sack. The woman moved out from behind the stall and leaned against one of the roofpoles. Half-smiling, she cocked her head, appraising Mingolla, and then – just as the silence between them began to get prickly – she said, 'My name's Debora.'

'David.' Mingolla felt as awkward as a fourteen-year-old; he had to resist the urge to jam his hands into his pockets and look away. 'Why'd you cheat?' he asked; in trying to cover his nervousness, he said it too loudly and it sounded like an accusation.

'I wanted to get your attention,' she said. 'I'm ... interested in you. Didn't you notice?'

'I didn't want to take it for granted.'

She laughed. 'I approve! It's always best to be cautious.'

He liked her laughter; it had an easiness that made him think she would celebrate the least good thing.

Three men passed by arm in arm, singing drunkenly. One yelled at

Debora, and she responded with an angry burst of Spanish. Mingolla could guess what had been said, that she had been insulted for associating with an American. 'Maybe we should go somewhere,' he said. 'Get off the streets.'

'After he's finished.' She gestured at the boy, who was now taking down the string of light bulbs. 'It's funny,' she said. 'I have the gift myself, and I'm usually uncomfortable around anyone else who has it. But not with you.'

'The gift?' Mingolla thought he knew what she was referring to, but was leery about admitting to it.

'What do you call it? ESP?'

He gave up the idea of denying it. 'I never put a name on it,' he said.

'It's strong in you. I'm surprised you're not with Psicorp.'

He wanted to impress her, to cloak himself in a mystery equal to hers. 'How do you know I'm not?'

'I could tell.' She pulled a black purse from behind the counter. 'After drug therapy there's a change in the gift, in the way it comes across. It doesn't feel as hot, for one thing.' She glanced up from the purse. 'Or don't you perceive it that way? As heat.'

'I've been around people who felt hot to me,' he said. 'But I didn't know what it meant.'

'That's what it means ... sometimes.' She stuffed some bills into the purse. 'So, why aren't you with Psicorp?'

Mingolla thought back to his first interview with a Psicorp agent: a pale, balding man with the innocent look around the eyes that some blind people have. While Mingolla had talked, the agent had fondled the ring Mingolla had given him to hold, paying no mind to what was being said, and had gazed off distractedly, as if listening for echoes. 'They tried hard to recruit me,' Mingolla said. 'But I was scared of the drugs. I heard they had bad side effects.'

'You're lucky it was voluntary,' she said. 'Here they just snap you up.'

The boy said something to her; he swung the burlap sack over his shoulder, and after a rapid-fire exchange of Spanish he ran off toward the river. The crowds were still thick, but more than half the stalls had shut down; those that remained open looked – with their thatched roofs and strung lights and beshawled women – like crude nativity scenes ranging the darkness. Beyond the stalls, neon signs winked on and off: a chaotic menagerie of silver eagles and crimson spiders and indigo dragons. Watching them burn and vanish, Mingolla experienced a wave of dizziness. Things were starting to appear disconnected as they had at the Club Demonio.

'Don't you feel well?' she asked.

'I'm just tired.'

She turned him to face her, put her hands on his shoulders. 'No,' she said. 'It's something else.'

The weight of her hands, the smell of her perfume, helped to steady him. 'There was an assault on the firebase a few days ago,' he said. 'It's still with me a little, y'know.'

She gave his shoulders a squeeze and stepped back. 'Maybe I can do something.' She said this with such gravity, he thought she must have something specific in mind. 'How's that?' he asked.

'I'll tell you at dinner ... that is, if you're buying.' She took his arm, jollying him. 'You owe me that much, don't you think, after all your good luck?'

'Why aren't *you* with Psicorp?' he asked as they walked.

She didn't answer immediately, keeping her head down, nudging a scrap of cellophane with her toe. They were moving along an uncrowded street, bordered on the left by the river – a channel of sluggish black lacquer – and on the right by the windowless rear walls of some bars. Overhead, behind a latticework of supports, a neon lion shed a baleful green nimbus. 'I was in school in Miami when they started testing here,' she said at last. 'And after I came home, my family got on the wrong side of Department Six. You know Department Six?'

'I've heard some stuff.'

'Sadists don't make efficient bureaucrats,' she said. 'They were more interested in torturing us than in determining our value.'

Their footsteps crunched in the dirt; husky jukebox voices cried out for love from the next street over. 'What happened?' Mingolla asked.

'To my family?' She shrugged. 'Dead. No one ever bothered to confirm it, but it wasn't necessary. Confirmation, I mean.' She went a few steps in silence. 'As for me ...' A muscle bunched at the corner of her mouth. 'I did what I had to.'

He was tempted to ask for specifics, but thought better of it. 'I'm sorry,' he said, and then kicked himself for having made such a banal comment.

They passed a bar lorded over by a grinning red-and-purple neon ape. Mingolla wondered if these glowing figures had meaning for guerrillas with binoculars in the hills: gone-dead tubes signaling times of attack or troop movements. He cocked an eye toward Debora. She didn't look despondent as she had a second before, and that accorded with his impression that her calmness was a product of self-control, that her emotions were strong but held in tight check and only let out for exercise. From the river came a solitary splash, some cold fleck of life surfacing briefly, then returning to its long ignorant glide through the darkness ... and his life no different really, though maybe less graceful. How strange it was to be walking beside this woman who gave off heat like a candle flame, with earth and sky blended into a black gas, and neon totems standing guard overhead.

'Shit,' said Debora under her breath.

It surprised him to hear her curse. 'What is it?'

'Nothing,' she said wearily. 'Just "shit."' She pointed ahead and quickened her pace. 'Here we are.'

The restaurant was a working-class place that occupied the ground floor of a hotel: a two-story building of yellow concrete block with a buzzing Fanta sign hung above the entrance. Hundreds of moths swarmed about the sign, flickering whitely against the darkness, and in front of the steps stood a group of teenage boys who were throwing knives at an iguana. The iguana was tied by its hind legs to the step railing. It had amber eyes, a hide the color of boiled cabbage, and it strained at the end of its cord, digging its claws into the dirt and arching its neck like a pint-size dragon about to take flight. As Mingolla and Debora walked up, one of the boys scored a hit in the iguana's tail and it flipped high into the air, shaking loose the knife. The boys passed around a bottle of rum to celebrate.

Except for the waiter – a pudgy young man leaning beside a door that opened onto a smoke-filled kitchen – the place was empty. Glaring overhead lights shined up the grease spots on the plastic tablecloths and made the uneven thicknesses of yellow paint appear to be dripping. The concrete floor was freckled with dark stains that Mingolla discovered to be the remains of insects. The food turned out to be decent, however, and Mingolla shoveled down a plateful of chicken and rice before Debora had half finished hers. She ate deliberately, chewing each bite a long time, and he had to carry the conversation. He told her about New York, his painting, how a couple of galleries had showed interest even though he was just a student. He compared his work to Rauschenberg, to Silvestre. Not as good, of course. Not yet. He had the notion that everything he told her – no matter its irrelevance to the moment – was securing the relationship, establishing subtle ties: he pictured the two of them enwebbed in a network of luminous threads that acted as conduits for their attraction. He could feel her heat more strongly than ever, and he wondered what it would be like to make love to her, to be swallowed by that perception of heat. The instant he wondered this, she glanced up and smiled, as if sharing the thought. He wanted to ratify his sense of intimacy, to tell her something he had told no one else, and so – having only one important secret – he told her about the ritual.

She laid down her fork and gave him a penetrating look. 'You can't really believe that,' she said.

'I know it sounds ...'

'Ridiculous,' she broke in. 'That's how it sounds.'

'It's the truth,' he said defiantly.

She picked up her fork again, pushed around some grains of rice. 'How is it for you,' she said, 'when you have a premonition? I mean, what happens? Do you have dreams, hear voices?'

'Sometimes I just know things,' he said, taken aback by her abrupt change of subject. 'And sometimes I see pictures. It's like with a TV that's not working right. Fuzziness at first, then a sharp image.'

'With me, it's dreams. And hallucinations. I don't know what else to call them.' Her lips thinned; she sighed, appearing to have reached some decision. 'When I first saw you, just for a second, you were wearing battle gear. There were inputs on the gauntlets, cables attached to the helmet. The faceplate was shattered, and your face ... it was pale, bloody.' She put her hand out to cover his. 'What I saw was very clear, David. You can't go back.'

He hadn't described artilleryman's gear to her, and no way could she have seen it. Shaken, he said, 'Where am I gonna go?'

'Panama,' she said. 'I can help you get there.'

She suddenly snapped into focus. You find her, dozens like her, in any of the R&R towns. Preaching pacifism, encouraging desertion. Do-gooders, most with guerrilla connections. And that, he realized, must be how she had known about his gear. She had probably gathered information on the different types of units in order to lend authenticity to her dire pronouncements. His opinion of her wasn't diminished; on the contrary, it went up a notch. She was risking her life by talking to him. But her mystery had been dimmed.

'I can't do that,' he said.

'Why not? Don't you believe me?'

'It wouldn't make any difference if I did.'

'Look,' he said. 'This friend of mine, he's always trying to convince me to desert, and there've been times I wanted to. But it's just not in me. My feet won't move that way. Maybe you don't understand, but that's how it is.'

'This childish thing you do with your two friends,' she said after a pause. 'That's what's holding you here, isn't it?'

'It isn't childish.'

'That's exactly what it is. Like a child walking home in the dark and thinking that if he doesn't look at the shadows, nothing will jump out at him.'

'You don't understand,' he said.

'No, I suppose I don't.' Angry, she threw her napkin down on the table and stared intently at her plate as if reading some oracle from the chicken bones.

'Let's talk about something else,' said Mingolla.

'I have to go,' she said coldly.

'Because I won't desert?'

'Because of what'll happen if you don't.' She leaned toward him, her voice burred with emotion. 'Because knowing what I do about your future, I don't want to wind up in bed with you.'

Her intensity frightened him. Maybe she *had* been telling the truth. But he dismissed the possibility. 'Stay,' he said. 'We'll talk some more about it.'

'You wouldn't listen.' She picked up her purse and got to her feet.

The waiter ambled over and laid the check beside Mingolla's plate; he pulled a plastic bag filled with marijuana from his apron pocket and dangled it in front of Mingolla. 'Gotta get her in the mood, man,' he said. Debora railed at him in Spanish. He shrugged and moved off, his slow-footed walk an advertisement for his goods.

'Meet me tomorrow then,' said Mingolla. 'We can talk more about it tomorrow.'

'No.'

'Why don't you gimme a break?' he said. 'This is all coming down pretty fast, y'know. I get here this afternoon, meet you, and an hour later you're saying, "Death is in the cards, and Panama's your only hope." I need some time to think. Maybe by tomorrow I'll have a different attitude.'

Her expression softened, but she shook her head, No.

'Don't you think it's worth it?'

She lowered her eyes, fussed with the zipper of her purse a second, and let out a rueful hiss. 'Where do you want to meet?'

'How 'bout the pier on this side? 'Round noon.'

She hesitated. 'All right.' She came around to his side of the table, bent down and brushed her lips across his cheek. He tried to pull her close and deepen the kiss, but she slipped away. He felt giddy, overheated. 'You really gonna be there?' he asked.

She nodded but seemed troubled, and she didn't look back before vanishing down the steps.

Mingolla sat awhile, thinking about the kiss, its promise. He might have stayed even longer, but three drunken soldiers staggered in and began knocking over chairs, giving the waiter a hard time. Annoyed, Mingolla went to the door and stood taking in hits of the humid air. Moths were loosely constellated on the curved plastic of the Fanta sign, trying to get next to the bright heat inside it, and he had a sense of relation, of sharing their yearning for the impossible. He started down the steps but was brought up short. The teenage boys had gone; however, their captive iguana lay on the bottom step, bloody and unmoving. Bluish-gray strings spilled from a gash in its throat. It was such a clear sign of bad luck, Mingolla went back inside and checked into the hotel upstairs.

The hotel corridors stank of urine and disinfectant. A drunken Indian with his fly unzipped and a bloody mouth was pounding on one of the doors. As Mingolla passed him, he bowed and made a sweeping gesture, a parody of welcome. Then he went back to his pounding. Mingolla's room was a windowless cell five feet wide and coffin-length, furnished with a sink and a cot and a chair. Cobwebs and dust clotted the glass of the transom, reducing the hallway light to a cold bluish-white glow. The walls were filmy with more cobwebs, and the sheets were so dirty that they appeared to have a pattern. He lay down and closed his eyes, thinking about Debora. About ripping off that red dress and giving her a vicious screwing. How she'd cry out. That both made him ashamed and gave him a hard-on. He tried to think about making love to her tenderly. But tenderness, it seemed, was beyond him. He went flaccid. Jerking off wasn't worth the effort, he decided. He started to unbutton his shirt, remembered the sheets and figured he'd be better off with his clothes on.

In the blackness behind his lids he began to see explosive flashes, and within those flashes were images of the assault on the Ant Farm. The mist, the tunnels. He blotted them out with the image of Debora's face, but they kept coming back. Finally he opened his eyes. Two ... no, three fuzzy-looking black stars were silhouetted against the transom. It was only when they began to crawl that he recognized them to be spiders. Big ones. He wasn't usually afraid of spiders, but these particular spiders terrified him. If he hit them with his shoe, he'd break the glass and they'd eject him from the hotel. He didn't want to kill them with his hands. After a while he sat up, switched on the overhead, and searched under the cot. There weren't any more spiders. He lay back down, feeling shaky and short of breath. Wishing he could talk to someone, hear a familiar voice. 'It's okay,' he said to the dark air. But that didn't help. And for a long time, until he felt secure enough to sleep, he watched the three black stars crawling across the transom, moving toward the center, touching each other, moving apart, never making any real progress, never straying from their area of bright confinement, their universe of curdled, frozen light.

II

In the morning Mingolla crossed to the west bank and walked toward the airbase. It was already hot, but the air still held a trace of freshness and the sweat that beaded on his forehead felt clean and healthy. White dust was settling along the gravel road, testifying to the recent passage of traffic; past the town and the cutoff that led to the uncompleted bridge, high walls of vegetation crowded close to the road, and from within them he heard monkeys and insects and birds: sharp sounds that enlivened him, making him conscious of the play of his muscles. About halfway to the base he spotted six Guatemalan soldiers coming out of the jungle, dragging a couple of bodies; they tossed them onto the hood of their jeep, where two other bodies were lying. Drawing near, Mingolla saw that the dead were naked children, each with a neat hole in his back. He had intended to walk on past, but one of the soldiers – a gnomish copper-skinned man in dark blue fatigues – blocked his path and demanded to check his papers. All the soldiers gathered around to study the papers, whispering, turning them sideways, scratching their heads. Used to such hassles, Mingolla paid them no attention and looked at the dead children.

They were scrawny, sun-darkened, lying facedown with their ragged hair hanging a fringe off the hood; their skins were pocked by infected mosquito bites, and the flesh around the bullet holes was ridged up and bruised. Judging by their size, Mingolla guessed them to be about ten years old; but then he noticed that one was a girl with a teenage fullness to her buttocks, her breasts squashed against the metal. That made him indignant. They were only wild children who survived by robbing and killing, and the Guatemalan soldiers were only doing their duty: they performed a function comparable to that of the birds that hunted ticks on the hide of a rhinoceros, keeping their American beast pest-free and happy. But it wasn't right for the children to be laid out like game.

The soldier gave back Mingolla's papers. He was now all smiles, and – perhaps in the interest of solidifying Guatemalan-American relations, perhaps because he was proud of his work – he went over to the jeep and lifted the girl's head by the hair so Mingolla could see her face. '*Bandida!*' he said, arranging his features into a comical frown. The girl's face was not unlike the soldier's, with the same blade of a nose and prominent cheekbones. Fresh blood glistened on her lips, and the faded tattoo of a coiled serpent centered her forehead. Her eyes were open, and staring into them – despite their cloudiness – Mingolla felt that he had made a connection, that she was regarding him sadly from somewhere behind those eyes, continuing to die past the point of clinical death. Then an ant crawled out of her nostril, perching on the crimson curve of her lip, and the eyes looked merely vacant. The soldier let her head fall and wrapped his hand in the hair of a second corpse; but before he could lift it, Mingolla turned away and headed down the road toward the airbase.

There was a row of helicopters lined up at the edge of the landing strip, and walking between them, Mingolla saw the two pilots who had given him a ride from the Ant Farm. They were stripped to shorts and helmets, wearing baseball gloves, and they were playing catch, lofting high flies to one another. Behind them, atop their Sikorsky, a mechanic was fussing with the main rotor housing. The sight of the pilots didn't disturb Mingolla as it had the previous day; in fact, he found their weirdness somehow comforting. Just then, the ball eluded one of them and bounced Mingolla's way. He snagged it and flipped it back to the nearer of the pilots, who came loping over and stood pounding the ball into the pocket of his glove. With his black reflecting face and sweaty, muscular torso, he looked like an eager young mutant.

'How's she goin?' he asked. 'Seem like you a little tore down this mornin'.'

'I feel okay,' said Mingolla defensively. '' Course' – he smiled, making light of his defensiveness – 'maybe you see something I don't.'

The pilot shrugged; the sprightliness of the gesture seemed to convey good humor.

Mingolla pointed to the mechanic. 'You guys broke down, huh?'

'Just overhaul. We're goin' back up early tomorrow. Need a lift?'

'Naw, I'm here for a week.'

An eerie current flowed through Mingolla's left hand, setting up a palsied shaking. It was bad this time, and he jammed the hand into his hip pocket. The olive-drab line of barracks appeared to twitch, to suffer a dislocation and shift farther away; the choppers and jeeps and uniformed men on the strip looked toylike: pieces in a really neat GI Joe Airbase kit. Mingolla's hand beat against the fabric of his trousers like a sick heart.

'I gotta get going,' he said.

'Hang in there,' said the pilot. 'You be awright.'

The words had a flavor of diagnostic assurance that almost convinced Mingolla of the pilot's ability to know his fate, that things such as fate could be known. 'You honestly believe what you were saying yesterday, man?' he asked. ''Bout your helmets? 'Bout knowing the future?'

The pilot bounced the ball on the concrete, snatched it at the peak of its rebound, and stared down at it. Mingolla could see the seams and brand name reflected in the visor, but nothing of the face behind it, no evidence either of normalcy or deformity. 'I get asked that a lot,' said the pilot. 'People raggin' me, y'know. But you ain't raggin' me, are you, man?'

'No,' said Mingolla. 'I'm not.'

'Well,' said the pilot, 'it's this way. We buzz 'round up in the nothin', and we see shit down on the ground, shit nobody else sees. Then we blow that shit away. Been doin' it like that for ten months, and we're still alive. Fuckin' A, I believe it!'

Mingolla was disappointed. 'Yeah, okay,' he said.

'You hear what I'm sayin'?' asked the pilot. 'I mean we're livin' goddamn proof.'

'Uh-huh.' Mingolla scratched his neck, trying to think of a diplomatic response, but thought of none. 'Guess I'll see you.'

He started toward the PX.

'Hang in there, man!' the pilot called after him. 'Take it from me! Things gonna be lookin' up for you real soon!'

The canteen in the PX was a big barnlike room of unpainted boards; it was of such recent construction that Mingolla could still smell sawdust and resin. Thirty or forty tables; a jukebox; bare walls. Behind the bar at the rear of the room, a sour-faced corporal with a clipboard was doing a liquor inventory, and Gilbey – the only customer – was sitting by one of the east windows, stirring a cup of coffee. His brow was furrowed, and a ray of sunlight shone down around him, making it look that he was being divinely inspired to do some soul-searching.

'Where's Baylor?' asked Mingolla, sitting opposite him.

'Fuck, I dunno,' said Gilbey, not taking his eyes from the coffee cup. 'He'll be here.'

Mingolla kept his left hand in his pocket. The tremors were diminishing, but not quickly enough to suit him; he was worried that the shaking would spread as it had after the assault. He let out a sigh, and in letting it out he could feel all his nervous flutters. The ray of sunlight seemed to be humming a wavery golden note, and that, too, worried him. Hallucinations. Then he noticed a fly buzzing against the windowpane. 'How was it last night?' he asked.

Gilbey glanced up sharply. 'Oh, you mean Big Tits. She lemme check her for lumps.' He forced a grin, then went back to stirring his coffee.

Mingolla was hurt that Gilbey hadn't asked about his night; he wanted to tell him about Debora. But that was typical of Gilbey's self-involvement. His narrow eyes and sulky mouth were the imprints of a mean-spiritedness that permitted few concerns aside from his own well-being. Yet despite his insensitivity, his stupid rages and limited conversation, Mingolla believed that he was smarter than he appeared, that disguising one's intelligence must have been a survival tactic in Detroit, where he had grown up. It was his craftiness that gave him away: his insights into the personalities of adversary lieutenants; his slickness at avoiding unpleasant duty; his ability to manipulate his peers. He wore stupidity like a cloak, and perhaps he had worn it for so long that it could not be removed. Still, Mingolla envied him its virtues, especially the way it had numbed him to the assault.

'He's never been late before,' said Mingolla after a while.

'So what, he's fuckin' late!' snapped Gilbey, glowering. 'He'll be here!'

Behind the bar, the corporal switched on a radio and spun the dial past Latin music, past Top Forty, then past an American voice reporting the baseball scores. 'Hey!' called Gilbey. 'Let's hear that, man! I wanna see what happened to the Tigers.' With a shrug, the corporal complied.

'... White Sox six, A's three,' said the announcer. 'That's eight in a row for the Sox ...'

'White Sox are kickin' some ass,' said the corporal, pleased.

'The White Sox!' Gilbey sneered. 'What the White Sox got cept a buncha beaners hittin' two hunnerd and some coke-sniffin' niggers? Shit! Every fuckin' spring the White Sox are flyin', man. But then 'long comes summer and the good drugs hit the street and they fuckin' die!'

'Yeah,' said the corporal, 'but this year ...'

'Take that son of a bitch Caldwell,' said Gilbey, ignoring him. 'I seen him coupla years back when he had a trial with the Tigers. Man, that nigger could hit! Now he shuffles up there like he's just feelin' the breeze.'

'They ain't takin' drugs, man,' said the corporal testily. 'They can't take 'em 'cause there's these tests that show if they's on somethin'.'

Gilbey barreled ahead. 'White Sox ain't gotta chance, man! Know what the guy on TV calls 'em sometimes? The Pale Hose! The fuckin' Pale Hose! How you gonna win with a name like that? The Tigers, now, they got the right kinda name. The Yankees, the Braves, the ...'

'Bullshit, man!' The corporal was becoming upset; he set down his clipboard and walked to the end of the bar. 'What 'bout the Dodgers? They gotta wimpy name and they're a good team. Your name don't mean shit!'

'The Reds,' suggested Mingolla; he was enjoying Gilbey's rap, its stubbornness and irrationality. Yet at the same time he was concerned by its undertone of desperation: appearances to the contrary, Gilbey was not himself this morning.

'Oh, yeah!' Gilbey smacked the table with the flat of his hand.

'The Reds! Lookit the Reds, man! Lookit how good they been doin since the Cubans come into the war. You think that don't mean nothin'? You think their name ain't helpin' 'em? Even if they get in the Series, the Pale fuckin' Hose don't gotta prayer against the Reds.' He laughed – a hoarse grunt. 'I'm a Tiger fan, man, but I gotta feelin' this ain't their year, y'know. The Reds are tearin' up the NL East, and the Yankees is comin' on, and when they get together in October, man, then we gonna find out alla 'bout everything. Alla 'bout fuckin' everything!' His voice grew tight and tremulous. 'So don't gimme no trouble 'bout the candyass Pale Hose, man! They ain't shit and they never was and they ain't gonna be shit 'til they change their fuckin' name!'

Sensing danger, the corporal backed away from confrontation, and Gilbey lapsed into a moody silence. For a while there were only the sounds of chopper blades and the radio blatting out cocktail jazz. Two mechanics wandered in for an early morning beer, and not long after that three fatherly looking sergeants with potbellies and thinning hair and quartermaster insignia on their shoulders sat at a nearby table and started up a game of rummy. The corporal brought them a pot of coffee and a bottle of whiskey, which they mixed and drank as they played. Their game had an air of custom, of something done at this time every day, and watching them, taking note of their fat, pampered ease, their old-buddy familiarity, Mingolla felt proud of his palsied hand. It was an honorable affliction, a sign that he had participated in the heart of the war as these men had not. Yet he bore them no resentment. None whatsoever. Rather it gave him a sense of security to know that three such fatherly men were here to provide him with food and liquor and new boots. He basked in the dull, happy clutter of their talk, in the haze of cigar smoke that seemed the exhaust of their contentment. He believed that he could go to them, tell them his problems, and receive folksy advice. They were here to assure him of the rightness of his purpose, to remind him of simple American values, to lend an illusion of fraternal involvement to the war, to make clear that it was merely an exercise in good fellowship and tough-mindedness, an initiation rite that these three men had long ago passed through, and after the war they would all get rings and medals and pal around together and talk about bloodshed and terror with head-shaking wonderment and nostalgia, as if bloodshed and terror were old lost friends whose natures they had not fully appreciated at the time... Mingolla realized then that a smile had stretched his facial muscles taut, and that his train of thought had been leading him into spooky mental territory. The tremors in his hand were worse than ever. He checked his watch. It was almost ten o'clock. *Ten o'clock!* In a panic he scraped back his chair and stood.

'Let's look for him,' he said to Gilbey.

Gilbey started to say something but kept it to himself. He tapped his spoon hard against the edge of the table. Then he, too, scraped back his chair and stood.

Baylor was not to be found at the Club Demonio or any of the bars on the west bank. Gilbey and Mingolla described him to everyone they met, but no one remembered him. The longer the search went on, the more insecure Mingolla became. Baylor was necessary, an essential underpinning of the platform of habits and routines that supported him, that let him live beyond the range of war's weapons and the laws of chance, and should that underpinning be destroyed ... In his mind's eye he saw the platform tipping, he and Gilbey toppling over the edge, cartwheeling down into an abyss filled with black flames. Once Gilbey said, 'Panama! The son of a bitch run off to Panama.' But Mingolla didn't think this was the case. He was certain that Baylor was close at hand. His certainty had such a valence of clarity that he became even more insecure, knowing that this sort of clarity often heralded a bad conclusion.

The sun climbed higher, its heat an enormous weight pressing down, its light leaching color from the stucco walls, and Mingolla's sweat began to smell rancid. Only a few soldiers were on the streets, mixed in with the usual run of kids and beggars, and the bars were empty except for a smattering of drunks still on a binge from the night before. Gilbey stumped along, grabbing people by the shirt and asking his questions. Mingolla however, terribly conscious of his trembling hand, nervous to the point of stammering, was forced to work out a stock approach whereby he could get through these brief interviews. He would amble up, keeping his right side forward, and say, 'I'm looking for a friend of mine. Maybe you seen him? Tall guy. Olive skin, black hair, thin. Name's Baylor.' He learned to let this slide off his tongue in a casual unreeling.

Finally Gilbey had had enough. 'I'm gonna hang out with Big Tits,' he said. 'Meet'cha at the PX tomorrow.' He started to walk off, but turned and added, 'You wanna get in touch 'fore tomorrow, I'll be at the Club Demonio.' He had an odd expression on his face. It was as if he were trying to smile reassuringly, but – due to his lack of practice with smiles – it looked forced and foolish and not in the least reassuring.

Around eleven o'clock Mingolla wound up leaning against a pink stucco wall, watching out for Baylor in the thickening crowds. Beside him, the sun-browned fronds of a banana tree were feathering in the wind, making a crispy sound whenever a gust blew them back into the wall. The roof of the bar across the street was being repaired; sheets of new tin alternating with narrow patches of rust that looked like enormous strips of bacon laid there to fry. Now and then he would let his gaze drift up to the unfinished bridge, a great sweep of magical whiteness curving into the blue, rising above the town and the jungle and the war. Not even the heat haze rippling from the tin roof could warp its smoothness. It seemed to be orchestrating the stench, the mutter of the crowds, and the jukebox music into a tranquil unity, absorbing those energies and returning them purified, enriched. He thought that if he stared at it long enough, it would speak to him, pronounce a white word that would grant his wishes.

Two flat cracks – pistol shots – sent him stumbling away from the wall, his heart racing. Inside his head the shots had spoken the two syllables of Baylor's name. All the kids and beggars had vanished. All the soldiers had stopped and turned to face the direction from which the shots had come: zombies who had heard their master's voice.

Another shot.

Some soldiers milled out of a side street, talking excitedly '... fuckin' nuts!' one was saying, and his buddy said, 'It was Sammy, man! You see his eyes?'

Mingolla pushed his way through them and sprinted down the side street. At the end of the block a cordon of MPs had sealed off access to the right-hand turn, and when Mingolla ran up, one of them told him to stay back.

'What is it?' Mingolla asked. 'Some guy playing Sammy?'

'Fuck off,' the MP said mildly.

'Listen,' said Mingolla. 'It might he this friend of mine. Tall, skinny guy. Black hair. Maybe I can talk to him.'

The MP exchanged glances with his buddies, who shrugged and acted otherwise unconcerned. 'Okay,' he said. He pulled Mingolla to him and pointed out a bar with turquoise walls on the next corner down. 'Go on in there and talk to the captain.'

Two more shots, then a third.

'Better hurry,' said the MP. 'Ol' Captain Haynesworth there, he don't put much stock in negotiations.'

*

It was cool and dark inside the bar; two shadowy figures were flattened against the wall beside a window that opened onto the cross street. Mingolla could make out the glint of automatic pistols in their hands. Then, through the window, he saw Baylor pop up from behind a retaining wall: a three-foot-high structure of mud bricks running between a herbal drugstore and another bar. Baylor was shirtless, his chest painted with reddish-brown smears of dried blood, and he was standing in a nonchalant pose, with his thumbs hooked in his trouser pockets. One of the men by the window fired at him. The report was deafening, causing Mingolla to flinch and close his eyes. When he looked out the window again, Baylor was nowhere in sight.

'Fucker's just tryin' to draw fire,' said the man who had shot at Baylor. 'Sammy's fast today.'

'Yeah, but he's slowin' some,' said a lazy voice from the darkness at the rear of the bar. 'I do believe he's outta dope.'

'Hey,' said Mingolla. 'Don't kill him! I know the guy. I can talk to him.'

'Talk?' said the lazy voice. 'You kin talk 'til yo' ass turns green, boy, and Sammy ain't gon' listen.'

Mingolla peered into the shadows. A big sloppy-looking man was leaning on the counter; brass insignia gleamed on his beret. 'You the captain?' he asked. 'They told me outside to talk to the captain.'

'Yes, indeed,' said the man. 'And I'd be purely delighted to talk with you, boy. What you wanna talk 'bout?'

The other men laughed.

'Why are you trying to kill him?' asked Mingolla, hearing the pitch of desperation in his voice. 'You don't have to kill him. You could use a trank gun.'

'Got one comin',' said the captain, 'Thing is, though, yo' buddy got hisself a coupla hostages back of that wall, and we get a chance at him 'fore the trank gun 'rives, we bound to take it.'

'But ...' Mingolla began.

'Lemme finish, boy.' The captain hitched up his gunbelt, strolled over, and draped an arm around Mingolla's shoulder, enveloping him in an aura of body odor and whiskey breath. 'See,' he went on, 'we had everything under control. Sammy there ...'

'Baylor!' said Mingolla angrily. 'His name's Baylor.'

The captain lifted his arm from Mingolla's shoulder and looked at him with amusement. Even in the gloom Mingolla could see the network of broken capillaries on his cheeks, the bloated alcoholic features. 'Right,' said the captain, 'Like I's sayin', yo' good buddy Mister Baylor there wasn't doin' no harm. Just sorta ravin' and runnin' round. But then 'long comes a coupla our Marine brothers. Seems like they'd been givin' our beaner friends a demonstration of the latest combat gear, and they was headin' back from said demonstration when they seen our little problem and took it 'pon themselves to play hero. Well sir, puttin' it in a nutshell, Mister Baylor flat kicked their ass. Stomped all over their *esprit de corps*. Then he drags 'em back of that wall and starts messin' with one of their guns. And ...'

Two more shots.

'Shit!' said one of the men by the window.

'And there he sits,' said the captain. 'Fuckin' with us. Now either the gun's outta ammo or else he ain't figgered out how it works. If it's the latter case, and he does figger it out ...' The captain shook his head dolefully, as if picturing dire consequences. 'See my predicament?'

'I could try talking to him,' said Mingolla. 'What harm would it do?'

'You get yourself killed, it's your life, boy. But it's my ass that's gonna get hauled up on charges.' The captain steered Mingolla to the door and gave him a gentle shove toward the cordon of MPs, ''Preciate you volunteerin', boy.'

Later Mingolla was to reflect that what he had done had made no sense, because – whether or not Baylor had survived – he would never have been returned to the Ant Farm. But at the time, desperate to preserve the ritual, none of this occurred to him. He walked around the corner and toward the retaining wall. His mouth was dry, his heart pounded. But the shaking in his hand had stopped, and he had the presence of mind to walk in such a way that he blocked the MPs' line of fire. About twenty feet from the wall he called out, 'Hey, Baylor! It's Mingolla, man!' And as if propelled by a spring, Baylor jumped up, staring at him. It was an awful stare. His eyes were like bull's-eyes, white showing all around the irises; trickles of blood ran from his nostrils, and nerves were twitching in his cheeks with the regularity of watchworks. The dried blood on his chest came from three long gouges; they were partially scabbed over but were oozing a clear fluid. For a moment he remained motionless. Then he reached down behind the wall, picked up a double-barreled rifle from whose stock trailed a length of flexible tubing, and brought it to bear on Mingolla.

He squeezed the trigger.

No flame, no explosion. Not even a click. But Mingolla felt that he'd been dipped in ice water. 'Christ!' he said. 'Baylor! It's me!' Baylor squeezed the trigger again, with the same result. An expression of intense frustration washed over his face, then lapsed into that dead man's stare. He looked directly up into the sun, and after a few seconds he smiled: he might have been receiving terrific news from on high.

Mingolla's senses had become wonderfully acute. Somewhere far away a radio was playing a country-and-western tune, and with its plaintiveness, its intermittent bursts of static, it seemed to him the whining of a nervous system on the blink. He could hear the MPs talking in the bar, could smell the sour acids of Baylor's madness, and he thought he could feel the pulse of Baylor's rage, an inconstant flow of heat eddying around him, intensifying his fear, rooting him to the spot. Baylor laid the gun down, laid it down with the tenderness he might have shown toward a sick child, and stepped over the retaining wall. The animal fluidity of the movement made Mingolla's skin crawl. He managed to shuffle backward a pace and held up his hands to ward Baylor off. 'C'mon, man,' he said weakly. Baylor let out a fuming noise – part hiss, part whimper – and a runner of saliva slid between his lips. The sun was a golden bath drenching the street, kindling glints and shimmers from every bright surface, as if it were bringing reality to a boil. Somebody yelled, 'Get down, boy!'

Then Baylor flew at him, and they fell together, rolling on the hard-packed dirt. Fingers dug in behind his Adam's apple. He twisted away, saw Baylor grinning down, all staring eyes and yellowed teeth. Strings of drool flapping from his chin. A Halloween face. Knees pinned Mingolla's shoulders, hands gripped his hair and bashed his head against the ground. Again, and again. A keening sound switched on inside his ears. He wrenched an arm free and tried to gouge Baylor's eyes; but Baylor bit his thumb, gnawing at the joint. Mingolla's vision dimmed, and he couldn't hear anything anymore. The back of his head felt mushy. It seemed to be rebounding very slowly from the dirt, higher and slower after each impact. Framed by blue sky, Baylor's face looked to be receding, spiraling off. And then, just as Mingolla began to fade, Baylor disappeared.

Dust was in Mingolla's mouth, his nostrils. He heard shouts, grunts. Still dazed, he propped himself onto an elbow. A short ways off, khaki arms and legs and butts were thrashing around in a cloud of dust. Like a comic-strip fight. You expected asterisks and exclamation points overhead to signify profanity. Somebody grabbed his arm, hauled him upright. The MP captain, his beefy face flushed. He frowned reprovingly as he brushed dirt from Mingolla's clothes, 'Real gutsy, boy,' he said. 'And real, real stupid. He hadn't been at the end of his run, you'd be drawin' flies 'bout now.' He turned to a sergeant standing nearby. 'How stupid you reckon that was, Phil?'

The sergeant said that it beat him.

'Well,' the captain said, 'I figger if the boy here was in combat that'd be 'bout Bronze-Star stupid.'

That, allowed the sergeant, was pretty goddamn stupid.

' 'Course here in 'Frisco' – the captain gave Mingolla a final dusting – 'it don't get you diddley-shit.'

The MPs were piling off Baylor, who lay on his side, bleeding from his nose and mouth. Blood thick as gray filmed over his cheeks.

'Panama,' said Mingolla dully. Maybe it was an option. He saw how it would be … a night beach, palm shadows a lacework on the white sand.

'What say?' asked the captain.

'He wanted to go to Panama,' said Mingolla.

'Don't we all,' said the captain.

One of the MPs rolled Baylor onto his stomach and handcuffed him; another manacled his feet. Then they rolled him back over. Yellow dirt had mired with the blood on his cheeks and forehead, fitting him with a blotchy mask. His eyes snapped open in the middle of that mask, widening when he felt the restraints. He started to hump up and down, trying to bounce his way to freedom. He kept on humping for almost a minute; then he went rigid and – his gone eyes fixed on the molten disc of the sun – he let out a roar. That was the only word for it. It wasn't a scream or a shout, but a devil's exultant roar, so loud and full of fury, it seemed to be generating all the blazing light and heat dance. Listening to it had a seductive effect, and Mingolla began to get behind it, to feel it in his body like a good rock 'n' roll tune, to sympathize with its life-hating exuberance.

'Whoo-ee!' said the captain, marveling. 'They gon' have to build a whole new zoo for that boy.'

After giving his statement, letting a Corpsman check his head, Mingolla caught the ferry to meet Debora on the east bank. He sat in the stern, gazing out at the unfinished bridge, this time unable to derive from it any sense of hope or magic. Panama kept cropping up in his thoughts. Now that Baylor was gone, was it really an option? He knew he should try to figure things out, plan what to do, but he couldn't stop seeing Baylor's bloody, demented face. He'd seen worse, Christ yes, a whole lot worse. Guys reduced to spare parts, so little of them left that they didn't need a shiny silver coffin, just a black metal can the size of a cookie jar. Guys scorched and one-eyed and bloody, clawing blindly at the air like creatures out of a monster movie. But the idea of Baylor trapped forever in some raw, red place inside his brain, in the heart of that raw, red noise he'd made, maybe that idea was worse than anything Mingolla had seen. He didn't want to die; he rejected the prospect with the impassioned stubbornness a child displays when confronted with a hard truth. Yet he would rather die than endure madness. Compared to what Baylor had in store, death and Panama seemed to offer the same peaceful sweetness.

Someone sat down beside Mingolla: a kid who couldn't have been older than eighteen. A new kid with a new haircut, new boots, new fatigues. Even his face looked new, freshly broken from the mold. Shiny, pudgy cheeks; clear skin; bright, unused blue eyes. He was eager to talk. He asked Mingolla about his home, his family, and said, Oh, wow, it must be great living in New York, wow. But he appeared to have some other reason for initiating the conversation, something he was leading up to, and finally he spat it out.

'You know the Sammy that went animal back there?' he said. 'I seen him pitted last night. Little place in the jungle west of the base. Guy name Chaco owns it. Man, it was fuckin' incredible!'

Mingolla had only heard of the pits third- and fourth-hand, but what he had heard was bad, and it was hard to believe that this kid with his air of home-boy innocence could be an aficionado of something so vile. And, despite what he had just witnessed, it was even harder to believe that Baylor could have been a participant.

The kid didn't need prompting. 'It was pretty early on,' he said. 'There'd been a coupla bouts, nothin' special, and then this guy walks in lookin' real twitchy. I knew he was Sammy by the way he's starin' at the pit, y'know, like it's somethin' he's been wishin' for. And this guy with me, friend of mine, he gives me a poke and says, "Holy shit! That's the Black Knight, man! I seen him fight over in Reunión a while back. Put your money on him," he says. "The fucker's an ace!"'

Their last R & R had been in Reunión. Mingolla tried to frame a question but couldn't think of one whose answer would have any meaning.

'Well,' said the kid, 'I ain't been down long, but I'd even heard 'bout the Knight. So I went over and kinda hung out near him, thinkin' maybe I can get a line on how he's feelin', y'know, 'cause you don't wanna just bet the guy's rep. Pretty soon Chaco comes over and asks the Knight if he wants some action. The Knight says, "Yeah, but I wanna fight an animal. Somethin' fierce, man. I wanna fight somethin' fierce." Chaco says he's got some monkeys and shit, and the Knight says he hears Chaco's got a jaguar, Chaco he hems and haws, says, "Maybe so, maybe not, but it don't matter 'cause a jaguar's too strong for Sammy." And then the Knight tells Chaco who he is. Lemme tell ya, Chaco's whole fuckin attitude changed. He could see how the bettin' was gonna go for somethin' like the Black Knight versus a jaguar. And he says, "Yes sir, Mister Black Knight, sir! Anything you want!" And he makes the announcement. Man, the place goes nuts. People wavin' money, screamin' odds, drinkin' fast so's they can get ripped in time for the main event, and the Knight's just standin' there, smilin', like he's feedin' off the confusion. Then Chaco lets the jaguar in through the tunnel and into the pit. It ain't a full-grown jaguar, half-growed maybe, but that's all you figure even the Knight can handle.'

The kid paused for breath; his eyes seemed to have grown brighter. 'Anyway, the jaguar's sneakin' 'round and 'round, keepin' close to the pit wall, snarlin' and spittin', and the Knight's watchin' him from up above, checkin' his moves, y'know. And everybody starts chantin', "Sam-mee, Sam-mee, Sam-mee," and after the chant builds up loud the Knight pulls three ampules outta his pocket. I mean, shit, man! Three! I ain't never been 'round Sammy when he's done more'n two. Three gets you clear into the fuckin' sky! So when the Knight holds up these three ampules, the crowd's tuned to burn, howlin' like they's playin Sammy themselves. But the Knight, man, he keeps his cool. He is *so* cool! He just holds up the ampules and lets 'em take the shine, soakin' up the noise and energy, gettin' strong off the crowd's juice. Chaco waves everybody quiet and gives the speech, y'know, 'bout how in the heart of every man there's a warrior-soul waitin' to be loosed and shit. I tell ya, man, I always thought that speech was crap before, but the Knight's makin' me buy it a hunnerd percent. He is so goddamn cool! He takes off his shirt and shoes, and he ties this piece of black silk 'round his arm. Then he pops the ampules, one after another, real quick, and breathes it all in. I can see it hittin', catchin' fire in his eyes. Pumpin' him up. And soon as he's popped the last one, he jumps into the pit. He don't use the tunnel, man! He jumps! Twenty-five feet down to the sand, and lands in a crouch.'

Three other soldiers were leaning in, listening, and the kid was now addressing all of them, playing to his audience. He was so excited that he could barely keep his speech coherent, and Mingolla realized with disgust that he, too, was excited by the image of Baylor crouched on the sand. Baylor, who had cried after the assault. Baylor, who had been so afraid of snipers that he had once pissed in his pants rather than walk from his gun to the latrine.

Baylor, the Black Knight.

'The jaguar's screechin' and snarlin' and slashin' at the air,' the kid went on. 'Tryin' to put fear into the Knight. 'Cause the jaguar knows in his mind the Knight's big trouble. This ain't some jerk like Chaco, this is Sammy. The Knight moves to the center of the pit, still in a crouch.' Here the kid pitched his voice low and dramatic. 'Nothin' happens for a coupla minutes, 'cept it's tense. Nobody's hardly breathin'. The jaguar springs a coupla times, but the Knight dances off to the side and makes him miss, and there ain't no damage either way. Whenever the jaguar springs, the crowd sighs and squeals, not just 'cause they's scared of seein' the Knight tore up, but also 'cause they can see how fast he is. Silky fast, man! Unreal. He looks 'bout as fast as the jaguar. He keeps on dancin' away, and no matter how the jaguar twists and turns, no matter if he comes at him along the sand, he can't get his claws into the Knight. And then, man ... oh, it was so smooth! Then the jaguar springs again, and this time 'stead of dancin' away, the Knight drops onto his back, does this half-roll onto his shoulders, and when the jaguar passes over him, he kicks up with both feet. Kicks up hard! And smashes his heels into the jaguar's side. The jaguar slams into the pit wall and comes down screamin', snappin' at his ribs. They was busted, man. Pokin' out the skin like tent posts.'

The kid wiped his mouth with the back of his hand and flicked his eyes toward Mingolla and the other soldiers to see if they were into the story. 'We was shoutin', man,' he said. 'Poundin' the top of the pit wall. It was so loud, the guy I'm with is yellin' in my ear and I can't hear nothin'. Now maybe it's the noise, maybe it's his ribs, whatever ... the jaguar goes berserk. Makin' these scuttlin' lunges at the Knight, tryin' to get close 'fore he springs so the Knight can't pull that same trick. He's snarlin' like a goddamn chain saw! The Knight keeps leapin' and spinnin' away. But then he slips, man, grabs the air for balance, and the jaguar's on him, clawin' at his chest. For a second they're like waltzin' together. Then the Knight pries loose the paw that's hooked him, pushes the jaguar's head back, and smashes his fist into the jaguar's eye. The jaguar flops onto the sand, and the Knight scoots to the other side of the pit. He's checkin' the scratches on his chest, which is bleedin' wicked. Meantime, the jaguar gets to his feet, and he's fucked up worse than ever. His one eye's fulla blood, and his hindquarters is all loosey-goosey. Like if this was boxin', they'd call in the doctor. The jaguar figures he's had enough of this crap, and he starts tryin' to jump outta the pit. This one time he jumps right up to where I'm leanin' over the edge. Comes so close I can smell his breath, I can see myself reflected in his good eye. He's clawin' for a grip, wantin' to haul hisself up into the crowd. People are freakin', thinkin' he might be gonna make it. But 'fore he gets the chance, the Knight catches him by the tail and slings him against the wall. Just like you'd beat a goddamn rug, that's how he's dealin' with the jaguar. And the jaguar's a real mess, now. He's quiverin'. Blood's pourin' outta his mouth, his fangs is all red. The Knight starts makin' these little feints, wavin' his arms, growlin'. He's toyin' with the jaguar. People don't believe what they're seein', man. Sammy's kickin' a jaguar's ass so bad he's got room to toy with it. If the place was nuts before, now, it's a fuckin' zoo. Fights in the crowd, guys singin' the Marine Hymn. Some beaner squint's takin' off her clothes. The jaguar tries to scuttle up close to the Knight again, but he's too fucked up. He can't keep it together. And the Knight, he's still growlin' and feintin'. A guy behind me is booin', claimin' the Knight's defamin' the purity of the sport by playin' with the jaguar. But hell, man, I can see he's just timin' the jaguar, waitin' for the right moment, the right move.'

Staring off downriver, the kid wore a wistful expression: he might have been thinking about his girlfriend. 'We all knew it was comin',' he said. 'Everybody got real quiet. So quiet you could hear the Knight's feet scrapin' on the sand. You could feel it in the air, and you knew the jaguar was savin' up for one big effort. Then the Knight slips again, 'cept he's fakin'. I could see that, but the jaguar couldn't. When the Knight reels sideways, the jaguar springs. I thought the Knight was gonna drop down like he did the first time but he springs, too. Feet first. And he catches the jaguar under the jaw. You could hear bone splinterin', and the jaguar falls in a heap. He struggles to get up, but no way! He's whinin', and he craps all over the sand. The Knight walks up behind him, takes his head in both hands, and gives it a twist. Crack!'

As if identifying with the jaguar's fate, the kid closed his eyes and sighed. 'Everybody'd been quiet 'til they heard that crack, then all hell broke loose. People chantin', "Sam-mee, Sam-mee," and people shovin', tryin' to get close to the pit wall so they can watch the Knight take the heart. He reaches into the jaguar's mouth and snaps off one of the fangs and tosses it to somebody. Then

Chaco comes in through the tunnel and hands him the knife. Right when he's 'bout to cut, somebody knocks me over and by the time I'm back on my feet, he's already took the heart and tasted it. He's just standin' there with the jaguar's blood on his mouth and his own blood runnin' down his chest. He looks kinda confused, y'know. Like now the fight's over and he don't know what to do. But then he starts roarin'. He sounds the same as the jaguar did 'fore it got hurt. Crazy fierce. Ready to get it on with the whole goddamn world. Man, I lost it! I was right with that roar. Maybe I was roarin' with him, maybe everybody was. That's what it felt like, man. Like bein' in the middle of this roar that's comin' outta every throat in the universe.' The kid engaged Mingolla with a sober look. 'Lotsa people go 'round sayin' the pits are evil, and maybe they are. I don't know. How you s'posed to tell 'bout what's evil and what's not down here? They say you can go to the pits a thousand times and not see nothin' like the jaguar and the Black Knight. I don't know 'bout that, either. But I'm goin' back just in case I get lucky. 'Cause what I saw last night, if it was evil, man, it was so fuckin' evil it was beautiful, too.'

III

Debora was waiting at the pier, carrying a picnic basket and wearing a blue dress with a high neckline and a full skirt: a schoolgirl dress. Mingolla homed in on her. The way she had her hair, falling about her shoulders in thick dark curls, made him think of smoke turned solid, and her face seemed the map of a beautiful country with black lakes and dusky plains, a country in which he could hide. They walked along the river past the town and came to a spot where ceiba trees with massy crowns of slick green leaves and whitish bark and roots like alligator tails grew close to the shore, and there they ate and talked and listened to the water gulping against the clay bank, to the birds, to the faint noises from the airbase that at this distance sounded part of nature. Sunlight dazzled the water, and whenever wind riffled the surface, it seemed to be spreading the dazzles into a crawling crust of diamonds. Mingolla imagined that they had taken a secret path, rounded a corner on the world and reached some eternally peaceful land. The illusion of peace was so profound that he began to see hope in it. Perhaps, he thought, something was being offered here. Some new magic. Maybe there would be a sign. Signs were everywhere if you knew how to read them. He glanced around. Thick white trunks rising into greenery, dark leafy avenues leading off between them ... nothing there, but what about those weeds growing at the edge of the bank? They cast precise fleur-de-lis shadows on the clay, shadows that didn't have much in common with the ragged configurations of the weeds themselves. Possibly a sign, though not a clear one. He lifted his gaze to the reeds growing in the shallows. Yellow reeds with jointed stalks bent akimbo, some with clumps of insect eggs like seed pearls hanging from loose fibers, and others dappled by patches of algae. That's how they looked one moment. Then Mingolla's vision rippled, as if the whole of reality had shivered, and the reeds were transformed into rudimentary shapes: yellow sticks poking up from flat blue. On the far side of the river, the jungle was a simple smear of Crayola green; a speedboat passing was a red slash unzippering the blue. It seemed that the rippling had jostled all the elements of the landscape a fraction out of kilter, revealing every object as characterless as a building block. Mingolla gave his head a shake. Nothing changed. He rubbed his brow. No effect. Terrified, he squeezed his eyes shut, He felt like the only meaningful piece in a nonsensical puzzle, vulnerable by virtue of his uniqueness. His breath came rapidly, his left hand fluttered.

'David? Don't you want to hear it?' Debora sounded peeved.

'Hear what?' He kept his eyes closed.

'About my dream. Weren't you listening?'

He peeked at her. Everything was back to normal. She was sitting with her knees tucked under her, all her features in sharp focus. 'I'm sorry,' he said. 'I was thinking.'

'You looked frightened.'

'Frightened?' He put on a bewildered face, 'Naw, just had a thought, is all.'

'It couldn't have been pleasant.'

He shrugged off the comment and sat up smartly to prove his attentiveness. 'So tell me 'bout the dream.'

'All right,' she said doubtfully. The breeze drifted fine strands of hair across her face and she brushed them back. 'You were in a room the color of blood, with red chairs and a red table. Even the paintings on the wall were done in shades of red, and …' She broke off, peering at him. 'Do you want to hear this? You have that look again.'

'Sure,' he said. But he was afraid. How could she have known about the red room? She must have had a vision of it, and … Then he realized that she might not have been talking about the room itself. He'd told her about the assault, hadn't he? And if she had guerrilla contacts, she would know that the emergency lights were switched on during an assault. That had to be it! She was trying to frighten him into deserting again, psyching him the way Christians played upon the fears of sinners with images of fiery rivers and torture. It infuriated him. Who the hell was she to tell him what was right or wise? Whatever he did, it was going to be his decision.

'There were three doors in the room,' she went on. 'You wanted to leave the room, but you couldn't tell which of the doors was safe to use. You tried the first door, and it turned out to be a façade. The knob of the second door turned easily, but the door itself was stuck. Rather than forcing it, you went to the third door. The knob of this door was made of glass and cut your hand.

After that you just walked back and forth, unsure what to do.' She waited for a reaction, and when he gave none, she said, 'Do you understand?'

He kept silent, biting back anger.

'I'll interpret it for you,' she said.

'Don't bother.'

'The red room is war, and the false door is the way of your childish ...'

'Stop!' He grabbed her wrist, squeezing it hard.

She glared at him until he released her. 'Your childish magic,' she finished.

'What is it with you?' he asked. 'You have some kinda quota to fill? Five deserters a month, and you get a medal?'

She tucked her skirt down to cover her knees, fiddled with a loose thread. From the way she was acting, Mingolla wondered whether he had asked an intimate question and she was framing an answer that wouldn't be indelicate. Finally she said, 'Is that who you believe I am to you?'

'Isn't that right? Why else would you be handing me this bullshit?'

'What's the matter with you, David?' She leaned forward, cupping his face in her hands. 'Why ...'

He pushed her hands away. 'What's the matter with me? This' – his gesture included the sky, the river, the trees – 'that's what's the matter. You remind me of my parents. They ask the same sorta ignorant questions.' Suddenly he wanted to injure her with answers, to find an answer like acid to throw in her face and watch it eat away her tranquility. 'Know what I do for my parents?' he said. 'When they ask dumb-ass questions like "What's the matter?" I tell 'em a story. A war story. You wanna hear a war story? Something happened a few days back that'll do for an answer just fine.'

'You don't have to tell me anything,' she said, discouraged.

'No problem,' he said. 'Be my pleasure.'

The Ant Farm was a large sugarloaf hill overlooking dense jungle on the eastern border of Fire Zone Emerald; jutting out from its summit were rocket and gun emplacements that at a distance resembled a crown of thorns jammed down over a green scalp. For several hundred yards around, the land had been cleared of all vegetation. The big guns had been lowered to maximum declension and in a mad moment had obliterated huge swaths of jungle, snapping off regiments of massive tree trunks a couple of feet above the ground, leaving a moat of blackened stumps and scorched red dirt seamed with fissures. Tangles of razor wire had replaced the trees and bushes, forming surreal blue-steel hedges, and buried beneath the wire was a variety of mines and detection devices. These did little good, however, because the Cubans possessed technology that would neutralize most of them. On clear nights there was scant likelihood of trouble, but on misty nights trouble could be expected. Under cover of the mist, Cuban and guerrilla troops would come through the wire and attempt to infiltrate the tunnels that honeycombed the interior of the hill. Occasionally one of the mines would be triggered, and a ghostly fireball would bloom in the swirling whiteness, tiny black figures being flung outward from its center. Lately some of these casualties had been found to be wearing red berets and scorpion-shaped brass pins, and from this it was known that the Cubans had sent in the Alacrán Division, which had been instrumental in routing the American forces in Miskitia.

There were nine levels of tunnels inside the hill, most lined with little round rooms that served as living quarters (the only exception being the bottom level, which was given over to the computer center and offices); all the rooms and tunnels were coated with a bubbled white plastic that looked like hardened sea-foam and was proof against antipersonnel explosives. In Mingolla's room, where he and Baylor and Gilbey bunked, a scarlet paper lantern had been hung on the overhead light fixture, making it seem that they were inhabiting a blood cell: Baylor had insisted on the lantern, saying that the overhead was too bright and hurt his eyes. Three cots were arranged against the walls, as far apart as space allowed. The floor around Baylor's cot was littered with cigarette butts and used Kleenex; under his pillow he kept a tin box containing a stash of pills and marijuana. Whenever he lit a joint he would always offer Mingolla a hit, and Mingolla always refused, feeling that the experience of the firebase would not be enhanced by drugs. Taped to the wall above Gilbey's cot was a collage of beaver shots, and each day after duty, whether or not Mingolla and Baylor were in the room, he would lie beneath them and masturbate. His lack of shame caused Mingolla to be embarrassed by his own secretiveness in the act, and he was also embarrassed by the pimply-youth quality of the objects taped above his cot: a Yankee pennant; a photograph of his old girlfriend and another of his senior-year high school basketball team; several sketches he had made of the surrounding jungle. Gilbey teased him constantly about this display, calling him 'the boy next door,' which struck Mingolla as odd, because back home he had been considered something of an eccentric.

It was toward this room that Mingolla was heading when the assault began. Large cargo elevators capable of carrying sixty men ran up and down just inside the east and west slopes of the hill; but to provide quick access between adjoining levels, and also as a safeguard in case of power failures, an auxiliary tunnel corkscrewed down through the center of the hill like a huge coil of white intestine. It was slightly more than twice as wide as the electric carts that traveled it, carrying officers and VIPs on tours. Mingolla was in the habit of using the tunnel for his exercise. Each night he would put on sweat clothes and jog up and down the entire nine levels, doing this out of a conviction that exhaustion prevented bad dreams. That night, as he passed Level Four on his final leg up, he heard a rumbling: an explosion, and not far off. Alarms sounded, the big guns atop the hill began to thunder. From directly above came shouts and the stutter of automatic fire. The tunnel lights flickered, went dark, and the emergency lights winked on.

Mingolla flattened against the wall. The dim red lighting caused the bubbled surfaces of the tunnel to appear as smooth as a chamber in a gigantic nautilus, and this resemblance intensified his sense of helplessness, making him feel like a child trapped within an evil undersea palace, He couldn't think clearly, picturing the chaos around him. Muzzle flashes, armies of antmen seething through the tunnels, screams spraying blood, and the big guns bucking, every shell burst kindling miles of sky. He would have preferred to keep going up, to get out into the open where he might have a chance to hide in the jungle. But down was his only hope. Pushing away from the wall, he ran full-tilt, arms waving, skidding around corners, almost falling, past Level Four, Level Five. Then, halfway between Levels Five and Six, he nearly tripped over a dead man: an American lying curled up around a belly wound, a slick of blood spreading beneath him and a machete by his hand. As Mingolla stooped for the machete, he thought nothing about the man, only about how weird it was for an American to be defending himself against Cubans with such a weapon. There was no use, he decided, in going any farther. Whoever had killed the man would be somewhere below, and the safest course would be to hide out in one of the rooms on Level Five. Holding the machete before him, he moved cautiously back up the tunnel.

Levels Five, Six, and Seven were officer country, and though the tunnels were the same as the ones above – gently curving tubes eight feet high and ten feet wide – the rooms were larger and contained only two cots. The rooms Mingolla peered into were empty, and this, despite the sounds of battle, gave him a secure feeling. But as he passed beyond the tunnel curve, he heard shouts in Spanish from his rear. He peeked back around the curve. A skinny black soldier wearing a red beret and gray fatigues was inching toward the first doorway; then, rifle at the ready, he ducked inside. Two other Cubans – slim bearded men, their skins sallow-looking in the bloody light – were standing by the arched entranceway to the auxiliary tunnel; when they saw the black soldier emerge from the room, they walked off in the opposite direction, probably to check the rooms at the far end of the level.

Mingolla began to operate in a kind of luminous panic. He realized that he would have to kill the black soldier. Kill him without any fuss, take his rifle, and hope that he could catch the other two off-guard when they came back for him. He slipped into the nearest room and stationed himself against the wall to the right of the door. The Cuban, he had noticed, had turned left on entering the room; he would have been vulnerable to someone positioned like Mingolla. Vulnerable for a split second. Less than a count of one. The pulse in Mingolla's temple throbbed, and he gripped the machete tightly in his left hand. He rehearsed mentally what he would have to do. Stab; clamp a hand over the Cuban's mouth; bring his knee up to jar loose the rifle. And he would have to perform these actions simultaneously, execute them perfectly.

Perfect execution.

He almost laughed out loud, remembering his paunchy old basketball coach saying, 'Perfect execution, boys. That's what beats a zone. Forget the fancy crap. Just set your screens, run your patterns, and get your shots down.'

Hoops ain't nothin' but life in short pants, huh, Coach?

Mingolla drew a deep breath and let it sigh out to rough his nostrils. He couldn't believe he was going to die. He had spent the past nine months worrying about death, but now when circumstances had arisen that made death likely, he had trouble taking that likelihood seriously. It didn't seem reasonable that a skinny black guy should be his nemesis. His death should involve massive detonations of light, special Mingolla-killing rays, astronomical portents. Not some scrawny little fuck with a rifle. He drew another breath and for the first time registered the contents of the room. Two cots; clothes strewn everywhere; taped-up Polaroids and pornography. Officer country or not, it was your basic Ant Farm decor; under the red light it looked squalid, long-abandoned. He was amazed by how calm he felt. Oh, he was afraid all right! But fear was tucked into the dark folds of his personality like a murderer's knife hidden inside an old coat on a closet shelf. Glowing in secret, waiting its chance to shine. Sooner or later it would skewer him, but for now it was an ally, acting to sharpen his senses. He could see every bubbled pucker on the white walls, could hear the scrape of the Cuban's boots as he darted into the room next door, could feel how the Cuban swung the rifle left to right, paused, turned …

He could!

He could feel the Cuban, feel his heat, his heated shape, the exact position of his body. It was as if a thermal imager had been switched on inside his head, one that worked through walls.

The Cuban eased toward Mingolla's door, his progress tangible, like a burning match moving behind a sheet of paper. Mingolla's calm was shattered. The man's heat, his fleshy temperature, was what disturbed him. He had imagined himself killing with a cinematic swiftness and lack of mess; now he thought of hogs being butchered and pile drivers smashing the skulls of cows. And could he trust this freakish form of perception? What if he couldn't? What if he stabbed too late? Too soon? Then the hot, alive thing was almost at the door, and having no choice, Mingolla timed his attack to its movements, stabbing just as the Cuban entered.

He executed perfectly.

The blade slid home beneath the Cuban's ribs, and Mingolla clamped a hand over his mouth, muffling his outcry. His knee nailed the rifle stock, sending it clattering to the floor. The Cuban thrashed wildly. He stank of rotten jungle air and cigarettes. His eyes rolled back, trying to see Mingolla. Crazy animal eyes, with liverish whites and expanded pupils. Sweat beads glittered redly on his brow. Mingolla twisted the machete, and the Cuban's eyelids flattered down. But a second later they snapped open, and he lunged. They went staggering deeper into the room and teetered beside one of the cots. Mingolla wrangled the Cuban sideways and rammed him against the wall, pinning him there. Writhing, the Cuban nearly broke free. He seemed to be getting stronger, his squeals leaking out from Mingolla's hand. He reached behind him, clawing at Mingolla's face; he grabbed a clump of hair, yanked it. Desperate, Mingolla sawed with the machete. That turned the Cuban's squeals higher, louder. He squirmed and clawed at the wall. Mingolla's clamped hand was slick with the Cuban's saliva, his nostrils full of the man's rank scent. He felt queasy, weak, and he wasn't sure how much longer he could hang on. The son of a bitch was never going to die, he was deriving strength from the steel in his guts, he was changing into some deathless force. But just then the Cuban stiffened. Then he relaxed, and Mingolla caught a whiff of feces.

He let the Cuban slump to the floor, but before he could turn loose of the machete, a shudder passed through the body, flowed up the hilt, and vibrated his left hand. It continued to shudder inside his hand, feeling dirty, sexy, like a postcoital tremor. Something, some animal essence, some oily scrap of bad life, was slithering around in there, squirting toward his wrist. He stared at the hand, horrified. It was gloved in the Cuban's blood, trembling. He smashed it against his hip, and that seemed to stun whatever was inside it. But within seconds it had revived and was wriggling in and out of his fingers with the mad celerity of a tadpole.

'*Teo!*' someone called. '*Vamos!*'

Electrified by the shout, Mingolla hustled to the door. His foot nudged the Cuban's rifle. He picked it up, and the shaking of his hand lessened – he had the idea it had been soothed by a familiar texture and weight.

'*Teo! Dónde estás?*'

Mingolla had no good choices, but he realized it would be far more dangerous to hang back than to take the initiative. He grunted '*Aqui!*' walked out into the tunnel, making lots of noise with his heels.

'*Date prisa, hombre!*'

Mingolla opened fire as he rounded the curve. The two Cubans were standing by the entrance to the auxiliary tunnel. Their rifles chattered briefly, sending a harmless spray of bullets off the walls; they whirled, flung out their arms, and fell. Mingolla was too shocked by how easy it had been to feel relief. He kept watching, expecting them to do something. Moan, or twitch.

After the echoes of the shots had died, though he could hear the big guns jolting and the crackle of firefights, a heavy silence seemed to fill in through the tunnel, as if his bullets had pierced something that had dammed silence up. The silence made him aware of his isolation. No telling where the battle lines were drawn ... if, indeed, they existed. It was conceivable that small units had infiltrated every level, that the battle for the Ant Farm was in microcosm the battle for Guatemala: a conflict having no patterns, no real borders, no orderly confrontations, but which, like a plague, could pop up anywhere at any time and kill. That being the case, his best bet would be to head for the computer center, where friendly forces were sure to be concentrated.

He walked to the entrance and stared at the two dead Cubans. They had fallen, blocking his way, and he was hesitant about stepping over them, half-believing they were playing possum, that they would reach up and grab him. The awkward attitudes of their limbs made him think they were holding a difficult pose, waiting for him to try. Their blood looked purple in the red glow of the emergencies, thicker and shinier than ordinary blood. He noted their moles and scars and sores, the crude stitching of their fatigues, gold fillings glinting from their open mouths. It was funny, he could have met these guys while they were alive and they might have made only a vague impression; but seeing them dead, he had cataloged their physical worth in a single glance. Maybe, he thought, death revealed your essentials as life could not. He studied the dead men, wanting to read them. Couple of slim, wiry guys. Nice guys, into rum and the ladies and sports. He'd bet they were baseball players, infielders, a double-play combo. Maybe he should have called to them, Hey, I'm a Yankee fan. Be cool! Meet'cha after the war for a game of flies and grounders. Fuck this killing shit. Let's play some ball.

He laughed, and the high, cracking sound of his laughter startled him. Christ! Standing around here was just asking for it. As if to second that opinion, the thing inside his hand exploded into life, eeling and frisking about. Swallowing back his fear, Mingolla stepped over the two dead men, and this time, when nothing clutched at his trouser legs, he felt very, very relieved.

Below Level Six there was a good deal of mist in the auxiliary tunnel, and from this Mingolla understood that the Cubans had penetrated the hillside, probably with a borer mine. Chances were the hole they had made was somewhere close, and he decided that if he could find it, he would use it to get the hell out of the Farm and hide in the jungle. On Level Seven the mist was extremely thick; the emergency lights stained it pale red, giving it the look of surgical cotton packing a huge artery. Scorch marks from grenade bursts showed on the walls like primitive graphics, and quite a few bodies were visible beside the doorways. Most of them Americans, badly mutilated. Uneasy, Mingolla picked his way among them, and when a man spoke behind him, saying, 'Don't move,' he let out a hoarse cry and dropped his rifle and spun around, his heart pounding.

A giant of a man – he had to go six-seven, six-eight, with the arms and torso of a weight lifter – was standing in a doorway, training a forty-five at Mingolla's chest. He wore khakis with lieutenant's bars, and his babyish face, though cinched into a frown, gave an impression of gentleness and stolidity: he conjured for Mingolla the image of Ferdinand the Bull weighing a knotty problem. 'I told you not to move,' he said peevishly.

'It's okay,' said Mingolla. 'I'm on your side.'

The lieutenant ran a hand through his thick shock of brown hair; he seemed to be blinking more than was normal. 'I'd better check,' he said. 'Let's go down to the storeroom.'

'What's to check?' said Mingolla, his paranoia increasing.

'Please!' said the lieutenant, a genuine wealth of entreaty in his voice. 'There's been too much violence already.'

The storeroom was a long, narrow L-shaped room at the end of the level; it was ranged by packing crates, and through the gauzy mist the emergency lights looked like a string of dying red suns. The lieutenant marched Mingolla to the corner of the L, and turning it, Mingolla saw that the rear wall of the room was missing. A tunnel had been blown into the hillside, opening onto blackness. Forked roots with balls of dirt attached hung from its roof, giving it the witchy appearance of a tunnel into some world of dark magic; rubble and clods of earth were piled at its lip. Mingolla could smell the jungle, and he realized that the big guns had stopped firing. Which meant that whoever had won the battle of the summit would soon be sending down mop-up squads. 'We can't stay here,' he told the lieutenant. 'The Cubans'll he back.'

'We're perfectly safe,' said the lieutenant. 'Take my word.' He motioned with the gun, indicating that Mingolla should sit on the floor.

Mingolla did as ordered and was frozen by the sight of a corpse, a Cuban corpse, lying between two packing crates opposite him, its head propped against the wall. 'Jesus!' he said, coming back up to his knees.

'He won't bite,' said the lieutenant. With the lack of self-consciousness of someone squeezing into a subway seat, he settled beside the corpse; the two of them neatly filled the space between the crates, touching elbow to shoulder.

'Hey,' said Mingolla, feeling giddy and scattered. 'I'm not sitting here with this fucking dead guy, man!'

The lieutenant flourished his gun. 'You'll get used to him.'

Mingolla eased back to a sitting position, unable to look away from the corpse. Actually, compared to the bodies he had just been stepping over, it was quite presentable. The only signs of damage were blood on its mouth and bushy black beard, and a mire of blood and shredded cloth at the center of its chest. Its beret had slid down at a rakish angle to cover one eyebrow; the brass scorpion pin was scarred and tarnished. Its eyes were open, reflecting glowing red chips of the emergency lights, and this gave it a baleful semblance of life. But the reflections made it appear less real, easier to bear.

'Listen to me,' said the lieutenant.

Mingolla rubbed at the blood on his shaking hand, hoping that cleaning it would have some good effect.

'Are you listening?' the lieutenant asked.

Mingolla had a peculiar perception of the lieutenant and the corpse as dummy and ventriloquist. Despite its glowing eyes, the corpse had too much reality for any trick of the light to gloss over for long. Precise crescents showed on its fingernails, and because its head was tipped to one side, blood had settled into that side, darkening its cheek and temple, leaving the rest of the face pallid. It was the lieutenant, with his neat khakis and polished shoes and nice haircut, who now looked less than real.

'Listen!' said the lieutenant vehemently. 'I want you to understand that I have to do what's right for me!' The biceps of his gun arm bunched to the size of a cannonball.

'I understand,' said Mingolla, thoroughly unnerved.

'Do you? Do you really?' The lieutenant seemed aggravated by Mingolla's claim to understanding. 'I doubt it. I doubt you could possibly understand.'

'Maybe I can't,' said Mingolla, 'Whatever you say, man. I'm just trying to get along, y'know.'

The lieutenant sat silent, blinking. Then he smiled. 'My name's Jay,' he said. 'And you are …?'

'David.' Mingolla tried to bring his concentration to bear on the gun, wondering if he could kick it away, but the sliver of life in his hand distracted him.

'Where are your quarters, David?'

'Level Three.'

'I live here,' said Jay. 'But I'm going to move. I couldn't bear to stay in a place where . .' He broke off and leaned forward, adopting a conspiratorial stance. 'Did you know it takes a long time for someone to die, even after their heart has stopped?'

'No, I didn't.' The thing in Mingolla's hand squirmed toward his wrist, and he squeezed the wrist, trying to block it.

'It's true,' said Jay with vast assurance. 'None of these people' – he gave the corpse a gentle nudge with his elbow, a gesture that conveyed to Mingolla a creepy sort of familiarity – 'have finished dying. Life doesn't just switch off. It fades. And these people are still alive, though it's only a half-life.' He grinned. 'The half-life of life, you might say.'

Mingolla kept the pressure on his wrist and smiled, as if in appreciation of the play on words. Pale red tendrils of mist curled between them.

'Of course you aren't attuned,' said Jay. 'So you wouldn't understand. But I'd be lost without Eligio.'

'Who's Eligio?'

Jay nodded toward the corpse. 'We're attuned, Eligio and I. That's how I know we're safe. Eligio's perceptions aren't limited to the here and now any longer. He's with his men at this very moment, and he tells me they're all dead or dying.'

'Uh-huh,' said Mingolla, tensing. He had managed to squeeze the thing in his hand back into his fingers, and he thought he might be able to reach the gun. But Jay disrupted his plan by shifting the gun to his other hand. His eyes seemed to be growing more reflective, acquiring a ruby glaze, and Mingolla realized this was because he had opened them wide and angled his stare toward the emergency lights.

'It makes you wonder,' said Jay. 'It really does.'

'What?' said Mingolla, easing sideways, shortening the range for a kick.

'Half-lives,' said Jay. 'If the mind has a half-life, maybe our separate emotions do, too. The half-life of love, of hate. Maybe they still exist somewhere.' He drew up his knees, shielding the gun. 'Anyway, I can't stay here. I think I'll go back to Oakland.' His tone became whispery. 'Where are you from, David?'

'New York.'

'Not my cup of tea,' said Jay. 'But I love the Bay Area. I own an antique shop there. It's beautiful in the mornings. Peaceful. The sun comes through the window, creeping across the floor, y'know, like a tide, inching up over the furniture. It's as if the original varnishes are being reborn, the whole shop shining with ancient lights.'

'Sounds nice,' said Mingolla, taken aback by Jay's lyricism.

'You seem like a good person.' Jay straightened up a bit. 'But I'm sorry. Eligio tells me your mind's too cloudy for him to read. He says I can't risk keeping you alive. I'm going to have to shoot.'

Mingolla set himself to kick, but then listlessness washed over him. What the hell did it matter? Even if he knocked the gun away, Jay could probably break him in half. 'Why?' he said. 'Why do you have to?'

'You might inform on me.' Jay's soft features sagged into a sorrowful expression. 'Tell them I was hiding.'

'Nobody gives a shit you were hiding,' said Mingolla, 'That's what I was doing. I bet there's fifty other guys doing the same damn thing.'

'I don't know,' Jay's brow furrowed. 'I'll ask again. Maybe your mind's less cloudy now.' He turned his gaze to the dead man.

Mingolla noticed that the Cuban's irises were angled upward and to the left – exactly the same angle to which Jay's eyes had drifted earlier – and reflected an identical ruby glaze.

'Sorry,' said Jay, leveling the gun. 'I have to.' He licked his lips. 'Would you please turn your head? I'd rather you weren't looking at me when it happens. That's how Eligio and I became attuned.'

Looking into the aperture of the gun's muzzle was like peering over a cliff, feeling the chill allure of falling. It was more out of contrariness than a will to survive that Mingolla popped his eyes at Jay and said, 'Go ahead.'

Jay blinked, but he held the gun steady. 'Your hand's shaking,' he said after a pause.

'No shit,' said Mingolla.

'How come it's shaking?'

'Because I killed someone with it,' said Mingolla, 'Because I'm as fucking crazy as you are.'

Jay mulled this over. 'I was supposed to be assigned to a gay unit,' he said finally. 'But all the slots were filled, and when I had to be assigned here they gave me a drug. Now I ... I . .' He blinked rapidly, his lips parted, and Mingolla found that he was straining toward Jay, wanting to apply Body English, to do something to push him over this agonizing hump. 'I can't ... be with men anymore,' Jay finished, and once again blinked rapidly; then his words came easier. 'Did they give you a drug too? I mean I'm not trying to imply you're gay. It's just they have drugs for everything these days, and I thought that might be the problem.'

Mingolla was suddenly, inutterably sad. He felt that his emotions had been twisted into a thin black wire, that the wire was frayed and spraying black sparks of sadness. That was all that energized him, all his life. Those little black sparks.

'I always fought before,' said Jay. 'And I was fighting this time. But when I shot Eligio ... I just couldn't keep going.'

'I really don't give a shit,' said Mingolla, 'I really don't.'

'Maybe I can trust you.' Jay sighed. 'I just wish you were attuned. Eligio's a good soul. You'd appreciate him.'

Jay kept on talking, enumerating Eligio's virtues, and Mingolla tuned him out, not wanting to hear about the Cuban's love for his family, his posthumous concerns for them. Staring at his bloody hand, he had a magical overview of the situation. Sitting in the root cellar of this evil mountain, bathed in an eerie red glow, a scrap of a dead man's life trapped in his flesh, listening to a deranged giant who took his orders from a corpse, waiting for scorpion soldiers to pour through a tunnel that appeared to lead into a dimension of mist and blackness. It was insane to look at it that way. But there it was. You couldn't reason it away; it had a brutal glamour that surpassed reason, that made reason unnecessary.

'... and once you're attuned,' Jay was saying, 'you can't ever be separated. Not even by death. So Eligio's always going to be alive inside me. Of course I can't let them find out. I mean' – he chuckled, a sound like dice rattling in a cup – 'talk about giving aid and comfort to the enemy!'

Mingolla lowered his head, closed his eyes. Maybe Jay would shoot. But he doubted that. Jay only wanted company in his madness.

'You swear you won't tell them?' Jay asked.

'Yeah,' said Mingolla. 'I swear.'

'All right,' said Jay. 'But remember, my future's in your hands. You have a responsibility to me.'

'Don't worry.'

Gunfire crackled in the distance.

'I'm glad we could talk,' said Jay. 'I feel much better.'

Mingolla said that he felt better, too.

They sat without speaking. It wasn't the most secure way to pass the night, but Mingolla no longer put any store in the concept of security. He was too weary to be afraid. Jay seemed entranced, staring at a point above Mingolla's head, but Mingolla made no move for the gun. He was content to sit and wait and let fate take its course. His thoughts uncoiled with vegetable sluggishness.

They must have been sitting a couple of hours when Mingolla heard the whisper of helicopters and noticed that the mist had thinned, that the darkness at the end of the tunnel had gone gray. 'Hey,' he said to Jay. 'I think we're okay now.' Jay offered no reply, and Mingolla saw that his eyes were angled upward and to the left just like the Cuban's eyes, glazed over with ruby reflection. Tentatively, he reached out and touched the gun. Jay's hand flopped to the floor, but his fingers remained clenched around the butt. Mingolla recoiled, disbelieving. It couldn't be! Again he reached out, feeling for a pulse. Jay's wrist was cool, still, and his lips had a bluish cast. Mingolla had a flutter of hysteria, thinking that Jay had gotten it wrong about being attuned: instead of Eligio's becoming part of his life, he had become part of Eligio's death. There was a tightness in Mingolla's chest, and he thought he was going to cry. He would have welcomed tears, and when they failed to materialize he grew both annoyed at himself and defensive. Why should he cry? The guy had meant nothing to him ... though the fact that he could be so devoid of compassion was reason enough for tears. Still, if you were going to cry over something as commonplace as a single guy dying, you'd be crying every minute of the day, and what was the future in that? He glanced at Jay. At the Cuban. Despite the smoothness of Jay's skin, the Cuban's bushy beard, Mingolla could have sworn they were starting to resemble each other the way old married couples did. And, yep, all four eyes were fixed on exactly the same point of forever. It was either a hell of a coincidence or else Jay's craziness had been of such magnitude that he had willed himself to die in this fashion just to lend credence to his theory of half-lives. And maybe he was still alive. Half alive. Maybe he and Mingolla were now attuned, and if that were true, maybe … Alarmed by the prospect of joining Jay and the Cuban in their deathwatch, Mingolla scrambled to his feet and ran into the tunnel. He might have kept running, but on coming out into the dawn light he was brought up short by the view from the tunnel entrance.

At his back, the green dome of the hill swelled high, its sides brocaded with shrubs and vines; an infinity of pattern as eye-catching as the intricately carved facade of a Hindu temple; atop it, one of the gun emplacements had taken a hit: splinters of charred metal curved up like peels of black rind. Before him lay the moat of red dirt with its hedgerows of razor wire, and beyond that loomed the blackish-green snarl of the jungle. Caught on the wire were hundreds of baggy shapes wearing bloodstained fatigues; frays of smoke twisted up from the fresh craters beside them. Overhead, half-hidden by the lifting gray mist, three Sikorskys were hovering. Their pilots were invisible behind layers of mist and reflection, and the choppers themselves looked like enormous carrion flies with bulging eyes and whirling wings. Like devils. Like gods. They seemed to be whispering to one another in anticipation of the feast they were soon to share.

The scene was horrid, yet it had the purity of a stanza from a ballad come to life, a ballad composed about tragic events in some border hell. You could never paint it, or if you could the canvas would have to be as large as the scene itself, and you would have to incorporate the slow boil of the mist, the whirling of the chopper blades, the drifting smoke. No detail could be omitted. It was the perfect illustration of the war, of its secret magical splendor, and Mingolla, too, was an element of the design, the figure of the artist painted in for a joke or to lend scale and perspective to its vastness, its importance. He knew that he should report to his station, but he couldn't turn away from the glimpse into the heart of the war. He sat down an the hillside, cradling his sick hand in his lap, and watched as – with the ponderous aplomb of idols floating to earth, fighting the cross-draft, the wind of their descent whipping up furies of red dust – the Sikorskys made skillful landings among the dead.

IV

Halfway through the telling of his story, Mingolla had realized that he was not really trying to offend or shock Debora, but rather was unburdening himself; and he further realized that by telling it he had to an extent cut loose from the past, weakened its hold on him. For the first time he felt able to give serious consideration to the idea of desertion. He did not rush to it, embrace it, but he did acknowledge its logic and understand the terrible illogic of returning to more assaults, more death, without any magic to protect him. He made a pact with himself: he would pretend to go along as if desertion were his intent and see what signs were offered.

When he had finished, Debora asked whether or not he was over his anger. He was pleased that she hadn't tried to offer sympathy. 'I'm sorry,' he said. 'I wasn't really angry at you ... at least that was only part of it.'

'It's all right.' She pushed back the dark mass of her hair so that it fell to one side and looked down at the grass beside her knees. With her head inclined, eyes half-lidded, the graceful line of her neck and chin like a character in some exotic script, she seemed a good sign herself. 'I don't know what to talk to you about,' she said. 'The things I feel I have to tell you make you mad, and I can't muster any small talk.'

'I don't want to be pushed,' he said. 'But believe me, I'm thinking about what you've told me.'

'I won't push. But I still don't know what to talk about,' She plucked a grass-blade, chewed on the tip. He watched her lips purse, wondered how she'd taste. Mouth sweet in the way of a jar that had once held spices. And down below, she'd taste sweet there, too: honey gone a little sour in the comb. She tossed the grass-blade aside. 'I know,' she said brightly. 'Would you like to see where I live?'

'I'd just as soon not go back to 'Frisco yet.' Where you live, he thought; I want to touch where you live.

'It's not in town,' she said. 'It's a village downriver.'

'Sounds good.' He came to his feet, took her arm, and helped her up. For an instant they were close together, her breasts grazing his shirt. Her heat coursed around him, and he thought if anyone were to see them, they would see two figures wavering as in a mirage. He had an urge to tell her he loved her. Though most of what he felt was for the salvation she might provide, part of his feelings seemed real and that puzzled him, because all she had been to him was a few hours out of the war, dinner in a cheap restaurant and a walk along the river. There was no basis for consequential emotion. Before he could say anything, do anything, she turned and picked up her basket.

'It's not far,' she said, walking away. Her blue skirt swayed like a rung bell.

They followed a track of brown clay overgrown by ferns, overspread by saplings with pale translucent leaves, and soon came to a grouping of thatched huts at the mouth of a stream that flowed into the river. Naked children were wading in the stream, laughing and splashing each other. Their skins were the color of amber and their eyes were as wet-looking and purplish-dark as plums. Palms and acacias loomed above the huts, which were constructed of sapling trunks lashed together by nylon cord; their thatch had been trimmed to resemble bowl-cut hair. Flies crawled over strips of meat hung on a clothesline stretched between two of the huts. Fish beads and chicken droppings littered the ocher ground. But Mingolla scarcely noticed these signs of poverty, seeing instead a sign of the peace that might await him in Panama. And another sign was soon forthcoming. Debora bought a bottle of rum at a tiny store, then led him to the hut nearest the mouth of the stream and introduced him to a lean white-haired old man who was sitting on a bench outside it. Tío Moisés. After three drinks Tío Moisés began to tell stories.

The first story concerned the personal pilot of an ex-president of Panama. The president had made billions from smuggling cocaine into the States with the help of the CIA, whom he had assisted on numerous occasions, and was himself an addict in the last stages of mental deterioration. It had become his sole pleasure to be flown from city to city in his country, to sit on the landing strips, gaze out the window, and do cocaine. At any hour of night or day, he was likely to call the pilot and order him to prepare a flight plan to Colón or Bocas del Toro or Penonomé. As the president's condition worsened, the pilot realized that soon the CIA would see he was no longer useful and would kill him. And the most obvious manner of killing him would be by means of an airplane crash. The pilot did not want to die alongside him. He tried to resign, but the president would not permit it. He gave thought to mutilating himself, but being a good Catholic, he could not flout God's law. If he were to flee, his family would suffer. His life became a nightmare. Prior to each flight, he would spend hours searching the plane for evidence of sabotage, and upon each landing he would remain in the cockpit, shaking from nervous exhaustion. The president's condition grew even worse. He had to be carried aboard the plane and have the cocaine administered by an aide, while a second aide stood by with cotton swabs to attend his nosebleeds. Knowing his life could be measured in weeks, the pilot asked his priest for guidance. 'Pray,' the priest advised. The pilot had been praying all along, so this was no help. Next he went to the commandant of his military college, and the commandant told him he must do his duty. This, too, was something the pilot had been doing all along. Finally he went to the chief of the San Blas Indians, who were his mother's people. The chief told him he must accept his fate, which – while not something he had been doing all along – was hardly encouraging. Nonetheless, he saw it was the only available path and he did as the chief had counseled. Rather than spending hours in a preflight check, he would arrive minutes before takeoff and taxi away without even inspecting the fuel gauge. His recklessness came to be the talk of the capitol. Obeying the president's every whim, he flew in gales and in fogs, while drunk and drugged, and during those hours in the air, suspended between the laws of gravity and fate, he gained a new appreciation of life. Once back on the ground, he engaged in living with a fierce avidity, making passionate love to his wife, carousing with friends, and staying out until dawn. Then one day as he was preparing to leave for the airport, an American man came to his house and told him be had been replaced. 'If we let the president fly with so negligent a pilot, we'll be blamed for anything that happens,' said the American, The pilot did not have to ask whom he had meant by 'we.' Six weeks later the president's plane crashed in the Darien Mountains. The pilot was overjoyed. Panama had been ridded of a villain, and his own life had not been forfeited. But a week after the crash, after the new president – another smuggler with CIA connections – had been appointed, the commandant of the air force summoned the pilot, told him that the crash would never have occurred had he been on the job, and assigned him to fly the new president's plane.

All through the afternoon Mingolla listened and drank, and drunkenness fitted a lens to his eyes that let him see how these stories applied to him. They were all fables of irresolution, cautioning him to act, and they detailed the core problems of the Central American people who – as he was now – were trapped between the poles of magic and reason, their lives governed by the politics of the ultrareal, their spirits ruled by myths and legends, with the rectangular computerized bulk of North America above and the conch-shell-shaped continental mystery of South America below. He assumed that Debora had orchestrated the types of stories Tío Moisés told, but that did not detract from their potency as signs: they had the ring of truth, not of something tailored to his needs. Nor did it matter that his hand was shaking, his vision playing tricks. Those things would pass when he reached Panama.

Shadows blurred, insects droned like tambouras, and twilight washed down the sky, making the air look grainy, the chop on the river appear slower and heavier. Tío Moisés' granddaughter served plates of roast corn and fish, and Mingolla stuffed himself. Afterward, when the old man signaled his weariness, Mingolla and Debora strolled off along the stream. Between two of the huts, mounted on a pole, was a warped backboard with a netless hoop, and some young men were shooting baskets. Mingolla joined them. It was hard dribbling on the bumpy dirt, but he had never played better. The residue of drunkenness fueled his game, and his jump shots followed perfect arcs down through the hoop. Even at improbable angles, his shots fell true. He lost himself in flicking out his hands to make a steal, in feinting and leaping high to snag a rebound, becoming – as dusk faded – the most adroit of ten arm-waving, jitter-stepping shadows.

The game ended and the stars came out, looking like holes punched into fire through a billow of black silk overhanging the palms. Flickering chutes of lamplight illuminated the ground in front of the huts, and as Debora and Mingolla walked among them, he heard a radio tuned to the Armed Forces network giving a play-by-play of a baseball game. There was a crack of the bat, the crowd roared, the announcer cried, 'He got it all!' Mingolla imagined the ball vanishing into the darkness above the stadium, bouncing out into parking-lot America, lodging under a tire where some kid would find it and think it a miracle, or rolling across the street to rest under a used car, shimmering there, secretly white and fuming with home-run energies. The score was three-to-one, top of the second. Mingolla didn't know who was playing and didn't care. Home runs were happening for him, mystical jump shots curved along predestined tracks. He was at the center of incalculable forces.

One of the huts was unlit, with two wooden chairs out front, and as they approached, the sight of it soured Mingolla's mood. Something about it bothered him: its air of preparedness, of being a little stage-set. He was just paranoid, he thought. The signs had been good so far, hadn't they? When they reached the hut, Debora sat in the chair nearer the door and looked up at him. Starlight pointed her eyes with brilliance. Behind her, through the doorway, he made out the shadowy cocoon of a strung hammock, and beneath it, a sack from which part of a wire cage protruded. 'What about your game?' he asked.

'I thought it was more important to be with you,' she said.

That, too, bothered him. It was all starting to bother him, and he couldn't understand why. The thing in his hand wiggled. He balled the hand into a fist and sat next to Debora. 'What's going on between you and me?' he asked, nervous. 'Is anything gonna happen? I keep thinking it will, but …' He wiped sweat from his forehead and forgot what he had been driving at.

'I'm not sure what you mean,' she said.

A shadow moved across the yellow glare, spilling from the hut next door. Rippling, undulating, Mingolla squeezed his eyes shut.

'If you mean … romantically,' she said, 'I'm confused about that myself. Whether you return to your base or go to Panama, we don't seem to have much of a future. And we certainly don't have much of a past.'

It boosted his confidence in her, in the situation, that she didn't have an assured answer. But he felt shaky. Very shaky. He gave his head a twitch, fighting off more ripples. 'What's it like in Panama?'

'I've never been there. Probably a lot like Guatemala, except without the fighting.'

Maybe he should get up, walk around. Maybe that would help. Or maybe he should just sit and talk. Talking seemed to steady him. 'I bet,' he said, 'I bet it's beautiful, y'know. Panama. Green mountains, jungle waterfalls. I bet there's lots of birds. Macaws and parrots. Millions of 'em.'

'I suppose so.'

'And hummingbirds. This friend of mine was down there once on a hummingbird expedition, said there was a million kinds. I thought he was sort of a creep, y'know, for being into collecting hummingbirds.' He opened his eyes and had to close them again. 'I guess I thought hummingbird collecting wasn't very relevant to the big issues.'

'David?' Concern in her voice.

'I'm okay.' The smell of her perfume was more cloying than he remembered. 'You get there by boat, right? Must be a pretty big boat. I've never been on a real boat, just this rowboat my uncle had. He used to take me fishing off Coney Island, we'd tie up to a buoy and catch all these poison fish. You shoulda seen some of 'em. Like mutants. Rainbow-colored eyes, weird growths all over. Scared the hell outta me to think about eating fish.'

'I had an uncle who …'

'I used to think about all the ones that must be down there too deep for us to catch. Giant blowfish, genius sharks, whales with hands. I'd see 'em swallowing the boat, I'd …'

'Calm down, David.' She kneaded the back of his neck, sending a shiver down his spine.

'I'm okay, I'm okay.' He pushed her hand away; he did not need shivers along with everything else. 'Lemme hear some more 'bout Panama.'

'I told you, I've never been there.'

'Oh, yeah. Well, how 'bout Costa Rica? You been to Costa Rica.' Sweat was popping out all over his body. Maybe he should go for a swim. He'd heard there were manatees in the Río Dulce. 'Ever seen a manatee?' he asked.

'David!'

She must have leaned close, because he could feel her heat spreading all through him, and he thought maybe that would help, smothering in her heat, heavy motion, get rid of this shakiness. He'd take her into that hammock and see just how hot she got. *How* hot *she got, how* hot *she got*. The words did a train rhythm in his head. Afraid to open his eyes, he reached out blindly and pulled her to him. Bumped faces, searched for her mouth. Kissed her. She kissed back. His hand slipped up to cup a breast. Jesus, she felt good! She felt like salvation, like Panama, like what you fall into when you sleep.

But then it changed, changed slowly, so slowly that he didn't notice until it was almost complete, and her tongue was squirming in his mouth, as thick and stupid as a snail's foot, and her breast, oh shit, her breast was jiggling, trembling with the same wormy juices that were in his left hand. He pushed her off, opened his eyes. Saw crude-stitch eyelashes sewn to her cheeks. Lips parted, mouth full of bones. Blank face of meat. He got to his feet, pawing the air, wanting to rip down the film of ugliness that had settled over him.

'David?' She warped his name, gulping the syllables as if she were trying to swallow and talk at once. Frog voice, devil voice.

He spun around, caught an eyeful of black sky and spiky trees and a pitted bone-knob moon trapped in a weave of branches. Dark warty shapes of the huts, doors into yellow flame with crooked shadow men inside. He blinked, shook his head. It wasn't going away, it was real. What was this place? Not a village in Guatemala, naw, un-unh. He heard a strangled wild-man grunt come from his throat, and he backed away, backed away from everything. She walked after him, croaking his name. Wig of black straw, dabs of shining jelly for eyes. Some of the shadow men were herky-jerking out of their doors, gathering behind her, talking about him in devil language. Faceless nothings from the dimension of sickness, demons in *peón* drag. He backed another few steps.

'I can see you,' he said. 'I know what you are.'

'It's all right, David,' she said, and smiled.

Sure! She thought he was going to buy the smile, but he wasn't fooled. He saw how it broke over her face the way something rotten melts through the bottom of a wet grocery sack after it's been in the garbage for a week. Gloating smile of the Queen Devil Bitch. She had done this to him, had teamed up with the bad life in his hand and done witchy things to his head. Made him see down to the layer of shit-magic she lived in.

'I see you,' he said.

He tripped, went backward flailing, stumbling, and came out of it running toward the town.

Ferns whipped his legs, branches cut at his face. Webs of shadow and moonlight fettered the trail, and the shrilling insects had the sound of a metal edge being honed. Up ahead, he spotted a big moonstruck tree standing by itself on a rise overlooking the water, a grandfather tree, a white-magic tree. It called to him. He stopped beside it, sucking air. The moonlight cooled him off, drenched him with silver, and he understood the purpose of the tree. Fountain of whiteness in the dark wood, shining for him alone. He made a fist of his left hand. The thing inside the hand eeled frantically as if it knew what was coming, he studied the deeply grooved, mystic patterns of the bark and found the point of confluence. He steeled himself. Then he drove his fist into the trunk. Brilliant pain lanced up his arm, and he cried out. But he hit the tree again, hit it a third time. He held the hand tight against his body, muffling the pain. It was already swelling, becoming a knuckleless cartoon hand; but nothing moved inside it. The riverbank, with its rustlings and shadows, no longer menaced him; it had been transformed into a place of ordinary lights, ordinary darks, and even the whiteness of the tree looked unmagically bright.

'David!' Debora's voice, and not far off.

Part of him wanted to wait, to see whether or not she had changed for the innocent, for the ordinary. But he couldn't trust her, couldn't trust himself, and he set out running once again.

Mingolla caught the ferry to the west bank, thinking that he would find Gilbey, that a dose of Gilbey's belligerence would ground him in reality. He sat in the bow next to a group of five other soldiers, one of whom was puking over the side, and to avoid a conversation he turned away and looked down into the black water slipping past. Moonlight edged the wavelets with silver, and among those gleams it seemed he could see reflected the broken curve of his life: a kid living for Christmas, drawing pictures, receiving praise, growing up mindless to high school, sex, and drugs; growing beyond that, beginning to draw pictures again, and then, right where you might expect the curve to assume a more meaningful shape, it was sheared off, left hanging, its process demystified and explicable. He realized how foolish the idea of the ritual had been. Like a dying man clutching a vial of holy water, he had clutched at magic when the logic of existence had proved untenable. Now the frail linkages of that magic had been dissolved, and nothing supported him: he was falling through the dark zones of the war, waiting to be snatched by one of its monsters. He lifted his head and gazed at the west bank. The shore toward which he was heading was as black as a bat's wing and inscribed with arcana of violent light. Rooftops and palms were cast in silhouette against a rainbow haze of neon; gassy arcs of blood-red and lime-green and indigo were visible between them: fragments of glowing beasts. The wind bore screams and wild music. The soldiers beside him laughed and cursed, and the one guy kept on puking. Mingolla rested his forehead on the wooden rail, just to feel something solid.

At the Club Demonio, Gilbey's big-breasted whore was lounging by the bar, staring into her drink. Mingolla pushed through the dancers, through heat and noise and veils of lavender smoke; when he walked up to the whore, she put on a professional smile and made a grab for his crotch. He fended her off. 'Where's Gilbey?' he shouted. She gave him a befuddled look; then the light dawned. 'Meen-golla?' she said. He nodded. She fumbled in her purse and pulled out a folded paper. 'Ees frawm Geel-bee,' she said. 'Forr me, five dol-larrs.'

He handed her the money and took the paper. It proved to be a Christian pamphlet with a pen-and-ink sketch of a rail-thin, aggrieved-looking Jesus on the front, and beneath the sketch, a tract whose first line read, 'The last days are in season.' He turned it over and found a handwritten note on the back. The note was pure Gilbey. No explanation, no sentiment. Just the basics.

I'm gone to Panama. You want to make that trip, check out a guy named Ray Barros in Livingston. He'll fix you up. Maybe I'll see you.

G.

Mingolla had believed that his confusion had peaked, but the fact of Gilbey's desertion wouldn't fit inside his head, and when be tried to make it fit he was left more confused than ever. It wasn't that he couldn't understand what had happened. He understood it perfectly; he might have predicted it. Like a crafty rat who had seen his favorite hole blocked by a trap, Gilbey had simply chewed a new hole and vanished through it. The thing that confused Mingolla was his total lack of referents. He and Gilbey and Baylor had seemed to triangulate reality, to locate each other within a coherent map of duties and places and events; and now that they were both gone, Mingolla felt utterly bewildered. Outside the club, he let the crowds push him along and gazed up at the neon animals atop the bars. Giant blue rooster, green bull, golden turtle with fiery red eyes. An advertising man's hellish pantheon. Bleeds of color washed from the signs, staining the air to a garish paleness, giving everyone a mealy complexion. Amazing, Mingolla thought, that you could breathe such grainy discolored stuff, that it didn't start you choking. It was all amazing, all nonsensical. Everything he saw struck him as unique and unfathomable, even the most commonplace of sights. He found himself staring at people – at whores, at street kids, at an MP who was talking to another MP, patting the fender of his jeep as if it were his big olive-drab pet – and trying to figure out what they were really doing, what special significance their actions held for him, what clues they presented that might help him unravel the snarl of his own existence. At last, realizing that he needed peace and quiet, he set out toward the airbase, thinking he would find an empty bunk and sleep off his confusion; but when he came to the cutoff that led to the unfinished bridge, he turned down it, deciding that he wasn't ready to deal with gate sentries and duty officers. Dense thickets buzzing with insects narrowed the cutoff to a path, and at its end stood a line of sawhorses. He climbed over them and soon was mounting a sharply inclined curve that appeared to lead to a point not far below the lumpish silver moon.

Despite a litter of rubble and cardboard sheeting, the concrete looked pure under the moon, blazing bright, like a fragment of snowy light not quite hardened to the material; and as he ascended he thought he could feel the bridge trembling to his footsteps with the sensitivity of a white nerve. He seemed to be walking into darkness and stars, a solitude the size of creation. It felt good and damn lonely, maybe a little too much so, with the wind lapping pieces of cardboard and the sounds of the insects left behind. After a few minutes he glimpsed the ragged terminus ahead. When he reached it, he sat down carefully, letting his legs dangle. Wind keened through the exposed girders, tugging at his ankles; his hand throbbed and was fever-hot. Below, multi-colored brilliance clung to the black margin of the east bank like a colony of bioluminescent algae. He wondered how high he was. Not high enough, he thought. Faint music was fraying on the wind – the inexhaustible delirium of San Francisco de Juticlan – and he imagined that the flickering of the stars was caused by this thin smoke of music drifting across them.

He tried to think what to do. Not much occurred to him. He pictured Gilbey in Panama. Whoring, drinking, fighting. Doing just as he had in Guatemala. That was where the idea of desertion failed Mingolla. In Panama he would be afraid; in Panama, though his hand might not shake, some other malignant twitch would develop; in Panama he would resort to magical cures for his afflictions because he would be too imperiled by the real to derive strength from it. And eventually the war would come to Panama. Desertion would have gained him nothing. He stared out across the moon-silvered jungle, and it seemed that some essential part of him was pouring from his eyes, entering the flow of the wind and rushing away past the Ant Farm and its smoking craters, past guerrilla territory, past the seamless join of sky and horizon, being irresistibly pulled toward a point into which the world's vitality was emptying. He felt himself emptying as well, growing cold and vacant and slow. His brain became incapable of thought, capable only of recording perceptions. The wind brought green scents that made his nostrils flare. The sky's blackness folded around him, and the stars were golden pinpricks of sensation. He didn't sleep, but something in him slept.

A whisper drew him back from the edge of the world. At first he thought it had been his imagination, and he continued staring at the sky, which had lightened to the vivid blue of predawn. Then he heard it again and glanced behind him. Strung out across the bridge, about twenty feet away, were a dozen or so children. Some standing, some crouched. Most were clad in rags, a few wore coverings of vines and leaves, and others were naked. Watchful; silent. Knives glinted in their hands. They were all emaciated, their hair long and matted, and Mingolla, recalling the dead children he had seen that morning, was for a moment afraid. But only for a moment. Fear flared in him like a coal puffed to life by a breeze and then died an instant later, suppressed not by any rational accommodation but by a perception of those ragged figures as an opportunity for surrender. He wasn't eager to die, yet neither did he want to put forth more effort in the cause of survival. Survival, he had learned, was not the soul's ultimate priority. He kept staring at the children. The way they were posed reminded him of a Neanderthal grouping in the Museum of Natural History. The moon was still up, and they cast vaguely defined shadows like smudges of graphite. Finally Mingolla turned away; the horizon was showing a distinct line of green darkness.

He had expected to be stabbed or pushed, to pinwheel down and break against the Río Dulce, its waters gone a steely color beneath the brightening sky. But instead a voice spoke in his ear: 'Hey, gringo.' Squatting beside him was a boy of fourteen or fifteen, with a swarthy monkeylike face framed by tangles of shoulder-length dark hair. Wearing tattered shorts. Coiled serpent tattooed on his brow. He tipped his head to one side, then the other.

Perplexed. He might have been trying to see the true Mingolla through layers of false appearance. He made a growly noise in his throat and held up a knife, twisting it this way and that, letting Mingolla observe its keen edge, how it channeled the moonlight along its blade. An army-issue survival knife with a brass-knuckle grip. Mingolla gave an amused sniff.

The boy seemed alarmed by this reaction, he lowered the knife and shifted away. 'What you doing here, gringo?' he asked.

A number of answers occurred to Mingolla, most demanding too much energy to voice; he chose the simplest. 'I like it here. I like the bridge.'

The boy squinted at Mingolla. 'The bridge is magic,' he said. 'You know this?'

'There was a time I might have believed you,' said Mingolla.

'You got to talk slow, man.' The boy frowned. 'Too fast, I can't understan'.'

Mingolla repeated his comment, and the boy said, 'You believe it, gringo. Why else you here?' With a planing motion of his arm he described an imaginary continuance of the bridge's upward course. 'That's where the bridge travels now. Don't have not'ing to do wit' crossing the river. It's a piece of white stone. Don't mean the same t'ing a bridge means.'

Mingolla was surprised to hear his thoughts echoed by someone who so resembled a hominid.

'I come here,' the boy went on. 'I listen to the wind, hear it in the iron. And I know t'ings from it. I can see the future.' He grinned, exposing blackened teeth, and pointed south toward the Caribbean. 'Future's that way, man.'

Mingolla liked the joke; he felt an affinity for the boy, for anyone who could manage jokes from the boy's perspective, but he couldn't think of a way to express his good feeling. Finally he said, 'You speak English well.'

'Shit! What you think? 'Cause we live in the jungle, we talk like animals? Shit!' The boy jabbed the point of his knife into the concrete. 'I talk English all my life. Gringos, they too stupid to learn Spanish.'

A girl's voice sounded behind them, harsh and peremptory. The other children had closed to within ten feet, their savage faces intent upon Mingolla, and the girl was standing a bit forward of them. She had sunken cheeks and deep-set eyes; ratty cables of hair hung down over her single-scoop breasts. Her hip bones tented up a rag of a skirt, which the wind pushed back between her legs. The boy let her finish, then gave a prolonged response, punctuating his words by smashing the brass-knuckle grip of his knife against the concrete, striking sparks with every blow.

'Gracela,' he said to Mingolla, 'she wants to kill you. But I say, some men they got one foot in the wort' of death, and if you kill them, death will take you, too. And you know what?'

'What?' said Mingolla.

'It's true. You and death' – the boy clasped his hands – 'like this.'

'Maybe,' Mingolla said.

'No "maybe." The bridge tol' me. Tol' me I be t'ankful if I let you live. So you be t'ankful to the bridge. That magic you don' believe, it save your ass.' The boy lowered out of his squat and sat cross-legged. 'Gracela, she don' care 'bout you live or die. She jus' go 'gainst me 'cause when I leave here, she going to be chief. She's, you know, impatient.'

Mingolla looked at the girl. She met his gaze coldly: a witch-child with slitted eyes, bramble hair, and ribs poking out.

'Where are you going?' he asked the boy.

'I have a dream I will live in the south; I dream I own a warehouse full of gold and cocaine.'

The girl began to harangue him again, and he shot back a string of angry syllables.

'What did you say?' Mingolla asked.

'I say, "Gracela, you give me shit, I going to fuck you and t'row you in the river."' He winked at Mingolla. 'Gracela she a virgin so she worry 'bout that firs' t'ing.'

The sky was graying, pink streaks fading in from the east; birds wheeled up from the jungle below, forming into flocks above the river. In the half-light Mingolla saw that the boy's chest was cross-hatched with ridged scars: knife wounds that hadn't received proper treatment. Bits of vegetation were trapped in his hair, like primitive adornments.

'Tell me, gringo,' said the boy. 'I hear in America there is a machine wit' the soul of a man. This is true?'

'More or less,' said Mingolla.

The boy nodded gravely, his suspicions confirmed, 'I hear also America has built a metal worl' in the sky.'

'They're building it now.'

'In the house of your president, is there a stone that holds the mind of a dead magician?'

Mingolla gave this due consideration. 'I doubt it,' he said. 'But it's possible.'

Wind thudded against the bridge, startling him. He felt its freshness on his face and relished the sensation. That – the fact that he could still take simple pleasure from life – startled him more than had the sudden noise.

The pink streaks in the east were deepening to crimson and fanning wider; shafts of light pierced upward to stain the bellies of some low-lying clouds to mauve. Several of the children began to mutter in unison. A chant. They were speaking in Spanish, but the way their voices jumbled the words, it sounded guttural and malevolent, a language for trolls. Listening to them, Mingolla imagined them crouched around fires in bamboo thickets. Bloody knives lifted sunward over their fallen prey. Making love in the green nights among fleshy Rousseau-like vegetation, while pythons with ember eyes coiled in the branches above their heads.

'Truly, gringo,' said the boy, apparently still contemplating Mingolla's answers. 'These are evil times.' He stared gloomily down at the river; the wind shifted the heavy snarls of his hair.

Watching him, Mingolla grew envious. Despite the bleakness of his existence, this little monkey king was content with his place in the world, assured of its nature. Perhaps he was deluded, but Mingolla envied his delusion, and he especially envied his dream of gold and cocaine. His own dreams had been dispersed by the war. The idea of sitting and daubing colors onto canvas no longer held any real attraction for him. Nor did the thought of returning to New York. Though survival had been his priority all these months, he had never stopped to consider what survival portended, and now he did not believe he could return. He had, he realized, become acclimated to the war, able to breathe its toxins; he would gag on the air of peace and home. The war was his new home, his newly rightful place.

Then the truth of this struck him with the force of an illumination, and he understood what he had to do.

Baylor and Gilbey had acted according to their natures, and he would have to act according to his, which imposed upon him the path of acceptance. He remembered Tío Moisés' story about the pilot and laughed inwardly. In a sense his friend – the guy he had mentioned in his unsent letter – had been right about the war, about the world. It was full of designs, patterns, coincidences, and cycles that appeared to indicate the workings of some magical power. But these things were the result of a subtle natural process. The longer you lived, the wider your experience, the more complicated your life became, and eventually you were bound in the midst of so many interactions, a web of circumstance and emotion and event, that nothing was simple anymore and everything was subject to interpretation. Interpretation, however, was a waste of time. Even the most logical of interpretations was merely an attempt to herd mystery into a cage and lock the door on it. It made life no less mysterious. And it was equally pointless to seize upon patterns, to rely on them, to obey the mystical regulations they seemed to imply. Your one effective course had to be entrenchment. You had to admit to mystery, to the incomprehensibility of your situation, and protect yourself against it. Shore up your web, clear it of blind corners, set alarms. You had to plan aggressively. You had to become the monster in your own maze, as brutal and devious as the fate you sought to escape. It was the kind of militant acceptance that Tío Moisés' pilot had not the opportunity to display, that Mingolla himself – though the opportunity had been his – had failed to display. He saw that now. He had merely reacted to danger and had not challenged or used forethought against it. But he thought he would be able to do that now.

He turned to the boy, thinking he might appreciate this insight into 'magic,' and caught a flicker of movement out of the corner of his eye. Gracela. Coming up behind the boy, her knife held low, ready to stab. In reflex, Mingolla flung out his injured hand to block her. The knife nicked the edge of his hand, deflected upward, and sliced the top of the boy's shoulder.

The pain in Mingolla's hand was excruciating, blinding him momentarily; and then as he grabbed Gracela's forearm to prevent her from stabbing again, he felt another sensation, one almost covered by the pain. He had thought the thing inside his hand was dead, but now he could feel it fluttering at the edges of the wound, leaking out in the rich trickle of blood that flowed over his wrist. It was trying to worm back inside, wriggling against the flow, but the pumping of his heart was too strong, and soon it was gone, dripping on the white stone of the bridge.

Before he could feel relief or surprise or in any way absorb what had happened, Gracela tried to pull free. Mingolla got to his knees, dragged her down, and dallied her knife-hand against the bridge. The knife skittered away. Gracela struggled wildly, clawing at his face, and the other children edged forward. Mingolla levered his left arm under Gracela's chin, choking her; with his right hand, he picked up the knife and pressed the point into her breast. The children stopped their advance, and Gracela went limp. He could feel her trembling. Tears streaked the grime in her cheeks. She looked like a scared little girl, not a witch.

'*Puta!*' said the boy. He had come to his feet, holding his shoulder, and was staring daggers at Gracela.

'Is it bad?' Mingolla asked, 'The shoulder?'

The boy inspected the bright blood on his fingertips. 'It hurts,' he said. He stepped over to stand in front of Gracela and smiled down at her; he unbuttoned the top of his shorts. Gracela tensed.

'What are you doing?' Mingolla suddenly felt responsible for the girl.

'I going to do what I tol' her, man.' The boy undid the rest of the buttons and shimmied out of his shorts; he was already half erect, as if the violence had aroused him.

'No,' said Mingolla, realizing as he spoke that this was not at all wise.

'Take your life,' said the boy sternly. 'Walk away.'

A long powerful gust of wind struck the bridge; it seemed to Mingolla that the vibration of the bridge, the beating of his heart, and Gracela's trembling were driven by the same shimmering. He felt an almost visceral commitment to the moment, one that had nothing to do with his concern for the girl. Maybe, he thought, it was an implementation of his new convictions.

The boy lost patience. He shouted at the other children, herding them away with slashing gestures. Sullenly, they moved off the curve of the bridge, positioning themselves along the miling, leaving an open avenue. Beyond them, beneath a lavender sky, the jungle stretched to the horizon, broken only by the rectangular hollow made by the airbase. The boy hunkered at Gracela's feet. 'Tonight,' he said to Mingolla, 'the bridge have set us together. Tonight we sit, we talk. Now, that's over. My heart say to kill you. But 'cause you stop Gracela from cutting deep, I give you a chance. She mus' make a judgmen'. If she say she go wit' you, we' – he waved toward the other children – 'will kill you. If she wan' to stay, then you mus' go. No more talk, no bullshit. You jus' go. Understan'?'

Mingolla wasn't afraid, and his lack of fear was not born of an indifference to life, but of clarity and confidence. It was time to stop reacting away from challenges, time to meet them. He came up with a plan. There was no doubt that Gracela would choose him, choose a chance at life, no matter how slim. But before she could decide, he would kill the boy. Then he would run straight at the others; without their leader, they might not hang together. It wasn't much of a plan, and he didn't like the idea of hurting the boy; but he thought he might be able to pull it off.

'I understand,' he said.

The boy spoke to Gracela; he told Mingolla to release her. She sat up, rubbing the spot where Mingolla had pricked her with the knife. She glanced coyly at him, then at the boy; she pushed her hair back behind her neck and thrust out her breasts as if preening for two suitors. Mingolla was astonished by her behavior. Maybe, he thought, she was playing for time. He stood and pretended to be shaking out his kinks, edging closer to the boy, who remained crouched beside Gracela. In the east a red fireball had cleared the horizon; its sanguine light inspired Mingolla, fueled his resolve. He yawned and edged closer yet, firming his grip on the knife. He would yank the boy's head back by the hair, cut his throat. Nerves jumped in his chest. A pressure was building inside him, demanding that he act, that he move now. He restrained himself. Another step should do it, another step to be absolutely sure. But as he was about to take that step, Gracela reached out and tapped the boy on the shoulder.

Surprise must have showed on Mingolla's face, because the boy looked at him and grunted laughter, 'You t'ink she pick you?' he said. 'Shit! You don' know Gracela, man. Gringos burn village. She lick the devil's ass 'fore she even shake hands wit' you.' He grinned, stroked her hair. ''Sides, she t'ink if she fuck me good, maybe I say, "Oh, Gracela, I got to have some more of that!" And who knows? Maybe she right.'

Gracela lay back and wriggled out of her skirt. Between her legs, she was nearly hairless. A smile touched the corners of her mouth. Mingolla stared at her, dumbfounded.

'I not going to kill you, gringo,' said the boy without looking up; he was running his hand across Gracela's stomach. 'I tol' you I won' kill a man so close wit' death.' Again he laughed. 'You look pretty funny trying to sneak up. I like watching that.'

Mingolla was stunned. All the while he had been gearing himself up to kill, shunting aside anxiety and revulsion, he had merely been providing an entertainment for the boy. The heft of the knife seemed to be drawing his anger into a compact shape, and he wanted to carry out his attack, to cut down this little animal who had ridiculed him; but humiliation mixed with the anger, neutralizing it. The poisons of rage shook him; he could feel every incidence of pain and fatigue in his body. His hand was throbbing, bloated and discolored like the hand of a corpse. Weakness pervaded him. And relief.

'Go,' said the boy. He lay down beside Gracela, propped on an elbow, and began to tease one of her nipples erect.

Mingolla took a few hesitant steps away. Behind him, Gracela made a mewling noise and the boy whispered something. Mingolla's anger was rekindled – they had already forgotten him! – but he kept going. As he passed the other children, one spat at him and another shied a pebble. He fixed his eyes on the white concrete slipping beneath his feet.

When he reached the midpoint of the curve, he turned back. The children had hemmed in Gracela and the boy against the terminus, blocking them from view. The sky had gone bluish-gray behind them, and the wind carried their voices. They were singing a ragged, chirpy song that sounded celebratory. Mingolla's anger subsided, his humiliation ebbed. He had nothing to be ashamed of; though he had acted unwisely, he had done so from a posture of strength and no amount of ridicule could diminish that. Things were going to work out. Yes, they were! He would make them work out.

For a while he watched the children. At this remove their singing had an appealing savagery, and he felt a trace of wistfulness leaving them behind. He wondered what would happen after the boy had done with Gracela. He was not concerned, only curious. The way you feel when you think you may have to leave a movie before the big finish. Will our heroine survive? Will justice prevail? Will survival and justice bring happiness in their wake? Soon the end of the bridge came to be bathed in the golden rays of the sunburst; the children seemed to be blackening and dissolving in heavenly fire. That was a sufficient resolution for Mingolla. He tossed Gracela's knife into the river and went down from the bridge in whose magic he no longer believed, walking toward the war whose mystery he had accepted as his own.

V

At the airbase Mingolla took a stand beside the Sikorsky that had brought him to San Francisco de Juticlan; he had recognized it by the painted flaming letters of the words *Whispering Death*. He rested his head against the letter *g* and recalled how Baylor had recoiled from the letters, worried that they might transmit some deadly essence. Mingolla didn't mind the contact. The painted flames seemed to be warming the inside of his head, stirring up thoughts as slow and indefinite as smoke. Comforting thoughts that embodied no images or ideas. Just a gentle buzz of mental activity, like the idling of an engine. The base was coming to life around him. Jeeps pulling away from barracks; a couple of officers inspecting the belly of a cargo plane; some guy repairing a forklift. Peaceful, homey. Mingolla closed his eyes, lulled into half-sleep, letting the sun and the painted flames bracket him with heat, real and imagined.

Sometime later – how much later, he could not be sure – a voice said, 'Fucked up your hand pretty good, didn'tcha?'

The two pilots were standing by the cockpit door. In their black flight suits and helmets they looked neither weird nor whimsical, but creatures of functional menace. Masters of the Machine. 'Yeah,' said Mingolla. 'Fucked it up.'

'How'd ya do it?' asked the pilot on the left.

'Hit a tree.'

'Musta been goddamn crocked to hit a tree,' said the pilot on the right. 'Tree ain't goin' nowhere if you hit it.'

Mingolla made a noncommittal noise. 'You guys going up to the Farm?'

'You bet! What's the matter, man? Had enough of them wild women?' Pilot on the right.

'Guess so. Wanna gimme a ride?'

'Sure thing,' said the pilot on the left. 'Whyn't you climb on to front. You can sit back of us.'

'Where your buddies?' asked the pilot on the right.

'Gone,' said Mingolla as he climbed into the cockpit.

One of the pilots said, 'Didn't think we'd be seein' them boys again.'

Mingolla strapped into the observer's seat behind the copilot's position. He had assumed there would be a lengthy instrument check, but as soon as the engines had been warmed, the Sikorsky lurched up and veered northward. With the exception of the weapons systems, none of the defenses had been activated. The radar, the thermal imager and terrain display all showed blank screens. A nervous thrill ran across the muscles of Mingolla's stomach as he considered the varieties of danger to which the pilots' reliance upon their miraculous helmets had laid them open; but his nervousness was subsumed by the whispery rhythms of the rotors and his sense of the Sikorsky's power. He recalled having a similar feeling of secure potency while sitting at the controls of his gun. He had never let that feeling grow, never let it empower him. He had been a fool.

They followed the northeasterly course of the river, which coiled like a length of blue-steel razor wire between jungled hills. The pilots laughed and joked, and the flight came to have the air of a ride with a couple of good ol' boys going nowhere fast and full of free beer. At one point the copilot piped his voice through the on-board speakers and launched into a dolorous country song.

> 'Whenever we kiss, dear, our two lips meet,
> And whenever you're not with me, we're apart.
> When you sawed my dog in half, that was depressin',
> But when you shot me in the chest, you broke my heart.'

As the copilot sang, the pilot rocked the Sikorsky back and forth in a drunken accompaniment, and after the song ended, he called back to Mingolla, 'You believe this here son of a bitch wrote that? He did! Picks a guitar, too! Boy's a genius!'

'It's a great song,' said Mingolla, and he meant it. The song made him happy, and that was no small thing.

They went rocking through the skies, singing the first verse over and over. But then, as they left the river behind, still mainlining a northeasterly course, the copilot pointed to a section of jungle ahead and shouted, 'Beaners! Quadrant Four! You got 'em?'

'Got 'em!' said the pilot. The Sikorsky swerved down toward the jungle, shuddered, and flame veered from beneath them. An instant later, a huge swath of jungle erupted into a gout of marbled smoke and fire. 'Whee-oo!' the copilot sang out jubilant, '*Whisperin' Death* strikes again!' With guns blazing they went swooping through blowing veils of dark smoke. Acres of trees were burning, and still they kept up the attack. Mingolla gritted his teeth against the noise, and when at last the firing stopped, dismayed by this insanity, he sat slumped, his head down. He suddenly doubted his ability to cope with the insanity of the Ant Farm and remembered all his reasons for fear.

The copilot turned back to him. 'You ain't got no call to look so gloomy, man,' he said. 'You're a lucky son of a bitch, y'know that?'

The pilot began a bank toward the east, toward the Ant Farm. 'How you figure that?' Mingolla asked.

'I gotta clear sight of you, man,' said the copilot. 'I can tell you for true you ain't gonna be at the Farm much longer. It ain't clear why or nothin'. But I 'spect you gonna be wounded. Not bad, though. Just a goin'-home wound.'

As the pilot completed the bank, a ray of sun slanted into the cockpit, illuminating the copilot's visor, and for a split second Mingolla could make out the vague shadow of the face beneath. It seemed lumpy and malformed. His imagination added details. Bizarre growths, cracked cheeks, an eye webbed shut. Like a face out of a movie about nuclear mutants. He was tempted to believe that he had really seen this; the copilot's deformities would validate his prediction of a secure future. But Mingolla rejected the temptation. He was afraid of dying, afraid of the terrors held by life at the Ant Farm, yet he wanted no more to do with magic ... unless there was magic involved in being a good soldier. In obeying the disciplines, in the practice of fierceness.

'Could be his hand'll get him home,' said the pilot. 'That hand looks pretty fucked up to me. Looks like a million-dollar wound, that hand.'

'Naw, I don't get it's his hand,' said the copilot. 'Somethin' else. Whatever, it's gonna do the trick.'

Mingolla could see his own face floating in the black plastic of the copilot's visor; he looked warped and pale, so thoroughly unfamiliar that for a moment he thought the face might be a bad dream the copilot was having.

'What the hell's with you, man?' the copilot asked. 'You don't believe me?'

Mingolla wanted to explain that his attitude had nothing to do with belief or disbelief, that it signaled his intent to obtain a safe future by means of securing his present; but he couldn't think how to put it into words the copilot would accept. The copilot would merely refer again to his visor as testimony to a magical reality or perhaps would point up ahead where – because the cockpit plastic had gone opaque under the impact of direct sunlight – the sun now appeared to hover in a smoky darkness: a distinct fiery sphere with a streaming corona, like one of those cabalistic emblems embossed on ancient seals. It was an evil, fearsome-looking thing, and though Mingolla was unmoved by it, he knew the pilot would see in it a powerful sign.

'You think I'm lyin'?' said the copilot angrily. 'You think I'd be bullshittin' you 'bout somethin' like this? Man, I ain't lyin'! I'm givin' you the good goddamn word!'

They flew east into the sun, whispering death, into a world disguised as a strange bloody enchantment, over the dark green wild where war had taken root, where men in combat armor fought for no good reason against men wearing brass scorpions on their berets, where crazy lost men wandered the mystic light of Fire Zone Emerald and mental wizards brooded upon things not yet seen. The copilot kept the black bubble of his visor angled back toward Mingolla, waiting for a response. But Mingolla just stared, and before too long the copilot turned away.

RADIANT GREEN STAR

Several months before my thirteenth birthday, my mother visited me in a dream and explained why she had sent me to live with the circus seven years before. The dream was a Mitsubishi, I believe, its style that of the Moonflower series of biochips, which set the standard for pornography in those days; it had been programmed to activate once my testosterone production reached a certain level, and it featured a voluptuous Asian woman to whose body my mother had apparently grafted the image of her own face. I imagined she must have been in a desperate hurry and thus forced to use whatever materials fell to hand; yet, taking into account the Machiavellian intricacies of the family history, I later came to think that her decision to alter a pornographic chip might be intentional, designed to provoke Oedipal conflicts that would imbue her message with a heightened urgency.

In the dream, my mother told me that when I was eighteen I would come into the trust created by my maternal grandfather, a fortune that would make me the wealthiest man in Vietnam. Were I to remain in her care, she feared my father would eventually coerce me into assigning control of the trust to him, whereupon he would have me killed. Sending me to live with her old friend Vang Ky was the one means she had of guaranteeing my safety. If all went as planned, I would have several years to consider whether it was in my best interests to claim the trust or to forswear it and continue my life in secure anonymity. She had faith that Vang would educate me in a fashion that would prepare me to arrive at the proper decision.

Needless to say, I woke from the dream in tears. Vang had informed me not long after my arrival at his door that my mother was dead, and that my father was likely responsible for her death; but this fresh evidence of his perfidy, and of her courage and sweetness, mingled though it was with the confusions of intense eroticism, renewed my bitterness and sharpened my sense of loss. I sat the rest of the night with only the eerie music of tree frogs to distract me from despair, which roiled about in my brain as if it were a species of sluggish life both separate from and inimical to my own.

The next morning, I sought out Vang and told him of the dream and asked what I should do. He was sitting at the desk in the tiny cluttered trailer that served as his home and office, going over the accounts: a frail man in his late sixties with close-cropped gray hair, dressed in a white open-collared shirt and green cotton trousers. He had a long face – especially long from cheekbones to jaw – and an almost feminine delicacy of feature, a combination of characteristics that lent him a sly, witchy look; but though he was capable of slyness, and though at times I suspected him of possessing supernatural powers, at least as regards his ability to ferret out my misdeeds, I perceived him at the time to be an inwardly directed soul who felt misused by the world and whose only interests, apart from the circus, were a love of books and calligraphy. He would occasionally take a pipe of opium, but was otherwise devoid of vices, and it strikes me now that while he had told me of his family and his career in government (he said he still maintained those connections), of a life replete with joys and passionate errors, he was now in the process of putting all that behind him and withdrawing from the world of the senses.

'You must study the situation,' he said, shifting in his chair, a movement that shook the wall behind him, disturbing the leaflets stacked in the cabinet above his head and causing one to sail down toward the desk; he batted it away, and for an instant it floated in the air before me, as if held by the hand of a spirit, a detailed pastel rendering of a magnificent tent – a thousand times more magnificent than the one in which we performed – and a hand-lettered legend proclaiming the imminent arrival of the Radiant Green Star Circus.

'You must learn everything possible about your father and his associates,' he went on. 'Thus you will uncover his weaknesses and define his strengths. But first and foremost, you must continue to live. The man you become will determine how best to use the knowledge you have gained, and you mustn't allow the pursuit of your studies to rise to the level of obsession, or else his judgment will be clouded. Of course, this is easier to do in theory than in practice. But if you set about it in a measured way, you will succeed.'

I asked how I should go about seeking the necessary information, and he gestured with his pen at another cabinet, one with a glass front containing scrapbooks and bundles of computer paper; beneath it, a marmalade cat was asleep atop a broken radio, which – along with framed photographs of his wife, daughter, and grandson, all killed, he'd told me, in an airline accident years before – rested on a chest of drawers.

'Start there,' he said. 'When you are done with those, my friends in the government will provide us with your father's financial records and other materials.'

I took a cautious step toward the cabinet – stacks of magazines and newspapers and file boxes made the floor of the trailer difficult to negotiate – but Vang held up a hand to restrain me. 'First,' he said, 'you must live. We will put aside a few hours each day for you to study, but before all else you are a member of my troupe. Do your chores. Afterward we will sit down together and make a schedule.'

On the desk, in addition to his computer, were a cup of coffee topped with a mixture of sugar and egg, and a plastic dish bearing several slices of melon. He offered me a slice and sat with his hands steepled on his stomach, watching me eat. 'Would you like time alone to honor your mother?' he asked. 'I suppose we can manage without you for a morning.'

'Not now,' I told him. 'Later, though ...'

I finished the melon, laid the rind on his plate, and turned to the door, but he called me back.

'Philip,' he said, 'I cannot remedy the past, but I can assure you to a degree as to the future. I have made you my heir. One day the circus will be yours. Everything I own will be yours.'

I peered at him, not quite certain that he meant what he said, even though his words had been plain.

'It may not seem a grand gift,' he said. 'But perhaps you will discover that it is more than it appears.'

I thanked him effusively, but he grimaced and waved me to silence – he was not comfortable with displays of affection. Once again he told me to see to my chores.

'Attend to the major as soon as you're able,' he said. 'He had a difficult night. I know he would be grateful for your company.'

Radiant Green Star was not a circus in the tradition of the spectacular traveling shows of the previous century. During my tenure, we never had more than eight performers and only a handful of exhibits, exotics that had been genetically altered in some fashion: a pair of miniature tigers with hands instead of paws, a monkey with a vocabulary of thirty-seven words, and the like. The entertainments we presented were unsophisticated; we could not compete with those available in Hanoi or Hue or Saigon, or, for that matter, those accessible in the villages. But the villagers perceived us as a link to a past they revered, and found in the crude charm of our performances a sop to their nostalgia – it was as if we carried the past with us, and we played to that illusion, keeping mainly to rural places that appeared on the surface to be part of another century. Even when the opportunity arose, Vang refused to play anywhere near large population centers because – he said – of the exorbitant bribes and licensing fees demanded by officials in such areas. Thus for the first eighteen years of my life, I did not venture into a city, and I came to know my country much as a tourist might, driving ceaselessly through it, isolated within the troupe. We traversed the north and central portions of Vietnam in three battered methane-powered trucks, one of which towed Vang's trailer, and erected our tents in pastures and school yards and soccer fields, rarely staying anywhere longer than a few nights. On occasion, to accommodate a private celebration sponsored by a wealthy family, we would join forces with another troupe; but Vang was reluctant to participate in such events, because being surrounded by so many people caused our featured attraction to become agitated, thus imperiling his fragile health.

Even today the major remains a mystery to me. I have no idea if he was who he claimed to be; nor, I think, did he know – his statements concerning identity were usually vague and muddled, and the only point about which he was firm was that he had been orphaned as a young boy, raised by an uncle and aunt, and, being unmarried, was the last of his line. Further, it's unclear whether his claims were the product of actual memory, delusion, or implantation. For the benefit of our audiences, we let them stand as truth, and billed him as Major Martin Boyette, the last surviving POW of the American War, now well over a hundred years old and horribly disfigured, both conditions the result of experiments in genetic manipulation by means of viruses – this the opinion of a Hanoi physician who treated the major during a bout of illness. Since such unregulated experiments were performed with immoderate frequency throughout Southeast Asia after the turn of the century, it was not an unreasonable conclusion. Major Boyette himself had no recollection of the process that had rendered him so monstrous and – if one were to believe him – so long-lived.

We were camped that day near the village of Cam Lo, and the tent where the major was quartered had been set up at the edge of the jungle. He liked the jungle, liked its noise and shadow, the sense of enclosure it provided – he dreaded the prospect of being out in the open, so much so that whenever we escorted him to the main tent, we would walk with him, holding umbrellas to prevent him from seeing the sky and to shield him from the sight of god and man. But once inside the main tent, as if the formal structure of a performance neutralized his aversion to space and scrutiny, he showed himself pridefully, walking close to the bleachers, causing children to shy away and women to cover their eyes. His skin hung from his flesh in voluminous black folds (he was African-American), and when he raised his arms, the folds beneath them spread like the wings of a bat; his face, half-hidden by a layering of what appeared to be leather shawls, was the sort of uncanny face one might see emerging from a whorled pattern of bark, roughly human in form, yet animated by a force that seems hotter than the human soul, less self-aware. Bits of phosphorescence drifted in the darks of his eyes. His only clothing was a ragged gray shift, and he hobbled along with the aid of a staff cut from a sapling papaya – he might have been a prophet escaped after a term in hell, charred and magical and full of doom. But when he began to speak, relating stories from the American War, stories of ill-fated Viet Cong heroes and the supernatural forces whose aid they enlisted, all told in a deep rasping voice, his air of suffering and menace evaporated, and his ugliness became an intrinsic article of his power, as though he were a poet who had sacrificed superficial glamour for the ability to express more eloquently the beauty within. The audiences were won over, their alarm transformed to delight, and they saluted him with enthusiastic applause ... but they never saw him as I did that morning: a decrepit hulk given to senile maundering and moments of bright terror when startled by a sound from outside the tent. Sitting in his own filth, too weak or too uncaring to move.

When I entered the tent, screwing up my face against the stench, he tucked his head into his shoulder and tried to shroud himself in the fetid folds of his skin. I talked softly, gentling him as I might a frightened animal, in order to persuade him to stand. Once he had heaved up to his feet, I bathed him, sloshing buckets of water over his convulsed surfaces; when at length I was satisfied that I'd done my best, I hauled in freshly cut boughs and made him a clean place to sit. Unsteadily, he lowered himself onto the boughs and started to eat from the bowl of rice and vegetables I had brought for his breakfast, using his fingers to mold bits of food into a ball and inserting it deep into his mouth – he often had difficulty swallowing.

'Is it good?' I asked. He made a growly noise of affirmation. In the half-dark, I could see the odd points of brilliance in his eyes.

I hated taking care of the major (this may have been the reason Vang put me in charge of him). His physical state repelled me, and though the American War had long since ceased to be a burning issue, I resented his purported historical reality – being half American, half Vietnamese, I felt doubly afflicted by the era he represented. But that morning, perhaps because my mother's message had inoculated me against the usual prejudices, he fascinated me. It was like watching a mythological creature feed, a chimera or a manticore, and I thought I perceived in him the soul of the inspired storyteller, the luminous half-inch of being that still burned behind the corroded ruin of his face.

'Do you know who I am?' I asked.

He swallowed and gazed at me with those haunted foxfire eyes. I repeated the question.

'Philip,' he said tonelessly, giving equal value to both syllables, as if the name were a word he'd been taught but did not understand.

I wondered if he was – as Vang surmised – an ordinary man transformed into a monster, pumped full of glorious tales and false memories, all as a punishment for some unguessable crime or merely on a cruel whim. Or might he actually be who he claimed? A freak of history, a messenger from another time whose stories contained some core truth, just as the biochip had contained my mother's truth? All I knew for certain was that Vang had bought him from another circus, and that his previous owner had found him living in the jungle in the province of Quan Tri, kept alive by the charity of people from a nearby village who considered him the manifestation of a spirit.

Once he had finished his rice, I asked him to tell me about the war, and he launched into one of his mystical tales; but I stopped him, saying, 'Tell me about the real war. The war you fought in.'

He fell silent, and when at last he spoke, it was not in the resonant tones with which he entertained our audiences, but in an effortful whisper.

'We came to the firebase in ... company strength. Tenth of May. Nineteen sixty-seven. The engineers had just finished construction and ... and ... there was still ...' He paused to catch his breath. 'The base was near the Laotian border. Overlooking a defoliated rubber plantation. Nothing but bare red earth in front of us ... and wire. But at our rear ... the jungle ... it was too close. They brought in artillery to clear it. Lowered the batteries to full declension. The trees all toppled in the same direction ... as if they'd been pushed down by the sweep ... of an invisible hand.'

His delivery, though still labored, grew less halting, and he made feeble gestures to illustrate the tale, movements that produced a faint slithering as folds of his skin rubbed together; the flickerings in his pupils grew more and more pronounced, and I half-believed his eyes were openings onto a battlefield at night, a place removed from us by miles and time.

'Because of the red dirt, the base was designated Firebase Ruby. But the dirt wasn't the color of rubies, it was the red of drying blood. For months we held the position with only token resistance. We'd expected serious opposition, and it was strange to sit there day after day with nothing to do except send out routine patrols. I tried to maintain discipline, but it was an impossible task. Everyone malingered. Drug use was rampant. If I'd gone by the book I could have brought charges against every man on the base. But what was the point? War was not truly being waged. We were engaged in a holding action. Policy was either directionless or misguided. And so I satisfied myself by maintaining a semblance of discipline as the summer heat and the monsoon melted away the men's resolve.

'October came, the rains slackened. There was no hint of increased enemy activity, but I had a feeling something big was on the horizon. I spoke to my battalion commander. He felt the same way. I was told we had intelligence suggesting that the enemy planned a fall and winter campaign building up to Tet. But no one took it seriously. I don't think I took it seriously myself. I was a professional soldier who'd been sitting idle for six months, and I was spoiling for a fight. I was so eager for engagement I failed to exercise good judgment. I ignored the signs, I ... I refused ... I ...'

He broke off and pawed at something above him in the air – an apparition, perhaps; then he let out an anguished cry, covered his face with his hands, and began to shake like a man wracked by fever.

I sat with him until, exhausted, he lapsed into a fugue, staring dully at the ground. He was so perfectly still, if I had come across him in the jungle, I might have mistaken him for a root system that had assumed a hideous anthropomorphic shape. Only the glutinous surge of his breath opposed this impression. I didn't know what to think of his story. The plain style of its narration had been markedly different from that of his usual stories, and this lent it credibility; yet I recalled that whenever questioned about his identity, he would respond in a similar fashion. However, the ambiguous character of his personal tragedy did not diminish my new fascination with his mystery. It was as if I had been dusting a vase that rested on my mantelpiece, and, for the first time, I'd turned it over to inspect the bottom and found incised there a labyrinthine design, one that drew my eye inward along its black circuit, promising that should I be able to decipher the hidden character at its center, I would be granted a glimpse of something ultimately bleak and at the same time ultimately alluring. Not a secret, but rather the source of secrets. Not truth, but the ground upon which truth and its opposite were raised. I was a mere child – half a child, at any rate – thus I have no real understanding of how I arrived at this recognition, illusory though it may have been. But I can state with absolute surety why it seemed important at the time: I had a powerful sense of connection with the major, and, accompanying this, the presentiment that his mystery was somehow resonant with my own.

Except for my new program of study, researching my father's activities, and the enlarged parameters of my relationship with Major Boyette, whom I visited whenever I had the opportunity, over the next several years my days were much the same as ever, occupied by touring, performing (I functioned as a clown and an apprentice knife thrower), by all the tediums and pleasures that arose from life in Radiant Green Star. There were, of course, other changes. Vang grew increasingly frail and withdrawn, the major's psychological state deteriorated, and four members of the troupe left and were replaced. We gained two new acrobats, Kim and Kai, pretty Korean sisters aged seven and ten respectively – orphans trained by another circus – and Tranh, a middle-aged, moonfaced man whose potbelly did not hamper in the slightest his energetic tumbling and pratfalls. But to my mind, the most notable of the replacements was Vang's niece, Tan, a slim, quiet girl from Hue with whom I immediately fell in love.

Tan was nearly seventeen when she joined us, a year older than I, an age difference that seemed unbridgeable to my teenage sensibilities. Her shining black hair hung to her waist, her skin was the color of sandalwood dusted with gold, and her face was a perfect cameo in which the demure and the sensual commingled. Her father had been in failing health, and both he and his wife had been uploaded into a virtual community hosted by the Sony AI – Tan had then become her uncle's ward. She had no actual performing skills, but dressed in glittery revealing costumes, she danced and took part in comic skits and served as one of the targets for our knife thrower, a taciturn young man named Dat who was billed as James Bond Cochise. Dat's other target, Mei, a chunky girl of Taiwanese extraction who also served as the troupe's physician, having some knowledge of herbal medicine, would come prancing out and stand at the board, and Dat would plant his knives within a centimeter of her flesh; but when Tan took her place, he would exercise extreme caution and set the knives no closer than seven or eight inches away, a contrast that amused our audiences no end.

For months after her arrival, I hardly spoke to Tan, and then only for some utilitarian purpose; I was too shy to manage a normal conversation. I wished with all my heart that I was eighteen and a man, with the manly confidence that, I assumed, naturally flowed from having attained the age. As things stood I was condemned by my utter lack of self-confidence to admire her from afar, to imagine conversations and other intimacies, to burn with all the frustration of unrequited lust. But then, one afternoon, while I sat in the grass outside Vang's trailer, poring over some papers dealing with my father's investments, she approached, wearing loose black trousers and a white blouse, and asked what I was doing.

'I see you reading every day,' she said. 'You are so dedicated to your studies. Are you preparing for the university?'

We had set up our tents outside Bien Pho, a village some sixty miles south of Hanoi, on the grassy bank of a wide, meandering river whose water showed black beneath a pewter sky. Dark green conical hills with rocky outcroppings hemmed in the spot, and it was shaded here and there by smallish trees with crooked trunks and puffs of foliage at the ends of their corkscrew branches. The main tent had been erected at the base of the nearest hill and displayed atop it a pennant bearing the starry emblem of our troupe. Everyone else was inside, getting ready for the night's performance. It was a brooding yet tranquil scene, like a painting on an ancient Chinese scroll, but I noticed none of it – the world had shrunk to the bubble of grass and air that enclosed the two of us.

Tan sat beside me, crossed her legs in a half-lotus, and I caught her scent. Not perfume, but the natural musky yield of her flesh. I did my best to explain the purpose of my studies, the words rushing out as if I were unburdening myself of an awful secret. Which was more-or-less the case. No one apart from Vang knew what I was doing, and because his position relative to the task was tutelary, not that of a confidante, I felt oppressed, isolated by the responsibility I bore. Now it seemed that by disclosing the sad facts bracketing my life, I was acting to reduce their power over me. And so, hoping to exorcise them completely, I told her about my father.

'His name is William Ferrance,' I said, hastening to add that I'd taken Ky for my own surname. 'His father emigrated to Asia in the Nineties, during the onset of doi moi (this the Vietnamese equivalent of perestroika), and made a fortune in Saigon, adapting fleets of taxis to methane power. His son – my father – expanded the family interests. He invested in a number of construction projects, all of which lost money. He was in trouble financially when he married my mother, and he used her money to fund a casino in Da Nang. That allowed him to recoup most of his losses. Since then, he's established connections with the triads, Malaysian gambling syndicates, and the Bamboo Union in Taiwan. He's become an influential man, but his money's tied up. He has no room to maneuver. Should he gain control of my grandfather's estate, he'll be a very dangerous man.'

'But this is so impersonal,' Tan said. 'Have you no memories of him?'

'Hazy ones,' I said. 'From all I can gather, he never took much interest in me … except as a potential tool. The truth is, I can scarcely remember my mother. Just the occasional moment. How she looked standing at a window. The sound of her voice when she sang. And I have a general impression of the person she was. Nothing more.'

Tan looked off toward the river; some of the village children were chasing each other along the bank, and a cargo boat with a yellow sail was coming into view around the bend. 'I wonder,' she said. 'Is it worse to remember those who've gone, or not to remember them?'

I guessed she was thinking about her parents, and I wanted to say something helpful, but the concept of uploading an intelligence, a personality, was so foreign to me, I was afraid of appearing foolish.

'I can see my mother and father whenever I want,' Tan said, lowering her gaze to the grass. 'I can go to a Sony office anywhere in the world and summon them with a code. When they appear they look like themselves, they sound like themselves, but I know it's not them. The things they say are always … appropriate. But something is missing. Some energy, some quality.' She glanced up at me, and, looking into her beautiful dark eyes, I felt giddy, almost weightless. 'Something dies,' she went on. 'I know it! We're not just electrical impulses, we can't be sucked up into a machine and live. Something dies, something important. What goes into the machine is nothing. It's only a colored shadow of what we are.'

'I don't have much experience with computers,' I said.

'But you've experienced life!' She touched the back of my hand. 'Can't you feel it within you? I don't know what to call it … a soul? I don't know …'

It seemed then I could feel the presence of the thing she spoke of moving in my chest, my blood, going all through me, attached to my mind, my flesh, by an unfathomable connection, existing inside me the way breath exists inside a flute, breeding the brief, pretty life of a note, a unique tone, and then passing on into the ocean of the air. Whenever I think of Tan, how she looked that morning, I'm able to feel that delicate, tremulous thing, both temporary and eternal, hovering in the same space I occupy.

'This is too serious,' she said. 'I'm sorry. I've been thinking about my parents more than I should.' She shook back the fall of her hair, put on a smile. 'Do you play chess?'

'No,' I admitted.

'You must learn! A knowledge of the game will help if you intend to wage war against your father.' A regretful expression crossed her face, as if she thought she'd spoken out of turn. 'Even if you don't … I mean …' Flustered, she waved her hands to dispel the awkwardness of the moment. 'It's fun,' she said. 'I'll teach you.'

I did not make a good chess player, I was far too distracted by the presence of my teacher to heed her lessons. But I'm grateful to the game, for through the movements of knights and queens, through my clumsiness and her patience, through hours of sitting with our heads bent close together, our hearts grew close. We were never merely friends – from that initial conversation on, it was apparent that we would someday take the next step in exploring our relationship, and I rarely felt any anxiety in this regard; I knew that when Tan was ready, she would tell me. For the time being, we enjoyed a kind of amplified friendship, spending our leisure moments together, our physical contact limited to hand-holding and kisses on the cheek. This is not to say that I always succeeded in conforming to those limits. Once as we lay atop Vang's trailer, watching the stars, I was overcome by her scent, the warmth of her shoulder against mine, and I propped myself up on an elbow and kissed her on the mouth. She responded, and I stealthily unbuttoned her blouse, exposing her breasts. Before I could proceed further, she sat bolt upright, holding her blouse closed, and gave me a injured look; then she slid down from the trailer and walked off into the dark, leaving me in a state of dismay and painful arousal. I slept little that night, worried that I had done permanent damage to the relationship; but the next day she acted as if nothing had happened, and we went on as before, except that I now wanted her more than ever.

Vang, however, was not so forgiving. How he knew I had taken liberties with his niece, I'm not sure – it may have been simply an incidence of his intuitive abilities; I cannot imagine that Tan told him. Whatever his sources, after our performance the next night he came into the main tent where I was practicing with my knives, hurling them into a sheet of plywood upon which the red outline of a human figure had been painted, and asked if my respect for him had dwindled to the point that I would dishonor his sister's daughter.

He was sitting in the first row of the bleachers, leaning back, resting his elbows on the row behind him, gazing at me with distaste. I was infuriated by this casual indictment, and rather than answer immediately I threw another knife, placing it between the outline's arm and its waist. I walked to the board, yanked the blade free, and said without turning to him, 'I haven't dishonored her.'

'But surely that is your intent,' he said.

Unable to contain my anger, I spun about to face him. 'Were you never young? Have you never been in love?'

'Love.' He let out a dry chuckle. 'If you are in love, perhaps you would care to enlighten me as to its nature.'

I would have liked to tell him how I felt about Tan, to explain the sense of security I found with her, the varieties of tenderness, the niceties of my concern for her, the thousand nuances of longing, the intricate complicity of our two hearts and the complex specificity of my desire, for though I wanted to lose myself in the turns of her body, I also wanted to celebrate her, enliven her, to draw out of her the sadness that sometimes weighed her down, and to have her leach my sadness from me as well – I knew this was possible for us. But I was too young and too angry to articulate these things.

'Do you love your mother?' Vang asked, and before I could respond, he said, 'You have admitted that you have but a few disjointed memories of her. And, of course, a dream. Yet you have chosen to devote yourself to pursuing the dictates of that dream, to making a life that honors your mother's wishes. That is love. How can you compare this to your infatuation with Tan?'

Frustrated, I cast my eyes up to the billow of patched gray canvas overhead, to the metal rings at the peak from which Kai and Kim were nightly suspended. When I looked back to Vang, I saw that he had gotten to his feet.

'Think on it,' he said. 'If the time comes when you can regard Tan with the same devotion, well ...' He made a subtle dismissive gesture with his fingers that suggested this was an unlikely prospect.

I turned to the board and hefted another knife. The target suddenly appeared evil in its anonymity, a dangerous creature with a wood-grain face and blood-red skin, and as I drew back my arm, my anger at Vang merged with the greater anger I felt at the anonymous forces that had shaped my life, and I buried the knife dead center of the head – it took all my strength to work the blade free. Glancing up, I was surprised to see Vang watching from the entrance. I had assumed that, having spoken his piece, he had returned to his trailer. He stood there for a few seconds, giving no overt sign of his mood, but I had the impression he was pleased.

When she had no other duties, Tan would assist me with my chores: feeding the exotics, cleaning out their cages, and, though she did not relish his company, helping me care for the major. I must confess I was coming to enjoy my visits with him less and less; I still felt a connection to him, and I remained curious as to the particulars of his past, but his mental slippage had grown so pronounced it was difficult to be around him. Frequently he insisted on trying to relate the story of Firebase Ruby, but he always lapsed into terror and grief at the same point he had previously broken off the narrative. It seemed that this was a tale that he was making up, not one he had been taught or programmed to tell, and that his mind was no longer capable of other than fragmentary invention. But one afternoon, as we were finishing up in his tent, he began to tell the story again, this time starting at the place where he had previously faltered, speaking without hesitancy in the deep, raspy voice he used while performing.

'It came to be October,' he said. 'The rains slackened, the snakes kept to their holes during the day, and the spiderwebs were not so thick with victims as they'd been during the monsoon. I began to have a feeling that something ominous was on the horizon, and when I communicated this sense of things to my superiors, I was told that according to intelligence, an intensification of enemy activity was expected, leading up to what was presumed to be a major offensive during the celebration of Tet. But I gave no real weight to either my feeling or to the intelligence reports. I was a professional soldier, and for six months I'd been engaged in nothing more than sitting in a bunker and surveying a wasteland of red dirt and razor wire. I was spoiling for a fight.'

He was sitting on a nest of palm fronds, drenched in a spill of buttery light – we had partially unzipped the roof of the tent in order to increase ventilation – and it looked as if the fronds were an island adrift in a dark void and he a spiritual being who had been scorched and twisted by some cosmic fire, marooned in eternal emptiness.

'The evening of the fourteenth, I sent out the usual patrols and retired to my bunker. I sat at my desk reading a paperback novel and drinking whiskey. After a time, I put down the book and began a letter to my wife. I was tipsy, and instead of the usual sentimental lines designed to make her feel secure, I let my feelings pour onto the paper, writing about the lack of discipline, my fears concerning the enemy, my disgust at the way the war was being prosecuted. I told her how much I hated Vietnam. The ubiquitous corruption, the stupidity of the South Vietnamese government. The smell of fish sauce, the poisonous greens of the jungle. Everything. The goddamn place had been a battlefield so long, it was good for nothing else. I kept drinking, and the liquor eroded my remaining inhibitions. I told her about the treachery and ineptitude of the ARVN forces, about the fuck-ups on our side who called themselves generals.

'I was still writing when, around 2100, something distracted me. I'm not sure what it was. A noise ... or maybe a vibration. But I knew something had happened. I stepped out into the corridor and heard a cry. Then the crackling of small arms fire. I grabbed my rifle and ran outside. The VC were inside the wire. In the perimeter lights I saw dozens of diminutive men and women in black pajamas scurrying about, white stars sputtering from the muzzles of their weapons. I cut down several of them. I couldn't think how they had gotten through the wire and the minefields without alerting the sentries, but then, as I continued to fire, I spotted a man's head pop up out of the ground and realized that they had tunneled in. All that slow uneventful summer, they'd been busy beneath the surface of the earth, secretive as termites.'

At this juncture the major fell prey once again to emotional collapse, and I prepared myself for the arduous process of helping him recover; but Tan kneeled beside him, took his hand, and said, 'Martin? Martin, listen to me.'

No one ever used the major's Christian name, except to introduce him to an audience, and I didn't doubt that it had been a long time since a woman had addressed him with tenderness. He abruptly stopped his shaking, as if the nerves that had betrayed him had been severed, and stared wonderingly at Tan. White pinprick suns flickered and died in the deep places behind his eyes.

'Where are you from, Martin?' she asked, and the major, in a dazed tone, replied, 'Oakland ... Oakland, California. But I was born up in Santa Cruz.'

'Santa Cruz.' Tan gave the name a bell-like reading. 'Is it beautiful in Santa Cruz? It sounds like a beautiful place.'

'Yeah ... it's kinda pretty. There's old-growth redwoods not far from town. And there's the ocean. It's real pretty along the ocean.'

To my amazement, Tan and the major began to carry on a coherent – albeit simplistic – conversation, and I realized that he had never spoken in this fashion before. His syntax had an uncustomary informality, and his voice held the trace of an accent. I thought that Tan's gentle approach must have penetrated his tormented psyche, either reaching the submerged individual, the real Martin Boyette, or else encountering a fresh layer of delusion. It was curious to hear him talk about such commonplace subjects as foggy weather and jazz music and Mexican food, all of which he claimed could be found in good supply in Santa Cruz. Though his usual nervous tics were in evidence, a new placidity showed in his face. But, of course this state of affairs didn't last.

'I can't,' he said, taking a sudden turn from the subject at hand; he shook his head, dragging folds of skin across his neck and shoulders, 'I can't go back anymore. I can't go back there.'

'Don't be upset, Martin,' Tan said. 'There's no reason for you to worry. We'll stay with you, we'll ...'

'I don't want you to stay.' He tucked his head into his shoulder so his face was hidden by a bulge of skin. 'I got to get back doin' what I was doin''

'What's that?' I asked him. 'What were you doing?'

A muffled rhythmic grunting issued from his throat – laughter that went on too long to be an expression of simple mirth. It swelled in volume, trebled in pitch, becoming a signature of instability.

'I'm figurin' it all out,' he said. 'That's what I'm doin'. Jus' you go away now.'

'Figuring out what?' I asked, intrigued by the possibility – however unlikely – that the major might have a mental life other than the chaotic, that his apparent incoherence was merely an incidental byproduct of concentration, like the smoke that rises from a leaf upon which a beam of sunlight has been focused.

He made no reply, and Tan touched my hand, signaling that we should leave. As I ducked through the tent flap, behind me the major said, 'I can't go back there, and I can't be here. So jus' where's that leave me, y'know?'

Exactly what the major meant by this cryptic statement was unclear, but his words stirred something in me, reawakened me to internal conflicts that had been pushed aside by my studies and my involvement with Tan. When I had arrived to take up residence at Green Star, I was in a state of emotional upheaval, frightened, confused, longing for my mother. Yet even after I calmed down, I was troubled by the feeling that I had lost my place in the world, and it seemed this was not just a consequence of having been uprooted from my family, but that I had always felt this way, that the turbulence of my emotions had been a cloud obscuring what was a constant strain in my life. This was due in part to my mixed heritage. Though the taint associated with the children of Vietnamese mothers and American fathers (dust children, they had once been called) had dissipated since the end of the war, it had not done so entirely, and wherever the circus traveled, I would encounter people who, upon noticing the lightness of my skin and the shape of my eyes, expressed scorn and kept their distance. Further fueling this apprehension was the paucity of my memories deriving from the years before I had come to live with Vang. Whenever Tan spoke about her childhood, she brought up friends, birthdays, uncles and cousins, trips to Saigon, dances, hundreds of details and incidents that caused my own memory to appear grossly underpopulated by comparison. Trauma was to blame, I reckoned. The shock of my mother's abandonment, however well-intended, had ripped open my mental storehouse and scattered the contents. That and the fact that I had been six when I left home and thus hadn't had time to accumulate the sort of cohesive memories that lent color to Tan's stories of Hue. But explaining it away did not lessen my discomfort, and I became fixated on the belief that no matter the nature of the freakish lightning that had sheared away my past, I would never find a cure for the sense of dislocation it had provoked, only medicines that would suppress the symptoms and mask the disease – and, that being so masked, it would grow stronger, immune to treatment, until eventually I would be possessed by it, incapable of feeling at home anywhere.

I had no remedy for these anxieties other than to throw myself with greater intensity into my studies, and with this increase in intensity came a concomitant increase in anger. I would sit at Vang's computer, gazing at photographs of my father, imagining violent resolutions to our story. I doubted that he would recognize me; I favored my mother and bore little resemblance to him, a genetic blessing for which I was grateful: he was not particularly handsome, though he was imposing, standing nearly six and a half feet tall and weighing – according to a recent medical report – two hundred and sixty-four pounds, giving the impression not of a fat man, but a massive one. His large squarish head was kept shaved, and on his left cheek was the dark blue and green tattoo of his corporate emblem – a flying fish – ringed by three smaller tattoos denoting various of his business associations. At the base of his skull was an oblong silver plate beneath which lay a number of ports allowing him direct access to a computer. Whenever he posed for a picture, he affected what I assumed he would consider a look of hauteur, but the smallness of his eyes (grayish blue) and nose and mouth in contrast to the largeness of his face caused them to be limited in their capacity to convey character and emotional temperature, rather like the features on a distant planet seen through a telescope, and as a result this particular expression came across as prim. In less formal photographs, taken in the company of one or another of his sexual partners, predominately women, he was quite obviously intoxicated.

He owned an old French Colonial in Saigon, but spent the bulk of his time at his house in Binh Khoi, one of the flower towns – communities built at the turn of the century, intended to provide privacy and comfort for well-to-do Vietnamese whose sexual preferences did not conform to communist morality. Now that communism – if not the concept of sexual morality itself – had become quaint, a colorful patch of history dressed up with theme-park neatness to amuse the tourists, it would seem that these communities no longer had any reason to exist; yet exist they did. Their citizenry had come to comprise a kind of gay aristocracy that defined styles, set trends, and wielded significant political power. Though they maintained a rigid exclusivity, and though my father's bisexuality was motivated to a great degree – I believe – by concerns of business and status, he had managed to cajole and bribe his way into Binh Khoi, and as best I could determine, he was sincere in his attachment to the place.

The pictures taken at Binh Khoi rankled me the most – I hated to see him laughing and smiling. I would stare at those photographs, my emotions overheating, until it seemed I could focus rage into a beam and destroy any object upon which I turned my gaze. My eventual decision, I thought, would be easy to make. Anger and history, the history of his violence and greed, were making it for me, building a spiritual momentum impossible to stop. When the time came, I would avenge my mother and claim my inheritance. I knew exactly how to go about the task. My father feared no one less powerful than himself – if such a person moved against him, they would be the target of terrible reprisals – and he recognized the futility of trying to fend off an assassination attempt by anyone more powerful; thus his security was good, yet not impenetrable. The uniqueness of my situation lay in the fact that if I were able to kill him, I would as a consequence become more powerful than he or any of his connections; and so, without the least hesitancy, I began to plan his murder both in Binh Khoi and Saigon – I had schematics detailing the security systems of both homes. But in the midst of crafting the means of his death, I lost track of events that were in the process of altering the conditions attendant upon my decision.

One night long after my seventeenth birthday, I was working at the computer in the trailer, when Vang entered and lowered himself carefully in the chair opposite me, first shooing away the marmalade cat who had been sleeping there. He wore a threadbare gray cardigan and the striped trousers from an old suit, and carried a thin folder bound in plastic. I was preoccupied with tracking my father's movements via his banking records and I acknowledged Vang's presence with a nod. He sat without speaking a while and finally said, 'Forgive my intrusion, but would you be so kind as to allow me a minute of your time.'

I realized he was angry, but my own anger took precedence. It was not just that I was furious with my father; I had grown weary of Vang's distant manner, his goading, his incessant demands for respect in face of his lack of respect for me. 'What do you want?' I asked without looking away from the screen.

He tossed the folder onto the desk. 'Your task has become more problematic.'

The folder contained the personnel file of an attractive woman named Phuong Anh Nguyen, whom my father had hired as a bodyguard. Much of the data concerned her considerable expertise with weapons and her reaction times, which were remarkable – it was apparent that she had been bred for her occupation, genetically enhanced. According to the file her senses were so acute, she could detect shifts in the heat patterns of the brain, subtle changes in blood pressure, heart rate, pupillary dilation, speech, all the telltales that would betray the presence of a potential assassin. The information concerning her personal life was skimpy. Though Vietnamese, she had been born in China, and had spent her life until the age of sixteen behind the walls of a private security agency, where she had received her training. Serving a variety of employers, she had killed sixteen men and women over the next five years. Several months before, she had bought out her contract from the security agency and signed on long-term with my father. Like him, she was bisexual, and, also like him, the majority of her partners were women.

I glanced up from the file to find Vang studying me with an expectant air. 'Well,' he said, 'what do you think?'

'She's not bad-looking,' I said.

He folded his arms, made a disgusted noise.

'All right.' I turned the pages of the file. 'My father's upgrading of his security implies that he's looking ahead to bigger things. Preparing for the day when he can claim my trust.'

'Is that all you're able to extract from the document?'

From outside came voices, laughter. They passed, faded. Mei, I thought, and Tranh. It was a cool night, the air heavy with the scent of rain. The door was cracked open, and I could see darkness and thin streamers of fog. 'What else is there?' I asked.

'Use your mind, won't you?' Vang let his head tip forward and closed his eyes – a formal notice of his exasperation. 'Phuong would require a vast sum in order to pay off her contract. Several million, at least. Her wage is a good one, but even if she lived in poverty, which she does not, it would take her a decade or more to save sufficient funds. Where might she obtain such a sum?'

I had no idea.

'From her new employer, of course,' Vang said.

'My father doesn't have that kind of money lying around.'

'It seems that he does. Only a very wealthy man could afford such a servant as Phuong Anh Nguyen.'

I took mental stock of my father's finances, but was unable to recall an excess of cash.

'It's safe to say the money did not come from your father's business enterprises,' said Vang. 'We have good information on them. So we may assume he either stole it or coerced someone else into stealing it.' The cat jumped up into his lap, began kneading his abdomen. 'Rather than taxing your brain further,' he went on, 'I'll tell you what I believe has happened. He's tapped into your trust. It's much too large to be managed by one individual, and it's quite possible he's succeeded in corrupting one of the officers in charge.'

'You can't be sure of that.'

'No, but I intend to contact my government friends and suggest an investigation into the trust. If your father has done what I suspect, it will prevent him from doing more damage.' The cat had settled on his lap; he stroked its head. 'But the trust is not the problem. Even if your father has stolen from it, he can't have taken much more than was necessary to secure this woman's services. Otherwise the man who gave me this' – he gestured at the folder – 'would have detected evidence of other expenditures. There'll be more than enough left to make you a powerful man. Phuong Anh Nguyen is the problem. You'll have to kill her first.'

The loopy cry of a night bird cut the silence. Someone with a flashlight was crossing the pasture where the trailer rested, the beam of light slicing through layers of fog, sweeping over shrubs and patches of grass. I suggested that one woman shouldn't pose that much of a problem, no matter how efficient she was at violence.

Vang closed his eyes again. 'You have not witnessed this kind of professional in action. They're fearless, totally dedicated to their work. They develop a sixth sense concerning their clients; they bond with them. You'll need to be circumspect in dealing with her.'

'Perhaps she's beyond my capacity to deal with,' I said after a pause. 'Perhaps I'm simply too thickheaded. I should probably let it all go and devote myself to Green Star.'

'Do as you see fit.'

Vang's expression did not shift from its stoic cast, but it appeared to harden, and I could tell that he was startled. I instructed the computer to sleep and leaned back, bracing one foot against the side of the desk. 'There's no need for pretense,' I said. 'I know you want me to kill him. I just don't understand why.'

I waited for him to respond, and when he did not, I said, 'You were my mother's friend – that's reason enough to wish him dead, I suppose. But I've never felt that you were my friend. You've given me … everything. Life. A place to live. A purpose. Yet whenever I try to thank you, you dismiss it out of hand. I used to think this was because you were shy, because you were embarrassed by displays of emotion. Now, I'm not sure. Sometimes it seems you find my gratitude repugnant … or embarrassing in a way that has nothing to do with shyness. It's as if' – I struggled to collect my thoughts – 'as if you have some reason for hating my father that you haven't told me. One you're ashamed to admit. Or maybe it's something else, some piece of information you have that gives you a different perspective on the situation.'

Being honest with him was both exhilarating and frightening – I felt as though I were violating a taboo – and after this speech I was left breathless and disoriented, unsure of everything I'd said, though I'd been thoroughly convinced of its truth when I said it. 'I'm sorry,' I told him. 'I've no right to doubt you.'

He started to make a gesture of dismissal such as was his habit when uncomfortable with a conversation, but caught himself and petted the cat instead. 'Despite the differences in our stations, I was very close to your mother,' he said. 'And to your grandfather. No longer having a family of my own, I made them into a surrogate. When they died, one after the other … you see, your grandfather's presence, his wealth, protected your mother, and once he was gone, your father had no qualms against misusing her.' He blew out a breath, like a horse, through his lips. 'When they died, I lost my heart. I'd lost so much already. I was unable to bear the sorrow I felt. I retreated from the world, I rejected my emotions. In effect, I shut myself down.' He put a hand to his forehead, covering his eyes. I could see he was upset, and I felt badly that I had caused these old griefs to wound him again. 'I know you have suffered as a result,' he went on. 'You've grown up without the affection of a parent, and that is a cruel condition. I wish I could change that. I wish I could change the way I am, but the idea of risking myself, of having everything ripped away from me a third time ... it's unbearable.' His hand began to tremble; he clenched it into a fist, pressed it against the bridge of his nose. 'It is I who should apologize to you. Please, forgive me.'

I assured him that he need not ask for forgiveness, I honored and respected him. I had the urge to tell him I loved him, and at that moment I did – I believed now that in loving my family, in carrying out my mother's wishes, he had established his love for me. Hoping to distract him from his grief, I asked him to tell me about my grandfather, a man concerning whom I knew next to nothing, only that he had been remarkably successful in business.

Vang seemed startled by the question, but after taking a second to compose himself, he said, 'I'm not sure you would have approved of him. He was a strong man, and strong men often sacrifice much that ordinary men hold dear in order to achieve their ends. But he loved your mother, and he loved you.'

This was not the sort of detail I'd been seeking, but it was plain that Vang was still gripped by emotion, and I decided it would be best to leave him alone. As I passed behind him, I laid a hand on his shoulder. He twitched, as if burned by the touch, and I thought he might respond by covering my hand with his own. But he only nodded and made a humming noise deep in his throat. I stood there for a few beats, wishing I could think of something else to say; then I bid him good night and went off into darkness to look for Tan.

One morning about a month after this conversation, in the little seaside town of Vung Tao, Dat quit the circus following an argument with Vang, and I was forced that same evening to assume the role of James Bond Cochise. The prospect of performing the entire act in public – I had previously made token appearances along with Dat – gave rise to some anxiety, but I was confident in my skill. Tan took in Dat's tuxedo jacket a bit, so it would hang nicely, and helped me paint my face with Native American designs, and when Vang announced me, standing at the center of our single ring and extolling my legendary virtues into a microphone, I strode into the rich yellow glow of the tent, the warmth smelling of sawdust and cowshit (a small herd had been foraging on the spot before we arrived), with my arms overhead, flourishing the belt that held my hatchets and knives, and enjoying the applause. All seven rows of the bleachers were full, the audience consisting of resort workers, fishermen and their families, with a smattering of tourists, mainly backpackers, but also a group of immensely fat Russian women who had been transported from a hotel farther along the beach in cyclos pedaled by diminutive Vietnamese men. They were in a good mood, thanks to a comic skit in which Tan played a farm girl and Tranh a village buffoon hopelessly in love with her, his lust manifested by a telescoping rod that could spring outward to a length of fourteen inches and was belted to his hips beneath a pair of baggy trousers.

Mei, dressed in a red sequined costume that pushed up her breasts and squeezed the tops of her chubby thighs like sausage ends, assumed a spread-eagled position in front of the board, and the crowd fell silent. Sitting in a wooden chair at ring center, Vang switched on the music, the theme from a venerable James Bond film. I displayed a knife to the bleachers, took my mark, and sent the blade hurtling toward Mei, planting it solidly in the wood an inch above her head. The first four or five throws were perfect, outlining Mei's head and shoulders. The crowd oohed and ahhed each time the blade sank into the board. Supremely confident now, I flung the knives as I whirled and ducked, pretending to dodge the gunshots embedded in the theme music, throwing from a crouch, on my stomach, leaping – but then I made the slightest of missteps, and the knife I hurled flashed so close to Mei, it nicked the fleshy portion of her upper arm. She shrieked and staggered away from the board, holding the injury. She remained stock-still for an instant, fixing me with a look of anguish, then bolted for the entrance. The crowd was stunned. Vang jumped up, the microphone dangling from his hand. For a second or two, I was rooted to the spot, not certain what to do. The bombastic music isolated me as surely as if it were a fence, and when Tranh shut it off, the fence collapsed, and I felt the pressure of a thousand eyes upon me. Unable to withstand it, I followed Mei out into the night.

The main tent had been erected atop a dune overlooking a bay and a stretch of sandy beach. It was a warm, windy night, and as I emerged from the tent the tall grasses cresting the dune were blown flat by a gust. From behind me, Vang's amplified voice sounded above the rush of the wind and the heavier beat of the surf, urging the audience to stay seated, the show would continue momentarily. The moon was almost full, but it hung behind the clouds, edging an alp of cumulus with silver, and I couldn't find Mei at first. Then the moon sailed clear, paving a glittering avenue across the black water, touching the plumes of combers with phosphorous, brightening the sand, and I spotted Mei – recognizable by her red costume – and two other figures on the beach some thirty feet below; they appeared to be ministering to her.

I started down the face of the dune, slipped in the loose sand and fell. As I scrambled to my feet, I saw Tan struggling up the slope toward me. She caught at the lapels of my tuxedo for balance, nearly causing me to fall again, and we swayed together, holding each other upright. She wore a nylon jacket over her costume, which was like Mei's in every respect but one – it was a shade of peacock blue spangled with silver stars. Her shining hair was gathered at the nape of her neck, crystal earrings sparkled in the lobes of her ears, her dark eyes brimmed with light. She looked made of light, an illusion that would fade once the clouds regrouped about the moon. But the thing that most affected me was not her beauty. Moment to moment, that was something of which I was always aware, how she flowed between states of beauty, shifting from schoolgirl to seductress to serious young woman, and now this starry incarnation materialized before me, the Devi of a world that existed only for this precise second ... No, it was her calmness that affected me most. It poured over me, coursing around and through me, and even before she spoke, not mentioning what had happened to Mei, as if it were not a potentially fatal accident, a confidence-destroyer that would cause me to falter whenever I picked up a knife – even before that I was convinced by her unruffled manner that everything was as usual, there had been a slight disruption of routine, and now we should go back into the tent because Vang was running out of jokes to tell.

'Mei ...' I said as we clambered over the crest of the dune, and Tan said, 'It's not even a scratch.' She took my arm and guided me toward the entrance, walking briskly yet unhurriedly.

I felt I'd been hypnotized – not by a sonorous voice or the pendulum swing of a shiny object, but by a heightened awareness of the ordinary, the steady pulse of time, all the background rhythms of the universe. I was filled with an immaculate calm, distant from the crowd and the booming music. It seemed that I wasn't throwing the knives so much as I was fitting them into slots and letting the turning of the earth whisk them away to thud and quiver in the board, creating a figure of steel slightly larger than the figure of soft brown flesh and peacock blue silk it contained. Dat had never received such applause – I think the crowd believed Mei's injury had been a trick designed to heighten suspense, and they showed their enthusiasm by standing as Tan and I took our bows and walked together through the entranceway. Once outside, she pressed herself against me, kissed my cheek, and said she would see me later. Then she went off toward the rear of the tent to change for the finale.

Under normal circumstances, I would have gone to help with the major, but on this occasion, feeling disconnected and now, bereft of Tan's soothing influence, upset at having injured Mei, I wandered along the top of the dune until I came to a gully choked with grasses that afforded protection from the wind, which was still gusting hard, filling the air with grit. I sat down amidst the grass and looked off along the curve of the beach. About fifteen meters to the north, the sand gave out into a narrow shingle and the land planed upward into low hills thick with vegetation. Half-hidden by the foliage was a row of small houses with sloping tiled roofs and open porches; they stood close to the sea, and chutes of yellow light spilled from their windows to illuminate the wavelets beneath. The moon was high, no longer silvery, resembling instead a piece of bloated bone china mottled with dark splotches, and appearing to lie directly beneath it among a hammock of coconut palms, was a pink stucco castle that guarded the point of the bay: the hotel where the tourists who had attended our performances were staying. I could make out antlike shapes scurrying back and forth on the brightly lit crescent of sand in front of it, and I heard a faint music shredded by the wind. The water beyond the break was black as opium.

My thoughts turned not to the accident with Mei, but to how I had performed with Tan. The act had passed quickly, a flurry of knives and light, yet now I recalled details: the coolness of the metal between my fingers; Vang watching anxiously off to the side; a fiery glint on a hatchet blade tumbling toward a spot between Tan's legs. My most significant memory, however, was of her eyes. How they had seemed to beam instructions, orchestrating my movements, so forceful that I'd imagined she was capable of deflecting a blade if my aim proved errant. Given my emotional investment in her, my absolute faith – though we'd never discussed it – in our future together, it was easy to believe she had that kind of power over me. Easy to believe, and somewhat troublesome, for it struck me that we were not equals, we couldn't be as long as she controlled every facet of the relationship. And having concluded this, as if the conclusion were the end of all possible logics concerning the subject, my mind slowed and became mired in despondency.

I'm not certain how long I had been sitting when Tan came walking down the beach, brushing windblown hair from her eyes. She had on a man's short-sleeved shirt and a pair of loose-fitting shorts, and was carrying a blanket. I was hidden from her by the grass, and I was at such a remove from things, not comfortable with but accepting of my solitude, I was half-inclined to let her pass; but then she stopped and called my name, and I, by reflex, responded. She spotted me and picked up her pace. When she reached my side she said without a hint of reproval, merely as if stating a fact, 'You went so far. I wasn't sure I'd find you.' She spread the blanket on the sand and encouraged me to join her on it. I felt guilty at having had clinical thoughts about her and our relationship – to put this sort of practical construction on what I tended to view as a magical union, a thing of fate and dharma, seemed unworthy, and as a consequence I was at a loss for words. The wind began to blow in a long unbroken stream off the water, and she shivered. I asked if she would like to put on my tuxedo jacket. She said, 'No.' The line of her mouth tightened, and with a sudden movement, she looked away from me, half-turning her upper body. I thought I must have done something to annoy her, and this so unnerved me, I didn't immediately notice that she was unbuttoning her shirt. She shrugged out of it, held it balled against her chest for a moment, then set it aside; she glanced at me over her shoulder, engaging my eyes. I could tell her usual calm was returning – I could almost see her filling with it – and I realized then that this calmness of hers was not hers alone, it was ours, a byproduct of our trust in one another, and what had happened in the main tent had not been a case of her controlling me, saving me from panic, but had been the two of us channeling each other's strength, converting nervousness and fear to certainty and precision. Just as we were doing now.

I kissed her mouth, her small breasts, exulting in their salty aftertaste of brine and dried sweat. Then I drew her down onto the blanket, and what followed, despite clumsiness and flashes of insecurity, was somehow both fierce and chaste, the natural culmination of two years of longing, of unspoken treaties and accommodations. Afterward, pressed together, wrapped in the silk and warmth of spent splendor, whispering the old yet never less than astonishing secrets and promises, saying things that had long gone unsaid, I remember thinking that I would do anything for her. This was not an abstract thought, not simply the atavistic reaction of a man new to a feeling of mastery, though I can't deny that was in me – the sexual and the violent break from the same spring – but was an understanding founded on a considered appreciation of the trials I might have to overcome and the blood I might have to shed in order to keep her safe in a world where wife-murder was a crime for profit and patricide an act of self-defense. It's strange to recall with what a profound sense of reverence I accepted the idea that I was now willing to engage in every sort of human behavior, ranging from the self-sacrificial to the self-gratifying to the perpetration of acts so abhorrent that, once committed, they would harrow me until the end of my days.

At dawn, the clouds closed in, the wind died, and the sea lay flat. Now and again, a weak sun penetrated the overcast, causing the water to glisten like an expanse of freshly applied gray paint. We climbed to the top of the dune and sat with our arms around each other, not wanting to return to the circus, to break the elastic of the long moment stretching backward into night. The unstirring grass, the energyless water and dead sky, made it appear that time itself had been becalmed. The beach in front of the pink hotel was littered with debris, deserted. You might have thought that our love-making had succeeded in emptying the world. But soon we caught sight of Tranh and Mei walking toward us across the dune, Kim and Kai skipping along behind. All were dressed in shorts and shirts, and Tranh carried a net shopping bag that – I saw as he lurched up, stumbling in the sand – contained mineral water and sandwiches.

'What have you kids been up to,' he asked, displaying an exaggerated degree of concern.

Mei punched him on the arm, and, after glancing back and forth between us, as if he suddenly understood the situation, Tranh put on a shocked face and covered his mouth with a hand. Giggling, Kai and Kim went scampering down onto the beach. Mei tugged at Tranh's shirt, but he ignored her and sank onto his knees beside me. 'I bet you're hungry,' he said, and his round face was split by a gap-toothed grin. He thrust a sandwich wrapped in a paper napkin at me. 'Better eat! You're probably going to need your strength.'

With an apologetic look in Tan's direction, Mei kneeled beside him; she unwrapped sandwiches and opened two bottles of water. She caught my eye, frowned, pointed to her arm, and shook her forefinger as she might have done with a mischievous child. 'Next time don't dance around so much,' she said, and pretended to sprinkle something on one of the sandwiches. 'Or else one night I'll put special herbs in your dinner.' Tranh kept peering at Tan, then at me, grinning, nodding, and finally, with a laugh, Tan pushed him onto his back. Down by the water Kai and Kim were tossing pebbles into the sea with girlish ineptitude. Mei called to them and they came running, their braids bouncing; they threw themselves belly first onto the sand, squirmed up to sitting positions, and began gobbling sandwiches.

'Don't eat so fast!' Mei cautioned. 'You'll get sick.'

Kim, the younger of the sisters, squinched her face at Mei and shoved half the sandwich into her mouth. Tranh contorted his features so his lips nearly touched his nose, and Kim laughed so hard she sprayed bits of bread and fried fish. Tan told her that this was not ladylike. Both girls sat up straight, nibbled their sandwiches – they took it to heart whenever Tan spoke to them about being ladies.

'Didn't you bring anything beside fish?' I asked, inspecting the filling of my sandwich.

'I guess we should have brought oysters,' said Tranh. 'Maybe some rhinoceros horn, some ...'

'That stuff's for old guys like you,' I told him. 'Me, I just need peanut butter.'

After we had done eating, Tranh lay back with his head in Mei's lap and told a story about a talking lizard that had convinced a farmer it was the Buddha. Kim and Kai cuddled together, sleepy from their feast. Tan leaned into the notch of my shoulder, and I put my arm around her. It came to me then, not suddenly, but gradually, as if I were being immersed in the knowledge like a man lowering his body into a warm bath, that for the first time in my life – all the life I could remember – I was at home. These people were my family, and the sense of dislocation that had burdened me all those years had evaporated. I closed my eyes and buried my face in Tan's hair, trying to hold onto the feeling, to seal it inside my head so I would never forget it.

Two men in T-shirts and bathing suits came walking along the water's edge in our direction. When they reached the dune they climbed up to where we were sitting. Both were not much older than I, and judging by their fleshiness and soft features, I presumed them to be Americans, a judgment confirmed when the taller of the two, a fellow with a heavy jaw and hundreds of white beads threaded on the strings of his long black hair, lending him a savage appearance, said, 'You guys are with that tent show, right?'

Mei, who did not care for Americans, stared meanly at him, but Tranh, who habitually viewed them as potential sources of income, told him that we were, indeed, performers with the circus. Kai and Kim whispered and giggled, and Tranh asked the American what his friend – skinnier, beadless, dull-eyed and open-mouthed, with a complicated headset covering his scalp – was studying.

'Parasailing. We're going parasailing ... if there's ever any wind and the program doesn't screw up. I woulda left him at the house, but the program's fucked. Didn't want his ass convulsing.' He extracted a sectioned strip of plastic from his shirt pocket; each square of plastic held a gelatin capsule shaped like a cut gem and filled with blue fluid. 'Wanna brighten your day?' He dangled the strip as if tempting us with a treat. When no one accepted his offer, he shrugged, returned the strip to his pocket; he glanced down at me. 'Hey, that shit with the knives ... that was part of the fucking plan! Especially when you went benihana on Little Plum Blossom.' He jerked his thumb at Mei and then stood nodding, gazing at the sea, as if receiving a transmission from that quarter. 'Okay,' he said. 'Okay. It could be the drugs, but the trusty inner voice is telling me my foreign ways seem ludicrous ... perhaps even offensive. It well may be that I am somewhat ludicrous. And I'm pretty torched, so I have to assume I've been offensive.'

Tranh made to deny this, Mei grunted, Kim and Kai looked puzzled, and Tan asked the American if he was on vacation.

'Thank you,' he said to Tan. 'Beautiful lady. I am always grateful for the gift of courtesy. No, my friend and I – and two others – are playing at the hotel. We're musicians.' He took out his wallet, which had been hinged over the waist of his trunks, and removed from it a thin gold square the size of a postage stamp; he handed it to Tan. 'Have you seen these? They're new ... souvenir things, like. They just play once, but it'll give you a taste. Press your finger on it until it you hear the sound. Then don't touch it again – they get extremely hot.'

Tan started to do as he instructed but he said, 'No, wait till we're gone. I want to imagine you enjoyed hearing it. If you do, come on down to the hotel after you're finished tonight. You'll be my guests.'

'Is it one of your songs?' I asked, curious about him now that he had turned out to be more complicated than he first appeared.

He said, yes, it was an original composition.

'What's it called,' Tranh asked.

'We haven't named it yet,' said the American; then, after a pause: 'What's the name of your circus?'

Almost as one we said, 'Radiant Green Star.'

'Perfect,' said the American.

Once the two men were out of earshot, Tan pressed her fingertip to the gold square, and soon a throbbing music issued forth, simply structured yet intricately layered by synthesizers, horns, guitars, densely figured by theme and subtle counter-theme, both insinuating and urgent. Kai and Kim stood and danced with one another. Tranh bobbed his head, tapped his foot, and even Mei was charmed, swaying, her eyes closed. Tan kissed me, and we watched a thin white smoke trickle upward from the square, which itself began to shrink, and I thought how amazing it was that things were often not what they seemed, and what a strange confluence of possibilities it had taken to bring all the troupe together – and the six of us were the entire troupe, for Vang was never really part of us even when he was there, and though the major was rarely with us, he was always there, a shadow in the corners of our minds ... How magical and ineluctable a thing it was for us all to be together at the precise place and time when a man – a rather unprepossessing man at that – walked up from a deserted beach and presented us with a golden square imprinted with a song that he named for our circus, a song that so accurately evoked the mixture of the commonplace and the exotic that characterized life in Radiant Green Star, music that was like smoke, rising up for a few perfect moments, and then vanishing with the wind.

Had Vang asked me at any point during the months that followed to tell him about love, I might have spoken for hours, answering him not with definitions, principles, or homilies, but specific instances, moments, and anecdotes. I was happy. Despite the gloomy nature of my soul, I could think of no word that better described how I felt. Though I continued to study my father, to follow his comings and goings, his business maneuvers and social interactions, I now believed that I would never seek to confront him, never try to claim my inheritance. I had all I needed to live, and I only wanted to keep those I loved safe and free from worry.

Tan and I did not bother to hide our relationship, and I expected Vang to rail at me for my transgression. I half-expected him to drive me away from the circus – indeed, I prepared for that eventuality. But he never said a word. I did notice a certain cooling of the atmosphere. He snapped at me more often and on occasion refused to speak; yet that was the extent of his anger. I didn't know how to take this. Either, I thought, he had overstated his concern for Tan or else he had simply accepted the inevitable. That explanation didn't satisfy me, however. I suspected that he might have something more important on his mind, something so weighty that my involvement with his niece seemed a triviality by comparison, and one day, some seven months after Tan and I became lovers, my suspicions were proved correct.

I went to the trailer at midafternoon, thinking Vang would be in town. We were camped at the edge of a hardwood forest on a cleared acre of red dirt near Buon Ma Thuot in the Central Highlands, not far from the Cambodian border. Vang usually spent the day before a performance putting up posters, and I had intended to work on the computer; but when I entered, I saw him standing by his desk, folding a shirt, a suitcase open on the chair beside him. I asked what he was doing and he handed me a thick envelope; inside were the licenses and deeds of ownership relating to the circus and its property. 'I've signed everything over,' he said. 'If you have any problems, contact my lawyer.'

'I don't understand,' I said, dumfounded. 'You're leaving?'

He bent to the suitcase and laid the folded shirt inside it. 'You can move into the trailer tonight. You and Tan. She'll be able to put it in order. I suppose you've noticed that she's almost morbidly neat.' He straightened, pressed his hand against his lower back as if stricken by a pain. 'The accounts, the bookings for next year … it's all in the computer. Everything else …' He gestured at the cabinets on the walls. 'You remember where things are.'

I couldn't get a grasp on the situation, overwhelmed by the thought that I was now responsible for Green Star, by the fact that the man who for years had been the only consistent presence in my life was about to walk out the door forever. 'Why are you leaving?'

He turned to me, frowning. 'If you must know, I'm ill.'

'But why would you want to leave. We'll just …'

'I'm not going to recover,' he said flatly.

I peered at him, trying to detect the signs of his mortality, but he looked no thinner, no grayer, than he had for some time. I felt the stirrings of a reaction that I knew he would not want to see, and I tamped down my emotions. 'We can care for you here,' I said.

He began to fold another shirt. 'I plan to join my sister and her husband in what they insist upon calling' – he clicked his tongue against his teeth – ' "Heaven." '

I recalled the talks I'd had with Tan in which she had decried the process of uploading the intelligence, the personality. If the old man was dying, there was no real risk involved. Still, the concept of such a mechanical transmogrification did not sit well with me.

'Have you nothing to say on the subject?' he asked. 'Tan was quite voluble.'

'You've told her, then?'

'Of course.' He inspected the tail of the shirt he'd been folding, and finding a hole, cast it aside. 'We've said our goodbyes.'

He continued to putter about, and as I watched him shuffling among the stacks of magazines and newspapers, kicking file boxes and books aside, dust rising wherever he set his hand, a tightness in my chest began to loosen, to work its way up into my throat. I went to the door and stood looking out, seeing nothing, letting the strong sunlight harden the glaze of my feelings. When I turned back, he was standing close to me, suitcase in hand. He held out a folded piece of paper and said, 'This is the code by which you can contact me once I've been …' He laughed dryly. 'Processed, I imagine, would be the appropriate verb. At any rate, I hope you will let me know what you decide concerning your father.'

It was in my mind to tell him that I had no intention of contending with my father, but I thought that this would disappoint him, and I merely said that I would do as he asked. We stood facing one another, the air thick with unspoken feelings, with vibrations that communicated an entire history comprised of such mute, awkward moments. 'If I'm to have a last walk in the sun,' he said at length, 'you'll have to let me pass.'

That at the end of his days he viewed me only as a minor impediment – it angered me. But I reminded myself that this was all the sentiment of which he was capable. Without asking permission, I embraced him. He patted me lightly on the back and said, 'I know you'll take care of things.' And with that, he pushed past me and walked off in the direction of the town, vanishing behind one of the parked trucks.

I went into the rear of the trailer, into the partitioned cubicle where Vang slept, and sat down on his bunk. His pillowcase bore a silk-screened image of a beautiful Vietnamese woman and the words HONEY LADY KEEP YOU COMFORT EVERY NIGHT. In the cabinet beside his bed were a broken clock, a small plaster bust of Ho Chi Minh, a few books, several pieces of hard candy, and a plastic key chain in the shape of a butterfly. The meagerness of the life these items described caught at my emotions, and I thought I might weep, but it was as if by assuming Vang's position as the owner of Green Star, I had undergone a corresponding reduction in my natural responses, and I remained dry-eyed. I felt strangely aloof from myself, connected to the life of my mind and body by a tube along which impressions of the world around me were now and then transmitted. Looking back on my years with Vang, I could make no sense of them. He had nurtured and educated me, yet the sum of all that effort – not given cohesion by the glue of affection – came to scraps of memories no more illustrative of a comprehensible whole than were the memories of my mother. They had substance, yet no flavor … none, that is, except for a dusty gray aftertaste that I associated with disappointment and loss.

I didn't feel like talking to anyone, and for want of anything else to do, I went to the desk and started inspecting the accounts, working through dusk and into the night. When I had satisfied myself that all was in order, I turned to the bookings. Nothing out of the ordinary. The usual villages, the occasional festival. But when I accessed the bookings for the month of March, I saw that during the week of the 17th through the 23rd – the latter date just ten days from my birthday – we were scheduled to perform in Binh Khoi.

I thought this must be a mistake – Vang had probably been thinking of Binh Khoi and my father while recording a new booking and had inadvertently put down the wrong name. But when I called up the contract, I found that no mistake had been made. We were to be paid a great deal of money, sufficient to guarantee a profitable year, but I doubted that Vang's actions had been motivated by our financial needs. He must, I thought, have seen the way things were going with Tan and me, and he must have realized that I would never risk her in order to avenge a crime committed nearly two decades before – thus, he had decided to force a confrontation between me and my father. I was furious, and my first impulse was to break the contract; but after I had calmed down, I realized that doing so would put us all at risk – the citizens of Binh Khoi were not known for their generosity or flexibility, and if I were to renege on Vang's agreement, they would surely pursue the matter in the courts. I would have no chance of winning a judgment. The only thing to do was to play the festival and steel myself to ignore the presence of my father. Perhaps he would be elsewhere, or, even if he was in residence, perhaps he would not attend our little show. Whatever the circumstances, I swore I would not be caught in this trap, and when my eighteenth birthday arrived I would go to the nearest Sony office and take great pleasure in telling Vang – whatever was left of him – that his scheme had failed.

I was still sitting there, trying to comprehend whether or not by contracting the engagement, Vang hoped to provide me with a basis for an informed decision, or if his interests were purely self-serving, when Tan stepped into the trailer. She had on a sleeveless plaid smock, the garment she wore whenever she was cleaning, and it was evident that she'd been crying – the skin beneath her eyes was puffy and red. But she had regained her composure, and she listened patiently, perched on the edge of the desk, while I told her all I'd been thinking about Vang and what he had done to us.

'Maybe it's for the best,' she said after I had run down. 'This way you'll be sure you've done what you had to do.'

I was startled by her reaction. 'Are you saying that you think I should kill my father ... that I should even entertain the possibility?'

She shrugged. 'That's for you to decide.'

'I've decided already,' I said.

'Then there's not a problem.'

The studied neutrality of her attitude puzzled me. 'You don't think I'll stand by my decision, do you?'

She put a hand to her brow, hiding her face – a gesture that reminded me of Vang. 'I don't think you have decided, and I don't think you should ... not until you see your father.' She pinched a fold of skin above the bridge of her nose, then looked up at me. 'Let's not talk about this now.'

We sat silently for half a minute or thereabouts, each following the path of our own thoughts; then she wrinkled up her nose and said, 'It smells bad in here. Do you want to get some air?'

We climbed onto the roof of the trailer and sat gazing at the shadowy line of the forest to the west, the main tent bulking up above it, and a sky so thick with stars that the familiar constellations were assimilated into new and busier cosmic designs: a Buddha face with a diamond on its brow, a tiger's head, a palm tree – constructions of sparkling pinlights against a midnight blue canvas stretched from horizon to horizon. The wind brought the scent of sweet rot and the less pervasive odor of someone's cooking. Somebody switched on a radio in the main tent; a Chinese orchestra whined and jangled. I felt I was sixteen again, that Tan and I had just met, and I thought perhaps we had chosen to occupy this place where we spent so many hours before we were lovers, because here we could banish the daunting pressures of the present, the threat of the future, and be children again. But although those days were scarcely two years removed, we had forever shattered the comforting illusions and frustrating limitations of childhood. I lay back on the aluminum roof which still held a faint warmth of the day, and Tan hitched up her smock about her waist and mounted me, bracing her hands on my chest as I slipped inside her. Framed by the crowded stars, features made mysterious by the cowl of her hair, she seemed as distant and unreal as the imagined creatures of my zodiac; but this illusion, too, was shattered as she began to rock her hips with an accomplished passion and lifted her face to the sky, transfigured by a look of exalted, almost agonized yearning, like one of those Renaissance angels marooned on a scrap of painted cloud who has just witnessed something amazing pass overhead, a miracle of glowing promise too perfect to hold in the mind. She shook her head wildly when she came, her hair flying all to one side so that it resembled in shape the pennant flying on the main tent, a dark signal of release, and then collapsed against my chest. I held onto her hips, continuing to thrust until the knot of heat in my groin shuddered out of me, leaving a residue of black peace into which the last shreds of my thought were subsumed.

The sweat dried on our skin, and still we lay there, both – I believed – aware that once we went down from the roof, the world would close around us, restore us to its troubled spin. Someone changed stations on the radio, bringing in a Cambodian program – a cooler, wispier music played. A cough sounded close by the trailer, and I raised myself to an elbow, wanting to see who it was. The major was making his way with painful slowness across the cleared ground, leaning on his staff. In the starlight, his grotesque shape was lent a certain anonymity – he might have been a figure in a fantasy game, an old down-at-heels magician shrouded in a heavy, ragged cloak, or a beggar on a quest. He shuffled a few steps more, and then, shaking with effort, sank to his knees. For several seconds he remained motionless, then he scooped a handful of the red dirt and held it up to his face. And I recalled that Buon Ma Thuot was near the location of his fictive – or if not fictive, ill-remembered – firebase. Firebase Ruby. Built upon the red dirt of a defoliated plantation.

Tan sat up beside me and whispered, 'What's he doing?'

I put a finger to my lips, urging her to silence; I was convinced that the major would not expose himself to the terror of the open sky unless moved by some equally terrifying inner force, and I hoped he might do something that would illuminate the underpinnings of his mystery.

He let the dirt sift through his fingers and struggled to stand. Failed and sagged onto his haunches. His head fell back, and he held a spread-fingered hand up to it as if trying to shield himself from the starlight. His quavery voice ran out of him like a shredded battle flag. 'Turn back!' he said. 'Oh, God! God! Turn back!'

During the next four months, I had little opportunity to brood over the prospect of meeting my father. Dealing with the minutiae of Green Star's daily operation took most of my energy and hours, and whenever I had a few minutes respite, Tan was there to fill them. So it was that by the time we arrived in Binh Khoi, I had made scarcely any progress in adjusting to the possibility that I might soon come face-to-face with the man who had killed my mother.

In one aspect, Binh Khoi was the perfect venue for us, since the town affected the same conceit as the circus, being designed to resemble a fragment of another time. It was situated near the Pass of the Ocean Clouds in the Truong Son Mountains some forty kilometers north of Da Nang, and many of the homes there were afforded a view of green hills declining toward the Coastal Plain. On the morning we arrived, those same hills were half-submerged in thick white fog, the plain was totally obscured, and a pale mist had infiltrated the narrow streets, casting an air of ominous enchantment over the place. The oldest of the houses had been built no more than fifty years before, yet they were all similar to nineteenth century houses that still existed in certain sections of Hanoi: two and three stories tall and fashioned of stone, painted dull yellow and gray and various other sober hues, with sharply sloping roofs of dark green tile, and compounds hidden by high walls and shaded by bougainvillea, papaya, and banana trees. Except for streetlights in the main square and pedestrians in bright eccentric clothing, we might have been driving through a hill station during the 1800s; but I knew that hidden behind this antiquated façade were state-of-the-art security systems that could have vaporized us had we not been cleared to enter.

The most unusual thing about Binh Khoi was its silence. I'd never been in a place where people lived in any considerable quantity that was so hushed, devoid of the stew of sounds natural to a human environment. No hens squabbling or dogs yipping, no whining motor scooters or humming cars, no children at play. In only one area was there anything approximating normal activity and noise: the marketplace, which occupied an unpaved street leading off the square. Here men and women in coolie hats hunkered beside baskets of jackfruit, chilies, garlic, custard apples, durians, geckos, and dried fish; meat and caged puppies and monkeys and innumerable other foodstuffs were sold in canvas-roofed stalls; and the shoppers, mostly male couples, haggled with the vendors, occasionally venting their dismay at the prices ... this despite the fact that any one of them could have bought everything in the market without blinking. Though the troupe shared their immersion in a contrived past, I found the depth of their pretense alarming and somewhat perverse. As I maneuvered the truck cautiously through the press, they peered incuriously at me through the windows – faces rendered exotic and nearly unreadable by tattoos and implants and caps of silver wire and winking light that appeared to be woven into their hair – and I thought I could feel their amusement at the shabby counterfeit we offered of their more elegantly realized illusion. I believe I might have hated them for the fashionable play they made of arguing over minuscule sums with the poor vendors, for the triviality of spirit this mockery implied, if I had not already hated them so completely for being my father's friends and colleagues.

At the end of the street, beyond the last building, lay a grassy field bordered by a low whitewashed wall. Strings of light bulbs linked the banana trees and palms that grew close to the wall on three sides, and I noticed several paths leading off into the jungle that were lit in the same fashion. On the fourth side, beyond the wall, the land dropped off into a notch, now choked with fog, and on the far side of the notch, perhaps fifty yards away, a massive hill with a sheer rock face and the ruins of an old temple atop it lifted from the fog, looming above the field – it was such a dramatic sight and so completely free of mist, every palm frond articulated, every vine-enlaced crevice and knob of dark, discolored stone showing clear, that I wondered if it might be a clever projection, another element of Binh Khoi's decor.

We spent the morning and early afternoon setting up, and once I was satisfied that everything was in readiness, I sought out Tan, thinking we might go for a walk; but she was engaged in altering Kai's costume. I wandered into the main tent and busied myself by making sure the sawdust had been spread evenly. Kai was swinging high above on a rope suspended from the metal ring at the top of the tent, and one of our miniature tigers had climbed a second rope and was clinging to it by its furry hands, batting at her playfully whenever she swooped near. Tranh and Mei were playing cards in the bleachers, and Kim was walking hand-in-hand with our talking monkey, chattering away as if the creature could understand her – now and then it would turn its white face to her and squeak in response, saying 'I love you' and 'I'm hungry' and other equally non-responsive phrases. I stood by the entranceway, feeling rather paternal toward my little family gathered under the lights, and I was just considering whether or not I should return to the trailer and see if Tan had finished, when a baritone voice sounded behind me, saying, 'Where can I find Vang Ky?'

My father was standing with hands in pockets a few feet away, wearing black trousers and a gray shirt of some shiny material. He looked softer and heavier than he did in his photographs, and the flying fish tattoo on his cheek was now surrounded by more than half-a-dozen tiny emblems denoting his business connections. With his immense head, his shaved skull gleaming in the hot lights, he himself seemed the emblem of some monumental and soulless concern. At his shoulder, over a foot shorter than he, was a striking Vietnamese woman with long straight hair, dressed in tight black slacks and a matching tunic: Phuong Anh Nguyen. She was staring at me intently.

Stunned, I managed to get out that Vang was no longer with the circus, and my father said, 'How can that be? He's the owner, isn't he?'

Shock was giving way to anger, anger so fulminant I could barely contain it. My hands trembled. If I'd had one of my knives to hand, I would have plunged it without a thought into his chest. I did the best I could to conceal my mood, and told him what had become of Vang; but it seemed that as I catalogued each new detail of his face and body – a frown line, a reddened ear lobe, a crease in his fleshy neck – a vial of some furious chemical was tipped over and added to the mix of my blood.

'Goddamn it!' he said, casting his eyes up to the canvas; he appeared distraught. 'Shit!' He glanced down at me. 'Have you got his access code? It's never the same once they go to Heaven. I'm not sure they really know what's going on. But I guess it's my only option.'

'I doubt he'd approve of my giving the code to a stranger,' I told him.

'We're not strangers,' he said. 'Vang was my father-in-law. We had a falling-out after my wife died. I hoped having the circus here for a week, I'd be able to persuade him to sit down and talk. There's no reason for us to be at odds.'

I suppose the most astonishing thing he said was that Vang was his father-in-law, and thus my grandfather. I didn't know what to make of that; I could think of no reason he might have for lying, yet it raised a number of troubling questions. But his last statement, his implicit denial of responsibility for my mother's death ... it had come so easily to his lips! Hatred flowered in me like a cold star, acting to calm me, allowing me to exert a measure of control over my anger.

Phuong stepped forward and put a hand on my chest; my heart pounded against the pressure of her palm. 'Is anything wrong?' she asked.

'I'm ... surprised,' I said. 'That's all. I didn't realize Vang had a son-in-law.'

Her make-up was severe, her lips painted a dark mauve, her eyes shaded the same color, but in the fineness other features and the long oval shape of her face, she bore a slight resemblance to Tan.

'Why are you angry?' she asked.

My father eased her aside. 'It's all right. I came on pretty strong – he's got every right to be angry. Why don't the two of us ... what's your name, kid?'

'Dat,' I said, though I was tempted to tell him the truth.

'Dat and I will have a talk,' he said to Phuong. 'I'll meet you back at the house.'

We went outside, and Phuong, displaying more than a little reluctance, headed off in the general direction of the trailer. It was going on dusk, and the fog was closing in. The many-colored bulbs strung in the trees close to the wall and lining the paths had been turned on; each bulb was englobed by a fuzzy halo, and altogether they imbued the encroaching jungle with an eerily festive air, as if the spirits lost in the dark green tangles were planning a party. We stood beside the wall, beneath the great hill rising from the shifting fogbank, and my father tried to convince me to hand over the code. When I refused, he offered money, and when I refused his money, he glared at me and said, 'Maybe you don't get it. I really need the code. What's it going to take for you to give it to me?'

'Perhaps it's you who doesn't get it,' I said. 'If Vang wanted you to have the code he would have given it to you. But he gave it to me, and to no one else. I consider that a trust, and I won't break it unless he signifies that I should.'

He looked off into the jungle, ran a hand across his scalp, and made a frustrated noise. I doubted he was experienced at rejection, and though it didn't satisfy my anger, it pleased me to have rejected him. Finally he laughed. 'Either you're a hell of a businessman or an honorable man. Or maybe you're both. That's a scary notion.' He shook his head in what I took for amiable acceptance. 'Why not call Vang? Ask him if he'd mind having a talk with me.'

I didn't understand how this was possible.

'What sort of computer do you own?' he asked.

I told him and he said, 'That won't do it. Tell you what. Come over to my house tonight after your show. You can use my computer to contact him. I'll pay for your time.'

I was suddenly suspicious. He seemed to be offering himself to me, making himself vulnerable, and I did not believe that was in his nature. His desire to contact Vang might be a charade. What if he had discovered my identity and was luring me into a trap?

'I don't know if I can get away,' I said. 'It may have to be in the morning.'

He looked displeased, but said, 'Very well.' He fingered a business card from his pocket, gave it to me. 'My address.' Then he pressed what appeared to be a crystal button into my hand. 'Don't lose it. Carry it with you whenever you come. If you don't, you'll be picked up on the street and taken somewhere quite unpleasant.'

As soon as he was out of sight, I hurried over to the trailer, intending to sort things out with Tan. She was outside, sitting on a folding chair, framed by a spill of hazy yellow light from the door. Her head was down, and her blouse was torn, the top two buttons missing. I asked what was wrong; she shook her head and would not meet my eyes. But when I persisted she said, 'That woman ... the one who works for your father ...'

'Phuong? Did she hurt you?'

She kept her head down, but I could see her chin quivering. 'I was coming to find you, and I ran into her. She started talking to me. I thought she was just being friendly, but then she tried to kiss me. And when I resisted' – she displayed the tear in her blouse – 'she did this.' She gathered herself. 'She wants me to be with her tonight. If I refuse, she says she'll make trouble for us.'

It would have been impossible for me to hate my father more, but this new insult, this threat to Tan, perfected it, added a finishing color, like the last brush stroke applied to a masterpiece. I stood a moment gazing off toward the hill – it seemed I had inside me an analog to that forbidding shape, something equally stony and vast. I led Tan into the trailer, sat her down at the desk, and made her tea; then I repeated all my father had said. 'Is it possible,' I asked, 'that Vang is my grandfather?'

She held the teacup in both hands, blew on the steaming liquid and took a sip. 'I don't know. My family has always been secretive. All my parents told me was that Vang was once a wealthy man with a loving family, and that he had lost everything.'

'If he is my grandfather,' I said, 'then we're cousins.'

She set down the cup and stared dolefully into it as if she saw in its depths an inescapable resolution. 'I don't care. If we were brother and sister, I wouldn't care.'

I pulled her up, put my arms around her, and she pressed herself against me. I felt that I was at the center of an enormously complicated knot, too diminutive to be able to see all its loops and twists. If Vang was my grandfather, why had he treated me with such coldness? Perhaps my mother's death had deadened his heart, perhaps that explained it. But knowing that Tan and I were cousins, wouldn't he have told us the truth when he saw how close we were becoming? Or was he so old-fashioned that the idea of an intimate union between cousins didn't bother him? The most reasonable explanation was that my father had lied. I saw that now, saw it with absolute clarity. It was the only possibility that made sense. And if he had lied, it followed that he knew who I was. And if he knew who I was …

'I have to kill him,' I said. 'Tonight … it has to be tonight.'

I was prepared to justify the decision, to explain why a course of inaction would be a greater risk, to lay out all the potentials of the situation for Tan to analyze, but she pushed me away, just enough so that she could see my face, and said, 'You can't do it alone. That woman's a professional assassin.' She rested her forehead against mine. 'I'll help you.'

'That's ridiculous! If I …'

'Listen to me, Philip! She can read physical signs, she can tell if someone's angry. If they're anxious. Well, she'll expect me to be angry. And anxious. She'll think it's just resentment … nerves. I'll be able to get close to her.'

'And kill her? Will you be able to kill her?'

Tan broke from the embrace and went to stand at the doorway, gazing out at the fog. Her hair had come unbound, spilling down over her shoulders and back, the ribbon that had tied it dangling like a bright blue river winding across a ground of black silk.

'I'll ask Mei to give me something. She has herbs that will induce sleep.' She glanced back at me. 'There are things you can do to insure our safety once your father's dead. We should discuss them now.'

I was amazed by her coolness, how easily she had made the transition from being distraught. 'I can't ask you to do this,' I said.

'You're not asking – I'm volunteering.' I detected a note of sad distraction in her voice. 'You'd do as much for me.'

'Of course. But if it weren't for me, you wouldn't be involved in this.'

'If it weren't for you,' she said, the sadness even more evident in her tone, 'I'd have no involvements at all.'

The first part of the show that evening, the entrance of the troupe to march music, Mei leading the way, wearing a red and white majorette's uniform, twirling – and frequently dropping – a baton, the tigers gamboling at her heels; then two comic skits; then Kai and Kim whirling and spinning aloft in their gold and sequined costumes, tumbling through the air happy as birds; then another skit and Tranh's clownish juggling, pretending to be drunk and making improbable catches as he tumbled, rolled, and staggered about … all this was received by the predominately male audience with a degree of ironic detachment. They laughed at Mei, they whispered and smirked during the skits, they stared dispassionately at Kim and Kai, and they jeered Tranh. It was plain that they had come to belittle us, that doing so validated their sense of superiority. I registered their reactions, but was so absorbed in thinking about what was to happen later, they seemed unreal, unimportant, and it took all my discipline to focus on my own act, a performance punctuated by a knife hurled from behind me that struck home between Tan's legs. There was a burst of enthusiastic cheers, and I turned to see Phuong some thirty feet away, taking a bow in the bleacher – it was she who had thrown the knife. She looked at me and shrugged, with that gesture dismissing my poor skills, and lifted her arms to receive the building applause. I searched the area around her for my father, but he was nowhere to be seen.

The audience remained abuzz, pleased that one of their own had achieved this victory, but when the major entered, led in by Mei and Tranh, they fell silent at the sight of his dark, convulsed figure. Leaning on his staff, he hobbled along the edge of the bleachers, looking into this and that face as if hoping to find a familiar one, and then, moving to the center of the ring, he began to tell the story of Firebase Ruby. I was alarmed at first, but his delivery was eloquent, lyrical, not the plainspoken style in which he had originally couched the tale, and the audience was enthralled. When he came to tell of the letter he had written his wife detailing his hatred of all things Vietnamese, a uneasy muttering arose from the bleachers and rapt expressions turned to scowls; but then he was past that point, and as he described the Viet Cong assault, his listeners settled back and seemed once again riveted by his words.

'In the phosphor light of the hanging flares,' he said, 'I saw the blood-red ground spread out before me. Beyond the head-high hedgerows of coiled steel wire, black-clad men and women coursed from the jungle, myriad and quick as ants, and, inside the wire, emerging from their secret warrens, more sprouted from the earth like the demon yield of some infernal rain. All around me, my men were dying, and even in the midst of fear, I felt myself the object of a great calm observance, as if the tiny necklace-strung images of the Buddha the enemy held in their mouths when they attacked had been empowered to summon their ribbed original, and somewhere up above the flares, an enormous face had been conjured from the dark matter of the sky and was gazing down with serene approval.

'We could not hold the position long – that was clear. But I had no intention of surrendering. Drunk on whiskey and adrenaline, I was consumed by the thought of death, my own and others, and though I was afraid, I acted less out of fear than from the madness of battle and a kind of communion with death, a desire to make death grow and flourish and triumph. I retreated into the communications bunker and ordered the corporal in charge to call for an air strike on the coordinates of Firebase Ruby. When he balked I put a pistol to his head until he had obeyed. Then I emptied a clip into the radio so no one could countermand me.'

The major bowed his head and spread his arms, as though preparing for a supreme display of magic; then his resonant voice sounded forth again, like the voice of a beast speaking from a cave, rough from the bones that have torn its throat. His eyes were chunks of phosphorous burning in the bark of a rotting log.

'When the explosions began, I was firing from a sandbagged position atop the communications bunker. The VC pouring from the jungle slowed their advance, milled about, and those inside the wire looked up in terror to see the jets screaming overhead, so low I could make out the stars on their wings. Victory was stitched across the sky in rocket trails. Gouts of flame gouged the red dirt, opening the tunnels to the air. The detonations began to blend one into the other, and the ground shook like a sheet of plywood under the pounding of a hammer. Clouds of marbled fire and smoke boiled across the earth, rising to form a dreadful second sky of orange and black, and I came to my feet, fearful yet delighted, astonished by the enormity of the destruction I had called down. Then I was knocked flat. Sandbags fell across my legs, a body flung from God knows where landed on my back, driving the breath from me, and in the instant before consciousness fled, I caught the rich stink of napalm.

'In the morning, I awoke and saw a bloody, jawless face with staring blue eyes pressed close to mine, looking as if it were still trying to convey a last desperate message. I clawed my way from beneath the corpse and staggered upright to find myself the lord of a killed land, of a raw, red scar littered with corpses in the midst of a charcoaled forest. I went down from the bunker and wandered among the dead. From every quarter issued the droning of flies. Everywhere lay arms, legs, and grisly relics I could not identify. I was numb, I had no feeling apart from a pale satisfaction at having survived. But as I wandered among the dead, taking notice of the awful intimacies death had imposed: a dozen child-sized bodies huddled in a crater, anonymous as a nest of scorched beetles; a horribly burned woman with buttocks exposed reaching out a clawed hand to touch the lips of a disembodied head – these and a hundred other such scenes brought home the truth that I was their author. It wasn't guilt I felt then. Guilt was irrelevant. We were all guilty, the dead and the living, the good and those who had abandoned God. Guilt is our inevitable portion of the world's great trouble. No, it was the recognition that at the moment when I knew the war was lost – my share of it, at least – I chose not to cut my losses but to align myself with a force so base and negative that we refuse to admit its place in human nature and dress it in mystical clothing and call it Satan or Shiva so as to separate it from ourselves. Perhaps this sort of choice is a soldier's virtue, but I can no longer view it in that light.' He tapped his chest with the tip of his staff. 'Though I will never say that my enemies were just, there is justice in what I have endured since that day. All men sin, all men do evil. And evil shows itself in our faces.' Here he aimed the staff at the audience and tracked it from face-to-face, as if highlighting the misdeeds imprinted on each. 'What you see of me now is not the man I was, but the thing I became at the instant I made my choice. Take from my story what you will, but understand this: I am unique only in that the judgment of my days is inscribed not merely on my face, but upon every inch of my body. We are all of us monsters waiting to be summoned forth by a moment of madness and pride.'

As Tranh and I led him from the tent, across the damp grass, the major was excited, almost incoherently so, not by the acclaim he had received, but because he had managed to complete his story. He plucked at my sleeve, babbling, bobbing his head, but I paid him no mind, concerned about Tan, whom I had seen talking to Phuong in the bleachers. And when she came running from the main tent, a windbreaker thrown over her costume, I forgot him entirely.

'We're not going directly back to the house,' she said. 'She wants to take me to a club on the square. I don't know when we'll get to your father's.'

'Maybe this isn't such a good idea. I think we should wait until morning.'

'It's all right,' she said. 'Go to the house and as soon as you've dealt with your father, do exactly what I told you. When you hear us enter the house, stay out of sight. Don't do a thing until I come and get you. Understand?'

'I don't know,' I said, perplexed at the way she had taken charge.

'Please!' She grabbed me by the lapels. 'Promise you'll do as I say! Please!'

I promised, but as I watched her run off into the dark I had a resurgence of my old sense of dislocation, and though I had not truly listened to the major's story, having been occupied with my own troubles, the sound of him sputtering and chortling behind me, gloating over the treasure of his recovered memory, his invention, whatever it was, caused me to wonder then about the nature of my own choice, and the story that I might someday tell.

My father's house was on Yen Phu Street – two stories of pocked gray stone with green vented shutters and a green door with a knocker carved in the shape of a water buffalo's head. I arrived shortly after midnight and stood in the lee of the high whitewashed wall that enclosed his compound. The fog had been cut by a steady drizzle, and no pedestrians were about. Light slanted from the vents of a shuttered upstairs window, and beneath it was parked a bicycle in whose basket rested a dozen white lilies, their stems wrapped in butcher paper. I imagined that my father had ridden the bicycle to market and had forgotten to retrieve the flowers after carrying his other purchases inside. They seemed omenical in their glossy pallor, a sterile emblem of the bloody work ahead.

The idea of killing my father held no terrors for me – I had performed the act in my mind hundreds of times, I'd conceived its every element – and as I stood there I felt the past accumulating at my back like the cars of a train stretching for eighteen years, building from my mother's death to the shuddering engine of the moment I was soon to inhabit. All the misgivings that earlier had nagged at me melted away, like fog before rain. I was secure in my hatred and in the knowledge that I had no choice, that my father was a menace who would never fade.

I crossed the street, knocked, and after a few seconds he admitted me into a brightly lit alcove with a darkened room opening off to the right. He was dressed in a voluminous robe of green silk, and as he proceeded me up the stairway to the left of the alcove, the sight of his bell-like shape and bald head with the silver plate collaring the base of his skull ... these things along with the odor of jasmine incense led me to imagine that I was being escorted to an audience with some mysterious religious figure by one of his eunuch priests. At the head of the stair was a narrow white room furnished with two padded chrome chairs, a wallscreen, and, at the far end, a desk bearing papers, an ornamental vase, an old-fashioned letter opener, and a foot-high gilt and bronze Buddha. My father sat down in one of the chairs, triggered the wall screen's computer mode with a penlight, and set about accessing the Sony AI, working through various menus, all the while chatting away, saying he was sorry he'd missed our show, he hoped to attend the following night, and how was I enjoying my stay in Binh Khoi, it often seemed an unfriendly place to newcomers, but by week's end I'd feel right at home. I had brought no weapon, assuming that his security would detect it. The letter opener, I thought, would do the job. But my hand fell instead to the Buddha. It would be cleaner, I decided. A single blow. I picked it up, hefted it. I had anticipated that when the moment arrived, I would want to make myself known to my father, to relish his shock and dismay; but I understood that was no longer important, and I only wanted him to die. In any case, since he likely knew the truth about me, the dramatic scene I'd envisioned would be greatly diminished.

'That's Thai. Fifteenth century,' he said, nodding at the statue, then returned his attention to the screen. 'Beautiful, isn't it?'

'Very,' I said.

Then, without a thought, all thinking necessary having already been done, and the deed itself merely an automatic function, the final surge of an eighteen-year-long momentum, I stepped behind him and swung the statue at the back of his head. I expected to hear a crack but the sound of impact was plush, muffled, such as might be caused by the flat of one's hand striking a pillow. He let out an explosive grunt, toppled with a twisting motion against the wall, ending up on his side, facing outward. There was so much blood, I assumed he must be dead. But then he groaned, his eyes blinked open, and he struggled to his knees. I saw that I'd hit the silver plate at the base of his skull. Blood was flowing out around the plate, but it had protected him from mortal damage. His robe had fallen open, and with his pale mottled belly bulging from the green silk and the blood streaking his neck, his smallish features knitted in pain and perplexity, he looked gross and clownishly pitiable. He held up an unsteady hand to block a second blow. His mouth worked, and he said, 'Wait ...' or 'What ...' Which, I can't be sure. But I was in no mood either to wait or to explain myself. A clean death might not have affected me so deeply, but that I had made of a whole healthy life this repellent half-dead thing wobbling at my feet – it assaulted my moral foundation, it washed the romantic tint of revenge from the simple, terrible act of slaughter, and when I struck at him again, this time smashing the statue down two-handed onto the top of his skull, I was charged with the kind of fear that afflicts a child when he more-or-less by accident wounds a bird with a stone and seeks to hide the act from God by tossing his victim onto an ash heap. My father sagged onto his back, blood gushing from his nose and mouth. I caught a whiff of feces and staggered away, dropping the Buddha. Now that my purpose had been accomplished, like a bee dying from having stung its enemy, I felt drained of poison, full of dull surprise that there had been no more rewarding result.

The penlight had rolled beneath the second chair. I picked it up, and, following Tan's instructions, I used the computer to contact a security agency in Da Nang. A blond woman with a brittle manner appeared on the screen and asked my business. I explained my circumstances, not bothering to characterize the murder as anything other than it was – the size of my trust would guarantee my legal immunity – and also provided her with the number of Vang's lawyer, as well as some particulars concerning the trust, thereby establishing my bona fides. The woman vanished, her image replaced by a shifting pattern of pastel colors, and, after several minutes, this in turn was replaced by a contract form with a glowing blue patch at the bottom to which I pressed the ball of my thumb. The woman reappeared, much more solicitous now, and cautioned me to remain where I was. She assured me that an armed force would be at the house within the hour. As an afterthought, she advised me to wipe the blood from my face.

The presence of the body – its meat reality – made me uncomfortable. I picked up the letter opener and went down the stairs and groped my way across the unlit room off the alcove and found a chair in a corner from which I could see the door. Sitting alone in the darkness amplified the torpor that had pervaded me, and though I sensed certain unsettling dissonances surrounding what had just taken place, I was not sufficiently alert to consider them as other than aggravations. I had been sitting there for perhaps ten minutes when the door opened and Phuong, laughing, stepped into the alcove with Tan behind her, wearing a blue skirt and checkered blouse. She kicked the door shut, pushed Tan against the wall, and began to kiss her, running a hand up under her skirt. Then her head snapped around, and although I didn't believe she could see in the dark, she stared directly at me.

Before I could react, before I could be sure that Phuong had detected me, Tan struck her beneath the jaw with the heel of her left hand, driving her against the opposite wall, and followed this with a kick to the stomach. Phuong rolled away and up into a crouch. She cried out my father's name: 'William!' Whether in warning or – recognizing what had happened – in grief, I cannot say. Then the two women began to fight. It lasted no more than half-a-minute, but their speed and eerie grace were incredible to see: like watching two long-fingered witches dancing in a bright patch of weakened gravity and casting violent spells. Dazed by Tan's initial blows, Phuong went on the defensive, but soon she recovered and started to hold her own. I remembered the letter opener in my hand. The thing was poorly balanced and Phuong's quickness made the timing hard to judge, but then she paused, preparing to launch an attack and I flung the opener, lodging it squarely between her shoulderblades. Not a mortal wound – the blade was too dull to bite deep – but a distracting one. She shrieked, tried to reach the opener, and, as she reeled to the side, Tan came up behind her and broke her neck with a savage twist. She let the body fall and walked toward me, a shadow in the darkened room. It seemed impossible that she was the same woman I had known on the beach at Vung Tau, and I felt a spark of fear.

'Are you all right?' she asked, stopping a few feet away.

'All right?' I laughed. 'What's going on here?'

She gave no reply, and I said, 'Apparently you decided against using Mei's herbs.'

'If you had done as I asked, if you'd stayed clear, it might not have been necessary to kill her.' She came another step forward. 'Have you called for security?'

I nodded. 'Did you learn to fight like that in Hue?'

'In China,' she said.

'At a private security company. Like Phuong.'

'Yes.'

'Then it would follow that you're not Vang's niece.'

'But I am,' she said. 'He used the last of his fortune to have me trained so I could protect you. He was a bitter man … to have used his family so.'

'And I suppose sleeping with me falls under the umbrella of protection.'

She kneeled beside the chair, put a hand on my neck, and gazed at me entreatingly. 'I love you, Philip. I would do anything for you. How can you doubt it?'

I was moved by her sincerity, but I could not help but treat her coldly. It was as if a valve had been twisted shut to block the flow of my emotions.

'That's right,' I said. 'Vang told me that your kind were conditioned to bond with their clients.'

I watched the words hit home, a wounded expression washing across her features, then fading, like a ripple caused by a pebble dropped into a still pond. 'Is that so important?' she asked. 'Does it alter the fact that you fell in love with me?'

I ignored this, yet I was tempted to tell her, No, it did not. 'If you were trained to protect me, why did Vang discourage our relationship?'

She got to her feet, her face unreadable, and went a few paces toward the alcove; she appeared to be staring at Phuong's body, lying crumpled in the light. 'There was a time when I think he wanted me for himself. That may explain it.'

'Did Phuong really accost you?' I asked. 'Or was that ...

'I've never lied to you. I've deceived you by not revealing everything I knew about Vang,' she said. 'But I was bound to obey him in that. As you said, I've been conditioned.'

I had other questions, but I could not frame one of them. The silence of the house seemed to breed a faint humming, and I became oppressed by the idea that Tan and I were living analogs of the two corpses, that the wealth I was soon to receive as a consequence of our actions would lead us to a pass wherein we would someday lie dead in separate rooms of a silent house, while two creatures like ourselves but younger would stand apart from one another in fretful isolation, pondering their future. I wanted to dispossess myself of this notion, to contrive a more potent reality, and I crossed the room to Tan and turned her to face me. She refused to meet my eyes, but I tipped up her chin and kissed her. A lover's kiss. I touched her breasts – a treasuring touch. But despite the sweet affirmation and openness of the kiss, I think it also served a formal purpose, the sealing of a bargain whose terms we did not fully understand.

Six months and a bit after my eighteenth birthday, I was sitting in a room in the Sony offices in Saigon, a windowless space with black walls and carpet and silver-framed photographs of scenes along the Perfume River and in the South China Sea, when Vang flickered into being against the far wall. I thought I must seem to him, as he seemed to me, like a visitation, a figure from another time manifested in a dream. He appeared no different than he had on the day he left the circus – thin and gray-haired, dressed in careworn clothing – and his attitude toward me was, as ever, distant. I told him what had happened in Binh Khoi, and he said, 'I presumed you would have more trouble with William. Of course, he thought he had leverage over me – he thought he had Tan in his clutches. So he let his guard down. He believed he had nothing to fear.'

His logic was overly simplistic, but rather than pursue this, I asked the question foremost on my mind: why had he not told me that he was my grandfather? I had uncovered quite a lot about my past in the process of familiarizing myself with Vang's affairs, but I wanted to hear it all.

'Because I'm not your grandfather,' he said. 'I was William's father-in-law, but ...' He shot me an amused look. 'I should have thought you would have understood all this by now.'

I saw no humor in the situation. 'Explain it to me.'

'As you wish.' He paced away from me, stopped to inspect one of the framed photographs. 'William engineered the death of my wife, my daughter, and my grandson in a plane crash. Once he had isolated me, he challenged my mental competency, intending to take over my business concerns. To thwart him, I faked my suicide. It was a very convincing fake. I used a body I'd had cloned to supply me with organs. I kept enough money to support Green Star and to pay for Tan's training. The rest you know.'

'Not so,' I said. 'You haven't told me who I am.'

'Ah, yes.' He turned from the photograph and smiled pleasantly at me. 'I suppose that would interest you. Your mother's name was Tuyet. Tuyet Su Vanh. She was an actress in various pornographic media. The woman you saw in your dream – that was she. We had a relationship for several years, then we drifted apart. Not long before I lost my family, she came to me and told me she was dying. One of the mutated HIVs. She said she'd borne a child by me. A son. She begged me to take care of you. I didn't believe her, of course. But she had given me pleasure, so I set up a trust for you. A small one.'

'And then you decided to use me.'

'William had undermined my authority to the extent that I could not confront him directly. I needed an arrow to aim at his heart. I told your mother that if she cooperated with me I'd adopt you, place my fortune in the trust, and make you my heir. She gave permission to have your memory wiped. I wanted you empty so I could fill you with my purpose. After you were re-educated, she helped construct some fragmentary memories that were implanted by means of a biochip. Nonetheless, you were a difficult child to mold. I couldn't be certain that you would seek William out, and so, since I was old and tired and likely not far from Heaven, I decided to feign an illness and withdraw. This allowed me to arrange a confrontation without risk to myself.'

I should have hated Vang, but after six months of running his businesses, of viewing the world from a position of governance and control, I understood him far too well to hate – though at that moment, understanding the dispassionate requisites and protocols of such a position seemed as harsh a form of judgment as the most bitter of hatreds. 'What happened to my mother?' I asked.

'I arranged for her to receive terminal care in an Australian hospital.'

'And her claim that I was your biological son ... did you investigate it?'

'Why should I? It didn't matter. A man in my position could not acknowledge an illegitimate child, and once I had made my decision to abdicate my old life, it mattered even less. If it has any meaning for you, there are medical records you can access.'

'I think I'd prefer it to remain a mystery,' I told him.

'You've no reason to be angry at me,' he said. 'I've made you wealthy. And what did it cost? A few memories.'

I shifted in my chair, steepled my hands on my stomach. 'Are you convinced that my ... that William had your family killed? He seemed to think there had been a misunderstanding.'

'That was a charade! If you're asking whether or not I had proof – of course I didn't. William knew how to disguise his hand.'

'So everything you did was based solely on the grounds of your suspicions.'

'No! It was based on my knowledge of the man!' His tone softened. 'What does it matter? Only William and I knew the truth, and he is dead. If you doubt me, if you pursue this further, you'll never be able to satisfy yourself.'

'I suppose you're right,' I said, getting to my feet.

'Are you leaving already?' He wore an aggrieved expression. 'I was hoping you'd tell me about Tan ... and Green Star. What has happened with my little circus?'

'Tan is well. As for Green Star, I gave it to Mei and Tranh.'

I opened the door, and Vang made a gesture of restraint. 'Stay a while longer, Philip. Please. You and Tan are the only people with whom I have an emotional connection. It heartens me to spend time with you.'

Hearing him describe our relationship in these terms gave me pause. I recalled the conversation in which Tan had asserted that something central to the idea of life died when one was uploaded into Heaven – Vang's uncharacteristic claim to an emotional debt caused me to think that he might well be, as she'd described her parents, a colored shadow, a cunningly contrived representation of the original. I hoped that this was not the case; I hoped that he was alive in every respect.

'I have to go,' I said. 'Business, you understand. But I have some news that may interest to you.'

'Oh?' he said eagerly 'Tell me.'

'I've invested heavily in Sony, and, through negotiation, I've arranged for one of your old companies – Intertech of Hanoi – to be placed in charge of overseeing the virtual environment. I would expect you're soon going to see some changes in your particular part of Heaven.

He seemed nonplused, then a look of alarm dawned on his face. 'What are you going to do?'

'Me? Not a thing.' I smiled, and the act of smiling weakened my emotional restraint – a business skill I had not yet perfected – and let anger roughen my voice. 'It's much more agreeable to have your dirty work handled by others, don't you think?'

On occasion, Tan and I manage to rekindle an intimacy that reminds us of the days when we first were lovers, but these occasions never last for long, and our relationship is plagued by the lapses into neutrality or worse – indifference that tends to plague any two people who have spent ten years in each other's company. In our case these lapses are often accompanied by bouts of self-destructive behavior. It seems we're punishing ourselves for having experienced what we consider an undeserved happiness. Even our most honest infidelities are inclined to be of the degrading sort. I understand this. The beach at Vung Tau, once the foundation of our union, has been replaced by a night on Yen Phu Street in Binh Khoi, and no edifice built upon such imperfect stone could be other than cracked and deficient. Nonetheless, we both realize that whatever our portion of contentment in this world, we are fated to seek it together.

From time to time, I receive a communication from Vang. He does not look well, and his tone is always desperate, cajoling. I tell myself that I should relent and restore him to the afterlife for which he contracted; but I am not highly motivated in that regard. If there truly is something that dies when one ascends to Heaven, I fear it has already died in me, and I blame Vang for this.

Seven years after my talk with Vang, Tan and I attended a performance of the circus in the village of Loc Noi. There was a new James Bond Cochise, Kai and Kim had become pretty teenagers, both Tranh and Mei were thinner, but otherwise things were much the same. We sat in the main tent after the show and reminisced. The troupe – Mei in particular – were unnerved by my bodyguards, but all in all, it was a pleasant reunion.

After a while, I excused myself and went to see the major. He was huddled in his tent, visible by the weird flickerings in his eyes ... though as my vision adapted to the dark, I was able make out the cowled shape of his head against the canvas backdrop. Tranh had told me he did not expect the major to live much longer, and now that I was close to him, I found that his infirmity was palpable, I could hear it in his labored breath. I asked if he knew who I was, and he replied without inflection, as he had so many years before, 'Philip.' I'd hoped that he would be more forthcoming, because I still felt akin to him, related through the cryptic character of our separate histories, and I thought that he might once have sensed that kinship, that he'd had some diffuse knowledge of the choices I confronted, and had designed the story of Firebase Ruby for my benefit, shaping it as a cautionary tale – one I'd failed to heed. But perhaps I'd read too much into what was sheer coincidence. I touched his hand, and his breath caught, then shuddered forth, heavy as a sob. All that remained for him were a few stories, a few hours in the light. I tried to think of something I could do to ease his last days, but I knew death was the only mercy that could mend him.

Mei invited Tan and I to spend the night in the trailer – for old times sake, she said – and we were of no mind to refuse. We both yearned for those old times, despite neither of us believing that we could recapture them. Watching Tan prepare for bed, it seemed to me that she had grown too vivid for the drab surroundings, her beauty become too cultivated and too lush. But when she slipped in beside me, when we began to make love on that creaky bunk, the years fell away and she felt like a girl in my arms, tremulous and new to such customs, and I was newly awakened to her charms. She drifted off to sleep afterward with her head on my chest, and as I lay there trying to quiet my breath so not to wake her, it came to me that future and past were joined in the darkness that enclosed us, two black rivers flowing together, and I understood that while the circus would go its own way in the morning and we would go ours, those rivers, too, were forever joined – we shared a confluence and a wandering course, and a moment proof against the world's denial, and we would always be a troupe, Kim and Kai, Mei and Tranh, Tan and I, and the major ... that living ghost who, like myself was the figment of a tragic past he never knew, or – if, indeed, he knew it – with which he could never come to terms. It was a bond that could not save us, from either our enemies or ourselves, but it held out a hope of simple glory, a promise truer than Heaven. Illusory or not, all our wars would continue until their cause was long-forgotten under the banner of Radiant Green Star.

VACANCY

CHAPTER 1

Cliff Coria has been sitting in a lawn chair out front of the office of Ridgewood Motors for the better part of five years, four nights a week, from midafternoon until whenever he decides it's not worth staying open any longer, and during that time he's spent, he estimates, between five and six hundred hours staring toward the Celeste Motel across the street. That's how long it's taken him to realize that something funny may be going on. He might never have noticed anything if he hadn't become fascinated by the sign in the office window of the Celeste. It's a No Vacancy sign, but the No is infrequently lit. Foot-high letters written in a cool blue neon script: they glow with a faint aura in the humid Florida dark:

VACANCY

That cool, blue, halated word, then ... that's what Cliff sees as he sits in a solitude that smells of asphalt and gasoline, staring through four lanes of traffic or no traffic at all, plastic pennons stirring above his head, a paperback on his knee (lately he's been into Scott Turow), at the center of gleaming SUVs, muscle cars, minivans, the high-end section where sit the aristocrats of the lot, a BMW, a silver Jag, a couple of Hummers, and the lesser hierarchies of reconditioned Toyotas, family sedans with suspect frames that sell for a thousand dollars and are called Drive-Away Specials. He's become so sensitized to the word, the sign, it's as if he's developed a relationship with it. When he's reading, he'll glance toward the sign now and again, because seeing it satisfies something in him. At closing time, leaving the night watchman alone in the office with his cheese sandwiches and his boxing magazines, he'll snatch a last look at it before he pulls out into traffic and heads for the Port Orange Bridge and home. Sometimes when he's falling asleep, the sign will switch on in his mind's eye and glow briefly, bluely, fading as he fades.

Cliff's no fool. Used car salesman may be the final stop on his employment track, but it's lack of ambition, not a lack of intellect, that's responsible for his station in life. He understands what's happening with the sign. He's letting it stand for something other than an empty motel room, letting it second the way he feels about himself. That's all right, he thinks. Maybe the fixation will goad him into making a change or two, though the safe bet is, he won't change. Things have come too easily for him. Ever since his glory days as a high school jock (wide receiver, shooting guard), friends, women, and money haven't been a serious problem. Even now, more than thirty years later, his looks still get him by. He's got the sort of unremarkably handsome, rumpled face that you might run across in a Pendleton catalog, and he dyes his hair ash brown, leaves a touch of gray at the temples, and wears it the same as he did when he was in Hollywood. That's where he headed after his stint in the army (he was stationed in Germany near the end of the Vietnam War). He figured to use the knowledge he gained with a demolition unit to get work blowing up stuff in the movies, but wound up acting instead, for the most part in B-pictures.

People will come onto the lot and say, 'Hey! You're that guy, right?' Usually they're referring to a series of commercials he shot in the Nineties, but occasionally they're talking about his movies, his name fifth- or sixth-billed, in which he played good guys who were burned alive, exploded, eaten by monstrous creatures, or otherwise horribly dispatched during the first hour. He often sells a car to the people who recognize him and tosses in an autographed headshot to sweeten the deal. And then he'll go home to his beach cottage, a rugged old thing of boards and a screened-in porch, built in the forties, that he bought with residual money; he'll sleep with one of the women whom he sees on a non-exclusive basis, or else he'll stroll over to the Surfside Grill, an upscale watering hole close by his house, where he'll drink and watch sports. It's the most satisfying of dissatisfying lives. He knows he doesn't have it in him to make a mark, but maybe it's like in the movies, he thinks. In the movies, everything happens for a reason, and maybe there's a reason he's here, some minor plot function he's destined to perform. Nothing essential, mind you. Just a part with some arc to the character, a little meat on its bones.

THE CELESTE MOTEL is a relic of Daytona Beach as it was back in the Sixties: fifteen pale blue stucco bungalows, vaguely Spanish in style, hunkered down amidst a scrap of Florida jungle – live oaks, shrimp plants, palmettos, Indian palms, and hibiscus. Everything's run to seed, the grounds so overgrown that the lights above the bungalow doors (blue like the Vacancy sign) are filtered through sprays of leaves, giving them a mysterious air. Spanish moss fallen from the oaks collects on the tile roofs; the branches of unpruned shrubs tangle with the mesh of screen doors; weeds choke the flagstone path. The office has the same basic design and color as the bungalows, but it's two stories with an upstairs apartment, set closer to the street. Supported by a tall metal pole that stands in front of the office is an illuminated square plastic sign bearing the name of the motel and the sketch of a woman's face, a minimalist, stylized rendering like those faces on matchbook covers accompanied by a challenge to Draw This Face and discover whether you have sufficient talent to enroll in the Famous Artist's School. Halfway down the pole, another, smaller sign to which stick-on letters can be affixed. Tonight it reads:

> WELCOME SPRING BEAKERS
> SNGL/DBL 29.95
> FREE HBO

The Celeste is almost never full, but whenever Number Eleven is rented, the No on the No Vacancy sign lights up and stays lit for about an hour; then it flickers and goes dark. Once Cliff realized this was a reoccurring phenomenon, it struck him as odd, but no big deal. Then about a month ago, around six o'clock in the evening, just as he was getting comfortable with Turow's *Presumed Guilty*, Number Eleven was rented by a college-age girl driving a Corvette, the twin of a car that Cliff sold the day before, which is the reason he noticed. She parked at the rear (the lot is out of sight from the street, behind a hedge of bamboo), entered eleven, and the No switched on. A couple of hours later, after the No had switched back off, a family of three driving a new Ford Escape – portly dad, portly mom, skinny kid – checked in and, though most of the cabins were vacant, they, too, entered eleven. The girl must be part of the family, Cliff thought, and they had planned to meet at the motel. But at a quarter past ten, a guy with a beard and biker colors, riding a chopped Harley Sportster, also checked into eleven and the No switched on again.

It's conceivable, Cliff tells himself, that a massive kink is being indulged within the bungalow. Those blue lights might signal more than an ill-considered decorating touch. Whatever. It's not his business. But after three further incidents of multiple occupancies, his curiosity has been fully aroused and he's begun to study the Celeste through a pair of binoculars that he picked up at an army surplus store. Since he can detect nothing anomalous about Number Eleven, other than the fact that the shades are always drawn, he has turned his attention to the office.

For the past four years or thereabouts, the motel has been owned and operated by a Malaysian family. The Palaniappans. The father, Bazit, is a lean, fastidious type with skin the color of a worn penny, black hair, and a skimpy mustache that might be a single line drawn with a fine pencil. Every so often, he brings a stack of business cards for Jerry Muntz, the owner of the used car lot, to distribute. Jerry speaks well of him, says that he's a real nice guy, a straight shooter. Cliff has never been closer to the other Palaniappans than across a four-lane highway, but through his binoculars he has gained a sense of their daily routines. Bazit runs the office during the morning hours, and his wife, a pale Chinese woman, also thin, who might be pretty if not for her perpetually dour expression, handles the afternoons. Their daughter, a teenager with a nice figure and a complexion like Bazit's, but with rosy cast, returns home from school at about four PM, dropped off by a female classmate driving a Honda. She either hangs about the office or cleans the bungalows – Cliff thinks she looks familiar and wonders where he might have seen her. Bazit comes back on duty at six PM and his wife brings a tray downstairs around eight. They and their daughter dine together while watching TV. The daughter appears to dominate the dinner conversation, speaking animatedly, whereas the parents offer minimal responses. On occasion they argue, and the girl will flounce off upstairs. At ten o'clock the night man arrives. He's in his early twenties, his features a mingling of Chinese and Malaysian. Cliff supposes him to be the Palaniappan's son, old enough to have his own place.

And that's it. That's the sum of his observations. Their schedules vary, of course. Errands, trips to Costco, and such. Bazit and his wife spend the occasional evening out, as does the daughter, somewhat more frequently. In every regard, they appear to be an ordinary immigrant family. Cliff has worked hard to simplify his life, though the result isn't everything he hoped, and he would prefer to think of the Palaniappans as normal and wishes that he had never noticed the Vacancy sign; but the mystery of Number Eleven is an itch he can't scratch. He's certain that there's a rational explanation, but has the sneaking suspicion that his idea of what's rational might be expanded if he were to find the solution.

CHAPTER 2

When Cliff was eighteen, a week after his high school graduation, he and some friends, walking on the beach after an early morning swim, came upon a green sea turtle, a big one with a carapace four feet long. Cliff mounted the turtle, whereupon she (it was a female who, misguidedly, had chosen a populated stretch of beach as the spot to lay her eggs) began trundling toward the ocean. His friends warned Cliff to dismount, but he was having too much fun playing cowboy to listen. Shortly after the turtle entered the water, apparently more flexible in her natural medium, or feeling more at home, she extended her neck and snapped off Cliff's big toe.

He wonders what might have happened had not he and the turtle crossed paths, if he kept his athletic scholarship and, instead of going to Hollywood, attended college. Now that he's contemplating another foolhardy move – and he thinks taking his investigation to a new level is potentially foolhardy – he views the turtle incident as a cautionary tale. The difference is that no pertinent mystery attached to the turtle, yet he's unsure whether that's a significant difference. When he gets right down to it, he can't understand how the Celeste Motel relates to his life any more than did the turtle.

Cliff's scheduled for an afternoon shift the following Saturday. Jerry thinks it'll be an exceptionally high-traffic weekend, what with the holiday, and he wants his best salesman working the lot. This irritates the rest of the sales staff – they know having Cliff around will cut into their money – but as Jerry likes to say, Life's a bitch, and she's on the rag. He says this somewhat less often since hiring a female salesperson, the lovely Stacey Gerone, and he's taken down the placard bearing this bromide and an inappropriate cartoon from inside the door of the employee washroom … Anyway, Cliff comes in early on Saturday, at quarter to eleven, and, instead of pulling into Ridgewood Motors, parks in the driveway of the Celeste Motel. He pushes into the office, the room he's been viewing through his binoculars. The decor all works together – rattan chairs, blond desk, TV, potted ferns, bamboo frames holding images of green volcanoes and perfect beaches – canceling the disjointed impression he's gained from a distance.

'Good morning,' says Bazit Palaniappan, standing straight as if for inspection, wearing a freshly ironed shirt. 'How may I help you?'

Cliff's about to tell him, when Bazit's pleasant expression is washed away by one of awed delight.

'You are Dak Windsor!' Bazit hurries out from behind his desk and pumps Cliff's hand. 'I have seen all your movies! How wonderful to have you here!'

It takes Cliff a second or two to react to the name, Dak Windsor, and then he remembers the series of fantasy action pictures he did under that name in the Philippines. Six of them, all shot during a three-month period. He recalls cheesy sets, lousy FX, incredible heat, a villain called Lizardo, women made-up as blue-skinned witches, and an Indonesian director who yelled at everyone, spoke neither Tagalog nor English, and had insane bad breath. Cliff has never watched the movies, but his agent told him they did big business in the Southeast Asian markets. Not that their popularity mattered to Cliff – he was paid a flat fee for his work. His most salient memory of the experience is of a bothersome STD he caught from one of the blue-skinned witches.

'Au Yong!' Bazit shouts. 'Will you bring some tea?'

Cliff allows Bazit to maneuver him into a chair and for the next several minutes he listens while the man extols the virtues of *Forbidden Tiger Treasure*, *Sword of the Black Demon*, and the rest of the series, citing plot points, asking questions Cliff cannot possibly answer because he has no idea of the films' continuity or logic – it's a jumble of crocodile men, cannibal queens, wizards shooting lurid lightning from their fingertips, and lame dialog sequences that made no sense at the time and, he assumes, would likely make none if he were to watch the pictures now.

'To think,' says Bazit, wonderment in his voice. 'All this time, you've been working right across the street. I must have seen you a dozen times, but never closely enough to make the connection. You must come for dinner some night and tell us all about the movies.'

Mrs Palaniappan brings tea, listens as Bazit provides an ornate introduction to the marvel that is Dak Windsor ('Cliff Coria,' Cliff interjects. 'That's my real name.'). It turns out that Bazit, who's some ten-twelve years younger than Cliff, watched the series of movies when he was an impressionable teenager and, thanks to Dak/Cliff's sterling performance as the mentor and sidekick of the film's hero, Ricky Sintara, he was inspired to make emigration to the United States a goal, thus leading to the realization of his golden dream, a smallish empire consisting of the Celeste and several rental properties.

'You know George Clooney?' she asks Cliff. That's her sole reaction to Bazit's fervent testimony.

'No,' says Cliff, and starts to explain his lowly place in hierarchy of celebrity; but a no is all Mrs Palaniappan needs to confirm her judgment of his worth. She excuses herself, says she has chores to do, and takes her grim, neutral-smelling self back upstairs.

Among the reasons that Cliff failed in Hollywood is that he was not enough of a narcissist to endure the amount of stroking that accompanies the slightest success; but nothing he has encountered prepares him for the hand job that Bazit lovingly offers. At several points during the conversation, Cliff attempts to get down to cases, but on each occasion Bazit recalls another highlight from the Dak Windsor films that needs to be memorialized, shared, dissected, and when Cliff checks his watch he finds it's after eleven-thirty. There's no way he'll have time to get into the subject of Number Eleven. And then, further complicating the situation, the Palaniappan's daughter, Shalin, returns home – her school had a half-day. Bazit once again performs the introductions, albeit less lavishly, and Shalin, half-kneeling on the cushion of her father's chair, one hand on her hip and the other, forefinger extended, resting on her cheek, says, 'Hello,' and smiles.

That pose nails it for Cliff – it's the same pose the Malaysian actress (he knows she had a funny name, but he can't recall it) who gave him the STD struck the first time he noticed her, and Shalin, though ten-fifteen years younger, bears a strong resemblance to her, down to the beauty mark at the corner of her mouth; even the mildness of her smile is identical. It's such a peculiar hit coming at that moment, one mystery hard upon the heels of another, Cliff doesn't know whether the similarity between the women is something he should be amazed by or take in stride, perceive as an oddity, a little freaky but nothing out of the ordinary. It might be that he doesn't remember the actress clearly, that he's glossing over some vital distinction between the two women.

After Shalin runs off upstairs, Bazit finally asks the reason for Cliff's visit, and, fumbling for an excuse, Cliff explains that some nights after work he doesn't want to drive home, he has an engagement this side of the river, he's tired or he's had a couple of drinks, and he wonders if he can get a room on a semi-regular basis at the Celeste.

'For tonight? It would be an honor!' says Bazit. 'I think we have something available.'

Suddenly leery, Cliff says, 'No, I'm talking down the road, you know. Next weekend or sometime.'

Bazit assures him that Dak Windsor will have no problem obtaining a room. They shake hands and Cliff's almost out the door when he hears a shout in a foreign language at his back. '*Showazzat Bompar!*' or something of the sort. He turns and finds that Bazit has dropped into a half-crouch, his left fist extended in a Roman salute, his right hand held beside his head, palm open, as if he's about to take a pledge, and Cliff recalls that Ricky Sintara performed a similar salute at the end of each movie. He goes out into the driveway and stands beside his car, an '06 dark blue Miata X-5 convertible, clean and fully loaded. The April heat is a shock after the air-conditioned office, the sunlight makes him squint, and he has a sneaking suspicion that somehow, for whatever reason, he's just been played.

CHAPTER 3

Sunday morning, Cliff puts on a bathing suit, flip-flops, and a Muntz Mazda World T-shirt, and takes his coffee and OJ into his Florida room, where he stands and watches, through a fringe of dune grass and Spanish bayonet, heavy surf piling in onto a strip of beach, the sand pinkish from crushed coquina shells. The jade-colored waves are milky with silt; they tumble into one another, bash the shore with concussive slaps. Out beyond the bar, a pelican splashes down into calmer, bluer water. Puffs of pastel cloud flock the lower sky.

Cliff steps into his office, goes online and checks the news, then searches the film geek sites and finds a copy of *Sword of the Black Demon*, which he orders. It's listed under the category, Camp Classics. Still sleepy, he lies down on the sofa and dreams he's in a movie jungle with two blue-skinned witches and monkeys wearing grenadier uniforms and smoking clove cigarettes. He wakes to the sight of Stacey Gerone standing over him, looking peeved.

'Did you forget I was coming over?' she asks.

'Of course not.' He gets to his feet, not the easiest of moves these days, given the condition of his back, but he masks his discomfort with a yawn. 'You want some coffee?'

'For God's sake, take off that T-shirt. Don't you get enough of Muntz World during the week?'

Stacey drops her handbag on the sofa. She's a redhead with creamy skin that she nourishes with expensive lotions and a sun blocker with special cancer-eating bacteria or some shit, dressed in a designer tank top and white slacks. Her body's a touch zaftig, but she is still, at thirty-eight, a babe. At the lot, she does a sultry Desperate Housewife act that absolutely kills middle-aged men and college boys alike. If the wife or girlfriend tag along, she changes her act or lets somebody else mother the sale. Jerry plans to move her over to his candy store (the new car portion of his business) in Ormond Beach, where there's real money to be made. For more than a year, he's tried to move Cliff to Ormond as well, but Cliff refuses to budge. His reluctance to change is inertial, partly, but he doesn't need the money and the young couples and high school kids and working class folk who frequent Ridgewood Motors are more to his taste than the geriatric types who do their car-shopping at Muntz Mazda World.

As Cliff makes a fresh pot, Stacey sits at the kitchen table and talks a blue streak, mostly about Jerry. 'You should see his latest,' she says. 'He's got a design program on his computer, and he spends every spare minute creating cartoons. You know, cartoons of himself. Little tubby, cute Jerrys. Each one has a slogan with it. Every word starts with an M. What do you call that? When every word starts with the same letter?'

'Alliteration,' says Cliff.

'So he's doing this alliteration. Most of it's business stuff. Muntz Millennium Mazda Make-out. Muntz Mazda Moments. Trying to find some combination of M-words that make a snappy saying, you know. But then he's got these ones that have different cartoons with them. Muntz Munches Muff. MILF-hunting Muntz. He took great pains to show them to me.'

'He's probably hoping to get lucky.'

Stacey gives him a pitying look.

'You did it with Jerry?' he says, unable to keep incredulity out of his voice.

'How many women do you see in this business? Grow up! I needed the job, so I slept with him.' Stacey waggles two fingers. 'Twice. Believe me, sleep was the operative word. Once I started selling ...' She makes a brooming gesture with her hand. 'Does it tick you off I had sex with him?'

'Is that how you want me to feel?'

'How do I want you to feel? That's a toughie.' She crosses her legs, taps her chin. 'Studied indifference would be good. Some undertones of resentment and jealousy. That would suit me fine.'

'I can work with that.'

'That's what I love most about you, Cliff.' She stands and puts her arms about his waist from behind. 'You take direction so well.'

'I am a professional,' he says.

Later, lying in bed with Stacy, he tells her about the Celeste and Number Eleven, about Shalin Palaniappan, expecting her reaction to be one of indifference – she'll tell him to give it a rest, forget about it, he's making a mountain out of a molehill, and just who does he think he is, anyway? Tony Shaloub or somebody? But instead she says, 'I'd call the cops if I was you.'

'Really?' he says.

'That stuff about the girl ... I don't know. But obviously something hinkey's happening over there. Unless you've lost your mind and are making the whole thing up.'

'I'm not making it up.' Cliff locks his hands behind his head and stares up at the sandpainted ceiling.

'Then you should call the cops.'

'They won't do anything,' he says. 'Best case, they'll ask stupid questions that'll make the Palaniappans shut down whatever's going on. As soon as the pressure's off, they'll start up again.'

'Then you should forget it.'

'How come?'

'You're a smart guy, Cliff, but sometimes you space. You go off somewhere else for a couple hours ... or a couple of days. That isn't such a great quality for a detective. It's not even a great quality for a salesman.'

Slitting his eyes, Cliff turns the myriad bumps of paint on the ceiling into snowflake patterns; once, when he was smoking some excellent Thai stick, he managed to transform them into a medieval street scene, but he hasn't ever been able to get it back. 'Maybe you're right,' he says.

After a therapy day with Stacey, Cliff thinks he might be ready to put *l'affaire* Celeste behind him. She's convinced him that he isn't qualified to deal with the situation, if there is a situation, and for a few days he eschews the binoculars, gets back into Scott Turow, and avoids looking at the Vacancy sign, though when his concentration lapses, he feels its letters branding their cool blue shapes on his brain. On Thursday evening, he closes early, before nine, and drives straight home, thinking he'll jump into a pair of shorts and walk over to the Surfside, but on reaching his house he finds a slender package stuck inside the screen door. *Sword of the Black Demon* has arrived from Arcane Films. A Camp Classic. He tosses it on the sofa, showers, changes, and, on his way out, decides to throw the movie in the player and watch a little before heading to the bar – refreshing his memory of the picture will give him something to talk about with his friends.

It's worse than he remembers. Beyond lame. Gallons of stage blood spewing from Monty-Pythonesque wounds; the cannibal queen's chunky, naked retinue; a wizard who travels around on a flying rock; the forging of a sword from a meteorite rendered pyrotechnically by lots of sparklers; the blue witches, also naked and chunky, except for one ... He hits the pause button, kneels beside the TV, and examines the lissome shape of, it appears, Shalin Palaniappan, wishing he could check if the current incarnation of the blue witch has a mole on her left breast, though to do so would likely net him five-to-ten in the slammer. He makes for the Surfside, a concrete block structure overlooking the beach, walking the dunetops along A1A, hoping that a couple of vodkas will banish his feeling of unease, but once he's sitting at the bar under dim track lighting, a vodka rocks in hand, deliciously chilled by the AC, embedded in an atmosphere of jazz and soft, cluttered talk, gazing through the picture window at the illuminated night ocean (the beach, at this hour, is barely ten yards wide and the waves seem perilously close), he's still uneasy and he turns his attention to the Marlins on the big screen, an abstract clutter of scurrying white-clad figures on a bright green field.

'Hey, Cliffie,' says a woman's voice, and Marley, a diminutive package of frizzy, dirty blond hair and blue eyes, a cute sun-browned face and jeans tight as a sausage skin, lands in the chair beside his and gives him a quick hug.

She's young enough to be his daughter, old enough to be his lover. He's played both roles, but prefers that of father. She's feisty, good-hearted, and too valuable as a friend to risk losing over rumpled bed sheets.

'Hey, you,' he says. 'I thought this was your night off.'

'All my nights are off.' She grins. 'My new goal – becoming a barfly like you.'

'What about … you know. Tyler, Taylor …'

She pretends to rap her knuckles on his forehead. 'Tucker. He gone.'

'I thought that was working out.'

'Me, too,' she says. 'And then, oops, an impediment. He was wanted for fraud in South Carolina.'

'Fraud? My God!'

'That's what I said … except I cussed more.' She neatly tears off a strip of cocktail napkin. 'Cops came by the place three weeks ago. Guns drawn. Spotlights. The whole schmear. He waived extradition.'

'Why didn't you tell me sooner?'

She shrugs. 'You know how I hate people crying in their beer.'

'God. Let me buy you a drink.'

'You bet.' She pounds the counter. 'Tequila!'

They drink, talk about Tucker, about what a lousy spring it's been. Two tequilas along, she asks if he's all right, he seems a little off. He wants to tell her, but it's too complicated, too demented, and she doesn't need to hear his problems, so he tells her about the movies he did in the Philippines, making her laugh with anecdotes about and impersonations of the director. Five tequilas down and she's hanging on him, giggly, teasing, laughing at everything he says, whether it's funny or not. It's obvious she won't be able to drive. He invites her to use his couch – he'd give her the bed, but the couch is murder on his back – and she says, suddenly tearful, 'You're so sweet to me.'

After one for the road, they start out along the dunes toward home, going with their heads down – a wind has kicked up and blows grit in their faces. The surf munches the shore, sounding like a giant chewing his food with relish; a rotting scent intermittently overrides the smell of brine. No moon, no stars, but porch lights from the scattered houses show the way. Marley keeps slipping in the soft sand and Cliff has to put an arm around her to prevent her from falling. The tall grasses tickle his calves. They're twenty yards from his front step, when he hears the sound of boomerang in flight – he identifies it instantly, it's that distinct. A helicopter-ish sound, but higher-pitched, almost a whistling, passing overhead. He stops walking, listening for it, and Marley seizes the opportunity to rub her breasts against him, her head tipped back, waiting to be kissed.

'Is this going to be one of those nights?' she asks teasingly.

'Did you hear that?'

'Hear what?'

'A boomerang, I think. Somebody threw a boomerang.'

Bewildered, she says, 'A boomerang?'

'Shh! Listen!'

Confused, she shelters beneath his arm as he reacts to variations in the wind's pitch, to a passing car whose high beams sweep over the dune grass, lighting the cottage, growing a shadow from its side that lengthens and then appears to reach with a skinny black arm across the rumpled ground the instant before it vanishes. He hears no repetition of the sound, and its absence unsettles him. He's positive that he heard it, that somewhere out in the night, a snaky-jointed figure is poised to throw. He hustles Marley toward the cottage and hears, as they ascend the porch steps, a skirling music, whiny reed instruments, and a clattery percussion, like kids beating with sticks on a picket fence, just a snatch of it borne on the wind. He shoves Marley inside, bolts the door, and switches on the porch lights, thinking that little brown men with neat mustaches will bloom from the dark, because that's what sort of music it is, Manila taxicab music, the music played by the older drivers who kept their radios tuned to an ethnic station – but he sees nothing except rippling dune grass, pale sand, and the black gulf beyond, a landscape menacing for its lack of human form.

He bolts the inner door, too. Resisting Marley's attempts to get amorous, he opens out the couch bed, makes her lie down and take a couple of aspirin with a glass of water. He sits in a chair by the couch as she falls asleep, his anxiety subsiding. She looks like a kid in her T-shirt and diaphanous green panties, drowsing on her belly, face half-concealed by strings of hair, and he thinks what a fuck-up he is. The thought is bred by no particular chain of logic. It may have something to do with Marley, with his deepened sense of the relationship's inappropriateness, a woman more than twenty years his junior (though, God knows, he's championed the other side of that argument), and she's younger than that in her head, a girl, really ... It may bear upon that, but the thought has been on heavy rotation in his brain for years and seems to have relevance to every situation. He's pissed away countless chances for marriage, for success, and he can't remember what he was thinking, why he treated these opportunities with such casual disregard. He recalls getting a third callback to test for the Bruce Willis role in *Die Hard*. Word was that the studio was leaning toward him, because Willis had pissed off one of the execs, so on the night before the callback he did acid at some Topanga cliff dwelling and came in looking bleary and dissolute.

Looking at Marley's ass, he has a flicker of arousal, and that worries him, that it's only a flicker, that perhaps his new sense of morality is merely a byproduct of growing older, of a reduced sex drive. He has the sudden urge to prove himself wrong, to wake her up and fuck her until dawn, but he sits there, depressed, letting his emotions bleed out into the sound of windowpanes shuddering from constant slaps of wind. Eventually he goes to the door and switches off the lights. Seconds later, he switches them back on, hoping that he won't discover some mutant shape sneaking toward the porch, yet feeling stupid and a little disappointed when nothing of the sort manifests.

CHAPTER 4

He's waked by something banging. He tries to sleep through it, but each time he thinks it's quit and relaxes, it starts up again, so he flings off the covers and shuffles into the living room, pauses on finding the couch unoccupied, scratches his head, trying to digest Marley's absence, then shuffles onto the porch and discovers it's the screen door that's banging. Thickheaded, he shuts it, registering that it's still dark outside. He walks through the house, calling out to Marley; he checks the bathroom. Alarm sets in. She would have left a note, she would have shut the front door. He dresses, shaking out the cobwebs, and goes out onto the porch steps, switching on the exterior lights. Beyond the half-circle of illumination, the shore is a winded confusion, black sky merging with black earth and sea, the surf still heavy. The wind comes in a steady pour off the water, plastering his shorts and shirt against his body.

'Marley!'

No response.

With this much wind, he thinks, his voice won't carry fifty feet.

He grabs the flashlight from inside the door, deciding that he'll walk down to the Surfside and make sure her car's gone from the lot. She probably went home, he tells himself. Woke up and was sober enough to drive. But leaving the door open ... that's just not Marley.

He strikes out along A1A, keeping to the shoulder, made a bit anxious by the music he heard earlier that evening, by the boomerang sound, though he's attributed that to the booze, and by the time he reaches the turn-off into the lot, his thoughts have brightened, he's planning the day ahead; but on seeing Marley's shitbox parked all by its lonesome, a dented brown Hyundai nosed up to the door of the Surfside, his worries are rekindled. He shines the flashlight through the windows of the Hyundai. Fast-food litter, a Big Gulp cup, a crumpled Kleenex box. He bangs on the door of the bar, thinking that Marley might have changed her mind, realized she was too drunk to drive and bedded down in the Surfside. He shouts, bangs some more. Maybe she called a cab from his house. She must have felt guilty about coming on to him. If that's the case, he'll have to have a talk with her, assure her that it's not that she isn't desirable, it's got nothing to do with her, it's him, it's all about how he's begun to feel in intimate situations with her, and then she'll say he's being stupid, she doesn't think of him as a dirty old man, not at all. It's like the kids say, they're friends with benefits. No big deal. And Cliff, being a guy, will go along with that – sooner or later they'll wind up sleeping together and there they'll be, stuck once again amid the confusions of a May-September relationship.

As he walks home, swinging the flashlight side-to-side, he wonders if the reason he put some distance between him and Marley had less to do with her age than with the fact that he was getting too attached to her. The way he felt when she popped up at the Surfside last night – energized, happy, really happy to see her – is markedly different from the way he felt when Stacy Gerone came over the other morning. He's been in love a couple of times, and he seems to recall that falling in love was preceded on each occasion by a similar reaction on his part, a pushing away of the woman concerned for one reason or another. That, he concludes, would be disastrous. If now he perceives himself to be an aging roué, just imagine how contemptible he'd feel filling out Medicare forms while Marley is still a relatively young woman – like a decrepit vampire draining her youth.

His cottage in view, he picks up the pace, striding along briskly. He'll go back to bed for an hour or two, call Marley when he wakes. And if she wants to start things up again ... It's occurred to him that he's being an idiot, practicing a form of denial that serves no purpose. In Asia, in Europe, relationships between older men and young women – between older women and young men, for that matter – aren't perceived as unusual. All he may be doing by his denial is obeying a bourgeoisie convention. He gnaws at the problem, kicking at tufts of high grass, thinking that his notion of morality must be hardening along with his arteries, and, as he approaches the cottage, verging on the arc of radiance spilling from the porch, he notices a smear of red to the left of the door. It's an extensive mark, a wide, wavy streak a couple of feet long that looks very much like blood.

Coming up to the porch, he touches a forefinger to the redness. It's tacky, definitely blood. He's bewildered, dully regarding the dab of color on his fingertip, his mind muddled with questions, and then the wrongness of it, the idea that someone has marked his house with blood, and it's for sure an intentional mark, because no one would inadvertently leave a two-foot-long smear ... the wrongness of it hits home and he's afraid. He whirls about. Beyond the range of the porch lights, the darkness bristles, vegetation seething in the wind, palmetto tops tossing, making it appear that the world is solidifying into a big, angry animal with briny breath, and it's shaking itself, preparing to charge.

He edges toward the steps, alert to every movement, and starts to hear music again, not the whiny racket he heard earlier, but strings and trumpets, a prolonged fanfare like the signature of a cheesy film score, growing louder, and he sees something taking shape from the darkness, something a shade blacker than the sky, rising to tower above the dunes. The coalsack figure of a horned giant, a sword held over its head. He gapes at the thing, the apparition – he assumes it's an apparition. What else could it be? He hasn't been prone to hallucinations for twenty years, and the figure, taller now than the tallest of the condominiums that line the beach along South Atlantic Avenue, is a known quantity, the spitting image of the Black Demon from his movie. Somebody is gaslighting him. They're out in the dunes with some kind of projector, casting a movie image against the clouds. Having established a rational explanation, albeit a flimsy one, Cliff tries to react rationally. He considers searching the dunes, finding the culprit, but when the giant cocks the sword, drawing it back behind its head, preparing to swing a blade that, by Cliff's estimate, is easily long enough to reach him, his dedication to reason breaks and he bolts for the steps, slams and locks the inner door, and stands in the center of his darkened living room, breathing hard, on the brink of full-blown panic.

The music has reverted to rackety percussion and skirling reeds, and it's grown louder, so loud that Cliff can't think, can't get a handle on the situation.

Many-colored lights flash in the windows, pale rose and purple and green and white, reminding him of the lights in a Manila disco created by cellophane panels on a wheel revolving past a bright bulb. He has a glimpse of something or someone darting past outside. A shadowy form, vaguely anthropomorphic, running back and forth, a few steps forward, slipping out of sight, then racing in the opposite direction, as if maddened by the music, and, his pulse accelerated by the dervish reeds and clattering percussion, music that might accompany the flight of panicked moth, Cliff begins to feel light-headed, unsteady on his feet. There's too much movement, too much noise. It seems that the sound-and-light show is having an effect on his brain, like those video games that trigger epileptic seizures, and he can't get his bearings. The floor shifts beneath him, the window frame appears to have made a quarter-turn sideways in the wall. The furniture is dancing, the Mexican throw rug fronting the couch ripples like the surface of a rectangular pond. And then it stops. Abruptly. The music is cut off, the lights quit flashing … but there's still too much light for a moonless, starless night, and he has the impression that someone's aiming a yellow-white spot at the window beside the couch. Cliff waits for the next torment. His heart rate slows, he catches his breath, but he remains still, braced against the shock he knows is coming. Almost a full minute ticks by, and nothing's happened. The shadows in the room have deepened and solidified. He's uncertain what to do. Call the police and barricade himself in the house. Run like hell. Those seem the best options. Maybe whoever was doing this has fled and left a single spotlight behind. He sees his cell phone lying on an end table. 'Okay,' he says, the way you'd speak to a spooked horse. 'Okay.' He eases over to the table and picks up the phone. Activated, its cool blue glow soothes him. He punches in Marley's number and reaches her voicemail. 'Marley,' he says. 'Call me when you get this.' Before calling the police, he thinks about what might be in the house – he's out of pot, but did he finish those mushrooms in the freezer? Where did he put that bottle of oxycodone that Stacy gave him?

A tremendous bang shakes the cottage. Cliff squawks and drops the phone. Something scrabbles on the outside wall and then a woman's face, bright blue, reminiscent of those Indian posters of Kali you used to be able to buy in head shops, her white teeth bared, her long black hair disheveled and hanging down, appears in the window, coming into view from the side, as if she's clinging to the wall like a lizard. Her expression is so inhuman, so distorting of her features, that it yields no clue as to her identity; but when she swings down to center the window, gripping the molding, revealing her naked body, he recognizes her to be what's-her-name, the witch who gave him the STD. The mole on her left breast, directly below the nipple gives it away. As does her pubic hair, shaved into a unique pattern redolent of exotic vegetation. Even without those telltales, he'd know that body. She loved to dance for him before they fucked, rippling the muscles of her inner thighs, shaking her breasts. But she's not dancing now, and there's nothing arousing about her presence. She just hangs outside the window, glaring, a voluptuous blue bug. Her teeth and skin and red lips are a disguise. Rip it away, and you would see a horrid face with a proboscis and snapping jaws. Only the eyes would remain of her human semblance. Huge and dark, empty except for a greedy, lustful quality that manifests as a gleam embedded deep within them. It's that quality that compels Cliff, that roots him to the floorboards. He's certain if he makes a move to run, she'll come through the window, employing some magic that leaves the glass intact, and what she'll do then … His imagination fails him, or perhaps it does not, for he feels her stare on his skin, licking at him as might a cold flame, tasting him, coating his flesh with a slimy residue that isn't tangible, yet seems actual, a kind of saliva that, he thinks, will allow her to digest him more readily. And then it's over. The witch's body deflates, shrivels like a leathery balloon, losing its shape, crumpling, folding in on itself, dwindling in a matter of four or five seconds to a point of light that – he realizes the instant before it winks out, before the spotlight, too, winks out – is the same exact shade of blue as the Vacancy sign at the Celeste Motel.

It's a trick, a false ending, Cliff tells himself – she's trying to get his hopes up, to let him relax, and then she'll materialize behind him, close enough to touch. But time stretches out and she does not reappear. The sounds of wind and surf come to him. Still afraid, but beginning to feel foolish, he picks up his cell phone, half-expecting her to seize the opportunity and pounce. He cracks the door, then opens it and steps out into the soft night air. Something has sliced through the porch screen, halving it neatly. He imagines that the amount of torque required to do such a clean job would be considerable – it would be commensurate with, say, the arc of an enormous sword swung by a giant and catching the screen with the tip of its blade. He retreats inside the house, locks and bolts the door, realizing that it's possible he's being haunted by a movie. Thoughts spring up to assail the idea, but none serve to dismiss it. Understanding that he won't be believed, yet having nowhere else to turn, he dials 911.

CHAPTER 5

Detective Sergeant Todd Ashford of the Port Orange Police Department and Cliff have a history, though it qualifies as ancient history. They were in the same class at Seabreeze High and both raised a lot of hell, some of it together, but they were never friends, a circumstance validated several years after graduation when Ashford, then a patrolman with the Daytona Beach PD, displayed unseemly delight in busting Cliff on a charge of Drunk and Disorderly outside Cactus Jack's, a biker bar on Main Street. Cliff was home for a couple of weeks from Hollywood, flushed with the promise of imminent stardom, and Ashford did not attempt to hide the fact that he deeply resented his success. Nor does he attempt to hide his resentment now. Watching him pace about the interrogation room, a brightly lit space with black compound walls, a metal table and four chairs, Cliff recognizes that although Ashford may no longer resent his success, he has new reason for bitterness. He's a far cry from the buzz-cut young cop who hauled Cliff off to the drunk tank, presenting the image of a bulbous old man with receding gray hair, dark, squinty eyes, a soupstrainer mustache, and jowls, wearing an off-the-rack sport coat and jeans, his gun and badge half-hidden by the overhang of his belly. Cliff looks almost young enough to be his son.

'Why don't you tell me where her body is?' Ashford asks for perhaps the tenth time in the space of two hours. 'We're going to find her eventually, so you might as well give it up.'

Cliff has blown up a balloon, peed in a cup, given his DNA. He's fatigued, and now he's fed up with Ashford's impersonation of a homicide detective. His take on the man is that while he may drink his whiskey neat and smoke cigars (their stale, pungent stench hangs about him, heavy as the scent of wet dog) and do all manner of grownup things, Ashford remains the same fifteen-year-old punk who, drunk on Orbit Beer (six bucks a case), helped him trash the junior class float the night before homecoming, the sort of guy no one remembers at class reunions, whose one notable characteristic was a talent for mind-fucking, who has spent his entire adult life exacting a petty revenge on the world for his various failures, failures that continue to this day, failures with women (no wedding ring), career, self-image ... Another loser. There's nothing remarkable about that. It is, as far as Cliff can tell, a world of six billion losers. Six billion and one if you're counting God. But

Ashford's incarnation of the classic loser is so seedy and thin-souled, Cliff is having trouble holding his temper.

'I want to call my lawyer,' he says.

Ashford adopts a knowing look. 'You think you need one?'

'Damn right I do! You're going to pick away at me all day, because this doesn't have anything to do with my guilt or innocence. This is all about high school.'

Ashford grunts, as though disgusted. 'You're a real asshole! A fucking egomaniac. We got a woman missing, maybe dead, and it's all about high school.' He pulls back a chair and sits facing Cliff. 'Let's say I believe someone's trying to set you up.'

'The Palaniappans. It has to be them! They're the only ones who know about the movie.'

'The movie. Right.' Ashford takes a notebook from his inside breast pocket and flips through it. '*Sword Of The Black Demon*.' He gives the title a sardonic reading, closes the notebook. 'So you had one conversation with the Planappans …'

'Palaniappans!'

'Whatever. You had the one conversation and now you think they're out to get you, because the daughter looks like a woman you caught the clap from back in the day.'

'It wasn't the clap, it was some kind of … I don't know. Some kind of Filipino gunge. And that's not why they're doing this. It's because, I think, I started sniffing around, trying to figure out what's going on with Bungalow eleven.'

Ashford grunts again, this time in amusement. 'Man, I can't wait to get your drug screen back.'

'You're going to be disappointed,' Cliff says. 'I'm not high; I'm not drunk. I'm not even fucking dizzy.'

Ashford attempts to stare him down, doubtless seeking to find a chink in the armor. He makes a clicking noise with his tongue. 'So tell me again what happened after you and Marley left the Surfside.'

'I want a lawyer.'

'You go that way, you're not doing yourself any good.'

'How much good am I doing myself sitting here, letting you nitpick my answers, trying to find inconsistencies that don't exist? Fuck you, Ashford. I want a lawyer.'

Ashford turtles his neck, glowers at Cliff and says, 'You think you're back in Hollywood? The cops out there, they let you talk to them that way?'

Cliff gays up his delivery. 'They're lovely people. The LAPD is renowned for its hospitality. As for where I think I am, I trust I'm among guardians of the public safety.'

Ashford's breathing heavies and Cliff, interpreting this as a sign of extreme anger, says, 'Look, man. I know what I told you sounds freaky, but you're not even giving it a chance. You've made up your mind that I did something to Marley, and nothing I say's going to talk you out of it. Lawyering up's my only option.'

Ashford settles back in his chair, calmer now. 'All right. I'll listen. What do you think I should do about the Palnappians?'

'That's Palaniappans.'

Ashford shrugs.

'If it were me,' says Cliff, 'I'd have a look round Bungalow Eleven. I'd ask some questions, find out what's happening in there.'

'What do you think is happening?'

'Jesus Christ!' Cliff throws up his hands in frustration, and closes his eyes.

'Seriously,' says Ashford. 'I want to know, because from what you've told me, I don't have a clue.'

'I don't know, okay?' says Cliff. 'But I don't think it's anything good.'

'Do you allow for the possibility that nothing's going on? That given everything you've said, the multiple occupancies, the sign, the vehicles disappearing …' Ashford pauses. 'Can you remember any of the vehicles that disappeared? The makes and models?'

'I'm not sure they've disappeared. I haven't been able to check. But if not, they must be piling up back there. But yeah, I remember most of them.'

Ashford tears a clean page from his notebook, shoves it and a pen across the table. 'Write them down. The model, the color … the year if you know it.'

Cliff scribbles a list, considers it, makes an addition, then passes the sheet of paper to Ashford, who looks it over.

'This is a pretty precise list,' he says.

'It's the job. I tend to notice what people drive.'

Ashford continues to study the list. 'These are expensive cars. The Ford Escape, that's one of those hybrids, right?'

'Uh-huh. New this year.'

Ashford folds the paper, sticks it in his notebook. 'So. What I was saying, do you think there could be a reasonable explanation for all this? Something that has nothing to do with a witch and a movie? Something that makes sense in terms someone like me could accept?'

This touch of self-deprecation fuels the idea that Ashford may be smarter than Cliff has assumed. 'It's possible,' he says, but after a pause he adds, 'No. Fuck, no. You had …'

A peremptory knocking on the door interrupts Cliff. With a disgruntled expression, Ashford heaves up to his feet and pokes his head out into the corridor. After a prolonged, muttering exchange with someone Cliff can't see, Ashford throws the door open wide and says flatly, 'You can go for now, Coria. We'll be in touch.'

Baffled, Cliff asks, 'What is it? What happened?'

'Your girlfriend's alive. She's out by the front desk.'

Cliff's relief is diluted by his annoyance over Ashford's refusal to accept that he and Marley are not lovers, but before he can once again deny the assertion, Ashford says, 'Your house is still a crime scene. You might want to hang out somewhere for a few hours until we've finished processing.'

Cliff gives him a what-the-fuck look, and Ashford, with more than a hint of the malicious in his voice, says, 'We have to find out who that blood belongs to, don't we?'

CHAPTER 6

In the entryway of the police station, Marley mothers Cliff, hugging and fussing over him, attentions that he welcomes, but once in the car she waxes outraged, railing at the cops and their rush to judgment. Christ Almighty! She woke up and couldn't get back to sleep, so she went to a diner and did some brooding. You'd think the cops would have more sense. You'd think they would look before they leaped.

'It's my fault,' Cliff says. 'I called them.'

She shoots him a puzzled glance. 'Why'd you do that?'

He remembers that she knows nothing about the Black Demon, the blood, the slit porch screen.

'You left the door open,' he says. 'I was worried.'

'I did not! And even if I did, that's no reason to call the cops.'

'Yeah, well. There was weird shit going on last night. I got hit by vandals, and that made me nervous.'

They stop at a 7-11 so Cliff can buy a clean t-shirt – it's a tough choice between a white one with a cartoon decal and the words Surf Naked, and a gray one imprinted with a fake college seal and the words Screw U. He settles on the gray, deciding it makes a more age-appropriate statement. They go for breakfast at a restaurant on North Atlantic, and then to Marley's studio apartment, which is close by. The Lu-Ray Apartments, a brown stucco building overlooking the ocean and the boardwalk – with the windows open, Cliff can hear faint digital squeals and roars from a video arcade that has a miniature golf course atop its roof. It's a drizzly, overcast morning and, with its patched greens and dilapidated obstacles, a King Kong, a troll, a dragon that spits sparks whenever someone makes a hole-in-one, etcetera, the course has an air of post-apocalyptic decay. The dead Ferris wheel beside it emphasizes the effect.

Marley's place is tomboyishly Spartan, a couple of surfboards on the wall, a Ramones poster, a wicker throne with a green cushion, a small TV with some Mardi Gras beads draped over it, a queen-size box spring and mattress covered by a dark blue spread. The only sign of femininity is that the apartment is scrupulously clean, not a speck of dust, the stove and refrigerator in the kitchenette gleaming. Marley tells Cliff to take the bed, she has to do some stuff, and sits cross-legged in the wicker chair, pecking at her laptop. He closes his eyes, surrendering to fatigue, fading toward sleep; but his thoughts start to race and sleep won't come. He tries to put a logical spin on everything that happened, works out various theories that would accommodate what he saw. The only one that suits is that he's losing it, and he's not ready to go there. Finally, he opens his eyes. Marley's still pecking away, her face concentrated by a serious expression. In her appearance and mien, she reminds him of girls he knew in LA in the eighties, many of them weekend punkers, holding down a steady job during the week, production assistants and set dressers and such, and then, on Friday night, they'd dress down, wear black lipstick and too much mascara, and go batshit crazy. But those girls were all fashion punks with a life plan and insurance and solid prospects, whereas Marley's a true edge-dweller with a punk ethos, living paycheck to paycheck, secure in herself, a bit of dreamer, though her practical side shows itself from time to time – for a week or two she'll binge on schemes to resurrect her fiscal security; then, Pffft!, it all goes away and she's carefree and careless again.

These thoughts endanger Cliff's resolve to remain friends with her, and more dangerous yet is his contemplation of her physical presence. Frizzy blond hair framing a gamin's face; braless breasts, her nipples on full display through the thin fabric of her t-shirt; she's his type, all right. He understands that part of what's at play here is base, that whenever he's at a loss or anxious about something or just plain bored, he relies on women to sublimate the feeling.

Marley glances up, catching him staring. 'Hey! You all right?'

'Yeah,' he says. 'Why?'

'You were looking weird is all.' She closes the laptop. 'You want anything?'

'No,' he says, a reflex answer, but thinks about the things he wants. They're all momentary gratifications. Sex; surcease; to stop thinking about it. He suspects that the real curse of getting older is a certain wisdom, the tendency to reflect on your life and observe the haphazard path you've made, and then he decides that what he wants above all is to want something so badly that he stops second-guessing himself for a while. Just go after it and damn the consequences ... though in reality, that's only another form of surcease.

'What do you want?' he asks.

She tips her head to one side, as if to see him more clearly. 'I don't think I'm getting the whole picture here. Did something happen last night? You know, something more than what you told me? Because you're not acting like yourself.'

'I'll tell you later.' He shifts onto his side. 'So what do you want? What would make you happy?'

She sets the laptop on the floor and comes over to the bed and makes a shooing gesture. 'Scoot over. If this is going to be a deep conversation, I want to lie down.'

He's slow to move, but she pushes onto the bed beside him and he's forced to accommodate her. She plumps the pillow, squirms about, and, once she's settled facing him, arms shielding her breasts, hands together by her cheek, she says, 'I used to want to be a singer. I was in love with Tori Amos, and I was going to be like her. Different, but one of those chicks who plays piano and writes her own songs. But I didn't want it badly enough, so I just bummed around with music, gigged with a few bands and like that. One of my boyfriends was a bartender. He taught me the trade, and I started working bar jobs. It was easy work, I met some nice guys, some not so nice. I was coasting, you know. Trying to figure it out. Now I think, I'm pretty sure, I want to be a vet. Not the kind who prescribes pills for sick cats and treats old ladies' poodles for gout. I'd like to work out in the country. Over in DuBarry, maybe, or down south in Broward. Cattle country. That would make me content, I think. So I'm saving up for veterinary college.' She grins, fine squint lines deepening at the corners of her eyes. 'Someday they'll be saying stuff like, "Reckon we better call ol' Doc Marley."'

He's shamed, because this is all new information; he's known her for three years and never before asked about her life. He recalls her singing about the house and being struck by her strong, sweet voice, how she bent notes that started out flat into a strange countrified inflection. He doesn't know what to say.

'You look perplexed,' she says. 'You thought I was just an aging beach bunny, is that it?'

'That's not it.'

'I suppose I am, technically, an aging beach bunny. But I'm making a graceful transition.'

A silence, during which he hears cars pass. The beach is extraordinarily quiet, all the spring breakers sleeping in, waiting out the rain. He remembers a morning like this when he was eleven, he and some friends rode their bikes down past the strip of motels between Silver Beach and Main, hoping to see girls gone wild, and seeing instead spent condoms floating in the swimming pools like dead marine creatures, a lone girl crying on the sidewalk, crushed beer cans, the beach littered with party trash and burst jellyfish and crusts of dirty foam, all the residue of joyful debauch. It never changes. The gray light lends the furnishings, the walls, a frail density and a pointillist aspect – it seems the room is turning into the ghost of itself, becoming a worn, faded engraving.

'Why do you always act scared around me, Cliffie?' Marley asks. 'Even when we were together, you acted scared. I know the age thing bothers you, but that's no reason to be scared.'

'It's complicated,' he says.

'And you don't want to talk about it, right? Guys really suck!'

'No, I'll talk about it if you want.'

She looks at him expectantly, face partly concealed by dirty blond strings of hair.

'It's partly the age thing,' he says. 'I'm fifty-four and you're twenty-nine.'

'Close,' she says. 'Thirty.'

'All right. Thirty. Turning a year on the calendar doesn't change the fact it's a significant difference. But mostly it's this ... blankness I feel inside myself. It's like I'm empty, and growing emptier. That's what I'm scared of.'

'Well, I don't pretend to know much,' Marley says. 'I could be wrong, but sounds to me like you're lonely.'

Could it be that simple? He's tempted to accept her explanation, but he's reluctant to accept what that may bring. Rain begins to fall more heavily, screening them away from the world with gray slanting lines.

'What do you see in me?' he asks. 'I mean, what makes someone like you interested in a fifty-something used car salesman with a bad back. I don't get it.'

'Wow. Once you start them up, some guys are worse than women. Out comes the rotten self-image and everything else.' She glances up to the ceiling, as if gathering information written there. 'I'll tell you, but don't interrupt, okay?'

'Okay.'

'We're friends. We've been friends for going on four years, and I like to think we're good friends. I can count on you in an emergency, and you can count on me. True?'

He nods.

'You make my head quiet,' she says. 'Not last night, not when I'm in party mode. But most of the time, that's how I feel around you. You steady me. You treat me as an equal. With guys my age or close, I can tell what's foremost on their mind, and it's always a battle to win their respect. Like with Tucker. That may explain why I've got this thing for older men. They don't just see tits and a pussy, they see all of me. I'm speaking generally, of course. I get lots of horny old goats hitting on me, but they're desperate. You're not desperate. You don't have a need to get over on me.'

'That might change,' he says.

She puts a finger to his lips, shushing him. 'Everything changes, everybody's kinky for something. Some guy shows up at my door with a muskrat, a coil of rope, and three pounds of lard, that's where I draw the line. But normal, everyday kinks ... They're cool.' She shrugs. 'So it changes? So you're fifty-four with a bad back? So I'm kinky for older men? So what? And in case you're going to tell me you don't want to be a father figure, don't worry. When I'm around you, I'm always wet. Some times more than others, but it's pretty much constant. I don't think of you as my dad.' She blows air through her pursed lips, as if wearied by this unburdening. 'Fucking is just something I do with guys, Cliff. It doesn't require holy water and a papal dispensation. It's not that huge a deal.'

'That's a lie,' he says.

'Yeah,' she says after a pause. 'It's a fairly huge deal. All right. But what I'm trying to say is, if it doesn't work out, I'll cry and be depressed and hit things. My heart may even break. But it won't kill me. I heal up good.'

The rain beats in against the window, spraying under the glass, drenching the ledge, spattering on the floor, yet Marley doesn't bother to close it. She sits up and, with a supple movement, shucks her t-shirt. The shape of a bikini top is etched upon her skin and in the half-light her high, smallish breasts, tipped by engorged nipples, are shockingly pale in contrast to her tan. It strikes Cliff as exotic, a solar tattoo, and he imagines designs of pale and dark all over her body, some so tiny they can only be detected by peering close, others needing a magnifying glass to read the erotic message that they, in sum, comprise. She lies down again, an arm across her tight, rounded stomach. Sheets of rain wash over the window, transforming it into a smeary lens of dull green and silvered gray, seeming to show a world still in process of becoming.

'So,' Marley says. 'You going in to work today?'

'Probably not,' he says.

CHAPTER 7

Before going into work the following day, Cliff stops by the cottage. It's a sunny, breezy afternoon and all should be right with the world, but the stillness of the place unnerves him. He peels police tape off the doors, hurriedly packs a few changes of clothes and, an afterthought, tosses his copy of *Sword Of The Black Demon* into his bag. If things get uncomfortable at Marley's, he'll move to a motel, but he has determined that he's not going to spend another night in the cottage until the situation is resolved, until he can be assured that there'll be no reoccurrence of blue witches and flashing lights and two-hundred-foot tall swordsmen.

He pulls into Ridgewood Motors shortly before two and, from that point on, he's so busy that he scarcely has a chance to glance at the Celeste. Jerry's in a foul mood because Stacey Gerone has run off and left him shorthanded.

'She's been screwing some rich old fart from Miami,' Jerry says. 'I guess she blew him so good, he finally popped the question. That bitch can suck dick like a two-dollar whore in a hurricane.'

Dressed in his trademark madras suit and white loafers, Jerry cocks an eye at Cliff, doubtless hoping to be asked how he knows about Stacey's proclivities; he's brimming over with eagerness to divulge his conquest.

Jerry's pudgy, built along the lines of Papa Smurf, with a tanning-machine tan like brownish orange paint and a ridiculous toupee – he cultivates this clownish image to distract from his nasty disposition. Thanks to this and an endless supply of dirty jokes, ranging from the mildly pornographic to X-tra Blue, he's in demand as a speaker at Rotary Club and Chamber of Commerce dinners and has acquired a reputation for being crusty yet loveable. He acknowledges Cliff as a near-equal, someone who has the worldliness to understand him, someone in whom he can confide to an extent, and thus Cliff, knowing that Jerry will vent his temper on the other salesmen if he doesn't listen to him brag, is forced to endure a richly embroidered tale of Jerry's liaisons with Stacey, culminating with an act of sodomy described in such graphic detail, he's almost persuaded that it might have happened, although it's more likely that the verisimilitude is due to Jerry's belief that it happened, that through repetition his fantasy has become real.

This is the first Cliff has heard of the 'rich old fart,' but he's aware that Stacey played her cards close to the vest and there was much he did not know about her. He tries to nudge the conversation in that direction, hoping to learn more; but Jerry, made grumpy by his questions, orders him out onto the lot to sell some fucking cars.

A little after five o'clock, he's about to close with a young couple who've been sniffing around a two-year-old Bronco since the previous Friday, when Shalin Palaniappan strolls onto the lot. She walks up to Cliff, ignoring another salesman's attempt to intercept her, and says, 'Hi.'

Cliff excuses himself, steers Shalin away from the couple, and says, 'I'm in the middle of something. Let me get somebody else to help you.'

'I want you,' Shalin says pertly.

'You're going to have to wait, then.'

'I've waited this long. What's a few minutes more?'

With her baggy shorts and a pale yellow T-shirt, her shiny black eyes, her shiny black hair in a ponytail, her copper-and-roses complexion, she looks her age, fifteen or sixteen, a healthy, happy Malaysian teenager; but he senses something wrong about her, something also signaled by her enigmatic comment about waiting, an undercurrent that doesn't shine, that doesn't match her fresh exterior, like that spanking new Escalade with the bent frame they had in a few weeks before. He leaves her leaning against a Nissan 350-Z and goes back to the couple who, given the time to huddle up, have decided in his absence that they're not happy with the numbers and want more value on the toad they offered as a trade-in. Cliff feels Shalin's eyes applying a brand to the back of his neck and grows flustered. He grows even more so when he notices a young salesman approach her and begin chatting her up, bracing with one hand on the Nissan, leaning close, displaying something other than the genial manner that is form behavior for someone who pushes iron – then, abruptly, the salesman scurries off as if his tender bits have been scorched. Most teenage girls, in Cliff's experience, don't have the social skills to deal efficiently with the two-legged flies that come buzzing around, yet he allows that Shalin may be an exception. The couple becomes restive; now they're not sure about the Bronco. Cliff, aware that he's blowing it, passes them off to John Sacks, a decent closer, and goes over to Shalin.

'How can I help you?' he asks, and is startled by the harshness, the outright antipathy in his voice.

Shalin, looking up at him, shields her eyes against the westering sun, but says nothing.

'What are you looking to spend?' he asks.

'How much is this one?' She pats the Nissan's hood.

He names a figure and she shakes her head, a no.

'Do you have a car?' he asks. 'We can be pretty generous on a trade-in.'

'That's right. You always take it out in trade, don't you?'

Her snide tone is typical of teenagers, but her self-assurance is not, and her entire attitude, one of arrogance and bemusement, causes him to think that there's another purpose to her visit.

'I'm busy,' he says. 'If you're not looking for a car, I have other customers.'

'Did you know I'm adopted? I am. But Bazit treats me like his very own daughter. He caters to my every whim.' She reaches into a pocket, extracts a platinum Visa card and waggles it in his face. 'Why don't we look around? If I see something I like, you can go into your song-and-dance.'

He's tempted to blow her off, but he's curious about her. They walk along the aisles of gleaming cars, past salesmen talking with prospective buyers, pennons snapping in the breeze. She displays no interest in any of the cars, continuing to talk about herself, saying that she never knew her parents, she was raised by an aunt, but she's always thought of her as a mother, and when the aunt died – she was nine, then – Bazit stepped in. Not long afterward, they moved to America and bought the Celeste.

'There!' She stops and points at a silver Jag, an XK coupe. 'I like that one. Can I take a test drive?'

'That's a sixty-thousand dollar car,' says Cliff. 'You want a test drive, I'll have to clear sixty thousand on your credit card.'

'Do it.'

He goes into the office and runs the card – it's approved. What, he asks himself, is a sixteen-year-old doing with that much credit? He knocks on Jerry's door and tells him that he has a teenage girl who wants to test-drive the SK.

'Fuck her,' says Jerry without glancing up. 'I've got a dealer who'll take it off our hands.'

'Her card cleared.'

'No shit? A rich little cunt, huh?' Jerry clasps his hands behind his head and rocks back in his swivel chair. 'Naw. I don't want a kid driving that car.'

'It's the girl from the Celeste.'

'Shalin?' Jerry's expression goes through some extreme changes – shock, concern, bewilderment – that are then paved over by his customary. 'What the hell. He throws a lot of business our way.'

Cliff doubts that a man who rents motel rooms for twenty-nine bucks a night could be boosting Jerry's profits to any consequential degree, and he wonders what shook him up … if, indeed, he was shaken, if he wasn't having a flare-up of his heartburn.

Shalin, it turns out, knows her way around a stick shift and drives like a pro, whipping the SK around sharp corners, downshifting smoothly, purring along the little oak-lined back streets west of Ridgewood Avenue, and Cliff's anxiety ebbs. He points out various features of the car, none of which appear to impress Shalin. It's clear that she enjoys being behind the wheel and, when she asks if she can check out what the SK is like on the highway, he says, 'Yeah, but keep it under sixty-five.'

Soon they're speeding south on Highway 1 toward New Smyrna, passing through a salt marsh that puts Cliff in mind of an African place – meanders of blue water and wide stretches of grass bronzed by the late sun, broken here and there by mounded islands topped with palms; birds wheeling under a cloudless sky; a few human structures, dilapidated cabins, peeling billboards, but not enough to shatter the illusion that they're entering a vast preserve.

After a minute or two, Shalin says, 'My mother and I … I mean, my aunt. We shared an unique connection. We resembled each other physically. Many people mistook us for mother and daughter. But the resemblance went deeper than that. We had a kind of telepathy. She told me stories about her life, and I saw images relating to the stories. When I described them to her, she'd say things like, "Yes, that's it! That's it exactly!" or "It sounds like the compound I stayed at on Lake Yogyarta." I came to have the feeling that as she died – she was sick the whole time I was with her, in dreadful pain – she was transferring her substance to me. We were becoming the same person. And perhaps we were.' She darts a glance toward Cliff. 'Do you believe that's possible? That someone can possess another body, that they can express their being into another flesh? I do. I can remember being someone else, though I can't identify who that person was. My head's too full of my aunt's memories. It certainly would explain why I'm so mature. Everyone says that about me, that I'm mature for my age. Don't you agree?'

Scarily mature, Cliff says to himself. He doesn't like the direction of the conversation and tells her they'd better be heading back to the lot.

'Certainly. As soon as I see a turn-off.'

She gooses the accelerator, and the SK surges forward, pushing Cliff back into the passenger seat. The digital readout on the speedometer hits eighty, eighty-five, then declines to sixty-five. She's putting on a little show, he thinks; reminding him who's in control.

'Aunt Isabel spoke frequently about the man who made her ill,' Shalin goes on. 'He was handsome and she loved him, of course. Otherwise she wouldn't have risked getting pregnant. He said he couldn't feel her as well when he wore a condom, and since this was at a time when protection wasn't considered important – nobody in Southeast Asia knew about AIDS – she allowed him to have his way.'

A queasy coldness builds in Cliff's belly. 'Isabel. Was she an actress?'

'You remember! That makes it so much easier. Isabel Yahya. You cracked jokes about her last name. You said you were getting your ya-yas out when you were with her. She didn't understand that, but I do.'

She swings the SK in a sharp left onto a dirt road, a reckless maneuver; then she brakes, throws it into reverse, backs onto the highway, raising dust, and goes fishtailing toward Daytona.

'Take it easy! Okay?' Cliff grips the dashboard. 'I didn't give her anything. She gave it to me. And it obviously wasn't AIDS, or I'd be dead.'

'No, you're right. It wasn't AIDS, but you definitely gave it to her.'

'The hell I did!'

'Before you became involved with Isabel, you slept with other women in Manila, didn't you?'

'Sure I did, but she's the one …'

'You were her first lover in more than a year!'

Shalin settles into cruising speed and Cliff, sobered by what she's told him, says, 'Even if that's true …'

'It's true.'

'… she could have seen a doctor.'

'She did,' says Shalin. 'If you hadn't gotten her fired, perhaps she could have seen the doctor who attended you.'

'What are you talking about? I didn't get her fired! She vanished off the set. I didn't know what had happened to her.'

Shalin makes a dismissive noise. 'As it was, Aunt Isabel went to a *bomoh*. A shaman. I can't blame you for that. She was a country girl and still put her trust in such men. But when he failed her, she wrote you letters, begging for help, for money to engage a western doctor. You never replied.'

'I never got any letters.'

'I don't believe you.'

'She didn't have my address. How could she have written me?'

'She mailed them in care of your agent.'

'That's like dropping them into a black hole. Mark … my agent. He's not the most together guy. He probably filed them somewhere and forgot to send them along.'

They flash past a ramshackle fishing camp at the edge of the marsh, wooden cabins and a pier with a couple of small boats moored at its nether end. Their speed is creeping up and Cliff tells her to back it down.

'It's an astonishing coincidence that we bought the Celeste and you started working for Uncle Jerry,' she says. 'It almost seems some karmic agency is playing a part in all this.'

Cliff doesn't know what troubles him more, the idea that the coincidence is not a coincidence, a thought suggested by her sly tone, or the implication that an intimate relationship exists between Jerry Muntz and the Palaniappans. Now that he thinks about it, he's seen Jerry, more than once, stop at the motel for a few minutes before heading home. He has no reason to assign the relationship a sinister character, yet Jerry wouldn't befriend people like the Palaniappans unless he had a compelling reason.

'All of what?' he asks.

'Aunt Isabel was a woman of power,' says Shalin. 'By nature, she was trusting and impractical, not at all suited for life in Manila or Jakarta. She ended up in Jakarta, you know. In a section known as East Cipinang, a slum on the edge of a dump. We survived by scavenging. I'd take the things we found and sell them in the streets to tourists. We had enough to eat most days. Tourists bought from me not because they wanted the things we found, but because I was very pretty little girl.' Her lips thin, as if she's biting back anger. 'Isabel could only work a few hours a day, and sometimes not that. Her insides were rotting. She received medicine from a clinic, but the disease had progressed too far for the doctors to do anything other than ease her pain. She'd lost her beauty. In the last years before she died, she looked like an old, shriveled hag.'

'I'm sorry,' Cliff says. 'I wish I had known.'

'Yes, you would have flown to her side, I'm sure. She often spoke of your generosity.'

'Look, I didn't know. I can't be held responsible for something I didn't know was happening.'

'Is that what it is to you? A matter of whether or not you can be held responsible? Are you afraid I'm going to sue you?'

'No, that's not ...'

'Rest assured, I'm not going to sue you.'

Her voice is so thick with menace, Cliff is momentarily alarmed. They're within the city limits now, driving in rush hour traffic past fruit stands and motels and souvenir shops, not far from the lot – he can't wait to get out of the car.

'Isabel, as I told you, was a woman of power,' says Shalin. 'In another time, another place, she would have been respected and revered. But ill, buried in the slums, power of the sort she possessed could do her no good.'

'What the hell are you getting at?' he asks.

She flashes a sunny smile and goes on with her narrative. 'Isabel loved you until the end. I know she hated you a little, too, but she maintained that you weren't evil, just profligate and vain. And slight. She said there wasn't much to you. You were terribly immature, but she had hopes you'd grow out of that, even though you were in your thirties when she knew you. She was basically a decent soul and power was something she used judiciously, only in cases where she could produce a good effect. It was among the last things she transferred to me.' She sighs forlornly. 'Taking control of me was the one selfish act she committed in her life. You can't blame her. The streets had left me damaged beyond repair and she was terrified of death. Of course these transfers are a bit like reincarnation, so it's not exactly Isabel who's alive. I mean, she is alive, but she's a different person now. There are things that are left behind during a transfer, and things added that belonged to the soul who once inhabited this body.'

'You're out of your tree.' He says this without much conviction. 'All you're doing is screwing with me.'

'Right on both counts.'

She slows and eases into the turning lane across from the lot, waiting for a break in the traffic.

'Now,' she says, 'I use my power to get the things I want, to make my family secure. Sometimes I use it on a whim. You might say I use it profligately.'

She edges forward, but brakes when she realizes she can't make the turn yet. A semi roars past, followed by a string of cars.

'One thing Isabel didn't transfer to me was her love for you,' she says. 'I imagine she wanted to keep that for herself, to warm her final moments. She was almost empty. All that was left was a shell, a few memories. Or maybe she didn't want me to love you. You know, in case I ever saw you again. Do you suppose that's it? She wanted me to hate you?'

'You can get by after that red pick-up,' he says.

'I see it.' She makes the turn, pulls into the lot and parks. 'If that's so, if that's really what Isabel wanted, she got her wish,' she says. 'No child should have to endure East Cipinang. You have no idea of the things I was forced to do as a result of your nonchalance, your triviality. Your shallowness.'

She looks as if she's about to spit on him, climbs out of the SK and then bends to the window, peering in at him. 'This car won't do, I'm afraid,' she says, blithely. 'It corners horribly.'

'What're you trying to pull?' he asks. 'You were at my house the other night, weren't you?'

'If you say so.'

'What the hell do you want from me?'

She straightens, as though preparing to leave, but then leans in the window again, her teeth bared and black eyes bugged. Except for the color of her skin, it's the face of the witch, vividly insane, without a single human quality, and Cliff recoils from it.

'If you want answers, watch Isabel's movie,' she says, her face relaxing into that of a teenage girl. 'I believe you have a copy.'

CHAPTER 8

Cliff sits in his office for an hour, hour and a half, not thinking so much as brooding about Shalin's story. It's absurd, impossible, yet elements of it ring true, especially the part about him giving Isabel the STD. He digs deep, mining his memories, trying to recall how she was, how he felt about her, and remembers her as a simple girl, not simple in the sense of stupid, but open and unaffected, though it may be he's prompted by guilt to gild the lily. She didn't seem at all 'a woman of power,' but then he didn't take the time to know her, to look beneath the surface. His clearest memories relate to her amazing breasts, her dancer's legs and ass, and to what a great lay she was. He wishes he could remember a moment when he loved her, an instance in which he saw something special about her, but he was a superficial kind of guy in those days, and maybe still is.

Thoughts buzz him like mosquitoes, a cloud of tiny, shrill thoughts that swarms around his head, diving close just long enough to nettle his brain, questions about Shalin's story, more memories of Isabel (once a trickle, their flow has become a flood, but all relating to how she looked, smelled, felt, tasted), and disparaging thoughts, lots of them, remarking on, as Shalin put it, his triviality, his nonchalance, his shallowness. If he could go an entire day without his life being captioned by this dreary self-commentary …

The phone rings, and he picks it up, grateful for the interruption. His agent's mellow tenor brings all the infectious banality of SoCal to his ear. After an exchange of pleasantries, his agent says, 'Listen, Cliff. I was in New York last week. I had this crazy idea and you know me, what the hell, I pitched it to a couple of publishers. I said, What if Cliff Coria wrote a book, a memoir, about his life in the movies. This guy's acted all over, I told them. Spain, Southeast Asia, Czechoslovakia. You name it. And he's smart. And he's seen celebrities in unguarded moments. He's kind of an insider-slash-outsider. He can give you a view from the fringes of Hollywood, and maybe that's the clearest view of all.'

'I don't know, Mark.'

'Don't you want to hear how they reacted?'

'Yeah.'

'They were excited, Cliff. There could be serious money for you in this. And if the book does what I think it will, it'll generate significant heat out here.'

The Celeste's Vacancy sign switches on in the twilight, seeming like a glowing blue accusation. Cliff lowers the Venetian blinds.

'I believe there'll be interest in you as a character actor,' Mark goes on. 'Not just cheesy parts. I think I'd be able to get you serious work. I know you can do this, Cliff. Remember those letters you used to send me? Like the one about Nicholson's ass hanging out of the car when he was banging that bit player? That was fucking hilarious! Come on! All I need is a few chapters and a rough outline.'

Cliff assures his agent that he'll give it a try. He leaves a note for Jerry, saying he's going to take a few days off to deal with some personal problems, and then heads for Marley's place. Crossing the Main Street Bridge over the Halifax River, which bisects Daytona, he sees several old men fishing off the bridge, half in silhouette, motionless, with buckets at their feet, the corpses of blowfish and stingrays bloodily strewn along the walkway, and thinks that if he were ever to take up fishing, this is where he'd like to drop his line. The idea of joining those sentinel figures appeals to him, as does the thought of hauling up little monsters from the deep.

At the apartment Cliff pours a vodka from a bottle chilled in the freezer, turns on the TV, and pops *Sword Of The Black Demon* into the DVD player. While the opening credits roll, he calls Marley and tells her he's coming up to the Surfside sometime between nine and ten. He fast-forwards through the movie until he finds the entrance of the witch queen and her chunky blue retinue; then he sits on the edge of the bed, sipping vodka, watching Isabel Yahya and the other women attending a ceremony in a torchlit cave made of acrylic fiber painted to look like rock – it involves the queen choosing a new fuck toy, a young Filipino youth with oiled muscles. She leads him to the royal chamber, where a bed with blue satin sheets awaits, screws his brains out and, while he's helpless, limp, and nearly unconscious from her amorous assault, she drains him of his soul, laughing as she coaxes it forth by means of a lascivious dance. The soul resembles a stream of pale smoke from which faces surface. Cliff assumes them to be the youth's memories. The smoke dwindles to a trickle and at long last, after much eye-rolling and twitching, the youth dies.

In another scene, Ricky Sintara, a striking young man with even larger muscles, also oiled, and Dak Windsor enter the cave, seeking to capture the queen and persuade her to divulge the whereabouts of the wizard who has loosed the black demon; but they are themselves captured by the royal guard. The queen drags Ricky off to suffer the same fate as the youth, but once in the sack, Ricky proves to be no ordinary man – his incomparable lovemaking renders the queen *hors de combat*. This is all shown tastefully – no actual penetration; only full frontal female nudity – and dredges up a chuckle from Cliff, because Ricky, a fine fellow and terrific drinking companion, would on occasion wear women's clothing when relaxing during the shoot and had a boyfriend who was prettier than the majority of the actresses.

Meanwhile, in another part of the cave, Dak is chained to the wall and Isabel is preparing to scourge him with an S&M dream of a whip whose lashes appear to be fashioned of live scorpions. He takes a few strokes, writhes in pain, calls out to God for assistance, using a specific phrase that causes Isabel to realize that he is the son of the doctor who saved her village from a cholera outbreak years before – she was a little girl at the time, but developed a crush on the teenage Dak that lasts to this day. Turned aside from the path of evil by the power of love, she frees Dak and they kiss, a miracle of osculation that changes her skin from blue back to a pleasing caramel, and together, along with Ricky, they flee the cave, carrying with them the comatose queen.

Lashed to a bed in Ricky's shack (the hero has hewed to his humble village origins), the queen strains mightily against her ropes, mimicking her earlier struggles in the act of love, breasts heaving, hips thrusting, tormented by Ricky's questions, and eventually she yields up her secrets. But that night, while Dak and Ricky are reconnoitering the wizard's lair, she calls out to Isabel, whom she still controls to an extent. By means of her occult powers and a cross-eyed, beetling stare, she coerces Isabel into untying her bonds. She then knocks her to the ground and stands over her, waggling her fingers and projecting dire energies from their tips, bursts of blue light that cause her former minion to shrivel, to grow desiccated and wrinkled, dying of old age in a matter of seconds.

Is that, Cliff asks himself, what Shalin wants him to believe may be in store for him? He recalls her talk about Isabel's premature aging, her comment regarding a karmic agency being involved in all of this – a sudden withering would be an apt punishment according to karmic law. But he refuses to believe Shalin capable of doling out such a punishment.

He goes to the refrigerator, pours another vodka, and watches the rest of the movie. The queen escapes through the surrounding jungle, but is killed by Ricky, who throws his magical dagger at her. It tumbles end over end, traveling hundreds of yards through the darkness, swerving around clumps of bamboo, tree trunks, bushes, and impales the fleeing queen through her malignant heart. Dak grieves for Isabel, but is bucked up by Ricky and rises to the moment with renewed zeal. With the help of a friendly shaman, they plot the attack: Dak will lead the simple villagers (there are always simple villagers in Filipino fantasy movies) in an assault on the wizard's palace, distracting the evil one so that Ricky can sneak inside and do him in.

The battle goes badly for Dak at first. The villagers are being hacked to pieces by the wizard's guard. All seems lost, but the ghost of Isabel appears, wreathed in swirling mist to disguise the fact the actress is no longer Isabel (a love scene between her ghost and Dak was intended for the night before the battle, but she vanished from the project and a rewrite was necessary), and she inspires him with a message of undying love and tells him of a secret tunnel into which they can lure the guard and fight them in a narrow confine, thus neutralizing their superior numbers. As this is happening, the Black Demon accosts Ricky outside the palace and all, again, seems lost. Not even he can defeat a giant. But the ancient gods, played by white-bearded men wearing silk robes and several busty Filipina babes in brocaded halters, intervene. They whisk Ricky and the Black Demon away to a cosmic platform surrounded by a profusion of stars and clouds of nebular gas (glowing, Cliff notices, rose and purple, green and white, like the lights he saw outside his cottage), shrink them to almost equal size (the demon still has a considerable advantage), and let them fight. Fending off blows with a magic bracelet given him by his dying father, a silvery circlet wrought from the stuff of a dying star, Ricky bests the demon and takes his sword – it is, by chance, the only weapon that can slay the wizard. He is returned to planet Earth where, after a torrid chase, the wizard changes into a huge serpent that Ricky chops into snake sushi.

In the final scene, also rewritten late in the game, a big celebration, Ricky wanders about the village, a girl on each arm, searching for his pal. Following an intuition, he divests himself of the ladies and enters the local temple, where he finds Dak on his knees, praying for the soul of Isabel at an altar surmounted by her portrait. He puts his hand on Dak's shoulder. The two men exchange sober glances. Then Ricky kneels beside him and adopts a prayerful attitude. Solemn music rises, changing to a bouncy disco theme as the screen darkens and the end credits roll.

Cliff thinks now that the last scene might have been intentionally ironic. He recalls that the director dogged Isabel throughout the shoot and seemed miffed when she got together with Cliff. He may have fired her because she wouldn't sleep with him and rewrote the scene to make a point. Not that this bears upon anything relevant to his current problem. He drains his vodka, idly gazing at the credits, puzzling over the film, wondering what Shalin wanted him to take from it. Maybe nothing. Maybe she just wanted him to endure the pain of watching it again. And then he spots something. A name. It flips past too quickly and he's not sure he saw it. He hits reverse on the remote, plays it forward, and there it is, the logical explanation he's been seeking, the answer to everything:

Special Effects: Bazit Palaniappan

He knew it! They've been trying to gaslight him the whole time. He remembers the F/X guy, a thin man in his fifties with graying hair who bore a passing resemblance to the owner of the Celeste. He must be Bazit the elder's son and dropped the Jr. after his father died. Why didn't he mention the connection? Surely he would have, unless he was too excited at seeing

Dak Windsor. No, he would have mentioned it. Unless he had a reason to keep quiet about it ... which he did. It occurs to Cliff that Bazit might be one of those soul transfers such as Shalin claimed to have undergone, but he's not buying that. With knowledge gained from his father, Bazit tricked up the dunes around Cliff's cottage and put on a show. Shalin must have assumed that he wouldn't watch the end credits.

Exhilarated, Cliff starts to pour another drink, then decides he'll have that drink with Marley. She gets off at ten – he'll take her out for a late supper, somewhere nicer than the Surfside, and they'll celebrate. She won't know what they're celebrating, but he's glad now that he didn't burden her with any of this. He trots down the stairs and out into the warm, windless night, into squeals and honks and machine gun fire from the arcades, happy shouts from the Ferris wheel, now lit up and spinning, and the lights on the miniature golf course glossing over its dilapidation, providing a suitable setting for the family groups clumped about the greens. The bright souvenir shops selling painted sand dollars and polished driftwood, funny hats and sawfish snouts, and the sand drifting up onto the asphalt from The World's Most Famous Be-atch (as an oft-seen t-shirt design proclaims), and the flashing neon signs above strip clubs and tourist bars along Main Street, the din of calliope music, stripper music, tavern music, and voices, voices, voices, the vocal exhaust of vacationland America, exclamations and giggles, drunken curses and yelps and unenlightened commentary – it's all familiar, overly familiar, tedious and unrelentingly ordinary, yet tonight its colors are sharper, its sounds more vivid, emblematic of the world of fresh possibility that Cliff is suddenly eager to engage.

CHAPTER 9

It's a good week for Cliff and Marley, a very good week. There is no recurrence of demons, no witches, no bumps in the night. Jerry is furious with him, naturally, and threatens to fire him, but he has no leverage – the job is merely a pastime for Cliff and he tells Jerry to go ahead, fire him, he'll find some other way to occupy his idle hours. He works on the book and is surprised how easily it flows. He hasn't settled on a title yet, but anecdotal material streams out of him and he's amazed by how funny it is – it didn't seem that funny at the time; and, though he's aware that he has a lot of cleaning up to do on the prose, he's startled by the sense of bittersweet poignancy that seems to rise from his words, even from the uproarious bits. It's as if in California, those years of struggle and fuck-ups, he realized that the dream he was shooting for was played-out, that the world of celebrity with its Bel Air mansions and stretch limos and personal chefs masked a terrible malformation that he hated, that he denied yet knew was there all along, that he didn't want badly enough because, basically, he never wanted it at all.

The relationship, too, flows. Cliff has his concerns, particularly about their ages, but he's more-or-less convinced himself that it's all right; he's neither conning Marley nor himself. He can hope for ten good years, fifteen at the outside, but that's a lifetime. After that, well, whatever comes will come. It's not that he feels young again. His back's still sore, he's beginning to recognize that he needs more than reading glasses, but he no longer feels as empty as he did and he thinks that Marley was spot-on in her diagnosis: he was lonely.

They make love, they go to the movies, they walk on the beach, and they talk about everything: about global warming, the NBA (Marley's a Magic fan; Cliff roots for the Lakers), about religion and ghosts and salsa, about dogs versus cats as potential pets, about fashion trends and why he never married, and veterinary school. Cliff offers to help with the tuition and, though reluctant at first, Marley says there's a well-regarded school in Orlando and she's been accepted, but doesn't know if she'll have enough saved to go for the fall term. Cliff has major problems with Orlando. There's no beach, no ocean breeze to break the summer heat, and he dreads being in such close proximity to the Mouse and the hordes of tourists who pollute the environment. Rednecks of every stamp, the blighted of the earth, so desperate in their search for fun that they make pilgrimages to Disneyworld and commingle with one another in a stew of ill-feeling that frequently results in knuckle-dragging fights between hairy, overweight men and face-offs between grim-lipped parents and their whiny kids. But he says, 'Okay. Let's do it.'

He's scared by what he's beginning to feel for her, and he's not yet prepared to turn loose of the pool ladder and swim out into the deep end; but his grip is slipping and he knows immersion is inevitable. At times, in certain lights, she seems no older than twenty. She's got the kind of looks that last and she'll still be beautiful when they cart him off to the rest home. That afflicts him. But then she'll say or do something, make a move in bed or offer a comment about his book or, like the other night at the movies, the first movie he's attended in years, reach over and touch his arm and smile, that causes him to recognize this is no girl, no beach bunny, but a mature woman who's committed her share of sins and errors in judgment, and is ready for a serious relationship, even if he is not. That liberates him from his constraints, encourages him to lose himself in contemplation of her, to see her with a lover's eye, to notice how, when she straddles him, she'll gather her hair behind her neck and gaze briefly at the wall, as if focusing herself before she lets him enter; how her lips purse and her eyebrows lift when she reads; how when she cooks, she'll stand on one foot for a minute at a time, arching her back to keep on balance; how when she combs out her hair after a shower, bending her head to one side, her neck and shoulder configure a line like the curve of a Spanish guitar. He wants to understand these phrasings of her body, to know things about her that she herself may not know.

The ninth morning after Cliff quit working for Jerry (he hasn't made it official yet, but in his mind he's done), he's lying in bed when Marley, fresh from a shower, wearing a bathrobe, tells him she's going to visit her mother in Deland; she'll be gone two or three days.

'I meant to tell you yesterday,' she says. 'But I guess I've been in denial. My mom's sort of demented. Not really, though sometimes I wonder. She never makes these visits easy.'

'You want me to come along?'

'God, no! That would freak her out. Totally. Not because you're you. Any man would freak her out ... any woman, for that matter. She'd hallucinate I'm having a lesbian affair, and then all I'd hear the whole time is stuff about the lie of the White Goddess and how we're in a time of social decline. It's going to be hard enough as it is.' She hoists a small suitcase out from the back of the closet. 'I want this visit to be as serene as possible, because the last day I'm there, I'm going to tell her about Orlando.'

'It's not that big a move,' he says. 'You'll still be within an hour's drive.'

'To her, it'll be an extinction event, believe me.' She rummages through her underwear drawer. 'One day you'll have to meet her, but you want to put that day off as long as you can. I love her, but she can be an all-pro pain in the butt.'

Gloomily, he watches her pack for a minute and then says, 'I'll miss you.'

'I know! God, I'm going to miss you so much!' She turns from her packing and, with a mischievous expression, opens her robe and flashes him. 'I've got time for a quickie.'

'Come ahead.'

She leaps onto the bed, throws a leg across his stomach, bringing her breasts close to his face; he tastes soap on her nipples. She rolls off him, onto her back, looking flushed.

'Better make that a long-ie,' she says. 'It's got to last for two days.'

After she's gone, Cliff mopes about the apartment. He opens a box of Wheat Thins, eats a handful, has a second cup of coffee, paces. At length, he sits on the bed, back propped up by pillows, and, using Marley's laptop, starts working on the book. When he looks up again, he's surprised to find that four hours have passed. He has a late lunch at a Chinese restaurant on South Atlantic, then drives home and works some more. Around eight-thirty, Marley calls.

'This has to be brief,' she says, and asks him about his day.

'Nothing much. Worked on the book. Ate lunch at Lim's. How about you?'

'The usual. Interrogation. Field exercises. Advanced interrogation.'

'It can't be that bad.'

'No, it's not … but I don't want to be here. That makes it worse.'

'Are you coming back tomorrow?'

'I don't know yet. It depends on how much aftercare mom's going to need.' A pause. 'How's the book coming?'

'You can judge for yourself, but it feels pretty good. Today I wrote about this movie I did with Robert Mitchum and Kim …'

'Shit! I have to go. I'll call tomorrow if I can.'

'Wait …'

'Love you,' she says, and hangs up.

He pictures her standing in her mother's front yard, or in the bathroom, a little fretful because she didn't intend to say the L word, because it's the first time either of them have used it, and she's not sure he's ready to hear it, she's worried it might put too much pressure on him. But hearing the word gives him a pleasant buzz, a comforting sense of inclusion, and he wishes he could call her back.

He falls asleep watching a Magic game with the sound off; when he wakes, a preacher is on the tube, weeping and holding out his arms in supplication. He washes up but chooses not to shower, checks himself in the mirror, sees a heavy two-day growth of gray stubble, and chooses not to shave. He breakfasts on fresh pineapple, toast, and coffee, puts on a t-shirt, bathing suit, and flip-flops, and walks down to the beach. It's an overcast morning, low tide, the water placid and dark blue out beyond the bar. Sandpipers scurry along the tidal margin, digging for tiny soft-shelled crabs that have burrowed into the muck. People not much older than himself are power-walking, some hunting for shells. One sixty-something guy in a Speedo, his skin deeply tanned, is searching for change with a metal detector. During spring and summer, Cliff reflects, Daytona is a stage set, with a different cast moved in every few weeks. After the spring breakers, the bikers come for Bike Week. Then the NASCAR crowd flocks into town and everywhere you go, you hear them display their thrilling wit and wisdom, saying things like, 'I warned Charlene not to let him touch it,' and, 'Damn, that Swiss steak looks right good. I believe I'll have me some of that.' But the elderly are always present, always going their customary rounds.

Being part of the senior parade makes Cliff uncomfortable. In the midst of this liver-spotted plague, he fears contagion and he goes up onto the boardwalk. Most of the attractions are closed. The Ferris wheel shows its erector set complexity against a pewter sky; many of the lesser rides are covered in canvas; but one of the arcades is open, its corrugated doors rolled up, and Cliff wanders inside. Behind a counter, a short order cook is busy greasing the grill. Three eighth- or ninth-graders, two Afro-Americans and one white kid dressed hip-hop style, backward caps and baggy clothes, are dicking around with a shooter game. As he passes, they glance toward him, their faces set in a kind of hostile blankness. He can read the thought balloon above their heads, a single balloon with three comma-like stems depending from it: Old Fucking Bum. Cliff decides he likes playing an old fucking bum. He develops a limp, a drunk's weaving, unsteady walk. The kids whisper together and laugh.

At the rear of the arcade, past the row of Ski Ball machines, where they keep the older games, the arcade is quiet and dark and clammy, a sea cave with a low ceiling, its entrance appearing to be a long way off. Cliff scatters quarters atop one of the machines, Jungle Queen, its facing adorned with black panthers and lush vegetation and a voluptuous woman with black hair and red lips and silicon implants, her breasts perfectly conical. When he was a kid, he'd lift the machine and rest its front legs on his toes so the surface was level and the ball wouldn't drop, and he'd rack up the maximum number of free games and play all day. It didn't take much to entertain him, and he supposes it still doesn't.

He plays for nearly an hour, his muscle memory returning, skillfully using body English, working the flippers. He's on his way to setting a personal best, the machine issuing a series of loud pops, signifying games won, when someone comes up on his shoulder and begins watching. Ashford. Cliff keeps playing – he's having a great last ball and doesn't want to blow it. Finally the ball drops. He grins at Ashford and presses the button to start a new game.

Ashford says, 'Having fun?'

'I can't lose,' says Cliff.

Ashford looks to be wearing the same ensemble he wore during the interview, accented on this occasion by a fetching striped tie. The bags under his eyes are faintly purple. Cliff's surprised too see him, but not deeply surprised.

'Have you guys been watching my building?' he asks.

'You didn't answer the buzzer. I took a chance you'd be somewhere close by.' Ashford nods toward the counter at the front of the arcade. 'Let's get some coffee.'

'I've got twelve free games!'

'Don't mess with me, Coria. I'm tired.'

The two men take stools at the counter and Ashford sits without speaking, swigging his coffee, staring glumly at the menu on the wall, black plastic letters arranged on white backing, some of them cockeyed, some of the items misspelled ('cheseburgers,' 'mountin dew'), others cryptically described ('Fresh Fried Shrimp'). The counterman, a middle-aged doofus with a name badge that reads Kerman, pale and fleshy, his black hair trimmed high above his ears, freshens Ashford's coffee. Even the coffee smells like grease. The arcade has begun to fill, people filtering up from the beach.

'Are we just sharing a moment?' asks Cliff. 'Or do you have something else in mind?'

For a few seconds, Ashford doesn't seem to have heard him; then he says, 'Stacey Gerone.'

'Yeah? What about her?'

'You seen her lately?'

'Not for a couple of weeks. Jerry said she ran off to Miami with some rich guy.'

'I heard about that.'

A shorthaired peroxide blonde in a bikini, her black roots showing in such profusion, the look must be by design, hops up onto a stool nearby and asks for a large Pepsi. She has some age on her, late thirties, but does good things for the bikini. Ashford cuts his eyes toward her breasts; his gaze lingers.

'Ain't got no Pepsi,' Kerman says in a sluggish, country drawl. 'Just Coke.'

'This morning around five-thirty, one of your neighbors found a suitcase full of Stacey Gerone's clothes in the dunes out front of your house.' Ashford emits a small belch, covering his mouth. 'Any idea how it got there?'

Alarmed, Cliff says, 'I didn't put it there!'

'I didn't say you put it there. You're not that stupid.'

'I haven't been to the house for three days. I just drove by to see if everything was all right.'

The blonde, after pondering the Pepsi problem, asks if she can have some fries.

'You want a large Coke with that?' asks Kerman.

Again the blond ponders. 'Small diet Coke.'

Kerman, apparently the genius of the arcade, switches on the piped-in music, and metal-ish rock overwhelms the noises of man and nature. Ashford, with a pained expression, tells him to turn it off.

'Got to have the music on after nine o'clock,' says Kerman.

'Well, turn it fucking down!'

'You got no call to be using bad language.' Kerman sulks, but lowers the volume; following Ashford's direction, he lowers it until the music is all but inaudible.

Ashford rubs his stomach, scowls, and then gets to his feet. 'I have to hit the john. Don't go away.'

As he walks off, the blonde leans the intervening stool and taps Cliff on the arm. 'Do I know you? I believe I do.'

Cliff mentions that he was once an actor, movies and commercials, and the blond says, 'No, that's not it. At least, I don't think.' She taps her chin and then snaps her fingers. 'The Shark! You used to come in. You were seeing Janice for a while last year. I'm Mary Beth.'

All the women at the Shark Lounge, waitresses and dancers alike, are working girls and, after hearing about how Janice has been doing, Cliff has an idea.

'Have you got time for a date this morning?' he asks.

That puts a hitch in Mary Beth's grin, but she says coolly, 'Anything for you, sweetie.'

'It's not for me, it's for my friend. He needs to get laid. He's a cop and the job's beating him up.'

'You want me to ball a cop?'

'He'll welcome it, I swear. Make out you're a police groupie and you saw his gun or something. And don't let on I had anything to do with it.'

'Whatever. It's two hundred for a shave and a haircut. You know, the basics.'

'Shit! I don't have two hundred in cash.'

'What about a credit card? I do Visa and Master.'

She hauls up a voluminous purse from the floor beside her stool and digs out a manual imprinter.

'Hurry!' he says, looking toward the bathroom door as she imprints his card.

Once they've completed their transaction, he says, 'I didn't mean to go all business on you. It was …'

'It's no thing. I do a lot of business with older guys this time of day. It beats night work. They're usually not freaks, so it's easy money.'

'I know, but you were being friendly and I …'

'Oh, was I?' The blonde shoulders her purse and smiles frostily. 'You must have me confused for somebody else. I was working the room, Clifford.'

'Cliff,' he says in reflex.

'Okay. Cliff. I'm going to move to another stool so I can make eye contact with your buddy. But I'm down here most every morning, so if you need me for anything else, you just sing out.'

Cliff doesn't know why he does this type of thing, plays pranks for no reason and without any point. He wonders if had it mind to compromise Ashford, to get something on him; but he doesn't believe it's about manipulating people. He figures it's like with the sea turtle – he's showing off, only for himself alone, his audience reduced to one. Another instance, he thinks, of his nonchalance.

Ashford returns and tells Kerman to bring him a glass of water. He swallows some pills, wipes his mouth, and says, 'They should blow up that john. It's a fucking disaster area.'

'I can help you with that.'

'Huh?'

'I was in a demolition unit during Vietnam.'

Ashford's eye snags on something – Mary Beth is sitting across from him, eating her French fries, giving each one a blowjob, licking off the salt and sucking them in. He tears himself away from this vision and says to Cliff, 'We haven't been able to locate Miz Gerone, so officially you're a person of interest. If that blood on your house matches DNA the lab extracted from her hair brush, I'm going to have to bring you in.'

Cliff offers emphatic denials of any involvement with her disappearance. 'We fucked occasionally,' he says, 'but that was it. We didn't have much of an emotional connection.'

'I know this is a frame. But the way you've handled everything, telling that story, lying about your girlfriend, it …'

'That wasn't a lie. I couldn't get back into my house because you were processing it. So I went over to Marley's after you released me, and things got deep. I swear to God that's the truth.'

'Doesn't matter. It looks bad. You want to know something else that looks bad? I got a copy of one of your movies in the mail the other day. Jurassic Pork. Came in an envelope with no return address.'

'Aw, Christ. I did that picture for the hell of it. I was curious to see what it was like.'

'Somebody's trying to besmirch your character.' Ashford chuckles. 'They're doing a hell of a job, too, because you were definitely the shortest man in the movie.'

'Yeah, yeah!'

'Prosecutors love to drop that sort of detail into a trial. Juries down here tend to think poorly of pornography. But the frame is so goddamn crude. The person doing the framing must have no comprehension of evidentiary procedure.'

'So you believe me?'

'I wouldn't go that far, but I believe something's going on at the Celeste.' Ashford has a sip of water, sneaks a peek at Mary Beth, who returns a wave, which he brusquely acknowledges. 'You know of any way a used car can be given a new car smell?'

'Polyvinyl chloride,' Cliff says. 'The stuff they make dashboards out of. It comes in a liquid form, too. The manufacturers use it as a sealant. When a dealer has to take a car back on warranty, some have been known to slap on a coat of PVC and resell the car as new.'

Ashford takes out his notebook. 'What was that? The sealant?'

Cliff repeats the name. 'The stuff's poison. Every time America has a whiff of a new car interior, they're catching a lungful of carcinogens.'

Apparently unconcerned by this threat to the nation's health, Ashford says, 'I might have found that Ford Escape. About five years ago, we were investigating a stolen car ring and we thought Muntz could be involved. We put a man into his service center in South Daytona. Nothing came of it, but I still had my suspicions. I went up there Tuesday and there was a red Ford Escape sitting out back under a tarp. I had one of our people take a look at it. It had that new car smell, but the engine number had been taken off with acid and the paint job wasn't the original. The car was originally gray, like the one you saw.'

'If Jerry was chopping cars, they would have cut it up within an hour or two of bringing it into the shop,' Cliff says. 'It's been a month.'

'He might have a special order for an Escape. It might be a present for one of Muntz's bimbos. Maybe he had a buyer and the guy has a cash flow problem. Who knows? Maybe it slipped his mind. Muntz is no Einstein.' Ashford's cough is plainly an attempt to disguise the fact that he's taking yet another look at Mary Beth. 'He's got papers, but the name on them doesn't check out. He claims the guy came in off the street and said he won the car on a quiz show. I haven't got enough to charge him, but my gut tells me that was your Escape.'

'So what's next?'

'I might check in to the Celeste tonight and see what's what. Vice has some expensive cars they use for undercover work. I can finagle one for the night, tell the guy on-duty at the yard I need it to impress some woman. That should get me into Room Eleven.'

'You think that's a good idea?'

'I can't see what else to do. I don't have much time. If Gerone's DNA comes back a match to the blood on your house, you're going to become the sole target of the investigation.'

'I thought you said you believed me!'

'I may buy your story. Some of it, anyway. But no one else does. The only reason you haven't been arrested is there's no evidence, no body. I'm on my own. The captain …' Ashford grimaces. 'He's a results kind of guy. He'd love to make this case. It would look good on his resume. You're about as close to a Hollywood celebrity as we got around here, and a trial would get him exposure. It'd be huge on Court TV. He won't authorize me to do diddley until after the DNA comes back. If it's a match, you're in the shit.'

'When's it due back?'

'Depends how far behind the lab's running. Maybe two-three days. Maybe tomorrow afternoon.'

'Fuck!' Cliff tries to concentrate on the problem, but he's too agitated – he flashes on scenes from prison movies, the wavy smear of blood on his porch, the face of the witch. 'You shouldn't do this alone.'

Amused, Ashford says, 'Yeah, it's going to be rough, what with demons and all.'

'You don't know what happened to all those people.'

'First of all, we don't know it's "all those people." We don't even know for sure about Gerone. Second …' He pushes back his coat to reveal his holstered weapon. 'I'm armed, and I have thirty years on the job. I appreciate your motherly concern, but nothing's going to happen that I don't want to happen.'

'Have you asked yourself why they only disappear people who rent Number Eleven?'

'Well,' says Ashford after pretending to contemplate the question. 'I guess because it has a magic stone buried underneath it.'

'You don't have an answer, huh?'

'Maybe there's a hidden entrance,' says Ashford, registering annoyance. 'Or you just didn't see the people leave. Maybe they take them out in little pieces. I got way too many answers. I got them coming out of my ass. That's why I'm going up there, man. That's how you work a case.'

Unhappy with this attitude, knowing he can't influence Ashford, Cliff says, 'I don't understand why you're doing this for me.'

'Jesus!' Ashford gives a derisive laugh. 'You think I'm doing this for you? I don't give a flying fuck about you. I'm doing this because I enjoy it. I dig being a cop. I hate to see bad guys get away. And that's what's going to happen if you become the focus of the investigation. We might get Muntz and the What's-the-fuck's-their-names for auto theft, but if they're guilty of murder, I want to make sure they don't slide.'

Cliff has new picture of Ashford as a rebel, a loner in the department who never advanced beyond the rank of sergeant because of his penchant for disobeying his superiors. He realizes this picture is no more complete than his original image of the man, but he thinks now that they're both part of Ashford's make-up. He wonders what pieces he's missing.

'Go on, get out of here,' Ashford says, still irritated. 'We're done. Go play your free games.'

Cliff hesitates. 'Give me your cell number.'

'What the hell for?'

'If you're in there more than two hours, I'll call you.'

Ashford glares at him, then extracts a card case from his jacket and flips a card onto the counter.

'Call me before you check in,' says Cliff. 'Right before. So I'll know when the two hours are up.'

'Fine.' Ashford signals Kerman, holds up his cup, and grins at Mary Beth. 'See you later.'

CHAPTER 10

As often happens when Cliff is under duress, he's inclined to put off thinking about crucial issues. He returns to Jungle Queen and finds that his place has been taken by a bald, sunburned, hairy-chested man in a bathing suit, a towel draped around his neck, who has frittered away all but two of his free games. Cliff watches for a bit, drawing a perturbed glance from the man, as if Cliff is the reason for his ineptitude.

He spends the rest of the morning pacing, puttering around the apartment, his mind crowded with thoughts about Stacey. They didn't care for each other that much, really. The relationship was based on physical attraction and sort of a mutual condescension – they both viewed the other as being frivolous and shallow. Nevertheless, the idea that she's been murdered makes him sick to his stomach. He switches on the TV, channel-surfs, and switches it off; he vacuums, washes dishes, and finally, at a quarter past one, needing to talk it out with someone, he calls Marley.

'I'm in the middle of something,' she says. 'I'll call you *tomorrow*.'

From her emphasis on the word, he understands that she probably won't be home tonight, that she's trapped by her mother's impending breakdown.

He drives to the Regal Cineplex in Ormond Beach, where a movie's playing that he wants to see, but after half an hour he regrets his decision. It's not that the movie is bad – he can't tell one way or another – but sitting in the almost-empty theater forces him to recognize his own emptiness. It's still there; it hasn't gone away. He's reminded of the first month after he returned to Daytona, when he attended matinee after matinee. He missed being part of the industry, and watching movies had initially been a form of self-punishment, a means of humiliating himself for his failure now that the work wasn't coming anymore; but before long those hours in the dark, staring at yet not really seeing those bright, flickering celluloid lives, brought home the fact that he was missing some essential sliver of soul. He hadn't always missed it – he was certain that prior to Hollywood he'd been whole. Yet somehow, somewhere along the line, show biz had extracted that sliver and left him distant from people, an affable sociopath with no particular ax to grind and insufficient energy to grind it, even if he had one. He hoped Marley could bring him back to life, and he still hopes for that, but hope is becoming difficult to maintain.

He walks out into the empty lobby and stands at the center of movie displays and posters. Pitt and Clooney, Will Smith and Matthew McConaughey, posed heroically, absurdly noble and grim. He buys a bag of popcorn at the concession stand from a pretty blond teenager who, after he moves away, leans on the counter, gazing mournfully at the beach weather beyond the glass. Thinking that it was the violence of the film that started him bumming, he tries a domestic melodrama, then a bedroom farce, but they all switch on the Vacancy sign in his head. He drives back to Marley's apartment in the accumulating twilight, a stiff off-shore wind beginning to bend the palms, and waits for Ashford to call.

By the time the call comes at ten past nine, Cliff's a paranoid, over-caffeinated mess, but Ashford sounds uncustomarily ebullient.

'Black Dog, Black Dog! This is Dirty Harry Omega. We're going in! Pray for us!'

Cliff hears high-pitched laughter in the background. 'Is someone with you? I thought you didn't have any back-up.'

'I brought along the hoo …' He breaks off and asks his companion is it okay he refers to her as a hooker. Cliff can't make out the response, and then Ashford says, 'I brought along the *beautiful, sexy* hooker you set me up with.'

More laughter.

'Are you crazy?' Cliff squeezes the phone in frustration. 'You can't …'

'He wants to know if I'm crazy,' says Ashford.

An instant later, a woman's voice says, 'Ash is *extremely* crazy. I can vouch for that.'

'Mary Beth? Listen! I want you to have him pull over. Right now!'

'Everything's under control, Coria,' says Ashford. 'I'm on top if it.'

'And behind it, too. And on the bottom.' Mary Beth giggles.

'You can't take her in there!' says Cliff. 'It's dangerous! Even if there's nothing …'

''Bye,' says Ashford, and breaks the connection.

Stunned, Cliff calls him back, but either Ashford has switched off his phone or is not picking up.

There's the missing piece to the Ashford puzzle, the one that explains why he never rose higher than sergeant: He's a fuck-up, likely a drunk. He didn't sound drunk, but then he didn't sound sober, either. His friends on the force probably have had to cover for him more than once. He has to be drinking to pull something like this. Cliff tells himself that Ashford has survived this long, he must be able to handle his liquor; but that won't float. He should go over to the Celeste … but what if he fucks up Ashford by doing so? He puts his head in his hands, closes his eyes, and tries to think of something that will help; but all he manages to do is to wonder about Mary Beth. Recalling how she slipped into business mode this morning, he's certain Ashford is paying for her company. Six or seven hundred dollars, plus dinner and drinks – that would be the going rate for an all-nighter with an aging hooker. Ashford, he figures, must earn thirty-five or forty K a year. Spending a week's wage for sex would be doable for him, but he couldn't make a habit of it. But what if this is his farewell party and he's crashing out? Unwed, unloved by his peers, facing a solitary retirement – it's a possibility. Or what if he's on the take and this sort of behavior is commonplace with Ashford? Cliff has a paranoid vision of Jerry Muntz slipping Ashford a fat envelope. He rebukes himself for this entire line of speculation, realizing there's nothing to do except wait.

Thirty minutes ooze past. Wind shudders the panes, rain blurring the lights of the boardwalk, and he calls again. Ashford answers, 'Yeah ... what?'

He's slurring, his voice thick.

'Just checking on you,' Cliff says.

'Don't fucking call me, okay? Call when it's been two hours ... or I'll call.'

'Are you in Number Eleven?'

'Yeah. Goodbye.'

To ease the strain on his back, Cliff lies down on the bed and, perhaps as a result of too much adrenaline, mental fatigue, he passes out. On waking, he sits bolt upright and stares at the alarm clock. Almost midnight. If Ashford called, he didn't hear it, but he's so attuned to that damn ring ... He fumbles for the phone and punches in Ashford's number. Voicemail. After a moment's bewilderment, panic wells up in him and he can't get air. Once his breathing is under control he tries the number again, and again is shunted to voicemail.

He talks out loud in an attempt to keep calm. 'He's fucking me around,' he says. 'Motherfucker. He's twisting my brains like in high school. Or he forgot. He forgot, and now he and Mary Beth Hooker are passed out in bed at the Celeste.'

Hearing how insane this monologue sounds, he shuts it down before he can speak the third possibility, the one he believes is true – that Ashford and Mary Beth are no more, dead and done for, presently being carted off to wherever the Palaniappans dispose of the bodies.

He flirts with the notion of calling the police, but what would be the point? If they're alive, all it would achieve is to attract more attention to him and that he doesn't need. If they're dead and he calls, he'll instantly become a suspect in multiple murders and they'd most likely pick him up. But he still has an out. He calls Marley. Voicemail. He leaves an urgent message for her to call him back. If he knew where her mother lived, the street address, he'd drive to Deland and pick her up, and they'd get the hell out of Dodge. Where they would go, that's a whole other question, but at least they'd be away from Shalin and Bazit. That's okay, that's all right. Tomorrow will be soon enough.

He tries Ashford a third time, to no avail, and lies down again. He doesn't think he can sleep, but he does, straight through to morning, a sleep that seems an eventless dream of a dark, airless confine in which insubstantial monsters are crawling, breeding, killing, speaking in a language indistinguishable from a heavy, fitful wind, coming close enough to touch.

CHAPTER 11

It's not unreasonable to think, Cliff tells himself, that Marley's still into it with her mother and that's why she hasn't called; but it's nine AM and he's growing edgy. He calls the police, asks to speak with Sgt. Ashford, and is put through to a detective named Levetto who says that Ashford's always late, he should be in soon, do you want to leave a message?

'No, thanks,' says Cliff.

Screwing up his courage, he does something he should have done last night – call the motel.

'Celeste Motel,' says Bazit. 'How may I be of service?'

Cliff rasps up his voice to disguise it. 'Number Eleven, please.'

'Number Eleven is vacant, sir.'

'I'm looking for some friends, the Ashfords. I could have sworn they were in Eleven.'

A pause. 'I'm afraid we have no one of that name with us. A Mister Larry Lawless and his wife occupied Number Eleven last night.' Cliff thinks he detects a hint of amusement in Bazit's voice as he says, 'They checked out quite early.'

After trying Marley again, Cliff sits in his underwear, eating toast and jam, drinking coffee, avoiding thought by watching Fox News, when an idea strikes. He throws on shorts and a shirt, and heads for the arcade where he met Ashford the previous morning; he stakes out a stool at the counter, orders an orange juice from Kerman, and waits for Mary Beth to appear.

Last night's deluge has diminished to this morning's drizzle, but the wind is gusting hard. It's a nasty day. Churning surf ploughs the beach, massive, ugly slate-colored waves larded with white, like the liquidinous flesh of some monstrosity spilling onto shore, strands of umber seaweed lifting on its muddy humps. The bruised clouds bulge downward, dragging tendrils of rain over the land. A mere scatter of senior citizens are braving the weather; in the arcade, a handful of debased souls, none of them kids, are feeding coin slots with the regularity of casino habitués. If she's alive, the chances of Mary Beth putting in an appearance are poor, but Cliff sticks it out for more than an hour, scanning every approaching figure, prospecting the gray backdrop for a glint of whitish gold with black roots. His thoughts grab and stick like busted gears, grinding against each other, and the low music of the arcade, a muttering rap song, seems to be issuing from inside his head.

He reaches for his cell phone, thinking to try Marley, and realizes he has left it on the kitchen counter. He hurries back to the apartment and finds a message from Marley. 'Hi, Cliffie,' she says. 'I'll be home soon. Mom's no longer threatening suicide. Of course, there could always be a relapse.' A sigh. 'I miss you. Hope you're missing me.'

The message was left five minutes ago, so he calls her back, but gets her voicemail. It's twenty-three miles to Deland, a twenty-minute drive at Marley's usual rate of speed. At worst, he expects her to walk through the door in a couple of hours. But two o'clock comes and she's not yet back. He calls obsessively for the better part of an hour, punching in her number every few minutes. At three o'clock, he calls the police again and asks for Ashford. A different detective says, 'I don't see him. You want to leave a message?'

'Is he in today?'

'I don't know,' says the detective impatiently. 'I just got here myself.'

Cliff is astonished by how thoroughly the circumstance has neutralized him. He knows nothing for certain. There's no proof positive that Stacey is dead, no proof at all concerning the fates of Mary Beth and Ashford. There is some evidence that Jerry is involved in criminal activity, perhaps with the Palaniappans, but nothing you can hang your hat on. He has every expectation that Marley is safe, yet he's begun to worry. He can't raise the alarm, because no one will believe him and the police think he's a murderer. If truth be told, he's not sure he believes Shalin's story – events have gone a long way toward convincing him, but it's perfectly possible that she's playing mind games with him and that's all there is to it. When the DNA results come back, as they could any minute, at least according to Ashford, then there may be some proof, but if the DNA doesn't match Stacey's ... *Nada*. Yet it's the very nebulousness of the situation that persuades him that his life has gone and is going horribly wrong, that he's perched atop a mountain of air and, once he recognizes that nothing is supporting him, his fall will be calamitous. He should do something, he tells himself. He should leave before the DNA comes back, pack a few things and put some miles between him and the Palaniappans whom – irrationally – he fears more than the police. He can call Marley from the road, though God knows what he'll say to her.

In the end, he takes a half-measure and drives to the cottage, deciding that he'll pack and wait there for Marley to call. The surf in Port Orange is as unlovely as that in Daytona, the sky as sullen. Wind flattens the dune grass, and the cottage looks vacant, derelict, sand drifted up onto the steps and porch. When he unlocks the inside door, a strong smell rushes out, a stale, sweet scent compounded of spoilage and deodorizers. Eau de Cliff. He tiptoes about nervously, peering into rooms, and, once assured that no one is lying in wait, he grabs a suitcase and begins tossing clothes into it. In a bottom drawer, underneath folded jeans, he finds his old army .45 and a box of shotgun shells. The shotgun has long since been sold, but the .45 might come in handy. He inspects the clip, making certain it's full, and puts it in the suitcase. Headlines run past on an imaginary crawl. Actor Slain In Deadly Shoot-out – details at eleven. He finishes packing, goes into the living room, and sits on the couch. A cloud seems to settle over him, a depressive fog. He can't hold a thought in his head. It's been years since he felt so unsound, as if the fluttering of a feather duster could disperse him.

The overcast turns into dusk, and for Cliff it's an eternal moment, a single, seamless drop of time in which he's embedded like an ancient insect, suspended throughout the millennia. He feels ancient; his bones are dry sticks, his skin papery and brittle. The phone rings. Not his cell, but his landline. He reacts to it sluggishly – he doubts Marley would call him at this number – but the phone rings and rings, a piercing note that reverberates through the house, disruptive and jarring. He picks up, listens, yet does not speak.

'Mister Coria? Hello?'

Cliff remains silent.

'This is Bazit Palaniappan, the owner of the Celeste Motel. How are you today?'

'What do you want?'

'I have someone here who wishes to speak with you.'

Marley's voice comes on the line, saying, 'Cliff? Is that you?'

'Marley?'

'I'm afraid she's too upset to talk further. I've arranged for her to have a lie-down in one of our bungalows.'

'You fuck! You hurt her, I swear to God I'll kill you!'

Unperturbed, Bazit says, 'Perhaps you could come and get her. Shall we say, within the next half-hour?'

'You bet your ass I'm coming! You'd better not hurt her!'

'Within the next half-hour, if you please. I can't tie up the room longer than that. And do come alone. She's very upset. I don't know what will happen if you should bring people with you. It might be too much for her.'

His cloud of depression dissolved, Cliff slings the receiver across the room. He's furious, his thoughts flurry; he doesn't know where to turn, what to do, but gradually his fury matures into a cold, fatalistic resolve. He's fucked. The trap that the Palnaniappans set has been sprung, but Marley ... He removes the .45 from the suitcase, sticks it in his waist, under his shirt, and thinks, no, that won't be enough. They'll be watching for him, they'll expect a gun or a knife. His mind muddies. Then, abruptly, it clears and he remembers a trick he learned in blow-it-up school. He goes to the drawer in which he found the .45; he takes out two shotgun shells, hustles back to the living room, rummages through his desk and finds thumbtacks, strapping tape, and scotch tape. He makes a package of the shells, the scotch tape, a few thumbtacks, and a length of string; he drops his shorts and tapes the package under his balls. He's clumsy with the tape – his hands shake and it sticks to his fingers. The package is unstable. One wrong move and everything will spill onto the ground. He adds more tape. It's uncomfortable; it feels as if he shit his pants. He stands at the center of the room, and the room seems to shrink around him, to fit tightly to his skin like plastic wrap. He's hot and cold at the same time. A breath of wind could topple him, yet when he squeezes his hand into a fist, he knows how strong he is. 'I love you,' he says to the shadows, and the shadows tremble. 'I love you.'

CHAPTER 12

Cliff burns across the Port Orange Bridge. It's not yet full dark when he reaches the Celeste, but the Vacancy sign has been lit. Across the way, with its strings of lights bobbing in the wind and clusters of balloons and people milling everywhere, the used car lot might be a tourist attraction, a carnival without rides. He pulls up to the motel office and spots Bazit standing at the window, his arms folded. Bazit must see him, but he remains motionless, secure – Cliff thinks – with his hole card. He jumps out, heads for the door and, as he's about to open it, feels something hard prod his back.

'You stop there,' says Au Yong, stepping back from him. She's training a small silver hangun on him and scowling fiercely. Cliff's right hand sneaks toward the .45, but Bazit emerges from the office and steers him into the shadows, where he pats him down. On discovering the .45, he makes a disapproving noise.

'I want to see Marley,' Cliff says.

'You will see her,' Bazit says. 'In due course.'

Au Yong says something in Cantonese; Bazit responds in kind, then addresses Cliff in English. 'My wife says for such a negligible man, you have a very powerful weapon.'

'Fuck your wife,' Cliff says. 'I want to see Marley now.'

Bazit continues patting him down, but does not check under his balls. 'You will see her,' he says. 'And when you do, let me assure you, she will be unharmed. She is resting. Shalin is with her.'

'You tell that bitch, if she …'

Bazit slaps him across the face. 'I apologize, sir, for striking you. But you mustn't call my daughter a bitch or say anything abusive to my wife.'

Again, he speaks to Au Yong in Cantonese – she looks at Cliff, spits on the grass, and goes into the office.

'This way, please.' Bazit gestures with the .45, indicating that Cliff should precede him toward the rear of the motel, toward Bungalow Eleven. 'Don't worry about your car. It will be taken care of.'

As he moves along the overgrown path that winds back among palmettos, Number Eleven swelling in his vision, Cliff's throat goes dry and he feels a weakness in his knees, as might a condemned prisoner on first glimpsing the execution chamber. 'Come on, man,' he says. 'Let me see Marley.'

'I hope you will find your accommodations suitable,' says Bazit. 'At the

Celeste, we encourage criticism. If you have any to offer, you'll find a card for that purpose on the night table. Please feel free to write down your thoughts.'

At the entrance to Number Eleven, he unlocks the door and urges Cliff inside. 'There's a light switch on the wall to your left. Is there anything else I can do before I bid you goodnight?'

Cliff opens the door and steps in. Of the hundred questions he needs answered, only one occurs to him. 'Was it your father who did the special effects for *Sword Of The Black Demon*?'

'No, sir. It was not.' Bazit smiles and closes the door.

Cliff switches on the overhead and discovers that the lights of Bungalow Eleven are blue. It doesn't look as bad as he imagined. No dried blood, no spikes on the walls. No bone fragments or ceilings that open to reveal enormous teeth. He tries the door. Locked from without – it appears to be reinforced. He fends off panic and goes straight to work, dropping his shorts and unpeeling the tape that holds the package. The entrance to the room is a narrow alcove, perfect for his purposes. He tapes a shotgun shell to the back of the door, the ignition button facing out. Then he tapes a thumbtack to the wall slightly less than head-high, the point sticking through the tape, aligning it so that the door will strike it when opened. He has to use the string to sight the job, but he's confident that he's managed it. The bathroom door slides back into the wall, so it's no good to him. He searches for a hidden entrance. Discovering none, he tapes the second shell to the front door, a foot-and-a-half lower than the first, and lines it up with a second thumbtack.

An easy chair occupies one corner of the room. He drags it around, angles it so that it faces the door, and sits down. Booby-trapping the door has taken it out of him. He thinks that the adrenaline rush wearing off is partly to blame for his fatigue, but he's surprised how calm he feels. He's afraid – he can almost touch his fear, it's so palpable – but overlying it, suppressing it, is a veneer of tranquility that's equally palpable. He supposes that this is what some men feel in combat, a calmness that permits them to function at a high level.

The blue light, which annoyed him at first, has come to be soothing, so much so that he finds himself getting sleepy, and he thinks that the Vacancy sign may have had a similar effect when he stared at it from the used car lot. He wants to stay alert and he looks around the room, hoping to see something that will divert him. The windows are covered by sheets of hard plastic dyed to resemble shades. Except for them, everything in Number Eleven is blue. The toilet, the rugs, the bed table coated in blue paint. The sheets on the bed are blue satin, like the witch queen's sheets in the movie. That bothers him, but not sufficiently to worry about it. He tries to estimate how long he's been here. Maybe thirty, forty minutes ... The sheets seem to ripple with the reflected light, gleams flowing along them as if they're gently rippling, and he passes the time by watching them course the length of the bed.

He thinks this could be it, the sum of the Palaniappans' vengeance – they've finished with their games, and in the morning they'll reunite him and Marley. They appear to know everything about him, where he is at any given moment ... all that. Perhaps they know he's basically decent and that he didn't intend to injure Isabel. That thought planes into others about Isabel, and those in turn plane into memories of the movie they made together. He can't recall its name, but it's right on the tip of his tongue. Devil Something. Something Sword. She flirted brazenly with him on the set, but there was an untutored quality to her brazenness, as if she didn't have much experience with men and knew no other way to achieve her ends. He recalls seeing her off the set, in a Manila hotel, room service on white linen, high windows that opened onto a balcony, how she danced so erotically he thought his cock would explode, but once he was inside her, that part of him calmed down and he could go all night. It's a wonder he didn't notice she loved him, because all these years later he sees it with absolute clarity. She would lie beside him, stroking his chest, gazing into his eyes, waiting for him to reciprocate. He thought she was trying to impress him with her devotion, to trap a rich American for her husband, and, while that might have been true, he failed to recognize the deeper truth that underscored her actions. It's the same with Marley, and he understands that, at least in the beginning, he treated her with equal deference, dealing with her as one might a sexy puppy that was eager to bounce and play. It was convenient to feel that way, because it absolved him of responsibility for her feelings.

Other memories obtain from that initial one, and he becomes lost, living in a dream of Isabel, and when a point of blue light begins to expand in midair, right in front of him, he thinks it's part of the movie he's replaying, part of the dream, and watches from a dreamlike distance as it expands further, unfolds and grows plump in all the right places, evolving into the spitting image of Isabel as she was in *The Black Devil's Sword* or whatever, blue skin, black nipples, lithe and curvy, her secret hair barbered into exotic shapes, and she's dancing for him, only this dance is different from the one she used to do, more aggressive, almost angry, though he knows Isabel didn't have an angry bone in her body ... it's as though she has no bones at all, her movements are so sinuous and supple, bending backwards to trail her hair along the floor, then straightening with a weaving motion, hips and breasts swaying, a sheen of sweat upon her body as she flings her fingers out at him, like the queen ... in the movie ... when she danced ...

Cliff feels pain, not an awful pain, but pain like he's never felt before, as if an organ of which he has been unaware, a special organ tucked away beneath the tightly packed fruits of heart, liver, spleen, kidneys, and intestines, insulated by their flesh, has been opened and is spilling its substance. It's not a stabbing pain, neither an ache nor a twinge, not the raw pain that comes from a open wound or a burning such as eventuates from an ulcer; but though comparably mild, not yet severe enough to combat his arousal, it's the worst pain he has known. A sick, emptying feeling is the closest he can come to articulating it, but not even that says it. He understands now that this is no movie and that something vital is leaking out, being drawn from his body in surges, in trickles and sudden gushes, conjured forth by blue fingers that tease, tempt, and coax. He tries to relieve the pain by twisting in the chair, by screaming, but he's denied the consolation of movement – he cannot convulse or writhe or kick, and when he attempts to scream, a scratchy whisper is all he can muster. It's not that he's being restrained, but rather it seems that as the level of that vital essence lowers, he's become immobilized, his will shriveled to the point that he no longer desires to move, he no longer cares to do anything other than to suffer in silence, to stare helplessly at the beautiful blue witch with full breasts and half-moon hips, sweat glistening on her thighs and belly, who is both the emblem and purveyor of his pain.

His vision clouds, his eyes are failing or perhaps they are occluded by a pale exhaust, a cloud-like shadow of the thing draining from him, for he glimpses furtive shapes and vague lusters within the cloud; but they are unimportant – the one wish he sustains, the one issue left upon which he can opine, is that she be done with him, and he knows that she is nearly done. His being flickers like a shape on a silent screen, luminous and frail. But then she dwindles, she folds in upon herself, shrinking to a point of blue light, and is gone. Her absence restores to him an inch of will, an ounce of sensitivity, yet he's not grateful. Why has she left him capable of feeling only a numb horror and his own hollowness? He wants to call her back, but has no voice. In frustration, he strains against his unreal bonds, causing his head to wobble and fall, and sits staring at his feet. Sluggish, simple thoughts hang like drool from the mouth of whatever dead process formed them, the final products of his mental life.

After a while, an eon, a second, he realizes that the pain has diminished, his vitality is returning, and manages to lift his head when he hears a click and sees the door being cautiously opened. A woman with frizzy blond hair peeks in. He knows her – not her name, but he knows her and has the urge to warn her against something.

'Cliff!' she says, relief in her voice, and starts toward him, bursting through the door.

Two explosions, two blasts of fire, splinter the wood and fling her against the wall, painting it with a shrapnel of blood, hair, scraps of flesh and bone. She flops onto the floor, an almost unrecognizable wreckage, face torn away, waist all but severed, blood pooling wide as a table around her. But Cliff recognizes her. He remembers her name, and he begins to remember who she was and why she was here and what happened to her. He remembers nights and days, he remembers laughter, the taste of her mouth, and he wants to turn from this grisly sight, from the burnt eye and the gristly tendons and the thick reddish black syrup they're steeping in. He wants to yell until his throat is raw, until blood sprays from his mouth; he wants to shake his head back and forth like a madman until his neck breaks; he wants very badly to die.

From outside comes the sound of voices, questioning voices, muted voices, and then a scream. Cliff understands now how this will end. The police, a murder trial, and a confinement followed by an execution. As Marley recedes from life, from the world, he is re-entering it, reclaiming his senses, his memories, and he struggles against this restoration, trying with all his might to die, trying to avoid an emptiness greater than death, but with every passing moment he increases, he grows steadier and more complete in his understanding. He understands that the law of karma has been fully applied. He understands the careless iniquity of humankind and the path that has led him to this terrible blue room. With understanding comes further increase, further renewal, yet nonetheless he continues to try and vomit out the remnant scrapings of his soul before Shalin returns to gloat, before one more drop of torment can be exacted, before his memories become so poignant they can pierce the deadest heart. He yearns for oblivion, and then thinks that death may not offer it, that in death he may find worse than Shalin, a life of exquisite torment. That in mind, he forces himself to look again at Marley's disfigured face, hoping to discover in that mask of ruptured sinews and blackened tissue, with here and there a patch of skull, and, where her neck was, amidst the gore, the blue tip of an artery dangling like a blossom from a flap of scorched skin ... hoping to discover an out, a means of egress, a crevice into which he can scurry and hide from the light of his own unpitying judgment. He forces himself to drink in the sight of her death; he forces himself and forces himself, denying the instinct to turn away; he forces himself to note every insult to her flesh, every fray and tatter, every internal vileness; he forces himself past the borders of revulsion, past the fear-and-trembling into deserts of thought, the wastes where the oldest monsters howl in the absence; he forces himself to persevere, to continue searching for a key to this doorless prison until thick strands of saliva braid his lips and his hands have ceased to shake and cracked saints mutter prayers for the damned and blood rises in clouds of light from the floor, and in a pocket of electric quiet he begins to hear the voice of her accusatory thoughts, to respond to them, defending himself by arguing that it was she who originally forced herself on him, and how could he have anticipated any of this, how can she blame him? You should have known, she tells him, you should have fucking known that someone like you, a jerk with a trivial intelligence and the morals of a cabbage and a blithe disregard for everything but his own pleasure, must have broken some hearts and stepped on some backs. You should have known. Yeah, he says, but all that's changed. I've changed. With a last glimmer of self-perception, he realizes this slippage is the start of slide that will never end, the opening into a hell less certain than the one that waits upon the other side of life. He feels an unquiet exultation, a giddy merriment that makes him dizzy and, if not happy, then content in part, knowing that when they come for him, the official mourners, the takers under, the guardians of the public safety, those who command the cold violence of the law, they'll find him looking into death's bad eye, into the ruined face of love, into the nothing-lasts-forever, smiling bleakly, blankly …

Vacantly.

GATEWAY

If you've enjoyed these books and would like to read more, you'll find literally thousands of classic Science Fiction & Fantasy titles through the **SF Gateway**

✲

*For the new home of
Science Fiction & Fantasy . . .*

✲

*For the most comprehensive collection
of classic SF on the internet . . .*

✲

Visit the SF Gateway

www.sfgateway.com

Lucius Shepard (1947–2014)

Lucius Taylor Shepard was born in Lynchburg, Virginia, in 1947. He travelled extensively in his youth, and has held a wide assortment of occupations in the United States, Europe, Southeast Asia and Latin America, including rock musician and night club bouncer. He attended the Clarion Writers' Workshop in 1980 and made his first commercial sale a year later. His work covers many areas of fantastic fiction and has recently encompassed non-fiction, as well. For over a decade, he has contributed a regular column on SF cinema for *The Magazine of Fantasy and Science Fiction*. Lucius Shepard has won numerous prizes for his work, including the Hugo, Nebula, World Fantasy, Theodore Sturgeon and International Horror Guild awards. He died in 2014.